HOUSE
OF
STEEL
THE
HONORVERSE
COMPANION

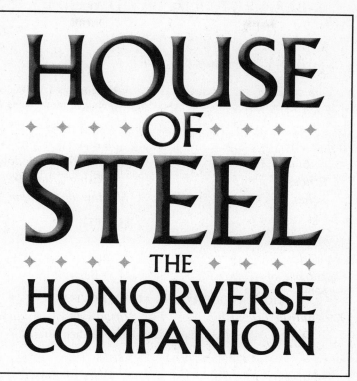

HOUSE OF STEEL

THE HONORVERSE COMPANION

DAVID WEBER
with BuNine

BAEN

HOUSE OF STEEL: THE HONORVERSE COMPANION

A Baen Books Original

Baen Publishing Enterprises
P.O. Box 1403
Riverdale, NY 10471
www.baen.com

ISBN: 978-1-4516-3875-2

Cover art by David Mattingly
Interior art by Thomas Marrone

First printing, May 2013

Distributed by Simon & Schuster
1230 Avenue of the Americas
New York, NY 10020

Library of Congress Cataloging-in-Publication Data

Weber, David, 1952–
    House of steel : the Honorverse companion / David Weber with BuNine.
       pages cm
    ISBN 978-1-4516-3875-2 (hc) — ISBN 978-1-4516-3893-6 (trade pb) 1. Harrington, Honor (Fictitious character) 2. Space warfare—Fiction. 3. Science fiction. I. Title.
    PS3573.E217H74 2013
    813'.54—dc23

                                                                2013004493

10 9 8 7 6 5 4 3 2 1

Design and layout by Thomas Pope and Joy Freeman
Printed in the United States of America

For my wife and children, who put up with far
too many weekend absences and sleepless nights.

For the members of BuNine, without whom
none of this would have been possible.

. . . and for David, who invited us inside
to play in his sandbox.

Thank you all.

—Thomas Pope

Fans are a storyteller's
greatest reward, and his greatest blessing.
Sometimes they become even more than that.
They become friends and collaborators as well,
as involved in the storytelling as the author himself.
I've been lucky enough to have that happen in my case,
and this book is the result of endless hours of work on
the part of some very special people. I can't possibly
thank them enough . . . and I hope those who read it
will realize how extraordinarily fortunate I've been.
Thanks, guys. You really pulled it off.

—David Weber

CONTENTS

I WILL BUILD MY HOUSE OF STEEL

DAVID WEBER

Although King Roger III's role in the prewar buildup of the Royal Manticoran Navy from what was essentially a system defense and commerce protection force into an interstellar navy capable of projecting massive combat power over hundreds of light-years has been well chronicled, the true depth of his contribution to the Star Kingdom of Manticore's survival has been under-appreciated for far too many years. His farsighted preparations, so ably continued by his daughter, the present Queen Elizabeth III, following his untimely death, were, in fact, absolutely essential to that survival, as were the tireless, equally under-appreciated labors of Admiral Jonas Adcock, his able collaborator, friend, and brother-in-law. These two remarkable men were instrumental in achieving an unparalleled and decisive transformation of modern warfare whose ramifications are even now only imperfectly appreciated by the navies of the Haven Sector and largely unguessed at beyond that sector.

The author of the present work is indebted to Her Majesty the Queen for her gracious permission to explore previously sealed archives and the many hours of her personal time which she has given to interviews with the author, not to mention the insight into events of her father's and her uncle's lives which no other source could possibly have provided. Clearly, the security aspects of the present work must also be considered, and the author wishes to express his gratitude to the office of the First Lord of Admiralty and to the office of the First Space Lord for their assistance in this regard.

The truth is that, even today, few people realize just how early in his own naval career then Crown Prince Roger became aware of the depth of the peril his Star Kingdom would one day face. However...

—from the preface to *To Stand Against the Tempest: An Authorized Biography of Roger III*, Sir Donald Keegan Morrison, Landing University of Manticore Press, Landing, 1921 PD

+ + + + +

December 1844 PD

LIEUTENANT R. WINTON—Commander Janofsky ("Commerce Protection and Societal Disintegration," *Proceedings*, No. 3673) is to be commended for the clarity with which he makes his points. The continuing slide into even more pronounced and widespread civil disorder, privateering, terrorism, and outright piracy in the territory of the Silesian Confederacy must give any navy pause. Commander Janofsky rightly points out the increasing cost, not simply in financial terms but also in terms of manpower and platform availability, inherent in maintaining existing levels of security for Manticoran merchant traffic in and through the Confederacy. Indeed, his arguments assume even more cogency when one considers the still greater costs associated with any expansion of our secured trading zones, patrol regions, and roving piracy suppression missions.

Where Commander Janofsky's analysis may break down, however, is in its intense focus on commerce protection as the Navy's primary mission. I would suggest that it would be appropriate for Her Majesty's Navy to consider the potential requirements of additional missions. Not to put too fine a point upon it, we in the Navy have narrowed our professional focus to a potentially dangerous degree, concentrating upon the mission in hand rather than stretching our imaginations to consider other challenges and threats.

The function of the Royal Manticoran Navy, as currently defined (see "Naval Security and the Star Kingdom's Fundamental Interests," Office of the First Space Lord, 01-15-249 AL) is to "(1) defend and secure the Manticore Binary system, its planets, its population, and its industrial base; (2) defend and secure the central terminus of the Manticoran Wormhole Junction and the industrial and economic base associated with it; (3) defend, protect, and expand Manticoran commerce and the Manticoran merchant marine; and (4) in conjunction with (3) enforce the Cherwell Convention for the suppression of the interstellar genetic slave trade." It should be noted that, in fact, this formulation establishes that commerce protection comes only *third* in the hierarchy of the Navy's missions. In addition, it is, I think, significant that in Commander Janofsky's article the first two of these four objectives are taken as givens. That is, Commander Janofsky's emphasis is on how to provide for the third and (by extension) fourth of them, which appears to assume that the first three are already adequately provided.

That assumption may be in error.

At this time, Her Majesty's Navy's wall of battle consists of eleven *Thorsten*-class battleships (the youngest 250 years old) and eleven *Ad Astra*-class dreadnoughts (the youngest of which is a century old and three of which are presently mothballed while awaiting long overdue repair and refit). The *Thorstens*, while fine ships in their day, are barely half the size of younger, more modern battleships, with far lighter armaments and much weaker defenses than their more recent counterparts, and as the *Ad Astras'* delayed and badly needed refits indicate, even they are far from the equal of more modern units. We are currently in the process of building the first three *Royal Winton*-class dreadnoughts, which will be superior vessels for their tonnage when completed, and a single superdreadnought: *Samothrace*. This ship will also be a modern, first-rate unit upon completion, but it is worth noting that the build number for the *Samothraces* was originally to have been a mere three ships . . . and—in the event—was actually reduced to only the name ship of the class with an "intent" to request additional units in later Naval Estimates.

While it is true that the *Royal Wintons* and the *Samothrace* will provide a significant boost in the defensive capacity of the Fleet against threats to the home system and, in conjunction with the Junction fortresses, to the security of the Manticoran Wormhole Junction, they can scarcely be classed as a true wall of battle when procured in such minute numbers. Moreover, it would appear that even less thought has been given to the development of proper doctrine for their employment than to developing a procurement policy which would maximize platform numbers and capability.

Nor would it appear that any thought has been devoted at this time to their potential usefulness for power *projection*. One cannot avoid the conclusion that the mere existence of this relative handful of new and powerful ships is regarded as adequately providing for "the Star Kingdom's fundamental territorial security" and the protection of its subjects. The question is whether or not that faith is merited.

At this time, the Navy has clearly adopted the traditional tactical, operational, and strategic paradigm which has been developed over the past several centuries by the Solarian League Navy. It is scarcely surprising that the largest, most powerful, and most successful naval force in galactic history should be seen as an appropriate model from which lessons and best-practices approaches might be drawn. It might, however, behoove the Star Kingdom of Manticore to bear in mind that, as the paucity of our wall of battle demonstrates, we are not the Solarian League. Despite the unquestionable prosperity and generally very high standard of living which the Star Kingdom has attained due to the many favorable factors stemming from its possession of the Junction, the Star Kingdom remains a single-system polity. As such, it must lack the population base, the sheer economic and industrial breadth, and—above all—astrographic *depth* of the Solarian League. The unpalatable truth is that we have only a single star system to lose in any confrontation with any potential adversary.

The Star Kingdom overlooks that vulnerability at its peril. While three hundred T-years have passed since Axelrod of Old Terra financed the attempt to seize the Manticore Binary System before the Junction had been plotted, surveyed, and mapped, it is a lesson we would do well to remember. The very source of our wealth and industrial and economic power must make the Star Kingdom an attractive target to any aggressive adversary who believes he possesses sufficient combat power to take it. If that conclusion is granted, then the Navy's primary mission—"to preserve the Star Kingdom's fundamental territorial security"—requires the creation and maintenance of a genuine battle fleet capable of deterring any such ambition. Moreover, that battle fleet cannot, as is the case for the Solarian League Navy, depend upon sheer, irresistible numbers and the strategic depth available to the League. It must be demonstrably and visibly capable of defeating any attack not simply short of the Manticore Binary System's hyper limit, but short of the Junction itself. And that leads inevitably to a requirement on the part of that battle force of the capacity to project power against—to take the war to—that hypothetical aggressor.

In light of that requirement, I would submit that Commander Janofsky's eloquent appeal for additional light units, the doubling of our cruiser force, the establishment of formal naval stations and forward enclaves within Silesian territory, and additional tactical, training, and financial support for the Confederacy Navy, while fully logical from the traditional commerce-protection perspective should be reconsidered. The Royal Manticoran Navy's record in commerce protection is second to none. It is a mission we fully understand, one which we have the training, the doctrine, and—for the most part—the means to carry out. Indeed, what we do, we do very well.

What we have *not* done, and what we must do, is to acquire the capability to discharge the rest of our mission and our obligation. We must recognize that we cannot, as a single star nation of extraordinary wealth, afford to ignore the temptation we must present to less prosperous but militarily powerful star nations. As the ancient pre-space philosopher Machiavelli pointed out, gold will not always get you good soldiers, but good soldiers can always get you gold. The Star Kingdom, and the Junction, are that gold, and it will require good soldiers—or, in our case, a qualitatively superior navy—to protect it. We cannot continue to embrace a vague, poorly articulated strategic and tactical doctrine based on an uncritical acceptance of the Solarian model as the best and highest available to us. We must accept instead that we will not be able to match the numbers of platforms an adversary may bring against us, and we must capitalize upon the most precious tactical resource we have: the tradition of independent judgment and responsibility taking we have inculcated into our officer corps ever since the days of Edward Saganami and Ellen D'Orville. We must value that initiative properly, cultivate it, and integrate it into our operational and tactical doctrine at every level. And we must provide that initiative with the tools it requires—the innovative approach to weaponry and war-fighting technologies—to make it fully effective.

Initiative thrives upon exploitable asymmetrical relationships, upon the ability to oppose qualitative superiority to quantitative predominance. It is not sufficient for us to accept that the gradual, stable evolution of war-fighting technologies which has typified naval doctrine and capabilities for the past several centuries is inevitable. It is time that we began significantly investing in an aggressive search for new capabilities, innovative applications, to provide an officer corps trained to think for itself with levers it can use to offset its almost inevitable numerical inferiority when confronted by a powerful aggressor. Our wall of battle's ship strength *must* be increased, but it will never be possible for the Star Kingdom to produce, man, and maintain naval forces on the scale of a star nation such as the Solarian League or even the People's Republic of Haven. Since we cannot have the most numerous navy in space, we must instead strive to have the most efficient one.

Commander Janofsky's call to bolster our forward deployed presence in Silesia is clear, logical, and concise. Despite that, however, one cannot avoid the conclusion that from the perspective of our *primary* mission, it is time and past time for the Navy to look to its wall of battle and the acquisition of the true *war-fighting* capability absolutely essential for any single-star system nation to adequately defend itself against a much larger multi-star system nation.

(ED: Lieutenant Winton is currently assigned to HMS *Wolverine*, serving as her executive officer.)

> —From "On the Event Horizon:
> Letters from the Deck Plates,"
> *Proceedings of the Royal
> Manticoran Navy Institute,*
> Issue number 3675, 12/10/249 AL

CAPTAIN E. JANACEK—Lieutenant Winton's comments on Commander Janofsky's article (see "On the Event Horizon," *Proceedings*, No. 3675) are as perspicacious and insightful as one might readily anticipate from a member of his family and an officer whose career to date has demonstrated not only intelligence and ability but diligence and dedication. Nonetheless, there are certain pragmatic realities to which he has attached insufficient weight.

While it is true that the Navy's current mission formulation rightly emphasizes the security of the home system, it is also true that the actual work of the Navy requires a concentration upon the mission in hand, and the mission in hand is, in fact, commerce protection, as Commander Janofsky so ably pointed out. At this time, there is no realistic threat to the security of the Manticore Binary System itself or to the Manticoran Wormhole Junction. The completion of the *Royal Winton* class will provide the Navy with a powerful, flexible deterrent force capable of holding its own against any projected threat. Lieutenant Winton is quite correct to underscore the invaluable advantage of our officer corps' flexibility, initiative, and independence of thought. That advantage, coupled with the enormous increase in combat power represented by the *Royal Wintons* and HMS *Samothrace* and backed up by our older but still perfectly serviceable dreadnoughts, is fully adequate to the mission of protecting our home space and our fellow subjects from any realistic threat. And while Lieutenant Winton is also correct to emphasize that initiative and operational innovation are most effective when provided with the tools they require to concentrate combat power as flexibly as possible, the diversion of funds needed for critical expansion of our commerce protection capabilities into problematic quests for some sort of technological "equalizer" must be considered a questionable policy. The Royal Manticoran Navy is well informed upon the capabilities of other navies, including that of the Solarian League itself. At this time, it would be both rash and, in this writer's opinion, quixotic to believe that what Lieutenant Winton correctly points out is a single-system polity could somehow single-handedly devise or discover a technological breakthrough (one hesitates to call it a panacea) which has hitherto evaded all of the galaxy's other naval powers.

The wall of battle we now possess—or will possess, when all units of the *Royal Winton* class are completed—will be fully adequate to our immediate security needs. Those security needs may, indeed, change in the future, as Lieutenant Winton suggests, and at that time a reexamination of our posture and capabilities may well be in order. Surely, however, considering that no navy in history has ever possessed an unlimited budget and that the fiscal realities (which must include a realistic appreciation of Parliament's willingness to spend money) are unlikely to change in that regard in the case of Her Majesty's Navy, it makes little or no sense to spend scarce dollars on capital ships we do not presently need. Nor can we afford to expend dollars urgently required for pressing presence mission requirements in Silesia on problematical, ill-defined, unpredictable, and dubious efforts to somehow short-circuit or telescope the inevitable and steady evolution of war-fighting technologies which has been clearly established over the last three T-centuries.

With all due respect to Lieutenant Winton's persuasively and eloquently argued position, it is neither reasonable nor appropriate for a single star system of ultimately limited resources to divert its focus from the provision of the best-tailored and most operationally potent force it can *practically* provide in order to pursue hypothetical technological "equalizers" to be employed against a theoretical adversary fleet which does not even currently exist.

(ED: Captain Janacek is currently attached to the Admiralty, serving as Second Space Lord Havinghurst's deputy chief of staff for Intelligence.)

—From "On the Event Horizon: Letters from the Deck Plates," *Proceedings of the Royal Manticoran Navy Institute,* Issue number 3676, 13/10/294 AL

✦　✦　✦　✦　✦

"AND THAT'S ABOUT IT, Sir." Lieutenant Roger Winton flicked off his memo board and looked across the briefing room table at his commanding officer. "Better than I really expected it to be, but the delay on those missile pallets is . . . irritating." He grimaced. "'As soon as practicable' isn't what a good, industrious XO likes to tell his captain when we're pushing a deployment deadline."

"No, I suppose not," Commander Pablo Wyeth, HMS *Wolverine*'s commanding officer said judiciously. He tipped back in his chair, regarding his executive officer sternly, then smiled. "On the other hand, if that's the worst thing that happens to us, we'll be luckier than we deserve. And while I realize it's likely to undermine my slave-driving captain's reputation, I can't see how I can reasonably construe it as your fault, Roger."

"As always, I am awed by your restraint, Sir."

"I'm sure you are."

The treecat on the back of Lieutenant Winton's chair tilted his head, ears twitching in amusement, and Wyeth shook his head, and found himself—again—wondering just why his exec had decided to pursue a naval career. Part of it was obvious enough. Lieutenant Winton had the talent, drive, and innate ability to succeed at anything he'd cared to turn his hand to, and his love for the Queen's Navy was obvious. Yet he had to find it immensely frustrating, as well. Promotion was glacially slow, and likely to get more so as the prolong therapies began extending officers' careers. There was more cronyism than Wyeth liked to think about, as well, although it was nowhere near as much a problem in the Royal Manticoran Navy as in some navies. (The Solarian

13

League Navy came forcibly to mind, as a matter of fact.) And the RMN had its cliques, its little mutual-protection clubs, too many of them built on birth and privilege, which had to be especially frustrating for Winton.

Thirteen T-years out of the Island, and he's still only a lieutenant, Wyeth thought. *Of course, I was four T-years older than he is now before I made lieutenant, but not all officers are created equal, whatever the Island likes to pretend. I can think of at least a dozen of his classmates who're senior to him by now, and not one of them is as flat out good at his job as Roger is.*

And that, he reflected, was particularly ironic given the fact that cronyism, patronage, and raw nepotism accounted for most of those accelerated promotions . . . and that it was only the lieutenant's own fierce refusal to play those games which prevented him from being senior to *all* of them.

Once upon a time, I would've thought being Heir to the Crown would have to work in someone's favor, the commander mused. *But that was before I met Roger. I know some of the "upper crust" think this is some sort of silly hobby on his part—or that his refusal to trade on the family name is some kind of perverse hairshirt he's chosen to wear—but that only confirms their idiocy. The Navy's important to him, and at least he by God knows he's earned every promotion that came his way. It'd take someone with big brass ones to blackball Crown Prince Roger Winton when his name comes before a promotion board, however it got there, but I'm inclined to think it would probably take a pronounced lack of IQ to go ahead and promote him just because of whose son he is. He's going to be King himself one day not so far down the road, and Wintons have long memories. Somehow I don't think the career of any brown-noser who "helped" his career along in hopes of some kind of payback down the road is likely to prosper when that happens.*

Oddly, that thought gave Commander Wyeth a certain profound sense of satisfaction.

On the other hand, there was no point pretending Lieutenant Winton was just any old lieutenant . . . even if he *had* insisted his fellow officers address him as if he were.

"I read Captain Janacek's response to your letter to the *Proceedings*," Wyeth said after a moment, his tone carefully casual.

"So did I, Sir."

Winton's calm reply would have fooled most people, but Wyeth could watch his treecat, and Monroe's ears flattened instantly at the mention of Janacek's name. The captain was less than five years older than Roger Winton, but his family was deeply involved in politics, one of the movers and shakers of the Conservative Association, and they'd pulled strings mercilessly to speed along his promotions.

Probably never even gave it a second thought, either. Hard to blame them, some ways. Promotion's slow enough and plum command slots are thin enough on the ground to make just about anyone figure he'd better use whatever edge he can if he wants to get command of a major combatant before he's too old and senile to remember what to do with it when he's got it!

It was an ignoble thought, and Wyeth knew it. Worse, he'd found himself thinking it more often as more and more of the officer corps became prolong recipients. The therapies had reached the Star Kingdom barely fifteen T-years earlier, and Wyeth had been too old to receive them. In fact, Roger himself had been close to the upper age limit when the treatments became available. But Pablo Wyeth was already fifty-two T-years old; the chance that he would make flag rank before his age-mandated retirement was virtually nil, whereas an arrogant prick like Janacek—just young enough to sneak in under the wire for prolong—would probably make it within the next five or six T-years...and then have something like a century in which to enjoy it.

Calmly, Pablo, he told himself. *Remember your blood pressure, you antiquated old fart!*

The self-reminder made him snort mentally, and he saw Monroe's ears flick back upright as the telempathic 'cat picked up on his own amusement.

"I thought the good Captain went out of his way to be gracious while he was stomping all over your suggestion with both feet," the commander observed out loud.

"With all due respect for Captain Janacek's seniority, I've never been especially impressed by the scintillating brilliance of his intellect," Winton replied. "He *was* careful about exactly how he phrased himself, though, wasn't he?"

"Yes, he was," Wyeth agreed with a grin. Then his expression sobered slightly. "On the other hand, you realize he never would've written that if he didn't know quite a few other officers—especially *senior* ones—agree with him. I know you don't really like me to mention this, Roger, but it takes a fair amount of chutzpah to publicly sign your name to something likely to piss off your future monarch. I don't see Janacek doing that if he didn't figure there'd be more than enough senior officers around to back his view of things."

And if he didn't have a pretty shrewd idea of just how much you hate the family interest game, Wyeth added mentally. *You're right about his lack of brilliance, whatever he and his cronies think, but he's not really outright stupid, however he acts sometimes. He's got to know you're not going to use* your *"family interest" to step on him the way he probably deserves, or he never would've opened his mouth.*

"I know there are. That's the problem." Winton reached up, and Monroe flowed down from the chair back to curl in his lap, his buzzing purr loud as the lieutenant stroked his fluffy coat. "We've been thinking in one direction for so long that two-thirds of our senior officers are so invested in it they don't even realize they're not looking at what's really happening."

"Oh?" Wyeth cocked his head, raising one eyebrow.

"It doesn't take a genius to realize how juicy a target the Junction is," Winton said. "Hell, Sir! All it *really* takes is a working memory! There was a reason I mentioned Axelrod of Old Terra in my letter."

Wyeth nodded, yet he couldn't help wondering if there was more than simple historical memory involved in his executive officer's position. Unlike quite a few of their fellow officers, whose attention was focused almost exclusively on the Navy's commerce-protection duties, particularly in the face of the worsening situation in the Silesian Confederacy and the Andermani Empire's increasing interest in fishing in those troubled waters, Wyeth tried to keep an eye on the broader picture. He wasn't especially happy about what seemed to be happening in the Haven Quadrant these days, mainly because of the People's Republic's naval buildup, despite what most of the pundits believed had to be a rapidly disintegrating fiscal position. Still, there were possible explanations for that buildup that were relatively innocuous. It wasn't the way *he'd* go about creating jobs and pumping money back into the economy, but he wouldn't have done *most* things the way the People's Republic's political leaders had done them for the last, oh, two T-centuries or so. And whatever they might be thinking, nothing he'd seen so far suggested that Haven might be considering reprising Axelrod's attempt on the Manticoran Wormhole Junction. For that matter, even if it was, and much as it pained Pablo Wyeth to contemplate agreeing even conditionally with Edward Janacek, the Junction fortresses and the new *Royal Wintons* and *Samothraces*—assuming the idiots in Parliament actually did go ahead and built the rest of the originally requested SDs—should be able to handle the People's Republic's battleships if it came to it.

All of that made nice, logical, reassuring sense. Unfortunately, whatever his own attitude towards his birth, Lieutenant Winton was also Crown Prince Roger of Manticore, only a single heartbeat away from the crown. As such, he received regular in-depth intelligence briefings unavailable to any other junior officer. Or to the commanding officers of any of Queen Samantha's destroyers, if it came to that.

And he's not about to let a single classified word slip, either, is he? Wyeth reminded himself. *He wasn't even willing to suggest obliquely in his letter that he might know something Janofsky doesn't. He's going to make one hell of a King one day.*

"Well, you're young," he said out loud. "You'll have time to wear them down."

"I hope so, Sir." His executive officer sounded grimmer than usual, Wyeth thought. "At the moment, though, I'm feeling like a character out of an Old Earth fairy tale."

"Really?" The commander chuckled. Ancient fairy tales and fables happened to be a hobby of his, and Winton knew it. "Let me see... If we asked Captain Janacek, I'm sure he'd be able to come up with quite a few. Like the little boy who cried 'Wolf!' for example. Or did you have Chicken Little in mind?"

"Actually, Sir, I was thinking of the Three Little Pigs. Especially the last one."

"So you're trying to convince the rest of the Navy that it's time to build a house out of bricks instead of straw—is that it?"

"Mostly, Sir." Winton nodded, looking down at his hands as they stroked the purring cream-and-gray treecat in his lap. "Mostly." He looked up, brown eyes dark and very level. "Except that if *I'd* been the third Little Pig, I'd have held out for something even better. I think *steel* would've worked very nicely, actually."

◆　◆　◆　◆　◆

August 1850 PD

"SIR CASPER WAS TALKING about you just yesterday, Roger dear," Samantha Winton, Queen Samantha II of the Star Kingdom of Manticore, said as she looked across the breakfast table at her son.

"I'll just *bet* he was," her daughter Caitrin said, rolling her eyes, and the treecat perched in the highchair beside Samantha made a soft sound that echoed his person's mingled amusement and exasperation.

"Don't encourage her, Magnus," the Queen told him, and spared him a brief, quelling glance before she turned her gaze upon her younger offspring.

Almost twelve T-years younger than her brother, Caitrin looked absurdly young to someone her mother's age, thanks in no small part to how youthful she'd been when prolong reached the Star Kingdom. She and Roger both had the Winton look—the dark complexion, the brown eyes, the strong chin—but neither of them were quite as dark as Samantha, who looked remarkably like a throwback to the days of King Roger I. Yet as similar as her children were to one another physically, there was an enormous difference in their personalities, the Queen reflected. Roger was the serious, thoughtful worrier—the sort who was constantly look-ing to the future, trying to anticipate oncoming storms and shape his course to deal with them. Caitrin wasn't really the mental gadabout she often liked to portray, but there was no denying that she was far more inclined to take things as they came rather than rushing to meet them.

And she was far, far more...irreverent about the venerable traditions and responsibilities of the House of Winton. She took them seriously, but she refused to *admit* she did. Of course she wasn't even thirty T-years old yet; there was time for her to grow properly stodgy, Samantha supposed.

Not that *Roger* showed any signs of stodginess, but he'd always been a serious little boy, and he'd grown into a serious man. One his mother rather liked, as a matter of fact. She often wondered how much of that would have happened anyway and how much was due to the fact that he'd known all his life he'd one day be king? She'd tried to keep that from overshadowing his childhood, just as her parents had tried to prevent the same thing in her own case.

And, like them, she'd failed.

"And what, may I ask," Roger said now, delivering a quelling glance of his own to his unrepentant sister, "did your estimable Prime Minister have to say about your scapegrace eldest offspring, Mother? No, let me guess. He took the opportunity upon the occasion of my birthday to once more point out that it's time I began producing an heir to the throne. Annnnnd"—he drew the word out, considering his mother through slitted eyes—"he also took the opportunity to suggest it's time I stopped playing and settled down to a serious career in politics."

"I see you know how Sir Casper's mind works," Samantha said dryly.

"You mean he knows which ruts the mind in question—such as it is and what there is of it—stays stuck in."

Caitrin's tone was far more acid than it had been, and her mother's expression turned reproving. Not that she expected it to do much good. Sir Casper O'Grady, Earl of Mortenson, was *not* one of Caitrin Winton's favorite people.

"Oh, don't worry, Mom," her daughter said now. "I promise to be polite—or moderately civil, at least—to him in public. But he keeps *harping* on that!"

"Yes, he does," Samantha agreed, holding her daughter's eyes. "Of course, he's over seventy, isn't he? And his attitudes were formed before prolong came along, too, weren't they?"

Caitrin's expression sobered. She looked back at her mother for a heartbeat or two, then nodded.

"Point taken, Mom," she said much more quietly.

Roger sipped coffee, taking his time, letting the moment subside a bit before he lowered his cup again. Queen Samantha would be seventy in another T-year, herself... and she'd been far too old for prolong when it reached the Star Kingdom. It was as awkward as it was painful for any child to adjust to the thought that his parents had no more than ninety or a hundred years of life while he himself might well live twice or even three times that long. And it was awkward for the parents, too. Their attitudes and expectations had been shaped by the life expectancies they'd faced growing up. It was hard for many of them to stand back, realize how different their children's perspectives had to be, and it was even worse in Mortenson's case. He was a natural worrier, and Roger couldn't remember the last time—or the first—he'd ever heard the Prime Minister crack a joke, but that might not be such a bad thing in a chief minister. Even if it was a pain in the ass to have Mortenson looking over his shoulder and pressing tactfully (or that was how the Prime Minister probably would have put it; Roger had rather a different perspective on it) now that he was forty-one T-years old—or would be tomorrow, at any rate—for him to "find a nice girl," put aside his youthful enthusiasms like the Navy, and settle down to his *real* career in politics.

And while he was about it, produce an heir.

"I suppose I can't really blame him," Roger said now, setting his cup back on its saucer. "Hard to remember that, sometimes, but I do try, Mom. But I'm not really planning on becoming King for another—oh, thirty years or so, either—if it's all right with you. And I'm not really interested in giving up the Navy just yet. Especially now."

The atmosphere in the pleasant, sunlit dining room seemed to darken. Samantha sat back in her chair at the head of the table, and her treecat companion abandoned his own meal to flow down into her lap and croon to her softly.

"I'm doing all I can, Roger," she said quietly.

"I know that, Mom." Roger shook his head quickly. "And I know it might help in some ways to have me available to trot out for debates. But I'm not as good a horse trader yet as you are, and I think—at the moment, at least—that I can do more good arguing the case from inside the Service." He made a face, then took a piece of bacon from his plate and offered it to Monroe, seated in his own treecat-sized highchair beside him. "If we're really going to make the kinds of changes you and I both agree we've got to make, someone's got to . . . convince the Navy's senior officers it's a good idea."

"Have you tried a sledgehammer?" his sister asked more than a little bitterly. "It's been six *T-years* since that first letter of yours in the *Proceedings*, Rog, and I haven't noticed any radical realignments, have you?"

"At least some of them are starting to listen, Katie," he replied, and watched her quick, involuntary smile as he used the nickname only he had ever applied to her. "I admit it's an uphill fight, but since the Peeps finally started coming out into the open, a few of my seniors—and quite a few more of my contemporaries—are starting to actually *think* about it." He smiled mirthlessly. "In some ways, the timing on Janacek's response to that much-maligned letter of mine is working in our favor."

Caitrin laughed. It was a harsh sound, but there was at least some genuine humor in it, her mother thought. And Roger had a point. In fact, he had a much better point than she might have preferred.

It was hard for a lot of people, even now, to accept what had happened to the Republic of Haven. Partly, she supposed, that was because it hadn't happened overnight. In fact, it had been an agonizingly slow process, one drawn out for the better part of two T-centuries, long enough for it to turn into an accepted part of the backdrop of interstellar politics. And it had all been internal to the Republic, after all. If Havenite citizens wanted to reorder their political and economic systems, that was up to them and really wasn't anyone else's business. Unfortunately, the process—and its consequences—were no longer a purely internal matter. That minor change in the interstellar dynamic was (or *should* have been, anyway) becoming increasingly evident to anyone. Even her best analysts were still split over how and why it had happened, yet the consequences were clear enough for those who had eyes and were willing to use them. Unhappily, however, quite a few people *weren't* willing to do that, and too many of those people wielded political power in the Star Kingdom.

In her more charitable moments—which were becoming steadily fewer and farther between—she actually sympathized with those who failed to see the danger. *Haven* a threat to interstellar peace? Clearly the entire notion was ridiculous! Why, for almost three T-centuries, the Republic of Haven had been the bright, shining light, the example every system in and out of the Haven Quadrant wanted to emulate. A vibrant, participatory democracy, a steadily burgeoning economy serving the most rapidly expanding cluster of colonies in the galaxy, and a growing, energetic star nation whose future seemed to hold no limits. That was how *everyone*, including the Star Kingdom of Manticore, had seen it for ten or twelve generations.

And then, somehow, it had all gone wrong.

The critical moment, she thought, hugging Magnus' warm, comforting silkiness, had been the Havenite "Economic Bill of Rights" in 1680, with its declaration that all of the Republic's citizens had an "unalienable right" to a relative standard of living to be defined and adjusted as inflation required by statute by the Havenite legislature. It had sounded like such a good idea. Who could possibly argue with it? Yet there'd been a subtext to it, an agreement struck between corrupt politicians, self-serving bureaucrats, an entrenched civil service, and the professional political operatives who controlled the "Dolist" voting blocs. One that gave those politicians a permanent grip on power, patronage, and office—and on all the wealth, graft, and special privileges that came with them—in return for giving the new class of "Dolist managers" the power to distribute that legally defined standard of living. What should have been—what had been sold to the Republic as—an exercise in political fairness had become a license to steal and to corrupt as the sprawling machinery of governmental bureaucracy turned into a machine that churned out money and personal license for the powerful and the politically connected.

The insidious rot of that corrupt bargain had overwhelmed Haven's growing, energetic future and turned it into something ugly and dark and stagnant as an economic burden the Republic's economy might have been able to bear under other circumstances turned into a fiscal black hole. Effective oversight of spending had become a bad joke as civil service posts became lucrative licenses to swill at the public trough, handed out to cronies and sycophants by lifetime officeholders in return for kickbacks and favorable, mutually back-scratching interpretations of an ever swelling mountain of regulations and rules. More and more of the ever-swelling government's largess had been siphoned into fewer and fewer pockets through one bogus swindle after another even as that legally mandated standard of living required ever increasing expenditures, and deficit spending had become a way of life, gobbling up Haven's legendary productivity as the Republic plunged steadily deeper and deeper into debt.

Perhaps the slide could have been arrested, the rot could have been cleaned away, but that would have required an open commitment to reform, a willingness to admit it wasn't working. Unfortunately, those who'd come to depend on the existing system as the only game in town wouldn't have liked that very much, and no one could predict where that sort of reaction might lead. And worse even than that, admitting it wasn't working would inevitably have led to a public look into the *reasons* it wasn't, and too many powerful people and families had had far too much to lose to let anything like *that* happen.

Which meant they'd had to find another solution to their problem.

The galaxy at large knew very little about the top-secret meeting between the leaders of the Legislaturalists, the Republic's *de facto* hereditary political rulers, and the handful of most powerful Dolist managers at Nouveau Paris' Plaza Falls Hotel in 1791. Even Samantha knew far less about it than she wished she did, and it had taken years for Manticoran intelligence to piece together what she *did* know. There'd been a time when she'd wanted desperately to believe her gloomier analysts' fears had been paranoid fantasies, but everything which had happened since, especially in the last fifteen or twenty T-years, convinced her otherwise. In fact, she was coming to fear that even their gloomiest predictions had fallen short of the reality.

Twenty T-years ago, possibly as little as ten, she might have been able to convince herself that wasn't so. But the Havenite "Constitutional Convention" of 1795 had radically rewritten the Republic's Constitution, ostensibly to fix the government overreach which had produced the crumbling economy but actually to create the *People's* Republic. The new constitution had maintained the façade of democracy even while it limited eligibility requirements, office qualifications, and the franchise—officially in order to reduce voter fraud and restrict the political clout of special interest groups—so severely it had become literally impossible to elect a representative who wasn't a Legislaturalist. It had also just happened to abridge the old Republic's once robust guarantees of freedom of speech and assembly, although that clause had been very carefully worded. The actual language only authorized the government to punish "hate speech" and language which "attacked another's dignity on the basis of political, religious, or economic differences." Of course, the courts had taken a rather broader view of the government's authority in that regard than the letter of the constitution might have suggested, but it had really only been officially codifying what had gradually become the normal, accepted state of affairs over the previous T-century.

And then, with the new constitution safely in place to rescue the Republic from insolvency and ruin, the first budget passed under it had actually *increased* the deficits, raising them to a level which could only lead to outright collapse within the next fifty T-years. Everyone had believed that eventually the Legislatural-ists would be forced to bite the bullet, to reform their system before it fell apart under them, but the Legislaturalists had had another solution in mind, and the reason for those increased deficits had become clear as the Peoples Navy's tonnage began to increase steadily.

It hadn't happened overnight. In fact, they'd managed to hide their increased military spending well enough no one had even noticed for the first ten or fifteen T-years, and once people did start to notice, they'd managed to pass it off as a means to "prime the economic pump" through government funded "jobs production" and "skill training programs." Oh, there'd been "wild rumors" about huge numbers of Havenite battleships being secretly constructed, but no one had believed them.

Despite everything, Haven was still the golden image. Its economic and fiscal woes *had* to be only temporary, just until the Republic caught its breath and got its house back in order. It was impossible for it to work any other way, and despite any transitory fiscal dislocations, its laudable commitment to economic fairness remained the model everyone else wanted to emulate.

Several of the other star nations in the Haven Quadrant had done just that, following the Republic into statist economies and guaranteed standards of living. And to be fair, most of those other star nations' governments had avoided the death spiral of the People's Republic for the simple reason that they'd been rela-tively *honest* governments. They'd managed to provide their own equivalent of the Havenite Basic Living Stipend without completely destroying their economies' competitiveness and productivity, and they'd managed to pay for their social programs without plung-ing themselves ever further into debt, but they'd done it only by radically changing their spending goals and policies. Unable to pay for everything without destroying their own economies, they'd cut back even further on military spending, relying for protection against outside aggression on Haven, the traditional guarantor of interstellar peace and order in the Haven Quadrant. In fact, many of them had actually been *relieved* by the expansion of the Peoples Navy, since its ability to protect them provided such a hefty "peace dividend" for the rest of their national budgets.

Until 1846, that was.

Less than eighteen T-months after Roger's letter to the *Proceedings*, the rest of the Haven Quadrant—or as much of it as was willing to face reality, at least—had discovered the real reason for the People's Republic's military buildup.

In the last four T-years, the People's Republic had "annexed" no fewer than eleven independent star systems. Most of them had been Havenite daughter colonies, and the majority of them had "spontaneously sought" inclusion in the new, greater, *interstellar* People's Republic of Haven. The thing that amazed Samantha was that there were actually people—quite a lot of them, in fact—who accepted the "spontaneous" nature of those star systems' eagerness to join the PRH. Obviously even the analysts who'd worried about the Havenite military buildup had missed the Legislaturalists' accompanying investment in espionage and subversion, although they hadn't really needed all that much subtlety in many cases. A quiet ultimatum here, a private conversation between the Havenite ambassador and a system president there, an offhand reference to the heavy task forces waiting to sweep in and take control by force of arms if an invitation wasn't forthcoming in another case, had proved quite effective.

It wouldn't take very much longer for *all* of Haven's daughter colonies to be gathered to her bosom, Samantha Winton thought grimly, her mouth tightening despite Magnus' comforting, buzzing purr. And if there was anyone in the entire galaxy who believed the People's Republic would stop then, she had some magic beans she wanted to sell them.

"We're running out of time, Roger," she told her son quietly. Monroe stopped nibbling on his bacon and looked up, grass-green eyes dark, ears flattening as he, too, sensed Samantha's emotions. "Our Navy's bigger and stronger than anything else in the Quadrant, but it's not big enough to stand off the entire Havenite fleet, and I can't get those *idiots* in Parliament to realize it!"

"I know." Roger nodded, and it was a sign of his mother's

distress, he thought, that she should be telling *him,* of all people, that. "But that's why I have to stay where I am. I can't wrangle politics the way you can. I don't know how—yet—and I don't know where enough of the political bodies are buried. Worse, I'm only the Heir. Nobody in the House of Lords has to take me seriously yet any more than those fossilized jackasses in uniform do."

"Maybe not," Samantha said. "But however much all of us may think Sir Casper isn't the sharpest possible stylus in the box, he's a good man, and *he* does understand what we're up against. That's one of the reasons he's as worried as he is. And I think he does have a good point, as much as you're going to hate hearing this, about assignments that deploy you outside the home system."

Roger stiffened. He'd finally attained lieutenant commander's rank and command of his first hyper-capable ship. He was reasonably sure, despite his well-known attitude towards nepotism and "family interest," that who he'd been born helped explain why that first hyper-capable command had been a modern destroyer instead of one of the RMN's more elderly frigates, but he knew he'd done well in his two deployments to Silesia. Three pirates, one "privateer," and two slave ships would cause no more harm thanks to Captain Winton and HMS *Daimyo.*

"I said you weren't going to want to hear it," his mother continued, holding his eyes levelly across Magnus' prick-eared head, "but I'm afraid we don't have a choice. And part of the reason for that is the fact that you *don't* have an heir of your own, aside from Caitrin, of course. And since *she* hasn't married anyone yet, either," the Queen gave her daughter an only half-humorous glare, "Sir Casper's quite right to be worried about what might happen to the succession if you...suffered a mischief in Silesia."

Roger looked rebellious, and Monroe's tail twitched, his ears flat, as he tasted his person's emotions. But the crown prince kept his mouth firmly closed, and Samantha smiled at him, hoping he saw her gratitude.

"You're right, Mom," he said finally. "I don't like it one bit, but I don't suppose there's much point my arguing about it, is there?"

"No, there isn't," Samantha said. "I'm sorry, but it's one of those unpleasant consequences of the nice house and all the people so eager to take care of us." She smiled just a bit crookedly. "And I'm not asking you to resign your commission, or even to go onto half-pay. We just need to find something—something worthwhile, not just make work—you can do here in the home system. And I'm afraid that while you're doing it, Sir Casper's going to insist on your being a bit more hands-on in the political arena, as well."

"Wonderful," Roger muttered, his tone dark, although it seemed to his mother that his heart wasn't fully in it.

"I know you don't want me speaking directly about this to Abner Laidlaw or Sir Frederick," she went on, "but there's no point pretending this is really a 'routine' personnel decision."

"No, I suppose there isn't," he agreed, trying not to shudder at the thought of his mother talking to Sir Frederick Truman, the Star Kingdom of Manticore's First Space Lord. The uniformed head of the Royal Manticoran Navy was one of the "fossils" he'd mentioned earlier. Well into his seventies and facing mandatory retirement within the next four T-years, Truman wasn't fond of people who rocked the boat and threatened his own orderly plans for the expansion of the Navy's mission in Silesia. He'd be simply delighted to suggest—with infinite respect, of course—that perhaps the simplest solution would be for Crown Prince Roger to leave active duty entirely.

Sir Abner Laidlaw, the Baron of Castle Rock, on the other hand, was the First Lord of Admiralty which, given the Navy's primacy, made him the civilian cabinet officer responsible for the Star Kingdom's overall military posture. He was two T-decades younger than Truman, and he'd been Queen Samantha's choice for his present position for several reasons. She'd had to fight hard against entrenched opposition in the House of Lords, where an unlikely alliance of the Conservative Association and the Liberal Party had viewed him with dark suspicion. His earlier career as an intelligence officer, rising at last to head the Special Intelligence Service, would have been enough to make the Liberals distrust him. The fact that as a junior analyst he'd been one of the first to point out the shift in Havenite military spending only confirmed that distrust, and somehow people like Second Space Lord Havinghurst—who, as a far from junior analyst at ONI, had brushed off his "inconclusive and alarmist" analyses—weren't all that fond of him either. Nor did the Conservative Association, whose members' spinal reflex opposition to anything that threatened the stability of their own star nation—and their position within it—take kindly to the suggestion that it might be wise to start mucking about with that stability in the name of defensive preparedness. Besides, ships cost money. The Conservatives were against spending money on general principles, and the Liberals had all sorts of deserving social programs in direct competition with any increased military spending. The fact that quite a few of those deserving social programs had been inspired by progressive Havenite notions before the Republic's fiscal wheels started coming off only made them even more mulishly opposed to building up the Navy in the face of a purported *Havenite* threat.

Can't very well go around admitting their inspiration is in the process of turning Conquistador on them, can they? Roger thought with an edge of bitterness. *Why, that would require them to engage in at least twenty or thirty seconds of actual critical thought! God only knows where that might end!*

He knew he was being at least a little unfair, but he didn't really care. Most members of the Conservative Association were a selfish, small-minded waste of perfectly good oxygen, as far as he was concerned. He had much more sympathy for the rank-and-file members of the Liberal Party, but their refusal to look beyond their own narrow political horizons was eroding that steadily. Marisa Turner, the Earl of New Kiev's older daughter, was a case in point. The only thing wrong with her brain, in Roger's opinion, was her refusal to actually *use* it, yet her birth, her wealth, and her father's position in the party meant she was inevitably going to become one of the Liberals' leaders over the next ten or fifteen T-years, and she flatly refused to admit Haven could possibly have any territorial interests outside its immediate astrographic neighborhood. Which was, after all the better part of three *light-centuries* from the Manticore Binary System!

"It's going to be a little tricky, however we come at it," he told his mother. "Truman would love to see me dirt-side and out of uniform. If you bring it up with him, he'll jump at the opportunity to accomplish just that, and if we fight him on it, we'll be just as guilty of using patronage to get what we want as someone like Janacek or Low Delhi. But if Laidlaw makes the suggestion, it'll automatically put Truman's back up as yet another example of 'civilian interference' in the Service's internal affairs. He might go as far as making his opposition to that interference part of the public record. And even if he didn't do that, I wouldn't be surprised if he—or Havinghurst—leaked the fact that he and Spruance had been pressured by Laidlaw. At which point, the idiots in the Conservative Association and the Liberals who already don't like Sir Abner will start demanding all sorts of Parliamentary inquiries into it."

"Like everyone *else* isn't using family pull to get what they want?" Caitrin demanded, and Roger shrugged.

"I'm not in Mom's league as a politician yet, Katie, but since when has consistency dared to rear its ugly head where partisan politics are concerned? They don't care what *their* friends and families may be doing, but they'll scream to high heaven about Laidlaw's seeming to do it in *my* case if it lets them embarrass him."

"Roger's right, Caitrin," Samantha said, looking approvingly upon her son. "And don't overlook the possibility of embarrassing *me*, at least indirectly, as well. They won't come right out and say it, but anything they can use as an obstacle for those 'alarmist' policies I'm trying to 'ram through' without due respect for their own august views would be like manna from heaven."

"There's a reason I really, really don't want to have anything more to do with politics than I have to," Caitrin said sourly.

"Not an option, in our case, I'm afraid, Sis."

Roger's eyes were sympathetic, but his voice was firm before he turned back to their mother.

"Actually, I think the best way to do this might be to approach Sir William very quietly," he said.

Samantha cocked her head, eyebrows rising inquisitively, and he shrugged.

"I'm not saying Sir William isn't half convinced that I'm at least a third as much of an alarmist as Truman thinks I am, but he's also at least a little more receptive. And the truth is, it would make a lot of sense for him to come to the same view Sir Casper's come to. I think if he was properly approached he might be willing to claim ownership of the idea and play godfather for it."

"Really?" Samantha sounded just a bit skeptical, and Roger smiled.

Rear Admiral of the Green Sir William Spruance was Fifth Space Lord, the head of the Bureau of Personnel. As such, he'd have to sign off on any reassignment, especially one which cut short a programmed tour of command for someone as . . . visible as a member of the Winton dynasty, no matter where the idea for it had come from. And if *he* proposed the change, it would be impossible for Truman—or anyone else—to blame it on Laidlaw.

"I have reason to believe he's at least a bit more sympathetic to my wild-eyed lunacy than Sir Frederick," Roger said. "Captain Wyeth's his chief of staff these days. He's been, ah, priming the pump a bit for me, I think. And if I very quietly suggested to Pablo that it might be a good idea to have the heir to the throne closer to hand, and if *he* suggested it to Sir William, and if Sir William suggested it to Truman, well—"

He shrugged, and his mother nodded. Slowly at first, then with increasing approval.

"I see your father was right when he said you'd learn plenty about politics and infighting with the Fleet." She stopped nodding and smiled a bit bittersweetly, remembering her husband. Then she shook herself and her eyes narrowed as she contemplated her son. "On the other hand, why do I have the feeling you're planning to hit more than one bird with that particular rock?"

"Because you know me so well." His own smile was fleeting, but it was also much closer to a grin. "If I have to give up *Daimyo*, then I know what I want instead, and I think we can probably convince Sir William to give it to me."

"And that would be what, precisely?"

"Well, I don't want a dirt-side command, that's for sure. And I'm sorry, Mom, but I'd cut my throat if they tried to stick me in BuPlan."

His shudder was only partly feigned. Vice Admiral Bethany Havinghurst, as head of the Bureau of Planning, also headed ONI, which meant she was responsible for the intelligence analyses Admiral Truman used to justify his emphasis on Silesia, instead of worrying about "the remote possibility" that the People's Republic might someday become a threat to the Star Kingdom. The possibility of becoming a staff weenie shuffling papers somewhere in the bowels of BuPlan—and with an idiot like Edward Janacek as his direct superior—held no appeal at all.

"That's what you *don't* want," his mother observed. "What is it you *do* want, dear?"

"BuWeaps," he said, and his voice was suddenly very, very serious. "Lomax isn't who I'd have chosen to head BuWeaps, Mom, but she's at least a little more open-minded than Truman or Havinghurst. I think she's too conservative in her approach, under the circumstances, but she's not part of the 'old boy and girl network' the way Truman and Low Delhi are. I'd like to get more hands-on experience with our R and D programs, and BuWeaps is small enough—way *too* small, in fact, given what's going on—that a lieutenant commander would be at least a moderately middle-sized fish. I think I could actually do some good over there."

"More than at BuShips?" Samantha asked shrewdly.

"*Lots* more than at BuShips." Roger grimaced. "Low Delhi's an idiot. Or his policy recommendations are idiotic, at any rate."

That wasn't something he could have said to a fellow Navy officer, of course, nor was it anything he'd *ever* say in public, but that didn't make it untrue. Third Space Lord Robert Hemphill, the Baron of Low Delhi, headed the Bureau of Ships, responsible for the construction and maintenance of the Navy's space stations and vessels, and he did not respond well to criticism, however constructive.

"In fairness, I don't suppose he's any more of an idiot than a few other senior officers I could name," he continued. "The problem is he's got too much invested on a personal and a professional level in the building policies Truman's been driving for the last several T-years. He's not going to recommend any radical changes, and BuShips is too damned big. I'd disappear into it and never be seen again—professionally speaking, that is—until *my* coronation!"

"And you really think you could have some influence with Lomax?"

"I think it's at least possible," Roger replied. "Like I say, Dame Carrie's a little too conservative for my tastes, but I understand why she is. In fact, in some ways I have to agree with her."

"Excuse me?" His mother sat back in her chair, and Magnus bleeked a laugh as he tasted her emotions. "You actually *agree* with one of the space lords?"

"I *did* say 'in some ways,'" he pointed out with a smile. "And the truth is, Mom, none of them are malevolent, ill-intentioned manipulators. I'll admit I don't much *like* Truman, and I think Havinghurst is too much of a brown-noser where he's concerned, but he's absolutely sincere in what he believes the Navy's requirements are. Low Delhi's more concerned about keeping his skirts clean than I'd like—or than someone who's attained his superiority *needs* to be, for that matter. I mean, my God, the man's *Third Space Lord!* It's not like his career's going to turn into a dismal failure if he should slip up and do something innovative for a change. But despite that, I think his positions are sincere and I don't doubt that he'd put patriotism above career if he were genuinely convinced the situation required it. The problem is that he doesn't think there's anything *wrong* with the situation, and nobody's going to be able to change his mind about it, as far as I can see.

"As for Countess Mailey, she's doing an excellent job at BuMed. I don't think anyone could complain about her. Earl Three Pines is too much in lockstep with Truman over at the BuTrain, but that's inevitable. The First Space Lord has the overriding voice when it comes to formulating operational and strategic doctrine, and that's the way it ought to be, however . . . inconvenient I personally may find it at the moment. And I actually *like* Sir William."

"Well, that's nice to hear," Samantha said dryly. "But what's this business about agreeing with Lomax?"

"Mom," Roger's voice turned suddenly very serious, "you know how much I've been thinking about this ever since the intelligence types started warning us about Haven. And the truth is that just like I said in that first letter to the *Proceedings*, we can't go toe-to-toe with the kind of navy Nouveau Paris can build if it really puts its mind to it. We're a hell of a lot richer on a per-capita basis than almost anyone else in the galaxy, but we just not *big* enough, and unless we want to start conquering people ourselves, there's no way we're going to *get* big enough in the time I'm afraid we've got."

His mouth twisted as if he'd bitten into something sour.

"We've got what's probably the biggest, most efficient single-system shipbuilding infrastructure in known space, but it's over-whelmingly oriented around building civilian ships for private owners. *Hephaestus* and *Vulcan* can churn out freighters like nobody's business, but we don't have the scale of *military* building capacity Haven's already built up, and all of your reports suggest they're still increasing that capacity when we haven't even *started* increasing ours yet. And even if that weren't true, they're getting bigger with every system they gobble up. Even with the BLS' drain on their economy, they'll probably be able to lay down at least twice as many ships as we'll be able to, especially when we're stuck with peacetime budgetary constraints and they're already operating on a wartime footing."

Samantha's expression had darkened with every word her son said. Not because she disagreed with him, but because she *couldn't* disagree with him.

"I absolutely agree with what you and Sir Abner are trying to do," he continued. "We've *got* to build up our wall of battle, but even if Parliament was willing to give you the budgets you're asking for, we still couldn't match the Peoples' Navy's numbers. That means we've got to have *qualitative* superiority, and enough of it to offset their *numerical* superiority. I realize that's why Sir Abner's pushing for superdreadnoughts, although I don't think he's going to get them yet. Not with Truman still arguing about the need for increasing numbers of medium-weight platforms for Silesia and commerce protection and the Conservatives and Liberals denying Haven poses any sort of credible threat. So as far as I can see, we've got to find a way besides sheer tonnage to give us that qualitative edge, which is why I say Dame Carrie's more conservative than I'd really like. I think we need to be pushing the envelope, working to find some kind of technological equalizer, and she's not really in favor of blue-sky concepts.

"But I understand *why* she isn't, and it's hard to blame her. The *Proceedings* did an interview with her a few months back, talking about the *Samothrace*'s weapons suite, and she said something very interesting. 'A ship-of-the-wall is too important, too big a financial investment and too big a piece of our Navy's combat potential, to be an experiment.'" He looked at his mother across the table. "She's not about to go haring off after some elusive, technological silver bullet. Some sort of...of *panacea*, I suppose. Not unless and until she's convinced it's going to be a significant improvement on what she's already got, at any rate. With the Star Kingdom's military security at risk, it's her *job* to avoid buying into a fleet mix that turns out not to work, and she takes that seriously. But she's also still wedded to the notion that one lonely little star system can't possibly be capable of pushing R and D farther and faster than something like the Solarian League. That's why she's continuing the policy—the *long-standing* policy, to be fair; she's not the one who originated it—of emulating the SLN instead of pushing the envelope right here at home."

"And you seriously think we *could* push 'farther and faster' than the League?" Samantha asked.

"I think we damned well better find out whether or not we can, Mom," Roger said grimly. "I think we need to increase BuWeaps' R and D funding. I think we need to find the best talent we can to look at every conceivable way we can improve our war-fighting capability. I think we need to keep it as 'black' as possible while we do it. And I think that if we *can't* come up with some kind of 'equalizer,' then in the end, we're screwed, no matter what happens."

✦ ✦ ✦ ✦ ✦

September 1850 PD

"I'M SURE YOU CAN UNDERSTAND why I might have a few . . . reservations about this particular routine personnel transfer, Commander," Dame Carrie Lomax said dryly. Lomax was in her early sixties, her red hair going steadily gray, and her blue eyes were shrewd as she contemplated the newest addition to her command. "I can understand why it might have seemed like a good idea to Earl Mortenson and even to Admiral Spruance. I'm not too sure it's going to be a good idea from *my* perspective, however."

"I beg your pardon, Ma'am?" Roger Winton said respectfully, standing in front of her desk with Monroe on his shoulder.

"Just between the two of us, it's going to be difficult for most of my people to forget who your mother is, Commander Winton." Lomax leaned back in her chair. "Speaking for myself, I find your insistence on being treated like any other Queen's officer laudable, but I doubt there's much point pretending that everyone around you is *really* going to think you're just one more lieutenant commander. And that leads me to all of the waves I can't help thinking you're likely to send scudding across my own personal hot tub here at BuWeaps."

"It's not my intention to make waves, Ma'am. In fact—"

"Please." She raised one hand, interrupting him. "I didn't fall off the produce shuttle yesterday, Commander. And that wasn't intended as a criticism, really. But I *have* read your letters in the *Proceedings*, as well as reviewing your file, and your performance reports, and the systems critiques and analyses in your end-of-commission reports. With all of that rattling around in the back of my mind, I can't *quite* convince myself that Sir William just decided out of a clear blue sky that BuWeaps was the ideal place to

34

put you. And that suggests to my naturally suspicious personality that someone else might have suggested to him. Which, Commander"—she eyed him very levelly—"brings me back to *you*."

Roger Winton didn't need the tip of the treecat's tail brushing very gently against his lower back or the true-hand resting lightly on the top of his head for balance to realize he'd underestimated Admiral Lomax rather badly. He thought hard for a moment, then shrugged.

"I suppose there's some fairness in your point, Ma'am." He smiled briefly. "I didn't call in any favors to get what I wanted, but I did ... suggest BuWeaps to Sir William after the Prime Minister pointed out to my mother that the Star Kingdom can't really have me gadding about the Confederacy any longer. And I'll admit I had a bit of an ulterior motive."

"Wonderful," Lomax sighed. "Another one."

"I beg your pardon, Ma'am?" Roger said a second time, but she only shook her head and punched a combination into her desktop com.

"Yes, Admiral?" a baritone voice with an obviously foreign accent said from the com.

"Come in here, Jonas. I've got someone you need to meet."

"Yes, Ma'am."

Lomax sat back once more, regarding Roger with a somewhat odd expression. A few moments later, her office door slid open and a tallish, dark-haired, gray-eyed commander—obviously at least a few years older than Roger, without prolong—stepped through it. He glanced at Roger without apparent recognition, then came briefly to attention before Lomax's desk.

"Yes, Ma'am?"

"Commander Winton, I'd like you to meet Commander Adcock," Lomax said a bit dryly. "I think you're going to be working for him. Jonas, Commander Winton. I'm sure you're likely to recognize him from the HD and the 'faxes, but we're not supposed to know who he is. Or, since we actually have working brains, we're supposed to *pretend* we don't know who he is."

Her expression was humorous, but something in her blue eyes made it plain she was serious, and Adcock nodded. Then he turned to Roger and extended his right hand.

"Welcome aboard ... Commander Winton," he said.

✦   ✦   ✦

"Have a seat," Adcock invited, waving at the two bare-bones chairs sitting in front of his equally bare-bones desk in his small cubicle of an office.

Roger inspected the chairs for a moment, carefully removed the box stuffed with chip folios from the less cluttered one, and settled into it. Monroe hopped down from his shoulder and started rummaging curiously through another box—this one full of discarded folios—and Adcock smiled.

"First time I've actually met a treecat," he admitted. "He's bigger than I expected."

"Monroe's one of the larger 'cats I've ever met myself, Sir," Roger replied. "I hope there's nothing critically important in that box, but he won't damage them. He just likes to play with them. He's got half a dozen sets of building blocks at home, too."

"I see." Adcock studied him for a moment, then sighed. "I see you're serious about military formality, too. I appreciate that, but I have to tell you I'm not entirely comfortable with your calling *me* 'Sir.' I know that's been the tradition with your family for a long time, and I can appreciate it, but I didn't grow up on Manticore. I'm finding it's a bit difficult for me to pretend you aren't a prince."

"It's a problem sometimes," Roger acknowledged. "But the Navy's a military hierarchy, Sir." He emphasized the rank title very slightly. "That's the seniority that has to be observed, at least on the Navy's clock."

"I see," Adcock repeated, sitting back in his own chair. "Then I'll just have to learn to live with it." He smiled. It was a fleeting expression, but the twinkle in his eye seemed genuine to Roger. "I'm sure it won't be any harder than some of the other things I've had to adapt to over the years."

"I hope not, Sir. I don't want it to be a problem for anyone, but my family's found it's best to get started on the right foot. If we don't, then as sure as God made little green apples, we're going to find an ass-kisser screwing everything up at some point."

Adcock's lips twitched and he shook his head.

"I don't think you'll have that particular problem in our shop, Commander. Since at the moment, 'our shop' consists of you, me, a young fellow named Sebastian D'Orville, and half a dozen enlisted personnel."

Roger felt his lips tighten, and Monroe's head came up, looking in his person's direction. Adcock glanced at the treecat, then looked back at Roger with a shrewd expression.

"I'm guessing from your friend's reaction that you were less than delighted to hear that, Commander. And I don't really blame you. It does sound like one of those makework little offices that get attached like pre-space barnacles to every military organization. We're not going to get much done with that short a personnel list, are we?"

"Well, since you ask, Sir, I'd have to say that, no, it doesn't sound like we are," Roger replied slowly. "On the other hand, I don't think you *would* have asked if the answer was quite that simple."

"Indeed not," Adcock agreed. "You see, Commander Winton, I've been banished. I made a few too many noises about possible improvements in our hardware that no one wanted to hear—especially over at BuShips. I was coming along quite nicely as a yard dog before that happened; but then, somehow, I wasn't getting the duty slots that would have moved me up within BuShips. And then I was 'counseled' by a representative from BuPers who suggested someone with my talents and mindset might be more comfortable over at BuWeaps. That was when Admiral Hewitt was Fourth Space Lord."

He regarded Roger expressionlessly, and Roger stifled a wince. Adenauer Hewitt had been of the opinion that fire was still too radical an invention to be fully trusted. For all of Roger's own disagreements with Sir Frederick Truman, he had to admit Truman's decision to retire Hewitt had been a long overdue breath of fresh air at BuWeaps. Admittedly, he hadn't thought Lomax was all that much of an improvement, but he was coming to the conclusion that there were several minor points he was going to have to reconsider carefully.

"Now, there are a few things *I* can tell you that Dame Carrie can't," Adcock continued, and his eyes were very intent. "On the other hand, and bearing in mind that title I'm not supposed to be calling you by, there's a certain degree of . . . let's not call it 'risk,' but that's possibly a step in the right direction, in doing that. I don't think she would have handed you over to me if she didn't want me to brief you in fully, though."

He paused, and Roger wondered if he was supposed to say something. Since he couldn't think of anything especially brilliant, he kept his mouth shut, and Adcock snorted in what could have been amusement.

"Admiralty politics are as nasty as any politics in the known universe," he said after a moment. "There are a lot of powerful egos involved; nobody gets to be a space lord without paying his or her dues, regardless of family connections, and they expect people to do things *their* way; and the stakes are whether or not we're going to have an effective Navy, so people are disinclined to pull their punches. And I've been following your correspondence in the *Proceedings*. I imagine you're as well aware as I am of just how . . . irritating your comments have been in certain senior quarters?"

"Something of the sort *has* been intimated to me," Roger acknowledged. "Politely, of course, bearing in mind that title you're not supposed to be calling me by."

"I'm afraid they were a little less polite to me," Adcock said cheerfully. "And Dame Carrie's too good at playing the game to tilt at any windmills. Sir Frederick made it abundantly clear what his spending priorities are—both in terms of platform procurement and in terms of R and D—when he helped kill the rest of the *Samothrace* program. Given his seniority and his current position, locking horns with him would be . . . counterproductive. At best, it'd end up wasting a lot of energy, burning a lot of political capital, and not accomplishing a hell of a lot. Understand me, that's not because Sir Frederick has any ulterior motives; it's just that he knows what he knows that he knows, and as the man responsible for calling the shots, he's going to do it the way his own best judgment says he should. And God knows he was absolutely right about how many eighty thousand-ton cruisers we can build for every seven *million*-ton superdreadnought we *don't* build. I may not fully agree with the decisions he makes, and I have to say that I'd just as soon not have my kneecaps broken by someone as good at political infighting as he is, but I understand why he feels the way he does and I can follow his logic, even if I think it's flawed.

"So can Dame Carrie, and she's not about to wreck her personal working relationship with him and create the kind of general disruption that fighting with him about R and D direction in public would produce. Especially not"—he shot Roger a very level look—"when Sir Frederick's going to be retiring within the next three T-years. No one knows who'll be tapped to replace him as First Space Lord at this point, but with Baron Castle Rock as First Lord, it seems likely that whoever it is will be more supportive of the baron's policies. Which I presume must bear at least some faint resemblance to your *mother's* policies, given how firmly she's supported him."

"I think that would be a not unreasonable assumption, Sir," Roger said, picking his words slowly and carefully, and Adcock smiled crookedly.

"Well, what Dame Carrie's done is to create what she's rather grandiloquently dubbed the 'Concept Development Office.' Um, that's *us*, Commander. You, me, Lieutenant D'Orville, and a batch of remarkably senior and closemouthed ratings and petty officers from the various technical branches. We don't appear under that particular title on any of the BuWeaps organizational charts, and we don't have an actual R and D budget, and no one's letting us play with any hardware at the moment. But we *do* have direct access to Dame Carrie and quite a remarkable reach in terms of the information available to us. We're not being allowed to do any development, but we're doing one hell of a lot of *research*."

"What sort of research, Sir?"

"We're going through every technical report ONI's generated in the last twenty T-years, Commander," Adcock said flatly. "And we're going through every report any of our reservists serving in the merchant fleet might happen to file between voyages. We're also auditing every current R and D project BuWeaps is being allowed to pursue and looking back at all the ones BuWeaps *wasn't* allowed to pursue, and we have subscriptions to all of the Manticoran—and Beowulfan—*civilian* technical journals, as well as the SLN's *Naval Quarterly*. And the reason we're doing that, Commander Winton, is because it's our job to look at *everything*, whatever the source, and assume *nothing* about practicality or feasibility until we've put it under a microscope and looked at it molecule by molecule. For example, this"—he tapped the reader on his desk—"is Aberu and Harmon's internal report on that 'laser head' they tested back in '33. The Sollies turned it down, and I can see why, based on the tests. But we're not going to simply take their word for how useless it was, because that's our job: to come up with blue-sky ideas, concepts, possibilities—and they can be pretty screwy ones, I'll grant you—for brand-new research projects. *Off the books* ideas and concepts that Dame Carrie doesn't have to fight with Admiral Truman or Admiral Low Delhi about because none of them are official. I expect most of them to turn out to be just as impractical and unworkable as Admiral Truman would expect, but it's just possible we might turn up a few worthwhile nuggets, while we're at it. And I wouldn't be so very surprised, actually, knowing Dame Carrie as well as I've come to know her, if she didn't see your assignment to our little workshop as a way to generate friends in high places—possibly even *very* high places—when the time comes to dust off some of those more preposterous ideas and see what happens."

He fell silent, swinging his chair gently through a back-and-forth arc while he allowed Roger to digest what he'd just said. Then he smiled again more crookedly than ever.

"So, tell me, Commander—does that sound like something you might be interested in?"

June 1852 PD

"JONAS, HAVE YOU SEEN this article on fusion bottle density?" Roger Winton was looking down at the reader's display, scrolling for the specific reference he wanted to discuss as he followed a scampering Monroe into Jonas Adcock's familiar office. "It says here that Grendel University's getting some unexpected results, and I'm wondering if that ties into what Grierson's been doing on Raiden. If it *does*, then—"

He looked up from the display as he navigated the doorway itself, and whatever he'd been about to say chopped off in midsentence as he saw Adcock's guest. Monroe skidded to a halt, as well, his ears pointing straight up and his tail kinking in an exclamation point behind him, and Adcock turned from his visitor with an undeniably wicked smile.

"Oh, hi, Rog!" he said in a sunny tone. "I'd like to introduce you to someone. This is my baby sister, Angelique. Angelique, my friend Roger."

Angelique Adcock had to be one of the most attractive women Roger Winton had ever seen, and the crown prince saw *many* attractive women. She wasn't classically beautiful, no, but "classically beautiful" women (and men) were a dime a dozen in the Star Kingdom, where personal affluence made biosculpt and genetic beauty mods readily obtainable. And she didn't need classic beauty, he thought. He'd actually seen imagery of her before, although Jonas might or might not be aware of that, yet that imagery hadn't done her justice. In person, face-to-face, she had a unique, fresh, gray-eyed attractiveness which was wholly her own, and an oval face which had clearly been designed for the laughter and zest which lurked in those gray eyes. Her natural skin tone was far lighter than Roger's, but she had the deeply tanned, bronzed complexion of someone who clearly spent a lot of time outdoors. Her kinship to her brother was obvious, but Jonas' strong features had been softened in her, and she turned with a quick, friendly smile of her own, automatically holding out her hand, as her brother introduced her.

"Hi," she said. "Pleased to meet—"

Her voice died in a peculiar sort of half-squeak, her mouth froze half-open, her eyes flew wide, and Jonas chuckled in obvious delight.

"Hello," Roger said, reaching out to grasp the hand which had stopped halfway to him. The imp of the perverse touched him abruptly, and he bent over the hand, brushing its back with his lips before he straightened. "Your brother has a peculiar sense of humor, Ms. Adcock."

She stared at him for several more heartbeats, and then seemed to come back to life again. She shook herself, smiled more than a little crookedly at Roger, and turned her head to glare at Jonas.

"No," she said tartly. "He *thinks* he has a sense of humor... Your Highness."

She looked back at Roger as she addressed him by his title, and he shook his head, still holding her hand.

"This isn't a social occasion, Ms. Adcock," he told her with a smile of his own. "I'm perfectly well aware Jonas deliberately threw me at you cold, but I really don't use any of that long, dreary list of titles when I'm on duty. Or with friends. Which, somehow, despite your entirely accurate observation on the state of his sense of humor, Jonas has become. For now, at least." He turned his gaze on Adcock. "You do realize, don't you, that any Machiavellian monarch worth his salt has hordes of sinister retainers lurking in the shadows at his beck and call to visit retribution on those who irritate him? Retainers who could make you disappear just like *that*!"

He snapped the fingers of his free hand sharply, and a soft little chuckle spurted out of Angelique Adcock.

"True. Too true, I'm sure," Jonas replied. He'd long since gotten over any uncertainty about addressing his future monarch on such familiar terms. "Fortunately, you're not King, only crown prince, and your mother doesn't like to have people disappeared." His expression darkened suddenly, and his lips tightened. "Unlike some," he finished in a far harsher voice, and Roger felt the slender fingers still clasped in his tighten, as well.

"Sorry, Jonas," he said quietly. He gave those fingers a small squeeze, without really noticing what he was doing, before he released them. "Probably not the best time to be making jokes about people disappearing after all, I guess."

"Actually," Adcock inhaled deeply, "there's no reason you shouldn't." He glanced at his sister, then back at Roger. "As Dad always said, shit happens. Sometimes it even happens for a reason. And whatever else, Angel and I aren't Maslowans any-more. Haven't been for thirty-five T-years now, and glad of it."

Roger nodded, but he was watching Angelique from the corner of his eye as he did, and he saw how carefully she was watching her brother, in turn.

Roger had learned a lot about Jonas Adcock over the last two T-years. He'd learned that Adcock had to be one of the most brilliant men he'd ever met, although it was a peculiar form of brilliance. Adcock would have been hopelessly miscast in the role of a research scientist, but he had a phenomenal gift for synthe-sis. For looking at other people's work, often in totally different fields, and seeing connections, possibilities, which would never have occurred to the people doing the actual research. He was a generalist, not a specialist, yet he was capable of talking to—and understanding—specialists in wildly diverse areas, and young Sebastian D'Orville had told Roger on more than one occasion, only half jokingly, that Adcock's middle name should have been "Serendipity," not Sebastian. It wasn't simply that he could *talk* to those different specialists; it was that he could get them to *listen* to him and start listening to each *other*, as well.

That ability of his was even more remarkable given his family background. For all his friendliness and approachability, Adcock was also a very private person, and it had taken a while for him to feel comfortable enough with Roger to discuss that background. On the other hand, much as Roger frequently detested it, Palace Security and the Queen's Own weren't about to let someone get as close to the heir to the throne as Adcock had without doing a complete—*very* complete—background check on him, and Roger had been briefed on what they'd discovered.

He hated that sort of intrusion into other people's privacy just because they'd come into proximity with him, and he generally refused to listen to anything more than very general information about them. He hadn't had a choice about hearing rather more than that in this case, however, because what Palace Security had discovered had triggered enough internal alarm bells for them to approach Queen Samantha with an urgent recommendation that Roger be removed from Adcock's vicinity.

Samantha, aware of how much Roger had discovered he liked Adcock, had refused to take their advice without discussing the situation with Roger, first, and that was how Roger had come to know that Jonas Adcock's family was from the Maslow System, deep in the Haven Quadrant. In fact, Maslow had been a staunch ally of the Republic of Haven for over three hundred T-years, and in light of Haven's current expansionism, the mere notion of the heir associating with a Maslowan expatriate had produced instant paranoia within the bowels of Palace Security.

A paranoia, Roger had pointed out acidly after sitting through an excruciatingly total dissection of a friend's life, which was as stupid as it was irrational.

Jonas' father Sebastian had been a prominent Maslowan engineer, a highly successful specialist in deep space infrastructure design and development. Normally, that would have been considered a good thing, but Maslow had followed its treaty partner, friend, and mentor into exactly the same sort of economic system Haven had developed. Unfortunately, Maslow's economy had never been as large and robust as Haven's, and despite its later start, it had started drifting towards the reefs of insolvency quickly. Nor had it helped that professionals like Sebastian Adcock had been given the chance to see the writing on the Havenite wall. In particular, they'd seen the Republic's Technical Conservation Act of 1778, which had classified an entire series of professions and skill sets as "national assets" and made any attempt to emigrate by someone who possessed them an act of treason. The TCA had been Haven's answer to its economy's steady hemorrhaging of people with marketable skills as that economy crunched into decline, and more than one Maslowan professional had feared their own government would follow suit, probably sooner, rather than later.

Sebastian's first wife, Angelique, had died shortly after giving birth to her daughter, but his second wife, Annette, had told him flatly that it was time for him to go. Time for him to find a star nation which still valued and rewarded individualism, hard work, and ability. Unfortunately, they'd waited just too long, and Maslow had, indeed, passed its own Technical Conservation Act in 1815. Sebastian Adcock had become a "national resource" who had no right to use his skills and abilities except as directed by his government.

Not even Palace Security or the SIS had been able to determine exactly how the Adcocks managed it, but two years later, in 1817, Sebastian, Annette, and their four children—Jonas, Angelique, Jeptha, and Aidan—had reached Manticore. How they'd gotten out of Maslow was a mystery, and one they'd refused to discuss with anyone, which led Roger to suspect there were people still on Maslow who'd helped them. But what was clear was that they'd left everything they owned behind, arriving in the Star Kingdom literally with nothing more than the clothing on their backs.

Jonas had been nineteen, the son of penniless immigrants with no family or friends to help them get their feet under them. Despite which, after a two-year intensive personal study program, he'd won admission to Saganami Island in 1819 and graduated four years later, eighth in his class. His father had found work, at first, as little more than a common laborer on *Hephaestus*, the planet Manticore's primary orbital industrial platform. By the time of his death, thirty years later, Senior Station Operations Manager Adcock had *run* the space station, and no nativeborn Manticoran could possibly have matched the Adcock family's passionate devotion to the Star Kingdom.

Roger had made that point to the security briefers. He'd made it at some length, in a tone which he'd later realized sounded remarkably like his mother's upon certain particularly frustrating occasions. He'd pointed out the Adcock family's contributions to the Star Kingdom. He'd pointed out that Jonas had passed every security check the Navy had ever thrown at him with flying colors. He'd suggested that when the analysts concerned over Jonas Adcock's patriotism and loyalty had demonstrated their own patriotism and loyalty one half as clearly he might be more inclined to listen to them. And he'd finished by pointing out that treecats' ability to identify anyone who harbored ill will towards their human partners was proverbial... and that Monroe *liked* Jonas immensely.

And that, as his mother had observed rather dryly into the ringing silence which followed his explanation, had been that.

Still, Jonas *had* been nineteen when his family left Maslow behind forever. However passionately loyal he might be to his new homeland, that was where he'd been born, where the childhood friends he'd left behind still lived. And that was why his usual sense of humor had become more than a little strained when the People's Navy occupied the Maslow System and it, too, was "voluntarily associated" into the People's Republic of Haven.

Not, unfortunately, without a certain degree of bloodshed among Maslowans who didn't want to become Havenites. That much had leaked out before the news blackout slammed down completely. No open reports were getting out at this point, but Manticoran intelligence still had some assets on the planet, and Roger suspected that he knew more about just how ugly the situation on Jonas' original homeworld actually was at the moment than Jonas himself did.

"Now," Jonas went on a bit more briskly, putting the moment firmly behind him, "I've been following some of that research at Grendel U for a month or so now, Rog, and if you're here to talk about what I think you're here to talk about, I'm definitely interested. I think we may need to get Chief Thompson in to discuss it with us, as well, since it's going to fall into her bailiwick, unless I'm mistaken. But before we do that, Angel happened to be in town and decided to drop by to drag her ancient and decrepit brother off to lunch. Under the circumstances, I'd like to invite you to accompany us . . . *if* you'll leave that reader right here on my desk and *promise* not to say a single word about it until we get back. Deal?"

Roger started to refuse politely. He knew Angelique lived on Gryphon, the single habitable planet of Manticore-B, where she was one of the planet's leading silviculturalists. She didn't get to Manticore all that often, and he had no business intruding into a family lunch. But then he glanced at Angelique and noticed her quick, fleeting smile at Jonas' stern tone.

It was a very attractive smile, he thought, bending over to scoop up Monroe and lift him to his shoulder perch.

"Deal . . . Sir," he said with a smile of his own, and dropped the reader on Jonas' desk.

✦ ✦ ✦ ✦ ✦

July 1852 PD

"—SO I'M AFRAID I CAN'T quite agree with you there, My Lord," Roger Winton said politely, looking across the palatial conference table at Jackson Denham, the Baron of Seawell and the Star Kingdom's Chancellor of the Exchequer.

"Indeed, Your Highness?" Seawell arched his eyebrows, then let his eyes flick very briefly—so briefly it was *almost* unnoticeable—towards the head of the table before he focused intently on Roger's expression. "I'm afraid I don't follow your logic. Perhaps you could explain it a bit more clearly?"

Roger made himself smile calmly, despite a frission of anger. He kept his own eyes on Seawell, without so much as a glance in his mother's direction.

"I'm not questioning your current figures, My Lord," he said. "My problem is with the basis for some of your projected *future* numbers. Specifically, the ones you're showing for trade in the Haven Quadrant. I think the underlying assumptions are far too optimistic given what we've seen out of the People's Republic's current economy."

"Those assumptions are based on quite a few decades worth of computer time, Your Highness, Seawell pointed out. "And the analysis they support is the product of some highly experienced analysts."

You have *heard of "Garbage In-Garbage out," haven't you?* Roger didn't quite ask out loud. *And those "highly experienced analysts" of yours know exactly what* you *wanted to hear out of them. Don't you think that might have helped them ... shave their analyses just a bit? Besides, we wouldn't want them to entertain a fresh thought and strain their brains, now would we?*

47

"I understand that, My Lord, but I'd also like to point out that everything coming out of our human intelligence sources in the People's Republic suggests Haven is in the process of adopting highly protectionist economic policies, and I don't see any mention of that in this analysis." He tapped the display in front of him, still smiling pleasantly. "Instead, it assumes current trend lines will continue, rather than dip sharply, and I think that's highly unlikely. According to Dame Alice's *current* figures, for example, our carrying trade to the People's Republic has fallen by almost nine percent over just the last three quarters. Would you care to comment on that, Dame Alice?"

He looked at the pleasant faced, silver haired woman sitting two seats down from Seawell. Dame Alice Bryson was the Star Kingdom's Minister of Trade, and she and Seawell didn't exactly see eye to eye on quite a few topics these days. At sixty-nine, she was only five T-years younger than he was, but she often seemed half his age when it came to mental flexibility, in Roger's opinion. Of course, that might be because she was a Centrist while Seawell was a card-carrying member of the Conservative Association.

"I think the figures speak for themselves, Your Highness," she said now, never even glancing in the Queen's direction. Instead, she turned her head to smile at Seawell. "His Highness is quite correct about the People's Republic's protectionist tendencies, I'm afraid, Jackson. Their government is steadily nationalizing the independent shipping houses of each of their new member systems. As they shut down the independents, they're also freezing out everyone else's carriers... including ours. It may not show up as much in your projections because our shipping lines are taking up the slack in Silesia and the League and at the moment the People's Republic's still buying plenty of Manticoran *goods*, so the trade balance is still a long way from tanking. They're simply sending their own ships to collect them—and to deliver what little we're buying from them. But everything we're hearing at Trade suggests they probably won't be doing that much longer."

"That's ridiculous," Seawell said testily. "It's going to cost them at least twenty percent more, possibly even more than that, to try to produce locally what they've been buying from us! And unless they want to cut their defense budgets, where are they going to get the investment capital to build the production facilities in the first place?"

"I'm afraid you're missing my point, My Lord," Roger said. Seawell looked back at him, and Roger shrugged. "At the moment, and increasingly, Havenite policies are being driven by ideology, not rational analysis. I don't say the Legislaturalists really buy into the ideology they're selling to everyone else in the PRH, but they have to at least *act* as if they do. And some of them probably do believe everything they're saying. What matters from our perspective is less the *why* than the *what* of what they're doing, however, and the problem is that they're buying more and more deeply into the notion of a command economy. And what their economic analysts are seeing at this moment isn't the opportunities of selling to an external market, but the opportunities of exploiting an *internal* market for Haven's benefit even at the expense of the economies of the People's Republic's other member systems.

"They see the star systems they control as a closed internal market, one they can lock other producers out of with protectionist measures to create a situation in which market demand can be satisfied only out of their domestic industry. Protectionism is supposed to create a situation in which market pressures will support the development of the industry their top-down system hasn't generated, and they don't *care* if that drives their subjects' standard of living down by driving prices *up*. And they intend to concentrate all of that new industry in the Haven System and their older daughter colonies. I believe they used to call that sort of thinking 'mercantilism' back on Old Earth."

The crown prince shook his head, his expression grim.

"I think your analysts are missing that because from the perspective of the PRH and its citizens as a whole, it's very, very bad policy. But from the perspective of the Haven System—which is all the Legislaturalists are actually concerned about at the moment, when all's said—it makes good *short-term* sense. In essence, they're looting the economies of the systems they're conquering—excuse me, peacefully annexing—" his irony was withering "in order to prop up and grow their own domestic economy in Nouveau Paris. In the end, it's going to wind up costing them far more for manufactured goods and they're going to take a hammering on lost foreign markets for their own products, but it *will* force the growth of their own heavy industry in the systems which are most important to them. And because it's an ultimately *irrational* policy from the perspective of the PRH as a whole, your rational analysts missed it."

Seawell started to say something, then made himself stop and closed his mouth firmly. He sat that way for several seconds before he nodded grudgingly.

"You may—*may*, I say—have a valid point there, Your Highness. I'll certainly sit down with my staff and examine all of our models in the light of what you and Dame Alice have just said. Having said that, however," he continued, rallying gamely, "the fact remains that increasing the Navy budget yet again is going to place a very serious strain on the economy as a whole. Because of that—"

✦ ✦ ✦

"You did well, Roger. Very well," Samantha Winton said, sipping her tea. "I was particularly impressed when you didn't reach across the table and pull his tonsils out through his nose."

"I thought I concealed my unhappiness rather well, actually, Mom," he replied, sitting back with a tankard of cold beer while Monroe purred across the back of his chair. "Besides, if I wanted his tonsils, I'd ask Monroe to extract them. His claws are a lot better equipped for that kind of surgery."

Samantha chuckled, and Monroe reached out to smack Roger gently on top of the head with a true-hand. Roger smiled, but there was a carefully hidden darkness behind that smile as he looked at his mother. She'd aged noticeably over the last couple of years, and something inside him raged at her increasing frailty, the slight bend in her spine that defied everything the doctors could do. It wasn't right—it wasn't *fair*!—for her to be visibly fading in front of him when she was barely thirty T-years older than *he* was.

"Don't go giving Monroe any ideas," she said sternly after a moment. "'Cats are very direct souls. If you give him the idea that he can go around dissecting cabinet ministers, it's going to get very messy."

"Not if he and I make a few salutary examples right up front, surely!" Roger replied. "Just one or two. I'm sure the others would get the idea and begin deferring suitably to my tyrannical whims."

"I wish," Samantha said with rather less humor.

She set down her teacup and leaned back in her chair, closing her eyes for a moment, and Roger felt a fresh pang as Magnus looked down at her protectively. The older treecat no longer rode his person's shoulder the way he had for as long as Roger could remember, and he was constantly at her side, watching over her. Roger could read his concern, his worry, in his body language, and another strand of concern of his own went through him.

Treecats almost never survived their companions' deaths. That had made their practice of adopting the shorter-lived humans a virtual death sentence for centuries, and the idea of losing Magnus, who'd been a part of his own life from the day he learned to walk, at the same time he lost his mother was almost insupportable.

At least that's not likely to be a problem for Monroe. The thought tasted much bleaker than usual at the moment. *That's one good thing about prolong. Not that it's going to help Mom or Magnus.*

"I think I'm getting too worn out for this, Roger," Samantha said without opening her eyes. "I just don't have the energy to beat up on them the way I used to. It helps—if that isn't an obscene use of that particular verb—that the Havenites are getting increasingly blatant. People can still argue about how much of a threat they are to *us*, but nobody can simply deny that they pose a threat to *anyone* anymore."

"I wouldn't go quite that far, Mom," he said dryly. "There's always Lady Helen."

"Oh, God." Samantha opened her eyes and looked at him. "I could've gone all day without thinking about her. Thank you, Roger. Thank you ever so much."

Roger snorted and took a long pull at his beer. Lady Helen Bradley was the current leader of the Liberal party in the House of Lords, and her insulation from the electoral process also seemed to insulate her from rationality, in Roger's opinion. She got to live in her own little echo chamber, where the only people she ever spoke to were those—from all sides of the aisle, he had to acknowledge—who agreed with her, and the electorate couldn't even punish her at the ballot box, because she never had to stand for office.

The good news (from Roger's perspective, at least) was that the Conservative Association had never had much representation in the House of Commons to begin with and that the isolation from reality of peers like Bradley was steadily eroding the Liberals' popular support, which was actively costing them seats in the lower house, as well. Allen Summervale, the Duke of Cromarty, who'd assumed the leadership of the Centrist Party with Earl Mortenson's resignation last year, was gathering up quite a few of those disaffected Liberals. The *bad* news was that the Star Kingdom's constitution gave the House of Lords disproportionate power, which meant a sufficient number of nobly born drooling idiots could still hamstring the government's policy badly.

The fact that Leonard Shumate, the Earl of Thompson, was Prime Minister instead of Cromarty was a demonstration of that unhappy truth. Roger had nothing against Thompson. In fact, he liked the earl a great deal, and Thompson was a Crown Loyalist. As such, his support for the House of Winton could be taken as a given. But everyone knew that, and putting together a majority in the House of Lords—essential for any prime minister—had required some unhappy horsetrading. That was how Jackson Denham had ended up as Chancellor of the Exchequer, traditionally the second most powerful seat in the Cabinet, and how Alfredo Maxwell, a Liberal, had ended up as Home Secretary while a Centrist like Dame Alice had been forced to settle for Trade.

But at least we got White Haven as First Space Lord. That's something, he told himself.

In fact, it was quite a lot. Murdoch Alexander, the twelfth Earl of White Haven, wasn't exactly a Centrist; he was too stubbornly independent to embrace *any* party label, and peers didn't require party support to defend their seats. He wasn't what Roger would have called a *flexible* man, either, but he was about as easy to deflect as Juggernaut, and he had a brain that *worked*. He hadn't been in the First Space Lord's chair long enough to have thoroughly cleaned house, but he was working on it, and his appreciation of the Star Kingdom's strategic realities was far better than Admiral Truman's had been.

Or it's closer to mine, *at least. Of course, that's the dictionary definition of "better," isn't it?*

That thought brought him a much-needed chuckle, and he grinned at his mother.

"We're getting them trimmed down and shaped up, Mom. All we need is a bigger, sharper machete."

"And two or three years to work on them," his mother agreed. "I just hope the Havenites give us the *time* for it, Roger."

"It's going to be a while yet," Roger told her, and she looked at him. She let him see the worry in her eyes, and he smiled gently. She'd been worrying about it too long, he thought. And she was afraid she was going to run out of time—that *she* was going to run out of time—before she accomplished everything her responsibilities to her kingdom and her people required of her.

"We've got at least another twenty or thirty T-years, I think," he continued. "That's part of the problem, actually. The people who want to pretend the sky isn't falling can do exactly what Janacek and Truman have been doing for the *last* ten or twelve T-years and point out that there's no *immediate* threat. The problem is they keep acting as if we've got some kind of unlimited savings account of time. That if the threat isn't 'immediate' right this moment we'll always have time to prepare before it *becomes* 'immediate.'" He shook his head, then shrugged. "The good news is that we're starting to get the people we need in place to do something about it. Like Admiral White Haven and Admiral Lomax."

"That's what Abner said last week," Samantha admitted. "And he also complimented me on my choice of White Haven for First Space Lord. He thinks the earl is going to work out very well. Of course, I smiled and accepted his praise with becoming humility without ever pointing out that *you* were the one who'd recommended him."

"Thank God!" Roger grimaced. "Even hinting to anyone that a lowly commander is 'recommending' flag officers for appointment as space lords would be the kiss of death for any Navy career I might still hope to cling to! I'm sure quite a lot of people have figured out you're going to ask me for advice on questions like that, but the longer we can keep even a whisper of it from becoming official knowledge, the better *I'll* like it!"

"I suppose I can understand that," she said with a crooked smile, opening her arms to invite Magnus into her lap. The treecat hopped down and curled into a silken oval, purring loudly as she stroked him while she gazed at her son.

"I'm afraid your career—your *Navy* career, at least—is on borrowed time, though, Roger," she said softly, and he froze in his chair, looking at her. Her smile reappeared, but this time it was gentle, almost compassionate. "I don't seem to be wearing quite as well as I could wish. I'm afraid you may find yourself sitting in my chair sooner than you'd like, love. I wish it weren't so, but—"

She shrugged, and Roger drew a deep, deep breath.

"You're not going anywhere for a while," he told her. "I don't care what anyone else says; *I* say you're not going anywhere for a while. I'll step up the time earmarked for Cabinet meetings and even—God help us—sessions of Parliament to take more of the weight off your shoulders, but you've still got too much to teach me to go traipsing off and leave me stuck with the job!"

"I'll try to bear that in mind. And while I'm bearing it in mind, Earl Thompson made a rather pointed suggestion to me last week. The same sort Earl Mortenson used to make."

"You know, I really don't think of myself primarily in terms of *breeding* stock," Roger said.

"Well, to some extent, you *should*. It comes with the Crown, unfortunately. And the truth is, Roger, that you've been able to wait a lot longer than any of the rest of us have because of prolong. But it really is time you were settling down. And"—her eyes sharpened suddenly, impaling him the same way they'd once impaled an adolescent Roger Winton when his "explanations" had started shedding their wheels—"it's not as if you didn't have a perfectly lovely young lady in mind, now is it?"

"No," he admitted after a moment. "No, but . . . it's not that simple, either, Mom. I mean, I'm delighted that the Constitution requires me to marry a commoner. There were times, when I was younger, it really pissed me off, but not now. Unfortunately, this particular commoner doesn't want to be queen."

"She doesn't *want* to marry you?" Samantha's surprise showed in her tone, and she shook her head. "Roger, nobody's been spying on you—or, at least, not spying on you for *me*—but I *have* seen the two of you together. I can't believe she doesn't love you!"

"That's not what I said. I didn't even say she didn't want to marry me. The problem is that she doesn't want to marry the *King*."

"Oh."

Samantha's hands stilled on Magnus' coat. The constitutional requirement that the heir to the throne wed outside the aristocracy had produced its share of unhappiness over the centuries. She was convinced it was one of the monarchy's greatest strengths, yet more than one potential consort had backed away from the thought of becoming prince consort or queen consort and plunging themselves—and their children—into the fishbowl of the Star Kingdom's politics.

"I think she'll come around," Roger said. "I wish I were certain I didn't think that mainly because of how badly I *want* it, but you're right. She *does* love me, and I love her, and Monroe adores her. Jonas is on my side, too, and that counts. But I'm not going to pressure her on it." He met his mother's gaze steadily. "From a cold-blooded political perspective, a marriage that turned out... unhappily could blow up in the entire Star Kingdom's face. But even more importantly, for me at least, is that I don't *want* her to be unhappy. I want her to marry me because that's what *she* wants to do. And I think it is. It's not even the political side of it that concerns her, I think. It's that she's afraid she doesn't have the background for it. That she'll *embarrass* me somehow. And that unmitigated asshole Bannister sure as hell isn't helping."

His expression turned ugly for a moment, and Samantha's mouth tightened. Godfrey Bannister, the senior social columnist for the *Landing Times*, had a well-deserved reputation for steeping his columns in acid from time to time. She didn't really think that was what he'd done this time, but the consequences were just as bad as if he had.

"The Little Beggar Girl."

That was what he'd dubbed Angelique Adcock.

Samantha was almost certain he'd actually meant it as a compliment. She'd read the column when he'd used it for the first time, and its tone had been admiring, almost celebratory, a reminder that in the Star Kingdom of Manticore the Crown married the Commons in every generation. And that even someone who'd arrived in Manticore as a penniless refugee could find himself or herself elevated to the very highest level of Manticoran society.

But it hadn't been taken that way. Perhaps it was because he'd used so much carefully distilled vitriol over the decades. Perhaps the sorts of people who read his column had simply become so accustomed to it that they'd read the appellation as a sneering comment on the Angelique's origins when that wasn't what he'd intended at all.

"I really think she hadn't even considered the possibility of my proposing until Bannister opened his mouth and 'outed' her," Roger continued harshly. "That's probably partly my fault. I was trying to be gradual about it, trying to avoid scaring her off, and I think I waited too long. She's thinking about it *now*, though, and what she really wants to do is run away back to Gryphon and hide in those woods of hers! But I'm not going to give up on her, Mom." His expression firmed. "She's the one I want, the one I love, and she damned well loves me, too. I'm not letting that get away from me. I know how much you and Dad loved each other, and I want that, as well. And we've both had the prolong therapies." He looked straight into his mother's eyes. "I've found the one I want, and I'm willing to be patient. You and Dad had forty-three T-years, and I know how good they were. But I want *more* than that, and I can have it, and nobody and nothing is going to take that away from Angelique and me. *Nobody.*"

His mother looked back at him for several long, silent moments, and then she nodded slowly.

"And I want you to have it, too," she told him softly. "So you go ahead, take your time, make sure what you have is strong enough to handle the Bannisters and the society backbiters. And when it is, you marry that girl, Roger. You marry her, and you love her, and you have children with her, and you remember me—and your dad—when you do. You do that."

"I will, Mom," he told her equally softly. "I will."

✦ ✦ ✦ ✦ ✦

March 1855 PD

"I'M TELLING YOU, ROGER, she's brilliant. We agree on that, all right?! But she *knows* she's brilliant, and she has about as much tact as . . . as—"

Jonas Adcock shook his head, obviously unable to come up with the simile he wanted, then threw up both hands.

"Hell, she doesn't have *any* tact! In fact, I don't think she's ever even *heard* the word!"

"Now, now, Jonas!" Roger shook his own head reprovingly. "You know perfectly well she has to have heard the word used at least in passing as much as, oh, two or three times just at the Island!"

"Then she sure as hell wasn't paying attention," Adcock growled.

"Should I assume from your obvious despair that she's . . . stepped on someone's toes again?"

"I'm astonished young Alexander didn't wring her neck," Adcock said bluntly. "Or that the two of them didn't spend their lunch hour down at the dueling grounds, for that matter!"

"Oh? And what was the source of their . . . mutual discontent *this* time?"

"The usual," Adcock sighed. "Mind you, this time it was all Sonja's own fault. Not that she was prepared to *admit* it! She ran into him when he dropped by Section Thirteen to discuss the latest 'burn' settings on the Mark Ten."

He paused, raising his eyebrows, and Roger nodded his understanding. Section Thirteen was internal Navy-speak for "Bureau of Weapons, Missile Development Command, Warhead Division," which happened to be housed in Section 13-065-9 of HMSS *Hephaestus*, and the Mark Ten was the latest-generation heavy

57

shipkiller warhead of the RMN. Like all such modern weapons, it could be used in "boom" or "burn" mode: as a contact nuke or as a sidewall "burner," designed to take down that critical defense before warships closed for the decisive energy duel. The Mark Ten was a very advanced warhead—markedly superior to current-generation Solarian warheads, in fact—which had raised the standoff range in sidewall-burning mode to almost eleven thousand kilometers.

"Well, Sonja was over there to see Commander Mavroudis about something completely separate, but she overheard the question and made some remark about how 'obsolescent dual mode warheads' are becoming."

He looked at Roger again, this time expressionlessly, and Roger groaned.

"Tell me she didn't say anything about Python!" he begged.

"No," Adcock said judiciously. "Not in so many words, anyway. But she'd said enough to make Alexander curious, and he asked her what she was talking about. At which point she realized she wasn't supposed to be talking about Python to *anyone*—Mavroudis was doing everything but send her semaphore messages from behind Alexander's back to shut up about it—and fell back on simply giving him a smug, Sonja, I-know-something-you-don't-know look. Which convinced him she didn't have a clue what she was talking about—that it was just Sonja being Sonja again—and he made a relatively scathing observation about people who happened to be obsessed with shiny toys and what a *pity* it was they couldn't spend the same amount of mental effort on *weapons*, instead."

"Oh, Lord."

Roger's tone was almost mild, his expression that of a man watching two ground cars slide unstoppably towards one another on a sheet of ice, and Adcock chuckled sourly.

Project Python was a top secret effort being pursued by Section Thirteen with very quiet, under-the-radar input from the Concept Development Office's researchers. Based on the original, failed effort by Abreu and Harmon, a Solarian defense contractor, Python represented an attempt to develop a workable "laser head": a weapon which would generate bomb-pumped X-ray lasers and punch them straight through sidewalls from far greater standoff ranges than any sidewall burner had yet attained. If it worked, it would enhance the lethality of missile combat enormously and offer the possibility of radically altering accepted tactics. Unfortunately, it was still a completely black program no one was supposed to know a thing about.

"Give her her due," Adcock said after a moment. "She obviously realized she should never have opened her mouth about it, and she wasn't about to breach security, even when Alexander whacked her up aside the head. But that doesn't mean her temper was any better than usual. She let him have it right back, and they were off to the races in a bloodbath that didn't have one single thing to do with hardware or weapon systems anymore. One of the little drawbacks of having known each other since they were weaned, I suppose." He shook his head. "Mavroudis says it took him ten minutes to separate them...and it felt like ten *hours*! He also asked me if I could put her on a leash in the future."

"Oof!"

Roger grinned. Commander Anders Mavroudis was one of the easiest-going officers in the Queen's Navy. The fact that *he'd* made a request like that spoke volumes about how...interesting the discussion must have become.

"He commed me while she was still in transit," Adcock continued, "so I took the opportunity to give her a few quality moments of my own time on her arrival and then sent her off to Sebastian for a refresher review on Security 101, and I'll just let you guess how well she took *that*. For a minute there, I thought *he* was going to invite her out for a little pistol practice this afternoon!"

Adcock grimaced disgustedly. Despite a degree of patriotism which made the most fervent nativeborn Manticorans' look positively anemic, there were some aspects of the Star Kingdom of which he'd never fully approved. One of those was the persistence of its Code Duello...which didn't mean there weren't times he could understand how useful people might find it in certain situations.

Roger chuckled, although he had to sympathize with his friend. Lieutenant Commander Sonja Hemphill, the granddaughter of Vice Admiral *Robert* Hemphill (who'd finally been forced into a long overdue retirement at BuShips), was just as brilliant as Adcock had suggested. And while she wasn't *quite* as socially tone deaf as the other captain's diatribe might suggest, she *did* have a pronounced gift (which she had obviously inherited from her grandfather) for stepping on toes. It didn't help that she and Commander Sebastian D'Orville didn't like each other very much, and the fact that she obviously thought D'Orville—who happened to be senior to her—was slightly denser than battle steel helped even less.

Lieutenant Commander Hamish Alexander, on the other hand, was just as smart and at least moderately more tactful than Hemphill. How someone with his mindset had ended up on Bethany Havinghurst's staff over at BuPlan was one of life's little mysteries, but Roger suspected Admiral White Haven (who happened to be Hamish's father) had probably had a little something to do with it. And in this instance, little though Roger cared for the patronage game, he was prepared to admit it was a good thing, although he was also prepared to admit that Hamish's occasional . . . lively disagreements with Edward Janacek probably helped explain his own approval in this instance. Fortunately for all concerned—*except, of course,* he reminded himself grimly, *for the* rest *of the Star Kingdom*—Janacek had become a professional intelligence specialist whereas Alexander remained firmly wedded to the tactical track which had always been the fast path to starship command and senior fleet command in the RMN. The good news was that Janacek was unlikely ever to command a fleet in battle and get a few thousand people killed; the *bad* news was that he had acquired sufficient seniority to be a serious obstacle to efforts to convince the Admiralty and, especially, Parliament that Manticore needed a true battle fleet.

The friction with Janacek was also driven by the fact that Alexander was advancing almost as rapidly towards Captain of the List and eventually flag rank as Janacek had . . . and doing it on the basis of proven ability in command positions, not just who he happened to know. The two men had never liked one another, and Roger forsaw the development of one of the Navy's truly legendary personal feuds looming inevitably on the horizon. Given their family and political connections, it was likely to be a particularly messy and vicious one, as well. Especially if Janacek ever made the mistake of getting Alexander's dander up in a public setting. Given the younger man's rapid advancement, he was going to overtake Janacek's rank sometime very soon, at which point Janacek was going to discover just how much interest he'd accrued on the numerous barbed, venomous comments he'd made about Alexander in "private conversations" he knew would be circulated through the officer corps. That sort of tactic was typical of his spiteful, coup-counting nature, especially since he could always claim he'd been misquoted or that the anonymous source who'd passed along the comment had garbled it or gotten it wrong. And since it hadn't been made in any *official* setting or on the record, no one in the Navy could take official cognizance of it and call him to account.

Unfortunately, young Hamish had inherited the White Haven temper from his father in all its glory. The First Space Lord's ability to totally demolish some unfortunate soul with a handful of carefully chosen, icily furious words was famous throughout the service. Hamish had the same gift, and one fine day, when Janacek could no longer hide behind the protective rampart of his superior rank and Article Twenty's prohibition of actions or language "of an insubordinate nature, tending to undermine the authority of a superior officer," Hamish Alexander was going to demonstrate that to him in full. Roger only wished he could be a fly on the wall when it happened.

Even more unfortunately, Hamish and Sonja were *already* equal in rank, which took Article Twenty off the table in her case. Worse, the two of them had known one another since childhood, and Roger was of the opinion that they'd probably had their first fight in a kindergarten sandbox.

Be fair, he scolded himself. *The real problem is that he thinks she's a "panacea merchant." He's not the only one, either, and the fact that she can't tell him what's really going on in Jonas' shop isn't making things any better. Whatever her other failings, she takes her security clearance and its restrictions seriously, God bless her ornery little soul, which forces her to talk in generalities, rather than specifics, in public. Her frustration quotient's getting bigger, too, now that she sees all those tantalizing possibilities she can't talk about, which is undermining whatever effort towards tactfulness she might otherwise make. In fact, that's probably what set this one off, and in some ways I can't really blame her. But if this keeps up, or gets even worse, a* lot *of people are going to start sharing Hamish's opinion, and that really* could *be a problem farther down the line.*

Lieutenant Commander Alexander was already recognized as one of the more capable—and sneakier—tacticians of his generation. Roger wasn't certain he was going to develop into an equally good *strategist*, but he had hopes. In addition to one of the most beautiful and glamorous wives in the entire Star Kingdom, Alexander had a scalpel-sharp, analytical brain and a deep and abiding interest in history. It was abundantly clear that he was one of the Queen's officers who recognized the long-term threat potential of the People's Republic of Haven, as well, and there were still far fewer of those than Roger could have wished... especially on Havinghurst's staff. He was too well aware of proper military discipline to publically voice his opinions of his nominal boss's intelligence analyses, however, and fortunately he worked directly for Rear Admiral Trenton Shu at Planning and Development, responsible for analyzing, developing, and disseminating operational and tactical doctrine. That kept him out of Havinghurst's hair (and vice-versa) on a daily basis and also insulated him and Janacek from one another at least somewhat.

Unfortunately, his very interest in history made him far more conservative than Hemphill where the potential for a true technological "equalizer" was concerned, especially without any access to the sorts of projects Adcock's small, secretive command was contemplating. It wasn't that Alexander opposed R&D; it was simply that he felt Hemphill had far too much faith in pie-in-the-sky future super weapons which threatened to prevent concentration on the improvement of *existing* technologies. He'd pointed out more than once that the best was the worst enemy of good enough, and argued that the Navy had to build innovative tactical and operational doctrines around hardware it *knew* was attainable if it was going to confront an opponent like the PRH. It couldn't afford to depend on stumbling across some radical transformation of war-fighting technology which had somehow managed to elude the rest of the galaxy for the past couple of T-centuries; instead (as he'd told Sonja on more than one scathing occasion), the emphasis should be on improvement of *known* technologies. Pure, speculative R&D had a place in his view, but primary emphasis should be placed on *applied* research to provide the greatest possible qualitative edge in existing offensive and defensive systems.

The problem, Roger thought, *is that we need* both *of them because both of them are making very valid arguments. Sonja really is too convinced she's going to come up with a silver bullet if she just throws enough ideas at the bulkhead until one of them sticks. She's not interested in how we get the best use out of the systems we've already got, because she's so confident she's going to be able to replace them with something so much better. And Hamish is too stubborn—and smart, and outside the loop of what we're looking at over here—to pin his hopes on something that may well never materialize. No wonder the two of them are at each other's throats! But at least he doesn't think Sonja's a cretin with delusions of godhood the way he sees Janacek. Or not yet, anyway. I suppose that's always subject to change if this . . . spirited discussion of theirs goes on long enough.*

"So what are you going to do about them?" he asked.

His tone darkened with the question. It was a small thing, but Adcock knew him well and gave him a sudden, sharp look. Roger saw it and shrugged with a crooked smile. There was a reason he'd asked Adcock what *he* was going to do about it instead of asking what *they* were going to do about it.

"There's not much I *can* do about young Alexander, since he's not under my command," Adcock pointed out after a moment. "For that matter, I doubt he and I have even spoken to one another more than three or four times, so I can hardly sit him down and 'reason' with him on any personal basis." He shrugged. "I *have* talked to Sonja . . . again. And she promises to behave better—hah! What she means is she'll *try* to behave better for at least a couple of weeks, but then she's going to get buried in something and step on somebody's toes—again—without even realizing she's done it. And I'm going to try to make the fact that we're losing Sebastian back to fleet duty an advantage. I'll have him sit down and 'counsel' her—bluntly—before he leaves. Maybe that'll keep her on the straight and narrow at least long enough for Stovalt to settle in at his desk before *he* has to separate any fractious children!"

Roger nodded, Commander Gerald Stovalt was Admiral Lomax's hand-picked successor to Sebastian D'Orville. He was older than D'Orville, although young enough to have received prolong, and Dame Carrie obviously hoped his calmer personality would be an asset as Adcock's executive officer. Roger didn't think Hemphill was the *only* reason Lomax thought a calmer personality might be in order, but she had to be *one* of the reasons.

And at least Dame Carrie's not going to have to play hide-the-pea about our shop much longer, he reminded himself, reaching up to scratch Monroe's ears as the treecat leaned against the side of his neck. *With Low Delhi gone at BuShips, Truman retired, and*

Havinghurst on her way out at ONI, the internal politics are going to be a lot smoother at Admiralty House. Now if only we could convince Parliament to at least open its damned eyes!

Unfortunately, not even the fact that the People's Republic had acquired two new member star systems in the last half T-year alone, neither of whom had joined remotely voluntarily, seemed capable of getting through to the Star Kingdom's career politicians. The intelligence reports Roger was seeing on the pacification measures adopted in the Rutgers System were enough to turn a man's stomach, but that wasn't enough to awaken Parliament's sense of urgency. Oh, heavens, no! In his darker moments, he was beginning to wonder if *anything* could accomplish that miracle.

Well, that's why we're a monarchy, Rog, he told himself. *I guess it's going to be up to you to do the waking up, one way or the other. And,* he thought more grimly, *whatever it takes.*

Monroe made a soft, distressed sound in his ear as he picked up the emotions which went with that thought, and Roger stroked the 'cat's head gently.

"May I ask how your mother is?"

Adcock's voice was quiet, and Roger looked at him sharply. The captain looked back, then twitched his head in Monroe's direction.

Of course. Jonas has been around us long enough to read the two of us like a book, hasn't he?

"Not good," he admitted in an equally quiet voice. "We're trying to keep it as quiet as we can, but she's not responding well." His jaw tightened. "Damn it, Jonas! She's not even *eighty*, and we've got the best medical establishment in the damned galaxy just through the Junction at Beowulf!"

Adcock nodded silently, and Roger felt a flush of shame. Jonas was fifty-eight already, himself...and without prolong he had perhaps another forty years of life left to look forward to.

"I'm sure they *are* doing their best, Roger," the other man said after a moment. "Sometimes that isn't good enough, but it's still the best they can do."

"I know, and I shouldn't complain, either. I know that, too." Roger summoned a smile which was only slightly off center. "Knowing doesn't help, sometimes, though."

"No, it doesn't," Adcock agreed. "And from a purely selfish viewpoint, I'm going to really miss you around here."

"I'm going to miss *being* around here."

Roger looked around the small, cluttered office which still housed Adcock's files and desk and very little else. At least they'd be able to move him and the rest of the shop into better quarters. Too bad Roger wasn't going to get to make the move with them. Unfortunately...

"If I could figure out away to avoid it, I would," he continued, looking back at Adcock. "But, as Mom's always said, it comes with the nice house and all the servants."

"I suppose it does."

Adcock snorted gently, although the joke wasn't as funny as it once had been—or as it was going to become in about another three planetary months, for that matter, when *he* started having to deal with those self-same servants any time he wanted to visit his sister. Still, little though he knew Roger would have enjoyed hearing it, there *were* upsides from his perspective to Roger's effective retirement. He hated the fact that it was his mother's failing health which was forcing the crown prince who'd also become one of the closest friends he'd ever had to take up his full-time political duties so soon, and he hated how much he knew Roger was going to miss active duty. Yet having an experienced naval officer, one who was fully committed to bolstering the Star Kingdom's defensive posture, effectively running the government from Mount Royal Palace was going to have a salutary effect on the battle Jonas Adcock had been fighting for so long. And on a more personal level—

"And where," he asked in a deliberately brisker voice, "is that gadabout sister of mine? I thought she was supposed to be dragging you off to lunch?"

"And so she is." Roger checked his chrono. "I might point out, however, that while she isn't quite as compulsive about clock-watching as *you* are, she still has over four full minutes before she's late. The odds are that she's—"

The opening door interrupted him, and he turned with a smile as Angelique Adcock and his sister Caitrin came through it.

"You *cheated*!" Adcock said indignantly, standing to greet the two women and bowing respectfully to Princess Caitrin. "Security told you they were on the way up, didn't they?"

"I have no idea what you're talking about."

Roger's innocent expression would have done justice to any lawyer, con man, politician, newsie, or other professional liar.

Unfortunately, he couldn't quite hold it when Monroe plucked the almost invisible earbug out of his right ear and held it up for all to see.

"Traitor!" he told the treecat as Monroe bleeked in amusement, and Angelique hit him on the 'cat-less shoulder.

"You did so cheat," she told him firmly. "And you *promised* me all those security people wouldn't spy on me for you!"

"They didn't," he said virtuously, putting his arm around her and kissing her firmly. "They were spying on *Caitrin*!" He shook his head, brown eyes gleaming at his sister. "They've been spying on *her* for us ever since she discovered boys."

Angelique laughed, but there was an edge to the laughter, and he hugged her a bit tighter in acknowledgment. She still wasn't really comfortable with the notion of becoming his queen, given all the monumental changes it would demand of her. She was one of Gryphon's most respected forestry experts, in constant demand for the forest regeneration and management concerns of the planet's huge (and hugely profitable) ski resorts, and she was never happier than when she was outdoors *doing* something in wind and weather. Which was probably a good thing for him, he admitted. He'd always enjoyed sports, but he'd spent far too much of his life in artificial environments since graduating from Saganami Island. Angelique had dragged his sorry butt back out into the open air, though, and he'd shared his rediscovered youthful passion for grav skiing with her, while she'd shown him the joys of forest hikes, camping trips, and whitewater kayaks.

Of course, the two of them couldn't enjoy those camping trips as much as they might have, given who he was and the intense watchfulness of Palace Security and the Queen's Own, and Angelique wasn't quite able to hide her awareness of that, however gamely she tried. And that, he conceded unhappily, was a problem which wasn't going away. The knowledge that the position of Queen Consort of Manticore was a full-time job that would leave no time or space for the career she'd built and loved was a heavy price to pay, and he knew it. In fact, he hated asking her to pay it almost as much as she did the thought of *paying* it . . . just as he knew the pervasive presence of her own security detail was part of her discomfort with the entire notion. It underscored the monumental change which would envelop her—and which would never release her, for the remainder of her life—when she married him in one hundred and three days.

"Well, I hope you've enjoyed reading their reports, brother mine," Caitrin told him now. "And I hope you realize Mom was keeping an eye on *you*, too. Of course, she'd never've shared those reports with me. But I always was a better hacker than you, wasn't I?"

She smiled sweetly, and Roger reached out his other arm to give her a hug, as well. She and Angelique had become fast friends, and he knew he owed a lot of Angelique's eventual willingness to accept his proposal of marriage to that friendship. Despite the decade-plus difference in their ages—Angelique was actually a T-year older than Roger—Caitrin had been her sponsor, confidante, mentor, and bulwark as she found herself thrust into the very highest levels of Manticoran society. And whether or not Angelique would ever admit it to Roger—or any other member of the human race—she was deeply grateful Caitrin had agreed to delay her own marriage to Edward Henke, the Earl of Gold Peak for over six T-months. The Star Kingdom of Manticore wasn't accustomed to double weddings in the royal family, but they weren't unheard of, either, and Roger knew Angelique would take enormous comfort from having Caitrin endure the ordeal right beside her.

Of course, "ordeal" is hardly the right word for how Katie's *going to be feeling about it,* Roger thought with a grin.

Palace Security most emphatically did *not* report to him on his sister's love life, although he was depressingly well aware that Security knew everything about everyone in the royal family, *including* who was sleeping with whom. On the other hand, he knew his sister well. Unlike Angelique, Caitrin thrived on social events and affairs, and she would be *delighted* to . . . regularize her relationship with young Gold Peak, too.

"Well," he said out loud, turning back to Adcock with a smug expression as he extended one elbow to each of the women, "it would seem there are some advantages to becoming an idle civilian, after all." He elevated his nose and sniffed loudly. "Unlike those uniformed menials whose ranks I shall soon be departing, *I* am free to go take a long, slow, luxurious lunch break." He smiled sweetly. "Should we bring you the leftovers, Sir?"

October 1857 PD

KING ROGER WINTON sailed into the Admiralty House conference room like a thunderstorm, and Jonas Adcock felt a sinking sensation as he absorbed the gale warning signals flying in his brother-in-law's eyes.

The last couple of months would have tried the patience of a saint, and whatever manifold virtues Roger III of Manticore might possess, sainthood was not among them. He was impeccably polite as he shed the three-man security detail from the King's Own Regiment—which had been the *Queen's* Own, until about six T-weeks ago—at the conference room door, strode to the head of the table, and seated himself. No one was fooled, however; one look at Monroe's flattened ears and twitching tail was enough to warn even the densest that His Majesty was *not* amused.

Allen Summervale, the Duke of Cromarty and the Star Kingdom's new Prime Minister, had followed him through the door. Now he nodded a greeting to the others seated around the table—First Lord Castle Rock, Second Lord Jerome Pearce, First Space Lord White Haven, Second Space Lord Big Sky, Fourth Space Lord Lomax, and sitting at the very foot of the table, monumentally junior to everyone else present, Captain (JG) Jonas Adcock—before he found his own seat and slipped into it.

Roger let Cromarty settle, then smiled (more or less) and planted his forearms firmly on his comfortable chair's armrests.

"Allen and I have just come from a Cabinet meeting," he said in a dismayingly pleasant tone. "At that Cabinet meeting, I was informed that while everyone deeply regrets my mother's death, they're simply delighted with the superlative degree of training, insight, and experience, gained at her side, which I bring to the Throne. My ministers inform me that Parliament has total faith in my judgment and that my people's hearts are with me as I take up the weight of government. And I have personal messages from the leaders of every political party promising cooperation and support as I take up the burden of government."

He showed his teeth in what was technically a smile.

"And I can go piss up a rope as far as increasing the Navy budget is concerned."

He leaned back in his chair amid a total, ringing silence. No one broke it for several moments—several very *long* moments. Then, finally, Cromarty cleared his throat.

"That's not *precisely* what they said, Your Majesty," he observed with laudable courage. The King looked at him icily, and the Prime Minister shrugged. "I agree that you've just summarized the *sense* of the discussion with admirable clarity, Your Majesty. They were a *little* more polite than that, though."

Most of the uniformed personnel present held their breath as Roger glowered at Cromarty. But then the King snorted in harsh amusement.

"Point taken, Allen," he acknowledged. "I'm beginning to understand, however, why there were so many times Mom just needed to vent. She didn't want anyone to offer solutions or advice; she just needed to rip off some heads—figuratively, at least—where it wouldn't do any political damage. I'm still working on that. And I've discovered there are times I really regret the fact that I don't have any royal headsmen in reserve!"

The naval officers relaxed visibly, and Baron Castle Rock actually chuckled quietly. The King's eyes tracked to him, and the first lord shrugged.

"You may not have headsmen, Your Majesty, but you do have the King's Own, and most of its personnel have actually seen Parliament in action."

"Don't tempt me, My Lord."

Roger's tone was distinctly frosty, but his lips twitched and Monroe's tail stopped twitching quite so vigorously.

The King sat for a moment longer, then inhaled deeply.

"All right," he said. "Allen is quite correct; no one told me outright that I can't have what I want, whatever they may have had to say about 'potentially insuperable difficulties' and the desirability of considering 'scaling back' my perhaps 'overly ambitious' plans. The short version of it is that Parliament in general and the House of Lords in particular remains unconvinced that the People's Republic of Haven poses a credible threat to the Star Kingdom. This despite eleven T-years of steady military conquest, the creation of an old-fashioned police state that routinely 'disappears' its own citizens and 'pacifies' new conquests with pulser darts and old fashioned torture, a covert action arm responsible for an estimated thousand assassinations and acts of 'domestic terrorism' a year to destabilize intended victims, and a steadily increasing rate of expansion. Indeed, it was pointed out to me by Mr. Lebrun—*tactfully*, I assure you—on behalf of the Liberal Party that the closest edge of Havenite-claimed space is still better than two hundred and fifty light-years from the Manticore Binary System. It may *amaze* all of you to discover that I was already in possession of that astonishing information. Oddly enough, however, neither Mr. Lebrun nor the rest of the Opposition leadership seemed to be aware that that meant the People's Republic is now *less* than fifty-four light-years from *Trevor's Star.*"

Some of the uniformed personnel's relaxation seemed to depart, and Shadwell Turner, the Baron of Big Sky, who'd replaced Bethany Havinghurst as Second Space Lord grimaced. Roger looked a question at him, and Big Sky shrugged ever so slightly.

"Sometimes I think some of *my* people haven't quite twigged to that yet, either, Your Majesty. We're working on it, but there's what I can only call an entrenched unwillingness to consider new truths. I've ordered a complete top-down review of all of our existing analyses where the Peeps are concerned, but it's going to take a while, and there are a lot of professional rice bowls involved." He shrugged again. "I've got a feeling some fairly drastic housecleaning's going to be in order in the aftermath."

"I'm sure you're right," Roger half-grunted. "And we need a lot better coordination between your people and the San Martinos than we've been getting under the old management, too." He shook his head, his expression frustrated. "Havinghurst dragged her heels over it for years, but we've got to establish some kind of information exchange with them, even if they're not about to do anything to tick off the Peeps. We need a look inside their thinking, not just what their diplomats are saying openly!"

Heads nodded soberly around the table. The people of San Martin, the single habitable planet of Trevor's Star, had traded with Manticore for over three hundred T-years. That relationship had not always been particularly close or amicable—in fact, they'd come perilously close to a shooting war a T-century ago—and things could have turned very ugly following the "San Martin War" of 1752.

When a radicalized San Martin government had sought to cure its fiscal ills by "nationalizing" the Trevor's Star Terminus of the Manticoran Wormhole Junction and seized it by force in blatant violation of the Junction Treaty of 1590, a powerful task force under the command of Vice Admiral Quentin Saint-James had been dispatched to get it back again. Saint-James' masterful strategy had diverted the entire San Martin Navy to hold the terminus it had seized... only to leave San Martin itself, three light-hours from the terminus, fatally exposed. Saint-James had pounced, forcing the planet (and the system government) to surrender after a "war" in which fewer than eighty people had been killed or wounded, and his terms had been remarkably compassionate. In the name of Queen Caitrin, he had demanded the return to the terms and conditions of the Junction Treaty, return of all private property seized, and restitution for damages done to the owners. In return for that and a pledge from the planetary government to put its fiscal house in order, Saint-James had negotiated a major reduction in transit fees for San Martin-flagged merchantmen using any of the Junction termini for a period of twenty-five T-years.

The San Martinos, astounded by the generosity of their "conqueror," had done just that, restoring their economy to solvency and, in the process, forging a very close and amicable relationship with the Star Kingdom. Over the last century those reforms and that relationship had made Trevor's Star the most economically powerful star system in the entire Haven Quadrant, outside Manticore itself... which, unfortunately, had to make it especially tempting to any expanding, imperialistic neighbor. Now, threatened by the approaching wave of Havenite conquest and far closer to the Haven System than Manticore, the current San Martin government was deliberately distancing itself—or its official foreign policy, at any rate—from the Star Kingdom lest it arouse the People's Republic's ire prematurely. Roger was privately certain the San Martinos wanted no part of the PRH, but they didn't

think they could afford to say so openly, which made it imperative that the Royal Manticoran Navy establish some sort of quiet,
under-the-radar conduit with the San Martin Navy.

"I agree, Your Majesty," Big Sky said, "but given the interstellar
situation and the San Martinos'...unpleasant neighbors, something
like that's going to have to be handled very carefully. Their civilian government probably won't approve, although I'm pretty sure
some of them will be willing to make it a case of deliberately
not seeing something so they don't have to take cognizance of
it. Even some of their naval officers are going to have serious
reservations, though, and I'm afraid Admiral Havinghurst didn't
exactly inspire confidence on the part of people who'd be taking serious risks to pass information on to us. For that matter,
no one's going to want the possibility that *anyone's* feeding us
information to make it into the 'faxes, and I'm not at all sure—
yet—that I could be confident we wouldn't have a few potential
deliberate leakers still inside ONI, at least until I've had a chance
to deal with that housekeeping. And then there's the question
of how much information we're willing to give back to them in
return for whatever they give us. I'm afraid I might have to wield
a somewhat bigger broom than I'd actually been planning on if
I'm going to feel comfortable about our ability to handle that as
discreetly as it would need to be handled."

Roger regarded him thoughtfully for a moment, then glanced
at the First Space Lord.

"Admiral White Haven?"

"It's Shadwell's shop, Your Majesty. I'd prefer he not be any
more draconian than he has to be, but you're right about the
necessity of opening some back channels to San Martin. That's
going to fall squarely into his court, and he's clearly entitled to
make whatever changes he deems necessary after his review."
White Haven shook his head. "There won't be any heel-dragging
on the uniformed side when he does it, I assure you. And I don't
care *whose* cousins, nephews, or nieces get stepped on in the
process, either. You're right about the need to get our foot down
on all that nepotism, Your Majesty. Especially if we're going to
be expanding our officer corps anytime soon."

"Don't expect any heel-dragging on the civilian side, either,"
Castle Rock said firmly, and Roger nodded.

"Good," he said. "But even if ONI starts producing chapter and verse, hard numbers to substantiate what we all already know is going on, we're still going to be looking at—what was it you called it, My Lord? 'An entrenched unwillingness to consider new truths,' I believe?—by the Parliamentary leadership. Given the fact that Allen doesn't have an outright majority in the Lords, the Opposition peers have too much clout for me to simply fire the cabinet ministers who're going to be expressing that unwillingness. None of them are about to come out into the open and actively oppose my policies, you understand. They'll just drag their heels when it comes to *supporting* those policies before Parliament. Allen, unfortunately, is going to have the exquisite pleasure of dealing with that, and I'm afraid there's going to have to be a lot of horse trading to get what I want out of them. In fact, I'm probably *not* going to get what I want out of them—not all of it, at any rate—but I damned well intend to get everything I can."

The King looked around the conference room, his expression unwontedly bleak.

The thought of the People's Republic getting close enough to threaten Trevor's Star should have been a wake-up call for *anyone*, he thought harshly. Manticorans understood—or damned well *ought* to understand—the realities of warp bridges. Trevor's Star might be close to two hundred light-years from Manticore, but it was also only a single, virtually instantaneous jump away through the Manticoran Wormhole Junction, and the People's Republic's plan to plunder its way to prosperity had become painfully evident. That being the case, how could anyone with a single functioning brain cell fail to grasp the temptation the Junction had to present? It was the Junction which gave the citizens of the Star Kingdom of Manticore the highest per capita income of any star nation—*including* the Solarian League—in history. Of course, the Solarian League was so huge, had so many more citizens, that the Star Kingdom's absolute income was minute in comparison, but even in purely economic terms, the Junction would be worth at least a dozen—more probably two or *three* dozen—star systems like the ones the Peeps had already gobbled up. And that didn't even consider the opportunities for future expansion the strategic mobility and reach the Junction would provide for any imperialistically inclined regime! Even if no one in Nouveau Paris was thinking in those terms *now*, they would be by the time they got close enough. That was as inevitable as the next day's sunrise, and whatever Parliament and the Opposition might be thinking, the House of Winton knew its duty.

I said I'd build my house of steel, Pablo, he thought, remembering a long-ago day aboard HMS *Wolverine* in Manticore orbit, *and I damned well meant it.*

"All right," he said again. "Here's what's going to happen. Allen, you and I are going to find the cash to increase our shipbuilding budgets by a minimum of twenty-five percent over the next fiscal year. When we present the Estimates to Parliament next year, that will be part of them. And if our good friend Baron Seawell doesn't believe he can support that, then I will regretfully accept his immediate resignation and find a new Chancellor of the Exchequer. If the Conservative Association doesn't like that, all they have to do is get behind my budget proposal. And if they want to find out just how prepared I am to get down and dirty over this, you invite them to make a fight over it, instead. They won't like what happens if they do."

Duke Cromarty didn't look very surprised, but neither did he look particularly happy, and Roger smiled thinly before he turned his attention to Castle Rock, Pierce, and White Haven.

"I want our construction schedules revised, starting right now, in accordance with that increase in budget. I want medium and light platform construction cut back hard. We've had the better part of two decades of fat years where our commerce protection programs are concerned; now it's time we build ourselves some wallers. I don't know if we'll be able to squeeze out the budget for superdreadnoughts, so I want you to plan a fallback budget—for at least the first couple of fiscal years—to build dreadnoughts, instead, but I don't want to hear about battleships. They're too small to be survivable, and I'm not sending our people out to die in fleet engagements because we couldn't be bothered to build effective warships for them."

He let his eyes sweep over them for several heartbeats, waiting for their nods, then continued.

"In addition to the new construction, we're about to start investing heavily in our infrastructure. You're not going to be able to use the full budget increase Allen and I are going to hammer out of Parliament just on superdreadnoughts and dreadnoughts, because we don't have enough building slips. So we're going to fix that, too. I can probably count on the Conservatives and the

Progressives to support at least that much, if only because of all of the porkbarrel contracts they'll think they're going to steer to their cronies." He smiled again, even more thinly than before. "They're perfectly welcome to think that way, as long as the money gets appropriated. Of course, they may be just a little surprised by the degree of personal oversight I intend to exercise on where that money goes afterward. And the King's Bench will be exercising it right along with me. So will the Judge Advocate General and the Inspector General from your side. And understand me about this: if the Opposition—or anyone else, including anyone in uniform—wants to drag his feet or try to feather his own nest out of this, he *will* be hammered. Nor am I above using the threat of indictments to...leverage the support we need in Parliament. I'll cheerfully send any bastard who tries to embezzle or misappropriate to prison for a long, long time, but I'm less concerned about prison sentences than I am about *stopping* malfeasance and graft and driving this building program through. I want that clearly understood by every investigator and prosecutor assigned to look for criminal activity."

He tapped the conference table top with his forefinger in slow, measured emphasis, and Monroe's ears were flattened once more. Silence hovered for a moment, but no one in that conference room thought for a moment that he was done yet.

"The other thing that's going to happen is that we're going to take advantage of all the spadework Dame Carrie's had Captain Adcock doing over at BuWeaps and the CDO. I know a lot of people are skeptical about the feasibility of our financing an independent R and D program on the scale Captain Adcock and I have been talking about."

He looked directly at White Haven. The First Space Lord had been supportive of Lomax's under-the-radar efforts, and he'd backed Project Python firmly enough, but he clearly continued to cherish some doubts. Not about the idea of improving existing systems—like his son, he had an acute appreciation of the need to do that—but about the idea that the Star Kingdom, however wealthy it might be on a per capita basis, could possibly somehow develop breakthrough war-fighting technologies which had evaded the Solarian League's R&D efforts.

"I know that skepticism exists," Roger continued, "but I think it's misplaced for several reasons. First, our general tech base here in the Star Kingdom is every bit as good as the Solarian League's. Our relationship with Beowulf gives us a close enough look at current-generation Solly tech for anyone to realize that's the case, despite our physical separation from the rest of the League.

"Second, everyone seems to keep forgetting that the League has a strong vested interest in *preventing* significant changes in military technology. It has the biggest navy in existence, and a real technological game changer might make that navy obsolete overnight. When you add that to the corruption and inefficiency generated by all of *their* nepotism and crony capitalism, I strongly question the universal assumption that somehow the SLN's technology has to be the end-all and be-all of military hardware. We damned well know our *merchant*ships are better than theirs; I intend for our *war*ships to be better, as well.

"And third, speaking of merchies, our merchant fleet is *everywhere*, My Lords, and it's expanding every year. It's Crown policy to *push* that expansion as hard as we can, for a lot of reasons, but one of them is its sheer reach. Our skippers and our crews and our shipping agents see *everything* eventually, and it's time we started taking advantage of that. At least a third and more probably half of all our civilian ship masters are ex-Navy or hold current Reserve commissions. We've always had the advantage of feedback, of reports on things that catch the interest of some of those veterans and reservists; now we're going to systematize that. We're going to send out orders for them to keep their eyes open, we're going to give them direction about things we're particularly interested in, and we're going to encourage them to look for anything they think we *ought* to be interested in. I know it's going to generate a huge increase in paperwork for your people at ONI, My Lord," he told Big Sky, "but I want the finest-meshed net we can produce. If anybody anywhere is doing *anything* where weaponized or potentially weaponizable technology is concerned, I want us to hear about it as soon as humanly possible. The Junction gives us more reach in that respect than anyone else in the galaxy. I want that reach *used*."

Big Sky nodded soberly, and Roger shifted his attention back to Truman and Jerome Pearce. As Second Lord of Admiralty, Pierce was the Navy's chief financial officer, and he looked mildly apprehensive, to say the least, as the King's gaze swiveled in his direction.

"In addition to that, we're going to take all of the work Captain Adcock and his people have done and put it to work," Roger said, seeing no need to mention that *he'd* been one of Adcock's people, since everyone sitting around that table already knew it. "We're going to stand up a new, completely black command. We're going to hide it on *Weyland*, we're going to call it 'Gram,' and Captain Adcock will command it."

White Haven's eyes narrowed, and Roger nodded. HMSS *Weyland* was the smallest, least capable, and least conveniently located of the Star Kingdom's three major infrastructure platforms. It also orbited the planet Gryphon, the rather less-than-hospitable habitable planet of Manticore-B, the G2 secondary component of the Manticore Binary System, however. That put it *very* conveniently out of sight of the enormous volume of traffic passing through the Junction, which was associated with Manticore-A, better than twelve light-hours away.

And just as *Weyland* was the best place to put it, Adcock was the best man to head it. He certainly had the technical credentials for it, and despite his sister's marriage to Roger, he'd managed to stay well hidden in the background. He wasn't exactly totally unknown, but his relatively junior rank and the fact that he hadn't held a space-going command in close to thirty T-years meant he was almost completely off everyone else's radar. He wouldn't even have to drop out of sight, because he'd *been* "out of sight" ever since Lomax set up her own covert think tank.

And if there was one man in the entire galaxy in whom Roger Winton could repose complete and total confidence, that man was Jonas Adcock.

"It's going to be off the books, My Lords," he said, looking around the table, his expression grim. "*Nobody* is going to know about it, and we'll do whatever we have to do to keep it that way. Hopefully, the name's obscure enough to conceal what we're doing if it should leak, but we *are* going to be forging a sword, and if Sigurd could kill Fafnir with the original, I intend for us to do the same thing to *our* dragon with its namesake.

"I suspect that eventually a lot of money's going to flow into it, and I want you to begin socking away cash for it now, Lord Pierce. Every loose dollar you can find gets earmarked for Gram, and I intend to press Parliament for a substantial increase in discretionary covert spending to come up with even more funding.

This is going to be completely separate from BuWeaps' open R and D programs, but any funding we can skim off the open R and D and funnel into Gram, gets skimmed. Understand me on this—if I have to dispose of Crown Lands and fund this out of the Privy Purse, that's what I'll do. We're looking at the short end of a disastrous war of attrition unless we come up with a qualitative equalizer. I don't know what we'll find, and for that matter I can't guarantee we *will* find our own Gram, but I *can* guarantee that if we *don't* find it, we lose. And, My Lords, the House of Winton does not lose when the security and the freedom of the Star Kingdom of Manticore and its citizens are at stake."

The final sentence came out with slow, dreadful emphasis, and Monroe sat up on his true-feet, ears flat, baring his white, needle sharp fangs as King Roger III of Manticore looked around the Admiralty House conference room's silence.

"Are there any questions?" he asked softly.

April 1867 PD

"YOUR MAJESTY," the Duke of Cromarty's tone was a bit more formal than it was in his private working sessions with King Roger, "the Liberals and the Conservatives will pitch three kinds of fit if you force the issue at this point. You know they will."

"Then they'll just have to get over it," Roger said flatly. "This sh—" He paused, glancing at Dame Rachel Nageswar, the Foreign Secretary. "This *crap*," he continued after a moment, "has dragged on too long already, Allen. I want it settled. We *need* it settled."

"I don't disagree, Your Majesty. I'm just saying that it's going to be one hell of a fight, one we may not win in the end, and that there are going to be potential costs down the road. As your Prime Minister, it's my responsibility to point all of that out before I go out and fight like hell to get it done, anyway."

Cromarty smiled faintly, and Roger snorted and sat back in his chair, feeling Monroe's familiar, comforting, warmth against the back of his neck. He reached up over his shoulder, opening his hand, and the treecat bumped his head affectionately against it. Then the King looked back at the two-footed people in the Mount Royal Palace conference room.

Cromarty sat across the table in his usual place. Jacob Wundt, Roger's Lord Chamberlain and one of his closest advisers, as he'd been Queen Samantha's, sat to the King's left; Dame Rachel sat to Cromarty's left; and Dame Elisa Paderweski, Roger's tough as nails ex-Marine chief of staff, sat to the King's right. It was a small group, all of its members drawn from Roger's most trusted inner circle, and every single one of them was looking back at him.

And I don't blame them, he thought grumpily. *If I had the choice,* I'd *be looking at someone else, too!*

The problem ought to have been an absurdly simple no-brainer, but could the Liberals and the Conservatives see it that way? No, of course they couldn't!

The math on the Manticoran Wormhole Junction had always insisted it had additional termini which had not yet been discovered. The fact that it was already the biggest junction in known space actually made finding those additional termini more difficult, not less, however, because the ones already discovered masked their undiscovered fellows' much fainter signatures. Some hyper-physicists had even claimed the math was wrong—that the real reason none of those hypothetical additional termini had never been found was because they simply didn't exist. Other hyper-physicists pointed out that over seventy T-years had elapsed between the rapid-fire discovery of the Junction's first three termini in Beowulf, Trevor's Star, and Hennesy and the discovery of the Gregor Terminus in 1662 . . . and that the Matapan Terminus hadn't been discovered until 1796, a hundred and thirty T-years after that! Those hyper-physicists had been confident in the existing math and, shortly after Roger had assumed the throne, their confidence had been justified by the discovery of a sixth terminus, associated with the G5 star Basilisk, two hundred and ten light-years from the Manticore Binary System.

At the moment, there wasn't much human settlement out that direction, but warp bridges had a tendency to change things like that, and Basilisk's position offered some very interesting possibilities where trade with Silesia and the Andermani was concerned. In fact, those possibilities were already in a fair way to being realized as what the economists had dubbed "the Triangle Route" gathered speed. Ships could now depart Manticore to the Gregor System, move normally through hyper-space from Gregor throughout the Silesian Confederacy or the Andermani Empire, then swing "north" to Basilisk and return directly to Manticore. The savings in time—and thus overhead—loomed large, the reduction in turnaround time meant a ship could make more voyages in a given time window, and the extra reach was opening still more markets.

But there was a kicker in Basilisk's case. The Basilisk System had an inhabitable planet . . . and that planet, Medusa, was already inhabited. Worse, it was inhabited by an alien species, not colonized by humans, and the aliens in question were decidedly pre-space. That minor fact had created a furor in the ranks of the Manticoran Liberal Party, and it had also spawned a bizarre alliance between the Liberals, the Conservative Association, the Progressive Party, and Sir Sheridan Wallace's so-called "New Men." In the Liberals' case, he was at least tentatively willing to admit that something remotely like principle played a part. The Conservatives and the Progressives, however, wouldn't have recognized a genuine principle if it jumped out of the underbrush and bit them . . . and the "New Men's" principle quotient was somewhere south of there.

Well south.

"I appreciate that it's going to be a problem," he said now, meeting Cromarty's eyes across the table. "I also think we've only made it worse by pussyfooting around it up till now, though. And I think it may be time to remind the Star Kingdom in general about some ancient history and Axelrod. You know damned well that things haven't changed *that* much where human greed is concerned over the last three hundred T-years!"

Cromarty smiled in unhappy agreement. The Axelrod Corporation had been one of the very first Solarian transtellers to recognize the true significance of warp bridges after their discovery in 1447 PD, and its Astro Survey Division had gone back and systematically recrunched the numbers on every surveyed star, looking for the gravitic markers no one had previously known to watch for. Axelrod's management had been willing to spend the manhours because it had believed those markers might well be buried in the old data if it was reexamined, and that belief had proved well founded. The various termini the search had uncovered within the territory of the Solarian League had, of course, been recognized as the League's property and duly reported to Old Terra for lucrative finder's fees, but those outside the League had enjoyed rather a different status in Axelrod's opinion—especially in cases where the recrunched data suggested the possibility of true junctions, with multiple termini.

Cases like, oh, the Manticore Binary System, for example.

Axelrod's boldfaced attempt to use its mercenary-manned fleet to seize the Manticoran Wormhole Junction by naked force before the then-Star Kingdom even realized it might exist could well have changed galactic history, and—given the typical Solarian transstellar's modus operandi—not for the better. Only courage, an officer named Carlton Locatelli, and a lot of luck had prevented the attempt from succeeding, although very few Manticorans seemed to think about that very much today. Not too surprisingly, perhaps. Looking around at the prosperity and the commercial and economic power the Junction had bestowed upon them, it was difficult to remember the sleepy, peaceful, isolated star nation Manticore had once been.

And life would probably be simpler if we still were *sleepy, peaceful, and isolated,* the Prime Minister reflected. *Unfortunately, we're not. Roger's right about that. And he's also right that what almost happened to us then can still happen to us* now *if the people opposed to his buildup don't realize our neighborhood isn't sleepy, peaceful,* or *isolated any longer.*

"Your Majesty," Nageswar said after a moment, "like Allen, I support your policy. But I'm not sure this is the best time to push."

She met Roger's gaze unflinchingly, with the confidence of the lifelong, career diplomat she'd been before rising to her present post in the latest Cabinet reorganization. One of the things he most valued about her, almost more than her indisputable expertise as the Star Kingdom's chief diplomat, was her willingness to disagree with him when she thought he was wrong, and he sat back with a courteous nod for her to continue.

Nageswar was a Crown Loyalist, part of Roger's ongoing—and frustratingly gradual—remaking of his Cabinet. Cromarty's Centrists, unfortunately, still couldn't command a majority in the House of Lords, even with Crown Loyalist support. That meant sharing out cabinet posts among the major political parties... and that Cromarty's premiership hung in perpetual jeopardy, at least in theory. Officially, with both Conservatives and Liberals in the Cabinet, there *was* no Opposition in Manticore at the present time; in fact, the restiveness of the other parties meant that political analysts routinely spoke of the Conservatives and Liberals as being in opposition even while they sat in a "coalition" Cabinet.

Unfortunately for them, the monarch was head of government in the Star Kingdom, not simply head of state. In theory, Roger didn't need the Cabinet at all, although God only knew what sort of political crisis he could provoke by deciding to rule by decree! But while he couldn't compel the House of Lords to support a prime minister not of its choosing, neither could the House of

Lords compel him to accept a prime minister not of *his* choosing. That sort of standoff would lead to effective paralysis of government in the Star Kingdom, of course, but the Opposition had realized early on that Roger, unlike his mother, was perfectly prepared to accept that paralysis in the short term if he had to. There was a steeliness behind those calm brown eyes of his that was already reminding some historians of Queen Adrienne, and he had the traditional weapon of the House of Winton—the powerful support of his subjects—tucked away in his hip pocket.

That connection of the Winton Dynasty with the Star Kingdom's commoners had been renewed with his marriage to Queen Consort Angelique, who'd won Manticore's collective heart by her beauty and obvious love for their King...and it had been underscored afresh by the birth of Crown Princess Elizabeth Adrienne Samantha Annette Winton, exactly one T-year ago next month. If the Opposition pushed him to it, if its leaders provoked a government shutdown, there wasn't much question what would happen in the House of Commons in the next general election. It might take a year or two, but the outcome would be the decimation of the Opposition parties' representation in the lower house. And while that might not much concern the Conservative Association, which was overwhelmingly a party of the aristocracy, it definitely loomed large in the thinking of Sir Orwell Lebrun's Liberals and Janice MacMillan's Progressives.

Roger didn't much like to contemplate that sort of constitutional crisis, either, although part of him was tempted to go ahead and embrace it, even *provoke* it. At the moment, the People's Republic of Haven was still the better part of two hundred light years away from the Manticore Binary System. There were moments—and this was one of them—when it seemed to him that taking on the Opposition and breaking it once and for all *now*, however bloody the political infighting, would be preferable to finding himself hamstrung at some more critical moment farther down the road, with the Peeps close at hand and the situation too critical for facing down domestic opposition. But that was the nasty, bloody-minded side of him talking, he told himself. Far better to continue gradually nibbling away at the Opposition parties' power without risking a constitutional fight he might not, after all, win.

Not that he intended to back away from that fight if it came, he reminded himself grimly.

"We're just about to wrap up our current negotiations with Beowulf, and everybody in Parliament knows it," Nageswar reminded him now. "If we add this to the mix, it might throw a spanner into those talks, as well. Or at least into the Lords' willingness to ratify whatever treaty modification we emerge with."

"That's a valid point, Rachel," Roger acknowledged. Obviously she'd been thinking the same thing he had.

"At the moment, Beowulf's going to agree to everything we've requested," she continued, "and Hennesy actually welcomes the changes. Gregor's going to be less enthusiastic, but it's also not going to have much choice when we get around to the Republic. But it would be a public relations debacle if after getting *Beowulf* to agree, the Lords rejected the treaty, and you know the Conservatives are opposed to it anyway, whatever Summercross may have to say."

Matthäus Routhier, the Earl of Summercross, was the current leader of the Conservative Association, and a more xenophobic isolationist would have been difficult to imagine. The only good thing about his paranoia, from Roger's perspective, was that he was at least marginally willing to support a Navy powerful enough to protect his isolationism.

"The Beowulf Planetary Board of Directors is going out of its way to meet our requests," Nageswar pointed out. "In some respects, they're courting the risk of a significant backlash from their own voters, and the League government's not going to be delighted when it hears about it, either. I don't think the Directors need—or deserve—to be kicked in the teeth because someone decides to mount a domestic resistance to the treaty modifications from *our* side. We could burn a lot of goodwill that way."

Roger nodded again. Once upon a time, the Beowulf System had enjoyed excellent relations with both the Star Kingdom and the Republic of Haven. The three of them had always been the strongest supporters of the Cherwell Convention to suppress the interstellar genetic slave trade, among other things, and Beowulfers worshiped at the shrine of meritocracy. The original Republic's emphasis on individual freedoms and opportunities had been a good fit with that Beowulfan attitude, but the PRH was something else entirely. The Technical Conservation Act had been a direct slap in the face, as far as Beowulf was concerned, and Manticore—with whom relations had been even closer, given the Junction's direct connection to the Beowulf System—had profited by the cooling of the Beowulf-Haven relationship over the last T-century. That was a major part of Beowulf's willingness to revisit the Junction Treaty of 1590, but there were limits in everything. However willing the Board of Directors might be to work with Manticore, Beowulfers in general were just as capable as anyone of getting pissed off at a star nation which had insulted *their* star nation.

"We *could* burn a lot of goodwill," Roger acknowledged, "but only if the Opposition's stupid enough to pick a fight over the treaty negotiations, and I don't think even Summercross is that dumb. If he is, someone like North Hollow or High Ridge will sit on him in this instance, I think."

Nageswar looked faintly dubious and glanced at Cromarty.

"I think His Majesty has a point, Rachel," the Prime Minister said. "Mind you, I'd rather not push it so far we find out whether or not he does, but even the Conservatives would realize they'd have trouble convincing anyone else to agree with them."

The foreign secretary looked at him for a moment longer, then sat back. She still didn't seem convinced, but Roger agreed with Cromarty.

The Junction Treaty had been negotiated by Queen Elizabeth II's government shortly after the initial discovery of the Junction and its first three known termini, associated with Beowulf, San Martin, and Hennesy. There were times Roger wished his great-great-great-great-great-great-great-great-great grandmother had been just a little more ruthless when that treaty was signed, but he supposed he really couldn't complain about how well it had served the Star Kingdom's interests for the last three hundred T-years.

The problem was that Manticore had ceded shared sovereignty over the termini to Beowulf, San Martin, and Hennesy. There'd been no legal requirement for Elizabeth to do that. While any star system was free to claim sovreignty over anything within a six light-hour radius of its primary, claims to anything more than twelve light-minutes from the primary were conditional. In order to establish sovereignty, the system's claim was subject to challenge under international law unless it could demonstrate its ability to maintain "a real and persistent police power" over it. All known warp termini lay well outside the twelve-minute limit (some, like the Junction itself, lay outside the six-hour limit, but they were rare), which meant they belonged to whoever could maintain that "real and persistent" police power. Essentially, whoever had the military wherewithal to hold it got to keep it, and if that whoever happened not to be the local star system, that was simply too bad.

The Beowulf System, as a member of the Solarian League, would probably have been in a position to produce that wherewithal. Neither Trevor's Star nor Hennesy, which had only recently been colonized at the time, would have, yet Elizabeth's government had opted to grant all three star systems an identical share of the Junction revenues, the same discounted transit fees, and the same shared sovereignty over the terminus. Roger had always suspected that Manticore's own experience with Axelrod had played a part in her decision, although there'd never been any formal mention of that in the negotiations. And given the smallness of the Royal Manticoran Navy at that time, it had undoubtedly made lots of sense not to go around heaping additional missions on it. Now, when the Star Kingdom's economic power absolutely depended upon the Junction, and when Roger's ability to prepare his kingdom against the Havenite threat absolutely depended upon that economic power, it didn't. His mother had quietly amended the RMN's strategic mission requirements to include providing for the Junction's secondary termini even before general commerce protection as long ago as 1850, but no one had gone out of the way to underscore that to the rest of the galaxy at the time, given the state of the Star Kingdom's wall of battle. For that matter, Roger had no desire to pick fights over the issue with anyone even now, yet times had changed (and not for the better) over the last seventeen years. Now he needed the authority—the recognized authority, domestically as well as abroad—to act unilaterally, in whatever fashion seemed necessary, to ensure the Junction's security, and that included ensuring the security of those secondary termini of it, as well.

Beowulf and Hennesy had recognized that, and both of them had specifically recognized Manticore's *undivided* sovereignty over their associated termini. Roger had sweetened the deal by increasing their percentage of transit fees and adding a secret clause which amounted to a mutual defense treaty, but in return he had the right to deploy Manticoran warships to protect either of those termini by force if he felt it was necessary. He doubted very much that it ever *was* going to be necessary in Beowulf's case, but Hennesy was another matter. That system had already required Manticoran assistance once, in the Ingeborg incident which had cost the RMN the life of Admiral Ellen D'Orville in 1710 PD, after all. But whether either of them ever actually needed Manticoran assistance to defend their termini, the precedent was important to establish, since he fully intended to extend it to Basilisk and any of those other as-yet-undiscovered termini the math predicted. And as Nageswar had just pointed out, the Republic of Gregor wasn't going to make much of a stink when he "requested" the same terms from it. It had far too many internal domestic problems to court a confrontation with a major trading partner. And the Matapan System, thank God, had neither habitable planets nor inhabitants, so there'd never been any question over who *that* terminus belonged to, lock, stock, and barrel.

Trevor's Star was another matter, of course. Already half-surrounded by Havenite conquests or proxies, San Martin wasn't about to risk pissing off the PRH, despite its traditional friendship with Manticore—or perhaps *because* of that friendship—by signing an agreement which would give the Star Kingdom the unilateral right to forward deploy battle squadrons to the Trevor's Star Terminus whenever it felt like it. The San Martinos were working hard to build a navy which would hopefully be big enough to at least give the People's Republic pause, but not even the contacts Baron Big Sky had managed to cultivate in the SMN were optimistic about their ability to do so. And there was no way in the universe San Martin was going to look like it was cozying up to Manticore when that was likely to convince the PRH to go ahead and nip the potential threat of its military in the bud.

"With all due respect, Dame Rachel," Jacob Wundt said in his calm, quiet voice, "I agree with His Majesty in this instance, as well. I think Summercross, at least, would prefer for the Junction Treaty to remain unaltered. I really don't think he's going to complain too much about the Beowulf or Hennesy aspect of it, but he's going to resent its precedent, especially when we press Gregor to concede the same status to the terminus there. He's going to see it as the first step down that 'slippery slope to imperialism' he's been whining about for as long as even *I* can remember!"

The Lord Chamberlain grimaced, and Nageswar's lips twitched. Not that it was really all that humorous. The Conservative Association was opposed to anything that might draw the Star Kingdom into territorial expansion. Its members had nothing at all against Manticore's burgeoning economic reach, the steady growth of its merchant marine, or its enormously active financial sector, but anything which might entangle the Star Kingdom in interstellar power rivalries was anathema to the Conservatives. Even worse from their perspective, Roger suspected, would be the possibility of actually adding additional voters to the Star Kingdom. The constitutional mechanisms which had been crafted to conserve political power in the House of Lords when the Star Kingdom was created were beginning to wear uncomfortably thin, in their opinion. The last thing they wanted was to open the door to "outsiders and foreigners who don't understand how our system works" . . . and who might have the effrontery to side with the Commons against them. That was the real reason they'd never raised a stink about Manticoran sovereignty in Matapan; no people meant no voters to screw up their treasured status quo.

"But however *he* feels about Gregor—and even Basilisk—too many of his fellow Conservatives are making too much money out of their business relationships with Beowulf for him to risk alienating the Planetary Directors" Wundt continued, "and he can't really make much of a stink about Hennesy, given how enthusiastically President O'Flaherty's embraced the idea. No," the Lord Chamberlain shook his head, "he'll reserve any open opposition for Gregor and Basilisk, exactly the way he's been doing."

"Jacob's put his finger on it, Rachel," Roger said. "Which rather brings us back to my original point, I suppose."

"And leaves us with the problem of Lebrun," Cromarty pointed out sourly.

The Conservatives' opposition to annexing Basilisk reflected their basic isolationism, but despite Summercross' personal rabidness on that particular issue, it didn't rally enormous amounts of resistance among their rank-and-file in Basilisk's case. The *Liberals'* opposition, on the other hand, was ideology and emotion-driven, and Sir Orwell Lebrun's followers were far more adamantly opposed to "imperialism" because that sort of "jingoistic aggression against weaker star nations" affronted their principles. That was especially true, unfortunately, in the case of the Medusans, who were somewhere in the equivalent of the early Bronze Age. That automatically made them "noble savages" and made it the Star Kingdom's moral responsibility to ensure their independence and guarantee the security of their natural resources—like the Basilisk terminus—rather than using an iron fist to despoil the native sentients itself.

Never mind the fact that neither Roger nor anyone else on Manticore had the least interest in "despoiling" the Medusans. Never mind the fact that interstellar law granted Manticore prima facie sovereignty over the terminus as its discoverer . . . or that there was no way in the universe the Medusans could have utilized, managed, *or* protected that terminus.

"We could settle for simply claiming the *terminus*," Nageswar suggested. "I know that would be less than ideal, but it would give us the authority we needed to develop it and—if necessary—defend it without interfering with the Medusans at all."

"If *we* don't claim sovereignty over the entire star system, then someone else is going to," Roger said flatly. "That's the whole reason we claimed the *Matapan* System as well as the Terminus. It's not as if we really *needed* an M-4 without a single planet of its own, after all! But we couldn't leave the system just hanging, either, and that's what that idiot Lebrun is systematically ignoring. It's all very well for him to proclaim that the Medusans must be left alone in undisputed possession of their planet and their star system, but even if *I* agreed with him, someone like Gustav Anderman or Hereditary President Harris wouldn't lose a minute's sleep over trampling all over a planet full of aborigines. Gustav would claim the system to use as leverage against us in Silesia and as a base to harass us—and anyone using the terminus—in order to get a bigger piece of the trade moving through the Triangle Route. And Harris would claim the system because he's a Peep who's damned well figured out we're going to be the biggest long-term threat to his expansion, and because when—not *if*, as far as he's concerned—he takes out Trevor's Star, that would allow him to threaten us militarily through two of the Junction's termini simultaneously."

"I agree that's probably how he'd think about it, Your Majesty," Paderweski said, "but I hope you'll forgive an ex-jarhead for pointing out that it would be a really, really stupid thing for them to try."

"Of course it would, Elisa," Roger agreed. "That doesn't mean they *won't* try it, though. Have any of you noted any particular signs of restraint on the Peeps' part?"

He looked around, answered only by silence, and snorted.

"That's what *I* think, too. And the problem is that whether an assault through the Junction worked or not, it would still be an act of war, and we'd still find ourselves fighting the Peoples Navy. At the moment, we're not in a position to do that, and we can't afford a situation in which Harris and his admirals screw us all over by starting a war neither side's really ready for. Besides, there's still that matter of future precedents to worry about. I want it established right now that if we do manage to locate, survey, and open any additional Junction warp bridges, both ends of them belong to *us*, no matter *what's* at the other end."

"All right, Your Majesty," Cromarty said, "as long as you understand that this could get really ugly."

"Oh, believe me, I understand that! But I've got an ace up my sleeve."

Roger smiled thinly, and Cromarty experienced a distinct sinking sensation. He'd seen that smile before.

"An ace up your sleeve?" he repeated carefully.

"Oh, yes. She's called Elizabeth."

"Your Majesty?" Cromarty blinked at the total non sequitur, and Roger chuckled. But then the King's expression turned hard.

"You tell Lebrun that if he wants a fight over this, he can have one," he said coldly. "And you tell Summercross that if he really wants to piss off the House of Winton, he should have at it. We're close to having the votes we need in the Lords with just your Centrists and Rachel's Crown Loyalists, and Janice Macmillan and Sheridan Wallace are for sale to the highest bidder. We can outbid Summercross or Lebrun, and just this once, I'm willing to do it if I have to. And if we bring the Progressives—or even just the 'New Men,' probably—on board, we'll have the votes."

"Assuming they'd stay bought, Your Majesty," Cromarty said with a grimace of distaste, and Roger nodded.

"Oh, I wouldn't expect them to stay bought forever, Allen. But I wouldn't need them to, either—I'd just need them long enough to sign off on my solution to the problem. And, frankly, this time around I'd be willing to buy whatever shiny new toy we had to give Macmillan or Wallace."

"And just what solution did you have in mind, Your Majesty?" Nageswar asked, her tone even more cautious than Cromarty's had been.

"I'm willing to throw Lebrun a bone if that's what it takes," Roger replied. "So I'm willing to specifically not claim sovereignty over the planet Medusa itself, to recognize the Medusans as the original inhabitants and rightful owners of the star system, precisely as the Ninth Amendment recognizes the treecats on Sphinx, and to set aside, say, five percent of all revenues generated by traffic through the Basilisk Terminus for the benefit of the Medusans. At the same time, however, we're going to assert sovereignty over the star system as a whole, and directly—*officially*—annex the terminus itself."

"I'm...not certain how that would stand up under interstellar law, Your Majesty." Nageswar's eyes were half-slitted in intense thought. "I don't think I've ever heard of anyone claiming a star system while specifically *not* claiming the only habitable planet in it. I doubt there's any precedent to support it."

"Then we'll *make* precedent," Roger told her.

"Lebrun will argue that it's easy to promise not to take over the planet *now*," Cromarty pointed out. "Then he'll trot out that aphorism about power corrupting and suggest that while, of course *you* wouldn't do any such thing, Your Majesty, that's not to say some *future* Manticoran government wouldn't."

"He can suggest anything he damn well wants," Roger said flatly. "We're going to do this, and in case anyone thinks we're not, I'm taking advantage of Beth's birthday to make a statement...and apply a little pressure of my own."

"I beg your pardon, Your Majesty?" Paderweski looked at him, one eyebrow raised. "Is this something that simply slipped your mind the last time you were discussing plans with, oh, your chief of staff?"

"I discussed it last night with the only person who'd actually have a veto right over it, Elisa." Roger smiled crookedly at her. "Angel said it's all right with her."

"I see. And just what did you have in mind for Beth's birthday, Sir?"

"Oh, it's very simple." Roger showed his teeth. "I'm going to exercise one of the Crown's—and Commons'—prerogatives. We're going to make Elizabeth Duchess of Basilisk."

Despite decades of political experience, Cromarty's jaw dropped, and Nageswar's eyes widened. Roger tipped back in his chair, listening to the buzzing purr from the treecat draped over its back.

"Between the Centrists and the Crown Loyalists, we have a clear majority in the Commons," he pointed out, "and patents of nobility are created by the Crown with the *Commons'* approval, not the Lords. I intend to make Beth Duchess of *Basilisk*—not Medusa—and I intend to enfeoff her with a percentage of all transit fees through the terminus. Only a tiny one, just enough to give her a *personal* claim on the terminus. But when we draw the patent of nobility, we'll include the entire star system *except* for Medusa. The Lords can't reject the patent, although they might theoretically refuse to seat her *as* Duchess of Basilisk, I suppose, if they're feeling really stupid. But since they can't, as far as everyone here in the Star Kingdom is concerned, the baby princess they adore will be the rightful duchess of the star system in question. Now," he looked around the conference room with that same, thin smile, "does anyone sitting around this table really think even Summercross would be stupid enough to buck that kind of public attitude? *Lebrun* might, but Summercross' advisers will insist he drop the issue like a hot rock." He shook his head. "I imagine we'll still have to do some horse trading, make some concessions to assuage the Liberals' concerns over the Medusans, but tell my daughter she can't have her first-birthday present when everyone else in the Star Kingdom wants to give it to her?"

He shook his head again, his smile positively sharklike.

"*Nobody*'s going to want to come across like that kind of Scrooge, people. Nobody."

May 1870 PD

"JONAS!" An obviously pregnant Queen Consort Angelique Winton threw her arms about her brother. "Roger didn't tell me you were coming, the stinker!"

She turned her head to glare at her husband and the treecat bleeking with laughter on his shoulder, and Roger grinned.

"I shouldn't have *had* to tell you, Angel. He *is* your brother, and you know how he dotes on Elizabeth! Besides, it's barely a forty-hour hop on one of the regular shuttle flights. Did you really think he was going to miss her fourth birthday party?"

"He could've told me he was coming, though!" Angelique pointed out. "And *you* could've told Beth when she was worrying about whether Uncle Jonas was going to make it."

"I told Jacob and I told Elisa, so they made all the arrangements with an eye towards his being here. But they were the *only* people I was going to tell, since he'd sworn me to secrecy."

"Jacob and Elisa both knew and neither of them told me, either?" Angelique glared even more ferociously. "That has to come under the heading of high treason!"

"Nonsense, there's an ancient Old Earth tradition—goes all the way back to something called the 'Wars of the Roses,' I think—that no one can be convicted of treason as long as he obeyed the orders of a legitimately crowned king. And that, my dear," he elevated his nose, "is *me*."

"You have to sleep sometime," his wife replied darkly.

"Yes, but I know you wouldn't really murder the father of your daughter and your unborn son." He put his arm around her, hugging her firmly. "That romantic center of yours is far too mushy for you to do anything like that, love."

"Don't think you can turn *me* up sweet, spacer!" she growled, kissing his ear.

"If it gets any mushier in here, I'm heading for the nursery and my niece," Jonas announced, and the King and Queen smiled at him.

"Actually, I think it would be a good idea if we *all* headed for the nursery and let Beth know her favorite uncle made it after all," Roger suggested, reaching out with his free right hand to shake Jonas'. "It really is going to be her best surprise present of the day, Jonas," he went on more seriously, "and Katie and Edward'll be here in about another hour. Let's go let Beth spend some time greeting you properly before you have to start sharing her."

◆ ◆ ◆

"She's growing like a weed," Jonas said several hours later, leaning back in the comfortable chair in Roger's Mount Royal Palace office.

Elisa Paderweski had warned them both that they had no more than ninety minutes before they had to be on stage for Elizabeth's official cake cutting. Given the fact that Crown Princess Elizabeth had inherited her father's temper to go along with her mother's beauty, that was not a time limit to be lightly ignored by any mere uncle, father, or king.

"You probably notice it more than I do, actually, given the intervals between your visits." Roger settled behind his desk, tipped his chair back, and rested his heels inelegantly on the blotter. "I expect it'll be more noticeable to me again in a month or so, once Michael arrives and I have that newborn meter stick to compare her to again."

"How does she feel about not being an only child anymore?"

"It's up for grabs." Roger smiled. "One day she's excited about having a baby brother; the next, she's worried Mommy and Daddy may love him more because he's newer. She told Jacob she hoped she wouldn't have to run away to the circus because we loved him more . . . and then, in the same conversation, she told him she hoped 'Mikey' would be comfortable in her old crib."

Jonas laughed. Elizabeth had Jacob Wundt wrapped as firmly around her finger as she did most of the rest of the Mount Royal staff.

"She'll be fine," he said. "I remember Angel worrying exactly the same way about Jeptha and Aidan."

"I don't doubt it."

Roger glanced around surreptitiously, then opened a desk drawer, extracted a hand rubbed ironwood humidor, and took out a cigar. Monroe instantly hopped down from the back of his chair, climbed up onto the perch on the opposite side of the office, and made a scolding sound, and Jonas shook his head.

"Angel's going to smell it on you," he warned. "And when she does—!"

"No, she *won't* smell it," Roger said smugly. "Lieutenant Givens brought me a little present last month." Lieutenant Patricia Givens was Roger's personal liaison to Admiral Big Sky, in charge (among other things) of seeing to it that the King got regular summaries of new technologies being reported by the network of merchant spacers ONI had created at Roger's suggestion. "One of our skippers brought back a new nanotech they developed in Footstep. It can be tuned to go after particular odors and clean them out of your clothes—or off your skin, for that matter—but leave everything else strictly alone and as stinky as you like, and it works just fine on tobacco smoke, thank you very much."

"And you really think she won't find out about it?" Jonas looked skeptical and Monroe's bleek and half-flattened ears seconded the motion, but Roger shrugged.

"I figure I've got at least another three or four weeks before she does, and I plan to enjoy it while I can." He clipped the cigar's end, put it into his mouth, lit it, and blew a fragrant cloud of smoke in Jonas' direction. "And I figure I deserve it. At least until she does find out."

"Can't argue with that, I suppose."

Jonas studied his brother-in-law surreptitiously for a moment. After thirteen T-years on the throne, there was an additional . . . solidity to him. It was as if his shoulders had broadened to bear the weight, and he seemed *tougher*, somehow. He wore the RMN uniform to which he was entitled, with the commodore's twin gold planets he'd earned. Eventually, he'd rise to admiral's rank by simple seniority, even officially on half-pay, but Jonas knew that he would never don an admiral's star until he *had* attained to that rank.

He wasn't the first Manticoran monarch to have served in the Navy, by any means, but he *was* the first to habitually appear in uniform rather than civilian dress. It wasn't simply to maintain his personal link to the service he'd loved, either. His drive to build up the Navy's fighting strength had gained momentum steadily over the past decade, and he was the deliberate, public face of that buildup. Opposition cartoonists had fastened upon that uniform in their caricatures. It was suggested in some quarters—especially those of the Liberal Party—that the real reason for the buildup was simply King Roger's desire to play with toy boats, and some had gone so far as to compare him to the original Gustav Anderman, who insisted that the members of his personal bodyguard all had to be at least two meters tall. Of course, the political cartoonists who *supported* his policies had also fastened on the uniform, although they seldom festooned it with all of the oversized rank badges and the chest full of medal ribbons the Opposition appended to it.

But he looked tired, too, Jonas thought. Not exhausted, nowhere near defeated, but ... weary. Like a man who knew he still had a long way to go.

Well, at least he's got prolong to get him to the end of the race, that's something! he told himself. At seventy-three, even with modern medical care and a vigorous exercise regimen, Jonas was finding it just a bit harder to maintain the pace he'd set since first becoming a King's officer.

"I've been following your reports," Roger said after a moment, apparently oblivious to his brother-in-law's examination. "It sounds like you're making some progress."

"In several directions, I think," Jonas agreed. "It's still early days, though, I'm afraid. Earlier days than I'd like."

"Yes, but Rodriguez tells me Section Thirteen's expecting a fully successful run of test shots on Python next month, and you and I both know how much your boys and girls contributed to that from behind the scenes. We're going to be first on the scene with an all-up laser head, Jonas." Roger showed his teeth. "The Peeps aren't going to like *that* one bit when they find out about it!"

"No," Jonas acknowledged. "But it's not going to take them all that long to duplicate it—or buy it from the Sollies—as soon as the rest of the galaxy figures out we've got it and goes after it in earnest. Don't forget ONI's reports on Astral. It took them thirty damned T-years to get A and H's basic model to work, but they've got it now!"

"And they can't convince the Sollies to buy it because of all the scandal over the original A and H tests, either," Roger pointed out, then waved his cigar. "Oh, they'll find a buyer eventually—maybe even the Peeps, though I'd put my money on the Andermani coming up to scratch for it first—but Rodriguez says our throughput numbers are already better than anything Astral has, and we're just at the very start of the development and upgrade process. It's going to get a hell of a lot better by the time Section Thirteen's done tweaking it, and that doesn't even consider all the other little goodies you and Gram are going to produce for us while BuWeaps is doing the tweaking!"

"We'll certainly try," Jonas promised.

His smile was less than completely happy, and he twitched a shrug when Roger gave him a sharp look.

"We've got several promising possibilities opening up, but that's the problem. Stuff is coming in from Big Sky and our open source avenues even faster than anyone could've anticipated. Just sorting it is eating up more manhours than I ever expected, which means I don't have enough capable people left over to follow up the leads we're generating. And I'm afraid quite a bit of what we *are* getting done at this point is probably duplicating work someone else's done somewhere else, if we only knew it."

"Best to put our own knowledge platform in place," Roger responded. "New advances, thy name is Synergy." He grinned. "I've noticed several places where the basic research you're doing—even if it is a case of catching up with someone else—is suggesting new possibilities, Jonas. That's exactly what Gram is supposed to be doing."

"I know, but we still don't—"

"You still don't have the manpower or the budget you need," Roger interrupted. "I know. And Allen and I are about to fix that."

"You are?"

"Yes." Roger smiled unpleasantly. "Haskins caught Summercross and that loathsome piece of work Dmitri Young involved in a kickback scheme with the Treadwell Yard. A rather lucrative one."

Jonas straightened in his chair as the cast of characters registered. Sir Sherwood Haskins was the current Chancellor of the Exchequer, the late, unlamented Baron Seawell's Centrist successor; Dmitri Young, the Earl of North Hollow, was an ex-Navy officer—of sorts, anyway—turned politician, lobbyist, and general all round slime merchant, serving as one of the Conservative Association's kingmakers, which gave him plenty of clout with Summercross; and the Treadwell Yard was one of the Navy's major contractors.

"Without going into all the sordid details," Roger continued, "Treadwell had been paying Summercross and the Conservative Association political action committee a tidy little piece of change in return for the Association's votes on appropriations bills, and Summercross and North Hollow—although we can't pin North Hollow to it as definitively as I'd like; say what you will, the man's slicker than pond scum—had been laundering the PAC contributions through straw donors to keep anyone asking just exactly why Treadwell might have been feeling so generous. And pocketing a bit of it for their personal use on the way past, for that matter. So that's embezzlement, bribery, illegal political contributions, money laundering, and conspiracy for the lot of them."

The King blew another streamer of smoke, his eyes dreamy.

"I'd really rather send Summercross and North Hollow to prison, all things being equal, but Judge Fitzgibbons says North Hollow could probably actually beat the charges in court. We've got Summercross and Treadwell dead to rights, though, and the campaign laws violation would be especially devastating to the Conservatives."

Jonas nodded in understanding. Havel Fitzgibbons was the Justice Minister of the Star Kingdom of Manticore, but he'd been a justice on the Queen's Bench for ten years before Samantha's death, and he far preferred the simpler title of "Judge." More to the point, he'd been a prosecutor before he ever became a judge, he knew his law, and he hated political corruption cases above all others.

Especially cases like *this* one, assuming Roger had summarized the details with his customary accuracy.

Under the Star Kingdom's campaign laws, there were no limits on anyone's individual or corporate political contributions. There was, however, an ironclad obligation for the *sources* of all contributions to be matters of public record. The Star Kingdom's constitution didn't care where a candidate got his money, but it cared quite strongly whether or not voters *knew* where that money had come from, in what amounts, and how it was actually spent, and the disclosure requirement was incumbent upon the giver and the receiver alike.

"After consultation with Fitzgibbons, however, Allen and I hit on a more fitting punishment for the crime. Just between you and me, I can't really complain too loudly about the vote-buying. Oh, I'm pissed off as hell that Treadwell was paying Summercross specifically to throw juicy contracts its way, but at least they were helping inspire him to vote in favor of our armament program. It needs to be whacked, if only to discourage such shenanigans in the future, but I don't see any reason to turn it into a full blown auto-da-fé at this point, so Treadwell's going to get a quiet plea bargain that means it'll be subsisting on a somewhat leaner profit margin for the next several years. Just long enough to pay back its illegal contributions at a modest little, oh, four hundred percent interest or so." The King smiled thinly. "As for the Conservatives, let's just say our good friend Summercross and his friends are going to lend Allen their full-blooded and energetic support in the next Estimates debate when he pushes for a ten percent increase in the Navy's R and D budget. A lot of that'll go into the open projects, but Admiral Rodriguez is going to funnel a goodly chunk of it to Gram. And Admiral Styler and Dame Lynette will be increasing the personnel—military and civilian—assigned to your shop, as well."

Jonas nodded slowly. Sir Franklyn Dodson, Baron Styler, had replaced First Space Lord White Haven upon his retirement. Admiral Dame Lynette Tillman had succeeded William Spruance at the Bureau of Personnel as Fifth Space Lord, following Spruance's long-delayed retirement. And Admiral George Rodriguez had replaced Dame Carrie Lomax as Fourth Space Lord. Adcock missed both White Haven and Spruance, but not as much as he missed Lomax, whose unexpected death had taken all of them by surprise. None of the current space lords were political virgins, though, and he had to suppress a smile as he pictured Styler's glee, especially. He and Summercross were cousins who thoroughly detested one another, and no one in the King's uniform could feel anything but satisfaction if someone stepped on North Hollow! Still . . .

"I'd imagine this isn't going to make Summercross any more cheerful," he said.

"I've come to the conclusion that *nothing*'s likely to make him 'any more cheerful,'" Roger replied. "And, frankly, I don't really give a damn. In fact, my one real regret is that I didn't have this in my pocket when we were negotiating over Basilisk. I could've avoided half the crap he and the Liberals demanded to cover their asses with their bases." He shrugged. "I can live with Summercross' resentment. Mom always said you can tell more about someone from his enemies than his friends, after all."

"You're the King around here, not me. Thank God!" Jonas said fervently, and Roger chuckled. Then he frowned.

"Of course," he said, "that leaves us with another minor problem. I think it's time to move you to the List, Jonas."

"No," Jonas said firmly. Roger looked at him, and he shrugged. "I want to stay hands-on at *Weyland*, Roger. If you make me a senior-grade captain, seniority's going to push me up into flag rank, especially at the rate we're expanding, and then they'll pull me away from Gram. Besides, I'm your brother-in-law. If I suddenly make List after 'languishing' all these years as a captain JG, people are going to figure it's because of who my sister married. The last thing we need is for the Opposition to 'out' Gram because they started digging for dirt about me because of my promotion!"

Roger regarded him thoughtfully. He didn't really buy into any of Jonas' arguments entirely, although the one about "outing" Gram was probably the most pointed. If Jonas was promoted, his name would appear on the official "Navy Promotion Selection Register (Captains, Senior Grade)," and it *would* be just like one of the Opposition's staffers to keep an eye on the Register and start digging if Jonas appeared there. At which point he really might start finding out about things Roger had gone to great lengths to keep very, very "black." And Jonas was right about how hard they'd worked to keep him under cover and in the background despite their close family relationship. "Captain Adcock" was widely regarded as the queen consort's well-intentioned but uninspired brother—"They don't like to talk about it, but the truth is he's probably just a bit dim, you know, given how junior his rank is at *his* age, darling"—which angered Angelique but actually amused Jonas. He'd even managed to avoid the courtesy titles Parliament had bestowed upon Angelique's younger brothers, which only added to the perception (outside certain carefully chosen circles, at least) that he was simply spinning out the last few years of an uninspired, pre-prolong naval career, probably on his sister's coattails.

But the real reason he doesn't want on the List is that he's afraid flag rank might make him a suitable candidate for Fourth Space Lord, Roger thought. *He doesn't want to give up Gram and get stuck with the Bureau of Weapons, instead. Sooner or later, he's going to* have *to move over there, though. We're going to reach the point where someone needs to turn the research into real weapons, and*

I want him in charge of that. But we're probably still at least ten T-years from that, so there's still some time . . . even without prolong.

He felt a familiar pang of regret as he looked at Adcock's snow white hair and lined face and remembered that his friend was barely twelve T-years older than he was.

"All right," he said after a moment. "I'll let you off this time. But Gram's going to get a lot bigger over the next couple of T-years, Jonas. If things work out the way I expect, you're going to have at least a handful of captains—some of them probably senior-grade, themselves—turning up over there, and you need the seniority to handle that. So instead of getting you onto the Captains' List the way I ought to, I'm going to have Styler and Tillman list Gram as carrying acting commodore's rank for whoever's in command. That'll give you the seniority you need and keep you off the Captains List, and as black as Gram is, no one's going to be seeing anything about your *acting* rank in the open press. And"—he raised an index finger when Jonas opened his mouth—"if you argue with me about it, I *will* have you put on the List."

Jonas closed his mouth again, and Roger smiled.

"Better," he said. "And while we're on the subject of personnel, what's this I hear about Sonja?"

"She's just being Sonja," Adcock sighed. "Tactless, brilliant, opinionated, tactless, irritating, energetic, tactless, bouncy, confident, tactless, over enthusiastic, overly focused—did I mention tactless?"

Roger laughed and shook his head.

"Tactless I can stand, but your latest memo said something about polarizing?"

His tone had become more serious and his eyebrows rose, and Adcock sighed again, more deeply.

"I'm afraid that's true," he said. "It's not that I think she's wrong, you understand. In fact, I'm positive she's *right* most of the time, at least theoretically. The problem is that where she sees glittering possibilities, a lot of my other people see harebrained notions produced by someone without any real tactical experience of her own. No one's done it explicitly yet, but sometime soon someone's going to bust her chops on exactly that issue, at which point things are going to get . . . lively. And even if we weren't having that problem in-house, eventually we'll have to come out into the open with at least some of our notional hardware. We'll have to sell whatever we come up with to a lot of thick-skinned dinosaurs, most of whom have backgrounds as 'shooters' themselves, and they're going to feel exactly the same way about it. For that matter, *I* feel that way sometimes. The woman really is brilliant, Roger, but she needs a bigger dose of... reality? Experience? I don't know the exact word, but something to... temper that enthusiasm of hers."

"I agree, and I've been thinking about it." Roger took another pull on his cigar, then waved it once more. "She's going to hate it, and you can blame it on me or Rodriguez to take the heat off you, but we're going to put her back into shipboard command. I know she'll feel like a square peg in a round hole, at least at first, but you're right—she needs that experience for her own perspective, and she needs her ticket punched if she's going to have credibility with those dinosaurs of yours."

"You're right, she *won't* like it," Jonas said. "But you're also right that she needs it." He grinned. "And it'll do her good to have to put on her big girl panties and get out there in the trenches with the rest of us mere mortals!"

"I don't think I'd be too quick to use that last sentence when you explain the situation to her," Roger said dryly.

"Oh, I'm *far* too wise to do *that*!" Jonas reassured him. "But it really will do her maturity quotient some good."

"I think it will, too," Roger agreed. Then he glanced at his chrono, set his cigar regretfully aside, and stood. "In the meantime, and speaking of maturity quotients, I believe you and I have a date with your favorite niece. I've noticed that she's not exceptionally patient at moments like this. Can't imagine where she gets it from."

"Neither can I," Jonas agreed straightfaced, climbing out of his own chair as Monroe thumped down from his perch. "But, considering her *mother's* 'maturity quotient,' and speaking as one of your loyal and admiring subjects, Your Majesty, I'd earnestly recommend using a *lot* of that new nanotech air freshener of yours. And while you're at it, you better squirt me and Monroe, too, or she's going to wonder what trash incinerator we got downwind of!"

✦ ✦ ✦ ✦ ✦

February 1877 PD

"—so while no one can possibly fault His Majesty's willpower, moral courage, and determination to do the right thing, I think it *is* legitimate to ask whether or not his commitment to confronting the People's Republic militarily is the best option available to us." Joseph Dunleavy looked into the pickup, his expression suitably serious and just a touch troubled. "Obviously, when a star nation has been expanding its borders by force of arms, as well as voluntary annexations, for so long, it's necessary, as one Old Earth politician expressed it over two thousand T-years ago, to 'Speak softly, but carry a big stick.' My concern, and that of those who approach these things from the same perspective as I do, is that His Majesty is giving too much emphasis to the stick and not enough to speaking softly."

"'Speaking softly' hasn't done any of the rest of the Peeps' victims a single bit of good, as far as I'm aware."

Hillary Palin's crisp Sphinxian accent was a sharp contract to Dunleavy's cultured, uppercrust Landing accent. She sat across the table from him on the deliberately old-fashioned, face-to-face set of the recently created yet already incredibly popular syndicated Into the Fire. That set was designed to bring guests into direct physical proximity rather than through a safely insulated electronic format (which helped generate more than a few of the fireworks for which the program was already famous), and her expression was far more scornful than his had been.

"I'll agree with you that a big stick is necessary to get the Peeps' attention," she went on, "but I'm pretty sure the two of us differ on whether the best negotiating ploy is to simply keep it handy or break their kneecaps with it."

Dunleavy rolled his eyes. A onetime professor of political science at Landing University, he'd been associated with any number of liberal-leaning think tanks for over forty T-years and served as one of Sir Orwell Lebrun's senior foreign policy advisers for the last decade or so. Palin, on the other hand, had exactly zero academic credentials in the social sciences. Instead, she'd been trained as a nano and materials engineer and founded an industrial application firm specializing in the development of advanced composites and (according to unconfirmed reports) radically advanced anti-energy weapon armors. No one had ever been able to prove the reports were true—the RMN was fiendishly good at protecting its technology, after all—but Palin, Holder, and Mitchell, Ltd., had sold its patents to the Navy for upwards of seven billion dollars almost twenty-five T-years ago, when she first stood for election to the House of Commons as the Liberal Party's candidate for the Borough of South Thule on Sphinx. She'd won that election quite handily, but she'd never had a great deal of patience with ivory tower theorists who'd never won election to anything in their entire lives and refused to acknowledge inconvenient truths that clashed with their own preconceptions. That was quite enough to explain why she and Dunleavy had thoroughly detested one another from the moment they first met, and the fact that she'd shifted her membership from the Liberals to the Centrists eleven T-years ago over the Basilisk annexation—and won reelection quite handily two more times since, despite the change in party affiliation—only made her even more irritating to him.

Besides, if those rumors about the nature of her patents were true, he thought now, she had a vested interest—all that Navy money in her accounts—in supporting the knuckle-draggers who thought warheads were the answer to any problem whenever they demanded yet another superdreadnought.

"That's precisely the sort of attitude which can be guaranteed to preclude the possibility of any rational resolution of the tensions which have been mounting between the People's Republic and the Star Kingdom over the last twenty T-years, Hillary," he more than half snapped now.

"Ah? Since His Majesty's coronation, you mean?" Palin shot back in dulcet tones, and Dunleavy's expression darkened.

Manticoran politicians always had to be careful about how they criticized the royal family. The Star Kingdom had a lively tradition of freedom of speech and even livelier political debate, and as the head of government as well as head of state, the monarch was expected to take his or her lumps along with everyone else. But there were limits to how those lumps could be administered. The sort of character assassination by innuendo and the politics of personal destruction which tended to rear their ugly heads from time to time in Parliamentary contests could not be applied to the reigning king or queen. Not unless the person foolish enough to make the attempt was prepared to kiss his own political career goodbye, at any rate. The Manticoran voting public was sufficiently cynical—or pragmatic, perhaps—to recognize the often sordid realities of political ambition, careerism, and what was still known as "spin doctoring," and it put up with a great deal in the political arena, but there were some things it was *not* prepared to tolerate.

Which, in Joseph Dunleavy's opinion, was completely irrational and gave people like Hillary Palin a grossly unfair advantage when it came to the reasoned debate of public policy issues. All she had to do was tar him by implication with attacking Roger III personally, and his argument was cut off at the knees so far as anyone but the Party's fully committed base was concerned. And that, Dunleavy thought, was as unfortunate as it was unfair, given the fact that King Roger was clearly...significantly less than rational where the People's Republic of Haven was concerned.

"His Majesty's ascension to the Throne is scarcely the only thing that's happened in the last twenty T-years, Hillary," he said after a moment. "I believe his policy and his attitudes have clearly played a role in creating the...dynamic we face today, but they're hardly the *only* factors involved. And I trust you'll do me the courtesy of remembering that I've never argued the People's Republic isn't expansionist—or, for that matter, that its foreign policy isn't being driven by its own militaristic clique. Obviously a star nation of that size and that power, with the military establishment virtually dictating to its civilian leadership, is a very, *very* serious threat to the interstellar community in general. I am not now and never have been one of those idealistic but unfortunately misguided souls who favor some sort of unilateral disarmament on our part as the best way to defuse the tension between Nouveau Paris and Landing. In the face of a major star nation with a powerful fleet and a clear commitment to using that fleet in the furtherance of its expansionist policies, discarding that 'big stick' I spoke of a moment ago would be the height of foolishness."

"Then, forgive me, Mr. Dunleavy," Patrick DuCain, one of *Into the Fire*'s cohosts, said, "but what exactly are the policy points on which you differ with Prime Minister Cromarty and Foreign Secretary Nageswar?"

Dunleavy showed his teeth for a moment. DuCain was the program's conservative voice, whereas Minerva Prince, his cohost, provided its liberal viewpoint. Another thing that made their broadcasts so popular, however, was that neither DuCain nor Prince were ideologues. Both were actually registered independents, eschewing party labels (although Dunleavy suspected they both probably *voted* Centrist, though he was less certain in Prince's case), and while DuCain was substantially more hardline on foreign policy issues, he was actually closer to the Liberals on many social issues than Prince. Of course, Prince made up for her foreign policy rationality by being somewhere to the right of Adam Smith on matters of fiscal policy, he thought resentfully.

And both of them had elevated their gift for choosing guests with...lively differences of opinion—and injecting plenty of blood into the political water when they did—to a fine art. That was yet another reason for their program's high viewership.

"The Prime Minister and the Foreign Secretary are, as I'm fully aware, intelligent, patriotic, and experienced servants of the Star Kingdom," he said, wishing with all his heart that he dared to speak the truth. They weren't servants of the *Star Kingdom*; they were servants of Roger Winton and his dangerously militant foreign policy. Could none of them see the holocaust—the millions of dead—which *had* to result from a headlong clash with the People's Republic?

"Obviously, however, I and other members of the Liberal Party don't see eye-to-eye with them on all matters," he continued. "Specifically, in terms of foreign policy, we believe the Star Kingdom has a moral responsibility—to itself and to the galaxy at large—to go the extra kilometer in its efforts to avoid what would inevitably be the biggest, bloodiest, and most destructive war in the last millennium of human history. It's entirely possible, little though any of us like to contemplate such an outcome, that war is inevitable. That the so-called 'Big Navy' advocates are correct, and that only the actual *use* of military force will be sufficient in the end to bring a halt to the People's Republic's expansion. Given that possibility, one cannot but be grateful for His Majesty's unflagging efforts to build the military wherewithal which will be so sorely needed on that grim and terrible day."

Dunleavy's expression was sober, solemn, and he inhaled deeply.

"Yet, granting all of that, do we not have a responsibility— indeed, given the difference between our open, representative political system and the closed, military-dominated system which has plunged the once bright beacon of the Republic of Haven into darkness, do we not have a *greater* responsibility than Haven—to do all we can to prevent such a hugely destructive, bloody con- flict? Whatever we may think of the People's Republic's leadership, *we* are an open system which believes in freedom, the worth of the individual, opportunity, the value of hard work and talent, and freedom of choice. As such, we owe the galaxy better than to simply abandon any hope of stopping short of war. It doesn't matter what the *People's Republic* does or doesn't owe to itself or to anyone else; we owe *ourselves* the knowledge that we didn't simply follow a brutish, militaristic, repressive regime into the maw of warfare without first making every possible effort to avert that outcome."

"Ms. Palin?" DuCain looked at his other guest. "I have to say that doesn't sound all that unreasonable. Surely Mr. Dunleavy is correct that every alternative should be considered before we resort to brute force."

"No one's advocating resorting to 'brute force' if any other alternative presents itself, Patrick." Palin shook her head, her expression just as sober as Dunleavy's. "The problem is that the *Peeps*—and I include their civilian leadership in this, as well as the military; Joe's mistaken if he thinks there's any actual dif- ference between them—*believe* in the use of 'brute force.' And, on the face of it, it's hard to argue with their view that it's been working pretty well for them for the last thirty T-years or so. They've built an enormous military machine, and that military power and their acceptance that they have no choice but to expand or die—politically and economically speaking, at any rate—has developed a momentum that isn't going to stop before it runs into something it can't devour. I'm afraid that by this time the Legislaturalists are completely captive to the so-called 'Duquesne Plan.' I would love, more than anyone—including Joe—might be prepared to believe, for him to be right that it's possible to stop the Peeps short of direct military conflict. Unfortunately, I'm no longer confident anyone can...or that it's even *possible* for them to stop, which is why I shifted my party affiliation to the Centrists. That wasn't an easy decision for me to make, but I believe I owe my constituents and the Star Kingdom as a whole support for the best available foreign and military policy."

She looked directly across the table at Dunleavy, and this time there was nothing in her eyes but somber sincerity.

"I don't say I think the Prime Minister's policy options are *good* ones, Joe. I only say they're the best of the *bad* options available to him. Don't think for a moment that he likes them any better than you do, either. But we live in the same galaxy, and the same tiny part of it, as the Peeps, and Duke Cromarty would be grossly derelict in his responsibilities to the Star Kingdom if he didn't prepare for the one argument he knows the Peeps will *have* to listen to if and when the time comes."

"It sounds to me," Minerva Prince said, "as if the disagreement here is more a matter of degree than kind." She looked back and forth between Palin and Dunleavy. "Would the two of you agree with that?"

"Not without some significant qualifications, I'm afraid," Dunleavy said heavily. "I have to agree with Hillary that if worse eventually comes to worst, the existence of the battle fleet Prime Minister Cromarty—and His Majesty—are committed to building is, indeed, an argument the People's Republic will be forced to 'listen to.' As I've said from the beginning, the Star Kingdom must have a big stick in reserve if it expects soft speech to accomplish anything.

"But, with all due respect, Hillary, the very way in which you state your argument only underscores the extent to which Cromarty and the Centrists have already abandoned—ruled out—any 'argument' that *isn't* based on raw force and brute firepower. Have you actually listened to yourself? I don't believe I've heard you refer to the Havenites by anything other than the pejorative, jingoistic label of 'Peep' since this broadcast began. That kind of polarization reveals a demonization of our potential adversaries which is symptomatic of the Cromarty Government's tunnel vision where the People's Republic is concerned. It's very possible, perhaps even probable, that the simplistic view of the PRH's entire leadership as jackbooted thugs isn't as invalid as I would like it to be. But at this time we have to find some means of engaging them in debate, some way to build a constructive dialogue that allows us to show them how much more valuable stable relations between our star nations would be. They can gain so much more by trading with us, by opening their borders to our technology and investment bankers, by relying on peaceful commerce rather than the inevitable cost in both blood and treasure war must exact from both of us! We need to find a way to convince them to take *that* path, demonstrate where their true self interest lies, rather than continuing blindly on the road of conquest and repression.

"I'm not naïve enough to believe we can do that simply by appealing to their better natures! For that matter, I'm not at all confident the current military-dominated clique running the People's Republic has anything remotely *like* a 'better nature.' But rather than simply abandoning the effort, we have to choose an 'all of the above' approach to our foreign policy. We have to be willing to be at least modestly accommodating to them where opportunities for peaceful interaction present themselves. Without that willingness on our part, there genuinely *is* no hope for any sort of constructive engagement which might lead to something less cataclysmic than a head-on clash of arms."

"If the last thirty T-years of the *People's Republic's* existence have demonstrated a single thing," Palin said flatly, "it's that anything remotely like 'constructive engagement' is seen as a sign of weakness, an opportunity to push for still more advantage before the hapless victim slides down the Peeps' throat."

She shook her head, and when she spoke again her tone was regretful, almost gentle.

"We've *tried* talking to them, Joe. For that matter, there was a time when we had a very close, cordial relationship with the Republic of Haven. When our naval units cooperated with theirs in the enforcement of the Cherwell Convention, for example. When we traded openly and freely with them. But that relationship is gone. Their markets are closed, sealed off by a combination of trade restrictions and punitive import duties, and the thought of Manticoran and Peep naval units cooperating to accomplish anything—short of one another's destruction, at any rate!—is about as realistic as expecting a planet to reverse its rotation. It's possible we may be able to talk them into stopping short of our own frontier, short of the Junction, but the only way we'll convince them is by presenting an argument they can't ignore. And that, Joe, is why the Cromarty Government is so focused on continuing the Navy's buildup, stitching together an alliance of independent star systems in a collective security arrangement intended to give even the Peeps pause, and drawing an unmistakable line in the sand that tells them—tells them in terms clear enough, stark enough, not even they can misinterpret our resolve—that we are *not* simply another juicy target, bigger and richer than any of the others they've already engulfed. These people have persuaded themselves they have a manifest destiny to continue their expansion indefinitely, and they've built a military machine big enough and strong enough to convince them nothing short of the Solarian League itself could possibly stop them. And the truth is that, on the basis of their record to date, they're right."

She shook her head again, her expression grim.

"The most dangerous error a foreign policy maker can commit is to assume the people on the other side of a confrontation, whether it's a peaceful competition or an active war, are 'just like us.' That, under the surface, they share the same basic values, the same view of the galaxy. And, even more dangerous, that they interpret events, relationships, and opportunities the same way *we* do. Because the truth is, Joe, that not everyone does... and the Peeps *don't*. In more ways than I can count, they live in a completely different galaxy from ours simply because their starting position, their objectives, and the way they see events are so different from ours. They're perfectly capable of doing things you and I would both agree—agree without any reservations at all—are insane, given the alternatives, the advantages of dealing openly and peacefully with their interstellar neighbors. And they're capable of that because they're starting from a different place and operating under a totally different set of constraints. Constraints and objectives—and beliefs—which make what you and I would agree are fundamentally irrational decisions completely rational, even inevitable.

"You're right that it takes a big stick to allow someone to speak softly—and be heard—by a masked thug who makes his living through armed robbery. Unfortunately, you also have to convince the thug in question that you not only *have* a big stick, but that you're prepared to *use* it. And sometimes, more often than you or I would like, the only way you can convince someone who's willing to make a living through armed robbery and mayhem to worry about your stick is to actually *hit* him with it, because until you do, he won't believe you're willing to."

◆　◆　◆

"She's doing quite well, I think," Allen Summervale said judiciously as the broadcast went to commercial break. He looked across the comfortable sitting room at his monarch. "In fact, she's doing better than I would, given the fact that I can't stand Dunleavy." The Prime Minister smiled without much humor. "Unlike a lot of his fellows, I think he's completely sincere in his beliefs. Arrogant and closed-minded, perhaps, and totally convinced of his own rectitude, but sincere and genuinely concerned about how many people will get hurt in any war against the Peeps. He's desperately determined to prevent that from happening—I have to give him credit for that, however irritating I personally find him. The problem is that he's walled that sincerity of his in with so many preconceptions reality just can't get through to him, and this in a man who's been shaping the Liberals' foreign policy for *decades*! Not to mention how damned supercilious he can be with anyone who *dares* to disagree with him, given his own indisputable brilliance. In his presence, I have a tendency to forget about our splendid traditions of freedom of speech and open, civil debate. In fact, I might as well admit he tends to make my pistol hand twitch."

Roger snorted harshly, then tipped his chair back and shrugged.

"You're right, she is doing well," he agreed. "On the other hand, both of them are doing what Mom used to call preaching to the choir. I'd like to think Hillary's going to convince at least a few more people to see reason, but I'm afraid most people have already chosen their positions on this issue."

"Yes and no," Cromarty disagreed. Roger looked at him, and the Prime Minister shrugged. "There's a lot in what you've just said, but I don't think opinion's as set in ceramacrete as quite a few pundits predict. All our polling suggests there's still an ongoing, gradual shift in our direction, and the Star Kingdom's support for you personally is stronger than it's ever been. Even those who'd be happier if we were 'less confrontational' trust you to make the right call in the end more than they trust Lebrun, or Summercross, or Macmillan, or any of the others. There's a lot of dissatisfaction about how much the Fleet's costing, and the tension between us and the Peeps has been growing long enough there's a lot of fear and a lot of pessimism, but according to all our data, a clear majority—not a very *big* one, I'll admit, but a majority—of registered voters agree with you."

"Oh?" Roger cocked a sardonic eyebrow at his chief minister. "That's why the treaty with Zanzibar sailed through so easily, is it?"

"There's less support for building this 'Manticoran Alliance' of yours," Cromarty conceded. "Rachel and I both told you there would be. An unfortunately large percentage of your subjects agree with the Conservative Association that entangling ourselves in defensive commitments to small star nations that could never hope to resist Peep aggression on their own is dangerously provocative and actually weakens our own position by burdening us with additional strategic commitments. And, of course, there's another largish—although smaller—percentage that agrees with Dunleavy, at least where the Alliance is concerned. If we persist in drawing that 'line in the sand' Hillary mentioned, aren't we simply daring the Peeps to step across it? Those who disapprove, disapprove for a whole host of different reasons, though. They may constitute the majority, but it's an ... incoherent majority, while a plurality—and a *growing* plurality, at that, according to all our tracking data—agrees with your reasoning on the Alliance."

"Which isn't helping us one bit where the Association and Liberals are concerned."

"If the Liberals weren't feeling the heat, Your Majesty, Lebrun wouldn't have sent Dunleavy to carry water for him like this." Cromarty waved at the HD, where the commercial break had just ended. "They have access to the same polling data we do. I think they're interpreting some of it rather differently from the way I would, but they know their base in the Commons is continuing to erode on this issue. That's why they're arguing the point so passionately, and I expect Lebrun to try to make his opposition to the Alliance's 'dangerous entanglements' the keynote of his foreign policy position in the next election. The Conservatives don't care about public opinion, you're right about that, because by this time they don't have *any* representation to lose in the Commons, and peers don't have to stand for election. But Macmillan and Sheridan can both see the writing on the wall as clearly as Lebrun can, and unlike him, they're not willing to ride their Commons seats down in flames over a matter of doctrinaire ideology."

"Maybe so," Roger acknowledged after a moment. "But I don't like the way Macmillan's backing Lebrun over the notion of giving the Peeps 'more access' to Basilisk. And I'm not especially confident that the reason she is doesn't have a little something to do with under the table outside encouragement."

The King raised his right hand, rubbing thumb and first two fingers together in an ancient gesture Cromarty wished he could misinterpret. Or disagree with, for that matter.

"On the face of it, it's not an unreasonable request on the Peeps' part," he observed in a carefully neutral tone. "They *are* sending a lot of freighters back and forth to the League through the Junction, even if they aren't trading with *us* very much. And they probably do have a legitimate interest in the Silesian trade if they're going to be passing through the Junction in the first place."

"*Sure* they do." Roger grimaced. "And for that matter, Summercross is right that every ship they send through the Junction pays us the transit fees we're using to help build up the Navy against them. But you know as well as I do that one of the reasons they're 'passing through the Junction' is to keep as close an eye as they can on what's going on here in the Star Kingdom. For that matter, both ONI and SIS are sure they're snagging data dumps from agents right here on Manticore in the process. And that doesn't even consider how much they want to keep the San Martinos aware of their presence by routing a few billion tons of shipping through Trevor's Star every year. Not to mention the fact that those freighters they're sending back and forth to the League are basically payoffs to people like Technodyne in return for the technology they can't produce anymore. They're nervous about the R and D they know about, and they'd be a hell of a lot *more* nervous if they knew about Gram. That's the reason they're grabbing every bit of tech from Technodyne they can, whatever that asshole Kolokoltsov is saying. You know *that* as well as I do, too. Their so-called *legitimate trade* in Silesia's a money loser for them, too, now isn't it? In fact, it's basically only a way for them to cover at least the majority of their information-gathering expenses as they go swanning through Manticoran space with those remarkably sensitive 'civilian grade' sensor suites their freighters mount!"

Cromarty was forced to nod. The People's Republic was so short of interstellar currency reserves that it had resorted to what amounted to a barter relationship with several of the larger Solarian transstellars. As Roger had pointed out, Technodyne of Yildun was an excellent case in point. As one of the Solarian League Navy's major contractors, Technodyne had access to virtually all of the SLN's latest hardware. And, despite the League's stringent controls on the export of first-line technology, even the "export" tech the SLN had signed off on was substantially better than anything the People's Republic could have produced internally after so many decades of self-inflicted infrastructure damage.

And, unfortunately, the PRH seemed to be waking up—some, at least—to the fact that Manticore's warfighting technology was better than its was. Manticoran intelligence, civilian and military alike, suggested the Peoples Navy still hadn't figured out how far behind the RMN's actually *deployed* hardware it was, far less how far behind Gram and the rest of the Star Kingdom's "black" R&D it was, yet it was clearly making a push to improve its position.

Possibly the fact that the Andermani Empire had finally bought the Astral Energetics' version of the laser head and put it into service in 1872 had something to do with that. All indications were that Astral's weapon was markedly inferior to Section Thirteen's latest variant, yet the mere fact that the Andermani possessed it at all represented a closing of their capability gap vis-à-vis the Star Kingdom. Fortunately, Emperor Gustav appeared to have little interest in distracting Manticore from its concentration on Haven, at least at the moment, but the IAN's introduction of the weapon into open service had to have spurred Havenite interest in acquiring an equivalent capability. At the moment, there was no evidence Technodyne had a laser head design to sell, but like most Solarian transstellars, Technodyne had never worried all that much over abiding by export restrictions if the customer could meet its price. That being the case, there was no reason to think it would hesitate to acquire a licensed version of Astral's design and happily sell it to the PRH, especially since the SLN didn't even seem to have noticed its existence. The League certainly hadn't made any move to prevent its proliferation, at any rate. Yet.

Even if that changed, Technodyne wouldn't care as long as it didn't get caught by someone it couldn't buy off, and that sort of Solarian arms inspector no longer existed. And if the Peeps were short on hard currency, Technodyne could work with that, as well. After all, the Peeps had all those political prisoners to provide the labor force they needed, which meant they were actually able to deliver raw and semi-refined materials to Technodyne—via the

Junction, of course—more cheaply than Technodyne could have purchased the same materials from a source in the League. All indications were that Technodyne was bleeding the Peeps' ruthlessly, but it was a cost they could bear, at least for now.

The fact that the state owned every Havenite freighter in existence helped hold down costs, as well, he supposed. But Roger was right about the capability of the sensor suites built into the Peep freighters passing through the Junction or trundling about the Manticoran Binary System itself to deliver or pick up cargoes. They were spy ships, plain and simple, and their presence only underscored Roger's wisdom in setting up Project Gram on *Weyland*, where those sensor suites never got a peek at any of the hardware Jonas Adcock and his people were beginning to surreptitiously test in the Unicorn Belt.

And it helps that Klaus Hauptman's such a stiff-necked bastard, too, Cromarty reflected. *The man holds grudges like a Gryphon Highlander, and he absolutely* loathes *Summercross and Lebrun. Doesn't stop him from doing business with Summercross, or even North Hollow, but that's just business, and he doesn't trust any of them any farther than he could jump without counter-grav. The man might as well have the Star Kingdom's coat of arms tattooed across his backside when it comes to national security, and it'll be a cold day in hell before anybody in the Association or the Liberal Party hears a single word out of* him *about the toys he's been building for Gram over the last couple of T-years.*

"You're probably right, Your Majesty," he acknowledged out loud. "But unless we're prepared to call Nouveau Paris on it, it's going to be hard to make a case for denying them the access they're asking for. We don't have to give them favored-star nation status, but we're going to need something more than 'because you're rotten people' if we're not going to give them at least the same degree of access we give everyone else."

"Oh, we'll *give* it to them, all right," Roger said with an unpleasant smile. "But I'll have my kilo of flesh from Summercross and Lebrun first."

"Your Majesty?" Cromarty's expression was wary, and Roger's smile turned still colder.

"I should never have accepted all the stipulations and restrictions the two of them insisted on when we annexed the terminus," he said, and it was Cromarty's turn to grimace in agreement.

Roger had been right about the Opposition's inability to stop him from making his infant daughter the Duchess of Basilisk, but they'd held out for a generous grab bag of concessions before they'd agreed to acquiesce and make Parliament's approval unanimous. The offer to *make* that approval unanimous in return for those selfsame face-saving concessions had been more than Roger and his ministers had been able to resist, given the emphatic way it had countersigned the Crown's new policy where control of the Junction's termini was concerned. Unfortunately, no one had repealed the law of unintended consequences, and the restrictions which had resulted had grown steadily more irksome over the past decade.

"The infrastructure in Basilisk—in the system itself, especially in Medusa orbit, not just on the terminus—is growing even faster than I expected," Roger continued. "It's more valuable to our economy and more tempting to someone like the Peeps—or Gustav—than I anticipated, too, and thanks to the way we pussyfooted around with Summercross and Lebrun, we don't have the wherewithal in-system to look after it properly. So I think it's time we stamp the entire terminus with a big, shiny Manticore."

"In what way, Your Majesty?"

"I'm going to create a formal naval station in Basilisk. It's going to be a standing naval presence." Cromarty looked faintly alarmed, and the King shook his head quickly. "Oh, I'm not going to renege on our promise not to fortify the terminus, Allen! Not that I wouldn't *like* to, you understand, but there's only so much blood in the turnip, and if I have to choose between a few more ships-of-the-wall and fortifying the Basilisk Terminus, I'm afraid I'm going to have to opt for the wallers. But that doesn't mean we can't permanently station a division of cruisers and a squadron of destroyers or so in Basilisk to keep an eye on things. And on any 'civilian Peep freighters' that happen to pass through. And if people like Summercross and Lebrun happen to get the message that we're through rolling over for the Peeps because we're somehow responsible for being the 'reasonable' ones, I'm just fine with *that*, too."

Cromarty managed not to wince, but it was hard as he contemplated the screams of protest bound to come at him from both left and right when he announced *this* little decision. On the face of it, it should have been a complete nonissue, but both the

Conservatives and the Liberals were going to recognize Roger's challenge, his warning that he was through deferring to their sensibilities, and that was going to guarantee an ugly reception. But over the past twenty T-years, he'd learned to recognize when there was no point trying to talk Roger Winton out of something.

Besides, he thought, *he's right. It is time we made that message of his crystal clear, and not just to the Peeps.*

"Very well, Your Majesty," he said aloud, "I'll have a word about it with Abner and Admiral Styler this afternoon."

May 1878 PD

"SO," KING ROGER III SAID, reaching down to ruffle Crown Princess Elizabeth Adrienne Samantha Annette Winton's feathery curls gently, "was it a good birthday?"

"Oh, yeah," Elizabeth replied emphatically, leaning back against her tall, broad-shouldered father and smiling up at him. She was a slender, small-boned child—she took after her mother in that respect—but muscular, with a passion for soccer and horses. As far as he could tell that equestrian fixation was something every girl child ever born shared, but she seemed to have caught a more intense case than most.

"I missed Uncle Jonas this year," she continued, "but everyone else was great. And I really liked the new grav ski. I can hardly wait to try it out!"

"Oh?" Something devilish glinted in Roger's eyes. "Well, just be sure you take Sergeant Proctor along when you do."

"*Daaaddy!*" Elizabeth rolled her huge, expressive eyes with a martyred expression. Her devastating eleven-year-old crush (well, *twelve*-year-old now, he supposed, if he was going to be accurate) on Sergeant Bynum Proctor of the King's Own Regiment was something of a sore point with her at the moment.

"Roger," Queen Consort Angelique said, never looking up from the forestry journal on her reader, "don't tease your daughter. I believe we've discussed that."

"*Tease* my daughter?" Roger looked at her with wide eyed innocence. "I am shocked—*shocked*, I tell you!—that you could *possibly* accuse me of such a thing, Angel! I'm innocent as the new fallen snow."

118

"There *is* no new fallen snow in Landing, even in the middle of winter," Angelique pointed out, looking up at last. "And if there were, you wouldn't be as innocent as it...if that sentence makes any sense at all." She furrowed her brow for a moment, considering it, then shrugged. "You're about as 'innocent' as that fellow from Old Earth you were telling me about the other day. Who was it? Macky somebody?"

"That was *Machiavelli*," Roger said severely, fully aware that Angelique had remembered the name perfectly well. Elizabeth realized it too, judging from her chortle, and he looked down at her sternly.

"Don't you go around laughing at Niccolò di Bernardo dei Machiavelli, Missy! He wasn't a very nice person, but any ruler worth his—or her—unscrupulous salt should at least be familiar with his advice."

"You obviously are, anyway," his daughter replied in a voice which was just slightly undutiful. "If you've got that entire name memorized, anyway!"

She made a face, and Roger shook his head. Elizabeth was an excellent student, but at this point in her life she saw no reason why anyone should expect her to remember names and dates. They were boring. Besides, that was the sort of thing uni-links were for storing. Still, judging by the questions she'd been asking lately, she was beginning to develop some of that deep interest in history her grandmother had taken pains to inculcate into her own heir. It wouldn't be much longer, Roger estimated, before *she* was the one rattling off names and dates and watching carefully from the corner of her eye to be sure her father was suitably impressed with her erudition.

Monroe made a soft, amused sound from his shoulder, and Elizabeth looked up suspiciously.

"You're thinking something funny about me again," she accused.

"*Never!*" her father assured her.

"Oh, yes you are. I can always tell by watching Monroe."

"I have absolutely no responsibility for the peculiar things 'cats find humorous, Beth. Some of them have very strange senses of humor, as far as I can tell. In fact, *he* was probably the one thinking something 'funny' about you, now that I think about it."

"You might want to remember, Bethie," Angelique observed, "that one of the first things any successful politician has to learn is how to lie convincingly."

"You're not helping here, Angel," Roger said, as their daughter grinned triumphantly at him. "And I'm going to remember this conversation the next time I hear Michael asking you what kind of nuts he needs to plant in the palace garden to grow a crown oak."

"Don't you *dare* put him up to that again, Roger Winton!"

Angelique shuddered, and Roger chuckled.

Michael was still shy of eight T-years old, but he was obviously at least as smart as his sister, in a tunnel vision, narrowly focused, seven-year-old sort of way, and that could have . . . interesting consequences in the strangest places. Like where crown oaks were concerned.

His mother remained active in the Star Kingdom's Royal Society of Silviculture, and Michael had accompanied her to Sphinx two years ago when she went to dedicate a new Sphinx Forestry Service preserve in East Slocum. It was the first time he'd actually seen a crown oak—eighty meters tall, with arrow-shaped leaves broader than his own chest had been at the time—and he'd instantly wanted one for his very own. He'd been even more impressed by that than by the treecats who always seemed to turn up to inspect members of the royal family whenever they visited Sphinx, and he'd pestered his mother to buy one for him all the way back to Landing. Expense had been no object, as far as he was concerned, since he'd had the same attitude towards money all five-year-olds—and politicians—seemed to possess. There was always plenty of it in someone else's pockets; all they had to do was pry it loose for their *own* pockets. His parents were working hard on convincing him otherwise (for a lot of reasons), but they'd made far more progress with his older sister than with him. So far, at least.

Angelique had stepped on the "But *why* won't you buy it for me?" semi-whine, only to have him hit on the brilliant inspiration of growing one of his own. After all, there was plenty of room in the palace gardens, wasn't there? And his mother had her own personal landscaping projects of her own, didn't she? And a crown oak *nut* had to cost a *lot* less than a whole tree, didn't it, Mommy?

It had taken her the better part of an hour, but she'd finally gotten him to understand that a crown oak that size was at least the better part of four or five hundred T-years old. In fact, it was probably two or three times that age, and that meant it wasn't exactly something even a queen could just whistle up whenever she wanted one.

That was the point at which Roger had come on the scene, and, unaware of the ordeal his wife had just been through at the hands of their focused, maddeningly persistent five-year-old extortionist, laughingly suggested to Michael (who'd recently discovered the Old Earth fairy tale about Jack and the Beanstalk) that if they just planted the right kind of nut in the garden, they could probably have a proper crown oak by next Tuesday.

He'd thought for a while that Angelique was going to commit regicide—not that any court would have convicted her, once the jury heard the extenuating circumstances—when Michael turned triumphantly around to his mother and said "*Daddy* says I can have one!"

"I won't put him up to that, if you'll stop undermining my aura of truth and virtue in my daughter's eyes," he said now.

"Too late, Dad," Elizabeth told him with twelve-year-old cynicism. "I wasn't going to mention this, but you and I need to have a talk about the Tooth Fairy, too."

"Oh, no, you don't!" He slid an index finger under her chin, tipping her head back to smile down at her and shook the other index finger under her nose. "Don't you go disillusioning me with your cynical skepticism!"

"All right, I won't," she said, but there was a calculating look in her eye, and he raised one eyebrow as he saw it.

"And just what is this unusual restraint on your part going to *cost* me?" he inquired.

"I want to start learning about your job," she told him with unusual seriousness, looking suddenly considerably older than her age. "*Really* learning, I mean, not just reading about it and watching holos. I mean, I know it'll be years and years before *I* have to be Queen, but Jacob and Elisa have been telling me how much help you were to Grandmama way before you ever had to be King yourself. And I know how hard you're working—and how *worried* you are, Dad." She put her arms around his waist, hugging him tightly, pressing her cheek against his chest. "You try not to show it, but I know. And I want to help."

"Beth," Angelique said softly, setting aside her book reader at last, "you just turned twelve, for goodness sake, and your Dad's going to be King for decades yet. Probably at least another

T-century! I know you want to help, honey, but there's no need to be rushing *that* hard to grow up."

"I didn't say I want to grow up, Mom," Elizabeth turned her head to look at her mother without releasing her hug on her father. "And I know there's a lot of stuff I wouldn't understand even if you and Dad explained it to me. But I *do* know how worried Dad is, and I know he's doing stuff with Uncle Jonas that we're not supposed to tell anybody about. I'm sure he's doing lots of other stuff we're not supposed to mention, either. I know I'm just a kid. I can't fix the things that are worrying him—and *you*, even if you don't want Mikey and me to know about it. But I do want to understand as much of it as I can, and if there's any way I can help Dad—even if it's just letting him talk to me the way he does to you when he says he's 'bouncing ideas off you'—then I want to do it."

"But you're so young."

Angelique glanced at Roger, her distress obvious, and he knew what she was thinking. Her marriage to him had turned her own life inside out; she didn't want to see her daughter rushing to discard her childhood and embrace the same sacrifices. Not yet. Not when she was still their little girl, despite the odd bursts of maturity that wandered through her from time to time . . . and despite what the destiny of her birth was going to demand of her one day.

"You're right when you say you probably wouldn't understand some of the stuff we grown-ups worry about," Angelique continued, her gray eyes dark. "But some of it's pretty scary, Bethie. There are parts of it I wish *I* didn't know, and I'm sure your Dad feels the same way about it. Can't you just let the grown-ups deal with it for at least a *few* more years?"

Roger looked back and forth between his wife and his daughter, seeing Angelique's worry and a familiar stubbornness in Elizabeth's eyes. He knew where she'd gotten that, just as he knew where she'd gotten her temper, and his lips twitched for a moment as he wondered how his subjects would have reacted to the knowledge that their monarch, the man proposing to build a military capable of defeating the second largest navy in the entire galaxy, recognized defeat when he saw it in a *twelve-year-old's* eyes. But that didn't mean he had to surrender without a fight or that he couldn't wage a valiant delaying action first, he reminded himself.

"Your Mom's right, Beth," he said. "I think I understand what you're saying. Of course, when I was your age, learning to be King was the last thing I was interested in! It was the *Navy* I wanted, but I was just as stubborn. Well, maybe not *just* as stubborn; I don't think there's anyone this side of Monroe who's really as stubborn as you are. But I was *pretty* stubborn, and your grandmother had a terrible time dealing with me. It was kind of like Mikey and the crown oak, I guess."

Elizabeth giggled, and he smiled and ruffled her hair again.

"I'll make a deal with you," he said. "This isn't one of those we'll-argue-back-and-forth-about-the-terms-of-the-deal deals, either—it's one of those take-it-or-leave-it, nonnegotiable, Daddy-decree deals. Got it?"

She looked at him for a moment, obviously considering the terms, then nodded, and he nodded back.

"I don't think you're ready to start going off to Cabinet meetings and diplomatic conferences with me just yet. In fact, I seem to remember someone who fell asleep halfway through her very first state dinner about a year ago. I wonder who that might have been?"

He raised his eyebrows at her, and she giggled again, looking suddenly much more like a twelve-year-old than someone twice that age.

"So here's the deal. If you have any questions you want answered about current events, or what I'm discussing with Duke Cromarty, or something you've seen on HD, like *Into the Fire*, or on the public boards, or any of that kind of stuff, I'll answer them. And Elisa and Jacob will answer questions for you, too. But I'm not going to haul you in to listen to all of those endless conferences and arguments and planning sessions a king has to deal with. Not yet. I think Mom's absolutely right about your being too young just yet, even though I know you're already tired of hearing that. Trust me, you'll be even *more* tired of it by the time you hit high school...and we'll be pretty darned tired of telling you so. But if you're still interested when you turn fifteen, I'll let you start sitting in on at least some of those boring conferences then.

"I'm pretty sure you'll decide they're nowhere near as interesting as you thought they might be, but you're right. One day you will be Queen, and even though Mom's right that it's not going to happen anytime soon, you're going to be Heir for a long time, and the Heir has a lot of responsibilities of her own, including ribbon cuttings, really tedious speeches, and smiling and being polite and attentive at political rallies the King can't make it to—and is just *delighted* to send someone else off to in his place! A lot of it's more boring than anyone who isn't the Heir—or the queen consort—" he looked up again to give Angelique a flashing smile "—could possibly believe, but it *is* going to be your job, and however boring it may be, it really is important, too. So I guess it won't hurt to let you start sort of easing your way into it early."

She smiled hugely, and he smiled back, looking across her head at Angelique and seeing the resignation—and the gratitude that at least the moment had been deferred—in those gray, beloved eyes.

And let's face it, Beth really is only twelve, he told himself. *Twelve-year-olds have notions, and she's no different from any other twelve-year-old in* that *respect! In two weeks she's more likely than not to have forgotten all about this and be more worried about Sergeant Proctor or her next soccer game. So maybe it's not just "deferred," Angel. I'll do my damnedest to keep her out of the mess as long as I can, but I know that look in her eyes. I see one a lot like it in my eyes when I look in the mirror . . . and I see one just like it when I look into* your *eyes when you really, really want something, too.*

"Deal?" he asked his daughter.

"Deal!" she said firmly.

✦ ✦ ✦ ✦ ✦

August 1883 PD

"SO, IS MIKEY—I MEAN, *MICHAEL*—still pissed off with me?" Roger Winton asked as the armored air limo, accompanied by the sting ships in the blue and silver livery of the House of Winton, descended sedately towards Admiralty House's rooftop pad.

"I wouldn't say he was *'pissed'* at you, Dad," Elizabeth replied, wrinkling her nose in thought. "I'd say he was more...intensely irritated by circumstances beyond his control."

"You've been spending too much time with Allen and Elisa. Or with your Uncle Ed, at least." Her father grinned at her, and the treecats sprawled across their laps bleeked in their species' equivalent of laughter. "No, I detect Allen's fell hand. He's the diplomat spinmeister—comes with being Prime Minister, I suppose. Ed's still a staff weenie; he hasn't learned how to weasel-word his way around unpleasant issues yet. And Elisa can't quite forget she used to be a Marine, so she just swings straight from the shoulder. Usually with a lead-loaded clue stick, now that I come to think of it."

"I guess that's at least a *little* fair." Elizabeth held up her right hand, thumb and forefinger perhaps a half-centimeter apart. "I stand by my original diagnosis, though. It's not so much you personally he's mad at, Dad. He's mad at the fact that he's not in control, not in a position to make his own decisions."

Roger crooked a thoughtful eyebrow, one hand stroking smoothly and reflexively down Monroe's silky spine. She was probably right, he decided, although it was a bit hard for a harassed parent— especially a harassed *male* parent—to remember that when teen-aged angst reared its ugly head in all its passionate glory.

125

"I have to say I wish the two of you wouldn't keep...locking horns this way, though," Elizabeth continued. "I know there've been times I was just as upset as he is about how little choice either of us have in our lives, but I really don't remember having had this kind of...of—what is it Mom calls it? War in the camp?—with either of you when I was his age."

"All of four whole T-years ago! Gosh!" Roger shook his head in astonishment. "You know, sometimes I forget what an ancient and decrepit sort you are, Beth."

His daughter stuck out her tongue at him, and the treecat in her lap—over twenty T-years younger than Monroe, with four fewer age bands around his tail—bared needle fangs in a long, laughing yawn.

"That doesn't make it untrue," she pointed out after a moment, and he nodded.

"No, it doesn't. But you and Mikey have always been different, honey. That's not a slam at him, either, but there's no point pretending you weren't pretty darned...precocious, even for a Winton. Probably your mom's genetic contribution, now that I think about it." Her eyes twinkled at him, and he shrugged. "Even so, though, you were only a year or so younger than he is now when you decided you wanted to get involved in the 'family business.' He's got time to make up his mind about what he wants to do—or, at least, how graciously he wants to do it." Roger grimaced. "I won't lie about it and say I don't wish both of you had more options, but there wasn't anything I could do about that. Except for your mom and me never to have had either of you, and, frankly, I'm too selfish a man to've put up with a world without the two of you in it."

Elizabeth's eyes softened, and he snorted.

"Don't worry! I'm not going all gooey on you. But it's true. And I think he's having a harder time with adolescence than you did. In fact, I'm sure he is. Your mom and I discussed it with Doctor Sugiyama earlier this year, and Mikey's having heavier sledding with the prolong therapies than you did. Frankly, I was a little surprised by some of what Sugiyama had to say about it, to be honest. Your mom and I are both first-generation prolong, and we didn't have to go through the hormone adjustment and monitoring you and Mikey have—we were both pretty much through that phase before we got the initial treatments in the first place, and I don't think either of us really understood just how different it was going to be for someone like you, with the third-gen therapies. They *explained* it to us, but there's a big difference between having it explained and actually experiencing it, and, unfortunately, Mikey's experiencing it right along with us. Sugiyama's working on balancing dosages, but he doesn't want to medicate Mikey's mood swings if he doesn't have to. And, so far, it's nothing we can't cope with...even if it does seem to Mikey sometimes that I've turned into a slave driver instead of a father!"

"Dad, he doesn't—"

"Oh, yes he does, honey." Roger's chuckle carried only the thinnest trace of sourness, and he reached out to touch the tip of his daughter's nose the way he had when she'd been far younger. "But he'll get over it. And there are times when parents can't be their children's friends. It comes with the responsibility of raising them, and one of these days Mikey's going to realize no one was really deliberately trying to make his life miserable. Best of all, your mom and I both have prolong, which means we may actually live long enough to *see* it!"

Elizabeth smiled, but she also shook her head. In a way, she was most frustrated with Michael because the very thing he was rebelling against was something *she'd* very much wanted. She'd *wanted* to go into the Navy, but she'd had to choose between that and learning her responsibilities and duties as Heir in the face of a situation radically different from the one her father had faced when he'd been her age. As Heir, she wasn't going to be allowed a combat assignment if war came, and she'd known it, which had also factored into the choice she had to make. Did she commit to a naval career under those restrictions, knowing she could never really be more than a glorified staff officer, or did she accept that she'd have to leave physically defending her people to someone else and concentrate on preparing herself to help her father as effectively as possible *outside* the Navy? It had been her own decision in the end, but she'd chosen Landing University of Manticore over Saganami Island because LUM had the best—and toughest—political science curriculum in the Star Kingdom.

And I'm glad I did...for a lot *of reasons,* she admitted, her smile softening. *I wouldn't have met Justin if I hadn't!*

Justin Zyrr was four years older than she was. That wasn't very much in a prolong society, but it meant he was old enough to have completed his graduate degree in chemistry before she enrolled at

LUM. Given who she was and the security considerations involved, LUM had been more than willing to provide freshwoman Elizabeth Winton with a private orientation tour, rather than sending her along with the rest of the thundering herd. And—also given who she was, she thought with an inner chuckle—she'd strayed from the assigned path and somehow ended up in Trantham Hall, the main chemistry building, and wandered into one of the research labs associated with the school. Where she had interrupted a very intense young man fully focused on his current research project. She had, in fact, distracted him at a most inopportune moment, which had resulted in the loss of over three hours of painstaking work, and he'd responded by ripping her head off and handing it to her. He'd just been revving up for the second round when the bodyguard she'd eluded had caught up with her, hurried into the lab, and addressed her as "Your Highness."

Elizabeth Winton had her father's—and her mother's—temper. She'd been trying very hard to put up with the incredibly rude young man's tirade with good grace, acknowledging her trespass, but that temper had been about to slip its steadily fraying leash when Sergeant Bradley turned up. Fortunately, the expression on Justin's face when he heard her title, realized who he'd just been ripping up on side and down the other *was*, had been priceless. He'd looked so *stricken*—not afraid of the consequences, but horrified by his own disrespect—that she'd burst out laughing. And then, after a moment, *he'd* started laughing, as well.

Probably as a result of how they'd met, Justin had become one of the few people remotely her own age who'd managed to conceal any awe he might feel in her royal presence. She'd liked that. Besides, he'd been so *cute*. Even better looking than her preadolescent memories of Sergeant Proctor! And there *had* been that constitutional requirement that she marry a commoner.

Not that Justin had entertained any such notion the first time they met. That was one thing Elizabeth had been able to be absolutely certain of, thanks to Ariel, she thought, stroking her treecat companion affectionately.

She'd been adopted by Ariel when she was only fifteen, which was on the young side, even for the House of Winton. No one pretended to understand even now how the treecats who bonded with humans made their selections, but the fact that all but two Manticoran monarchs since Queen Adrienne had been adopted before they ever took the throne certainly suggested the process wasn't quite as random as it might otherwise appear. Indeed, that pattern had caused some alarm over the centuries, and at least some people believed it wasn't really the treecats' decision at all.

Wintons knew better than that, although they didn't go out of their way to make the point. By this time, the situation was so well-established that no one was likely to raise any concerns, but more than one of the security personnel responsible for the dynasty's safety had worried about it in earlier days. Anyone who'd ever been adopted knew that people who argued treecats were no more than clever animals were completely and totally wrong, and the notion that an intelligent, empathic, and at least potentially *telepathic* alien species was deliberately attaching itself to the human monarchs of the Star Kingdom in what could only be described as a bond of emotional dependency was enough to make any good conspiracy theorist paranoid. No one in the House of Winton was concerned about that—which the aforementioned conspiracy theorist would simply have pointed out meant the conspiracy was working, she guessed—and the 'cats had saved the lives of members of her family at least three times, starting with then-Crown Princess Adrienne. Under the circumstances, if anyone wanted to believe the 'cats were somehow being influenced by humans using the well-worn paths of wealth, patronage, and political power to push the Sphinx Forestry Service into "encouraging" the bonds with the royal house, the Wintons were entirely in favor. And so was Palace Security, given the anti-assassin early warning system the 'cats provided. Not that Security went out of its way to mention the instances when that had happened. Having potential *assassins* regard treecats as little more than cute, adorable, exotic pets no self-respecting killer had to worry his head over was all to the good, as far as the royal family's bodyguards were concerned.

They also provided other, less readily apparent advantages, however. Like everyone who'd ever been adopted, Elizabeth was convinced Ariel helped her balance her own anxieties and worries, and she was virtually certain the 'cat had saved her on more than one occasion from what her cousin Michelle irreverently referred to as her "temper from hell." And 'cats were infallible barometers of the emotions of people around their human companions. It took a while for those companions to learn to read the 'cats' responses, but even if Ariel was physically incapable of human speech, he understood Elizabeth just fine. He was fully capable of responding to "yes/no" queries by nodding or shaking his head, too, and she'd become almost as adroit as a good customer service AI when it came to asking questions to refine whatever he was trying to tell her.

And what he'd told her about Justin Zyrr was that she'd have to be very cautious about how she approached him if she didn't want him to immediately back off and run lest someone think he was attempting to "take advantage" of her. That would've been enough all by itself to convince her to look at him very, very closely, given how many theoretically eligible males she'd run into who'd done everything in their power to convince her they were the perfect answer to any nubile maiden's prayers. So she'd specifically requested him as her chemistry mentor for the required basic course. It had been, she cheerfully admitted, at least a tiny case of abuse of power, since she'd known perfectly well that the university would never dream of *not* giving her the mentor she'd requested. She hadn't much cared about that, either, because it had given her the opportunity for that closer look, and what she'd found when she took it had been even better than she'd expected...even if he had been skittish as an Old Earth rabbit downwind of a treecat when he realized she was taking it.

He's coming along quite nicely at the moment, though, she reflected. *And Mom and Dad both approve of him immensely.* She quirked a smile. *I always knew they had excellent judgment.*

But the smile faded as the armored limo drifted towards touchdown and her thoughts returned to her younger brother.

I don't want Mikey to be unhappy, and I know it bothers Dad more than he's willing to admit. Mom, too, but this one's between him and Dad a lot more than between him and her.

"I really do wish he didn't get so wound up about it," she said, watching the sting ships through the side window. "He hates it afterward, too, you know. I think he knows he's being unfair when he gets so mad, and he doesn't *like* being mad at you, Dad."

"I know that, honey. And *I* don't like being mad at *him*, either." He touched her hair lightly and smiled when she looked back at him. "But, fortunately, Mikey's a really good kid, whatever rough patch we're going through right now. And part of it, you know, is the difference between the way boys' and girls' heads work."

"Oh?"

Elizabeth looked at him just a bit suspiciously, and his smile broadened.

"Boys don't do 'subtle' very well, Beth. Especially when those hormones kick in, but it starts earlier than that, really. They know what they know, they're stubborn as the day is long, and they don't handle limits very well. They're geared to solve problems—like disputes with parental authority—by doing things *their* way, with all the finesse of an Old Earth rhino, and they come at you head on. That's the reason Mikey and I lock horns so much more often than he and your mom do. As Doctor Sugiyama says, Mikey's a lot more like *me* than he is like your mom, and that makes these little...lively moments between us inevitable, I'm afraid."

And, he chose not to add out loud, *the way I'm stressing over the situation in Trevor's Star isn't helping just at the moment. I try not to let it affect the way I react when he and I don't see eye-to-eye, but I know it's leaking over sometimes. In fact, I think it was probably a major contributory factor in our last blow up.*

"So, if *boys* don't do 'subtle' very well, is that another way of saying girls *do*?" Elizabeth demanded, pulling him away from that unhappy thought before his smile could fade.

"Well, of course!" He shook his head at her. "Girls tackle problems more consensually than boys do, they'd rather spend their energy doing things they don't know from the outset is going to get them lectured by their elders, and they figure out early that the males in their lives are only there to get in the way and mess things up, so they start out by practicing on their parents. They smile, they promise to do exactly what their parents tell them to do, and then they go out to do precisely what they were going to do anyway, on the theory that if they're lucky—and good—their parents will never find out about it. And, the way they see it, they're actually doing their parents a favor, aren't they? By keeping them from worrying about the consequences of all those things they promised they wouldn't do, I mean."

Elizabeth's eyes widened, and Ariel bleeked with laughter as he tasted her chagrin.

"I didn't—I mean," she said, "*I*—"

"Didn't realize I'd figured that out?" her father suggested helpfully, and chuckled at her expression. Then his smile faded slightly.

"Beth, I never worried about the venal sins your mom and I knew you were committing, because—like Mikey, but maybe even more so—you were always a good kid. You're turning into a remarkable young woman, as well, and I knew the whole time you were manipulating and evading your way around me in those venal things you were up to, that you'd never lie to me about anything important." He rested his hand on her shoulder as the limo settled onto its skids. "I wasn't worried then, I'm not worried now, and I doubt there's another father anywhere in the entire Star Kingdom who's more satisfied—more *delighted*—than I am with the way his daughter's turned out. I'm sure Mikey'll turn out just as well—in his own stubborn, male, mule headed, obstinate, *determined* way—as you did. And as for the rest of it, I console myself with an ancient Old Earth proverb."

"And which proverb would that be?" Elizabeth asked as a lieutenant of the King's Own began to open her limo door for her.

"The one that says 'This too shall pass,'" her father told her wryly. "'This too shall pass.' Even male adolescence, thank God!"

◆　◆　◆

Jonas Adcock and the other people gathered in the briefing room rose respectfully as King Roger and Crown Princess Elizabeth walked through the door.

They were a striking pair, Adcock thought yet again, his brother-in-law and his niece. Elizabeth was above average height for a woman, but her father had his own father's height. At a hundred and ninety-four centimeters, Roger was far taller than his daughter, whose slender, not quite delicate frame clearly favored her mother's side of the family. Her complexion was just a shade lighter than her father's, as well, but she had the Winton chin and her father's steady brown eyes. And if her head didn't top Roger's shoulder, her spine was just as straight, her head regally raised, despite the weight of the treecat riding on her shoulder.

She'll make a wonderful queen someday, he thought, *even if I'll be long gone before that ever happens. No system of government's proof against throwing up idiots, incompetents, thieves, or charlatans as head of state, and monarchy's got more potential for it than some others I could think of. But Manticore's been lucky as hell in that regard over the centuries. I imagine an awful lot of that's due to the requirement that the Heir marry a commoner—avoids inbreeding, anyway!—but I think a lot more has to do with that whole Winton concentration on "servant of the people" when they start raising their kids. Wouldn't be surprised if the 'cats have more than a little to do with it, too, now that I think about it, but the childhood training . . . that's the big factor. And Roger and Angel are smart—smart—to get Beth involved in Roger's plans as deeply as possible, as early as possible.*

He knew more than a few people, even among Roger's closer advisers, wouldn't have agreed with him. People who felt that a young woman—a girl—barely three T-months past her eighteenth birthday was *not* a suitable recipient for the sorts of heavily classified information which routinely came her way. And even many who'd learned not to worry that she was going to start posting classified documents on her personal blog continued to cherish reservations about an eighteen-year-old's insight, judgment, and ability to truly understand the Star Kingdom's steadily deteriorating relations with the People's Republic of Haven.

Jonas thought those people were fools. He was willing to admit *he* might be just a little prejudiced, as well, but still—!

Hadn't they been *listening* to her? She clearly remembered one of her mother's favorite adages, learned from Jonas' stepmother—"A wise man speaks because he has something to say; a fool speaks because he has to say something." Elizabeth didn't open her mouth all that often in the meetings she attended with her father, but whenever she did, what she had to say was worth listening to. There'd even been a time or two when she'd disagreed with Roger, at least in part, and it had been instructive to see how carefully *Roger* listened to her when she did.

Yep, a wonderful queen, he told himself as her father pulled back her chair and seated her before taking his own place. *I hope she doesn't get to demonstrate that for decades and decades after I'm gone, but when the time comes, she'll be ready.*

◆   ◆   ◆

Roger noticed Jonas' small smile, and he was glad to see it, although he hated how lined his brother-in-law's face was getting, how thin his snowy hair had turned. It was even more striking at today's meeting, since Roger's other brother-in-law, Edward Henke, was also present, looking absurdly—painfully—young beside Jonas. The Earl of Gold Peak was an up-and-coming assistant undersecretary in the Foreign Office, although he was still more than a little junior for this sort of stratospheric session, despite his close relationship to the Crown. He was also, however, one of Foreign Secretary Nageswar's specialists where San Martin was concerned, and that was rather the point of today's meeting.

In fact, it would probably be a good idea to get that part of the meeting out of the way now so they could move on to the material Gold Peak and most of the other Foreign Office representatives had no need to know.

"All right," he said, "at least part of this is going to be brutally short, simple, and to the point. According to all our information," he nodded in Big Sky's direction, "the Peeps are going to move on Trevor's Star within the next six T-months. Possibly even sooner."

Most of the civilians around the table stiffened as they abruptly realized why this meeting was taking place at Admiralty House instead of Mount Royal Palace, and Roger smiled thinly.

"Yes, you're absolutely right," he told those civilians, sparing a slight, additional nod in Gold Peak's direction. "As soon as we can shove all of you civilians—except you and Abner, Allen—" he smiled a bit more naturally at Prime Minister Cromarty and First Lord Castle Rock "—out the door, the uniformed types and I are going to be looking very closely at all of our military hole cards. But before we get to that, we have to decide what we're going to tell President Ramirez and his government."

"At the moment, Your Majesty," Baron Big Sky said, "I'm not sure there's much we *can* tell the President." His expression was unhappy. "I don't doubt he and his intelligence people are picking up on the same straws in the wind we are—in fact, I know their navy's intelligence officers are. President Ramirez's assessment may be somewhat different from ours, but he has to realize what's building. The problem is that they're painted into a corner. Not only have they been looking down the barrel of the Peeps' pulser for damned close to thirty T-years, but they've pursued that 'nonaligned' policy of theirs for so long that trying to reverse course would be bound to create all sorts of confusion within their own government. And that completely ignores the question of how the Peeps would react!"

"Admiral Big Sky's correct, I'm afraid, Your Majesty," Gold Peak put in. He was careful to speak formally, under the circumstances, even if Roger was his brother-in-law. "I hate to say it, but there's a huge degree of...fatalism, I guess I'd have to call it, in the San Martin leadership. They've been trying to build up their military, but everyone knows they've got the chance of a snowball in hell if—when—the Peeps come after them. I think they'll probably fight, even knowing they can't win, but that's the problem. They'll hurt the Peeps a lot worse than the Peeps probably think they can, but the San Martinos *know* they can't win in the end, and they've got their heads so far down, leaning so hard into the wind, that they just aren't open to any other possibilities. In fact, it's almost as if they're afraid to *consider* any other possibilities because of how much worse it will hurt when they find out they were right to be pessimistic all along."

"I'm aware of that, Ed," Roger replied. "And I think your estimate's a very good one. For that matter, more than one member of the *Alliance* is going to have serious reservations about what I have in mind. They agree with Ramirez's advisers: Trevor's Star is going down, and there's nothing anyone can do about it. Not when the Peeps outgun the San Martinos as badly as they do, and not when Trevor's Star is effectively completely surrounded by Peep territory. To be brutally realistic about it, they see no benefit to tying the Alliance to a walking corpse, especially if it's likely to embroil the entire Alliance in a shooting war with the PRH. We're a hell of a lot better off than we were a couple of decades ago, but so are the Peeps, and they're still a hell of a lot bigger than we are. We have seventy-six of the wall; *they* have twice that many. And they've got somewhere north of three hundred and fifty battleships for rear area security...while we don't have *any* anymore."

He paused for a moment, long enough to let all of that sink in, then leaned forward, folding his hands on the table in front of him, looking around the faces of his most trusted advisers, feeling his daughter sitting at his elbow.

"I understand why they feel we can't risk facing down the Peeps over a single star system that isn't even a member of the Alliance, but they're wrong," he said flatly. "Completely ignoring any moral questions or how long San Martin's been a Manticoran trading partner, we can't afford to let the Trevor's Star Terminus go down without at least trying to save it. And we can't put defensive forces on it without the San Martinos' permission. And San Martin isn't about to give us permission to defend the *terminus* if they believe doing so will move up the Peeps' schedule for seizing the *star system*. We have to convince them to...see the situation differently, and we also need to deliver a shock to Nouveau Paris. They've gotten too complacent, too sure of themselves, and that's part of the problem. We need to make them back off and rethink, really *consider* how serious a threat our own Navy's become and whether or not they *really* want to risk opening the ball with us. At the very least we need to change the game in a way which can buy us another five, even ten extra T-years before the missile actually does go up."

It was very quiet in the conference room, and Roger let his eyes circle the table again, his gaze making contact with that of every other person around it.

"The Queen and I are scheduled for a state visit to San Martin in October," he continued finally. "That was set up almost a year ago, and all indications are that the Peeps' planners want to let us get that visit out of the way before they move. Our analysts think that letting us go ahead with 'business as usual' with San Martin is supposed to lull both us and President Ramirez's administration into not noticing what's about to happen. And I think we can safely assume the Peeps aren't going to pull the trigger while Queen Angelique and I are actually in Trevor's Star. That gives us at least a brief window, and I intend to take advantage of it by personally proposing to President Ramirez, during our visit, a mutual defense treaty between Trevor's Star and the Star Kingdom of Manticore. Exactly the same sort of treaty we have with every other member of the Alliance—one that obligates us to protect *their* territory, as well as simply guarding our own assets on the terminus."

There was something suspiciously like a muted gasp, and his smile turned feral.

"Don't misunderstand me. I don't think we're fully prepared for war against the People's Republic at this point. On the other hand, I'm pretty sure we'll never feel like we're *fully* prepared, even when the shooting actually starts. I don't think *they're* ready to take *us* on directly yet, either, though. I think that if they suddenly realize we're serious about meeting them head on if they go after Trevor's Star, they'll blink. I don't think we'll stop them *permanently*, but I do think we'll knock them off stride, at least slow them down, inspire them to run an entirely new set of risk assessments based on our obvious determination to stop trying to *avoid* a confrontation and actually court one on our own terms. And if we do have to fight them now, then so be it. There's no point building a sword"—his eyes flitted sideways to Jonas for just a moment—"if you're never willing to use it. I'd rather not yet, but I'd also rather take the chance on having to than simply sit here and watch Trevor's Star and San Martin go down when we might have stopped it."

"Your Majesty, I don't know if that's even possible," Castle Rock said after a moment. "Coming at them cold, after so long—"

"It won't be coming at them *completely* cold, Abner," Roger said. "I actually met Ramirez on our last state visit to San Martin, eight years ago. Of course, he was only *Senator* Ramirez at the time, which is probably the main reason I got to talk to him in something like genuine privacy. And I liked him. I liked him a lot... and so did the Queen. Not only that, I think there's a lot more fire in that man's belly than anyone in Nouveau Paris—or most of the people in Ciudad San Marcos, for that matter—believe. That's what gave me the idea to try something this insane in the first place."

The King smiled briefly, then sobered.

"I apologize for not having brought you in on this sooner, but under the circumstances it had to be kept very, very quiet. Only Foreign Secretary Nageswar, Assistant Secretary Maxwell, and our ambassador to San Martin have been brought fully on board at this point. But Ambassador Mandelbaum has conveyed a personal message from me to Hector Ramirez, laying out the offer I'm prepared to make. And Ramirez has responded. I won't pretend he's positive he can pull it off, but he thinks there's a very, very good chance of it, especially if it comes spontaneously 'out of nowhere' and directly from me to him when I'm standing on San Martin's soil. The fact that I'm *personally* making it, putting the Crown of Manticore directly and explicitly behind it, without any of the customary diplomatic euphemisms, is critical to the calculus from San Martin's end. I intend to invoke Quentin Saint-James while I'm about it, too." The King's eyes glinted. "It won't hurt to remind the galaxy in general of the standards the Navy holds itself to, and the memory of how he handled things in 1752 should resonate with the San Martin electorate. And the sheer surprise of having it dropped on them with no previous leaks, no trial balloons, no diplomatic discussion at all, should give us at least the possibility of breaking through that 'fatalism' Ed just described."

He sat back again, looking at his advisors, tasting their shock as they grappled with his proposal, and his bared teeth would have done any treecat proud.

"Nobody wants a war against the People's Republic. But nobody in this conference room is foolish enough to think one isn't coming, anyway. All right, if it has to come, then let's fight it with a bridgehead right in the heart of the Peeps' own territory. Let's take away that complacent certainty that Trevor's Star is theirs for the taking whenever they get around to it. Let's make them think—*really* think—about facing a navy every bit as good or *better* than theirs and make them think about the Sword of Damocles that terminus represents where their own territorial integrity's concerned. They're the ones who've been marching in our direction for forty T-years now, and it's time someone showed them the error of their ways."

Those brown Winton eyes were ice, and his voice was colder still.

"If they want a war, we'll give them a war like none they've ever fought, and we'll by God give it to them *now.*"

September 1883 PD

"SO ARE YOU REALLY as full of fight as everyone in the Cabinet and at Admiralty House thinks you are?" Jonas Adcock asked, leaning back in the comfortable armchair and waving the brandy snifter appreciatively under his nose.

One of the few "upper crust" luxuries he'd come to enjoy was a good glass of brandy, and the Mount Royal Palace cellars' collection of brandies was his secret vice. One his sister and brother-in-law always remembered at Christmas and birthdays. And one which he pandered to shamelessly on his visits to the palace.

"In a way, yes," Roger replied, settling into his own chair with a sigh of comfort. Unlike Jonas, the King favored whiskey, and the glass in his hand contained Glenfiddich Grand Reserve. "I don't *want* to, not yet, but we genuinely can't afford to lose Trevor's Star at this point. A logistically secure forward base well behind the enemy's front lines? One we could reinforce faster than they could? One that would give us forward basing for raids on their shipping and infrastructure?" He shook his head, his expression grim. "I know we're still outgunned, but Gram and our open R and D have already given us a substantial qualitative edge. And much as I'd love to wait until we had more of Gram's programs into the developmental stage, or even ready to deploy, I just can't sacrifice the strategic advantage of being able to deploy that far forward. My God, Jonas! It would put our advanced fleet base less than two weeks from the Haven System itself, instead of almost two damned *months*! Think of the force multiplier that kind of reduction in turn around time would give us! If we can get our fleet to Haven in a quarter of the time, it'd be the same as giving

139

us four times the wallers... and *they'd* have to worry about us taking out *their* home system with a pounce through hyper rather than the other way around. For all intents and purposes, it gives us a hundred and fifty more light-years of strategic depth."

"And, conversely," Jonas said, nodding gravely, "*losing* the Trevor's Star Terminus puts the Peeps a lot closer to us than that hundred and fifty light-years would suggest."

"In a lot of ways," Roger agreed. He sipped from his glass, then looked up with a grimace which had nothing at all to do with the rich, honeyed fire of the whiskey. "Mind you, I think they'd be lunatics to try an assault through the Junction, especially with only one terminus in their possession. Unfortunately, there's nothing to guarantee they won't *be* lunatics about it, and as I've said more than once before, even a failed Junction assault on their part would result in a state of war between us, anyway. We won't have any choice but to upgrade and strengthen the Junction forts if we lose Trevor's Star, either, which won't help our naval budgets one bit. And that doesn't even consider the consequences for trade patterns or the implications for morale. Losing Trevor's Star would have to have a depressing effect on our people's psychology. By the same token, it would have to pump up domestic support for the Peeps. Not only would San Martin be the wealthiest single planet they've managed to pick off yet, but it would give them a claim—potentially, at least—on San Martin's share of the Junction transit fees under the Treaty of 1590. And if we don't let them cash in on the treaty, they can always withdraw from it and charge whatever damned fees they want. That would be a shot in the arm for their economy... and one that would only make them even hungrier to grab off the mother lode for themselves. It would also give us the choice between accepting whatever fee schedule they set or trying to do something about it by force, which would simply get us into that war we're all trying so hard to postpone. You know their propagandists would use the fact that they'd gotten away with punching out Trevor's Star as another way to suggest to their domestic news market that we're not willing to face them militarily, despite all our 'posturing' and 'unilateral hostility towards the peaceloving citizens of the People's Republic.' And if they got away with jacking up the terminus fees, they'd just use our restraint as another example of how frightened of them we are.'"

"Of course they would." Adcock's grimace was as sour as Roger's had been . . . and owed equally little to his beverage of choice. "And I'm sure they'd find all sorts of ways to use their possession of Trevor's Star and our proximity to it, thanks to the Junction, to stage-manage tensions—and incidents—between us and them for their advantage whenever they felt like it."

"Exactly." Roger took another sip of whiskey and shook his head. "Like I say, I don't *want* to fight them right now, but I'm a lot more willing to do that than to give up Trevor's Star. Of course, if this visit with Ramirez works out next month, we may be able to have our cake and eat it too."

"And if pigs had wings they'd be pigeons, Roger." It was Jonas' turn to shake his head. "You're not going to convert the Legislaturalists into pacifists just by standing up beside San Martin."

"No, but I genuinely believe from everything we're hearing out of ONI and the SIS that we'd at least cause them to rethink, and probably rethink hard. Big Sky's gotten better penetration than I think a lot of people realize. We don't have anyone actually inside the Octagon, but we've managed to recruit or place agents a lot more broadly at lower levels, and we've gotten a better look inside their hardware than I ever expected."

Roger sipped whiskey again, then shrugged.

"He's going to shoot a copy of our latest tech analysis over to you—top-secret, burn-before-reading, of course—and I think you'll find it interesting. Unless it's a really clever example of disinformation, we've opened an even bigger edge in conventional weapons systems—especially ECM and our missile targeting systems—than we'd realized. It looks like our current-generation laser head grav lensing's a lot better than theirs than we'd thought, too. They're basically using the straight Astral design, without any upgrades, and I know Rodriguez has routed Section Thirteen's latest through-put numbers to Gram. Our capital missile laser heads are almost twice as powerful as their current-generation hardware, assuming these numbers are good. And they're nowhere near deploying a cruiser or destroyer grade version, whereas *we—*"

He shrugged, and Jonas nodded in understanding. Gram's researchers had played a not insignificant role in pointing Section Thirteen at the component miniaturization which had permitted BuWeaps to engineer the newest laser heads down to something that would fit a missile body which could be launched from light units' tubes. And carried in sufficient numbers to be useful, he reminded himself. One disadvantage of the RMN's increasing emphasis on missiles was that magazine space had to be upsized to keep pace with the increase in launchers. That problem had already reared its head when the impeller drive counter-missile came into use, of course, and the increased standoff range of the laser head was only making that still worse. Last-generation sidewall burners had started the progression, but with laser heads, it became imperative to begin thinning the incoming salvos as early as possible, and only counter-missiles had that kind of reach.

And every counter-missile we carry uses up volume we can't *use on shipkillers,* he thought. *And if Mjølner works out the way we hope, that◻s going to get even worse. Or better depending on who else has the same capability!*

"I wish we had a better look inside their software," Roger went on, "but we've managed to get our hands on actual tech manuals, and the decrypt codes, for their current generation shipkillers, radar, and gravitic sensors."

Jonas' eyebrows rose respectfully.

"Somebody's damned well earned his pay, assuming they're really current," he observed. "Of course the fact that we got them also underscores one of my own worst nightmares!"

"And I'm not going to tell you our security hasn't been breached," Roger replied with a nod. "I don't think it has, and what ONI's been turning up suggests a lower level of tension among the Peeps than we'd be seeing if they had a clue about some of the things your people are working on at *Weyland*. If they knew about Gram, they'd either be running a lot more scared, or else they would've already launched a preemptive attack. The *last* thing they'd want to do would be to let us get the new systems through development and into deployment!" He shook his head again. "No, it looks to me like Shell Game's working, Jonas."

Jonas considered that for a moment, then nodded just a bit grudgingly. One thing which Roger had insisted upon fanatically from the very beginning was that Project Gram's security *had* to be absolute. Gram was his ace in the hole, his desperately needed equalizer, and for it to be those things, it also had to be completely black, completely hidden from the People's Republic of Haven's spies and analysts. It helped that all indications were that the Peeps saw espionage more as an offensive than a defensive tool. They appeared to be far more focused on gathering political information, looking for dissidents who could be subsidized to destabilize opponents, using blackmail, extortion, and even assassination to weaken their targets at the critical moment. Their covert operations people were among the best in the galaxy when it came to that sort of mission, but it did tend to give their intelligence people a form of tunnel vision. They focused on short-range, intensive efforts to penetrate, undermine, and critically weaken the objective immediately on their targeting screens, and they appeared to assign their very best people to those sorts of ops, which left only limited personnel, resources, and funding for their chronically understrength *long*-range operations.

None of which meant they didn't spend *any* effort on those sorts of operations, and they'd obviously realized long ago that Manticore was going to constitute their greatest challenge. Under the circumstances, they had to have assigned a substantial chunk of their intelligence efforts to "the Manticore Problem."

That was why Shell Game, the operation designed to protect Gram's secrecy, had been stood up over fifteen T-years ago. Gram's first fruits had been decanted into BuWeaps' openly maintained R&D programs, like Section Thirteen and Project Python, with carefully worked out and documented pedigrees designed to provide plausible origins for them which had nothing at all to do with top-secret R&D think tanks based on HMSS *Weyland*. In addition, BuWeaps had its own R&D staff, working independently of Gram, within the sorts of security safeguards anyone would have anticipated. That staff was doing good work, too, without ever realizing that much of its function was to serve as the Office of Naval intelligence's counterespionage staff's stalking horse—the "honeypot," as Roger had called it—designed to attract Peep espionage efforts. Nor was that staff aware that there were *Manticoran* "spies" seeded throughout its ranks, charged with making certain that every scrap of useful data it might turn up would be channeled to the even larger, carefully concealed R&D staff assigned to Gram. And even if anyone eventually figured out there was a research effort going on aboard *Weyland*, Gram itself was hidden behind a secondary level of BuWeaps' official research efforts which had been located on the station precisely to cover Gram and serve as a second level "honeypot" for anyone who got past the first one.

Which doesn't even consider the fact that Gram is under the command of that well-connected but clearly-something-of-a-dim-bulb, Captain Jonas Adcock, he thought wryly.

The House of Winton wasn't above using planted stories to help mislead and misdirect the Star Kingdom's enemies, and Roger's staff, under Elisa Paderweski's competent direction, had "leaked" several new stories subtly underscoring the point that King Roger and Queen Consort Angelique were "looking after" Captain Adcock until he was finally ready to be eased out into retirement. It was hard to conceal the kinds of information flow—in and out—a research effort like Gram required, but Shell Game had considered that aspect, as well, and Jonas' personal relationship with Roger gave him a perfect excuse to "take time off" from the sinecure in the Office of Fleet Logistics which had been created for him aboard *Weyland* for visits to his sister and his brother-in-law. Visits which just happened to let him deliver personal and highly comprehensive briefings to Roger, the space lords, and the two or three senior officers at BuWeaps who knew about Gram.

"I don't think our security's been broken, either, really, Roger," he said now. "That doesn't keep me from spending the occasional sleepless night worrying about it, of course. But I think you're right about how the Peeps would have reacted by now if they knew about it. That doesn't mean they couldn't have picked up at least a whiff, though, and simply not realized how far along we actually are."

"Probably not. But that brings up an interesting question, you know." Roger gave his brother-in-law a very level look. "We can't keep you hidden away in Gryphon orbit forever, Jonas. At some point, your research is going to be far enough along that we need to start major development, and there's no one currently at BuWeaps with the knowledge and the expertise you have. I'm not going to be able to leave you as a mere captain much longer."

Jonas' jaw tightened. He started to reply quickly, then made himself stop and draw a deep breath. The worst of it was that he knew Roger was right ... even though Roger was also *wrong*. The problem was that it all came down to a judgment call, and someone had to make it. Which, given the fact that Roger Winton was King of Manticore, meant *he* had to make it.

"I know you don't want to hear that, and I know you're not going to want to give up Gram," Roger continued, "but I don't think I have a choice. The new fusion bottles, the new shipboard armors, the new LAC notions Sonja's playing around with, and—*especially*—the new shipkillers, if we can get them to work, are going to be an even bigger game changer than I ever hoped for when we first established Gram. That's been your work since well before I ever came along, and I wish with all my heart that the rest of the Star Kingdom could know how very much we all owe to you and your people. But at the moment, it's all still theoretical, and you know it."

The King shook his head, waving one hand in a brushing away gesture.

"I know you've built small-scale proof of concept test rigs for a lot of it, Jonas, but you've been a King's officer even longer than I have. You know how true that old adage about 'many a slip betwixt cup and lip' really is, and the transition from experimental theory into *developmental* hardware and then into actual, deployable weapons systems—*reliable* weapons systems, with workable doctrine for their use—has one hell of a lot of possible potholes along the way. Not only that, but if Mjølner works out remotely as well as your current models suggest, every single ship-of-the-wall in the galaxy's going to turn obsolete overnight. *All* of them, Jonas . . . including ours. We're talking about a fundamental shift in the combat paradigm like nothing the human race has seen since the invention of the Warshawski sail itself. We're not only going to have to develop the weapons, we're going to have to design entirely new, fundamentally different warships to mount them, and then we're going to have to *build* the ships, and we're going to have to do all of that without letting the Peeps see what's coming. I'm sorry, but I can't think of anyone else I'm prepared to trust to see to all of that. You've got good deputies aboard *Weyland*; you're going to have to turn Gram over to them, because I need you here."

Jonas wanted—badly—to protest, but Roger's face told him protests would be useless. He knew that expression. He'd seen it more often than he could remember on the face of the man who'd set out to "build his house of steel" so many years before. And the clincher was that he couldn't argue with Roger's logic.

He doubted that even Roger fully grasped everything Gram had accomplished and was still accomplishing. Yet the King had fastened unfailingly on the most critical of all of Gram's potential products.

Every capital ship in the galaxy was optimized for the brutal savagery of the close-range energy weapon slugging match, because every admiral in the galaxy knew missiles were little more than nuisance weapons, employed against a modern ship-of-the-wall's missile defenses. Oh, with the emergence of the laser head-armed missile, the threat had begun to shift, over the last dozen years, but a ship-of-the-wall's armor was so massive, its defenses were so good, and laser heads (even the RMN's latest version) were so light compared to the throughput of shipboard energy batteries, that naval designers and builders had contented themselves with merely incremental improvements in missile defense. Wallers mounted a few more missile tubes and a lot more counter-missile launchers than they used to, and virtually every modern capital ship had upgraded by now to the longer ranged and more effective laser cluster for point defense. But nothing had changed the view that a solid core of graser-armed superdreadnoughts simply could not be stopped by anything short of a matching force of similarly armed ships.

But Mjølner was something else again: a true long-ranged shipkiller, not a mere "nuisance." The concept had actually first been suggested by Roger himself almost fifteen T-years ago, even before Section Thirteen had perfected its very first laser head, and on the face of it, it had been an impossible dream. Of course, Jonas had observed that quite a *few* of Roger Winton's notions had been "impossible dreams" when he tossed them out and then expected his loyal minions to make them work anyway.

The problems with Mjølner had been just a bit more...profound than usual, however, and lay primarily in the fundamental difference between starships', or even recon drones', impeller rings and those used for missiles. Getting the sort of acceleration effective impeller drive missiles required out of something which would fit into a practical-sized missile body required some substantial design tradeoffs. The sheer power load impeller nodes had to carry was one of them, both in terms of supplying the power in the first place—superconductor capacitors had undergone a significant upgrade when the modern missile came along—and in terms of *surviving* the power levels involved long enough to be worthwhile. Drones were larger than missiles, but even so they'd been required to accept *far* lower acceleration rates in order to get the service life their nodes required (and live within an energy budget they could meet) if they were going to have worthwhile range and endurance. Not that his people at Gram weren't convinced they couldn't make major improvements on existing drone limitations, of course.

Missiles were tougher, though, and the designers' solution had been to accept impeller drives which literally consumed themselves in flight. Their acceleration rates had to be preselected at launch, and they couldn't be turned off and turned back on—or even throttled back and then ramped up—the way drones could, because they were *designed* to operate at a self-destroying, overloaded level. The trick over the T-centuries since the impeller drive missile's introduction had been to match the rate of node destruction to the attainable power budget of the missile to gain the maximum possible range/accel before the nodes blew.

Roger's suggestion had been that they consider a staged approach, with multiple impeller rings which could be activated in sequence, and he'd only smiled blandly when Jonas and the rest of the Concept Development Office had goggled at him in disbelief. Even Jonas had been inclined to think he must have been smoking things he shouldn't have, but he'd been serious. The CDO had been forced to more or less file the idea away for future reference, since it hadn't had the budget or facilities to actually *do* anything with it, but Gram had started looking at the problems one by one with it from the day it opened its doors aboard HMSS *Weyland*.

There were a lot of them, those problems. If there hadn't been, someone else would surely have tried strapping extra drives onto a missile already, after all. And the more Jonas and his people had looked, the better they'd come to understand why no one had ever been crazy enough to attempt it before.

First, there was the problem of power supply. Even with the improvements in capacitor technology, just feeding the energy appetite of a multidrive weapon was going to require an enormous missile body. At the time they'd started what had become Project Mjølner, they couldn't have squeezed the thing into even the largest system defense missile ever built—they would have required something bigger than any existing recon drone, actually, which was far too large for anyone to consider carrying in the sorts of numbers which would be needed when waller met waller in missile-range combat.

Second, there'd been the question of node endurance. Design lifetimes had been increased markedly since the very first impeller drive missile was introduced in 1256, but it had taken all the weary years since just to get to where they'd been at the moment Roger had his inspiration. The notion that it could be pushed still higher in a relatively short time frame had seemed...unlikely, and they still hadn't managed to increase the drive's lifetime. They had, however, managed to increase the *power levels* it could sustain, which was going to lead to significant increases in missile acceleration rates. More importantly, at least in the short term, counter-missiles relied on their insanely over-powered impeller wedges, using those wedges as huge, immaterial brooms that destroyed anything they hit. With the new drive nodes, Manticoran CMs were about to become markedly more potent. Coupled with the RMN's already existing advantage in electronic warfare systems and fire control, that was going to increase Manticore's missile combat advantage still further. The trick, after all, was to hit the bad guy while he *couldn't* hit you, and one way to accomplish that was to kill his shipkillers short of their target more efficiently than he could do the same thing to you.

But the third problem—the really *killer* problem—had been that there were only so many places on a missile where you could *put* the impeller rings. They literally couldn't be put anywhere else without fatally compromising some other aspect of the weapon's design...which wouldn't have been so bad if an active impeller node didn't rip hell out of the basic matrix of any *other* impeller node in its immediate vicinity. The nodes of a single impeller ring were tuned to one another, and (at least in a missile drive) all of them were up and fully powered at the same time. In a starship, or even a purely sublight light attack craft, the rings themselves were far enough apart to obviate any problem of mutual interference, and the nodes were big enough to incorporate the tuners which synched the alpha and beta nodes of each individual ring to one another. Even a starship, however, had to bring *all* of the nodes in a ring online, whether it intended to power all of them to fully operational levels or not, in order to get all of their tuners synched into the ring at once. Otherwise, the gravitic stress pouring off the active nodes warped the molecular circuitry of the inactive nodes. They had the same effect on other molycircs in the vicinity, as well, which was the reason starship impeller node heads had to be kept well clear of the hull and any other important systems they might affect. LAC nodes were weak enough they didn't have to project very far, but superdreadnought nodes were enormous and required clearances—even from one another in the same ring, and even with the tuners in the circuit—which were measured in meters. The warping effect wasn't a huge, gross, easily observable thing, but it didn't have to be, because impeller node engineering tolerances were incredibly tight and demanding.

And, of course, there was no way to do that with a missile. There just wasn't anyplace else to put them, and you couldn't move them farther up, space them along the length of the missile body (even if that wouldn't have compromised sensors and lasing rod deployment), because of their effect on other critical systems. They *had* to be concentrated in a very narrow chunk of the missile's entire length and, by the same token, they *couldn't* be concentrated that way without the first ring activated eating any others you'd installed!

And, fourth, even if you could somehow get the range in the first place, what did you *do* with it? The existing single-drive missiles were already pushing the limits of effective light-speed telemetry and fire control hard; if ranges were extended as radically as Roger's idea suggested, the entire system would break down. Onboard sensors and AI could be improved to make each individual missile smarter and more capable, but there were limits to how far you could take that, especially with the new generations of decoys and ECM which were bound to confront them. One of Gram's major efforts was directed at producing exactly those better, more capable defensive systems, given the RMN's clear appreciation for just how dangerous laser heads were likely to prove, and it had to be assumed that any potential adversary would be thinking exactly the same way. That meant Manticoran missiles were going to have to go up against increasingly sophisticated countermeasures, in addition to thicker active defenses, and once they got beyond effective telemetry support range from the ships which had launched them, their effectiveness would decline sharply. And if that range was extended from the current shipkiller's maximum powered range of roughly twenty-five light-*seconds* into multiple light-*minutes*, hit percentages were bound to plummet.

That didn't mean it wouldn't still be worthwhile, of course, especially if the RMN could score *any* hits and no one else could reply in kind. The problem was that no current design of waller could carry enough missiles of the size Mjølner's multidrive progeny would require to score *enough* hits to be decisive against other capital ships at that sort of range. At the very least, the laser head itself would have to be substantially upgraded, well past any point Section Thirteen had currently envisioned, because the power of each individual hit would have to be increased to make up for how many fewer of them anyone could hope to score.

Every difficulty seemed to lead to two more problems, but Roger had insisted Gram could make it work, and the more he'd looked at it and all the advantages it would confer, the more Jonas had come to the conclusion that they *had* to make it work. And the really remarkable thing was that it was beginning to look as if perhaps—just perhaps—they actually could.

The most critical breakthrough was what Sonja Hemphill and some of Gram's other team leaders had dubbed simply "the baffle"—essentially, a very carefully designed generator which would project a tame plate of focused gravity to shield adjacent, inactive impeller rings from an active one. Doing it in a way that didn't slice the missile body into divots the moment it came online had turned out to be...moderately tricky, and they still hadn't quite licked the problem, but current results were promising. *Very* promising, actually...in an incremental, God-why-does-this-take-so-long, work-your-butt-off sort of way. And if they could only make the baffle work, all the rest of it was simply fiddly bits. Difficult, challenging, and *expensive* fiddly bits, perhaps, but still only fiddly bits; he was confident of that.

Some other interesting bits and pieces were emerging from the effort, as well. Sonja, for example, was intrigued by the implications of something she'd tentatively christened a "grav lance," although it looked to Jonas like something which would be useful mainly for capital ships that managed to get to knife-fighting range of one another. He couldn't really see anything lighter than a waller being able to make much use of it, but he was more than willing to let Sonja run with it.

The critical point, though, was that despite everything, it looked as if they might very well actually make Mjølner work after all. There were still more obstacles than he liked to think about, but he was confident his people on *Weyland* would overcome them in the end. And if they did—*when* they did—nothing would ever be the same again. Mjølner's range would be incredible, its attack velocities unlike anything the galaxy's navies had ever seen, its energy budget—and the penetration-aiding electronic warfare that would make possible—would make it far, far harder to intercept or spoof, and the new laser heads would be many times as destructive as any existing capital missile, even the RMN's current weapons. It truly would complete what the laser head had begun and shatter the centuries-old, short-ranged, energy weapon combat model which had gripped galactic warfare for as long as anyone could remember once and for all.

And it can't possibly be carried aboard any current design of capital ship, he thought. *Not in sufficient numbers, at any rate; not even my boys and girls are going to squeeze it down into something that'll change that minor problem! Which means we're going to have to completely rethink hull forms, weapons tonnages, launch methods and mechanisms, and ammunition stowage, just for a start. I'm thinking those new lightweight LAC launchers might be part of the answer, at least in the short term. Build ourselves an offensive version of the system defense missile pods and use it as a strap on, or tractor it astern or something, at least for an interim approach. We'll have to come up with something better in the long run though. Defining a new, workable operational doctrine's going to be a big enough pain in the ass all by itself, but I'm willing to bet we're going to have to redesign the ship-of-the-wall from the keel out, too, and then we're going to have to find the wherewithal to build the damned things. And Roger was right; no one at BuWeaps or BuShips had a clue what was about to be thrown at them. If, on the other hand, there was a single man in the RMN who did have a clue . . .*

"What exactly do you have in mind?" he asked.

"I've already talked to Castle Rock and Styler," Roger replied. "Sometime early next year, they're going to create a new command— we're calling it the Weapons Development Board—and you're going to be in charge of it. It'll be based in Manticore Beta, aboard *Weyland,* so it'll still be as much out-of-sight, out-of-mind as we can keep it, and if we can convince the newsies to think it's more makework for a beloved but not that bright brother-in-law, so much the better. You *will* be being bounced directly to flag rank—vice admiral of the red—when you take over as CO, I'm afraid. In fact, I've already signed your promotion, but we've classified it under the Official Secrets Act, at least for now. As far as anyone outside a certain very select circle is concerned, you'll still be a mere captain holding an acting commodore's slot as a way to let Angelique and me funnel a few extra perks and a better pension in your direction."

"I suppose I should be accustomed to being a drone by now," Jonas observed with a dry smile, and Roger chuckled.

"We've all worked hard enough to convince the galaxy at large that you are one, at any rate!"

"And the duties of this new entity would be—?"

"I'm not sure whether it's ultimately going to have to find a home under the BuShips or the BuWeaps umbrella, but for right now, it's not going to belong to either. You'll still be working out of Admiral Rodriguez's office, officially, but your real job is going to be to start creating the liaison between BuShips and BuWeaps we're going to need to move the new systems from pure research into development and then into volume production as early as possible. You'll be doing as much of the work as you can from *Weyland*, if only because our security arrangements there have been worked out in so much depth, but eventually you're going to have to have 'branch offices' aboard *Vulcan* and *Hephaestus*, as well. And in addition to the purely hardware side of things, you're also going to be responsible for developing tactics and operational doctrine to *use* the new systems."

"I see."

Jonas considered for a moment, then shrugged.

"I won't pretend I'm happy about the thought of giving up Gram. On the other hand, I see your logic, and I believe that somewhere around here it says that since you're the King, we all get to do things your way, anyway." He smiled briefly. "How much freedom am I going to have to request personnel?"

"Probably not as much as you'd like, at least initially." Roger made a face. "Obviously we're going to have to bring in additional manpower, which'll mean expanding the number of people who have at least some idea of what Gram's been working on all this time. We need to be careful about how we do that, though. And once anybody disappears into this Weapons Development Board, he won't be being released to the general population again anytime soon. We may have to make some exceptions here and there, and we're going to want people with the shooter's perspective in this up to their elbows, of course, but the security requirements are going to remain paramount for the foreseeable future, as well. We'll have to go public with it eventually, at least within the Service, if it's going to do its job, but I don't want to do that one instant before we have to. Call me paranoid, but I *really* don't want this leaking to the Peeps until we've got the hammer we need to hit them so hard they don't get up again. Why? Is there someone in particular you think you'd like?"

"I was thinking about young Alexander, as a matter of fact," Jonas admitted. "I understand he's just about finished with his current tour at BuPlan. The thought of getting him into harness with Sonja would probably make Sisyphus cringe, but this sounds like something we could really, really use his brain on, Roger. And you know a lot of senior officers're going to have major reservations about such radically new hardware. They know what already works, and they're going to fight like hell against risking the loss of proven weapon systems in favor of a batch of new, half-baked ideas which may end up not working and get us all killed, as a result. But Alexander's broadly enough respected that if we can get *him* signed on, it'll help enormously with the fleet's acceptance in general."

"Um."

Roger frowned, sipping more whiskey and looking into space while he considered. He sat that way for several moments, then blinked and refocused on Jonas.

"I'll think about it," he said, "but my initial thought is that we need him elsewhere even worse." He raised his free hand, forestalling any protest Jonas might have made. "God knows you're right about how good he is and how respected he is, and he's hit the ground running ever since he went back on active duty."

The King's expression went briefly bleak, recalling the horrendous air car accident which had crippled Lady Emily Alexander... and very nearly destroyed Hamish Alexander's naval career as he went on to half-pay in his desperately determined battle to somehow reverse the verdict of his beloved wife's catastrophic damage. He'd failed. Emily Alexander—actress, equestrienne, tennis player, and one of the Star Kingdom's most beloved public figures—would never leave her life-support chair again. The fact that she'd confronted that truth, accepted the physical wasteland her future had become, without even a trace of surrender—that she'd already become one of Manticore's premier HD producers, now that she could no longer take the stage herself—had only made her even more beloved, and she'd had the strength to encourage her husband's return to active duty, as well.

"The problem is, we *do* need him where he is, at the moment, and we need to get him rotated back through active fleet command ASAP, as well," Roger continued. "Your job is going to be to produce the next generation of weapons and the ships and doctrine we need to make them work. In the meantime, though, we have to have the very best commanders and doctrine we can get with *existing* weapons systems, and that describes Hamish perfectly. Eventually, we'll have to bring him on board, but for now, I think he'll be even more valuable to us in more...conventional roles. And let's face it, Jonas. You and I are busy planning for a future war in which Gram's weapons could prove decisive, but we can't be remotely certain the Peeps will hold off that long. One of the reasons I'm going to be talking to Hector Ramirez is my hope that a united front with San Martin will cause the Peeps to back off, buy us the time to get the Weapons Development Board fully up and running and actually bring the new systems to a deployable level. If it doesn't, though—if the Peeps don't blink, and do go ahead and pull the trigger—we'll have to fight with the ships and weapons we already have, and we'll need someone who can use those weapons as effectively as humanly possible. Again, that describes Hamish perfectly. So the bottom line is that I simply can't spare him at this time."

"But you think I can probably have him at some point in the future?" Jonas pressed.

"Assuming we're *not* actively at war with the People's Republic, yes," Roger said dryly.

"Good. I'll hold you to that," Jonas warned.

"Thanks for the warning."

Roger smiled, then glanced at his chrono and made another face. This one was considerably more cheerful than the last one, Jonas noticed.

"Well," the King stood, setting his empty whiskey glass on an end table, "I hate to drink and run, but Angel's waiting for me."

"Really?" Jonas stood as well. "Where are the two of you off to? I thought we were having supper together tonight?"

"Oh, we are," Roger reassured him. "But not here. In fact, we're—"

He broke off as the study door opened and Elizabeth stepped through it. The King's eyebrows rose, and his daughter laughed.

"I bribed Captain Trevor to let me burst in on you without notice, Dad," she said, then stepped past her father to hug Jonas tightly.

"They told me you were here, Uncle Jonas, and I wanted to be sure I got to see you before you disappeared back off to the Admiralty again. Especially since I won't be seeing you at supper tonight."

"You won't?" Jonas returned her embrace, then stood back, smiling at her. "And what have I done to offend you, Your Highness?"

She laughed again, the treecat on her shoulder tilting his head to regard Jonas with matching amusement.

"You haven't done a thing," she assured him. "Except for being guilty of bad timing, anyway. Mom and Dad are off to the Indigo Salt Flats for a little overdue recreation before heading off to Trevor's Star."

"I hadn't heard," Jonas said, looking across at Roger, and the King shrugged.

"We've kept it quiet. Angel and I are both worn out getting ready for this trip—especially her, I'm afraid." He shook his head, his brown eyes softening with the memory of all Angelique had put up with since wedding him. "No newsies, no press, no guests— just the two of us. Well, and you, for supper. Possibly Michael, too...assuming he's on speaking terms with me."

"Bad?" Jonas asked.

"No worse than usual." Roger rolled his eyes. "God, I love that boy, but there *are* times..."

"He'll get over it, Dad," Elizabeth assured him.

"And *you* won't be joining us because—?" Jonas inquired, and Roger laughed.

"Jonas, you'd better get used to it," the King said when his brother-in-law glanced back at him. "Ever since she and young Zyrr announced their engagement, she's taken every opportunity she can find to drag him off to some glitzy nightspot somewhere. Yes, and *pretended* she was just studying for *exams* with him." Roger shook his head, his expression mournful. "She thinks she's actually fooling her soft-headed old dad, too. It's sad, when you think about it."

"You need to work on making your lower lip quiver properly, Dad," his undutiful daughter said critically. "And, no, I don't think I'm fooling you and Mom a bit, given the way Security keeps an eye on all of us. Not to mention the fact that I know *you* know perfectly well that Justin really is helping me study for finals. Or the fact that I happen to know you get along with him just fine yourself."

"Respect," Roger sighed. "It says somewhere in the Constitution, that the King is supposed to be spoken to with respect. I *know* it does."

"By everyone except his family, Dad," Elizabeth said, rising slightly on her toes to kiss his cheek and smiling at him. "But Justin really is waiting for me, and I've got to run, that's the real reason I interrupted you and Uncle Jonas. I already talked to Mom, and I wouldn't keep her waiting, if I were you." She shook her head, brown eyes gleaming. "She's *really* looking forward to this."

"I know—I know!" Roger said repentantly. "She puts up with a lot."

"Oh, it's not *all* bad, Roger," Jonas told him.

"No, it isn't," Elizabeth agreed. "And let me know how that new grav ski works!"

◆　◆　◆

Roger smiled in delight, feeling the wind whip across his tightly curled hair as he rode the grav ski high above the blue sands which gave the Indigo Salt Flats their name. It really had been too long since he and Angel had taken the time to be just the two of them, treasuring one another properly, and the glorious afternoon offered them at least another three or four hours of daylight before they'd have to call it quits. He rather regretted the fact that the new ski Elizabeth had given him for his birthday had been downchecked by Planetary Security. The problem was minor enough he might have used it anyway, but as Major Dover had pointed out, there was no point taking chances with a brand new, possibly temperamental ski. They could always have it serviced for a later excursion, and the backup ski he kept here at the Flats was an old and trusted friend.

He came out of a perfect double spiral flip and looked over to see Angelique's reaction. She looked back at him, raising her hand in salute while her dark hair whipped behind her in the wind of her passage, then banked gracefully and swooped upward, executing exactly the same maneuver. She was a little slower, but her control was better, and Roger chuckled. If there'd been any judges watching them, they'd have given the round to her on points.

"Ready for a quad, Angel?" he asked over the com.

"Why not?" She laughed. "I can't remember when conditions've been more perfect."

"You go first."

"So you can study my technique?" She laughed again. "As Your Majesty commands."

Her quadruple spiral flip was perfect, of course. It always was, and Roger hand-signaled his appreciation, then checked his read-outs. If he was going to win *this* round, he needed every advantage he could get from the light wind and the thermal updrafts. He waited, until conditions were as close to ideal as they were going to get, then glided up into the first spiral.

Perfect!

The second went just as smoothly, and the third without a hitch. He was slightly ahead of her time, and he frowned in concentration, focused on the perfection of his technique, as he moved into the fourth spiral. He was just gathering velocity to imitate the flourish with which Angelique had ended her own flip, when the ski jumped under his feet.

It wasn't much of a jump, but he was far too experienced a grav skier to think he'd imagined it. Another light jolt kicked at the soles of his feet. Again, it wasn't particularly violent, and he was tempted to ride it out. He'd never competed professionally, but he knew he was among the Star Kingdom's best grav skiers, and he was still firmly in control of the ski. He could put it down safely rather than baling and simply letting it crash.

Don't be stupid, Roger. The thought flashed through his brain. *You can get a new ski a hell of a lot easier than you can get a new* neck, *and the last thing you need is to bang yourself up at a moment like this! Ramirez is expecting you in less than three T-weeks now, you dummy!*

He grimaced at the thought, but it was pure reflex and his left hand was already reaching for the tab to release him from the grav ski and onto the standby counter-grav pack. Then there was another jolt—this one a buck that must have been visible from the ground—and the shock shook his hand from the tab.

"I'm closing to help, Roger!" Angelique called over the com.

"I'm holding, love," he responded, continuing to fumble for the release.

And then, impossibly, the ski failed completely. The velocity he'd brought into his last spiral turned against him, ripping his hands away from the release tab. The wind howled around his ears, no longer a joy but a demon, bent on his destruction. Fear burned through him, but he didn't panic. He fought the slipstream, pulling his arms in close, sliding his hand down to the release tab even as he plummeted. His fingers found the tab once more, relief blossomed through the fear, and he pulled.

Nothing happened. Nothing at all.

Below him, the salt sands glittered bright, hard, and utterly unforgiving. He died with the sound of his wife's scream in his ears and the sensation of a distant heart breaking.

October 1883 PD

THE MEN AND WOMEN seated around the table rose as Elizabeth Adrienne Samantha Annette Winton—no longer Crown Princess or Heir, but Queen Elizabeth III of Manticore—walked into the cabinet room.

She moved with a regal, somber grace, a stateliness, few of the members of what had been her father's Cabinet and now was hers had ever seen from her, and the treecat on her shoulder sat very tall and still, his tail hanging down her back like the banner of an army in mourning. The members of her Cabinet rose as one and bowed deeply as she crossed to her place at the head of the table with her aunt and regent, Caitrin Winton-Henke, Countess of Gold Peak, at her side.

Elizabeth lifted Ariel from her shoulder and set him on the back of her chair, then seated herself, followed a moment later by Countess Gold Peak. The cabinet officers waited courteously, then took their own seats at the youthful Queen's gesture. It was the first time since her father's death, three days before, that they'd all been gathered in one place, and they would be going from this cabinet room to King Michael's Cathedral for Roger III's state funeral and burial.

Silence hovered for several seconds, and then Elizabeth drew a deep breath.

"I won't keep you long, My Lords and Ladies," she said with unwonted formality, and more than one of those cabinet officers winced in sympathy, recognizing the way she used that courtesy as a shield for the wound gaping within her. "All of us have a great many things to do, and my—"

Her voice quivered, hovering for a moment on the edge of breaking, and she cleared her throat.

"All of us have a great many things to do," she repeated huskily, "and my mother needs me." She inhaled deeply. "However there are certain things which need saying, and I want all of you to hear them before...before my father's funeral."

She looked around the table once more, and her brown eyes were dark—wounded and shadowed with grief, yes, but touched with something else, as well. Something cold and hard. Something...dangerous.

"It's obvious," she continued after a moment, "that my father's plan for a mutual defense treaty with San Martin is no longer possible. Its success would have depended on carrying the proposal in one, bold sweep, and whatever President Ramirez might want, he could never convince his legislature to approve an action which would necessarily infuriate the People's Republic of Haven"—her mouth seemed to tighten and Ariel's ears flattened—"at the invitation of a minor Queen who's worn her crown for less than a week. That means we're not going to find ourselves in a position to prevent the fall of Trevor's Star."

She made the admission bleakly, but for all the grief, all the anger, in that youthful voice, there was no despair, no hint of surrender, and those oddly hard brown eyes swept the members of her Cabinet once more.

"My father's plans, all he committed himself to for over forty T-years, twenty-five of them as King, will *not* perish with his death," she told them flatly. "His loss wounds us all—wounds the entire Star Kingdom, not just those of us who knew and loved him so very much—but I, My Lords and Ladies, I am his daughter, and I will not—I *will not*—let his life's work go for naught."

She shook her head once, sharply, and Ariel showed bone-white fangs for just a moment.

"I realize that at this moment the entire Manticoran Alliance is in a state of disarray, or will be, when all its members learn of Father's death. It will take time to restore order and confidence, for the other members of the Alliance to realize the Star Kingdom's policy hasn't changed, and for them to gain confidence in my own capability as head of state. I believe it's unlikely the People's Republic"—again, that tightness around the lips—"will move against the Alliance or any of its members in the immediate future." She smiled thinly. "The Peeps will be too busy digesting Trevor's Star, once they take it, and I suspect they'll find the San Martinos less than docile when they make the attempt. But in the end, the conflict my father saw *is* coming. Let no one delude herself over that point, because *I* most assuredly will not."

Those wounded eyes were flint now, overlaid with an edge of steel, and her nostrils flared.

"The day will come when we find ourselves at war with the People's Republic of Haven," she told them softly, almost terribly, "and when it does, the Navy *my* father built, the Star Kingdom *he* prepared, will meet the Peoples Navy anywhere in space it can be found, and ... we ... will ... *destroy* ... it."

Her forefinger tapped the table, in time with her last five words, and no one around that table breathed as the Queen sat back slowly in her chair.

"Over the next few days," she continued after a moment, "Aunt Caitrin and I will be meeting individually with each of you. I want to review all of our preparations, our policies, but understand me. The House of Winton does not forget its duties, or its responsibilities ... or its enemies. And in the fullness of time, I intend to demonstrate that to any who wish this Star Kingdom ill in terms the galaxy will never forget."

She sat for a moment longer, regarding the men and women who knew now that they would never think of her as a teenager again. And then, once more, she inhaled deeply.

"And now, My Lords and Ladies, your King requires your services one final time."

✦   ✦   ✦

"Beth."

Jonas Adcock turned quickly from the window towards the tall, slender young woman with the treecat on her shoulder. He still wore the dress uniform he'd worn to King Michael's Cathedral for Roger's funeral, but Elizabeth had shed her formal attire. She wore a simple white blouse and dark, tailored trousers.

And one more thing, Jonas thought. She wore the invisible weight of her crown, and those square young shoulders were unbowed by the burden.

He wrapped his arms around her, holding her, and she let her cheek rest against his shoulder for a moment. Then she straightened.

"Thank you for coming," she said. "Mom's waiting for you,

and Michael. But I wanted to see you for a minute, first. There's something I need to tell you. Something I don't want to discuss in front of them, especially Mikey."

Jonas stiffened at the somber note in her voice. He'd heard about the Cabinet meeting, and there was something...perilous about his niece's face. Something that actually frightened him, more than a little.

"Tell me what?" he asked.

"It wasn't an accident," she said, and that note in her voice had turned into edged steel. He frowned at her for a moment, trying to understand, and she showed her teeth. "It wasn't a grav skiing accident, Uncle Jonas—Dad was murdered."

"Beth!" He shook his head, trying to process what she'd just said. The words didn't make sense. If Roger's death hadn't been an accident, then surely—!

"I know," she said in that same, steely voice, as if she'd read his mind. "You're afraid I'm imagining things. After all, if there were any evidence, any proof, we'd already have acted, wouldn't we? We'd have someone under arrest. Unfortunately, there *is* evidence. In fact, there's *proof*. And the man who sabotaged Dad's grav ski, Padraic Dover—a major in Palace Security, Uncle Jonas; one of our *own*—tried to kill Justin, as well." Her lips twisted, and he saw a soul-deep revulsion flash through her eyes. "Apparently he thought he could convince me to marry *him*, instead, if Justin was gone, so he took it upon himself to murder him, too. Unfortunately for him, that was enough to bring Monroe out of his withdrawal to save Justin's life."

She looked at her uncle squarely, and her eyes glittered with a cold, hard light he'd never seen in them before.

"He didn't stop there, either," she said harshly. "Justin and Inspector Chu had been putting things together already, and Dover actually *confessed* when Justin confronted him. Which was the last and worst mistake he ever made in his miserable life, because when Monroe realized what he'd done, he ripped his fucking throat out."

Her voice was harsh, dark with hate and satisfaction. Her expression actually frightened him, and Ariel's ears were flat to his skull on her shoulder. The treecat's entire body bristled with vengeful hatred, and the soft, high snarl of his rage hung in the air like an echo of Elizabeth's own hatred.

For a moment, Jonas found it a difficult to breathe, but then her eyes softened and she reached up to touch Ariel's head gently.

"We were going to lose Monroe, too, Uncle Jonas. He was grieving himself to death, and none of us could convince him to eat or drink. But now... now he's going to make it. I think he's bonded with Justin, in fact. I could wish we'd taken Dover alive for interrogation and trial, but there's no question about his guilt, and I'll gladly give up his formal execution if that gives us back Monroe. Besides, even without his testimony, we know who else he was working with."

Jonas stared at her, and that soft, fierce snarl echoed from Ariel once more.

"'Working with'?" he repeated after a moment. "You mean he wasn't acting alone? It was some... some kind of plot against the Crown?"

"Oh, I think you could call it that," Elizabeth agreed icily. "Dover was too stupid—or too full of himself, at any rate—to come up with something like this all by himself, Uncle Jonas! Oh, no. Someone else recruited him and gave him the tech support he needed to make it work, and that 'someone else' was Marvin Seltman and Baroness Stallman, along with the Earl of Howell and Jean Marrou."

"I beg your pardon?"

Jonas shook himself, trying to understand. Those four names read like a Who's Who of the inner power circles of the Liberal and Progressive Parties! And *Howell*? The man was a *Crown Loyalist*! He'd been one of the leading candidates to serve as Elizabeth's regent before she chose her aunt!

"There's no question," Elizabeth said flatly. "Marrou's turned Crown's Evidence—she was... unaware of all of the ramifications of the plot—and when she realized how she'd been used, she brought us recordings of Stallman and Seltman *admitting* their guilt, and their motivations, which would be admissible in any court. No, Uncle Jonas. We have absolute, conclusive evidence of their guilt.

"And I can't do a thing about it."

"*What?*" Jonas stared at her. "But... but—" He sucked in a deep breath, feeling the sudden burn of tears in his eyes. "Damn it, Bethie—they killed *Roger*! They killed your father—my friend and my *King*! What do you mean you can't do anything about it?" He shook his head savagely, vaguely stunned by the fury he felt—fury directed at the grieving young woman in front of him because there was no one else *to* direct it at—and showed his teeth. "Maybe *you* can't, but *I* sure as hell can! I'll kill the bastards with my own two hands!"

"No, you won't," she told him in that same, flat voice of hammered iron. "And you won't for the same reasons Aunt Caitrin and Jacob convinced me *I* couldn't challenge them to duels and shoot them. There are...factors involved that you don't know about yet. Reasons we can't take any official cognizance of Marrou's evidence, whatever we want."

"'*Official* cognizance'?" He pounced on the qualifier like a wounded hexapuma, and she nodded.

"They won't get off scot-free, I promise," she told him. "They know I know *exactly* what happened, and all of them are going 'into retirement' starting tomorrow. They can give whatever reasons they damn well want, but if they ever so much as give another speech, far less ever try to enter politics again, it'll be the last mistake they ever make. I may not be able to move officially against them at this moment, but that won't be true forever, and they know it. If they ever give me the slightest excuse I'll have them *crushed*, and they know *that*, too. But the reason I can't take any open action against any of them now, Uncle Jonas, is because the whole thing was set up by the Peeps. Marrou and Howell didn't know that, but Seltman and Stallman most certainly did know they were being paid off by Peep agents. Finding that out was what pushed Marrou into turning the others in, and we've got times, dates, and amounts on their payments. Chu and the Ministry of Justice got complete copies of their bank records. I've ordered them sealed under the Defense of the Realm Act, but those bastards know I'll *un*seal them and use them to hang the lot of them if they push me.

"But we can't do it yet. We just can't go public, not when I know *exactly* how Parliament and public opinion would react. We don't have all the details even now, but it's obvious what the Peeps wanted, and they got it. Admiral Big Sky told me this morning that the People's Navy will be moving against Trevor's Star sometime within the next two weeks, and we're not in a position to do anything about it. Worse, if I make public accusations against the PRH, if the Star Kingdom's people find out who murdered their King, they won't leave the government any choice. We'd find ourselves at war with the Peoples Republic tomorrow... and we'd have to fight without the advantages of a forward position in Trevor's Star.

"I can't do that." Her eyes gleamed with tears over a core of frozen steel. "Much as I want to, much as everything inside me screams to accuse them, to rip out their black hearts for murdering my father, I *can't*. I can't commit my entire Star Kingdom to a war we'll probably lose, no matter how much I want to. So they're going to get away with it. They've *already* gotten away with it, and I can't stop them."

"Oh, Bethie," he whispered, reaching out to fold her in his arms once more, and he felt the grief and pain—and the bitter, driving will—in that tall, slim body.

"I can't stop them," she repeated in his ear. "Not now. Not *yet*. But we *will* stop them, Uncle Jonas."

She straightened once more, looking into his eyes.

"Dad told me about his plans for the Weapons Development Board, and nothing's changed as far as I'm concerned, except for this one thing. I can't openly accuse the Peeps of having murdered Dad, but when they take Trevor's Star, they're going to give me the card Dad didn't have. There won't be any more arguing, any more debate. Aunt Caitrin and I will use the threat of the fall of the Trevor's Star Terminus—the conquest of San Martin, one of our oldest trading partners, a single warp bridge from the Junction—to ram through the biggest increase in military spending in the history of the Star Kingdom. We're going to *double* our building rate, Uncle Jonas, and in the midst of all that budget, we're going to find the funding for the WDB and to push Gram even harder than we ever have before. We're going to do that—*you're* going to do that for me—and when the time comes, the two of us—you and I, Uncle Jonas—we're going to *destroy* the People's Republic of Haven. As God is my witness, I will take that murderous excuse for a star nation apart brick by brick. I will find whoever ordered my father's murder, and I will send that blackhearted bastard to hell with my own two hands."

Her brown eyes looked deep, deep into his, and Jonas Adcock shivered at what he saw in their depths.

"Trust me," she said very, very softly. "They think they've gotten away with it, but they're wrong, Uncle Jonas. They can't even *guess* how wrong they are about that."

✦ ✦ ✦ ✦ ✦

November 1914 PD

"STAND BY FOR TRANSLATION . . . *now.*"

Captain (Junior Grade) Jonathan Yerensky announced the return to normal-space, and Hamish Alexander, Earl of White Haven, grimaced as the familiar discomfort and disorientation lashed through him. That was one nice thing about being a senior admiral, he thought. By the time you acquired as much rank as he had, you no longer had to worry about impressing uppity juniors with your stoicism. If crossing the alpha wall made you feel like throwing up, you could go ahead and admit it . . . and nobody dared laugh.

He grinned at the reflection, but his eyes were already on his repeater plot on *Benjamin the Great*'s flag deck, waiting for CIC's updates while he listened to a murmured litany of background reports without really hearing them. His staff had been with him for over three T-years; after the next best thing to ten brutal T-years of war, they knew exactly what he needed to know immediately and what he expected them to handle on their own, and *he* knew he could rely on them to do just that.

Which freed White Haven to study his bland, uninformative plot and worry.

Well, uninformative from the *enemy's* side, he amended, for quite a few Allied icons burned on the display. First, there were the seventy-three superdreadnoughts and eleven dreadnoughts of his wall of battle, thirty of them the radically new, hollow-cored *Harrington/Medusa* class with their massive loads of multidrive missiles. Then there were the traditional screening elements, already spreading out to assume missile defense positions. And

166

last, there were the seventeen CLACs of Alice Truman's task group and *their* escorts—battlecruisers and heavy cruisers, with four attached dreadnoughts to give them a little extra weight—astern of the main formation. A blizzard of diamond chips erupted from the CLACs as he watched, and he smiled grimly as the deadly swarm of light attack craft began to shake down into formation even as they accelerated ahead of the main body. CIC had a tight lock on them when they launched, but their EW was already on-line, and within minutes even *Benjamin the Great*'s sensors began to lose them.

A second blizzard, almost as dense, sped outward at accelerations even a LAC could never hope to match, and White Haven tipped back his command chair as the FTL-capable recon drones darted in-system.

I actually feel almost as calm as I'm trying to look, he reflected with some surprise. *Of course, that's because I can be reasonably confident the Peeps don't have a clue as to what's coming at them. Whether or not that will be true—and whether or not it will matter if it isn't—the next time around are two different questions, of course.*

He watched the drones speeding steadily inward, and he smiled.

◆　◆　◆

Citizen Admiral Alec Dimitri and Citizen Commissioner Sandra Connors were in DuQuesne Base's war room for a routine briefing when an alarm buzzed. The tall, stocky citizen admiral turned quickly, trained eyes seeking the status board, and Citizen Commissioner Connors turned almost as quickly. Neither she nor Dimitri had ever expected in their worst nightmares that they would suddenly find themselves responsible for the Barnett System, the biggest and most powerful naval base the People's Republic had ever built, but they'd served as understudies to Thomas Theisman and Denis LePic for the better part of four T-years. Both were serious about their duty, and even if they hadn't been, Theisman and LePic would have made damned sure the two of them were intimately familiar with the system and its defenses. As a result, Connors' eyes were only fractionally slower than Dimitri's in finding the fresh datum, and her frown mirrored his own.

"Twenty-two light-minutes from the primary?" she murmured, and Dimitri turned his head to give her a tight smile.

"It does seem a bit...overly cautious of them. Especially on that broad a bearing from Enki," he agreed, and wondered what the hell the Manties thought they were up to. Barnett was only a G9 star, with a hyper limit of just a hair over eighteen light-minutes, so why were they turning up a full four light-minutes farther out than they had to? And on a bearing from the primary which added yet four more unnecessary light-minutes to their distance from their only possible objective?

The citizen admiral clamped his hands behind him and took a slow, deliberate turn around the command balcony above the enormous war room. His outermost sensor shell was seventeen light-minutes from the primary, far enough from the gravitational center of Barnett to give the enormous passive arrays a reach of almost two and a half light-weeks, over which they could expect to pick up the hyper transit of anything much bigger than a courier boat. That range put them nine light-minutes outside the planet Enki, and the actual range to the platform closest to the Manties was about thirteen light-minutes. Which meant it would be another—he checked the time—ten minutes and twenty-six seconds before he got a light-speed report from the sensors with the best look at whatever was coming at him. On the other hand, the inner-system arrays had more than enough reach to at least detect such a massive hyper translation. They'd picked up the faster-than-light ripple along the alpha wall as the Manties made transit, and they were picking up a confused clutch of impeller drive signatures now. But they were much too far away to see anything else, which meant Tracking's reports were going to be maddeningly vague until the Manties were a lot deeper in-system. Unfortunately, Tracking had already picked up enough for Dimitri to feel certain the enemy would be coming *in* a lot deeper. The estimate blinking on the main board said there were over seventy of the wall headed for Enki, and that was no raiding force.

"It's White Haven," he rasped. "It has to be their Eighth Fleet. Maybe with their Third Fleet along to side it, judging from the preliminary numbers. Which means we're probably screwed, Citizen Commissioner."

Connors' expression turned disapproving, but only briefly. And the disapproval wasn't really directed at Dimitri. She didn't like defeatism, but that didn't change what was going to happen, and she knew the citizen admiral was correct. Their own strength had been reduced to only twenty-two of the wall. Even with the new mines and missile pod deployment Theisman had devised, plus the forts and the LACs, that was highly unlikely to stop seventy or eighty Manty superdreadnoughts and dreadnoughts. And, she reminded herself, initial estimates at this sort of range were almost always low. On the other hand...

"We can still give them a fight, Citizen Admiral," she said, and he nodded.

"Oh, we can certainly do that, Ma'am, and I intend to make *them* aware of that fact, too. I just wish I knew why they made translation so far out...and why they're coming in so slowly. I don't object to an enemy who gives me time to assemble all my forces to meet him, but I do have to wonder why he's being so obliging."

"I had the same thought," Connors murmured, and the two of them turned as one to look out at the huge holo tank's light sculpture replica of the Barnett System.

The angry red pockmarks of a hostile fleet hung in that display, twenty-six-point-three light-minutes from Enki and headed for it at an unhurried six thousand KPS with an acceleration of only three hundred gravities. Preliminary intercept solutions were already coming up on a sidebar display, providing Dimitri with his entire menu of choices. Not that he intended to use any of the ones that involved sending his mobile units out to meet that incoming hammer. His outnumbered units would undoubtedly score a few kills if he was stupid enough to do that, but none would survive, and his fixed fortifications and LACs would be easy meat for an unshaken, intact wall of battle. Nor did he intend to waste his long-ranged mines. Those would wait until he could coordinate their attacks with those of his mobile units' missiles. Which narrowed the only numbers he really needed to think about to the ones which showed what the Manties could do to *him*.

Assuming they maintained their current acceleration all the way in and went for a passing engagement with Enki's close-in defenses, they could be on top of him in just under five hours. But they'd go ripping right on past him at over fifty-three thousand KPS, and he doubted they'd go for that option. It would get them to him a bit sooner, but that obviously wasn't a factor in their thinking, or they'd have made their translation farther in and be coming in under a higher acceleration. Besides, there was no point in their opting for a passing engagement. The fighting would be all over, one way or the other, by the time they reached

Enki's orbital position, and if they overshot, they'd simply have to decelerate to come back and occupy the ruins.

No, the way they were coming in, they meant to go for a leisurely but traditional zero/zero intercept. Which meant, assuming they stuck with their ridiculously low accel, that they would come to rest relative to Enki (and ready to land their Marines) in six and a half hours...by which time, all of his units would be so much drifting wreckage.

But that wreckage was going to have a lot of Manty company, he thought grimly. That was all he could really hope for, and if he could take a big enough chunk out of those slow-moving, overconfident bastards, they might just find themselves fatally weakened when Operation Bagration went in, took Grendelsbane away from them, and started rolling them up from the southeast.

He glanced at another display and grunted in approval. This one showed his mobile units, racing from their scattered patrol positions to form up with the forts. Another one showed the readiness states on his LACs, with squadron after squadron blinking from the amber of stand-by to the green of readiness, and he nodded sharply. He'd have plenty of time to assemble and prepare his forces, and the bastards didn't know about the new mines and pod arrangements he had to demonstrate for them.

His upper lip curled, showing just a flash of white teeth, and he turned back to the main board, waiting patiently for solid enemy unit IDs to appear.

✦　✦　✦

"Here comes the first info, My Lord."

Admiral White Haven looked up from a quiet conversation with his chief of staff, Captain Lady Alyson Granston-Henley, as the new data blinked onto his plot.

"I see it, Trev."

White Haven and Granston-Henley moved over beside Commander Trevor Haggerston, Eighth Fleet's dark-haired, heavy-set ops officer, and watched with him as the FTL drones began reporting in.

There were only a spattering of additional icons at first, but the initial spray grew quickly into a wider, deeper, brighter blur, and White Haven pursed his lips as CIC began evaluating the data. Unless the Peeps were trying to be sneakier than usual, they had considerably fewer ships of the wall than he'd anticipated. That probably indicated Caparelli's diversionary efforts down around Grendelsbane had worked, White Haven thought, with a mental nod of respect for the First Space Lord's efforts.

Of course, there was a downside to Caparelli's success. Under normal circumstances, fewer ships meant fewer opponents, which would have been a good thing. In *this* instance, however, fewer ships simply meant fewer *targets*.

"What do we make it so far, Trev?" he asked after a moment.

"CIC's calling it twenty-two of the wall, ten battleships—there could be a couple more of those hiding behind the wedge clutter—twenty to thirty battlecruisers, forty-six cruisers, and thirty or forty destroyers. Looks like they've got forty to forty-five of their forts on-line, as well, and there's one hell of a lot of LACs swanning around in that mess. CIC figures it for a minimum of seven hundred."

"Um." White Haven rubbed his chin. Seven hundred *was* a lot of LACs . . . for a navy that didn't have the RMN's *Shrikes* or *Ferrets*. Older style LACs simply weren't effective enough to build in huge numbers, and Esther McQueen must have scraped the bottom of the barrel to put that many in one system. Unless, of course, the PN had started building the things again themselves. Unlike Sonja Hemphill's brainchildren—his lips quirked as he remembered their monumental clashes . . . and the way a certain Steadholder by the name of Harrington had ripped his head off for being such a stiff-necked idiot about the new weapons mix—they'd be largely useless against hyper-capable warships, but enough of them could still inflict painful losses on the newer LAC types. The exchange rate would be ruinously in favor of the *Shrikes* and the *Ferrets*, but McQueen had already proved herself capable of playing the attrition game when that was her only option.

Not that seven hundred old-style LACs or even twice that many were going to be much of a problem for Alice Truman's boys and girls.

Assuming they had to fight them at all.

"Range to their forces?"

"We've been inbound for thirty-seven minutes, Sir. Range to zero/zero is roughly four hundred sixty-six million klicks—call it twenty-six light-minutes—and we're up to a smidge over seventy-two hundred KPS. Long way to go yet, even for Ghost Rider, Sir."

"Agreed. Agreed." White Haven rubbed his chin some more. The final—or *currently* "final"; the WDB was promising even better

ones soon—version of the long-range missiles could reach 96,000
gravities of acceleration. That gave them a powered attack range
from rest of almost fifty-one light-seconds at maximum acceleration. By stepping the drives down to 48,000 *g*, endurance could be
tripled, however, and that upped the maximum powered envelope
to well over three and a half light-*minutes* and a terminal velocity of .83 *c*. That was crowding the very limits of the fire control
technology available even to the Royal Manticoran Navy, however.

But given that the maximum possible engagement range from
rest for the *enemy,* even at low accel, was going to be on the
order of less than thirty light-*seconds*, things were about to get
very ugly for the Peeps.

Thank you, Vice Admiral Adcock, he thought quietly, thinking
about those numbers. *And you, too, I suppose, Sonja. Thank you
very, very much.*

◆   ◆   ◆

Citizen Admiral Dimitri accepted another cup of coffee from a
signals yeoman. It was good coffee, brewed just the way he liked
it, and it tasted like corrosion-strength industrial cleaner. Not
surprisingly, he supposed. Five hours and thirty-eight minutes had
passed since the Manties' translation, and the bastards had come
the next best thing to four hundred and sixty million kilometers
in that time. They were down to just a hair over fifteen million
klicks from Enki, decelerating now, and their velocity was back
down to a little over ninety-three hundred KPS.

He still didn't understand their approach, and his brain continued to pick at its apparent illogic like a tongue probing a
sore tooth. No doubt they were coming in heavy with missile
pods—*he* certainly would have been in their place!—but Manty
SDs could pull a lot more than three hundred gees, even with
full pod loads on tow. So why had they wasted so much time?
And why hadn't they gone for a least-time course at whatever
accel they were willing to use? The logical thing would have been
to translate into n-space on a heading that pinned Enki between
them and Barnett. As it was, they'd not only come in too far
out and too slowly, but they were approaching Enki's position
to intercept at a shallow angle. At the moment, their icons and
those of the mobile units positioned to intercept them weren't
even on anything approaching a direct line with the blue dot
that marked Enki's position.

It all looked and felt dreadfully unorthodox, which was enough to make Dimitri instantly suspicious, especially knowing that if that was Eighth Fleet out there, he was up against White Haven, who'd systematically kicked the crap out of every Republican CO he'd ever faced. Which suggested there had to be *some* reason for the Manties' apparently inept and clumsy approach, even if Dimitri couldn't come up with a single one that made sense. It was almost as if White Haven was intentionally giving the defenders plenty of time to concentrate their full forces to meet him, but that was ridiculous. Granted, Manty hardware was superior, but there were limits in all things. Not even *Manties* could be ballsy enough to deliberately throw away any chance of catching him before he concentrated. Any flag officer worth his braid schemed furiously in search of some way to catch the defenders with their forces spread out so he could engage and crush them in detail rather than facing all of them at once!

But that seemed to be exactly what White Haven wasn't doing, Dimitri thought irritably, then shrugged. In another twelve minutes it would no longer matter what the Manty CO thought he *was* doing, because the range would be down to six million klicks. Given the geometry of the Manties' approach vector, they'd be in his powered missile envelope—technically speaking—for at least two minutes before that, but against Manty electronic warfare, even six million klicks against a closing enemy might be a little optimistic. Which meant he and his people were going to have to take their lumps from the Manties before any of their own birds got home. But he'd be sending the mine-armed drones out in another four minutes, and at least he ought to be able to flush all of his pods before any of the incoming arrived, and—

A shrill, strident alarm sliced through the war room's tense calm like a buzz saw.

✦   ✦   ✦

"Coming down on fifteen million kilometers, Sir," Trevor Haggerston said quietly, and White Haven nodded.

"Anything more on those unidentified bogies?"

"We still can't be positive, but it looks like most of them are missile pods, Sir. We're a bit more puzzled by some of the others, though. They're smaller than pods, but they seem to be bigger than individual missiles ought to be. About the size of a recon drone, actually."

"I see." The earl frowned, then shrugged. Missiles or drones, a saturation pattern of heavy warheads should take them out with proximity kills handily enough...and before they could do anything nasty.

The Peeps obviously didn't know it, but they'd been in his powered missile range for well over an hour. Unfortunately, even with his RDs hovering just beyond the range of the Peeps' weapons, targeting solutions would have been very poor at sixty-five million kilometers...not to mention that flight time would have been the next best thing to nine minutes. That was plenty of time for an alert captain to roll ship and take the brunt of the incoming fire on his wedge, and even with Project Ghost Rider's EW goodies along for company, it might have given the defenders time to achieve effective point defense solutions.

Besides, there was no need to do any such thing. He still had over twelve minutes before he entered the *Peeps'* effective envelope, and each of his hollow-cored *Harrington/Medusas* could get off sixty six-pod salvos in that time. That was over a hundred and eleven thousand multidrive missiles from the SD(P)s alone.

But they *weren't* alone, and he checked his plot one last time.

Between the input from his drones and the long, unhurried time his fire control officers had been given to refine their data, his ships had tight locks on most of the Peep capital ships. Of course, "tight lock" at this sort of range didn't mean what it would have at lower ranges, and accuracy was going to suffer accordingly. On the other hand, the Peeps hadn't yet deployed a single decoy, and their jammers were only beginning to come on line.

"Very well, Commander Haggerston," he said formally. "You may fire."

✦ ✦ ✦

Citizen Admiral Dimitri's mug hit the floor, but he never noticed. Neither the sound of breaking china nor the sudden pool of steaming coffee registered even peripherally, for he could *not* be seeing what he saw.

But the sensors and the computers didn't care what their human masters thought was possible. They insisted on presenting the preposterous data anyway, and Dimitri heard other voices, several shrill with rising panic, as the war room's normal discipline disintegrated as completely as his broken cup. It was inexcusable. They were trained military men and women, manning the nerve center of the system's entire defense structure. Above all else, it was their duty to remain calm and collected, exerting the control over their combat units upon which any hope of victory depended.

But Dimitri couldn't blame them, and even if he could have, it wouldn't have mattered. No conceivable calm, collected response could have affected the outcome of this battle in the least.

No one in the history of interstellar warfare had ever seen anything like the massive salvo coming in on his ships. Those missiles were turning out at least ninety-six *thousand* gravities, launched from pods and shipboard tubes which were themselves moving at over nine thousand kilometers per second, and that didn't even consider the initial velocity imparted to them by their launchers' grav drivers. A corner of Dimitri's brain wanted to believe the Manties had gone suddenly insane and thrown away their entire opening salvo at a range from which hits would be impossible. That the incredible acceleration those missiles were cranking meant they couldn't possibly have more than a minute of drive endurance. That they would be dead, unable to maneuver against his evading units, when they reached the ends of their runs.

But one thing the Earl of White Haven was not was insane. If he'd launched from that range, his birds had the range to attack effectively . . . and none of Dimitri's did.

He watched numbly as the missiles roared down on his wall. The entire front of the salvo was a solid wall of jamming and decoys, and he clamped his jaw as he pictured the panic and terror crashing through the men and women on those ships. *His* men and women. He'd put them out there in the sober expectation that their ships would be destroyed, that many—even most—of them would be killed. But he'd at least believed they'd be able to strike back before they died. Now their point defense couldn't even *see* the missiles coming to kill them.

It seemed to take forever, and he heard someone groan behind him as the Manty wall belched a *second* salvo, just as heavy as the first. Which was also impossible. That *had* to be the firepower of a full pod load out for every ship in White Haven's wall. He *couldn't* have still more of them on tow! But apparently no one had told the Manties what they could and couldn't do, and yet a third launch followed.

The first massive wave of missiles crashed into his wall like the hammer of Thor itself, and his numb brain noted yet another difference from the norm. The tactical realities of towed pods meant each fleet had no real choice but to commit the full weight of its pods in the first salvo, because any that didn't fire in the first exchange were virtually certain to suffer proximity kills from the *enemy's* fire. They were normally concentrated on the enemy vessels for whom the firing fleet had the best firing solutions, as well, because firing at extreme range rather than waiting until the enemy had irradiated your weapons into uselessness meant even the best solutions were none too good.

All of that tended to result in massive overkill on a relatively low number of targets, but that wasn't happening this time. No, *this* time the Manties had allocated their fire with lethal precision. There were well over three thousand missiles in the first wave. Many were jammers or decoys, but many were not, and Hamish Alexander's fire plan had allocated a hundred and fifty laser heads to each Peep ship of the wall. His targets' hopelessly jammed and confused defenses stopped no more than ten percent of the incoming fire, and Havenite capital ships shuddered and heaved, belching atmosphere and debris and water vapor as massive, bomb-pumped lasers slammed into them. Hulls spat glowing splinters as massive armor yielded, and fresh, dreadful bursts of light pocked Citizen Admiral Dimitri's wall as fusion bottles began to fail.

But even as the SDs and DNs reeled and died under the pounding, a second, equally massive wave of missiles was on its way. This one ignored the surviving, mangled ships of the wall. Its missiles went for Dimitri's lighter, more fragile battleships and battlecruisers, even heavy and light cruisers. Fewer of them went after each target, but even a battleship could take no more than a handful of hits from such heavy laser heads...and none of them could begin to match the point defense capability of a ship of the wall.

The third wave bypassed the mobile units completely to swoop towards Enki's orbital defenses. They ignored the fortresses, but their conventional nuclear warheads detonated in a blinding, meticulously precise wall of plasma and fury that killed every unprotected satellite, missile pod, and drone in Enki orbit.

And then, as if to cap the insanity, a tidal wave of light attack craft—well over fifteen hundred of them—erupted from stealth, already in energy range of the broken wreckage which had once been a fleet. They swept in, firing savagely, and a single pass reduced every unit of Dimitri's wall to drifting hulks...or worse. The LACs were at least close enough that his fortresses could fire on them, but their EW was almost as good as the capital ships', and they deployed shoals of jammers and decoys of their own. Even the missiles which got through to them seemed to detonate completely uselessly. It was as if the impossible little vessels' wedges had no throat or kilt to attack!

The LACs had obviously planned their approach maneuver very carefully. Their velocity relative to their victims had been very low, no more than fifteen hundred KPS, and their vector had been designed to cross the base track of Dimitri's wall at an angle that carried them away from his forts and his own LACs. A few squadrons of the latter were in position to at least try to intercept, but those who did vanished in vicious fireballs as hurricanes of lighter but still lethal missiles ripped into their faces. Then the Manty LACs disappeared back into the invisibility of their stealth systems. And just to make certain they got away clean, that impossible Manty wall of battle blanketed the battle area with a solid cone of decoys and jammers which made it impossible for any of the surviving defenders to lock onto the fleet, elusive little targets.

Alec Dimitri stared in horror at the display from which every single starship of his fleet had been wiped without ever managing to fire a single shot. Not *one*. And as he stared at the spreading patterns of life pods, someone touched him on the shoulder.

He flinched, then turned quickly, and his com officer stepped back from whatever she saw in his eyes. But he stopped, made himself inhale deeply, and forced the lumpy muscles along his jaw to relax.

There was no more shouting, no more cries of disbelief, in the war room. There was only deep and utter silence, and his voice sounded unnaturally loud in his own ears when he made himself speak.

"What is it, Jendra?"

"I—" The citizen commander swallowed hard. "It's a message from the Manties, Citizen Admiral," she said then. "It was addressed to Citizen Admiral Theisman. I guess they don't know he's not here." She was rambling, and her jaw tightened as she forced herself back under control. "It's from their commander, Citizen Admiral."

"White Haven?" The question came out almost incuriously, but that wasn't the way he felt, and his eyes narrowed at her nod. "What sort of message?"

"It came in in the clear, Citizen Admiral," she said, and held out a message board. He took it and punched the play button, and a man in the black-and-gold of a Manticoran admiral looked out of the holographic display at him. He was dark haired and broad shouldered . . . and his hard eyes were the coldest blue Alec Dimitri had ever seen.

"Admiral Theisman," the Manty said flatly, "I call upon you to surrender this system and your surviving units immediately. We have just demonstrated that we can and will destroy any and all armed units, ships or forts, in this system without exposing our own vessels to return fire. I take no pleasure in slaughtering men and women who cannot fight back. That will not prevent me from doing precisely that, however, if you refuse to surrender, for I have no intention of exposing my own people to needless casualties. You have five minutes to accept my terms and surrender your command. If you have not done so by the end of that time, my units will resume fire . . . and we both know what the result will be. I await your response. White Haven, out."

December 1914 PD

THE BEDSIDE COM chimed softly, and the mahogany-skinned woman's eyes opened. The man beside her stirred, but her hand darted out and silenced the chimes before he fully waked. She looked at him for a moment, smiling gently in the light of the com's still flashing attention signal, then eased out of bed and padded across the bedroom floor on bare feet. He'd found himself awakened in the middle of the night just because she'd been far too often, and there was no need to do that to him yet again.

Something thumped behind her, and she looked over her shoulder with another smile as one of the cream-and-gray treecats hopped down from his perch and followed her. She could just see the green glow of the other 'cat's eyes, picked out by the blinking attention light as he curled on his perch on her husband's side of the bed, but he obviously had no intention of joining his companion, and she shook her head.

"Go back to sleep, Monroe," she told him very, very quietly, and closed the bedroom door behind her. She stooped to pick Ariel up in her arms and carried him across the study to her desk. The com light on her terminal was flashing there, as well, and she let Ariel ooze down onto her blotter and seated herself in her work chair. She took one more moment to rub her eyes, then keyed the com panel to accept the call audio-only from her end.

The attention light stopped blinking and the Admiralty House wallpaper appeared on her display. It lasted only a moment, then disappeared, and she found herself looking at Sir Thomas Caparelli, First Space Lord of the Royal Manticoran Navy. She knew he could see only *her* wallpaper, the coat of arms of the House of Winton, not the person to whom he was actually speaking, and she cleared her throat.

"Good evening, Sir Thomas," she said. "Or should I say 'good morning'?" she added a bit wryly, and he bobbed his head in an abbreviated bow of apology.

"I'm afraid it's 'morning,' Your Majesty—or will be in about another ten minutes," Caparelli said. "I apologize for waking you at this hour, but the dispatch from Admiral White Haven arrived about fifteen minutes ago."

Elizabeth Winton stiffened, nostrils flaring, and Ariel sat up abruptly, ears flat. The Queen of Manticore drew a deep, deep breath and ordered her voice to remain calm.

"In that case, Sir Thomas, no apologies are necessary. I believe I specifically directed that I was to be informed immediately when we heard back from Admiral White Haven."

"Yes, you did, Your Majesty." Caparelli inclined his head a second time, then looked straight into his com pickup. "Your Majesty," he said formally, "I have the honor to inform you that Admiral White Haven, commanding Eighth Fleet, reports the surrender of the star system of Barnett, with all military personnel and facilities therein, to his forces."

Elizabeth's eyes closed. She kept them that way for a moment, then drew another breath.

"And Admiral White Haven's losses, Sir Thomas?" she asked levelly.

"None, Your Majesty," Caparelli said simply.

"None?" Elizabeth repeated, her voice sharpening slightly around the edges, and Caparelli nodded.

"Your Majesty, generalizing from a single operation is usually as dangerous as it is foolish. In this instance, however, I think the conclusion is inescapable. We will, of course, provide you with a detailed analysis of Admiral White Haven's report as soon as there's been time to prepare one, but the principal aspects of that analysis are already clear. And so is the central conclusion—the People's Republic of Haven has just lost the war."

Elizabeth raised one hand to her lips, a hand which quivered with a tremor she would never have let another human being see.

"The technology which has come out of the Weapons Development Board, Project Gram, and—especially—Project Mjølner and Project Ghost Rider, has fundamentally transformed warfare," Caparelli continued in that same level, unflinching voice. "Thanks to your father's initiatives and your uncle's energy and inspiration, our fleet already outclassed the Peoples Navy in every aspect of war-fighting technology, even before Ghost Rider. Now, with the new multidrive missiles and the pod-layer capital ships actually in service, they can't even reply effectively to our fire. For all intents and purposes, their warships have just become *targets*, not threats, and I see no possible way for them to overcome their technological inferiority before we destroy their entire existing fleet."

It was the First Space Lord's turn to draw a deep breath, as if steeling himself for what he was about to say.

"Your Majesty, in my considered opinion as First Space Lord, the Manticoran Alliance will be in a position to dictate terms of surrender to the People's Republic of Haven within the next four to six T-months."

The single, uncompromising sentence hung between them for a long, silent moment, and a single tear glittered like diamond on Elizabeth Winton's cheek.

"Thank you for informing me, Sir Thomas."

Her voice sounded surprisingly level, but Sir Thomas Caparelli had come to know his monarch over the years he'd served her. He heard the emotion within it, and she saw a flicker of concern in his eyes, but she only continued in that same level, formal tone.

"Please pass my thanks—my deep and sincere gratitude—to Admiral White Haven and all of the other officers and enlisted personnel who have served the Star Kingdom so long and so well. Your devotion and theirs has been all any queen could ever have hoped for...and no less than my house has come to anticipate from you. I'll thank them all more publicly and more formally in the very near future, but for now I'll let you get back to the many decisions I know must be made in the wake of Eighth Fleet's victory. Thank you, Sir Thomas."

"Your Majesty," Caparelli said quietly, "no thanks are necessary. It's been my greatest honor and privilege to serve you." He looked into the pickup again, meeting her unseen eyes. "Not every officer is given the gift of knowing he serves a monarch worthy of every exertion or sacrifice which may be required of him or the people under his command. Anyone privileged to serve you or your father has been given that gift, and on behalf of every man and woman in Manticoran uniform, it's *my* privilege to thank *you*."

Elizabeth's lips quivered and she scooped Ariel up, holding him to her chest. It took a moment, but she made her voice serve her again at last.

"You're kinder and more generous than I deserve, Sir Thomas. But thank you. Clear."

She reached out and touched the disconnect key, then bent over the silken warmth in her arms, hugging the treecat while tears soaked his silken coat.

◆   ◆   ◆

"Wait here."

The fair-haired, blue-eyed colonel looked sharply at her monarch and started to open her mouth in protest. But Elizabeth only looked back and shook her head.

"Not this time, Ellen," she told the woman who'd headed her personal security detachment from the day she took the throne.

They stood alone in the silent, incense-scented, dimly lit nave of King Michael's Cathedral. The enormous cathedral never locked its doors, but at this still, quiet moment, five hours yet before the dawn, it was empty, deserted save for the presence light burning above the altar. The Palace Security detachment had been greeted by the night duty priest when Elizabeth arrived. Father O'Banion's astonishment at the Queen's unannounced, unscheduled, middle-of-the-night arrival had been obvious, but he'd recovered quickly. Now he stood at Elizabeth's elbow, waiting quietly, while she faced Colonel Shemais.

Elizabeth reached out and touched Shemais lightly on the shoulder.

"This is something I have to do myself," she told the colonel. "Just me. And Ariel, of course." She quirked a smile and reached up to touch the treecat's head. "I think you can trust him to look after me this once."

Shemais looked back at her stubbornly for perhaps ten seconds, but then the colonel's expression softened.

"All right, Your Majesty. This once," she said.

"Thank you."

Elizabeth squeezed the colonel's shoulder, then turned to O'Banion.

"And now, Father, if you please."

◆   ◆   ◆

Elizabeth descended the final three steps to the polished marble floor. Father O'Banion waited silently at the head of those steps, by the antique-looking grill whose door he had unlocked to allow her entrance. The bars of that grill looked like wrought iron, but they were actually battle steel, not that it mattered. Not now, at this moment.

She crossed the private family crypt silently, Ariel very still on her shoulder, and stopped before the carved marble plaque. It was very simple, that plaque, compared to the far more ornate one set into the cathedral floor above it:

Roger Michael Danton Maxwell Winton
August 19, 1809–October 7, 1883 PD
Beloved husband and father, who reigned too briefly
in this city and reigns forever in our hearts.
"I will build my house of steel."

Elizabeth stood before that plaque, looking at it, thinking about the seventy T-years between her father's first letter to the *Proceedings* and this moment. Thinking about her uncle, who hadn't lived to see this day yet had known it was coming. Thinking about all the sacrifices, all the pain, all the destruction and lost lives and shattered hearts. Thinking about how many had given so much to bring her here, to this place, on this still, quiet night.

Feeling the tears break loose.

They fell into the silence like lost, broken bits of crystal, those tears, kissing that marble floor. And then, finally, she reached out and touched the words. Let her fingertips run gently, tenderly across them, and leaned forward, resting her forehead against the cool, unyielding stone while Ariel crooned lovingly in her ear.

"We got them, Dad," she whispered into the stillness. "We got them."

STAR EMPIRE OF MANTICORE

Flag of the Star Empire of Manticore

ROYAL MANTICORAN NAVY

Crest of the RMN

MISCELLANEOUS INSIGNIA

Project Patch

Starship Crest (List of Honor)

Squadron Crest

RMN BUREAU CRESTS

AWARD RIBBONS

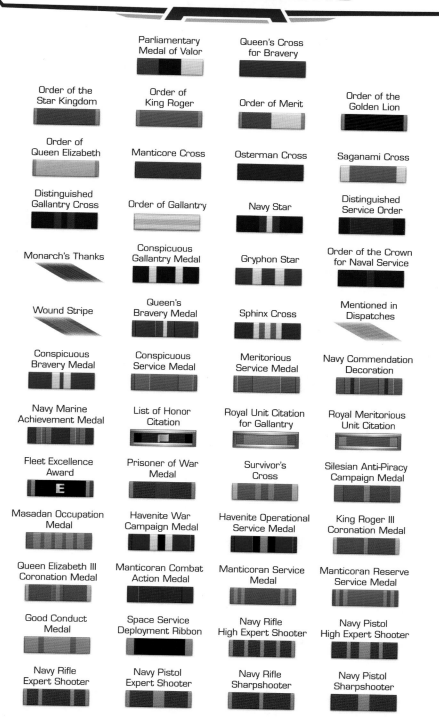

Parliamentary Medal of Valor

Queen's Cross for Bravery

Order of the Star Kingdom

Order of King Roger

Order of Merit

Order of the Golden Lion

Order of Queen Elizabeth

Manticore Cross

Osterman Cross

Saganami Cross

Distinguished Gallantry Cross

Order of Gallantry

Navy Star

Distinguished Service Order

Monarch's Thanks

Conspicuous Gallantry Medal

Gryphon Star

Order of the Crown for Naval Service

Wound Stripe

Queen's Bravery Medal

Sphinx Cross

Mentioned in Dispatches

Conspicuous Bravery Medal

Conspicuous Service Medal

Meritorious Service Medal

Navy Commendation Decoration

Navy Marine Achievement Medal

List of Honor Citation

Royal Unit Citation for Gallantry

Royal Meritorious Unit Citation

Fleet Excellence Award

Prisoner of War Medal

Survivor's Cross

Silesian Anti-Piracy Campaign Medal

Masadan Occupation Medal

Havenite War Campaign Medal

Havenite Operational Service Medal

King Roger III Coronation Medal

Queen Elizabeth III Coronation Medal

Manticoran Combat Action Medal

Manticoran Service Medal

Manticoran Reserve Service Medal

Good Conduct Medal

Space Service Deployment Ribbon

Navy Rifle High Expert Shooter

Navy Pistol High Expert Shooter

Navy Rifle Expert Shooter

Navy Pistol Expert Shooter

Navy Rifle Sharpshooter

Navy Pistol Sharpshooter

Shown at half size

OFFICER UNIFORM

Service Dress,
Fleet Admiral

Skinsuit,
Fleet Admiral

OFFICER RANKS

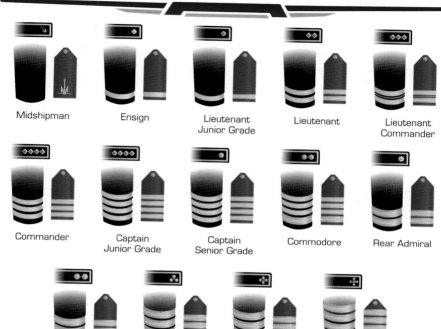

Midshipman   Ensign   Lieutenant Junior Grade   Lieutenant   Lieutenant Commander

Commander   Captain Junior Grade   Captain Senior Grade   Commodore   Rear Admiral

Vice Admiral   Admiral   Fleet Admiral   Admiral Of The Fleet

PATCHES & PINS

Unit Patch (Left Shoulder)

Navy Patch (Right Shoulder)

Space Warfare Pin (Enlisted, 4 deployments)

Space Warfare Pin (Officer)

ENLISTED RANKS

Spacer
3rd Class

Spacer
2nd Class

Spacer
1st Class

Petty Officer
3rd Class

Petty Officer
2nd Class

Petty Officer
1st Class

Chief
Petty Officer

Senior Chief
Petty Officer

Master Chief
Petty Officer

Senior Master
Chief Petty Officer

ENLISTED RATING PATCHES

Missile
Technician

Beam Weapons
Technician

Gunner's
Mate

Fire Control
Technician

Electronic Warfare
Technician

Tracking
Specialist

Data Systems
Technician

Sensor
Technician

Electronics
Technician

Environmental
Technician

Gravitics
Technician

Impeller
Technician

Hydroponics
Technician

Power
Technician

Damage Control
Technician

Helmsman

Communications
Technician

Plotting
Specialist

Corpsman

Sick Berth
Attendant

Operations
Specialist

Intelligence
Specialist

Steward

Yeoman

Storekeeper

Disbursing
Clerk

Ship's
Serviceman

Personnelman

Navy
Counselor

Coxswain

ENLISTED UNIFORM

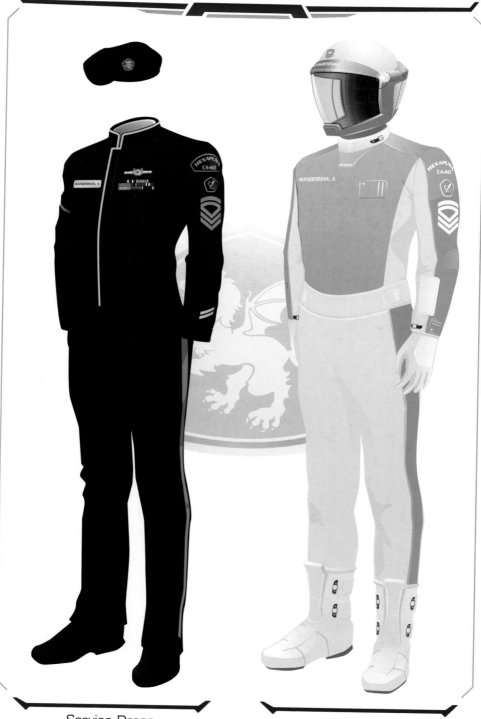

Service Dress,
Senior Chief Petty Officer

Skinsuit,
Senior Chief Petty Officer

ROYAL MANTICORAN NAVY STARSHIPS

Minotaur-class Light Attack Craft Carrier: HMS *Minotaur*, CLAC-01

Shrike-B Light Attack Craft

HMLAC "Cutthroat", LAC-1961

Nike-class Battlecruiser: HMS *Nike*, BC-562

Keyhole II Electronics Warfare Platform

Mk-30 "Condor II" Pinnace

Edward Saganami-C-class Heavy Cruiser: HMS *Hexapuma*, CA-412

All ships shown to approximate scale

GRAYSON SPACE NAVY STARSHIPS

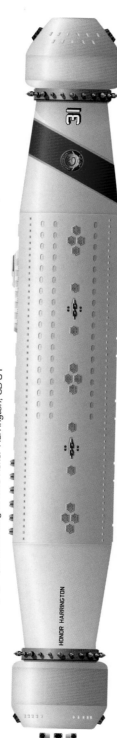

Honor Harrington-class Podlaying Superdreadnaught: GNS *Honor Harrington*, SD-31

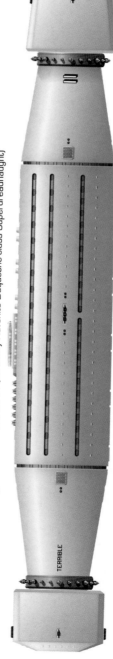

Manticore's Gift-class Superdreadnaught: GNS *Terrible*, SD-11 (Formerly Havenite *Duquesne*-class Superdreadnaught)

Mk-30 "Condor II" Pinnace (Grayson Livery)

Raoul Courvosier II-class Podlaying Battlecruiser: GNS *Raoul Courvosier II*, BC-44

All ships shown to approximate scale

PROTECTORATE OF GRAYSON

Flag of the Protectorate of Grayson

GRAYSON SPACE NAVY

Crest of the GSN

GRAYSON KATANA

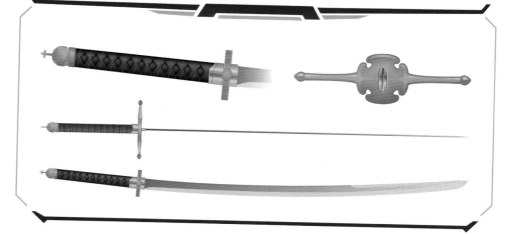

GSN OFFICE CRESTS

OFFICER UNIFORM

Service Dress,
Lieutenant Commander

Skinsuit,
Lieutenant Commander

OFFICER RANKS

Midshipman

Ensign

Lieutenant
Junior Grade

Lieutenant

Lieutenant
Commander

Starship Command

Commander

Captain

Commodore

Rear Admiral

Vice Admiral

Admiral

High Admiral

ENLISTED RANKS

Spacer
3rd Class

Spacer
2nd Class

Spacer
1st Class

Petty Officer
3rd Class

Petty Officer
2nd Class

Petty Officer
1st Class

Chief
Petty Officer

Senior Chief
Petty Officer

Master Chief
Petty Officer

Senior Master
Chief Petty Officer

DEVICES AND PATCHES

Unit Patch on Enlisted Cap
(Right Side)

Space Warfare Qualification Badge (Enlisted)

Space Warfare Qualification Badge (Officer)

ENLISTED UNIFORM

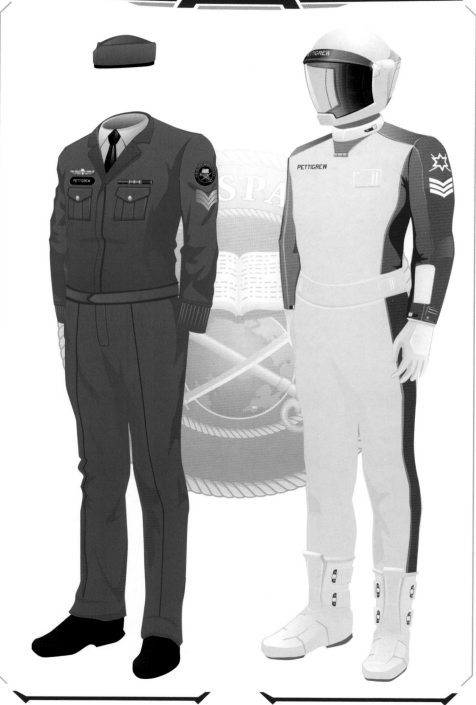

Service Dress,
Petty Officer 1st Class

Skinsuit,
Petty Officer 1st Class

GSN AWARD RIBBONS

Star of Grayson

Saint Austin's Cross

Protector's Cross

Sword's Cross with Diamonds

Armsman's Cross with Diamonds

Cross of Courage with Diamonds

Sword's Cross with Laurel Wreath

Armsman's Cross with Laurel Wreath

Cross of Courage with Laurel Wreath

Sword's Cross with Crossed Swords

Armsman's Cross with Crossed Swords

Cross of Courage with Crossed Swords

Sword's Cross in Gold

Armsman's Cross in Gold

Gold Cross of Courage

Sword's Cross in Silver
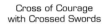

Armsman's Cross in Silver

Silver Cross of Courage

Sword's Cross in Bronze

Armsman's Cross in Bronze

Bronze Cross of Courage

Sword's Cross in Steel

Armsman's Cross in Steel

Steel Cross of Courage

Wound Medal

Survivor's Cross

Meritorious Service Cross

Meritorious Service Star

Meritorious Service Medal

Grayson Military Achievement Medal

Protector's Unit Citation for Gallantry

Meritorious Unit Award

Battle Efficiency Medal

Masadan War Campaign Medal

2nd Masadan War Campaign Medal

Havenite War Campaign Medal

Space Combat Action Badge

Good Conduct Medal

Reserve Forces Service Medal

Recruit Training Ribbon

NCO Senior Course Ribbon

Armed Forces Service Medal

Space Service Ribbon

Champion Shots Medal

Distinguished Weapons Qualification Medal

Weapons Qualification Medal

THE HONORVERSE COMPANION

DAVID WEBER
AND
BuNine

EDITED BY DAVID WEBER AND THOMAS POPE
Artwork by Thomas Marrone
Copy Edit by Christopher Weuve

WRITERS
David Weber
Scott Akers, Scott Bell, Ken Burnside, Derick Chan, Mark Gutis,
Joelle Presby, Thomas Pope, Gena Robinson, Christopher Weuve

CONTRIBUTORS
Pat Doyle, Bill Edwards, Rob Graham, Richard Hanck,
Bryan Haven, Robb Jackson, Barry Messina, Andrew Presby,
Greg Whitaker, Marcus Wilmes

CONTRIBUTING ARTISTS
Bob Bulkeley, Robert Graham, John O'Donnell, Thomas Pope

COPY EDITORS
Mark Gutis, Arius Kaufmann, Kay Shelton, Christopher Weuve

The Honorverse Companion
1921 PD

JAYNE'S INTELLIGENCE REVIEW

Letter from the Editor

For centuries, Jayne's has been the recognized authority on the ships, equipment, and personnel of navies across the explored galaxy. We at Jayne's have been proud to present the most accurate and comprehensive analyses of deployed military technology available. This is no mean task when one considers the sheer number of navies, breadth of technology, and volume of inhabited space. These difficulties are further compounded by the necessity of reliance on unclassified sources of information for the weapons, systems, and even hull features of combatants.

Due to the issues noted above as well as the constraints imposed by publication dates and production deadlines, some small errors are unavoidable. As our long-time readers are well aware, every new edition contains errata from the previous year as new information becomes available. Despite external appearances, units within a given class are rarely as homogeneous as the layman might imagine. Visual similarities across a class may conceal upgraded capabilities and shipyard inconsistencies and design changes can create vast differences between the first and last ship produced. Refits are common and ships still in service may not reflect the new realities of ships recently out of space-dock. Normally, these errors are minimal and we correct them without any additional commentary. Occasionally, however, significant errors creep in and we at Jayne's feel an obligation to call these to the attention of our readers.

Covering the wars in the Haven Sector has proven to be a particular challenge for our group. Nothing spurs the development and change of military technology like war. Therefore, keeping track of the many and rapid changes in the deployed systems occasioned by operational necessities is particularly challenging.

Given the remoteness of the Haven Sector and the exigencies of military secrecy, obtaining up-to-date and accurate information is often difficult.

Haven, especially the People's Republic but even the newly restored Republic, has always kept information on its shipbuilding and warship classes classified. Hull numbers are randomized among classes and shipyards and are even subject to occasional changes throughout the life of the ship. This purposeful randomization of these identifiers serves to obscure their build numbers, as readers will recall from editorials in our 1907 PD annex.

By comparison, information on the Royal Manticoran Navy has always been easier to collect. Although not entirely an open book, their construction programs, especially prewar, have largely been a matter of public record, often resulting from vicious debates in their Parliament. Other than their newest construction, many of their warships were regularly docked at their major space stations prior to the outbreak of open hostilities and thus subject to physical observation. Since the beginning of active operations, the RMN has drawn a very deliberate veil of secrecy over its new designs and construction, but that was not the case prior to 1905. This earlier ease of access may, in fact, have led to a degree of complacency on the part of our researchers, who have discovered, to our chagrin, that the Royal Manticoran Navy was not above exploiting that complacency, resulting in our most notable error: the *Star Knight*-class heavy cruiser.

When the *Star Knight* was commissioned in 1893 PD, it was believed to be an unremarkable design, merely a modern extension of their older heavy cruiser classes. Its weaponry was a matter of public record and was noted in our 1896 edition. This belief remained unquestioned for some years. It was not until a small skirmish in a fourth-tier star system where a *Star Knight* clashed with a Havenite *Sultan*-class battlecruiser that anyone realized there was anything special about the class.

Far from an evolutionary design of known parentage, the *Star Knight* was the first of a wave of revolutionary new Manticoran heavy cruisers. It was not only the first true two-deck heavy cruiser, it was also the first step taken by the Royal Manticoran Navy to build a heavy cruiser capable of surviving in the combat environment created by the rise of the laser head as the primary shipkiller.

Our failure to recognize this significant departure from established design philosophies stemmed from no mere clerical error.
It was an intentional campaign of misdirection by the RMN
to hide the capabilities of their new design. We at Jayne's had
become so accustomed to the public availability of information
about new Manticoran designs that, with only a small dose of
deception on their part, they were able to "hide in plain sight"
a specification that bore little resemblance to the actual design
information transmitted by requests for information from the
public. The RMN had announced that they were mounting some
experimental sensors and were therefore obscuring the upper
sections of hull with a combination of smart paint and shroud-
ing during port calls. While there were unconfirmed reports
of a heavier-than-expected broadside, they were dismissed as
inconsistent with known observations or even confirmation of a
new sensor suite.

As a civilian publication, *Jayne's* is limited to open source
research, without the benefits of dedicated intelligence agencies of
the Solarian League Navy. It would be a reasonable assumption
that ONI has been aware of the true nature of the *Star Knight*
for far longer than we have.

While perhaps not as extreme an error as the one we made on
the *Star Knight*, the published data in our 1920 edition on the
new *Nike*-class battlecruiser also appears to have been in error in
one significant respect. Our artist's conception of the class was
correct in most respects. All reports that the *Nike* class carried a
"larger than average" decoy system, however, significantly understated the issue. The new Mk20 "Keyhole" system appears to be
far more than a simple decoy. From analysis of visual records, it
appears to be virtually a parasite craft in its own right.

If the platform is indeed unmanned, it may well be more
massive than even a light attack craft, and the obvious sensor
and point defense installations indicate that it is far more than a
simple decoy. Exactly why the RMN has decided to build a decoy
and defensive installation so much larger than their previous
platforms remains unclear, and the purpose of the array panels
on the sides of the platform remains a mystery.

We at Jayne's feel a responsibility to you, our readers, to provide
information that is as accurate as possible. In the rare cases where
later access to information establishes that our earlier analysis was

incorrect, we feel it is our obligation to correct these analyses, even at the expense of admitting our fallibility. Our pledge of accuracy has always been the touchstone of our editorial policy. Our analysts continue to gather as much information as possible on these and other new warships to come out of the Haven Sector. We pledge to continue to work to provide the most accurate, up-to-date information for those whose lives depend on it.

Annette Konduru, Senior Editor
Jayne's Information Group
April 17, 1921 PD

The Star Empire of Manticore

7/24/1920 PD
Hamilton Hall,
Saganami Island

John—

I wish you could have been here to hear Duchess Harrington's address at Last View last month! There are so many things I've tried—we've all tried—so hard to teach them, impress upon them, but they're so damned young. They're so damned full of their own immortality, they still find it so hard to believe the universe could exist just fine without them in it. I know—I know! We were all like that once, and maybe it's just as well we were. If we'd known then what we know now, how many of us would have stuck it out? Worn the uniform? Seen so many of our friends die?

Sorry. I don't mean to be all doom-and-gloom or rain all over your parade. You know the score as well as I do, after all. One of the things I hate most about being Commandant—or even a Queen's officer, sometimes—is the way I have to keep my mouth shut, especially in front of the middies, about the sort of things that "undermine respect for civilian authority." When I think about the systematic way High Ridge and those other bastards threw away everything—everything, John!—that you and I and everyone else fought and died for. About the way we were right on the brink of outright military victory. We had them—we had them, and there wasn't a single damned thing they could do about it, and High Ridge and those other bastards decided to play politics instead. Damn it, you know as well as I do who was really behind the Cromarty Assassination. Hell, without Duchess Harrington, they'd have killed Her Majesty as well! Don't tell me for one stinking second High Ridge didn't know that just as well as you and I do. The son-of-a-bitch knew Saint-Just ordered it, and he still insisted on "negotiating" with the Peeps. He let them wiggle off the hook, when we could've dictated terms to Saint-Just in Nouveau Paris itself, because it was more important to him to break Her Majesty's kneecaps in the House of Lords to protect his own precious ass and political power, and God knows how many men and women in uniform have been killed because that was more important to him than winning the damned war. I don't know, anyway, and when the nightmares are especially bad, I try not to know how many of my midshipmen and midshipwomen are going to die for the same frigging reason. Kids, John—good kids, my kids—and they're going to be killed because a clutch of self-serving, conniving politicians didn't care what their actions were going to cost anybody else.

And I can't say a word about it in public without violating the Articles of War and my own oath as an officer of the Queen. Sorry. There I go again. I'll try to behave better.

Look, they're supposed to be pulling me out of the Academy, sending me back to the Fleet sometime in the next few months. I don't know where yet, although there's some talk about a task force in Home Fleet that needs looking after. Can't say I really like the thought of going up against the Peeps now that they've duplicated the MDM and built pod-layers of their own, but we're still better than they are, and we'll still kick their asses in the end. In fact, I think Duchess Harrington's on her way to do a little preliminary ass-kicking of her own right now, and the truth is, I wish I was with her. But remember what Mom always said, "If wishes were fishes, we never want food."

Anyway, I'll be seeing you and her and the kids next month, once I get the semester shut down and I can grab a little time for myself. I'll bring along a chip of Duchess Harrington's address. If you're still as much like me as you've always been before, it'll send a shiver down your spine, I promise. But they'll do good, my kids. It won't matter to them whose fault it is, or why so many of them are going to die. They believe, John. They believe in duty, and honor, and responsibility. They believe there are things in this universe worth dying for. And they believe in those things strongly enough to go out and do the dying for the people they love and the things they care about. That's what Last View is all about, really, and it's what Duchess Harrington put into words for them so well. She touched that belief of theirs because she believes, too.

And when you come down to it, John, so do I.

Gotta go. Kiss Martha for me, hug those kids, and tell Mom to get the grill fired up. I'll see you all in a couple of weeks, little brother.

Love,
Betty

—excerpt from a letter from Vice Admiral Lady Beatrice McDermott, Baroness Alb, Commandant, Naval Academy, Saganami Island, to her younger brother, Commodore John McDermott, one year before her death in the Battle of Manticore.

Introduction

The Star Empire of Manticore is a constitutional monarchy comprising twenty-one member star systems, thirty-four protectorate star systems, and a wormhole junction with seven mapped termini. The capital planet, Manticore, shares a binary star system with the planets of Sphinx and Gryphon.

Combined, the fifty-four star systems of the Star Empire of Manticore are ethnically diverse, the product of large-scale diaspora immigration from Old Earth and other Core Worlds. Manticore is also a xeno-diverse star nation, home to two sapient nonhuman species: the Treecats of Sphinx and the Medusans of the Basilisk System.

Humans migrated to the Manticore binary system in 1416 PD (Post Diaspora) aboard the sublight hibernation ship *Jason* and colonized three planets: Manticore (Manticore-A III), Sphinx (Manticore-A IV), and Gryphon (Manticore-B V). The colony's founder, the Manticore Colony Trust, consisted of shareholders primarily from Old Earth Western Europe, with a small number from the Ukraine and the North American Federation.

Following the death by plague of sixty percent of the original colonists, more colonists needed to be recruited and were subsidized heavily. Before inviting the second wave of colonists, Planetary Administrator Roger Winton and the Manticore Colony, Ltd., Board of Directors adopted the current Constitution of Manticore, which established a constitutional monarchy and ennobled the original colonists and their descendants. The Constitution of Manticore includes a Declaration of Fundamental Rights applicable to all citizens, although franchise is limited to those who have paid taxes for at least five consecutive years. With the offer of Manticoran nobility also available to those second wave emigrants who purchased sufficient land credits, the Kingdom of Manticore grew quickly in population and economy.

Manticoran territorial expansion was limited before the Second Havenite War. However, due to the discovery of the seventh terminus of the Manticore Wormhole Junction in 1919 PD, the admission of the Talbott Quadrant to the Kingdom, and the resumption of the War with Haven later that same year, the Star Kingdom of Manticore needed to adapt to be able to manage the wildly disparate star systems and populations that had come under its control. The Star Kingdom of Manticore formally became the Star *Empire* of Manticore (SEM) in 1921, forming an Imperial government that provided greater flexibility and increased ability to meet the needs of all member and protectorate star systems under their new government.

Astrography

The Manticoran Wormhole Junction has had a significant effect on the Star Kingdom of Manticore and, more recently, on the formation of the Star Empire. Due to the far-flung coverage of the Junction, the Star Empire has not followed any of the traditional models of expansion adopted by other star nations. While the Star Empire's borders stretch almost nine hundred light-years between its farthest systems, all of its members systems are clustered around the termini of the Junction.

The formal borders of the Star Empire include twenty-one member star systems, thirty-four protectorate star systems, and the wormhole junction, with seven mapped termini. The capital planet, Manticore, shares a binary star system with the planets of Sphinx and Gryphon.

With twenty-two habitable planets and over twenty-seven billion people, the Star Empire of Manticore is the largest by total area and, including the populations of the protectorate star systems, boasts the second largest population of the Verge star nations.

The Star Kingdom's transformation into the Star Empire began with the annexation of the Basilisk system in 1865 PD. Following the first phase of the Havenite Wars, Trevor's Star sought annexation in 1914, and the Lynx System sought membership in 1919 following the discovery of the Lynx Terminus of the Manticoran Wormhole Junction. These star systems, all

of which share access to the Junction, are collectively referred
to as the "Old Star Kingdom" and form a single territorial unit
within the Star Empire.

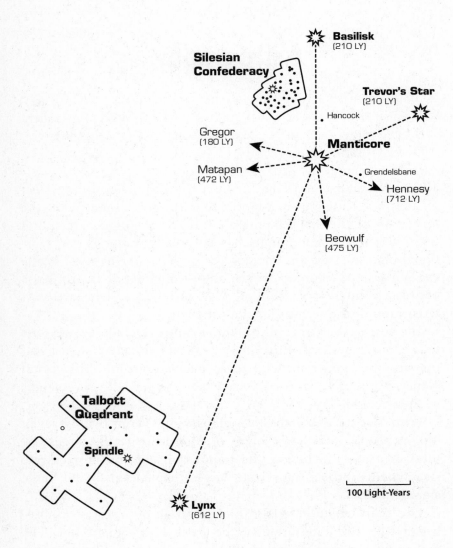

The Silesian protectorate systems became territories of the Star Kingdom in 1920 PD, following intense negotiations with the then Silesian government and the Andermani Empire. At this time, the protectorate systems do not hold voting membership in the Star Empire, although that may change in the future. The Star *Empire* actually came into existence in 1921 following the admission of the Talbott Quadrant, which was organized into a separate, federated territorial unit at the Constitutional Convention in the Split System.

Finally, a number of single system star nations are treaty signatories in the Manticoran Alliance. Some of these systems, such as the Marsh system just outside the borders of the old Silesian Confederacy, while not considered Manticoran territory, still have a significant Manticoran presence.

The Manticore Binary System

The Manticore System consists of a G0 star of 1.12 solar masses with a G2 binary companion of 0.92 solar masses. Both stars orbit a common center of gravity 333 light-minutes from the A component and 406 light-minutes from the B component. The apparent eccentricity of the pair approaches twelve percent, and results in distances between the stars that range from 650 light-minutes at periastron to 827 light-minutes at apastron.

The total system population is close to three billion, spread among its three Earth-like worlds and its main asteroid belt. The majority of the population resides in the Manticore-A subsystem, although the Manticore-B subsystem's Unicorn Belt's asteroid extraction operations produce the lion's share of the kingdom's raw ores. Perhaps because of this space-going orientation, Gryphon provides a quite disproportionate percentage of the Star Kingdom's merchant spacers and of the Royal Manticoran Navy's and Marines' personnel.

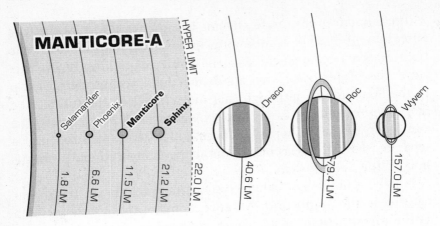

Manticore (Manticore-A III)

Radius: 6,496 km
Gravity: 1.01 G
Orbit Period: 629.83 T-days
Sidereal Day: 22.45 hours
Hydrosphere: 76%

Of the three worlds in the Manticore Binary System, Manticore was clearly the one with the most desirable real estate. Slightly larger than Earth but with a lower density, its surface gravity is almost exactly Earth standard. Manticore's climatic zones and regions are comparable to Earth, but cover a larger temperate zone, due to favorable ocean currents and a lower axial tilt. It has a single moon, Thorson, which is much smaller than Earth's moon, resulting in negligible tidal activity. Internal processes make Manticore moderately tectonically active. Like all life in the Manticore Binary System, Manticore's protein chirality is right-handed, making it digestible to humans. Manticoran life is similar enough to Terrestrial life that only minimal engineered adaptations were required for crops and livestock.

Manticore is the breadbasket of the Manticore Binary System and the most heavily populated planet in the system. It is also the seat of government and the capital city of Landing is home to Mount Royal Palace as well as the Hall of Parliament, Admiralty House, and Burke Tower, the home of the Queen's Bench Court. The University of Manticore, which is ranked in the top five percent of all university systems, galaxy wide, also maintains its primary campus in Landing. Major Manticoran industries include agriculture, aquaculture, mining, and a well-diversified industrial sector and research and development base. In addition, the corporate headquarters of over seventy-five percent of the financial houses and banks involved in the Star Kingdom's enormous investment and banking industry are located in Landing. The total planetary population is just under 1.5 billion people as of 1921 PD.

Her Majesty's Space Station *Hephaestus* serves as a combination shipyard, transfer station and living facility for nearly one million workers (both permanent and transient) and their families.

Sphinx (Manticore-A IV)

Radius: 6,953 km
Gravity: 1.35 G
Orbit Period: 1,903.65 T-days
Sidereal Day: 25.62 hours
Hydrosphere: 68%

Sphinx is a larger planet, with roughly a third again the mass of Earth and a denser atmosphere that can cause some adaptation sickness. It is tectonically less active than is typical of a planet of its mass but is more active than Earth. In recent geological times, it had a volcanic eruption at the Stubleford Traps that increased the CO_2 levels considerably.

Sphinx is blessed with extensive mineral resources. Utilizing those resources, however, is complicated by long seasons and a climate that starts out chilly at the equator and gets markedly colder from there. It is only by dint of its extremely active CO_2 cycle that Sphinx remains shirtsleeve-habitable to humans.

All major Sphinxian fauna are hexapeds, of which the most notable are the treecats, one of the few alien species thus far discovered that have approached human-level sentience. By the Ninth Amendment to the Star Kingdom's Constitution, approximately one-third of the planetary surface belongs to the treecat clans in perpetuity.

Sphinx's major industries are mining, forestry, and animal husbandry. Industry has been slow to develop but is now beginning to make considerable ground. Planetary population as of the 1920 PD census (291 AL) is approximately 1.1 billion humans and twelve million treecats.

Sphinx is orbited by Her Majesty's Space Station *Vulcan*, the second largest construction and commerce node in the home system, as well as two small moons, Perseus and Bellerophon.

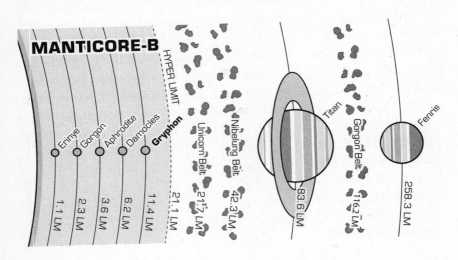

Gryphon (Manticore-B V)

Radius: 5,939 km
Gravity: 1.05 G
Orbit Period: 615.51 T-days
Sidereal Day: 22.71 hours
Hydrosphere: 51%

Of the three habitable planets in the Manticore Binary System, Gryphon's diameter, mass and planetary density are the closest to Earth's. It is only borderline habitable, however, due to the slight hydrosphere and parts of its continental interiors are nearly Martian in their arid beauty.

Gryphon is a world of extremes. While the hydrosphere covers a relatively small percentage of its surface, its oceans are comparatively deep, providing the thermal reservoir that makes Gryphon habitable even with the combination of extreme axial tilt and large orbital radius. The end result is a rugged "continental" climate with extremely cold winters and, relatively speaking, scorching summers.

Gryphon has trade-worthy concentrations of rare earth elements and fissionable materials, but is otherwise mineral-poor. More than two hundred kilometers from the coasts, the land is dry for half the local year, then drenched as the fall rains come, which are followed by a hard freeze. Gryphon's stark beauty, mountainous terrain, and excellent skiing make the recreation industry a primary contributor to the planetary economy. The planet is also home to a disproportionately robust planetary industrial infrastructure, partly because of ease of access to the Unicorn Belt and the Royal Manticoran Navy's policy of basing much of its primary R&D complex there and producing many of its prototypes in Gryphon's shipyards. As of 1920 PD, Gryphon had a planetary population of no more than six hundred million.

Her Majesty's Space Station *Weyland* orbits Gryphon. It is significantly smaller than both *Hephaestus* and *Vulcan*, with an average population of just over three hundred thousand. Since the beginning of the war it has been closed to all civilian traffic. Gryphon has a single large moon, named Egg, which produces extreme tides on its deep, narrow oceans.

Unicorn Belt

The Unicorn Belt is the primary resource extraction location in the Manticore Binary System, being both the innermost and richest of the three asteroid belts in the Manticore-B subsystem. Just outside the hyper limit, at any given time there are at least twenty resource extraction motherships working their way around the belt, each with dozens of ore boats serving its needs.

Total Belter population as of 1920 PD was approximately three hundred million.

The Manticore Wormhole Junction

The Manticore Wormhole Junction, the largest wormhole junction so far discovered, has secondary termini at no less than seven other star systems. The "reach" of those termini give the Junction a critical location in the wormhole network, which has made it indispensable to the Manticore System's thriving economy. A trip from the Core to the Verge via the wormhole, for example, could reduce travel time by upwards of six months as compared to making the same voyage through hyper-space. This generates substantial savings in operating costs and permits carriers to make many more voyages in the same time window.

Those advantages have allowed a star system with less than one-fifth the population of the Sol System to grow to a Gross System Product equal to seventy-eight percent that of the Sol System by 1900 PD and to exceed it comfortably by 1920, despite the strain of a major war against a far larger adversary. This is possible in no small part because the combined termini of the Junction directly cover an irregular volume of space over a thousand light-years across its widest point. The proximity to other wormholes and their warp bridges extends the Junction's "reach" still further, however. For example, it would take 18.5 T-months for a freighter in the delta bands to make the 1,680-light-year voyage from Basilisk to the system of Mullins on the far side of the Solarian League. By way of the Junction and the warp bridge connecting Mullins to the Titania System, 116 light-years from Beowulf, the same ship can make the same trip in only thirty-eight days, or less than seven percent of the longer time. The implications for the transport of freight and passengers are apparent, and those same implications apply to the transportation of information, helping to explain Manticore's emergence as the explored galaxy's premier banking and financial markets center.

The wormhole nexus lies 412 light-minutes from Manticore A. First transit was made in 1585 PD, to Beowulf, followed within a few years by Trevor's Star and Hennesy, and, over the years since by Gregor, Matapan, Basilisk, and most recently, Lynx.

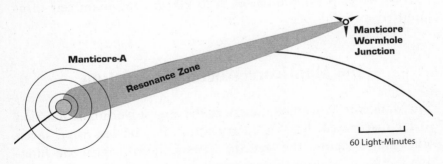

Substantial levels of Crown revenue are directly derived from Junction usage fees and service fees from infrastructure usage, but the Junction also underpins a banking and financial market, dependent upon information flow through the Junction, which constitutes a very significant percentage of the total Manticoran economy. Junction fees are computed based on a fixed base transit fee, applicable to all vessels and modified by type of ship, size of ship, cargo carried or passengers embarked, and the normal-space distance between the termini used. Maritime law currently recognizes three types of commercial vessels: courier, passenger carrier, and freighter. Couriers are charged the base fee at a small multiplier. Freighters and passenger carriers pay an additional fee based on the "empty" tonnage of the ship, plus a surcharge per ton of cargo or passenger embarked, and all vessels are assessed an additional fee equal to 2.5 percent per light-century of normal-space distance covered in the transit. (That is, for the four hundred seventy-five light-years between Manticore and Beowulf, the total fee multiplier would be roughly 15 percent.)

Even with the increase in usage fees due to the Star Empire's need to fund a war, the savings are still sufficiently compelling that traffic through the Junction has done nothing but increase. The expansion of the Junction's "reach" through its newly discovered termini, plus the opening of additional hyper bridges in several spots around the Solarian League's periphery, helps to account for much of the increased usage. At the same time, the sixty-percent discount on transit fees for Manticoran-owned and -registered vessels has simultaneously forced Solarian shipping houses to cut prices to remain competitive and driven more and more of the galaxy's shipping under the Manticoran flag, increasing Manticore's share of the galactic merchant marine. This has fanned long-standing resentment on the part of many Solarians, who feel that the Star Kingdom of Manticore has long used the Junction's leverage to increase the size of its own merchant fleet at the expense of other star nations, including the Solarian League.

In addition to usage fees, an entire sub-economy has sprung up specifically to service the activity tied to Junction traffic. While not flowing directly into the Crown's coffers, revenue is still generated indirectly via various taxes. A large number of platforms providing warehousing and transshipment stations, maintenance and refueling facilities, and financial offices are located in the vicinity of the Junction. The majority of these platforms (which must be equipped with station keeping drive capability in order to maintain position with the Junction) are owned by one or more of the Manticoran cartels, sometimes with participation by one or more of the Solarian transstellars, although the Star Kingdom has pursued a deliberate policy to discourage outright non-Manticoran ownership of such facilities. Despite that, there is room for smaller players who tend to specialized markets, such as the foodstuffs trade or environmentally controlled storage. In addition, the Junction makes the Manticore Binary System a logical shipbuilding hub, and the Star Kingdom's commercial shipyards are among the largest and most efficient in the known galaxy. Indeed, a sobering percentage of humanity's total merchant fleet, and especially of its more modern units, is the product of Manticoran builders.

The sheer volume of traffic through the Junction also means that even though emergencies are low-probability events, they nonetheless happen on a frequent basis. Junction search-and-rescue capabilities are among the galaxy's best, and its service platforms can handle virtually any urgent refit. For those without a pressing issue, the stations can provide environmental replenishment, and a large number of "rest and recreation" platforms offer temporary lodging and entertainment facilities for crews and passengers on layover.

Physical goods are not the only thing shipped through the wormhole. As already noted, the Junction is also a natural focal point for the galaxy's financial institutions. A number of banks and financial firms have major branches located on stations around the Junction, on one or more of the major inner-system habitats, or on the planet Manticore itself. A large fleet of dispatch vessels, many owned by the firms themselves, stand ready to carry encrypted fund transfers rapidly anywhere in the galaxy, via the wormhole network. The banks also facilitate credit voucher redemptions and currency exchanges. If money is the lifeblood of the galaxy, then the Manticoran Wormhole Junction could be considered its heart.

Management of the wormhole is provided by the Manticoran Astro Control Service (ACS). While responsible for all traffic in the Manticore System and its termini-connected systems, ACS is primarily concentrated around the Junction due to the high volume of traffic. While ACS is a civilian service, it does coordinate with the Royal Manticoran Navy in order to track traffic in the system, with the RMN enforcing ACS's traffic control and conducting customs inspections. As a secondary responsibility, ACS also controls intrasystem civilian search-and-rescue craft for any space-based emergency response.

The Old Star Kingdom

The Old Star Kingdom consists of the Manticore Binary System along with the Basilisk System, Trevor's Star System and Lynx System. All three secondary members anchor their respective ends of the Manticore Wormhole Junction and were added before the Star Kingdom formally became the Star Empire of Manticore.

The Basilisk System was annexed by Manticore in 1865 PD after the terminus was fully surveyed, but a vicious political squabble over the rights of the native sentient species of the planet Medusa delayed the formal declaration of sovereignty over the entire system. The political fallout after the Havenite attempt to seize the system in 1901 allowed the Cromarty Government to formally annex Basilisk as a member system, with the provision that formal admission of Medusans as full citizens of the Star Kingdom would occur after a fifty-year period. At that time they would be allowed to vote on whether to accept or refuse membership.

San Martin, in the Trevor's Star System, was a longtime ally of the Star Kingdom until it was conquered by the expanding People's Republic of Haven in 1883 PD. The system was liberated in 1911 during the First Havenite War and formally requested membership into the Star Kingdom in 1914.

Lynx was the fourth and final member of the Old Star Kingdom, having requested membership in 1919 PD, shortly after the first survey transit of what was eventually called the Lynx Terminus of the Manticore Wormhole Junction. The terminus is anchored near MQ-L-1792-46A, a planetless M8 star approximately four light-years from the Lynx System.

Silesian Confederacy

The decision to partition the Silesian Confederacy was, essentially, an understanding between Queen Elizabeth III and Emperor Gustav XI which recognized the ultimate failure of the Silesian Confederacy as a government.

Arguably, the annexations by the then-Star Kingdom and the Andermani were territory grabs. In the context of their individual and mutual experiences in the Confederacy, however, it is an understandable reaction to the chaos that has reigned almost since the Confederacy was founded. Manticore and the Andermani had provided most of what little stability was present in the area for many decades prior to the partition, expending a great deal of money and many lives in fighting piracy and "privateers" licensed by various breakaway governments. Moreover, the region remained a dangerous potential flashpoint for both star nations. While both have both profited enormously from trade and shipping, the Andermani have long coveted control of Silesia, in no small part because of the way in which Silesian instability tended to spill over onto the Andermani Empire, whose borders lie much closer to the Confederacy. Manticore, with the greater insulation provided by distance but only a single transit away via the Manticoran Wormhole Junction, has traditionally been less than sympathetic to that aspect of the Andermani's Silesian policy. This has been a source of considerable tension over the years as the Royal Manticoran Navy has traditionally served as the primary counterbalance to Andermani ambitions. Ultimately, Elizabeth realized that agreeing to a division which permitted Emperor Gustav to address those "spillover" issues once and for all was in the interest of the Star Kingdom, given its need to retain the Andermani as an ally. The Silesian government consented to the annexation in 1920 PD and assigned its powers to the respective star nations, although individual system governments were left in place.

The Andermani-administered portion of the former confederation has been subjected to typical Andermani policy. Using the Imperial Andermani Navy (IAN) as the steel fist inside the velvet glove, the Andermani have put an efficient, if not unduly gentle, stop to the piratic depredations and insurrectionary movements. While planetary governments have been left largely in place, the Empire has made it clear to them that membership in the Empire is a privilege they would do best to accept gracefully. Faced with Andermani firmness and the gratitude of system populations no longer subject to cronyism, corruption, and bloodshed, only the most foolish of system governments would dare disagree.

By contrast, the SEM-administered areas have been treated somewhat more gently. By and large, the Star Empire has allowed local governments to continue functioning, subject to the adoption of personal liberties laws matching those of the Manticoran constitution and monitoring by Manticoran Foreign Office advisors.

A small number, however, have been placed under direct Manticoran control, with appointive governors, due to special local circumstances, generally related to residual corruption, cronyism, human rights violations, and support for local brigandage. Each star system will be allowed an individual plebiscite on the decision to become full, permanent members of the Star Empire, on approximately the same terms as the Talbott Cluster, pending the completion of certain specifically defined milestones related to human rights, electoral participation, and government and law enforcement transparency. Under the Silesian Protectorate Act as adopted by Parliament, systems which decline to seek admission or fail to meet the required milestone will be retained permanently in protectorate status, although there is provision under the Act for this to be amended.

The occupation is under the jurisdiction of Royal Manticoran Navy (RMN) Admiral Mark Sarnow, serving as Queen Elizabeth's appointed civilian governor as well as the commanding officer of all RMN units in Silesian space, assisted by Lieutenant Governor Lord James Bannion, Baron Jurgenson, a career Foreign Office diplomat. Accounting for every Confederacy Navy hull has proved difficult due to a combination of the chaotic way in which records were kept and a tendency for Silesian "naval officers" with pre-partition connections to Silesian criminal enterprises to disappear with their ships into the ranks of pirates, smugglers, and other criminal actors. Sarnow has also met some passive resistance in decommissioning obsolescent units, yet the effort continues and has recently begun gathering speed under his skillful direction.

Both the RMN and IAN have been granted the right of hot pursuit into the other's respective jurisdictions in case of piracy or other military action. The Andermani have also fully recognized the treaty between the Sidemore Republic and the SEM as well as the RMN's Sidemore Station.

Talbott Quadrant

The Talbott Cluster was long regarded as a galactic backwater which must inevitably be incorporated into the Solarian League. League expansion was predicted to reach the Cluster sometime in the 1930s, and the League had considered it within its sphere of interest for well over half a century, since the Office of Frontier Security's (OFS's) establishment of the neighboring Madras Sector in 1862 PD. Due to its location, the Cluster was also of some immediate concern to Mesa, which had interests in the area if only because of simple proximity. Much to the irritation of both Mesa and the OFS, however, a terminus of the Manticoran Wormhole Junction was discovered near the Lynx System in 1919 PD.

This discovery quickly led to Lynx's successful application for inclusion into the Star Kingdom, followed shortly by plebiscites from each government in the Cluster to decide whether their star nation would also seek Manticoran annexation. Not all star systems within the volume of the Cluster voted to join the Star Kingdom, but representatives of those which did gather in the Spindle System in 1920 to draft a Clusterwide constitution. Although not without controversy or violence, the Talbott Constitutional Convention was relatively straightforward, despite alleged Mesan and OFS attempts to destabilize the cluster to prevent it joining the Manticoran system, and the new constitution was ratified in January 1921.

Because of the astrography and the distances involved (the Lynx Terminus is 612 light-years from the Manticore Binary System) the Cluster's annexation (as the Talbott Quadrant) prompted the change of the Star Kingdom of Manticore into the Star Empire and the introduction of a federal model of government. The Quadrant is administered by an Imperial Governor (in the person of Lady Dame Estelle Matsuko, Baroness Medusa) as the Crown's direct representative. It has its own Parliament and executive branch with the Spindle System as Quadrant capital and the location of the RMN's Talbott Station. By the standards of Manticore, the star nations in the Quadrant are somewhat backward, and income inequality is a problem in several of them. Local governmental forms range from democracies to nations controlled by ruling oligarchies, although most nations have democratically elected governments.

Other Systems

During the buildup and maneuvering preceding the Havenite Wars, the Star Kingdom constructed a number of military bases in both uninhabited and member systems of the Manticoran

Alliance. In addition, a number of star systems liberated from the People's Republic of Haven were occupied, some changing hands several times during the course of the conflicts.

Hancock and Grendelsbane bases are the most notable for their size and importance, though many smaller bases were also established along the front. These bases provide support structure and repair and resupply points as well as a nodal concentration of forces. Other bases, such as Sun-Yat, were captured Havenite forward bases, repurposed for Manticoran use.

Aside from purely military bases in uninhabited star systems, a number of other systems have their own unique treaty arrangements with Manticore, despite not being formal members of the Alliance. Marsh is one such system, with a Manticoran fleet base established originally to keep an eye on the Silesian Confederacy and Anderman Empire.

History

The original colony expedition to Manticore departed Old Earth on October 24, 775 PD, aboard the sublight hibernation ship *Jason* bound for the Manticore Binary System. Manticore, which lies approximately 512 light-years from Earth, was first confirmed to have planets in 562 PD by the astronomer Sir Frederick Clarke. Its distance was such that the voyage would take 640 years (just over 384 subjective years allowing for relativistic effects), requiring that each colonist be waked from cryosleep for exercise seven times. Accordingly, the colonists were investing about four and a half years of their lives and all their money in the voyage.

Sixty percent of the colonists were Western Europeans, with most of the remainder drawn from the North American Federation, the Caribbean, and a very small minority of ethnic Ukrainians. The total expedition consisted of ninety-three thousand adults and thirty-two thousand minor children.

The "rights" to the system had been purchased at auction from the survey firm of Franchot et Fils, Paris, France, Old Earth. FF, as the firm was known, had an excellent reputation, and its survey ship *Suffren* had made the same voyage in just twenty years. *Suffren*'s crew had done FF's usual professional job, although all data was accompanied by the caution that it would be 650 years out of date when the colonists arrived. FF sold its rights in the Manticore System to the Manticore Colony, Ltd., (MC) for approximately 5.75 billion EuroDollars. As part of the transfer of rights, FF expunged all data on the system from its memory banks, transferring the information to the Solarian International Data Bank's maximum security files. This was a standard safeguard to protect MC against the occupation of the planet by later expeditions with faster ships, as it was already apparent that advances in hyper travel might well make such protection necessary. It was also recognized that there was no way to guarantee that faster, more capable hyperships would not beat the colonists to Manticore anyway. Accordingly, Roger Winton, President and CEO of MC (who had already been elected Planetary Administrator) opted to establish the Manticore Colony Trust of Zurich (MCT).

The MCT's purpose was to invest all capital remaining to the MC after mounting the expedition (something under one billion EuroDollars) and use the accrued interest to watch over the colonists' rights to their new home. It was a wise precaution.

Landing and Early History
1416–1453 PD

When *Jason* finally arrived in the Manticore System on March 21, 1416 PD, her crew discovered a modest settlement on the planet Manticore, staffed by MCT personnel who also manned the four small Earth-built frigates that protected the system against claim-jumpers. Indeed, so well had the Trust done in the last six centuries, that Manticore found itself with a very favorable bank balance on Old Terra, and the frigates became the first units of the Manticoran System Navy. Moreover, the small MCT presence on Manticore included data banks and carefully selected and trained instructors assigned to update the colonists on the technical advances of the last six centuries. This last was a feature even Winton had not anticipated and he had very good reason to be pleased with his own decisions and the diligence, foresight, and imagination with which he and a succession of MCT managers had discharged their duties.

Two centuries later, the MCT funds on Old Terra provided the initial capitalization of the Royal Bank of Manticore, and it has been argued that the initial experience with the MCT had a great deal to do with the Star Kingdom of Manticore's farsighted enlightened self-interest where management of the Manticoran

Wormhole Junction is concerned. Despite occasional detours, the Star Kingdom has always had a tradition of long-term, forward-looking economic and fiscal policies. The MCT remains in existence even today, managing Manticoran economic and governmental affairs on Old Terra, although it is no longer the financial mega-giant it once was.

A notable side effect of the emergence of the impeller drive and Warshawski sail was the emergence of both interstellar piracy and warfare. The region in which Manticore was settled had few close neighbors, and the colony government used some of their bank balance to purchase a squadron of Solarian-built destroyers, and hire the personnel to crew them.

It was well that they had that foresight. Less than two decades later, the nascent Manticore System Navy fought its first battle against advanced units of the Free Brotherhood, a wandering band of nomads and raiders that had begun migrating through the galaxy aboard a fleet of huge hyper transports accompanied by a veritable horde of light warships. Although no match for a well-organized multi-star imperium, the Free Brotherhood had wreaked havoc with many single-system polities and made the error of thinking it could do the same thing to Manticore.

The first battle occurred in the uninhabited Megan System, 8.4 light-years from Manticore, when two Manticoran frigates on a survey mission were attacked by advance scouts for the Brotherhood. MSNS *Triumph* was destroyed with all hands, but her gallant resistance bought time for the badly damaged MSNS *Defiant* to escape back to Manticore. When an aroused Manticore proved to be a much tougher customer than their normal victims, the Brotherhood moved towards the Haven Sector in search of easier prey.

The Plague Years
1464–1496 PD

The initial bid for Manticore had been so high for two reasons. One was that the G0/G2 binary was highly unusual—indeed, unique—in having no less than three planets suitable for human life. The second was that Manticore and Sphinx, the two habitable planets orbiting the G0 stellar component, were extremely Earth-like. Although each had its own unique biosphere, survey reports indicated that terrestrial life forms would find it unusually easy to adapt, and so it proved. Terran food crops did well and while the local flora and fauna could not provide all essential dietary elements, much of it was digestible by terrestrial life forms. Thus, terraforming requirements were extraordinarily modest, consisting of little more than the need to seed food crops and selected terrestrial grasses to support imported herbivores. Unfortunately, that very ease of adaptation had a darker side and Manticore proved one of the very few extra-terrestrial systems to possess microorganisms which could prey on humans.

The culprit was a pathogen—or, rather, a small family of pathogens—that were similar to human coronaviruses and had been missed by the original survey team. Some virologists argue that it was not, in fact, missed but evolved in the six centuries between the initial survey and the arrival of the colonists. Whatever the truth of the matter, the pathogen, when it combined with human coronaviruses, was deadly, producing a condition analogous to simultaneous virulent influenza and pneumonia in its victims. Worse, it proved resistant to all existing medical technology and over thirty years were to pass before a successful vaccine was found.

In those three decades, almost sixty percent of the original colonists died. Their Manticore-born children fared better against the disease, experiencing a generally less severe manifestation of it. Without the cushion provided by the MCT funds on Old Earth and the evolution of the Warshawski sail hypership, the entire expedition would almost certainly have come to grief.

The Plague was initially restricted to Manticore itself. Colonization of Sphinx continued but under rigorously applied quarantine conditions as a "fallback" position for the colony as a whole. Sphinx was seen as a "citadel" from which the star system might be resettled, should worse come to worst, after the Plague was finally defeated. Unfortunately, the quarantine procedures failed, and in 1463 PD, the Plague "jumped" to Sphinx with equally catastrophic consequences for the colonists living there.

Founding of the Star Kingdom
1471–1542 PD

Under the circumstances, the colony found itself in urgent need of additional homesteaders. These were recruited from Old Earth, another process made much easier by the existence of the MCT, but the original colonists, concerned about retaining control of their own colony, adopted a radically new constitution before opening their doors to immigration.

Roger Winton had been reelected continuously to the post of Planetary Administrator and served superbly throughout the early settlement period and the Plague crisis. He was now an elderly man whose wife and two Terran-born sons had died of the Plague but he remained vigorous and his Manticore-born daughter Elizabeth showed promise at least equal to his. At fifty-three, she was President of the Board of Directors, making her effectively vice-president of the colony, and one of the young colony's preeminent jurists. Because she had a large and thriving brood of second-generation Manticoran children and her family had served so outstandingly, a convention of colony shareholders converted the Corporation's elective board into a constitutional monarchy and crowned Roger Winton King Roger I of Manticore on August 1, 1471 PD.

It was a post he was to enjoy for only three years before his death in one of the secondary outbreaks of the Plague, but his daughter succeeded him as Queen Elizabeth I in a smooth and popular transfer of power. The House of Winton has ruled the Manticore System ever since. Simultaneously, the surviving "First Shareholders" and their descendants, who held title to vast tracts of land, acquired patents of nobility to go with their wealth and the hereditary aristocracy of Manticore was born. (It should be noted that the term "lands," under the original colonial charter—and, indeed, under current Manticoran law—refers to much more than actual land on the surface of one of the Manticore Binary System's habitable planets. It also references mineral rights in the system's asteroid belts, portions of the broadcast spectrum, etc.)

The new wave of immigrants arriving in the wake of the Plague comprised three distinct classes of citizens. Each immigrant received a land rights credit, the value of which precisely equaled the cost of a second-class passenger ticket from his planet of origin to Manticore. Any individual capable of paying his own passage received the full credit upon arrival. Those unable to pay their passages could draw upon MCT for a dollar amount equal to their land rights credit to cover the difference between their own resources and the cost of passage. An immigrant whose resources exceeded the cost of his passage could invest the surplus, paying fifty percent of the "book" price for additional land. The most affluent immigrants thus became "Second Shareholders," with estates which, in some cases, rivaled those of the original shareholders and entitled them to patents of nobility junior only to those of the existing aristocracy. Those immigrants who were able to retain their base land right or perhaps enlarge upon it slightly became "yeomen," free landholders with voting rights beginning one Manticoran year (1.73 T-years) after their arrival. Those who completely exhausted their land rights credit to buy passage to Manticore were known as "zero-balance" immigrants and did not become full citizens until such time as they had become well-enough established to pay taxes for five consecutive Manticoran years (8.7 T-years). While all Manticoran subjects were equal in the eyes of the law, whether enfranchised or not, there were distinct social differences between shareholders, yeomen, and zero-balancers. Even today there is greater prestige in claiming a yeoman as a first ancestor than in claiming a zero-balance ancestor. And, of course, direct descent from a full shareholder is considered by many to be the most prestigious of all.

Despite the apparent stratification of the Star Kingdom's social classes, life was for the most part quiet, peaceful and productive. Nearly every member of society was dedicated to rebuilding the personnel infrastructure laid waste by the Plague. The physical plant was essentially untouched, and the massive holes left in the workforce by the disease allowed and encouraged people to rise to their highest skill levels, thus creating a self-reinforcing meritocracy for the young star nation. This growth in the civilian side of the economy was not matched with growth on the military side, however, as the Star Kingdom attempted to avoid many of the ills of other star nations. Parliament was more willing to spend money on education then on weapons. For many years this was not a problem as the Star Kingdom was able to grow unmolested due to the absence of hostile neighbors. This idyllic state, however, would not last forever.

Birth of the Royal Manticoran Navy
1543–1584 PD

The Navy's losses to the Plague, especially among shipboard personnel, were even higher than among the population at large and making those losses good was a long, hard task, even with the assisted immigration programs. Moreover, a time of relative peace and concentration on other priorities left the Manticoran public ambivalent, at best, about the Navy, and the first of what would be many bitter debates in Parliament concerning the fate of the post-Plague Navy began.

The Manticoran System Navy's strength was at its nadir due to lack of personnel when it formally became the Royal Manticoran Navy in 1504 PD. Half of the newly reorganized RMN's ships were in mothballs, those on active service were severely undermanned, and the Navy had to fight both to demonstrate its relevance and for the funding to train an entirely new core of officers and enlisted personnel.

At the end of the aided immigration period, many of the service's remaining warships were almost a century old. With no local shipbuilding programs to replace aging units as they were withdrawn from service, a decline in ship strength was inevitable, and the Navy's total effective strength was less than two dozen ships and falling. Even authorized construction was often delayed, as in the case of the laydown of the new *Burgundy* class of system defense destroyers originally scheduled for 1536 PD. Given the Navy's parlous state, Parliament granted the last six *Triumph*-class battlecruisers (later reclassified as heavy cruisers) a last-minute reprieve by allowing the service to retain them for an additional decade beyond their originally scheduled decommissioning date in light of the *Burgundy*'s delayed delivery.

That reprieve proved extremely fortunate barely two years later when a force of mercenaries hired by Axelrod of Terra attacked the Manticore home system. The attack came without warning and the Navy was hard pressed to mount an effective defense. The RMN's officer corps, hobbled by inexperience and a pre-attack sense of apathy, managed to drive off the attackers in a short, bloody engagement, but losses were high. Indeed, the defense probably would have failed had Axelrod's mercenaries not expected to meet a far weaker force.

Examination of one of the ships captured after the battle demonstrated that Axelrod had been unaware of the delayed disposal of the battlecruisers, and the surprise of finding six battlecruisers still in commission proved fatal to their plans. The same examination also revealed the true reason for the attack: Axelrod had realized the Manticore Binary System was almost certainly home to a major wormhole junction. Nobody in Manticore had ever anticipated that possibility, but the Navy grasped both the potential benefits (and drawbacks) almost immediately. It took somewhat longer for Parliament and the general public to realize the same things, but the attack proved the need for a strong Navy and reawakened public support for the fleet. Enlistment rates exploded almost overnight and the first major naval buildup in over a century began only a few years later.

The Manticore Wormhole Junction
1585–1723 PD

While the possible presence of a wormhole had been public knowledge ever since the Battle of Manticore, actually locating it and charting it took many years. Although the existence of wormholes had been theorized as early as 1391 PD, the possibility that they might be used as a means of effectively instantaneous faster-than-light (FTL) travel had not been realized until 1429 and the first successful manned transit had not occurred until 1447. Despite the century of research between their discovery and Axelrod's attack on the Star Kingdom in 1543 PD, no other multi-terminus wormhole had ever been discovered. Wormhole theory and astrogation were still in the early stages of formulation, and most theoreticians had dismissed the possibility of such phenomena as possessing a very low order of probability. Even after the Manticore Wormhole Junction's discovery had forced a reconsideration of that belief, its sheer size and strength made the task of properly surveying it a formidable one.

As a result, the first transit did not occur until 1585 PD, when the survey ship *Pathfinder* successfully passed through the Junction and emerged from its terminus in the Beowulf System. This direct link into the very heart of the Solarian League provided an almost overnight boost to the Manticoran economy. Discovery of the Trevor's Star and Hennesy termini followed shortly thereafter, expanding the reach of the Star Kingdom's merchant marine far in excess of its own import requirements. Within a few years Manticore went from relying on Solarian hulls to bring it the most basic of necessities to building its own ships and establishing a dominant position in the galaxy's carrying trade, transporting finished goods and passengers from the Core Worlds to the Verge—especially to the rapidly growing Haven Sector—and raw materials back to the core worlds. The Junction fees, while small per ship, quickly accumulated. Because they were virtually pure profit, the Star Kingdom's economy rapidly improved.

In 1647, the survey ship *Artemis* made a first transit through the Gregor Terminus, opening up yet another shipping route, this one providing access to both the Andermani Empire and the Silesian Confederacy. Four T-years later, in 1651 PD, King Roger II signed the Cherwell Anti-Slavery Convention, pledging the Star Kingdom, along with the Republic of Haven and other signatories, to cooperate in suppressing the genetic slave trade and the RMN added that obligation to its missions. The Navy had been in the process of steady expansion over the last century in response to the need to protect the growing merchant fleet as well as the home system. The opportunities and the threats posed by the existence of the Junction were being analyzed, understood and incorporated into naval thinking and planning, and it was just as well that was true.

In 1660 PD, Manticore became embroiled with the Ranier System near the Hennesy Terminus of the Manticore Junction. Ranier was little more than a pirate enclave which had been raiding commerce around the relatively unsettled Phoenix Cluster. No local star system had the power to deal with the Ranierians—indeed, Phoenix itself had been forced to pay tribute to them—and the pirates saw no reason they should not extort the same payments from Manticoran merchantmen. Faced with this situation, the RMN deployed heavy escort forces and fought numerous cruiser actions against Ranierian pirates between 1660 and 1662 PD. This effort culminated in Commodore Edward Saganami's punitive expedition against Ranier itself with the first five modern Manticoran battlecruisers under his command, which ended the Ranier War by terminating the government of the Ranier System later that same year.

In 1669 PD, Manticore began amassing evidence of governmental connivance in the growing piracy problem in Silesia. At this time, the RMN still thought of itself as primarily a system defense fleet and Saganami's Ranier expedition as something of a flash in the pan that was unlikely to be repeated. Queen Adrienne felt differently, however, and attacks by those pirates on trade with that region via the Gregor Terminus were costing not simply ships but the lives of her subjects, as well. In 1670 PD, she directed her Admiralty to take steps to protect the Star Kingdom's commerce in Silesia.

At the time, the involvement of Solarian interests with the region's pirates and their targeted attacks on Manticoran shipping was not suspected. The Office of Naval Intelligence (ONI) would learn only later that Manpower Incorporated, apparently out of an awareness of how the RMN's enforcement of the Cherwell Convention would hamper its slave-trading (and other illegal) activities in Silesia, had begun providing covert support through its Solarian transtellar associates in an effort to drive Manticoran trade out of the Confederacy. Should the pirates fail to fully accomplish that task, they might at least keep the still small RMN too preoccupied convoying merchant ships to go slaver-hunting.

Unaware of Solarian involvement, Saganami, the hero of the Ranier War, was ordered to assemble a force for the purpose of proactive, search-and-destroy operations against pirates in the Silesian Sector. His operations were an unqualified success, destroying dozens of pirate ships and many bases before the Silesian government—with heavy technical support from Manpower—made a covert attempt to either destroy or discredit him. These efforts resulted in the Battle of Trautman's Star and then in the Battle of Carson, in which Saganami and the entire crew of his flagship were lost in the successful defense of a convoy against overwhelming odds.

The SKM's response to the Battle of Carson, unfortunately for the Silesians (and Manpower), was the exact opposite of the one they had anticipated. Instead of being horrified and convinced Silesia was simply too dangerous an area for Manticoran trade, the public—and the Royal Manticoran Navy—had been given an iconic hero. HMS Nike's last action became a rallying point which galvanized the entire Star Kingdom into wholehearted support for the Silesia mission. In the end, the RMN dispatched a complete squadron of battleships to systematically locate and destroy pirate bases throughout the entire eastern portion of the Confederacy.

Following the successful eradication of piracy in the region, the battleships—supported by two divisions of dreadnoughts—made a "courtesy call" on the Confederacy's capital system to escort the new Manticoran ambassador to Silesia. In the face of that visit, the Confederacy signed a most-favored star nation trade agreement with the SKM—and the Cherwell Convention—in 1674.

Even as Manticore's economy expanded following the discovery of the Junction, the Star Kingdom's constitutional system of government prospered, blessed by a series of strong monarchs and a steadily growing population base. The constitution contained a strong "Declaration of Fundamental Rights," but the franchise remained limited to citizens who had paid taxes for at least five consecutive Manticoran years. The policies encouraging immigration with land rights credits were ended after a period of fifty years, having served their purpose most effectively, and it was no longer possible for an immigrant to become an instant shareholder or gain the franchise immediately upon arrival. The steadily expanding economy and one of the best educational systems in the explored galaxy continued to offer vast opportunity for the talented and the hardworking, however, and the SKM had become a bustling meritocracy which welcomed those eager to take advantage of the opportunities it offered. The result was a remarkably stable society, despite the rapid growth of its economy and the upswing in immigration following the discovery of the Junction.

The only real challenge to the Manticoran monarchy came in 1721 PD with the so-called "Gryphon Uprising," which remains the most serious internal dissent the Star Kingdom has been forced to confront. Gryphon, the least congenial of the three habitable planets of the Manticore System, had, by far, the smallest share of First Shareholder families. The bulk of its aristocracy came from the Second Shareholders, who, for the most part, had substantially less credit than First Shareholders and so received smaller "Clear Grants" (that is, land to which clear title was granted prior to improvements by the owner/tenant). The Crown, however, had established the principle of "Crown Range" (land in the public domain and free for the use of any individual) to encourage emigration to Gryphon. By 1715 PD, the population of Gryphon had grown to the level set under the Crown Range Charter of 1490, so the Crown began phasing out the Crown Range, granting title on the basis of improvements made. That's when the trouble began. Yeomen who hoped to become independent ranchers, farmers, or miners claimed that the planetary nobility was using strong-arm tactics to force them off the land. Something very like a shooting war erupted between these "squatters" and "the children of shareholders." After two years of increasingly bloody unrest, the Gryphon Range Commission was established in 1717 with extraordinary police powers and a mandate to suppress open violence and reach a settlement. Its final finding was that there was a sound foundation to the yeomen's original complaints and the Manticoran Army, having pacified and stabilized the situation, then oversaw a closely regulated privatization of the Crown Range. There remains some hostility between small landholders and certain of the noble families, although it has become something of a tradition rather than a source of active hostility for the majority of the population.

The Calm Before the Storm
1723–1857 PD

The period from 1723 to 1857 was a time of relative peace for the Star Kingdom although events beyond its borders were later to have profound consequences for the House of Winton and all its subjects. In particular, the Republic of Haven's official transformation into the People's Republic of Haven, although of little apparent concern to Manticore, would eventually present the SKM with a fundamental threat to its very existence.

For two centuries, the RMN's attention was directed primarily to commerce protection and anti-slavery operations. As the power that claimed sovereignty over the Manticore Junction, the Star Kingdom felt a degree of responsibility to protect the trade of other systems as well as its own, and the RMN found itself involved in several punitive expeditions (none on the scale of the Silesia Mission). Although some of the weaker star nations in Manticore's growing sphere of interest resented the SKM's "interference" in their affairs, most also recognized how much their own peace and prosperity during this period owed to Manticore's protection against outside threats.

In 1752 PD Manticore fought a brief, almost bloodless, war with Trevor's Star over the punitive tariffs the near-bankrupt

San Martin government had decided to impose on all traffic through its terminus of the Junction in violation of The Treaty of 1590 PD. The RMN followed a deep-space approach with half its battle fleet rather than using the wormhole route the Trevor's Star government on San Martin had assumed it would use. The war ended with a single, sharp engagement around the planet. As part of the peace terms, Manticore, recognizing the fiscal extremity which had driven San Martin to levy its tariffs, negotiated a "most favored star system" trade agreement with them. Shaken by its experience, the war government of San Martin brought the Trevor's Star budget under control and greatly reduced welfare payments, and the system became one of the few systems of the Haven Sector that had a sound, thriving economy.

Following the "war" with Trevor's Star, Manticore returned to the normal affairs of expanding and protecting its commerce and the Junction's ever-growing traffic. Over the course of the next century, the Manticoran shipbuilding industry became the most efficient and productive in the known galaxy, and the advantages of the Junction also transformed the Star Kingdom into one of the galaxy's largest and most important financial hubs. The resulting prosperity raised Manticoran per-capita income to a level unsurpassed even by the Sol System itself, and in 1829, first-generation prolong reached the Star Kingdom, with all its promises and implications for the future.

In many ways, this period was the "Golden Age" of Manticore, yet clouds were gathering on the horizon. In 1793 the People's Republic of Haven issued a new constitution which made the Legislaturalists its hereditary rulers, and in 1794 the PRH, despite a huge and growing national debt, began a systematic, sustained military expansion. Initially described as a "public works project," the enlarged People's Navy's actual purpose became clear in 1846, with the PRH's first forcible conquests of neighboring star systems.

King Roger's Buildup
1857–1883 PD

In early 1856 PD, survey ships successfully charted the Junction terminus in what became known as the Basilisk System, 210 light-years to galactic north of Manticore, and about the same distance from Havenite space. The following year the aging Queen Samantha II passed away in her sleep leaving her son Crown Prince Roger to ascend to the throne as King Roger III, the first prolong recipient to take the crown, on September 24, 1857 PD.

King Roger III was an astute student of galactic history and politics and it had been clear to him even before 1846 that the PRH posed a threat not only to its immediate neighbors but to Manticore as well. The SKM's wealth must make it an attractive target, and as the only star nation in the Haven Sector with the potential to match its military power it was a threat which must be neutralized. With two termini (Trevor's Star and Basilisk) already within reach of the PRH's expanding military the Star Kingdom's vulnerability was obvious to him, as was its need to build up its ability to protect not only its commerce and the Home System, but also to defend the Junction itself.

Roger, a gifted politician as well as an experienced naval officer, realized the Conservative Association and the alliance of the Liberals and Progressives in both houses of Parliament would oppose any rapid and massive expansion of the fleet. Queen Samantha had begun a gradual buildup, largely on Roger's advice, despite that opposition, and following his own coronation, he immediately began building on that foundation. Aware that Manticore would never be able to match the sheer tonnage the far larger PRH could produce and unwilling to accept the plateaued, virtually stagnant state of galactic naval technology and doctrine, he adopted a two-pronged approach.

The first prong was an open, public increase in the Navy's size, expanding the capacity of the major naval yards aboard the space stations *Hephaestus*, *Vulcan* and *Weyland* and slowly growing the number of ships available to it despite a number of often ugly confrontations with the Opposition. The second, highly secret prong was what became known as "Project Gram," a highly covert R&D program designed to overcome the Star Kingdom's quantitative disadvantage by providing it with a decisive qualitative superiority.

Thus began a fifty-year "cold war" between Manticore and the People's Republic. Roger's strategy for winning that cold war largely depended on three of the Star Kingdom's greatest strengths: the quality of its educational system and the innovative R&D it supported; its enormous, far-reaching merchant marine (with ties to both the Navy and to various industrial cartels throughout the Star Kingdom); and the vast wealth generated by Manticoran economy and from the transit fees from the Junction. Despite those advantages and his own role as head of government, as well as head of state, Roger was never able to move as quickly and decisively as he would truly have preferred. He was a powerful and effective monarch, but it took him almost twenty T-years to build the decisive political majority he required in Parliament, and especially in the House of Lords. It is a testimonial to his abilities as statesman and politician that he did achieve it and that he passed it intact to his daughter upon his own untimely death.

Despite opposition from some members of the aristocracy, King Roger's buildup increased the RMN from a mere twelve ships of the wall at the time of his coronation to nearly eighty ships of the wall by his death.

Queen Elizabeth III
1883–1905 PD

Roger III was killed in a grav ski accident on August 24, 1883 PD. His daughter was crowned Queen Elizabeth III, supported by a regency until she reached the majority age of twenty-one T-years in 1886. Contrary to the expectations of many members of Parliament, Queen Elizabeth not only continued but accelerated her father's naval expansion programs.

Over the next twenty T-years, hostility between Manticore and Haven deepened, especially after the Havenite conquest of Trevor's Star gave the PRH control of that system's Junction terminus. During the same time period, as the stakes and the inevitability of an eventual military confrontation became ever clearer, the SKM's internal political struggles intensified. The isolationism of the Conservative Association, which had initially generated at least grudging support for the Navy's buildup, turned into a sense of profound alarm as the Conservatives recognized Elizabeth's grim determination to continue her father's work, further strengthen the Navy, and expand the anti-Haven Manticoran Alliance Roger had envisioned and begun. They came to view her efforts and her obvious readiness to confront the PRH openly as a dangerous and provocative *eagerness* to do so. Their alarm brought them into alliance with the Liberals and Progressives in their efforts to block or slow military appropriations. Fortunately, Elizabeth proved as skilled a politician as her father had been. She and her prime minister, the Duke of Cromarty, maintained and strengthened the partnership, based on Cromarty's own Centrists and the Crown Loyalists, which Roger had forged and continued their war preparations despite the Opposition's vociferous resistance.

The first shooting incident between Manticoran and Havenite forces occurred in the Basilisk System in 1900 PD with the destruction of the armed merchant ship PMSS *Sirius* by the light cruiser HMS *Fearless* (Commander Honor Harrington, commanding) following a failed attempt by Havenite operatives to incite a general native uprising on the planet of Medusa. A second incident occurred two T-years later in the Yeltsin's Star System, when RMN forces (once again under Captain Honor Harrington's command) successfully stymied a Havenite-backed attack on the planet Grayson by the planet of Masada in the neighboring Endicott System. These incidents further increased the tensions between the two star nations.

The next few years saw a hardening of positions as Haven expanded into neighboring systems while Manticore continued to consolidate its alliance of smaller single-system star nations along the front. Both sides built a number of fleet bases and established nodal concentrations of warships and both realized it was only a matter of time before a shooting war began.

The First Havenite War
1905–1918 PD

The long-awaited catastrophe began in 1905 when the People's Republic launched a deliberate, widespread, undeclared series of attacks on the Star Kingdom designed to draw the RMN into dispersing its strength in response. The initial attacks were followed with a two-pronged offensive directed against Yeltsin's Star and the RMN fleet station in the Hancock System. The intention was to strike both of these nodal points in overwhelming strength in order to defeat the forces stationed there in detail, destroying them and substantially weakening the Navy before the decisive campaign. Both attacks were thrown back with heavy Havenite casualties, however, and the shock of the PRH's first serious military defeats had profound consequences. Acting quickly and decisively in the wake of the disastrous news from the front, Rob S. Pierre and his Committee of Public Safety were able to assassinate Hereditary President Sydney Harris and overthrow the Legislaturalist regime in a bloody coup.

For the next ten years, the war raged. Initially the RMN won battle after battle against the demoralized Havenite Navy, which had lost the bulk of its experienced senior officers to the Pierre Coup and was badly hampered by the control of "people's commissioners" who had little or no understanding of naval warfare. The RMN made deep inroads into Havenite territory, but the People's Republic gradually recovered and the Manticoran advances began to slow. Finally in 1910 PD, the RMN's Sixth Fleet under the command of Admiral White Haven was able to liberate the Trevor's Star System, thus regaining control of all of the termini of the Junction. Three T-years later, in 1913, a new president, Jesus Ramirez, was elected under the restored, prewar San Martin Constitution following his escape from the prison planet of Cerberus in company with Admiral Honor Harrington, and in June of 1914, Trevor's Star sought annexation by the Star Kingdom of Manticore.

In the meantime, however, a brief period of stability in the otherwise volatile political situation in the PRH resulted in the nomination of Admiral Esther McQueen to the post of Secretary of War. Under McQueen's guidance, the PN scored its first offensive victories of the war, unsettling the Alliance and throwing its military plans into chaos.

The momentum shifted once again, however, when White Haven's Eighth Fleet moved on Barnett in the final push towards the Haven System itself. A new generation of weapons, the fruit of Roger III's Project Gram and the much later Project Ghost Rider, heralded the final turning point of the war, and McQueen's death after a failed coup attempt threw the PN once again into disarray.

Following these successes Queen Elizabeth made a state visit to Grayson. During the visit, she survived an assassination attempt that claimed the life of Prime Minister Cromarty. With his death, the Centrists' alliance with the non-aligned peers in the House of Lords (which had depended in no small part on Cromarty's personal relationships) fell apart amid fears that Elizabeth planned to reduce and restrict the power of the Lords. Baron High Ridge was able to form a government of Conservatives, Liberals, and Progressives who were hostile to the Crown, and the new government immediately accepted a Havenite offer of a ceasefire in place. Shortly after the ceasefire has been signed, a second coup against the Committee of Public Safety, this one led by Admiral Thomas Theismann, succeeded. Theismann restored the old, pre-Legislaturalist Constitution and proclaimed the restoration of the old Republic, but fighting between forces loyal to the Constitution and State Security warlords asserting their loyalty to the Pierre Revolution continued for several years.

For the next five T-years the High Ridge Government deliberately failed to reach a formal peace agreement with the newly restored Republic. More fearful of Elizabeth's reported plans to reform Parliament than of a technologically outclassed and still divided Haven, High Ridge and his allies preferred to maintain a technical state of war in order to avoid a general parliamentary election and to justify the maintenance of wartime taxation rates. Taking advantage of that revenue stream, High Ridge and his allies diverted funding from the military into their "Building the Peace" initiative, which was intended to bolster the voting strength of their own parties when elections were finally held.

In 1917, a new Junction terminus was located and surveyed, linking the Manticore Binary System to the Talbott Cluster on the far side of the Solarian League.

Birth of an Empire and the Second Havenite War
1918 PD–PRESENT

The almost immediate request by the residents of most of the star nations in the Cluster to join the Star Kingdom, mirroring that of the San Martinos after the Trevor's Star's liberation, necessitated a modification of the Star Kingdom into the Star Empire. The process has been neither simple nor peaceful, however, and may well pose an existential threat to Manticore's very existence.

High Ridge and Edward Janacek, his First Lord of the Admiralty, had believed that Manticore's unchallengeable military lead meant they could not only negotiate in bad faith with Haven but simultaneously draw down the military to fund their efforts to buy public support at the polls.

They were incorrect.

Their fundamental misjudgment was made infinitely worse by a massive intelligence failure which permitted the Republic of Haven to secretly build an entirely new navy, with weapons which largely closed the gap between its own capabilities and those of Manticore. Faced with the evidence of the Republic's new military capability when that navy's existence was finally revealed, the High Ridge Government and Janacek Admiralty scrambled desperately to retrieve the situation, but events had taken on a momentum of their own. Following an acrimonious diplomatic exchange in which each side accused the other of negotiating in bad faith and of falsifying diplomatic correspondence, Haven renewed hostilities. Operation Thunderbolt, the Republic of Haven Navy's initial series of attacks, was devastatingly effective, allowing Haven to recover virtually every system—except Trevor's Star—which Manticore had taken in the First Havenite War. The same offensive destroyed hundreds of ships being built for the RMN, inflicted heavy losses on many of Manticore's alliance partners, and brought down the High Ridge Government in disgrace.

Following High Ridge's fall, the new Grantville Government under William Alexander (newly created Baron Grantville and current leader of the Centrist Party) took up the heartbreaking task of rebuilding the fleet and its technological edge. In an attempt to even the odds, the Star Empire entered into an agreement for the Andermani Empire to join the Alliance and to end the ongoing piracy, civil unrest, and loss of life in Silesia by partitioning the Confederacy between Manticore and the Empire.

In the three years since the resumption of hostilities, the war has shown no sign of abating. Indeed, it has become even more threatening with the Star Empire's discovery of direct Solarian interference in the annexation of the Talbott Cluster. Captain Aivars Terekhov's preemptive attack on the Republic of Monica, a Solarian ally, in February 1921 PD, prevented a Monican attempt to seize the entire Cluster and the Lynx Terminus of the Manticoran Wormhole Junction as a Solarian proxy, but only at the risk of open hostilities with the Solarian League, as well as the Republic. The thought of confronting the enormous power of the Solarian League Navy is somewhat mitigated by the evidence that the SLN has lagged far behind the navies of the Haven Sector in terms of weapons technology, but the League remains the largest and most powerful star nation ever to have existed.

Within the Haven Sector itself, however, the pace and scale of combat has only grown still more intense. While Haven held a huge initial quantitative edge at the time it launched Thunderbolt, the technological edge still belonged to Manticore. Although the gap had become far narrower than it had been at the time of Earl White Haven's offensive in Operation Buttercup, it began to widen once more as weapons research and production which had been stifled under High Ridge and Janacek was urgently resumed. The results of that resumption became manifest in the RMN's Cutworm Offensives and, especially, the introduction of the Apollo FTL missile control systems.

Government

Constitutional monarchies come in many varieties, with both written and unwritten constitutions, and with monarchs which possess widely varying degrees of actual power. For its part, the constitution of the Star Empire grants its empress very broad authority indeed.

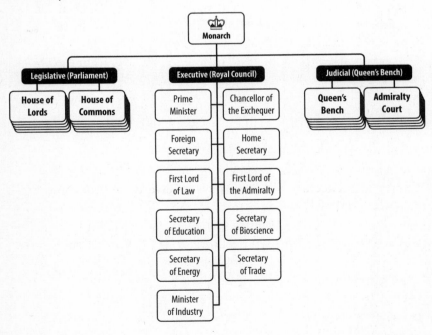

For example, the Constitution grants the Monarch the power to function as both head of state and head of government. Although the written Constitution enshrines a cabinet form of government, headed by a Prime Minister, the *unwritten* portion of the Constitution established during Queen Elizabeth I's reign (1489–1521 PD) holds that the Cabinet is the Monarch's servant and serves at his or her pleasure. The written Constitution provided her with several weapons which aided significantly in her ability to establish that point. Among those weapons, the Constitution specifically provides that when Parliament is hung and no party in the House of Lords can form a majority or coalition government, the Monarch may choose the Prime Minister and instruct him to form a minority government. In fact, under a strict interpretation of the written Constitution, the Monarch is not required to accept a Prime Minister even if he commands a majority in the Lords. In practice, that majority could refuse to support any other candidate for the office, creating an impasse which would paralyze government completely.

The supreme legislative body of the Star Empire will be the Imperial Parliament, which will meet in a new Imperial Hall of Parliament in Landing on Manticore. Based closely on the structure of the original Parliament of the Star Kingdom, but with membership drawn from the entire Empire, the Imperial Parliament is still in the early stages of formation. In the meantime, the Parliament of the Old Star Kingdom continues to act in a caretaker role for the Empire as a whole.

Parliament is bicameral, with an upper house (the House of Lords) and a lower house (the House of Commons). The Constitution requires the Prime Minister to be a member of the House of Lords (and hence a peer) who must receive the endorsement of a majority of his fellow peers to hold the office. This provides him with a base of political power which a wise Monarch does not challenge, since the Crown can accomplish little without the support of Parliament. As a consequence, despite the Monarch's status as head of government and despite the Crown's power to dismiss a Prime Minister at will, successful governance requires a partnership between Monarch and Prime Minister. The consequences when the Crown finds itself at odds with a Prime Minister not of its choosing, backed by a powerful majority in the Lords, can be disastrous, as demonstrated by the recent High Ridge Government.

Monarch

The present Monarch is Elizabeth III. Until late 1921 PD, Manticore was officially a kingdom and the Monarch was King or Queen. After the incorporation of the Talbott Quadrant and the formation of the Star Empire, the monarchy adopted the new title of Empress or Emperor while retaining the title of Queen or King of the Old Star Kingdom.

The constitution acknowledges a wide range of executive powers the Monarch may exercise without regard to elected government, collectively referred to as the "Royal Prerogative." Royal Prerogative is concerned with several areas critical to the government of the Star Empire, including the conduct of foreign affairs, defense, and national security. Most monarchs maintain the tradition of soliciting advice from the Prime Minister and the Cabinet, however, and rarely exercise Royal Prerogative in direct opposition to the will of the government.

Parliament

The Star Kingdom's House of Lords is the senior and upper house of Parliament. Membership is attained by appointment or letters patent. Membership is composed of three groups: the senior ranked hereditary peers, their immediate heirs, and life peers upon whom voting rights have been bestowed. All three groups may also designate a representative, of their choice, if they are unable to fulfill their rights and duty to the house. (The precise basis upon which peers in the new, Imperial House of Lords will be selected by previously independent star nations with no preexisting hereditary aristocracy is in the process of resolution at this time.) Membership of the Lords as of 1921 PD is 587, and the total membership may be increased by a maximum of only ten percent between general elections of the House of Commons, no newly created peer may assume his or her seat until after the first general election following his elevation, and grants of peerages may be confirmed only by the House of Commons. (Note, however, that the majority of these peerages are also granted "cadet" seats, held by the heir apparent to the peerage. Holders of cadet seats have no vote in their own right in the Lords but act as proxies for the actual peer in his or her absence.) The peers may vote to exclude any peer for any reason and at their own discretion, however.

The Prime Minister must come from among the peers in the House of Lords and command a majority within it. Arguably, an exception was made to this rule when William Alexander became Prime Minister, since although he had been named Baron Grantville he had not yet taken his seat in the Lords as Baron Grantville. The Queen, however, argued that since he had held the cadet seat in the Lords for his brother, Earl White Haven, for many years, he was *de facto* a member of the Lords and so eligible on that basis until he assumed his seat in his own right. Under the circumstances, no one was inclined to dispute her on this point.

When the Constitution was adopted, converting shareholders into peers of the realm, the membership of the House of Lords was fixed at fifty, with seats granted based on the order in which the original colonists had invested in the expedition. That is, a "baron" who had been among the very early investors (or whose parent or grandparent had been) would be seated in the Lords in preference to a "duke" whose investment had come later. This rule of seniority within the Lords continues to this day, which helps to explain the influence of Michael Janvier, who was "merely" Baron of High Ridge but whose direct ancestor had been only the sixth individual to invest in the colony expedition. In the years since the founding, the number of seats in both the Lords and the Commons have been adjusted several times to reflect the SKM's growing population base, but even today, not all peers hold seats in the House of Lords, by any means.

The old colonial territorial and administrative districts were also transformed at the time the Constitution was ratified. The existing geographically defined units were retained, but they became duchies, rather than the previous "districts" and the senior noble in each county became its hereditary governor. This created some problems, since the senior peer in one existing "duchy" might be an earl or even a baron, rather than a duke. The constitutional solution adopted was to create the title of "magister," which applies to the senior peer (and governor) of any duchy, regardless of his hereditary rank. Although one magister may take precedence over another when seated in the House of Lords, all magisters are equal before the law when acting as the administrators of their duchies.

The House of Commons is the junior and lower house of Parliament. Unlike the House of Lords, members of the House of Commons must sit for reelection every four T-years, although the ruling government may call an election anytime earlier. General elections may also be suspended in declared times of emergency, supported by a two-thirds majority in each house, or in time of war, at the discretion of the Government. For elections to the Commons, the planets of the Star Kingdom are divided into constituencies known as boroughs, with one Member of Parliament representing each borough. Membership in the House of Commons is limited to no more than eight hundred, apportioned on a population basis, and fights over boundaries when reapportionment requires boroughs to be redrawn have been among the most bitter of the Star Kingdom's domestic political battles. Peers cannot stand in elections in the House of Commons, although they may resign their titles of nobility in order to seek election.

Prior to 1919 PD, the House of Lords had the power of the purse, meaning that only it could introduce a finance or budget bill. The House of Commons could propose and pass amendments to the bill, but the House of Lords was empowered to strip them out again without the need for reconciliation, effectively relegating the House of Commons to an advisory role on budgetary matters. The House of Lords would then conduct a vote on the final bill which, if passed, would become law (subject to negation by royal prerogative). This constitutional provision was part of the deliberate effort to see to it that the original colonists and their descendants retained effective political control of the Star Kingdom and, in the view of many Manticorans (including the House of Winton) had long outlived its usefulness by the twentieth century PD. After 1919, the Lords lost the right to create budget or financial bills, which was transferred to the House of Commons, although the Lords have the right to amend and the upper house's assent is necessary to the final passage of any such bill introduced by the Commons.

Political Parties

The House of Lords was intended by the framers of the Constitution to be the most powerful organ of government in the Star Kingdom. While it has been the scene of many bitter factional fights over the centuries, historically it was not marked by the creation of formal political parties, although that has been gradually changing for some time now. Most (though by no means all) Manticoran aristocrats have possessed a fairly strong sense of *noblesse oblige*; those who have not, as exemplified by Baron High Ridge and his allies, are among the most self-centered and intolerant in the known universe. The aristocratic parties which have existed have tended to be working alliances of individuals with the same basic interests, but those alliances also tend to be flexible, elastic, and subject to change. This approach to party and faction has been changing for some time now, but the tradition of *ad hoc* alliances irrespective of formal party labels remains very much alive.

Formal political parties have always been very much a part of the House of Commons, on the other hand, and over the last hundred years or so, the parties of the Commons have been finding members in the House of Lords, as well, as alliances are forged across the house boundaries. The more powerful parties are the Centrist Party and its normal ally, the Crown Loyalists; the Liberal Party; the Conservative Association; the Progressive Party; and the so-called "New Men" Party. Traditionally, members of the Commons, as the peers, have been expected to vote their own consciences if they find themselves at odds with their parties' positions. A more collectivist approach, with tighter party discipline, has developed out of the bitter political battles marking Roger III and Elizabeth III's military buildup prior to the First Havenite War, but personal conviction is still expected to trump partisan politics on critical votes.

Ironically, it is not at all uncommon for the leader of a "party of the Commons" to be a member of the House of Lords. The reason for this apparent contradiction becomes evident when one considers the Lords' historical ascendency over the Commons. A party which sought to wield power or influence national policy absolutely required allies, at the very least, in the upper house, and the fact that peers need not stand for election gave them a huge advantage in terms of political tenure and effective power. By the same token, members of the Lords have come to recognize that they require allies in the Commons, which helps to explain the gradual "bleed over" of the parties of the Commons into the Lords.

Royal Council (Cabinet)

The Royal Council is the formal title of the Cabinet of the Star Kingdom of Manticore, although it is seldom used. The Royal Council functions as the executive branch of the Star Kingdom of Manticore. As of 1921 PD, membership includes:

Prime Minster: Lord William MacLeish Alexander, Baron Grantville
Chancellor of the Exchequer (Deputy Prime Minister): Lady Francine Maurier, Countess Mourncreek
Foreign Secretary: Sir Anthony Langtry
Home Secretary: Sir Tyler Abercrombie
First Lord of Law: Lord Sir Llywelyn St. John
First Lord of the Admiralty: Lord Hamish Alexander-Harrington, Earl White Haven
Secretary of Education: Lady Dame Melanie Howard, Countess Greenlake
Secretary of Bioscience: Dame Penelope Singh
Secretary of Energy: Dame Karen Witherings
Secretary of Trade: Bruce Wijenberg
Minister of Industry: Lady Dame Charlotte FitzCummings, Countess Maiden Hill

Judicial System

The Star Empire's judicial system, commonly referred to as the Queen's Bench, is a common-law system, which means that courts rely on the precedents set in past cases (*stare decisis*) unless and until there is a compelling reason for changing the law judicially. The courts are courts of general jurisdiction and may hear cases in both law (money damages) and equity (orders of the court) and are an adversarial system for both civil and criminal trials. All search warrants require the signature of a judge and criminal defendants are constitutionally entitled to a presumption of innocence.

The original structure of the court system was specified by the articles of incorporation of the Manticore Colony, Ltd. This structure was local courts, then planetary courts, then district courts with the Board of Directors as the *de facto* supreme court.

When the Constitution altered the corporate structure into a constitutional monarchy, the form and rules were retained but the names of the courts were changed. In addition, the highest court, the Queen's Bench Court, was vested with the power of final review of judicial decisions from below.

The Shareholders' Court (an ancient term carried over from the original articles of incorporation) is the first level of the Star Empire's court system and is organized on a duchy level. Misdemeanor criminal cases are heard in this court, as are most civil actions. The rule in civil actions for damages is that the loser is required to pay court costs as a way of reducing frivolous lawsuits. Judges for the Shareholders' Courts in any county are nominated by the County Magister, but final approval is given by the County Parliament. Local law and procedures govern the Shareholders' Courts as long as the law in question does not conflict with or is not superseded by national law. Within the duchy or county, the local lord has the power of commutation and pardon.

Parallel to the Shareholders' Courts is the Magister's Bench in each county. These, like the Shareholders' Courts, are courts of general and original jurisdiction. The difference is that in criminal cases, felonies are heard by these courts while in civil actions, these courts hear only cases where the amount in controversy exceeds a certain figure (which varies depending on the local jurisdiction).

The Duke's Bench is the second level of the Star Empire's court system. It is organized the same as the Magister's Bench but on a planetary level. Judges to the Duke's Bench are nominated by the planetary grand duke or duchess and confirmed by the Planetary Parliament.

The Crown District Court is the third level of Star Empire's court system. All serious felony criminal cases that fall under Crown law, as opposed to County or Planetary law, are heard in this court, as are all cases that have been appealed from the lower courts. These courts may also, on motion from a party, accept jurisdiction where there is a conflict between which local law should be applied to a case. They may, however, decline jurisdiction in any such case. A county will usually, depending on size, have four district courts. The senior judge in the Crown District Court is called the Chief Judge and her headquarters is in the capital of the county her district serves. Crown District courts are also organized on a county level, but judges are selected by the Monarch, with advice from the Prime Minister, rather than the County Magister.

The fourth level of the Star Empire's courts consists of the Crown Appellate Courts. In the Manticore Binary System, they are organized on a planetary level. These courts are purely appellate in nature and accept cases appealed from the Crown District Courts. They do not accept cases appealed from the Duke's Bench except in matters touching upon the constitutionality of planetary statutes. The number of circuits within each appellate court depend on the volume of cases handled. Judges are selected by the Monarch, with advice from the Prime Minister, and these courts sit *en banc* with three judges hearing each case.

The Queen's Bench refers to both the most senior court in the Star Empire and to the overall court system, depending upon context. The Queen's Bench *Court*, however, is the final level of appeal. The one and only Queen's Bench Court is seated in Landing City on Manticore. The Queen's Bench Court hears all cases that have been appealed by all courts below and is also the court of original jurisdiction for questions from the Monarch. The Bench consists of the eleven most senior judges in the Star Empire, known as the "Law Lords." They are selected by the Monarch and confirmed by the House of Lords. As members of the Queen's Bench Court, they are organized by seniority on the bench as Lords of Law and any hereditary peers are barred from the House of Lords during their tenure on the bench in order to prevent conflicts of interest when laws come before the Bench for review. The Second Lord of law (sometimes also referred to as the Lord Chief Justice) is the head of the Bench and the senior judge in the Star Empire. The First Lord of Law is a member of the Royal Council and serves as the Star Kingdom's minister of justice.

The Admiralty Court is a special court for the merchant shipping of the Star Empire. The Admiralty Court deals with shipping disputes such as collisions, salvage, carriage of cargo and limitation of tonnage of cargo. It also handles letters of marque and the awarding of prize money to warships and privateers.

The more recently added territories (Trevor's Star, Lynx, Talbott Cluster and Silesia) retain their own legal systems until they can be incorporated into the Queen's Bench system. While plans have not been finalized, it is likely that the local courts will retain their original jurisdiction as the first level of the system with the addition of Crown District Courts and Crown Appellate Courts. The only requirement imposed on the local courts is that their rulings cannot conflict with the law of the Star Empire once the systems have been formally incorporated.

Lawyers in the Star Empire are authorized to appear in any of the courts in the Star Empire with the exception of the Queen's Bench Court, which requires a separate certification. There is no division among lawyers who are authorized to perform any legal work, including litigation. The entry-level degree is a Bachelor of Laws (LLB). Academically-minded attorneys can achieve two more degrees, a Master of Laws (LLM) and a Juris Doctor (JD).

Imperial Government

Over the fifty-five T-years between the Basilisk Act of Annexation in 1867 and the addition of the Talbott Quadrant in 1921 PD, the Star Kingdom of Manticore has grown from a single system polity to a sprawling star empire. The governmental structure that had sufficed for a kingdom with a limited area was clearly inadequate for a widely dispersed empire, and Queen Elizabeth III and the Grantville Government were determined from the beginning not to repeat the mistakes of the Solarian League. They believed that empire needed to be "governed," rather than maintained by a bureaucracy that simply regulated, and they have set up a new, imperial constitution to do just that.

The Basilisk System, Trevor's Star, and the Lynx System were added directly to the original "Old Star Kingdom" which had previously consisted solely of the Manticore Binary System, because each of them is a single star system with or directly associated with a terminus of the Manticore Wormhole Junction. All of them were already members of the Star Kingdom when the Talbott Quadrant requested membership, even though Lynx predated the request by only a few months. The fact that each lies only a single Junction transit from Manticore makes their inclusion into a single unit of government feasible.

The Imperial Parliament is to be permanently seated on Manticore. At present, each member system will be permitted to send five peers to the House of Lords, with each federal unit (Old Star Kingdom,

Talbott Quadrant, and any subsequently added units) choosing the criteria for selection. All members of the Imperial House of Lords will hold lifetime peerages. Membership in the Imperial House of Commons must be elective, by all taxpayers of the planet for which he or she is seated, and seats will be apportioned on the basis of population. The total number of seats to be apportioned will be equal to twenty per star system, and each system, regardless of population, is guaranteed at least one seat. For the first fifteen years, seventy-five percent of the seats will be elected by the Old Star Kingdom. This will decrease to sixty percent after another fifteen years and then twenty-five percent after another twenty-five years. Thereafter, population will be the sole determinant.

When the Talbott Quadrant's draft constitution was ratified by the Old Kingdom's Parliament, the Quadrant's member systems were officially incorporated into the Star Empire of Manticore. Each system may retain its original form of government, so long as it enacts no laws that conflict with the law of the Star Empire; it may at its discretion create laws that afford greater citizen protections, but it may not infringe upon those set forth in the imperial constitution. A Quadrant Parliament has likewise been created to address Quadrantwide concerns on a "local" level, with the Imperial Governor permanently seated in the Quadrant Cabinet as the Empress' direct representative. Any individual member system of the Quadrant may grant the franchise on whatever basis it chooses, but all citizens are accorded the franchise for Quadrant elections if they can show that they have been citizens of the territory for at least five T-years. The exercise of the imperial franchise is dependent upon the payment of taxes, as per the original Manticoran constitution. The Manticoran dollar is the official currency and there are to be no internal trade restrictions or barriers. Member star systems' local court systems have been left intact, although they are required to amend local law as necessary to meet the requirements of imperial law. Quadrantwide courts are in the process of establishment, with Crown appointment of judges nominated by the Quadrant Parliament. Imperial judges will be appointed by the Crown from candidates nominated by the Imperial Parliament.

It is anticipated that the Silesian territories will officially join the Star Empire on a similar basis and will remain administered provinces until officially incorporated. Sentiment among the general population is highly favorable to inclusion in the Star Empire, due in no small part to the Silesian Confederacy's chaotic and bloody history and its people's familiarity with the Royal Manticoran Navy's longstanding peacekeeping role in Silesia.

House of Winton

The House of Winton can trace an unbroken line to the founder and CEO of the original Manticore colony expedition, and the first ruler of the Star Kingdom, Roger Winton I. Winton was the principal financier of the colony expedition and indisputably held the largest share of the initial land entitlements. However, quite intentionally, he took a large proportion of the least desirable real estate when the aristocracy was formed, in order to provide better lands for the other new aristocrats and additional lands for the new immigrants. From all accounts, this act was in keeping with his general conduct and has set the tone of the relationship between the Winton family and the Star Kingdom ever since.

Although not all monarchs have been equally capable or equally beloved (during the middle years of Roger II's reign, for example, the Crown's popularity was extraordinarily low), the Winton dynasty has always taken the long view, and this attitude has been, for the most part successfully, passed down through the generations. They have enshrined the adage that "privilege demands responsibility," and that philosophy has earned them the deep trust of their subjects. Combined with a deliberate policy of partnering with the House of Commons to balance the power of the Lords (in whose favor the Constitution was originally slanted) and the Constitutional requirement that the heir to the throne wed a commoner, it is a significant reason for the success of the Monarchy over the years.

LINE OF SUCCESSION

The Crown passes with each generation to the eldest child of the monarch upon death. The line of succession goes through the monarch's children before moving up to any of the monarch's living siblings.

Perhaps one of the most farsighted provisions of the Star Kingdom's Constitution was the requirement that the heir marry a commoner rather than a member of the aristocracy. The fact that in every generation "the Crown marries the Commons" is seen as a renewal of the social contract between monarch and subjects and insures that the commoners' perspective is always represented at the very head of this aristocratic form of government. In addition, this strengthens the Star Kingdom as a whole by the fashion in which it underscores the "open" nature of the Manticoran aristocracy.

The line of Wintons and their reign dates has progressed as follows (note: the symbol to the left of some names indicates those members of the House of Winton who have been adopted by a treecat):

	King Roger I	1485–1489 PD
	Queen Elizabeth I	1489–1521 PD
	King Michael I	1521–1542 PD
	King Edward	1542–1544 PD
	Queen Elizabeth II	1544–1601 PD
	King David	1601–1642 PD
	King Roger II	1642–1669 PD
🐾	Queen Adrienne	1669–1681 PD
	King William I	1681–1690 PD
🐾	King William II	1690–1741 PD
🐾	Queen Caitrin	1741–1762 PD
🐾	Queen Samantha	1762–1785 PD
	King Michael II	1785–1802 PD
🐾	Queen Samantha II	1802–1857 PD
🐾	King Roger III	1857–1883 PD
🐾	Queen Elizabeth III	1883 PD–present

The introduction of prolong into the Star Kingdom in 1829 PD has had—or ought to have had—a profound effect on the royal family, giving them not only longer reigns, but also a greater amount of time to prepare their heirs. In the case of Roger III, the first monarch to have received prolong, however, untimely death prevented him from taking full advantage of those benefits.

Fortunately, he had been careful to involve Elizabeth in affairs of state from a remarkably young age despite the fact that he anticipated a far longer reign, and his preparation was strongly tested after her youthful ascension to the throne upon his death. She has now reigned in her own right for thirty-seven T-years, with the expectancy of at least another century on the throne, and she has been training her own heir since his fourteenth birthday.

ROYAL FAMILY
1921 PD

The Winton dynasty has a strong tradition of its young scions going into public service. The normal career choice is military, usually with the RMN, or foreign office. Those with the inclination have joined the clergy. Public service among the young family members is seen as a way of preventing the next generation from becoming royal loafers, instilling in them a sense of duty, and giving them a satisfying personal career rather than condemning them to live solely in the shadow of the throne.

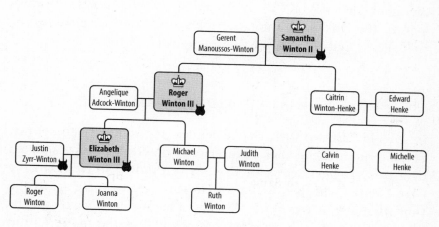

The present head of the Winton family, Queen Elizabeth III, is married to Prince Consort Justin Zyrr-Winton and bonded to the treecat Ariel. Zyrr, a Marine veteran and successful research scientist as well as prince consort, is the human companion of the treecat Monroe, who had originally adopted Elizabeth's father, Roger Winton III. Together, Elizabeth and Justin have two children, Crown Prince Roger Winton and Princess Joanna Winton.

Elizabeth's brother, Prince Michael Winton, Duke of Winton-Serisburg, an officer in the RMN, was still a midshipman when he met his wife, Judith, a kidnapped Grayson who had escaped her tyrant husband with other Masadan women and her unborn daughter Ruth. Michael and Judith married, and Michael adopted Ruth, who was raised as a Royal Princess. As a young adult, Ruth played a large part in the formation of the Kingdom of Torch, a new nation of freed slaves, and currently serves as the head of the new nation's Intelligence Service.

Angelique Adcock, the Queen Mother, is the widow of King Roger III, and has largely retired from public life. Although when she and Roger married Manticoran society gossip referred to her as the "Poor Little Beggar Maid," she was a well-loved Queen Consort for twenty-five years.

Elizabeth's uncle Edward Winton-Henke, the Earl of Gold Peak, and cousin Calvin were both killed in the Cromarty Assassination, leaving only her aunt, Caitrin Winton-Henke (Dowager Countess of Gold Peak), and cousin, Michelle Henke (Countess Gold Peak) alive on her father's side of the family. In case of the untimely death of Elizabeth III, next in line of succession for the monarchy will be Crown Prince Roger, followed by Princess Joanna, the Duke of Winton-Serisburg, the Dowager Countess of Gold Peak, and the current Countess of Gold Peak.

WINTONS AND TREECATS

In 1651 PD, Crown Princess Adrienne, on a state visit to Sphinx, became the first member of the House of Winton to be adopted by a treecat when Seeker of Dreams of the Red Leaves Dancing Clan bonded with her. Seeker of Dreams' approximate age at the time of adoption was thirty T-years, and Adrienne gave him the human name Dianchect, after a Greek god of the hunt. Within hours of the adoption, he foiled an attempt on the Crown Princess' life. Adrienne's father, King Roger II, who had been favoring changes which would strip treecats of many of their rights, abruptly changed his position and helped enact the Treecats Rights Bill later in his reign.

Although Seeker of Dreams was the first treecat to adopt a member of the Winton Royal Family, seven out of nine of the ruling monarchs since Queen Adrienne have been adopted by treecats. Various "treecat conspiracy theories" have been suggested, but having an adoption bond has become a tradition in the House of Winton. The family quickly discovered that a treecat bond offers the prospective monarch a confidant whose loyalty and trustworthiness are beyond question, a sense of balance and companionship, and a bodyguard who not only will fight to the death in his human companion's defense but is unfailingly capable of identifying any assassin who comes within range of his telempathic sense. Treecats are also considered a powerful aid to character building in young humans, since it is impossible to lie to or deceive a 'cat in any way and the disapproval of one's bonded companion is a punishment more severe than any other being could inflict. That early training in honesty has stood generations of Manticoran monarchs—and thus the entire Star Kingdom—in good stead, all of which explains the reason Crown Princes and Princesses are sent to Sphinx on frequent state visits in middle and late adolescence in the hope that they, too, will find the stability a treecat bond offers.

Although the first treecat adoption of a member of the House of Winton was quite by accident, eventually the clans themselves realized that having a treecat friend at court was to their benefit. This adoption trend also allowed them to help defend the two-legs who were helping to protect their society. Memory singers actively passed memories of the mind-glows of the prospective heirs around the clans, so that treecats who felt they might feel the call to bond might make themselves known. By the time of Elizabeth III, the treecats had begun appearing at the landing area in Sphinx when the heir arrived, to interview the heir for bonding.

William I, son of Queen Adrienne, was not adopted by a treecat because neither the treecats nor the Wintons had fully realized the benefits of the treecat bond at the time. Michael II, due to his rare and potentially fatal allergic reactions, was almost unable to travel, seldom left Mount Royal Palace, and never visited Sphinx, which kept him from being adopted as well.

People

Manticore is an aristocratic society but it is also a meritocracy, with great respect for the idea of people, selected on the basis of their ability, holding positions of power and authority. The aristocracy is not closed to new members, since the system was intentionally designed to encourage new membership based on talent and achievements.

Because membership in the Manticoran aristocracy is always open to new members based on personal ability and service to the Star Empire, Manticoran aristocrats attach little stigma to those born outside the ranks of the nobility. By the same token, because admission to the aristocracy is so open, very little friction exists between Manticoran social classes, in direct contrast to many another overtly aristocratic societies. There are exceptions to this general rule, of course, and when they occur, they tend to be extreme.

Manticoran culture as a whole is both traditional and innovative, and this unique world view has allowed them to remain flexible and grow as a society without losing sight of their roots. Historically, Manticore has always been a small nation, and some observers fear the sudden influx of new member systems may have an adverse effect on the longstanding stability of the Star Empire's social matrix.

Adcock-Winton, Angelique

Angelique Adcock immigrated to Manticore from the Maslow System with her family as a child while still young enough to receive first-generation prolong. Married to the future King Roger III prior to his ascension to the throne, she served her adopted star nation well but was never truly comfortable in such a public role. Following Roger's death and her daughter's coronation, Queen Mother Angelique chose to move back to Gryphon, where she lives in relative seclusion from the public eye as an instructor at the Gryphon Planetary University's School of Silviculture.

Adcock, Jonas (deceased)
Fourth Space Lord, Royal Manticore Navy

Jonas Adcock, brother of Queen Mother Angelique and uncle of Elizabeth Winton III, was too old for prolong treatments when his family immigrated to Manticore from the Maslow system. After graduating eighth in his class from the Royal Manticoran Naval Academy, Adcock played a pivotal (although deliberately understated) role in King Roger's naval buildup.

Adcock was instrumental in creating sweeping changes in the face of modern warfare throughout his tenure at BuWeaps both as Fourth Space Lord and head of the Weapons Development Board. The Ghost Rider project, LAC carrier, and pod superdreadnought were but a few of the projects brought to fruition on his watch. An outstanding synthesist rather than a researcher in his own right, his most outstanding contributions to the Manticoran Navy lay in his ability to visualize new possibilities and to create an environment in which "cutting edge" researchers like Sonja Hemphill literally revolutionized warfare under his guidance and direction. Jonas Adcock died in 1913 PD while serving as Fourth Space Lord.

Alexander, Lord William, Baron Grantville
Prime Minster, Star Empire of Manticore

William Alexander, the younger brother of Hamish Alexander and former Lord of the Exchequer under the Cromarty Government, became the Prime Minister and Baron of Grantville after the fall of the High Ridge Government. Although he possesses his own share of the famed "Alexander temper," his keen political insight and many years of experience at the highest level of Manticoran politics have made him an outstanding success as a wartime prime minister.

Alexander-Harrington, Lady Emily, Countess White Haven

Emily Alexander-Harrington, noted holodrama actress and senior wife of Hamish Alexander, suffered a full spinal severance in an aircar accident in 1862 PD. As she was unable to accept regeneration, much of the damage was unrepairable, leaving her confined to a life-support chair since the accident and effectively paralyzed below the neck, although she has retained seventy-five percent usage of one hand.

Lady Emily now works as a writer and producer in the Manticoran entertainment industry. She is regarded as a leading historian and a keen political analyst, especially in the role of semi-official biographer of the House of Winton.

In 1921 PD, Lady Emily, White Haven, and Honor Harrington married. They have two children, Katherine Allison Miranda Alexander-Harrington and Raoul Alfred Alistair Alexander-Harrington. Lady Emily is the genetic mother of Katherine Alexander-Harrington.

Alexander-Harrington, Lord Hamish, Earl White Haven
First Lord of the Admiralty, Royal Manticoran Navy

Hamish Alexander spent the majority of his career as a combat officer in the RMN. Many of the missions he commanded during the war were deciding factors in Manticoran victories, and he spent several years assigned to Home Fleet. In command of Sixth and then Eighth Fleets, he fought a grueling series of battles for control of Trevor's Star and its terminus of the Manticoran Wormhole Junction. After taking the PRH's largest advanced naval base in the Barnett System, the Earl of White Haven spearheaded Operation Buttercup, which proved a decisive blow to the People's Republic.

Although an able administrator and an innovative thinker, White Haven has been criticized for his initially slow acceptance of new technologies, although he has fully embraced them over the last decade.

In 1921 PD, Hamish and Emily Alexander married Honor Alexander-Harrington in a Grayson-inspired ceremony, making Hamish Steadholder Consort Harrington, the first male steadholder consort in Grayson history. He has one son by Honor, named Raoul Alfred Alistair, and a daughter by Emily, named Katherine Allison Miranda. After the fall of the High Ridge Government, his brother, William, was named Prime Minister. White Haven went on inactive duty with the RMN to serve as the (civilian) First Lord of the Admiralty.

Alexander-Harrington, Lady Dame Honor Stephanie, Duchess Harrington, Steadholder Harrington
Admiral, Royal Manticoran Navy

Honor Harrington, born on Sphinx in 1859 PD, was adopted during childhood by a treecat that she named Nimitz. As a young adult, she was admitted to the Royal Manticoran Naval Academy on Saganami Island for training. During that training, she began her long friendship with Michelle Henke, cousin to the Queen, and her conflict with Pavel Young, both of which shaped her early career.

Nicknamed "The Salamander" by the Manticoran press for her tendency to find herself in situations where battle was the hottest, Honor Harrington's service record is both long and distinguished. She holds the Parliamentary Medal of Valor, the Star of Grayson, and the Manticore Cross, among others, and has been awarded both a steading by Grayson and a knighthood and duchy by Manticore for her service.

She is married to Hamish Alexander and Emily Alexander and has a son, Raoul Alfred Alistair Alexander-Harrington, and a daughter, Katherine Allison Miranda Alexander-Harrington. Lady Harrington is the genetic mother of Raoul Alexander-Harrington.

Alquezar, Joachim
Prime Minister, Talbott Quadrant

Joachim Alquezar, a native of San Miguel, was the head of the Constitutional Union Party and the senior delegate from San Miguel to the Talbott Constitutional Convention. He became the prime minister of the Talbott Quadrant after its incorporation into the Star Empire of Manticore.

Arif, Adelina

Adelina Arif's life work has specialized in interspecies language and communication. As a member of the first contact team on Medusa, Dr. Arif was responsible for the breakthrough that enabled communication with the Medusans. She later developed and implemented a sign language enabling true two-way communication between humans and treecats and has continued working with the treecats to explore ways in which they can become more integrated into human society.

Babcock, Iris
Sergeant Major, Royal Manticoran Marine Corps

Iris Babcock, a native of Gryphon, is known for her perseverance and dedication to the Manticoran Marine Corps. In 1909, she married Horace Harkness. Babcock is currently command sergeant major at Saganami Island, the Royal Manticoran Naval Academy.

Brigham, Mercedes
Commodore, Royal Manticoran Navy

Mercedes Brigham, a native of Gryphon, was captured and endured horrific treatment at the hands of the Masadans at Blackbird Base. After her rescue, she was promoted to lieutenant commander and volunteered for the Endicott occupation force but was "loaned" to the Grayson Space Navy (GSN) shortly thereafter, where she rose to the rank of rear admiral. After serving as Honor Harrington's chief of staff during Harrington's Grayson service from 1906–1907 PD, she returned to Manticoran service in 1920 as Harrington's chief of staff with Task Force 34 and later Eighth Fleet.

Caparelli, Sir Thomas
First Space Lord, Royal Manticoran Navy

Thomas Caparelli became First Space Lord shortly before the beginning of the war with the People's Republic of Haven. Despite the Royal Manticoran Navy's prewar policy of rotating senior admirals between staff and fleet positions to keep them up to date in modern naval realities, he remained as First Space Lord for ten years. When the High Ridge Government came into power, Caparelli was placed on half-pay, but was recalled after the devastating Havenite attacks which led to the Second Havenite-Manticoran War.

Cardones, Rafael
Captain (SG), Royal Manticoran Navy

Rafael Cardones is a highly decorated RMN officer whose career has been intimately interwoven with that of Admiral Harrington. He served with her aboard the original HMS *Fearless* and was part of the team that won the First Battle of Basilisk against PMSS *Sirius*. Although his early career path intersected that of Admiral Harrington repeatedly, his later career shifted towards LAC operations, where he commanded one of the new LAC carriers in Eighth Fleet. After Harrington's return from Cerberus, Cardones' experience netted him the command of HMS *Werewolf* in Eighth Fleet in Operation Buttercup. Harrington requested him as her flag captain in Task Force 34, and he has continued in this position aboard HMS *Imperator* in Eighth Fleet.

Cortez, Sir Lucien
Fifth Space Lord, Royal Manticoran Navy

Lucien Cortez entered the RMN and rose through the ranks, earning a knighthood for conspicuous gallantry in action against a three-ship squadron of Silesian privateers. Seriously wounded in that engagement, he spent three T-years on medical inactive service. After his return to active service, he spent several years alternating between staff and command appointments. In 1898, he was appointed to serve as Fifth Space Lord, in charge of the Bureau of Personnel, and served in that capacity for over fifteen years. Cortez was placed on half-pay by the Janacek Admiralty but was recalled as Fifth Space Lord under the Alexander Admiralty.

Courvosier, Raoul (deceased)
Admiral of the Green, Royal Manticoran Navy

Raoul Courvosier spent much of his career teaching at Saganami Island and was a positive influence on a great number of RMN officers, including Honor Alexander-Harrington. In 1903 PD, he was named to head the diplomatic mission to Yeltsin's Star and to secure the Protectorate of Grayson as an ally of Manticore. When the Masadans attacked on 25 April, he was designated the second-in-command of the Grayson-Manticoran Combined Fleet and was killed in action at the First Battle of Yeltsin's Star.

Descroix, Lady Elaine
Former Foreign Minister, Star Kingdom of Manticore

Elaine Descroix, cousin of the Earl of Gray Hill and wife of Sir John Descroix, was a leader of the Progressive Party during the Cromarty Government. When the High Ridge Government was formed in 1915, she was appointed to the Cabinet as Foreign Minister. After the High Ridge Government fell, an investigation led to formal charges of bribery, corruption, malfeasance, and other criminal activities. Descroix transferred twenty million dollars to an account in the Stotterman System and left Manticore on a tourist visa. The money disappeared, and she has not been heard of again.

D'Orville, Sebastian
Admiral of the Fleet, Royal Manticoran Navy

Sebastian D'Orville is considered one of the premiere fleet commanders in the RMN—a distinction which has ironically kept him on the sidelines through much of the war. Although he began the war as commanding officer of Second Fleet, he was soon transferred back to Home Fleet, where he served as Sir James Bowie Webster's second-in-command. With the ascension of the High Ridge Government and the Janacek Admiralty in 1915, he was placed on half-pay and became a military analyst for the Opposition. In 1920, he was named to command Home Fleet.

Givens, Patricia
Second Space Lord, Royal Manticoran Navy

Patricia Givens has earned a high reputation in the Star Kingdom of Manticore's intelligence services in the course of her lengthy career. A career naval intelligence officer and highly regarded operational analyst, she served as Second Space Lord and Chief of the

Office of Naval Intelligence and the Bureau of Planning throughout the First Havenite War. Placed on half-pay by the Janacek Admiralty, she returned to her post shortly after the resumption of hostilities.

Harkness, Sir Horace
Chief Warrant Officer, Royal Manticoran Navy

Horace Harkness earned a towering—and fully justified—reputation as brawler, smuggler, and two-fisted drinker. Widely regarded as one of the Royal Manticoran Navy's most colorful characters, he was also too valuable, because of his leadership skills and acknowledged superior abilities as a missile technician, to dismiss from the service, and he was promoted and subsequently demoted numerous times prior to HMS *Fearless'* deployment to Basilisk Station. On that deployment, however, he took a very young ensign by the name of David Prescott "Scotty" Tremaine "under his wing," providing the enlisted mentor Tremaine required to become an outstanding officer. Harkness' relationship with Tremaine has continued throughout his subsequent career, reportedly thanks in no small part to certain unauthorized changes made to specific BuPers files. Although rated as a missile technician, he is also an excellent small-craft engineer, computer hacker, and cyberneticist—all skills that have served him well during his time in the RMN.

Harkness was awarded the Parliamentary Medal of Valor and knighted for his actions during the escape from PNS *Tepes* and the prison camp Hades. In 1920 PD he was assigned to Eighth Fleet along with Tremaine, who had been promoted to captain (junior grade), where Harkness served as the engineer on Tremaine's LAC, before being assigned as Captain (Senior Grade) Tremaine's staff electronic warfare officer with CruDiv 96.1.

Harrington, Alfred

During his service in the Royal Manticoran Marine Corps, Alfred Harrington earned the Osterman Cross for his actions on Clematis. Following that epic mission, he requested—and received—permission to transfer from the Corps to the Navy and returned to school to pursue medicine, meeting his future wife Allison as a student at Beowulf's Semmelweiss University.

After they married and moved to Sphinx, he became an RMN Surgeon Commander and was the Assistant Chief of Neurosurgery at Basingford Medical Center for many years. After leaving the RMN he became a partner in the Duvalier Medical Association.

Husband of Allison Chou Harrington and father of Honor, Faith, and James Harrington, Dr. Harrington is recognized as one of the finest neurosurgeons in the Star Kingdom of Manticore. After Honor's return from Hades, he personally performed the surgery to repair her arm and eye at his clinic on Manticore and established the Harrington Neurological Clinic in Harrington Steading on Grayson.

Harrington, Allison Chou

Allison Harrington, a native of Beowulf, is of almost pure Old Earth Oriental heritage. The wife of Alfred Harrington and the mother of Honor, Faith, and James Harrington, she is a descendant of one of the oldest and most prestigious Beowolf families, the Chou and Benton-Ramirez Clan. A brilliant geneticist, she took a leave of absence from her medical practice to accept the directorship of the Doctor Jennifer Chou Genetic Clinic on Grayson, where she resided with her husband for the next few years. During this time she discovered the genetic basis for the low male birthrate on Grayson and was able to develop a nanite to eliminate the damaged chromosomes.

Harrington, Lord Devon, Earl Harrington

Devon Harrington, a history professor and academic and Honor Harrington's cousin, inherited Honor's Manticoran title after her supposed execution by the People's Republic of Haven. Upon her return from Cerberus, he remained Earl Harrington when she was granted the title of Duchess Harrington.

Hauptman, Klaus
Chairman and CEO, Hauptman Cartel

Klaus Hauptman is the owner and principal of the Hauptman Cartel, the largest and most powerful of all of the Manticoran shipping and industrial cartels. The Hauptman family's business empire has built up over several generations, and Klaus Haupt-man is the single wealthiest individual in the entire Star Empire.

Hauptman, who is noted for his volcanic temper, has had many conflicts with the Navy over the years and some very personal confrontations with specific officers, most notably with Honor Harrington. He is also noted for intense personal loyalty, however, and has become a powerful political ally of Harrington following her 1910 Silesian cruise in HMAMC *Wayfarer*.

Hauptman is one of the galaxy's most bitter opponents of genetic slavery and quietly authorized the construction of a number of frigates for the Anti-Slavery League even before the liberation of Torch, in addition to funding early research on the Torch wormhole.

Hauptman, Stacey
Operations Director, Hauptman Cartel

Daughter of Klaus Hauptman and sole heir to the Haupt-man Cartel, Stacey Hauptman is the operations director of the Hauptman Cartel for Manticore-B and takes an active role in the Cartel management. She is also a personal friend of Honor Alexander-Harrington.

Hemphill, Lady Sonja, Baroness Low Delhi
Fourth Space Lord, Royal Manticoran Navy

Sonja Hemphill has consistently led the effort to push Manti-coran technology in new directions, although some of her critics have dismissed her as opposing traditional ideas simply because they were "old." As leader of the derisively dubbed "*jeune ecole*," she became a tireless advocate (with Jonas Adcock's support) of technical advancement and turned the dismissive label into something quite different. Although many of the *jeune ecole's* ideas ultimately failed, many others succeeded, and led directly to Manticoran victories.

Hemphill was instrumental in the development of the FTL grav-pulse com and of the hollow-cored, pod-laying superdreadnoughts and "super light attack craft" which made Operation Buttercup possible and which signaled a revolutionary change in traditional naval tactics. As Adcock's eventual successor at the Bureau of

Weapons, Hemphill has subsequently overseen the development of Project Mistletoe (stealthed recon drones with laser and nuclear warheads designed to kill fixed defenses) and Project Apollo (the development of a faster-than-light command link missile).

Henke, Lady Gloria Michelle Samantha Evelyn, Countess Gold Peak
Vice Admiral of the Red, Royal Manticoran Navy

Michelle Henke, daughter of Lord Edward Henke, Earl of Gold Peak, and Caitrin, Duchess Winton-Henke, and sister of Lord Calvin Henke, is Queen Elizabeth III's only living first cousin on the Queen's father's side. After the death of her father and brother, she became the Countess of Gold Peak and fifth in line of succession for the throne of Manticore.

Her close friendship with Honor Harrington began at Saganami Island, and she has served with Harrington a number of times throughout her career. As a rear admiral, she was wounded and captured during Operation Cutworm, when her flagship HMS *Ajax* was destroyed in the Solon system.

After Henke had recovered from her injuries, Havenite President Eloise Pritchart paroled her and sent her back to Manticore with an offer of truce for Queen Elizabeth. Under the terms of her parole, Admiral Gold Peak was prohibited from serving against the Republic of Haven for the remainder of the war. Accordingly, the Admiralty assigned her command of the newly created Tenth Fleet and sent her to the Talbott Quadrant to support Vice Admiral of the Red Augustus Khumalo and Baroness Medusa.

Hibson, Susan
Brigadier, Royal Manticoran Marine Corps

Susan Hibson, determined from a young age to become a Marine, survived a ski lift accident and was able to alert rescuers to her location, saving the lives of others. As a result, she became one of the youngest recipients of the Queen's Cross for Bravery and was guaranteed a spot in the OCS when she was old enough. Her career with the Royal Marines has been distinguished, starting with the assault on Blackbird Base in the Yeltsin System in 1903 PD. Promoted to brigadier in 1919 PD, Hibson is currently the commanding officer (designate) of the 19th Brigade (Independent), Royal Manticoran Marine Corps, earmarked for assignment to the Talbott Quadrant in support of Tenth Fleet.

Higgins, Allen
Admiral of the Red, Royal Manticoran Navy

Allen Higgins commanded the task force defending Grendelsbane Station in the face of Thomas Theismann's Operation Thunderbolt in 1918 PD. When he realized that his force was far too weak to defend the station he ordered the system's evacuation and destroyed all ships under construction. Placed on half-pay by the Janacek Admiralty pending a board of inquiry, he was fully exonerated and returned to active duty by the Alexander Admiralty in 1920.

Houseman, the Honorable Reginald
Second Lord of Admiralty, Royal Manticoran Navy (retired)

Reginald Houseman, an honors graduate of Mannheim University's College of Economics in 1891 PD, subsequently held a succession of minor government appointments and served as a Foreign Office advisor for the Courvosier Mission to Grayson in 1903.

Although his diplomatic service ended after the Queen expressed her displeasure at his actions during the Masadan attack on Grayson, Houseman was embraced by the Cromarty Government's political opponents and held several advisory positions for the Opposition. His political career seemed revitalized when he was named Second Lord of the Admiralty under First Lord Janacek, but his strong support for the build-down of the fleet proved unfortunately timed. His renewed career plummeted disastrously after Operation Thunderbolt (and the Navy's weakened posture) led to the fall of the High Ridge Government, and he is currently a guest lecturer at Mannheim University.

Janacek, Sir Edward *(deceased)*
Admiral of the Green, Royal Manticoran Navy (retired)
First Lord of Admiralty

Edward Janacek, having risen through the ranks in the Bureau of Planning, spent three years as First Lord of Admiralty before the war until his replacement by Baroness Mourncreek in the wake of the Basilisk Incident. Following the cease-fire in 1915 PD, the High Ridge Government named him First Lord again, during which time he was responsible for the downsizing of the Navy amid steadily worsening relations with the GSN and other member navies of the Manticoran Alliance. Janacek committed suicide after the disastrous opening battles of what became known as the Second Havenite War.

Janvier, Lord Michael, Former Baron High Ridge
Former Prime Minister, Star Kingdom of Manticore

Michael Janvier, head of the Conservative Association through-out the twentieth century, was one of the Cromarty Government's fiercest critics. Following the Duke of Cromarty's assassination in 1915 PD, High Ridge refused to agree to a coalition all-parties government until the war with the People's Republic of Haven could be concluded. Instead, he became Prime Minister of a government built from an alliance of the Conservative, Liberal, and Progressive parties when he managed to convince enough Independent peers to support him by playing upon the fear that Elizabeth III intended to curtail the power of the House of Lords. Needless to say, his support in the House of Commons was effectively non-existent.

In 1920 PD, following the news of Operation Thunderbolt, he asked the Queen for permission to form an all-parties govern-ment, which she denied. When news came of the disaster at Grendelsbane Station he resigned and his government fell. Fol-lowing a spectacular (and squalid) trial, High Ridge and several members of his government were convicted on charges of bribery, malfeasance, and corruption, and he himself was sentenced to twenty-nine years in prison and deprived of his seat in the Lords by a majority vote of his peers.

Jaruwalski, Andrea
Captain (JG), Royal Manticoran Navy

Andrea Jaruwalski's career was effectively destroyed by the spite of a senior officer who refused to listen to her advice and suffered a catastrophic defeat in 1913 PD. The following year, however,

Admiral Harrington asked Jaruwalski to be her aide at ATC, where Jaruwalski quickly gained the respect both of the midshipmen in Harrington's "Intro to Tactics" class and of the prospective starship COs passing through the "Crusher" under Harrington's auspices. In 1919, Jaruwalski was promoted to captain (jg) below the zone and Harrington selected her as operations officer in Task Force 34. Jaruwalski continues as Harrington's ops officer with Eighth Fleet.

Kare, Jordin
Chief Astrophysicist, RMAIA

One of the most brilliant astrophysicists in the Star Kingdom, Jordin Kare holds at least five degrees. He was the first chief astrophysicist of the Royal Manticoran Astrophysics Investigation Agency, and in 1918 PD he and a team at Valasakis University began working on a new approach to the mathematical model of the Manticoran Wormhole Junction that led directly to the discovery of the Lynx Terminus. Although he was ordered not to accompany the ship through the wormhole, he led the team that explored the Torch wormhole in 1921.

Khumalo, Augustus
Vice Admiral of the Red, Royal Manticoran Navy

Augustus Khumalo, a distant cousin of Queen Elizabeth III and Rear Admiral of the Green, became CO of Talbott Station in 1919 PD. He was appointed to the command mainly on the basis of his credentials with the Conservative Association, despite a reputation for being difficult to work with. However, he also had a reputation for working long hours and distinguished himself in the eyes of the Grantville Government by his strong support for Captain Aivars Terekov after the Battle of Monica. He was subsequently promoted to vice admiral and retained in command of Talbott Station and the overall defense of the Talbott Quadrant.

Krietzmann, Henri
Minister of War, Talbott Quadrant

Henri Krietzmann, a native of Dresden, was president of the 1920 Talbott Constitutional Convention. When the Quadrant approved its constitution and joined the Star Empire of Manticore, he became the Talbott Quadrant's minister of war, responsible for administration of the Quadrant's local defense military forces and coordination with Imperial Naval and Army authorities.

Kuzak, Theodosia
Admiral of the Green, RMN

Theodosia Kuzak performed admirably as second-in-command of Sixth Fleet and was placed in command of Third Fleet at Trevor's Star after the system was captured. Under the Janacek Admiralty, she was the only one of two admirals from the war left in command of a major unit. When war broke out again between the Republic of Haven and Manticore, she continued to lead the defense of San Martin and Trevor's Star.

Langtry, Sir Anthony
Foreign Secretary, Star Kingdom of Manticore

Anthony Langtry began his career in the Royal Manticoran Marine Corps, where he was a highly decorated officer. Following his retirement from the Corps, he moved to the Foreign Office. Shortly before the First Havenite War began, he was chosen as the first Manticoran ambassador to Grayson. His support of Honor Harrington's actions in that star system in 1903 PD led to a strong alliance between Grayson and Manticore. Under the Grantville Government, he was named Foreign Secretary in Grantville's cabinet.

Lewis, Ginger
Captain (JG), Royal Manticoran Navy

Ginger Lewis was assigned to HMAMC *Wayfarer* in 1910 PD as a gravitics specialist first class and quickly was promoted far outside the zone to acting senior chief. She received the Osterman Cross for her actions during the Battle of the Selkir Rift and was offered a position at Fleet Officer Candidate School, where she received a commission. In 1920, as a commander, she served as chief engineer on HMS *Hexapuma*, and in 1921 she was promoted to captain (jg) and assigned to HMSS *Weyland*.

MacGuinness, James
Senior Master Chief Petty Officer, Royal Manticoran Navy (retired)

Steward First Class James MacGuinness was assigned to Commander Harrington onboard HMS *Fearless* in 1900 PD, and has accompanied her from command to command throughout her career. In 1906, when Harrington moved to Grayson on half-pay, the servants at Harrington House accepted him as majordomo.

He remained Commander Harrington's steward when she was returned to active service in the RMN in 1910 PD. When Harrington was lost on HMS *Prince Adrian* and declared dead, she left him forty million dollars in her will with the proviso that he retire from the RMN and look after her treecat Samantha and the treekittens. Since Harrington's return from Hades, he has continued to serve as her steward, despite being the only steward in the RMN who isn't actually in the service of the RMN.

Matsuko, Lady Dame Estelle, Baroness Medusa
Imperial Governor, Talbott Quadrant

Estelle Matsuko was appointed the Resident Commissioner for Planetary Affairs of Medusa in 1897 PD, where she and the Native Protection Agency fought to preserve the rights and culture of the Medusan natives with limited assistance. Her work with Honor Harrington during the Havenite-inspired Mekoha Uprising and her ongoing efforts in its aftermath helped to resolve many of the issues which had previously endangered the native population.

For her tireless service in the Basilisk System, Matsuko was named a peer of the realm and awarded the newly created Barony of Medusa. In 1920, the Grantville Government chose her as Home Secretary. Following the discovery of the Lynx Terminus and the Talbott Cluster's request for annexation, she was named Provisional Crown Governor of the Talbott Cluster and then Imperial Governor of the Talbott Quadrant when it joined the Star Empire.

Maurier, Lady Francine, Countess Mourncreek
Chancellor of the Exchequer

Francine Maurier served as the First Lord of the Admiralty during the last ten years of the Cromarty Government. After Duke

Cromarty's death, she was replaced at the Admiralty by Admiral Janacek under the High Ridge Government. In 1920 PD in the new Grantville Government, she was appointed Chancellor of the Exchequer and elevated to Countess Mourncreek by the Queen.

Maxwell, Richard

Richard Maxwell, a former Royal Marine who was awarded the Manticore Cross, became one of the SKM's leading criminal defense lawyers following his retirement from military service. In 1914 PD, Willard Neufsteiler recommended him to Honor Harrington for her in-house counsel, a position which he accepted and has held continuously ever since.

McKeon, Alistair
Rear Admiral of the Red, Royal Manticoran Navy

Alistair McKeon served as Honor Harrington's executive officer on the original HMS *Fearless* at the time of the Basilisk Incident. Following the First Battle of Basilisk, he was promoted from lieutenant commander to commander as CO of HMS *Troubadour* and again served with Harrington during the First Battle of Yeltsin, in which *Troubadour* was destroyed. In 1903 PD, shortly before the outbreak of war with the PRH he was promoted to captain (jg) and assigned to command HMS *Prince Adrian*. By 1911 he was a captain (sg) and Harrington designated him as her tactical deputy in CruRon 18.

McKeon was among those captured during the surrender of HMS *Prince Adrian* and was held as a prisoner of war with Honor Harrington on the planet Hades. After the prisoner revolt led by Harrington, he served as president of the court that tried the surviving StateSec personnel. He commanded two separate ships in the Elysian Space Navy during the return to Manticore.

Promoted to Rear Admiral of the Red in 1915, he commanded a LAC-carrier division in Eighth Fleet before he was reassigned to command one of the task groups in Harrington's Task Force 34 on Sidemore Station. Since 1920, he has served as one of the senior commanders of Eighth Fleet and as the commanding officer of BatRon 61, once again under Harrington's command.

Montaigne, Catherine, former Countess Tor

Catherine Montaigne, a close childhood friend of Queen Elizabeth III, was a peer and a member of the Liberal Party and one of only three nobles ever excluded from the House of Lords. A long-time anti-slavery activist and a leader of the Anti-Slavery League, she moved to Old Earth following her exclusion from the Lords for her very vocal support of then Commander Honor Harrington's Casimir Raid. On Old Earth, she established direct contact with the Audubon Ballroom, considered a terrorist organization.

She reappeared in Manticore some years later with Anton Zilwicki, his genetic daughter Helen, and his adopted children Berry and Lars, all of whom had been rescued by the Audubon Ballroom from agents of Manpower Incorporated. At that time she provided Crown prosecutors documented evidence of the involvement of over a dozen prominent Manticorans in the genetic slave trade, which led to a series of spectacular trials. After the realization that her continual exclusion from the House of Lords had rendered her position as Countess of Tor as much a liability as an asset, she renounced her title and ran successfully for a seat in the House of Commons for the Borough of High Threadneedle. After the fall of the High Ridge Government, she became the leader of the Liberal Party.

Montoya, Fritz
Surgeon Captain, Royal Manticoran Navy

Fritz Montoya served on HMS *Fearless* (CL-56) as a surgeon lieutenant under Honor Harrington in 1900 PD. Promoted to surgeon commander by 1903, Dr. Montoya was the chief medical officer on HMS *Fearless* (CA-286). In 1904, he was the chief medical officer on HMS *Nike*. In 1910, he became the chief medical officer on GSN *Jason Alvarez* and Harrington considered him an adjunct to her squadron staff. In 1911, he accompanied Harrington to HMS *Prince Adrian* and was taken prisoner with her by the People's Navy.

Promoted to surgeon captain in 1913 after his return from Hades, he was selected as the senior medical officer for Task Force 34 by Harrington in 1920. Following TF 34's return from Silesia, he was promoted to surgeon commodore and selected to head the Combat Surgery Faculty at Bassingford Medical Center.

Neufsteiler, Willard
CFO, Grayson Sky Domes, Ltd.

Willard Neufsteiler was originally Honor Harrington's financial manager. By 1912 PD, he moved to Grayson and took over as Grayson Sky Domes' full-time chief financial officer.

Oversteegen, Michael
Rear Admiral of the Red, Royal Manticoran Navy

Michael Oversteegan, fourth in the line of succession for the Barony of Greater Windcombe, is son to Baron High Ridge's second cousin. In 1918 PD, as a captain (jg), he commanded the heavy cruiser HMS *Gauntlet* at the Battle of Tiberian, for which he was promoted to captain (sg) and received the Manticoran Cross. After repairs, his ship was deployed to Erewhon to "show the flag." In early 1920 PD, he and his crew took part in the liberation of the planet Verdant Vista (aka Congo) and assisted in establishing the Kingdom of Torch. In 1921, he received command of HMS *Nike* (BC-562) and participated in the Battle of Solon.

Ramirez, Jesus
President, Republic of San Martin

Jesus Ramirez, as the senior surviving officer of the San Martin Navy, inflicted three times his own losses on the People's Navy during his ultimately unsuccessful defense of his home system when People's Republic attacked Trevor's Star in 1883 PD. He was believed to have been killed in the battle until Harrington's escape from Hades brought him home, along with over a quarter-million other prisoners.

On his return to San Martin he was drafted without consultation into running for president. All but one opponent withdrew from the race and he received eighty-six percent of the vote.

Ramirez, Tomas Santiago
Major General, Royal Manticoran Marine Corps

Tomas Santiago Ramirez, a native of San Martin, is the son of President Jesus and Rosario Ramirez. He, his mother, and siblings escaped on the last transport before San Martin was conquered by the PRH. As a result, he grew up with a deep and abiding hatred of Haven. Ramirez has led an exemplary career, including positions as assault commander for the Blackbird Raid in 1903 PD and later as executive officer of the Allied occupation forces on his homeworld of San Martin, following its liberation from the People's Republic.

After his father's return from Hades, Ramirez resigned his Marine commission to become the commander of his homeworld's reconstituted army. Following Jesus Ramirez's election as president and San Martin's admission to the Star Kingdom of Manticore and the integration of its armed forces into the Star Kingdom's, Tomas Ramirez returned to the Royal Manticoran Marine Corps with the rank of major general. In 1920, Major General Ramirez was assigned as chief of staff to the Commandant of the Corps.

Reynaud, Michel
Admiral, Astro Control Service
Commanding Officer, RMAIA

Michel Reynaud, as a captain in the Royal Manticoran Astro-Control Service was CO, Basilisk Traffic Control, in 1900 PD at the time of the Basilisk Incident. In 1903, he was promoted to rear admiral, and in 1910 he was promoted to vice admiral, continuing to command Basilisk ACS. Promoted to admiral in 1915, he became the first commanding officer of the Royal Manticoran Astrophysical Investigation Agency in 1916, where he continues to serve after the successful navigation of the Lynx Terminus of the Manticore Wormhole Junction.

Sarnow, Mark
Admiral of the Red, Royal Manticoran Navy

Mark Sarnow commanded Battlecruiser Squadron Five in 1903 PD. During the First Battle of Hancock Station, Rear Admiral of the Red Sarnow was severely wounded. He was the only flag officer in the task force to survive the battle, but he lost both legs at the knee and suffered internal injuries. After an extensive medical rehabilitation period on Manticore, during which he served as an instructor at Saganami Island, Sarnow returned to fleet duty as the commanding officer of Grendelsbane Station. In 1911, he was promoted to vice admiral and became the CO of the RMN's Naval War College, where he was responsible for major revisions in RMN convoy and commerce protection doctrine following HMAMC *Wayfarer*'s Silesian deployment. In 1913, Sarnow was relieved at the War College and selected to command the diversionary attacks designed to clear the way for Hamish Alexander's Operation Buttercup, in which role he performed brilliantly. In 1915, he was placed on half-pay by the Janacek Admiralty but was one of the first flag officers recalled by the Alexander Admiralty. He is currently CO of 9th Fleet and governor of the Silesian Sector in the Queen's name.

Summervale, Lord Allen, Duke Cromarty *(deceased)*
Prime Minister, Star Kingdom of Manticore

Allen Summervale was the longtime leader of the Centrist Party. The Duke of Cromarty served as King Roger III's Prime Minister and continued in that role for Queen Elizabeth III. Over the course of his fifty-eight T-years as Prime Minister, he worked with both Roger III and Elizabeth III to prepare for what he realized would be a long, difficult war against the People's Republic of Haven. Gifted at balancing the interests of opposing political factions and possessed of great personal charisma, he managed to guide the government through the successive crises of the most dangerous periods of the First Havenite War.

He and several other influential political figures were killed on 19 February 1915 in the destruction of HMS *Queen Adrienne* in an attempt to assassinate Queen Elizabeth III. Because much of his governing coalition was based on personal loyalty, it fell apart and was replaced by the High Ridge Government.

Summervale, Denver *(deceased)*

Denver Summervale, a distant cousin of the Duke of Cromarty, was a former Marine captain who was cashiered from the Corps for killing a brother officer in a duel. In 1905 PD, he was hired by Lord Pavel Young to induce first Paul Tankersley and then

Honor Harrington into challenging him to a duel. Tankersley died, but Summervale was killed during his subsequent duel with Harrington.

Tankersley, Paul (deceased)
Captain (SG), Royal Manticoran Navy

Paul Tankersley began the war as a junior grade captain and the executive officer of the repair base at Hancock Station, where he and then-Captain Honor Harrington became lovers. After the Battle of Hancock Station, he was promoted to captain of the list and returned to Manticore, where he was assigned as a deputy constructor on HMSS *Hephaestus*. He was killed in a duel by Denver Summervale, a hired duelist in the employ of Pavel Young.

Terekhov, Sir Aivars Aleksovitch
Commodore, Royal Manticoran Navy

Aivars Terekhov began his career in the RMN, but after eleven T-years moved to the Foreign Office where he served for twenty-eight T-years. He returned to active duty at the start of the war and, as captain of HMS *Defiant*, was taken prisoner in the Hyacinth System after a convoy under his light cruiser division's escort was ambushed. After the truce, he returned to Manticore as part of a prisoner exchange and spent an extended period at Bassingford Medical Center rehabilitating and regenerating.

In 1920 PD, he was assigned to command HMS *Hexapuma* and directed to join the Manticoran squadron in the Talbott Cluster. He and his crew intercepted and captured several pirates and, in the course of suppressing terrorist activities in the Split and Montana Systems, uncovered an interstellar conspiracy to sabotage the Constitutional Convention. Terekhov assembled an *ad hoc* squadron and led an unauthorized incursion into the Monica System, which was clearly implicated in the conspiracy, to disrupt the delivery of modern warships to the Monican Navy. Although his squadron sustained serious losses, he destroyed three operational Monican battlecruisers and all those still being refitted for Monican service at Eroica Station. For his actions he was awarded the Parliamentary Medal of Valor, promoted to commodore, and given command of CruRon 94, attached to Tenth Fleet in the Talbott Quadrant.

Tremaine, Prescott David
Captain (SG), Royal Manticoran Navy

David "Scotty" Tremaine was assigned to HMS *Fearless* (CL-56) in 1900 PD as a boat bay control officer. During *Fearless'* deployment to Basilisk, Ensign Tremaine first met PO Horace Harkness when the two of them were assigned to customs enforcement. Tremaine provided primary air support for *Fearless'* Marines on Medusa. Promoted to lieutenant (jg) in 1901, he was assigned to HMS *Troubadour* in 1902 and survived that ship's destruction during the Second Battle of Yeltsin. Following Second Yeltsin, he was assigned to HMS *Prince Adrian* and promoted to lieutenant (sg) in 1905. In 1910, he was transferred to HMAMC *Wayfarer* as flight operations officer. In 1911, promoted to lieutenant commander, he served as Honor Harrington's staff electronics officer in CruRon 18 and was among the POWs who accompanied her to Cerberus. After serving as CO, ENS *Krashnark*, in the Battle of Cerberus, he returned with Harrington to Trevor's Star and was promoted to full commander in 1914, when he was assigned as COLAC in HMS *Hydra*. Promoted to captain (jg) in 1917, he served as COLAC for HMS *Werewolf* in Task Force 34 for the Battle of Sidemore in 1918. Promoted to captain (sg) in 1920, he served as COLAC of CarRon 3 in Eighth Fleet.

Truman, Dame Alice
Vice Admiral of the Red, Royal Manticoran Navy

Alice Truman was born into a family with a long and distinguished history in the RMN. By 1902 PD, Commander Truman was the commanding officer of HMS *Apollo* and served as Honor Harrington's second-in-command at the Battle of Blackbird, where her ship was severely damaged. After the engagement, she evacuated Manticoran wounded and nationals and alerted the Admiralty of the desperate need for reinforcements at Yeltsin's Star. In 1910, she accepted command of the armed merchantman *Parnassus* and participated in Commodore Harrington's anti-piracy operations in the Silesian Confederacy. In 1912, she received command of HMS *Minotaur* and proved the LAC carrier concept at the Second Battle of Hancock Station. She then commanded the LAC-carriers assigned to Eighth Fleet for Operation Buttercup. Like many, she was placed on half-pay by the High Ridge Government Admiralty, but on Harrington's insistence, she was returned to command the LAC-carrier task group in Task Force 34 during the Second Battle of Marsh. Once more designated to command Eighth Fleet's LAC-carriers in 1920, she became Harrington's second-in-command when Harrington assumed command of that fleet.

Van Dort, Bernardus
Minister without Portfolio, Talbott Quadrant

Bernardus Van Dort, a native of Rembrandt, was the founder, majority shareholder, and chairman of the Rembrandt Trade Union, as well as the primary moving force behind the Talbott Cluster's request for annexation by the Star Kingdom of Manticore. Van Dort is currently a minister without portfolio in the new Talbott Quadrant government.

Venizelos, Andreas *(deceased)*
Commander, Royal Manticoran Navy

Andreas Venizelos, as a lieutenant in 1900 PD, was the tactical officer on HMS *Fearless* (CL-56) and commanded the RMN personnel assigned to Basilisk Traffic Control. In 1902, as a lieutenant commander, he served as the executive officer on HMS *Fearless* (CA-286), and in 1905 was promoted to commander and served as CO, HMS *Apollo*. In 1911, as Honor Harrington's chief of staff in CruRon 18, he was one of the officers captured and taken aboard PNS *Tepes* and was killed during the escape from that vessel.

Wanderman, Aubrey
Senior Chief Petty Officer, Royal Manticoran Navy

Aubrey Wanderman joined the RMN after leaving Mannheim University, where he was a physics major. He finished second in his training class and was assigned to HMAMC *Wayfarer* as an electronics technician. In 1920, SCPO Wanderman was assigned to HMS *Hexapuma* at the time of the Battle of Monica. He is currently assigned to HMSS *Weyland*'s fabrication and materials division.

Webster, Lord Sir James Bowie, Baron New Dallas (deceased)
Fleet Admiral, Royal Manticoran Navy (retired)
Ambassador to the Solarian League

James Webster took command of Home Fleet as First Space Lord in 1903 PD. As one of the many officers placed on half-pay by Sir Edward Janacek, Admiral Webster became a military analyst for the Opposition. The Grantville Government named him ambassador to the Solarian League, where he orchestrated a remarkably successful public relations campaign on behalf of the Star Kingdom and the annexation of the Talbott Cluster until his assassination in 1921 PD.

Webster, Samuel Houston
Rear Admiral of the Green, Royal Manticoran Navy

Samuel Webster began his career as a communications officer, serving alongside Honor Harrington on multiple occasions, including his first hyper-capable command, HMAMC *Scheherazade* in 1909. As a Rear Admiral of the Red, he commanded Battle Squadron 16, TF 34, at the Battle of Sidemore in 1918. Promoted to Rear Admiral of the Green in 1920, he is currently attached to BuWeaps as Admiral Sonja Hemphill's senior departmental commander.

Winton, Elizabeth Adrienne Samantha Annette
Queen Elizabeth III, Star Kingdom of Manticore
Empress Elizabeth I, Star Empire of Manticore

Elizabeth Adrienne Samantha Annette Winton is the sixteenth monarch of the Star Kingdom of Manticore. Born the year Basilisk was annexed, she was named Duchess of Basilisk in 1867 PD on her first birthday. She became Queen at age eighteen, after the untimely death of her father. Although there have been rumors for many years that the death of King Roger III was more than a simple grav skiing accident, no proof has ever been made public. Ably assisted by her Aunt Caitrin (serving as her regent), the Duke of Cromarty (as her prime minister), and her Uncle Jonas (at BuWeaps), Elizabeth continued and expanded her father's labors to prepare the Star Kingdom for war against the People's Republic of Haven. From 1905, with the outbreak of active hostilities, until Operation Buttercup in 1914, Elizabeth led her star nation to a point of decisive military superiority over the PRH.

Following the destruction of HMS *Queen Adrienne* and the death of Allen Summervale in February 1915 PD, she was unable to convince the Opposition to agree to an all-parties government to fight the war to a conclusive victory. Despite her opposition, Baron High Ridge formed a coalition government which excluded the Centrists and Crown Loyalists and accepted Saint-Just's offer of a truce. When hostilities resumed with Haven in 1918, High Ridge asked her permission to form an all-parties government after all, in a bid to spread the blame for the disaster. Elizabeth, in an unprecedented decision, refused his request. Following the High Ridge Government's inevitable fall, she summoned William Alexander to form a new government and agreed to the division of the Silesian Confederacy between the SKM and Andermani in order to bring Emperor Gustav XI into the Manticoran Alliance against Haven.

Elizabeth Winton was adopted as a teenager by a treecat that she named Ariel. The treecats refer to her as "Soul of Steel." Elizabeth Winton's fiery temper is famous (or infamous, depending upon one's perspective), and she has a long memory for those who have wronged her, her family, or those she holds dear. She is also extremely loyal to people who serve the Star Kingdom well.

She is married to Justin Zyrr-Winton, a common-born native of Gryphon. Their children are Crown Prince Roger and Princess Joanna. She and Prince Consort Justin are two of Raoul Alexander-Harrington's godparents.

Winton, Crown Prince Roger Gregory Alexander Timothy

Roger Winton is the Crown Prince of Manticore and the eldest son of Queen Elizabeth III and Prince Consort Justin. He is currently engaged to Rivka Rosenfeld.

Winton, Lady Judith Newland, Duchess Winton-Serisburg

Judith Newland Winton is the daughter of Grayson merchants who were killed when their ship was taken by Masadan pirate Ephraim Templeton. She was taken by Templeton as his youngest "wife" at age twelve. She kept her literacy a secret out of fear, but Templeton's eldest wife, Dinah, realized she was literate and inducted her into the Sisterhood of Barbara, a secret resistance organization among Masadan women. Judith routinely hacked into the computers on Templeton's ships and taught herself to operate a starship. To save the life of her unborn daughter, she and Dinah led their "chapter" of the Sisterhood in the capture of one of Templeton's ships and escaped from Masada to Manticore in 1892 PD, with the assistance of Midshipman Michael Winton, then crown prince of Manticore and serving in HMS *Intransigent*. In 1894, Michael married her and adopted her daughter Ruth. Her past became public only after Grayson and Manticore became allied, at which time she became a national heroine on Grayson.

Winton, Prince Michael, Duke Winton-Serisburg
Rear Admiral of the Red, Royal Manticoran Navy

Michael Winton, the younger child of King Roger III and Queen Consort Angelique, was crown prince until the birth of Elizabeth III's children. He entered Saganami Island, the Royal Manticoran Navy's academy in 1888 PD, specializing in communications. In 1892 he was assigned to HMS *Intransigent* for his midshipman's cruise and was part of the diplomatic team sent to Masada. He assisted the members of the Sisterhood of Barbara, led by Dinah Templeton and Judith Newland, in their escape from Masada. Two years later, he proposed to Judith and married her, adopting her daughter Ruth. He continued his active service career, specializing in R&D with occasional diplomatic assignments. In 1914 he was promoted to commodore and became the commanding officer of BuShips Cyber and Communications Command. Although not placed on half-pay by the Janacek Admiralty, he refused to serve the High Ridge Government and voluntarily went on inactive duty, serving primarily as his sister the Queen's personal envoy to members of the Manticoran Alliance. In 1919, promoted to Rear Admiral of the Red, he returned to Cyber and Communications, which he currently commands.

Winton-Henke, Lady Caitrin, Duchess Winton-Henke, Dowager Countess Gold Peak

Caitrin Winton-Henke, younger sister of Roger III and wife of Edward Henke, the Earl of Gold Peak, is the mother of Calvin and Michelle Henke and Queen Elizabeth III's aunt. She served as Queen Elizabeth's regent from the time of her brother's death until Elizabeth's twenty-first birthday and was instrumental in Elizabeth's continuation and expansion of Roger's program of naval expansion. Upon the termination of the regency, she served as one of Elizabeth's senior councilors. When her husband became Foreign Secretary in the Cromarty Government, Caitrin was often selected as one of Elizabeth's personal diplomatic representatives. Following Gold Peak's death aboard HMS *Queen Adrienne* in 1915 PD, Caitrin largely withdrew from any official government role, although she remained one of Elizabeth's most trusted personal advisors. As Dowager Countess Gold Peak, she acts as her daughter Michelle's representative in the House of Lords and steward in Gold Peak, but the majority of her time is devoted to her role as CEO of the Edward Henke Memorial Trust, a charitable foundation set up by the House of Winton in her late husband's memory to assist and support the children and families of personnel serving in the Manticoran armed forces.

Young, Lord Dimitri, Earl North Hollow (deceased)

Dimitri Young, father of Pavel and Stefan Young, was a commander in the RMN before he inherited his title, resigned, and went into politics. He was reputed to have compiled blackmail information on a great many people and to have used it to maintain power through political extortion. He was extremely obese and required a life support chair for mobility. When the court-martial board announced his son Pavel's conviction and sentence, he died of a stroke.

Young, Lady Georgia Sakristos, Countess North Hollow

Georgia Sakristos worked for Dimitri Young as a security advisor, assistant and female companion. After Pavel Young became Earl, she remained in his employ, although there is some speculation she may have been involved in some of the machinations that led to his death. After Pavel's death, she married Stefan Young and was selected by Baron High Ridge to chair the Conservative Association's Policy Coordination Committee. After the destruction of the North Hollow mansion, she disappeared.

Young, Lord Pavel, Earl North Hollow (deceased)

Pavel Young was the eldest son of the Earl of North Hollow. At the Academy, he was issued a reprimand for sexually harassing Honor Harrington. He was relieved of command following the Battle of Hancock and placed under arrest for cowardice under fire. At his court-martial, he was found guilty of the non-capital charges against him and was dishonorably dismissed from the RMN. He attempted to have Honor Harrington killed via duel by proxy and by assassination, before he was himself challenged and killed by Harrington in a duel.

Young, Lord Stefan, Earl North Hollow
Minister of Trade, Star Kingdom of Manticore (retired)

Stefan Young became Earl after his older brother, Pavel, was killed by Honor Harrington in a duel. As the Earl of North Hollow, he was the only peer who actively opposed giving Honor Harrington command of the Q-ships to be deployed to the Silesian Confederacy. In the High Ridge Government, he was Minister of Trade but retired and went into relative seclusion after the destruction of his Landing mansion and the mysterious disappearance of his wife, Lady Georgia Sakristos Young.

Zilwicki, Anton
Captain (JG), Royal Manticoran Navy (retired)

Anton Zilwicki, a native Gryphon highlander, has a background in naval construction with a specialty in technical evaluation. After his wife Helen died in action against PN raiders, defending a convoy that included Zilwicki and his young daughter, he transferred to the Office of Naval Intelligence (ONI). While he was stationed on Old Earth and working for the ONI, his daughter Helen was kidnapped. In direct violation of orders to leave the entire investigation in Old Earth hands, he appealed to Lady Catherine Montaigne for help from the Audubon Ballroom and found himself working in collaboration with an agent of the PRH, Victor Cachat. Placed on half-pay for violating orders, he adopted Berry and Lars, who had aided Helen on Old Earth, returned to Manticore, opened an investigation company, became Montaigne's lover, and continued to represent the Anti-Slavery League. With the creation of the Kingdom of Torch, he became Queen Berry's senior intelligence analyst.

Zilwicki, Helen Angela (deceased)
Captain (JG), Royal Manticoran Navy

Helen Zilwicki, a native of Manticore, was an active member of the Anti-Slavery League. She was married to Anton Zilwicki and was Helen Zilwicki's mother. In 1904 PD, she commanded the badly outgunned naval escort for a convoy that was ambushed in hyper-space by a PN force. She sacrificed herself and the escort to protect the convoy, which contained over six thousand Naval technicians and their families, including her husband and daughter. For her actions she was posthumously awarded the Parliamentary Medal of Valor.

Zilwicki, Helen Antonia
Ensign, Royal Manticoran Navy

Helen Zilwicki is the daughter of Anton and Helen Zilwicki, and the adoptive sister of Lars Zilwicki and Queen Berry I of Torch. At age fourteen, she was kidnapped on Old Chicago, where she met and rescued two orphans, Lars and Berry, before the rescue of all three of the children by members of the Audubon Ballroom and the Havenite agent Victor Cachat.

Zilwicki was assigned to HMS *Hexapuma* for her midshipman's cruise and took part in the Battle of Monica. Despite her very junior rank, she was specifically requested by Commodore Terekhov as his flag lieutenant for his redeployment to the Talbott Quadrant.

Zyrr-Winton, Prince Justin
Prince Consort, Star Kingdom of Manticore

Justin Zyrr, a native of Gryphon, and Crown Princess Elizabeth III met when she was touring his research lab. They were engaged when she succeeded to the Crown in 1883 PD after the death of her father, Roger III. Zyrr helped Elizabeth investigate Roger's death. Roger III's treecat, Monroe, defended Zyrr's life and created a bond with him shortly after Roger's death. Zyrr's children with Elizabeth are Crown Prince Roger and Princess Joanna.

Nonhuman Sentient Species

The Star Empire of Manticore counts among its inhabitants two of the twenty-seven sentient nonhuman species discovered to date: the Sphinxian treecats and the Medusans. Like the Barthoni, treecats are one of the few nonhuman species to have established a multiple planetary presence, with small colonies on Grayson and Gryphon in addition to their native Sphinx. The Medusans remain limited to their planet of origin in the Basilisk system.

As a result of treecat-human bondings and the presence of treecats in the courts of several generations of Manticoran monarchs, the Sphinxian treecats now enjoy legal status as citizens of the Star Kingdom and the acceptance of most of her Majesty's subjects. However, they enjoy that citizenship only in the status of minor children, and until they began to communicate directly with humans through sign language, even many Manticorans dismissed them as intelligent animals rather than a true sentient species.

The Medusans, on the other hand, have had less exposure to the other members of the Star Empire and have, at times, found themselves the subject of uneasiness and ambivalence.

Treecats

Treecats are the native sentient species of Sphinx. As such, they are considered citizens of the Star Empire, albeit with protected status.

PHYSIOLOGY

Treecats are hexapedal like all of Sphinx's indigenous mammals. 'Cats are built long and lean, somewhat along the lines of a Terran ferret or weasel crossed with a lemur monkey. They average about sixty centimeters in body length or about one hundred thirty centimeters overall, including their tails. Their foremost limbs end in well-developed "true-hands," each with three fingers and a single opposable thumb. Their mid-limbs end in similar "hand-feet" that are considerably stronger but less agile, and their rearmost limbs end in "true-feet" that have toes, rather than fingers. All digits are tipped with retractable claws, approximately one centimeter in length. These claws are scimitar-shaped and formed of extremely dense, hard material, resembling terrestrial sharks' teeth much more than they do the claws of terrestrial cats. The back edge of each claw is extremely sharp, which turns them into quite lethal weapons. It is uncommon for a 'cat to shed a claw, but it can happen. When it does a new claw grows to replace it.

Treecats are covered in thick, fluffy coats that grow in three separate layers. The two outer layers are subject to seasonal variations in length and thickness, with a shedding process governed by a temperature-sensitive biological mechanism, and a treecat's full winter coat is almost twice as bulky as its summer coat. The outer surfaces of treecat tails are also very fluffy, but many people do not realize that those tails are actually flat, with a bare, leathery "gripping" surface on the "bottom." Under normal circumstances, powerful muscles keep the tail curled into a tube, showing only the outer, furry side. The tube relaxes into its flattened state in order to allow the 'cats to attain secure holds on limbs and branches that may be wet or coated in ice.

Treecats have definite muzzles, cat-like ears, and round heads that appear somewhat too large for their bodies in comparison to terrestrial cats. Their heads resemble that of a terrestrial bobcat or wildcat but with sharper muzzles, higher foreheads, and no tufts to the ears. Male treecats are universally gray in color, although there are gradations from 'cat to 'cat within that color range. This coloring allows them to blend well with the various colors of picketwood bark. Males also tend to be about fifteen to twenty percent larger than females and, unlike females, grow darker bands around their tails as they age. These "tail rings" make it possible to estimate a male's age with a fair degree of accuracy. The first ring appears at about four Sphinxian years of age and a new band appears every Sphinxian year thereafter.

In addition to being smaller than males and possessing no tail rings, females have dappled coats patterned in brown and white. This coloring allows them to blend in with the leaf-and-sunlight patterns of the upper branch level of the picketwood.

Treecats are similar to Terran mammals in that they give birth to live young. Multiple births are the norm for treecats. A treecat litter will contain three to seven treekittens, with an average of four being typical. The gestation period is approximately four and a half T-months (thirteen and a half T-weeks).

TELEMPATHY AND TELEPATHY

While many suspected that treecats were true, functional telempaths, the theory was unproven until 1914 PD, when Dr. Adelina Arif developed a sign language to enable direct human-treecat dialogue. Among themselves, treecats are also telepaths, which is undoubtedly how they managed to attain a high level of societal and cultural integration without ever developing the concept of a spoken language. They do use a few recognizable audio signals, such as cries of alarm, but other than that, they communicate directly mind-to-mind. The combined emotional aura and deliberate transmission of thoughts is what a treecat means by the term "mind-glow." To a treecat, another treecat appears as a bright beacon of emotion at all times. The transmission of thoughts, however, is a deliberate act.

Although it is normally accompanied by what might be thought of as "sideband transmissions" that deliver a great deal of additional, often subtle, information, a treecat's "mind-voice," unlike the emotional portion of his mind-glow, operates only when he chooses.

By human standards, 'cats are not naturally innovative. While they are problem solvers, they tend to solve specific problems without generalizing to other applications of the solution. This leads to a highly stable society and technological level, yet they are capable of making sudden, enormous intellectual leaps as a consequence of the existence of "memory singers." Female treecats' mind-voices are normally stronger than those of males, but a very small number of females also possess the telepathic equivalent of eidetic memory. Able to actually experience and reproduce the remembered thoughts and actions of other 'cats, these memory singers become their clans' repositories of history and knowledge. In addition, because a memory singer can pass actual experiences from one treecat to another, they are capable of transmitting new knowledge or new techniques throughout the entire 'cat population with astonishing speed.

SOCIAL ORGANIZATION

Treecats are organized into "clans." These are extended communities of closely related families that share a common range and the responsibilities of maintaining, expanding, and protecting their clan as a whole. Within any clan there are clearly differentiated responsibilities and tasks. Clans and their ranges tend to be extremely stable. In some cases a clan has maintained the same range literally for centuries. Because they are primarily carnivorous, the population density for any given clan range must be carefully maintained. Upon occasion, increases in population will force an expansion of a clan's range, although the more normal consequence is for the excess population to migrate outside the original range and establish an entirely new, though still closely related, clan.

Treecats seldom mate outside their own clans, although it does happen upon occasion. When it does, the male half of the mated pair normally becomes a member of his mate's birth clan. That pattern is not always followed, however, and whichever way it works out, the "moving" mate is readily adopted into and assimilated into his or her mate's clan.

Treecats mate for life. The union between two treecats is a telempathic as well as a physical one. The individual mind-glows of both halves of a mated pair grow considerably "brighter" and stronger than they were prior to the mating. Once a pair has mated, they become permanent parts of one another in a way that other individual treecats do not. Indeed, they are uncomfortable if circumstances part them. This need not rise to the level of acute pain, so long as both know the parting will be only temporary, but it is a source of stress and unhappiness during the period of separation. If one half of a mated pair dies, however, it is far more common than not for the other mate to follow into death. This may be the result of active suicide (although this is rare) or the result of what might be thought of as terminal depression. The surviving mate gradually sinks into a state of withdrawal in which he or she neither eats nor drinks until, eventually, death results. The most common countervailing influence is the existence of relatively youthful treekittens. The mind-glows of a 'cat's children will sometimes pull the surviving parent out of that dark death spiral.

Treecats who have adopted humans do not normally mate. In most cases, they may form temporary, primarily physical, attachments with other 'cats during their periodic return visits to their clan's home range, but the permanent mating bond is normally foreclosed by the strength and power of the treecat-human bond of adoption. According to the Sphinx Forestry Service, Nimitz and Samantha are the only mated pair both bonded to humans.

The rearing and education of treekittens, once they are old enough to begin exploring their world, is a communal experience. Adult 'cats, both male and female, contribute to incorporating the 'kittens into the social structure of the clan.

Because of their telempathic abilities, treekittens are familiar with their mother's mind-glow before they are born. This was believed to be the case once those telempathic abilities were recognized by humans and was subsequently confirmed by Dr. Arif from her discussions with Samantha and with 'cats on Sphinx. It is believed that, much as human babies take time to learn to speak, the growing 'kittens develop the ability to use their mind-voice over time.

TECHNOLOGY

Treecats are tool-users and fire-users, although the use and control of fire in an arboreal civilization poses certain obvious challenges and threats. Prior to contact with humanity, treecats made tools out of bone, wood, and stone, and wove fabrics and ropes out of the Sphinxian equivalent of hemp and also out of their own shed coats. Although clothing was never necessary for them, they created carry nets, tents, pillows, cushions, and similar textile items.

Following the establishment of contact with humanity and especially after the formation of the Sphinx Forestry Service, more sophisticated tools became available to treecats. By and large, especially during the period when treecat intelligence remained a hotly debated topic, efforts were made to prevent them from developing a dependency on humans for tools. Efforts concentrated on teaching them to make new tools out of the materials they'd always used rather than handing out "trade axes" which they would be unable to replace themselves.

RELATIONSHIP WITH THE CROWN

Treecats are legally considered citizens (albeit as minor children) of the Star Empire and have been since 1568 PD with the passage of the Ninth Amendment to the Constitution. By the same enactment, they hold permanent title to over one-third of the land area on Sphinx. Although it took over eighty T-years, that status as citizens was completely resolved by the passage of the Treecats Rights Bill in 1651. A subsequent decision by the Queen's Bench Court, the highest court in the Star Kingdom, in 1685 forever banned any legal challenge to the treecats' status as citizens. The Royal Manticoran Navy's regulations state that a treecat bonded to a serving member may not be separated for his or her adopted human. This applies to all ranks and all situations, including training.

In 1911 PD, a group of treecats from the same clan as Nimitz asserted that they wanted to emigrate to Grayson. Although the Sphinx Forestry Service opposed the move, the 'cats made it clear that they did not want to be "saved" by the SFS, and the move was allowed. After the RMN declined to provide transport, the 'cats were brought to Grayson on Lady Harrington's private yacht. An additional small colony from the same clan was recently established in Alexander-Harrington's duchy on Gryphon.

While adoptions have been occurring at a limited rate since 1518 PD, when Lionheart adopted Dame Stephanie Harrington, only in the last few years have most Manticoran citizens truly understood the intelligence level of the 'cats. This was due, at least in part, to a conscious policy of the treecats to downplay their own capabilities. Following the work of Dr. Arif, the 'cats have demonstrated a growing "comfort" in allowing humans to understand their level of intelligence. There appears to be a growing understanding among the treecat clans of the potential threat posed to the 'cats existence by warfare among humans. Some human researchers believe that the decision to emigrate to Grayson and Gryphon may have been one response to this understanding by the treecats, a fact that seems to be borne out by Dr. Arif's continuing discussions with the 'cats on Sphinx.

The fact that since the adoption of Crown Prince Adrienne so many monarchs of the Star Kingdom have been adopted by treecats has given rise to some conspiracy theories. Unquestionably, adopting a monarch or a potential monarch gives the treecats powerful protection at Court, but the Wintons have also recognized the benefits of human-treecat bonding, and heirs to the Crown routinely travel to Sphinx to meet the treecats and, hopefully, be adopted. The advantage of having a treecat as a constant companion has been demonstrated on a number of occasions by adoptees, and the Manticoran Palace Guard Service has long recognized the value of treecats as additional security "personnel." With the growth of direct communications between humans and the 'cats and their mutual recognition of the benefits to each other, it would be reasonable to conclude that 'cats will, more and more, be integrated into the fabric of human society.

NOTABLE TREECATS

Far Climber of Bright Water Clan (Farragut)

Far Climber of Bright Water Clan was one of the first wave of treecats to leave Sphinx and settle on Grayson. He formed an adoption bond with Miranda LaFollet shortly after arrival. He possesses a playful wit and a penchant for low humor, interacting with humans easily and comfortably. Far Climber is also one of the first treecats to learn the sign language developed by Doctor Arif.

Golden Voice of Sun Leaf Clan (Samantha)

Golden Voice is one of the very few female treecats, and the very first memory singer, to form an adoption bond. In addition, she is one of the only two memory singers ever to leave Sphinx. She originally bonded with George Tschu, an engineering officer in the Royal Manticoran Navy. During her and Tschu's deployment on HMAMC *Wayfarer*, she met and mated with Laughs Brightly. After Tschu's death at the Battle of Selkir Rift, she relocated to live with Laughs Brightly and Honor Harrington on Sphinx, where she gave birth to a healthy group of young.

Golden Voice was instrumental in the decision of Bright Water Clan to send a "colony expedition" of eight other adult treecats to Grayson with her and her four kittens, marking the first emigration of the treecat species to another world. Since that time the Grayson treecat population has risen to a total of forty-two thanks to additional births and emigration.

When Laughs Brightly returned from Cerberus with crippling damage to his telepathic transmitter, Golden Voice was influential in the work of Doctor Adelina Arif in teaching the treecats sign language. Golden Voice also formed a second adoption bond with Hamish Alexander-Harrington in 1919 PD, a highly unusual circumstance.

Laughs Brightly of Bright Water Clan (Nimitz)

Laughs Brightly was a member of the Bright Water Clan when he met and bonded with Honor Harrington, a young Sphinxian. His age at the time of adoption was approximately fifty T-years, making him a mature adult in his own right at the time of his adoption.

During his and Harrington's deployment on HMAMC *Wayfarer*, he met and mated with Golden Voice, fathering several healthy young treecats, who were later fostered with the clan that moved to Harrington Steading on Grayson.

Laughs Brightly sustained injuries to his telepathic transmitter during his capture by Havenite and, later, State Security Forces after the Battle of Adler. Only on his return did anyone realize the extent of the damage. While he can hear the mind-voices of other treecats and still sense their mind-glows, his own mind-voice has been rendered mute. His injury was the catalyst that led to the development of treecat sign language.

Leaf Catcher of Fire Runs Fast Clan (Ariel)

Leaf Catcher bonded with a very young Elizabeth Winton on her state visit to Sphinx in 1880 PD, while she was still the Crown Princess. While smaller and younger than Laughs Brightly, he is in many ways far more mature (or at least sober), as befitting the bondmate to the woman the treecats call "Soul of Steel."

According to Leaf Catcher's account, Clan memory singers had passed around images of Elizabeth Winton's mind-glow to all of the clan members, and Leaf Catcher felt drawn to Elizabeth immediately. When the young Crown Princess arrived in Sphinx for her visit, Leaf Catcher appeared at the edge of the landing pad to meet her, and their bonding was nearly immediate.

Sharp Claw of Moon Water Clan (Monroe)

King Roger III was adopted during a visit to Sphinx in 1827 PD. Sharp Claw presented himself to the Crown Prince Roger, and they bonded almost immediately. Sharp Claw and Roger's bond was shattered, however, when Roger was killed. After Roger's death, Sharp Claw entered the withdrawal pattern common to treecats who have lost their bonded partner, declining all food and water as he withdrew ever inward toward extinction. When Major Padraic Dover attempted to murder Queen Elizabeth's fiancé, Justin Zyrr, in his presence, however, Sharp Claw roused in Zyrr's defense. In the fight which ensued, Dover was killed and Sharp Claw formed a new adoption bond with Zyrr, thus becoming one of the very few treecats ever to survive the death of a bonded human.

Medusans

Medusans, or "Stilties" as they are often known to Manticorans, are the native species of the planet Medusa in the Basilisk System. Medusan civilization is based on autonomous bronze age city-states, although significant nomad populations exist. While birthrates in the cities are much higher than among the nomads, a combination of high infant mortality rates and primitive notions of public health and sanitation have kept population relatively stable in the cities. Periodic respiratory plagues also contribute to this stability, and total planetary population is estimated at well under seven hundred million.

PHYSIOLOGY

Medusans are trilaterally symmetrical with three legs and three arms. A typical Medusan stands 2.3 meters tall, although they can settle to less than a third of that height on their unique, tripedal legs. Joints are all ball-and-swivel, as is common for most of the animal life-forms on the planet. Medusans have the ability to splay their legs out on the ground and ride out a wind storm, or pull them in and set up a gamboling trot that can outpace a human in Medusan gravity.

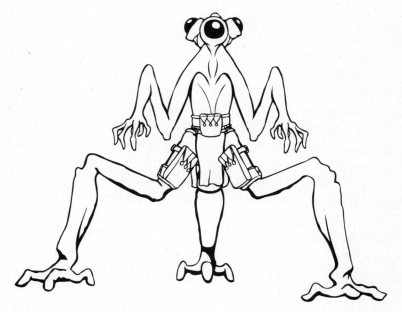

Each arm ends in a six-fingered hand, of which three fingers form dominant graspers and three smaller fingers provide a remarkable ability to manipulate objects. Legs end in feet with three toes also capable of grasping objects. A Medusan can pick up a rock with one foot, spin, and hurl it with remarkable accuracy, and can move at full speed in any direction.

The top of a Medusan's body case has three eyes, one over each of the arms, with three olfactory spiracles above the eyes. The mouth is under one of the three hip joints, the primary excretory apparatus is below the hip joint clockwise from the mouth, and the third hip joint protects the cloacal sex organs.

Medusan digestion obviates the need to cook most foods, as Medusans produce a strong "stomach acid" and expel it over their food, then massage it with their hands before squatting over it to eat it. Medusan culture elevates the touching and handing of partially digested food to other members of the social circle as a gesture of goodwill. They can go for longer periods without feeding than a human can, though they grow gradually more torpid as time passes.

Mating drives, which occur near the end of summer, are triggered both by the length of the day and by availability of food. Females eat ravenously and grow thick around their upper carapace both to prepare for a pregnancy and to signal their readiness for mating. Males use semaphoric threat displays and prepare a large ritual meal.

Medusan pregnancy is short, about a third of a local year, or nearly ninety T-days. They typically give birth to fraternal twins, and subsequent maturation is rapid. Sexual maturity occurs at eight local years (five T-years) and old age sets in at seventy local years (forty-eight T-years). Females are nearly impossible to distinguish from males unless they are preparing for mating.

Medusans communicate primarily by semaphoric body language, supplemented by vocalization through their spiracles, with scent changes for emphasis. A human linguist has described the polyphonic Medusan language as "singing operas through sneezing." Manticoran efforts to make a sign language system involved a holographic projector to overcome the shorthanded limitations of human physiology. A workable trade pidgin using two arms and exaggerated facial expressions and head motions has been in use since 1881 PD.

CULTURE

Prior to the arrival of humans, Medusan culture was dominated by nomadic grazers trading with city-states, with seven small clusters of city-states along marshlands and river deltas. The city-states trade worked metal, textiles, and other goods in exchange for wood and meat brought the nomads.

Among Medusan nomads, tribal conflicts consist of constant low-intensity warfare. Inter-city conflicts are much more serious and intensive, using armies composed primarily of militia organized around a much smaller core of regular, standing troops.

Medusan city-based culture was only an estimated seven or eight T-centuries old at the time of human contact, although this is far from certain. Turning an oral history of the birth of kings translated through semaphoric hand gestures into T-dates is fraught with speculation at best. The better analysis comes from carbon dating Medusan food storage pots.

Medusans consider fire to be a primarily industrial application; they are well suited to the climates in which they live and need little protection from the elements and rarely wear clothing other than kilts and equipment harnesses.

TECHNOLOGICAL ASSESSMENT

Medusan native technology had evolved to an ability to cast in bronze and copper alloys by the time of the planet's initial contact with humans. Most Medusan public works are huge constructs of dressed stone and the buildings can reach impressive heights for a culture without counter-grav. Although the Star Kingdom of Manticore has been trying to regulate the flow of offworld goods and devices to prevent the loss of the original Medusan culture through technological upheaval, technology transfer is happening between the humans and Medusans.

Prior to trade with off-worlders, the height of Medusan military armament was a form of bow, well suited to use from jhern-back, although it bore little resemblance to something a human could comfortably fire. Traditionally, Medusan foot soldiery used slings and stone-tipped spears, although bronze swords and spear and arrowheads were coming into use at the time of first contact.

Most of Medusa's flora is dominated by moss-like vegetation. Human residents on the planet refer to the entire planet as being covered in moss; this is only partially correct but, given humans' limited interaction with the planet, it is not an unfair characterization. Following contact with humans, Medusan agriculture has advanced by leaps and bounds, and output per hectare has increased dramatically with the introduction of fertilizers, crop rotation, and improved cultivation techniques, which is helping to fuel a modest population explosion among the city-based culture.

Manticoran efforts are underway to educate the Medusans in terms of technology, medicine, and public sanitation and hygiene, as well as issues in off-world affairs that may affect them. Manticoran schools for Medusans have full holographic communication suites and cover a wide range of topics. Medusan students may attend universities in the Manticore system within the forseeable future. While the process of bringing the Medusans into "interstellar adulthood" is ongoing, some issues cause friction. For example, while many Medusans would prefer to raze their Old Cities and build newer, more modern, durable, and comfortable cities, the Native Protection Agency is resistant to this idea, fearing that Medusan cultural treasures would be lost in the process.

RELATIONSHIP WITH THE CROWN

Medusa is held by the Medusan people, and all human enclaves are on T-century leases. The Star Kingdom has regulated contact with off-worlders much more tightly since the off-world-incited Mekoha Uprising in 1900. Following that incident and the First Battle of Basilisk, the Crown adopted an official policy under which Medusa may join the Star Kingdom as a member world or remain independent, following an eventual plebiscite. The creation of a coalition of city-states to act as the basis for a unified world government is a precondition for such a plebiscite, however, and it is uncertain if this will ever happen or if the Medusans even desire such an arrangement. Certain factions in the Manticoran Parliament also appear to be of two minds where the possibility of Medusan membership in the SKM is concerned, and most political analysts (and sociologists) estimate that it will be at least another thirty T-years—and probably much longer—before any such plebiscite might realistically be expected.

The Royal Manticoran Navy

The Royal Manticoran Navy (RMN) is a professional, career-oriented service. It began with only four small frigates, built in the Sol System for the Manticore Colony Trust of Zurich in 1389 PD, but has grown over the past five centuries into a potent fighting force with a solid core of ships of the wall supported by more numerous battlecruisers and smaller classes.

Prior to the discovery of the Manticoran Wormhole Junction, the Royal Navy was primarily a system defense force, its main function being to guard the Manticoran home system and deter potential threats from the generally small power blocs in Manticore's area of the galaxy. The expanding merchant marine and trade opportunities provided by the Junction required an equal expansion of the Navy and it grew into a powerful fighting and commerce protection force, although one that relied primarily on battlecruisers and lighter warships.

That orientation changed in the mid-nineteenth century when King Roger III began his great buildup in response to the Havenite wars of conquest. The Navy expanded exponentially into what is by any measure the third largest navy in the galaxy. Due to an aggressive R&D program, it is also by far the most technologically advanced and has been at the cutting edge of several revolutionary changes in warfighting, most notably the advent of the pod-layer and multi-drive missile.

Throughout its history, the RMN has maintained that the proper place for a naval officer to learn his trade is in space. While Saganami Island Naval Academy on Manticore is grueling and demanding, any line officer's career truly begins after graduation. An Academy graduate typically spends at least the next four or five Manticoran years (seven to nine Terran years) almost continuously in space in one shipboard assignment after another. Initiative and independence are encouraged along the way, in a process which produces seasoned, highly-experienced ship-handlers who are intimately familiar with their weapons, their personnel, and their mission. Traditionally, ninety percent of all officers have been graduates of the Academy, but that percentage has dipped during the recent decades of expansion, with a higher percentage of "mustangs" (an ancient term whose origin is lost in obscurity), non-commissioned personnel promoted to commissioned rank. This is more common in the RMN than in many other navies, and one reason for the practice is that Manticore's vast merchant marine, excellent education system, and extensive shipbuilding and orbital industries provide the Star Kingdom's Navy with non-commissioned and enlisted personnel of outstanding competence and quality.

Organization

The RMN is administered by the Board of Admiralty, which consists of three civilian Lords of Admiralty and seven Space Lords. Broadly speaking, the Lords of Admiralty are responsible for formulating policy while the Space Lords are responsible for implementing those policies.

The Lords of Admiralty are nominated by the Monarch, from a list of candidates selected by the Prime Minister. The final nominations must be confirmed by a majority vote in the House of Lords. The selection of the Space Lords follows the same procedure, nominated from a list provided by the First Lord of Admiralty.

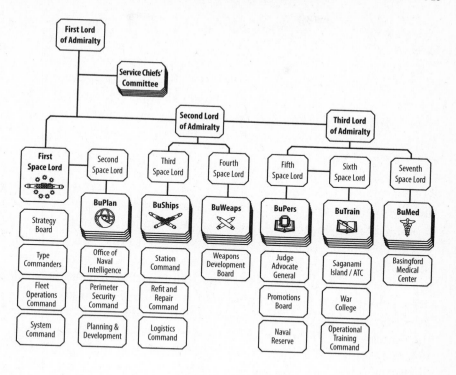

First Lord of the Admiralty
Lord Hamish Alexander-Harrington, Earl White Haven

The First Lord of the Admiralty is responsible for overall coordination of naval policy as directed by the Royal Council and the Crown. The First Lord acts as the *de facto* Minister of War for the Star Empire, and the senior uniformed commanders of the Navy, Marines and Army all report to him as the head of the senior Manticoran service through the Service Chiefs' Committee.

Second Lord of the Admiralty
Liam Guernicke

The Second Lord of the Admiralty is responsible for budgetary and fiscal management and reports directly to the First Lord. The Second Lord has direct administrative oversight of the Bureau of Ships and the Bureau of Weapons. The Second Lord is also called upon to work with Parliament during the annual budget review and has historically held the unenviable job of justifying the Navy's ever-growing costs.

Third Lord of the Admiralty
Dame Jessica Orbach

With an oversight role in the Bureaus of Personnel, Training and Medicine, the Third Lord of the Admiralty is responsible for the health and training of all Royal Naval personnel. She works closely with the Fifth Space Lord in particular to manage the growing manpower crunch that the Navy is experiencing as the war goes on.

First Space Lord
Admiral of the Green Sir Thomas Caparelli

The First Space Lord, regardless of his actual rank, is considered the senior uniformed officer in the RMN and is responsible for the overall strategic direction, force structure management, and deployment of the Navy. Immediately under the First Space Lord's direction are the Type Commanders (each an admiral charged with the management and training of a specific type of naval vessel) and the Strategy Board (consisting of the First, Second, and Sixth Space Lords plus the Type Commanders). Operationally, the Royal Manticoran Marine Corps also answers directly to the First Space Lord, although the Commandant of the Corps is seated with him and the Royal Army's Chief of Staff on the Service Chiefs' Committee.

While all RMN personnel are under the orders of the First Space Lord under the umbrella of Fleet Operations Command, the Admiralty has long understood that it cannot micromanage an interstellar war from the home system. The RMN generally follows the tradition of "mission type" orders, where a subordinate is given a mission and forces and is granted a great deal of discretion in how the mission is actually executed. Only on rare occasions (usually involving specific intelligence or policy concerns that a local commander may not know about) does the Admiralty override an officer on the spot.

Second Space Lord
Bureau of Planning (BuPlan)
Admiral of the Green Patricia Givens

The Second Space Lord reports to the First Space Lord and is responsible for operational planning and tactics. Everything from war plans to deployment patterns to doctrine are formulated by the Second Space Lord and her staff, working with the Strategy Board and other Space Lords as necessary.

The Second Space Lord is the *de facto* head of the Office of Naval Intelligence, although most of the administrative duties of the job are delegated. ONI is the clearinghouse for all of the Navy's intelligence operations, from intelligence gathered during routine naval operations to the human intelligence sources (spies) operating in enemy territory. The Criminal Investigation Division of ONI is its counterintelligence unit, working jointly with the Judge Advocate General's office on internal cases where there may have been a foreign influence. ONI works closely with the Bureau of Planning, which is responsible for analyzing, developing, and disseminating operational and tactical doctrine. In other words, ONI is responsible for determining adversary doctrine, while BuPlan develops RMN (and, through its liaison with allied navies, Allied) doctrine.

The other major commands that report to the Second Space Lord are Perimeter Security Command and Fortress Command. PSC maintains the huge system detection arrays, the network of reconnaissance platforms emplaced around the hyper limit as well as several Destroyer Squadrons to chase down possible contacts. Fortress Command is responsible for the network of fortresses, LACs, minefields and missile pods covering both the Manticore Wormhole Junction and its termini.

Third Space Lord
Bureau of Ships (BuShips)
Vice Admiral of the Red Anton Toscarelli

The Third Space Lord and BuShips oversee all construction and maintenance in association with the Second Lord's fiscal directions. The space stations *Hephaestus*, *Vulcan*, and *Weyland* are included in the Third Space Lord's purview, as well as the dispersed yards in planetary orbit.

Refit and Repair Command also reports to the Third Space Lord and oversees the shipyard portions of the stations, managing everything from routine maintenance to service life extension programs and major refits.

Logistics Command and its operational formation, Fifth Fleet, are jointly tasked with maintaining, organizing, and deploying all units of the fleet train (even if they are detached and assigned to other numbered fleets) and with meeting the logistics requirements of the other operational fleets.

Fourth Space Lord
Bureau of Weapons (BuWeaps)
Admiral of the Green Lady Sonja Hemphill, Baroness Low Delhi

The Fourth Space Lord is in charge of all research and development, specifically that of weapon systems in association with the Second Lord's fiscal directions.

Over the years the Weapons Development Board has served as a clearinghouse for the Navy's R&D efforts, with the specific tasking of creating weapons systems and technologies to offset the large and growing quantitative edge the People's Navy enjoyed over the RMN. The WDB was responsible not only for the majority of the new technologies seen in the Fleet today, but also for creating the environment where this kind of research could be performed and thrive.

In addition to the R&D side, BuWeaps is responsible for the construction and distribution of weapon systems, ordnance, and other consumables, working in concert with Logistics Command at BuShips.

Fifth Space Lord
Bureau of Personnel (BuPers)
Admiral of the Green Sir Lucian Cortez

The Fifth Space Lord is responsible for recruiting and manpower management, in association with the Third Lord's directions. This task includes not only finding crew for new construction and assuring adequate rotation, but also managing the personnel transfers to Alliance navies and management of the Naval Reserve.

BuPers is responsible for all aspects of a service member's career, which includes payment, housing, benefits and ensuring he or she meets the requirements for promotion. During peacetime, a typical career path would include a mixture of shipboard and "shore" commands appropriate to the career path of the officer or enlisted member in question. In wartime, those plans often change as the critical need for manning of new construction and replacement of injured or captured crew continues.

The Judge Advocate General's office reports directly to the Fifth Space Lord in matters of Admiralty law as well as maritime law, covering legal services both for individual service members as well as for the Navy as a whole.

Sixth Space Lord
Bureau of Training (BuTrain)
Vice Admiral of the Red Lord Sir Frederick Ormskirk, Earl Tanith Hill

The Bureau of Training is responsible for training and education in association with the Third Space Lord and Fifth Space Lord. He also coordinates with the Second Space Lord on training syllabuses and doctrine. All of the academic units maintained by the Navy (Saganami Island Naval Academy, Advanced Tactical Center, Fleet Officer's Candidate School and the War College) report to the Sixth Space Lord.

Operational Training Command also reports to BuTrain. Prior to the capture of Trevor's Star, units were frequently transferred to Second Fleet for their workup, especially the new pod super-dreadnoughts, LACs and carriers. Currently, Operational Training Command is attached to Third Fleet, and all workup takes place in Trevor's Star before assignment.

Seventh Space Lord
Bureau of Medicine (BuMed)
Vice Admiral of the Red Sir Allen Mannock
Surgeon General of the Star Kingdom

The Seventh Space Lord is responsible for the health and medical treatment of all Fleet personnel, including management of all Fleet hospitals (such as Basingford Medical Center), in coordination with the Third Space Lord. Auxiliary hospital ships in RMN service are jointly managed between the Third and Seventh Space Lords.

TACTICAL ORGANIZATION

The largest static combat organizational unit in the RMN is the fleet. Fleets are established to meet a specific need, which can be anything from defense of the home system (Home Fleet) to attacking a specific objective (Sixth Fleet) to patrolling a specific area of responsibility (Tenth Fleet).

Defense of the Manticore Home System was originally divided into two fleet districts, Manticore and Gryphon. Manticore was considered the senior fleet district, officially on the record as First Fleet, but always referred to simply as Home Fleet. Likewise, the much smaller Gryphon fleet district was officially Second Fleet.

Flag officers were originally rotated between fleet districts on the basis of seniority, Admirals of the Red (Gryphon) being junior to Admirals of the Green (Manticore). This system allowed senior officers to rotate frequently between districts and kept the Navy from stagnating. When the Gryphon Fleet was officially disestablished by Samantha II in 1828, the division of seniority remained but was no longer tied directly to duty station. Additional fleets (such as Third Fleet for the original attack on Trevor's Star) have been activated and deactivated as necessary over the years.

Fleets can be temporarily or permanently subdivided into *task forces* to perform specific missions. No strict requirements on the size or nature of a task force exist, other than that it consist of the assets necessary to fulfill the mission, which could be an offensive operation, defense of a sector, reserve, etc. Each task force is assigned a two-digit number, typically abbreviated as "TF ##." The first digit is the number of the fleet, while the second differentiates between task forces from the same fleet, so "TF 31," for example, refers to the first task force of Third Fleet. In addition, a task force can be broken into several *task groups*, identified by decimal points, as in TG 31.2.

Squadrons in the RMN are permanent administrative units, not necessarily tactical units, although there is a distinct tendency for squadrons of cruisers and larger warships to be kept together as much as possible. Thus a Destroyer Squadron might consist of sixteen destroyers operating in four separate divisions of four ships each, deployed light-years apart on an as-needed basis. The fact that light units routinely need to be detached as escorts, scouts, couriers, etc., helps to explain why their unit organization is so much more flexible than that for larger units, which are not so likely to be detached.

Cruisers fall into a special category as the medium combatant jack-of-all-trades. Cruisers very seldom operate as complete squadrons unless assigned to a task force or fleet organization, and, even there, the task force or fleet commanding officer has a distinct incentive to detach individual heavy cruisers or divisions of light cruisers for all sorts of tasks.

Prior to 1902 PD, both heavy cruisers and battlecruisers were organized more according to their mission than their type. The two most common squadron sizes are eight-ship squadrons integrated into the screen and twelve-ship squadrons tasked for independent operations, though recent years have seen frequent changes in these sizes, often to match the smaller battle squadrons.

Ships of the wall have historically been organized into eight-ship battle squadrons, a practice which was phased out in favor of a six-ship squadron during the Janacek Admiralty as a largely political maneuver, though (unlike most Janacek "reforms") the practice has been maintained due to the increased tactical flexibility the smaller squadrons offer.

Heroes of the Royal Manticoran Navy

The official motto of the Royal Manticoran Navy is "The tradition lives," but the motto of the Saganami Island Naval Academy is somewhat longer. Taken from a great pre-space political leader, it reads "In War: Resolution. In Defeat: Defiance. In Victory: Magnanimity. In Peace: Goodwill," and was chosen to enshrine the lessons gleaned from the RMN's three greatest heroes: Edward Saganami, Ellen D'Orville, and Quentin Saint-James.

COMMODORE EDWARD SAGANAMI
(1616–1672 PD)

If any one individual might be said to represent the heart and soul of the Royal Manticoran Navy, that individual would be Edward Saganami. Born of yeoman parents on the planet of Gryphon eighty T-years prior to the Gryphon Uprising, Saganami was a typical Gryphon Highlander: stubborn and passionately loyal to the Crown. Admitted to the Navy, he excelled on the basis of sheer talent, determination, and energy and had risen to commodore's rank by 1662 PD despite a complete lack of patronage or highly placed relatives. At that time, he was selected to command the successful punitive expedition against the Ranier System, whose piratical "navy" had been raiding commerce and infrastructure in the vicinity of the Hennesy Terminus of the Manticoran Wormhole Junction.

Having compelled the Ranierians' capitulation, Saganami, after a brief stint lecturing at the Academy, was selected by Queen Adrienne to command the squadron dispatched to the Silesian Confederacy in late 1671 PD to suppress piratical attacks on Manticoran commerce. Later evidence conclusively demonstrated that the "pirates" were supplied with ships, men, and weapons by Manpower of Mesa and elements within the Silesian government itself. Manticore's role as one of the original signatories of the Cherwell Convention (1651 PD), dedicated to the suppression of the interstellar genetic slave trade, explained Manpower's enmity; the opportunity for profit and to prune back Manticoran influence explained the Silesian element; and the chronic disorder of the Confederacy (already sliding into "failed state" status) provided the opportunity for both adversaries.

Those adversaries had anticipated neither the strength Queen Adrienne was prepared to commit nor the determination of its commander, however, and by April 1672 PD, Saganami's augmented battlecruiser squadron had destroyed four major "pirate" bases, and in the process captured intelligence pointing towards the involvement of the Silesian government. In the face of his embarrassing success, the Silesian Navy quietly transferred several of its more powerful units to the "pirates," who were also reinforced by additional Solarian-built cruisers and battlecruisers supplied by Manpower. In July 1672, at the Battle of Trautman's Star, Saganami's nine battlecruisers encountered nineteen "pirates." The RMN lost two ships in action, with four more damaged. Only two enemy vessels, both heavily damaged, escaped destruction or capture, but Saganami's own losses and damage reduced him to only three remaining battlecruisers. Until he could be reinforced, he was forced to suspend his offensive operations and revert to convoy escort, dispersing his remaining units for that purpose.

On August 11, 1672 PD, the surviving "pirate" fleet, guided by intelligence provided by the Silesian government, ambushed a convoy personally escorted by Commodore Saganami in his flagship, HMS *Nike*, in the Carson System. Given the geometry of the encounter, *Nike* could readily have avoided action but the merchant vessels under her escort could not have. Rather than flee, Commodore Saganami accepted action at six-to-one odds in an effort to destroy or so cripple the "pirates" that they would be unable to overtake the merchantmen. In the ensuing engagement, HMS *Nike* was lost with all hands, but not before she had destroyed three destroyers and one battlecruiser outright. A second heavy cruiser was severely damaged and only a single hostile battlecruiser survived uninjured. As a result of their losses, the "pirates" were unable to capture or destroy a single merchant ship and their remaining forces, weakened by the cumulative losses Saganami's squadron had inflicted, were easily defeated by the heavily reinforced fleet Queen Adrienne dispatched to avenge Saganami's death.

Posthumously awarded the very first Parliamentary Medal of Valor for the Battle of Carson, Commodore Edward Saganami, by his actions, established the tradition and the meter stick by which all subsequent Royal Manticoran Navy officers were to be judged.

REAR ADMIRAL ELLEN D'ORVILLE
(1650–1710 PD)

The second member of the triad of iconic Royal Manticoran Navy heroes, Ellen D'Orville was born to one of the Star Kingdom's most aristocratic families. After serving as a youthful lieutenant under Edward Saganami during his Silesian mission, D'Orville rose rapidly in rank, earning an enviable reputation as a tactician. In 1683, as commanding officer of the elderly light cruiser HMS *Unconquered*, Commander D'Orville intercepted and captured a four-ship convoy of slave ships, liberating approximately 24,000 genetic slaves. In 1687, Captain (acting Commodore) D'Orville was rotated to a teaching position at Saganami Island, the Royal Manticoran Navy's Academy, where she lectured in tactics, helped to reorganize the Naval War College, and created the Advanced Tactical Course (the commanding officer's course required for all starship captains of the RMN even today).

Returned to fleet duty in 1700 PD and promoted to Rear Admiral of the Red in 1705, D'Orville was dispatched with a small but powerful squadron to the Ingeborg System in 1710, in response to a request from the Terre Haute System government.

Terre Haute had received reports that the current Ingeborg regime was developing weaponized nanotech which it intended to employ against Terre Haute. D'Orville proceeded to Ingeborg, where the authorities initially denied any interest in nanotech research. D'Orville declined to believe them and pressed politely, but *very* firmly, for a face-to-face meeting with Ingeborg System President for Life Adrian Lipsky. After repeated attempts to delay, Lipsky agreed to meet with her aboard Ingeborg Alpha, the largest of the star system's three artificial habitats.

Unknown to D'Orville, the laboratory in which the weapon was being developed had lost containment, and the weapon had already contaminated and virtually depopulated the orbital habitat which had contained it, killing over 350,000 people. President for Life Lipsky, who had no intention of admitting that fact to D'Orville (primarily for fear that the Solarian League might construe the development of an obviously genocidal weapon as a violation of the Eridani Edict), hoped to meet with D'Orville, convince her that Terre Haute's fears had been misplaced, send her on her way, and then arrange a plausible "accident" to destroy the contaminated habitat and any evidence of his government's actions.

Unfortunately for Lipsky, Ingeborg Alpha had also been contaminated, although that fact became evident only after D'Orville and her security detachment had boarded the habitat to meet with the system president. Lipsky immediately attempted to flee the habitat, but was prevented by D'Orville, who took command of the frantic effort to rescue as many of Ingeborg Alpha's two-million-plus inhabitants as possible. Although urged by her flag captain to evacuate herself, she remained personally on-station, using her own fleet personnel, small craft, and every available civilian Ingeborgian vessel to evacuate personnel from the path of the nano weapon while simultaneously coordinating the effort to contain and confine the contagion.

Approximately two-thirds of Ingeborg Alpha's personnel had been removed from the habitat when the nanotech breached the final firewall and containment failed. D'Orville's final message to her flag captain was to destroy the entire habitat with a saturation nuclear strike to ensure the total destruction of the nano weapon. For her rescue of 1.4 million Ingeborgian civilians at the cost of her own life, Ellen D'Orville became the second recipient of the Parliamentary Medal of Valor.

ADMIRAL QUENTIN SAINT-JAMES
(1696–1769 PD)

Ensign Quentin Saint-James became the fifth and (to date) youngest recipient of the Parliamentary Medal of Valor (PMV) in 1719 PD, when in command of one of a flight of three assault shuttles from the heavy cruiser HMS *Black Rose* supporting a Marine landing party on the planet Jeremiah in the Hume System of the Breslau Sector of the Silesian Confederacy. The Hume Liberation Front (HLF), a Silesian separatist organization, had issued "letters of marque," commissioning "privateers" to prey on Silesian commerce. Unfortunately for the HLF, its privateers had turned pirate, preying on Manticoran commerce as well, prompting *Black Rose*'s intervention in the system.

As the assault shuttles deposited the Marines and lifted to provide fire support, they came under intense fire from the planetary surface. Simultaneously, concealed heavy weapons opened fire on the Marines. Two of the RMN assault shuttles were destroyed immediately. Saint-James' shuttle was severely damaged, his flight engineer was killed, and he and his copilot were both wounded. Rather than withdraw, Saint-James, with his unconscious copilot beside him, attacked into the teeth of the fire decimating the Marines he had landed. Hit twice more in the course of the next fourteen minutes, Saint-James' shuttle crash-landed outside the Marine perimeter, but not until he had inflicted massive losses on the HLF ambushers. Critically injured in the crash, Saint-James dragged his still-unconscious copilot clear of the wreckage and defended him with only his sidearm until the Marines fought their way to his position. As a consequence of his wounds, Quentin Saint-James lost his left arm and his left leg below the knee, but his fearless defense of the Marines he had landed allowed them to hold their position until reinforcements from *Black Rose* arrived to restore the position.

Despite the valor which won him his well-deserved PMV, however, Quentin Saint-James is best remembered for a "fleet battle" in which only seventeen people were killed and fewer than sixty were wounded.

In 1752 PD, the planet of San Martin in the Trevor's Star System acted unilaterally to abrogate the terms of the Treaty of 1590 between San Martin and the Star Kingdom of Manticore, governing usage and transit fees of the Trevor's Star Terminus of the Manticoran Wormhole Junction. By 1750 PD, the San Martin government, following the statist example of the Republic of Haven but without the size and broad diversity of Haven's original economy, was in dire fiscal straits. A coalition of radical minority parties gained control of the executive and legislative branches in the 1751 elections, and the following year "nationalized" the Trevor's Star Terminus, dispatching warships to seize control of it without warning in clear violation of the Treaty of 1590.

Surprised by the attack, Manticore was unable to prevent the terminus' seizure, but although Queen Caitrin was known as "Caitrin the Good," her government, under the leadership of Prime Minister Margo Thackeray, was unprepared to allow such aggression to stand. In particular, there were strong fears in Landing that the radicalized San Martin government would officially ally itself with relatively nearby Haven and give the People's Republic of Haven, with whom Manticoran relations had steadily worsened, control of the terminus.

Rather than attempt to fight its way through the terminus from the Junction (which would have been feasible, given the imbalance between the Royal Manticoran Navy's resources and those of the San Martin Space Navy, but would have resulted in very heavy casualties for both sides), the RMN chose instead to demonstrate its resolution to assault through the terminus while actually sending a powerful force of ships of the wall and battleships on a month-long voyage through hyper. That squadron, under the command of Vice Admiral Quentin Saint-James, struck not at the terminus, but at the star system three light-hours from the terminus. As Saint-James had hoped when he proposed the strategy, every heavy unit of the San Martin Space Navy had been drawn to the terminus by Manticore's ostentatious preparation to attack through it, leaving the home system covered only by light units. A single San Martin light cruiser, encountered as Saint-James' force advanced towards San Martin, was heavily damaged when it refused to strike its wedge, but personnel casualties were minimal. None of the San Martin units deployed to the terminus were in a position to intercept the Manticoran task force short of planetary orbit, and the San Martin government had no option but to surrender once Saint-James' ships controlled the space about it.

To the astonishment of the San Martinos, however, Saint-James, accredited as his monarch's plenipotentiary, imposed remarkably gentle terms. Rather than exacting punitive reparations, the vice admiral, on behalf of Queen Caitrin, demanded simply the restoration of all seized property, restitution to private owners for damage and losses, and a return to the terms of the 1590 Junction Treaty. In addition, recognizing the dire fiscal straits which had inspired the San Martinos, he proposed to the Queen, who accepted his recommendation, that San Martin be granted favored star nation status and that San Martin transit fees through all Junction termini be reduced by fifty percent for a period of twenty-five years in return for a pledge from the San Martin government of fiscal reforms designed to return the system to solvency. The fiscal reforms which San Martin adopted in compliance with his terms did, indeed, restore the system government to prosperity over the next thirty T-years. Indeed, until Trevor's Star's conquest by the People's Republic of Haven in 1883, San Martin enjoyed the most prosperous economy, outside the Star Kingdom itself, in the Haven Sector. In addition, the goodwill which Saint-James' firm but compassionate handling of the situation earned from San Martin was a significant factor in San Martin's decision to seek admission to the Star Kingdom of Manticore in 1914 PD at the end of the First Havenite War.

Quentin Saint-James continued to serve the Navy he loved for another twelve T-years, retiring in 1764 PD with the rank of Admiral of the Green. His final duty assignment was as Academy Commandant.

Uniforms and Equipment

OFFICER'S SERVICE DRESS

The RMN officer's service dress uniform consists of a black, double-breasted tunic which seals up the right side and falls to the upper thigh. Beneath the tunic, officers wear a white blouse and black trousers. The tunic collar is "Prussian" in style—high and round but loose enough for comfort—and the blouse collar is a turtleneck. Trousers are loose and straight cut to shin level, at which point they flare out and are bloused into low-topped space boots. The tunic's tailoring is slightly wasp-waisted, which can have unfortunate consequences for more portly officers, and bears thin gold piping on either side of the cross-over front panel. Trousers are untrimmed, with a smart-fabric closure.

Cuff stripes are bands, usually referred to as "rings," of gold braid. In addition to the cuffs, a matching number of thin gold stripes are carried on the tunic's shoulder board "epaulets." Epaulet stripes run front-to-back and are counted in from the outer end of the epaulet. The background color of the epaulet is red, not black.

The left shoulder of the tunic bears the name of the wearer's current assignment, with hull number if applicable, in an inverted horseshoe arrangement immediately below the shoulder seam. The right shoulder bears the gold-and-scarlet Manticore badge of the RMN. Collar insignia are worn on the tunic's collar, and the same insignia are worn on an embroidered patch on the left chest of the blouse, immediately above the pocket. Medal ribbons and qualification badges are worn on the left breast of the tunic, and a nameplate is worn on the right with any unit ribbons worn below the nameplate. Above their other ribbons officers wear one star, embroidered in gold thread, for each hyper-capable command they have held.

The standard headgear is a beret, which breaks to the right and bears the Kingdom's coat of arms as a flash on the left side. Starship commander's berets are white; all others are black.

ENLISTED SERVICE DRESS

The enlisted service dress uniform is considerably simpler than the officer's uniform. Built for comfort and range of motion, the uniform is a tailored, one-piece coverall, in standard Navy black with gold trim down the front. A nametag is worn on the left breast, with ribbons and qualification badges worn underneath. Unit ribbons are worn on the right side.

The same basic uniform is worn by noncomissioned officers (NCOs), but the trouser seams of petty officers and chiefs are picked out in piping color-coded by branch.

Rating insignia is worn on the left sleeve, color-coded by department. Additional specialist insignia is worn on the upper left sleeve as a shoulder patch, under the unit patch. Above the left cuff, one hash mark is displayed for every three Manticoran years (approximately five T-years) of service.

The beret is identical to that worn by the officers.

SKINSUITS

The RMN skinsuit consists of a single-piece body suit, boots, gloves and a helmet. A skinsuit is individually fitted to its wearer and varies in thickness from a minimum of about one centimeter to a maximum of twelve centimeters across the shoulders and upper back. The gloves are much thinner to allow manual dexterity.

The outer layer of the skinsuit consists of tightly woven anti-ballistic fabric. Underneath is a flexible matrix of storage vacuoles in which consumables are stored under immense pressure. The vacuoles are interwoven with the suit's air, waste management, heat management and power systems. The innermost layer is a porous padding, designed to wick away excess heat and moisture.

The joints of the skinsuit are equipped with strands of an electro-organic "muscle," which respond to the wearer's movements by biofeedback sensors. These enhancements provide a full range of motion and help to counteract the weight of the suit.

The body suit itself is a single-piece garment covering the legs, arms and torso. Along the left arm is a flexible control pad that features small waterfall displays and a trio of telltales providing information on the skinsuit power level, seal integrity, and oxygen level, designed to be readable at a glance while the helmet is off. Suit functions (including configuring the displays and adjusting the color of the smart fabric on the outside of the suit) are controlled by a panel built into the same sleeve.

The chest has a medical panel consisting of a biometric readout and controls for emergency stimulants and painkillers. In addition, the arms and legs are equipped with an emergency tourniquet system that activates automatically when critical damage to a limb is detected, both to reduce blood loss and retain pressure.

At waist level, the suit features two umbilical connection points, on the left and right sides. These umbilicals are used to connect the suit's life support and plumbing to the ship's systems, or to daisy chain with another suit in an emergency situation.

The primary suit thrusters are located across the shoulder blades, while a second pair of smaller thrusters is located in the kidney area. The thrusters are controlled (and can be locked out) by the suit's control panel. Using the thrusters requires a fair bit of coordination, and the body must be kept in a relaxed "sitting" position to balance the vectors properly. Total reaction mass for these thrusters is extremely limited, and it is by far and away the most sharply constrained consumable in the skinsuit, suitable only for short periods of EVA work.

The helmet has an opaque back and an armorplast faceplate with a 120-degree field of view, which opens upward for comfort. Unlike most navies, the RMN wears its headgear inside its helmets, accepting a slightly larger helmet as a consequence. Small spotlights for EVA and emergency use are located on both sides above eye level. A small magnetic clamp allows the helmet to mount in a shockframe, or be stowed on the chest of the skinsuit when not worn.

The inside of the faceplate contains a multifunction heads-up display used for status displays, communications and navigation. Inside to the left is a retractable water tube controlled by the arm keypad and to the right is the chin switch that connects the suit's communicator to the emergency channel.

Officers' skinsuits are solid white and display collar and cuff insignia in black similar to the service dress uniform. The helmet is marked with both rank insignia and a name stenciled across the top.

Enlisted and non-commissioned officers' skinsuits are white with arms, legs and chest color coded by department. Name and rate insignia are displayed on the helmet, as on the officers', and the arms display rating and specialist insignia in white or black contrasted against the departmental color.

Order of Battle

For all its current firepower and technological superiority, the Royal Manticoran Navy's origins were humble. From the date of landing until the formation of the Star Kingdom, what became the RMN never boasted more than thirty-five ships, the largest approximately the size of a modern light cruiser. The discovery of the Manticoran Wormhole Junction led directly and inevitably to a major expansion in the Navy's size, creating both a wall of battle and a numerous and powerful force of lighter units for commerce protection duties. In the middle decades of the nineteenth century PD, the future Roger III foresaw the coming clash with the People's Republic of Haven more clearly than virtually anyone else in the Star Kingdom's government, and began his life's work of building up the fleet.

The expansion driven by Roger's foresight lasted four decades, despite his own tragic, early death. The Navy's wall of battle grew from a mere three squadrons at the time of his coronation in 1857 to over eighty ships by the time of his death, thirty years later. By the end of the century, the RMN had become the third most powerful navy in existence; arguably, today, it is the galaxy's leading naval power in light of its numbers, technological superiority, and expertise. That position is no accident. It results directly from the policies of King Roger and his daughter Queen Elizabeth and the Navy's unwavering focus—driven by Roger's initial vision—on the R&D and technological imagination necessary to create a qualitatively as well as quantitatively superior fighting machine.

LIGHT ATTACK CRAFT (LAC)

Over the course of the last two decades the role of the LAC has evolved far more than that of any other type of vessel in the Manticoran Navy. By the time the Havenite Wars began officially in 1905 PD, the LAC had been completely phased out of Manticoran service. Too light to survive and too weakly armed to seriously threaten modern warships, the LAC had become a clearly obsolete type. Certain RMN theoreticians, however, led by Admiral Sonja Hemphill, had begun to consider the creation of an attrition unit built with the new technologies then becoming available. What began as a design study for an "expendable" unit (the *Series 282* LAC) evolved over the next several T-years into one designed to operate and survive even in heavy-threat environments.

Several experimental types were produced over the next five T-years, but the true renaissance of the light attack craft came in 1913 PD with the new *Shrike* class, built with almost entirely new technology. Small, fast, and more heavily armed than some prewar destroyers, this new breed of warship revolutionized the concept of LAC operations in the Manticoran Navy. While the original *Shrikes* were used as alpha-strike units against unsuspecting targets, LAC doctrine was in a constant state of evolution throughout the last battles of the First Havenite War. By the end of Operation Buttercup, the LAC wings were used in a counter-screening role, destroying scouting platforms to deny the enemy tactical data on the wall's formation, stripping off critical defenses from the Havenite walls of battle, and swarming and destroying cripples as they fell out of formation.

The sudden appearance of Havenite pod-layers and LACs forced a major reevaluation, and doctrine remains in a state of flux. Taking a page from the Republican Navy, the RMN has begun to use the LAC to replace the destroyer as one of the primary members of the antimissile screen, with LAC wings tightly integrated into the defensive network to blunt the initial massive salvoes that now characterize pod-layer warfare.

Highlander-class light attack craft

Mass: 11,250 tons
Dimensions: 138 × 23 × 21 m
Acceleration: 409.3 G (4.014 kps²)
80% Accel: 327.5 G (3.211 kps²)
Broadside: 12MB, 1L, 3PD
Chase: 1L
Service Life: 1843–1912

The *Highlander*-class light attack craft was commissioned in 1843 PD as a system defense picket and customs patrol unit. It had a heavier beam armament than most contemporary classes, though contrary to typical RMN doctrine of the time, the lasers were optimized for point defense fire as well as the antiship role. The one-shot missile launch cells were built directly into the hull, allowing for system checks and routine maintenance without vacuum gear by the crew, although this increased costs and made them somewhat less suited to rapid re-arming than previous external launchers.

When the *Highlander* class was first placed into service, light attack craft were primarily used as home system pickets and scouts, freeing up hyper-capable hulls for interstellar deployment or for concentrated rapid reaction system defense formations. As King Roger's naval buildup progressed, Manticore system hyper-limit picket duty was shifted to destroyers cued by reconnaissance satellites and the passive system arrays. Starting in 1887 PD, the *Highlander* class was retired. A number of hulls were stripped of armament, modified heavily and transferred to Astro Control Service as search and rescue platforms. An additional small number were retained purely as training craft attached to Saganami Island Naval Academy.

Series 282 light attack craft

Mass: 17,750 tons
Dimensions: 121 × 20 × 19 m
Acceleration: 573.2 G (5.621 kps^2)
80% Accel: 458.6 G (4.497 kps^2)
Broadside: 12MB, 1L, 1CM, 3PD
Chase: 1L, 2PD
Service Life: 1904–1918

The *Series 282* light attack craft was never given a formal class name because it was a prototype LAC, designed by the Weapon Development Board for the Trojan Horse program which saw extremely limited operational service.

While the *Highlander* class was a typical LAC design, built to very similar standards as a conventional warship, the *Series 282* took advantage of advances in both equipment miniaturization and automation to greatly decrease the volume necessary for critical systems. The result was a flattened hull that was slightly smaller than the *Highlander*, despite being half again the tonnage. The small size of the *Series 282*, along with the fact that its "on-paper" offensive capabilities were nearly identical to those of the old design, was cited numerous times by the program's many critics.

These critics uniformly failed to recognize the qualitative improvements behind the figures. The *282s* carried only twelve cell-launched missiles, but both the missiles and launch cells were far in advance of anything the *Highlander* mounted. Beam mounts were also more powerful, and the addition of a counter-missile launcher in each broadside more than doubled their survivability, as well as allowing them to perform an area defense mission in protection of their launch platform. Perhaps most notably, the *Series 282* was the first LAC to mount an impeller ring powerful enough to accelerate it to the limits of its inertial compensator. This class was the first to serve as testbeds for the early second generation compensator, raising its maximum acceleration to just over 600 G.

Despite the type's clear advantages, it was never able to overcome the opposition of its critics. Regarded as suitable solely for local defense and burdened with the anti-LAC attitudes of a navy philosophically committed to projecting combat power (and vehemently opposed to attrition-based tactics), it was produced in very small numbers. The number built provided valuable experience in the new technologies and were used as test beds for many of the systems incorporated into the early *Shrike*-class prototypes, however, and the *282s* provided a critical component in the combat power of the *Trojan*-class Q-ships until their final retirement in 1918.

Shrike-class light attack craft

Mass: 20,250 tons
Dimensions: 71 × 20 × 20 m
Acceleration: 636 G (6.237 kps^2)
80% Accel: 508.8 G (4.989 kps^2)
Forward: 4M, 1G, 4CM, 6PD
Service Life: 1912–1917

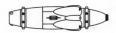

The *Shrike* revolutionized the concept of the LAC in many ways. Far from a simple evolutionary outgrowth of the *Series 282*, the *Shrike* has virtually nothing in common with a conventional LAC. Although the *Shrike* carried over many of the *282*'s technology innovations in terms of system miniaturization and increased automation, it represented a complete conceptual break with previous LACs. Earlier examples of the type had been seen as miniature warships equipped with traditional weapon systems; the *Shrike* was visualized as a single-weapon system, optimized for the sole purpose of getting its powerful graser into decisive range.

Historically, LACs have suffered from limited endurance driven by bunker space for fusion reactor hydrogen, so, unlike any warship in a millennia, the *Shrike* class carries a highly efficient fission pile as primary power. Inspired by Grayson developments in fission reactor technology, the fission plant means that the *Shrike's* cruise endurance is limited primarily by crew support consumables. Its combat endurance remains a factor of plasma feedstock for the gravitic subsystems (mostly graser and missile launch systems), but its ability to stay on station for months if necessary is a huge advantage in the system defense role. In addition, while a *Shrike* masses almost twice as much as a *Highlander* (in a hull less than half the size), its remotes and expert systems are some of the most advanced anywhere in space, simultaneously increasing lethality while decreasing crew requirements.

The *Shrike* class was also the first warship to be fitted with the new "beta-squared" impeller nodes, which by 1921 PD have become standard equipment on all new Manticoran construction. In addition to the mass savings the nodes provided, they also allowed the *Shrikes* to transmit FTL communications while under acceleration. The vastly more powerful impeller rings, second generation inertial compensators and enhanced electronic warfare and stealth systems made the *Shrikes* the fastest, stealthiest, and ton-for-ton most dangerous warships in space for their time.

Among all of the other advances seen on the *Shrike* class, perhaps the most notable was the introduction of the all-forward armament, combining the new off-bore launch technology with a bow wall and a powerful spinal-mounted graser for close range antiship strikes, all without relying on the traditional broadside armament carried by LACs up until this point.

For a program that was nearly cancelled by Navy before it could prove itself, the *Shrike*-class LACs performed far above expectations during the Second Battle of Hancock. Able to approach to far closer range of an enemy under stealth than anyone had predicted, their initial attacks were devastating. While their survivability against a prepared opponent was questionable, their ability to isolate and destroy cripples and the savage damage they could do to the enemy's screen proved their value.

Despite exceeding all expectations, the original *Shrike* was still a transitional design, with many flaws, some major and some minor, appearing during the early simulations, wargames, and battle experience. While the heavy demand for LACs kept many of them in service longer than expected, the last of the original production run was replaced in 1917 by the *Shrike-B*.

Shrike-B-class light attack craft

Mass: 21,250 tons
Dimensions: 72 × 20 × 20 m
Acceleration: 635.5 G (6.232 kps²)
80% Accel: 508.4 G (4.986 kps²)
Forward: 4M, 1G, 4CM, 6PD
Aft: 4CM, 6PD
Service Life: 1914–present

The *Shrike-B* class was a refinement of the original *Shrike* class, based on operational experience with the initial deployed prototypes. Almost before the first of what came to be known as the *Shrike-A* variant was commissioned, simulation data had begun to turn up weaknesses in the design. Its first trial by fire at Hancock provided all the evidence BuShips needed to finalize the new design. The aft hanger and cutter of the original *Shrike* were replaced by a duplicate set of counter-missile launchers and point defense facing aft, which provided much needed protection against the "up-the-kilt" fire which was responsible for the majority of the early losses. A small hanger was retained for deployment of the current generation of Ghost Rider reconnaissance drones or decoys.

Starting from 1915, all new construction added an external sternwall generator modeled on the one carried by the *Ferret* class. Like the *Ferret*'s generator, the power budget was tight enough to provide only enough power to run either the bow or sternwall but not both simultaneously.

Ferret-class light attack craft

Mass: 20,750 tons
Dimensions: 72 × 20 × 20 m
Acceleration: 635.8 G (6.235 kps²)
80% Accel: 508.6 G (4.988 kps²)
Forward: 4M, 4CM, 6PD
Aft: 4CM, 6PD
Service Life: 1914–present

The *Ferret* class was developed in parallel with *Shrike-B* as a screening unit, designed both to accompany squadrons of *Shrikes* on their strike missions and to thicken defenses for the wall of battle.

The *Ferret* is a pure missile-armed craft, with no antiship energy armament. The launch tubes remain in the same locations but the magazine is a far more traditional design, rather than the combination magazine and launch cell used in the *Shrikes*. The mass and volume freed up by the removal of the graser was enough to more than double the missile load of the *Shrikes*, thereby allowing the *Ferret* to carry dedicated electronic warfare (EW) drones as well as sophisticated decoys in addition to shipkillers. The counter-missile launchers remained similar to the *Shrike-B*, but their capacity was expanded as well, and the EW systems were upgraded still further. The addition of a dedicated sternwall generator marked the final difference between the *Ferret* and original *Shrike-B* classes, though the same power management limitations applied as on the *Shrike-B* refits.

Katana-class light attack craft

(for specification, see GSN Katana-class LAC)
Service Life: 1920–present

Shortly after the turnover at Admiralty House in 1920 PD, the RMN ordered several dozen squadrons of *Katanas* from the Graysons and put the design into Manticoran production, as well. Many of their frontline *Minotaur* and *Hydra*-class carriers are being refitted to carry a few squadrons of *Katanas* in addition to their regular complement of *Shrikes* and *Ferrets*.

DESTROYERS (DD)

From the earliest days of the Wormhole Junction and subsequent expansion of both the Navy and merchant fleet, the destroyer has been the workhorse of the Royal Manticoran Navy. The type itself remained almost unchanged in fundamental design for hundreds of years, but the roles it fills have been in a state of constant flux, especially over the course of King Roger's buildup.

Destroyer missions generally fit into one of two major roles: screening the wall of battle and fulfilling independent missions such as commerce protection. The primary choice facing designers has always been how—or even whether—to balance these roles.

The destroyer first came into its own as a screening unit because it was an inexpensive platform that could provide tactical reconnaissance duties as well as deny the enemy those same opportunities. A hyper-capable unit was needed to search in nearby sub-bands when a fleet or convoy was in hyper transit. Traditional cruising formations also deployed destroyers and light cruisers far out to the flanks upon emergence into real space to expand the sensor baseline of the formation and provide an outer picket to detect and destroy enemy scouting forces. Once battle was joined, the lighter units of the screen fell into position behind and around the wall, lending their support to the area defense without putting their fragile hulls in the line of fire.

The evolution of small, high-endurance drones began to erode the destroyer's operational reconnaissance roles, as these new drones were both faster and stealthier than any warship, in addition to being unmanned and therefore more expendable. The destroyer became a crewed node controlling formations of drones and the principle antiscouting platform, designed to localize and destroy recon drones as they approached the flanks of the formation. It still had a place as part of the wall's missile defense, but remained fragile and limited in that role compared to heavy cruisers and battlecruisers. On the other side of the coin, the traditional roles of a destroyer as an independent cruising unit were being eroded slowly as the Navy built up its inventory of light cruisers, a type that had been traditionally underrepresented in the Manticoran order of battle. The new light cruisers were more powerful, better defended and had longer endurance than any destroyer in service, which made them far better suited to the roles of strategic reconnaissance picket forces, commerce protection, or commerce raiding. The advent of the advanced LAC in 1914 PD, followed by the evolution of LAC antimissile doctrine in the early 1920s, removed the destroyer's last vestiges of utility as a screening unit. On a ton-for-ton basis, the new LACs were faster, better at localizing and killing recon drones, and far more effective in the missile defense role then destroyers had ever been.

At the present time, the future of the destroyer as a type is uncertain. On the one hand, there are those who predict that the destroyer will effectively disappear from the Navy in the not-too-distant future, with its independent operations role reverting to the cruiser and its fleet screening role going to the LAC groups. On the other hand, it is clear that the RMN sees a role for the destroyer today and into the future, as evidenced by the new *Roland* class. The advent of the multi-drive missile and the fact that the *Roland* appears to be the smallest hyper-capable ship type able to carry a meaningful number of these missiles indicate to many that the destroyer will be with us for a long time, even if it masses as much as an old-style light cruiser.

Noblesse-class destroyer

Mass: 68,250 tons
Dimensions: 351 × 41 × 24 m
Acceleration: 524.4 G (5.143 kps²)
80% Accel: 419.5 G (4.114 kps²)
Broadside: 4M, 3L, 2CM, 3PD
Chase: 2M, 1L, 1CM, 2PD
Number Built: 60
Service Life: 1819–1907

The *Noblesse*-class destroyer, a contemporary of the *Courageous*-class light cruiser, was the oldest destroyer still in service when the war with Haven began. In many ways, it was built as a scaled-down version of the *Courageous*, armed with the same outdated missile tubes and general weapon balance, though without the powerful beam armament carried by its larger cousin.

Although originally scheduled for decommissioning by the turn of the century, the RMN's need for light combatants extended the class beyond its planned operational life, and the many of the ships remained in service until 1907 PD. Although they were still suited for anti-piracy work, they had become obsolete with the rapid technological developments stimulated by the war and all were decommissioned as the *Culverin* class started coming off the building slips.

Falcon-class destroyer
Mass: 70,500 tons
Dimensions: 355 × 42 × 24 m
Acceleration: 523.6 G (5.134 kps²)
80% Accel: 418.8 G (4.108 kps²)
Broadside: 3M, 4L, 3CM, 4PD
Chase: 1M, 2L, 2CM, 2PD
Number Built: 88
Service Life: 1851–1916

The *Falcon*-class destroyer was a product of the same design study that yielded the *Apollo*-class light cruiser and *Lightning*-class frigate, the last frigate class to be built by the RMN. The notable feature of the *Falcon* class is that it is a beam-heavy platform relative to its contemporaries, designed to close quickly and engage an enemy at short range.

The first flight *Falcons* suffered from the same sub-standard construction practices which caused the *Apollo* class' structural weaknesses, and all but two required substantial refits.

Unlike the far more successful *Apollo*, both the *Falcons* and *Lightnings* were widely considered to be too fragile to survive an energy engagement (where a single lucky hit can do major damage). Although possessed of impressive firepower for their size, there were grave concerns about their ability to defeat something of their own rate. Although the last of the *Lightnings* was decommissioned before the turn of the century, the *Falcons* lasted until the fleet drawdown of 1916 PD.

Havoc-class destroyer

Mass: 84,500 tons
Dimensions: 377 × 44 × 26 m
Acceleration: 519.8 G (5.097 kps²)
80% Accel: 415.8 G (4.078 kps²)
Broadside: 5M, 3L, 3CM, 3PD
Chase: 2M, 1L, 2CM, 2PD
Number Built: 83
Service Life: 1861–present

The *Havoc* class was built as a successor to the *Falcon*-class destroyer. In many ways, its design presaged the move away from beam-heavy combatants to missile-heavy combatants. Designed as a general purpose destroyer, the *Havoc* class was able to perform all of the traditional destroyer missions and served many of them well. This was especially true in Silesia, where its mix of defensive armaments and adequate broadside made it a natural for anti-piracy operations. The skipper of a *Havoc* will generally attempt to keep the range open against its usual opponents, where the *Havoc*'s superior electronics and deep magazines provide it the greatest edge. Beam armament is modest at best, and a *Havoc* commander who approaches too aggressively places his command in danger.

As the buildup of light units accelerated and after hull numbers reached an unwieldy four digits, the RMN began to renumber its destroyers, with HMS *Havoc* being redesignated as DD-01 in 1873 PD. While the majority of the class are still in service, the combination of a small cramped hull and sub-par defenses have relegated the *Havocs* to rear-area duties and less important remote stations. With the latest round of EW refits, they remain well suited for anti-piracy operations, even if they are unsuited for combat against the Republic of Haven Navy.

Chanson-class destroyer

Mass: 78,000 tons
Dimensions: 367 × 43 × 25 m
Acceleration: 520.7 G (5.107 kps²)
80% Accel: 416.6 G (4.085 kps²)
Broadside: 3M, 3L, 4CM, 4PD
Chase: 2M, 1L, 2CM, 2PD
Number Built: 204
Service Life: 1867–present

With King Roger's naval expansion program in full swing, the RMN began a serious analysis of combat records from Silesia, and realized that ship defense needed significant improvement. The resulting destroyer, light cruiser, and heavy cruiser designs of the Enhanced Survivability Program all emphasized greater defensive armament and improved passive defenses. The destroyer design was the *Chanson* class.

By far the most numerous class of destroyer in the RMN, the *Chanson* is well suited to a variety of duties, from scouting and picket duty to the destroyer screen of a wall of battle, to independent operations "showing the flag" in smaller star polities. The class has long strategic endurance for a destroyer, making it popular with RMN planners, and its modern electronics suite and enhanced area defense capabilities make it better suited for convoy defense than the *Havoc*. Despite the reduction in launchers over the *Havoc* and *Noblesse* classes, the *Chanson* class remains strongest in a missile duel. Its heavy defenses and superior fire control allow it to hold its own against most destroyers and even some light cruisers as long as it can remain out of energy range. Still, it lacks the offensive punch of the *Havoc* class and its successor the *Javelin* class, a fact that was heavily criticized by opponents of the Enhanced Survivability Program.

When the *Culverin* class was delayed in the early 1900s, another flight of *Chansons* was ordered as a stop-gap. Other than incremental updates in electronics and fittings, these hulls are virtually identical to the older model *Chansons*, despite the ten-year gap in construction.

Javelin-class destroyer

Mass: 87,250 tons
Dimensions: 381 × 45 × 26 m
Acceleration: 519.7 G (5.096 kps²)
80% Accel: 415.7 G (4.077 kps²)
Broadside: 6M, 2L, 4CM, 3PD
Chase: 2M, 1L, 2CM, 2PD
Number Built: 65
Service Life: 1883–present

The *Javelin*-class destroyer is a contemporary of the *Chanson* class but has a fundamentally different design philosophy. Where the *Chanson* focused on cramming as much defense as possible into as small a hull as possible, the *Javelin* favors a heavier offensive punch, at the cost of some defense. It was intended to serve mostly as a fast screening unit for battlecruiser squadrons and has seen less independent command than its more survivable cousins.

While in simulation it seems like a highly effective design, its heavy offensive punch came at a price. Magazine space to support the larger broadside was one limitation, and the fact that all six launchers shared only two magazines made the design particularly vulnerable to damage. Missile tubes and magazines also had to be placed nearer to the sidewall generator spaces than normal and as a result the class has been plagued by feedback issues between grav drivers and sidewall generators for its entire service life. Compared to the *Chanson* and even the much maligned *Culverin* class, the *Javelins* were never particularly popular among either RMN planners or their crews. Most of them were relegated to reserve duty by 1920 even though some much older *Chanson*-class hulls were still in active service.

Culverin-class destroyer

Mass: 104,000 tons
Dimensions: 404 × 48 × 27 m
Acceleration: 547.4 G (5.368 kps²)
80% Accel: 437.9 G (4.294 kps²)
Broadside: 5M, 4L, 5CM, 4PD
Chase: 2M, 1L, 2CM, 2PD
Number Built: 72
Service Life: 1899–present

The *Culverin* class was designed as a powerful, general purpose destroyer to replace both the *Havoc* and *Chanson* classes. Although a bold design in terms of intent, the first units to be delivered came in over budget, late, and "overweight." Changes in requirements during the design process resulted in an increase in the offensive throw weight and a decrease in crew size, dictating the use of automation more commonly seen in merchant ships. In the end, the automation project was abandoned after the first two ships, but not before these changes delayed the commissioning of the first ship by two years and resulted in software and hardware glitches that were all but impossible to work out. The armament changes caused the *Culverin* to grow by nearly eight thousand tons and to lengthen by almost ten meters. Some point to these early problems as the reason that it took the Admiralty another ten years to try again to reduce crew requirements through increased automation.

When all was said and done however, the *Culverin* class was nearly as good as its design simulations said it should be. It has significant electronic warfare assets, an impressive broadside for a destroyer, and solid defensive capabilities that mesh perfectly with the latest generation of Manticoran hardware. The primary complaint about the *Culverin* is its reputation as a maintenance headache, although part of this reputation resulted from periodic shortages of spare parts during the initial construction phase. The peculiar internal layout brought on by the design changes has caused a great deal of trouble for damage control teams, a fact that wasn't fully appreciated until the first units began to see combat.

Wolfhound-class destroyer

Mass: 123,500 tons
Dimensions: 428 × 51 × 29 m
Acceleration: 784.7 G (7.695 kps^2)
80% Accel: 627.7 G (6.156 kps^2)
Broadside: 6M, 3G, 6CM, 5PD
Chase: 2G, 4PD
Number Built: 19
Service Life: 1919–present

The *Wolfhound*-class destroyer is a general purpose destroyer originally designed during the Janacek Admiralty to replace the entire RMN inventory of older model destroyers. Eighteen percent heavier than the *Culverin* class, the *Wolfhound* takes full advantage of the new technologies that enabled the RMN to build a destroyer that is more effective than many prewar light cruisers. The class has a limited off-bore capability and carries the latest generation of single drive missiles in RMN service, far longer ranged and more powerful than anything in service at the start of the war. With a crew of only eighty-seven, the complement of an old-style destroyer can be spread across nearly four *Wolfhounds*, freeing up manpower for other new construction without reducing the total number of destroyers in service.

While the *Wolfhound* is an effective platform by any prewar standard, once the performance numbers began to appear for the new *Roland*-class destroyers, the RMN substantially revised their building schedules. Given the missions that it would be assigned, the *Wolfhound* would not be significantly more capable than the hulls already in service, at least not enough to warrant the cost of replacing almost four hundred of them in wartime. Only nineteen *Wolfhounds* are currently in service; the other twenty of the original flight were destroyed in the Grendelsbane raids. While there are plans to put the *Wolfhound* into limited series production to start slowly replacing the oldest surviving destroyer classes, currently all of the smaller building slips have been dedicated to building *Rolands* and *Avalon*-class light cruisers.

Roland-class destroyer

Mass: 188,750 tons
Dimensions: 446 × 54 × 45 m
Acceleration: 780 G (7.649 kps^2)
80% Accel: 624 G (6.119 kps^2)
Broadside: 5L, 10CM, 9PD
Chase: 6M, 2G, 6PD
Number Built: 46+
Service Life: 1920–present

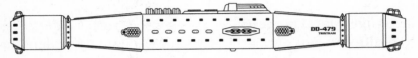

The *Roland* class reflects much of what the RMN has learned in the course of the war against Haven. In terms of sheer size, it is the largest destroyer ever produced, rivaling the size of other navies' light cruisers.

The RMN had been caught short of suitable flagships for cruiser and destroyer service during the First Havenite War, and the *Rolands* were one attempt to address that shortage. Every member of the class was fitted with extensive command and control capability and, in essence, each can operate as the flagship of a destroyer squadron.

The *Roland* is also the smallest warship to carry the Mark 16 dual-drive missile, mounting a cluster of six launchers in each hammerhead. Using off-bore fire, it can bring all missiles to bear on a single target. The obvious downside of this arrangement is that a single hammerhead hit can take out half the total missile armament.

The *Roland* is a match for any conventional light or even heavy cruiser without multi-drive missiles of its own. The *Roland* is able to engage at a range far outside the opponent's and is fast enough to make a run for it if its Mk16s are unable to penetrate the enemy's defenses. As with the *Wolfhound*, the *Roland* class has no place in the modern RMN wall of battle, and all of the units thus far deployed have been sent to either the Talbott Quadrant or Silesia for use as pickets, system defense, and convoy protection. The *Roland*'s use as a commerce raider has yet to be proven but extensive simulations reportedly have shown that the *Roland* will excel in that role should it be necessary.

LIGHT CRUISERS (CL)

Historically, the frigate was the primary RMN cruising unit, not the light cruiser. Designed for independent, long-endurance interstellar operations, frigates frequently engaged in commerce protection, anti-piracy operations, and strategic intelligence gathering. They became a common sight in many Verge systems as the Manticoran merchant fleet expanded, and as the first independent commands for many outstanding Manticoran officers of the war years, these tiny ships may rightly claim to have played a major part in the RMN's subsequent successes.

The RMN's longtime predilection for this type, despite its known disadvantages, stemmed from the need for numbers of platforms to deal with relatively low-level threats. Frigates were cheaper than destroyers, although their crew sizes and operating costs were very nearly equal, and they were capable of trouncing almost any pirate they were likely to meet. The ability to deploy them in greater numbers made them more desirable to a Navy whose primary business was just that—trouncing pirates—despite the always marginal combat power imposed by the heavy demands life-support, power rooms, and hyper generators placed upon the available mass and volume of such small hulls.

It took the looming war against Haven to knock the frigate out of favor due to its inability to face any regular warship, regardless of tonnage, and one of King Roger's major initiatives was the gradual replacement of the large inventory of frigates with light cruisers for long-range interstellar missions.

Light cruisers were seen as interstellar units, intended to operate for long periods of time without outside support, primarily for strategic and tactical scouting missions. Substantially larger than current-generation destroyers, they were also more potent combat units, capable of dealing with the increasing numbers of heavily armed "privateers" operated by various Silesian separatist movements in the Confederacy. Despite this, Manticore never had more than a couple of dozen light cruisers in service prior to King Roger's naval expansion program. Lacking neighbors with ill intent and with a battle fleet geared primarily towards home system defense rather than power projection, the RMN's limited wall of battle had little need for strategic scouting, and the tactical scouting role was filled by LACs and destroyers in the home system. Roles had begun to shift within the RMN in the 1820s, however, due to the ever-expanding reach of the Manticoran merchant marine. As conditions worsened in Silesia, missions normally assigned to destroyers began to be filled by the limited number of RMN light cruisers, and tasks normally assigned to frigates began to be filled by destroyers and light cruisers alike. The success of both the merchant marine and the light cruisers assigned to protect it prompted an acceleration of CL building programs, which were already underway when Roger began to increase the size of the battle fleet. The expansion of the battle fleet substantially accelerated the process, and as increasing numbers of cruisers became available, the remaining frigates were steadily taken out of service, both to free up manpower for the king's "New Navy" and to increase the combat power and survivability of individual units.

The best known light cruiser in RMN history is certainly HMS *Unconquered* (CL-16), built in 1649 PD, which served as the first hyper-capable command for both Edward Saganami and Ellen D'Orville. *Unconquered* has been restored and kept in permanent commission as a living museum in orbit around Manticore.

Courageous-class light cruiser

Mass: 88,250 tons
Dimensions: 389 × 40 × 31 m
Acceleration: 519.6 G (5.096 kps^2)
80% Accel: 415.7 G (4.076 kps^2)
Broadside: 7M, 2L, 2G, 3CM, 3PD
Chase: 2M, 1L, 2CM, 2PD
Total Built: 62
Service Life: 1820–1909

The *Courageous*-class light cruiser was the oldest light cruiser class in the RMN's inventory at the start of the war. These cruisers were originally scheduled to be decommissioned in 1897 PD, but remained on the active list for another ten years in light of the Navy's growing demand for light combatants in Silesia, coupled with a shortage of yard space for the construction of replacements. The *Courageous* class was designed for commerce escort and anti-piracy duties, where it could make best use of its heavy offensive armament. Although scarcely larger than a modern destroyer, the *Courageous* mounts a broadside of seven lightweight missile tubes and was one of the few units of its size to mount grasers in its beam broadside.

The heavy offensive armament of the class came at a cost, however. It is virtually unarmored, even by light cruiser standards, and the designers opted to save even more mass by reducing crew spaces and bunkerage to levels well below current standards. The reduction in cruise duration between resupply evolutions has rendered the *Courageous* less suited to its intended role than its weapons fit might indicate, and in that respect it was a disappointing replacement for the classes it superseded.

Despite the age of its offensive systems and its endurance issues, the *Courageous* class has a good performance record. It was still a strong performer in missile combat and, if it could keep the range open, was a match for most contemporary light cruisers. However, the combination of reduced endurance and cramped crew accommodations make it unpopular with crews. The surviving ships had a series of major upgrades over the years, but hardware supply constraints have caused them to fall behind the more modern classes. They were being replaced on a hull-for-hull basis by the *Valiant* class as the war began, and the last unit was decommissioned in 1909 PD.

Apollo-class light cruiser
Mass: 126,000 tons
Dimensions: 438 × 46 × 35 m
Acceleration: 517.8 G (5.078 kps^2)
80% Accel: 414.2 G (4.062 kps^2)
Broadside: 5M, 6L, 4CM, 4PD
Chase: 2M, 1L, 3CM, 3PD
Total Built: 132
Service Life: 1856–present

The *Apollo* class is a beam-centric light cruiser designed for anti-piracy operations. Built as the result of an 1846 design study, the focus of the design was overall protection and antimissile defenses on extended duration deployments far from resupply, primarily in places like Silesia, but also with an eye towards future fleet scouting requirements.

The first seven ships built to the design study's specifications were delivered between 1851 and 1856 PD. The RMN had awarded the Jordan Cartel a production contract lasting through the 1860s, but three of the first twelve ships failed their full power trials due to structural flaws. The subsequent scandal forced the cancellation of all naval contracts with the Jordan Cartel, following a lengthy investigation of charges of fraud and substandard building practices. Even before the investigation concluded, the Navy had turned construction over to the Hauptman Cartel. Following the investigation, Hauptman was also awarded possession of the remaining Jordan hulls for salvage of parts and systems. Aside from the first two, all of the remaining hulls have been built by the Hauptman Cartel, which received contract renewals in the mid 1860s and early 1870s.

The *Apollos* are designed to fight a closing battle while maneuvering into beam range, and have electronic countermeasures and sidewalls as strong as some older heavy cruisers. They also boast heavier armor than most light cruisers. At close quarters, nimble maneuvering and a heavy energy broadside should make an *Apollo* more than a match for any ship of its type. However, the beam armament has come at the expense of the missile broadside, leaving only five tubes in each broadside, with disadvantages that became truly obvious only after the widespread introduction of the laser head towards the end of the nineteenth century. The *Apollos* have undergone three major refit cycles to update their electronics and fire control systems. The remaining units in the class are expected to be decommissioned soon, though wartime requirements may extend their service life yet again.

Talisman-class light cruiser

Mass: 124,250 tons
Dimensions: 438 × 46 × 35 m
Acceleration: 517.9 G (5.079 kps^2)
80% Accel: 414.3 G (4.063 kps^2)
Broadside: 5M, 2L, 4CM, 4PD
Chase: 2M, 1L, 3CM, 3PD
Number Built: 16
Service Life: 1871–present

The *Talisman*-class light cruiser is a dedicated intelligence-gathering cruiser built on the versatile *Apollo* hull. With most of the Admiralty convinced that war with Haven was a near certainty, plans were put in place to shadow Havenite units in neutral space and picket Havenite systems with *Talismans*, in order to capture as much data as possible on Havenite propulsion, sensor, and fire control systems. In the event that war broke out, the *Talisman*-class ships were to be assigned to screening formations, using their upgraded sensors to provide a direct data feed to the wall's fire control computers in real time as the battle progressed.

Four broadside lasers were removed and magazine space was reduced to make room for an extensive suite of passive sensors, analysis gear and room for the crew required to run the systems. The entire forward half of the boat bay was dedicated to launch and recovery equipment for a variety of reconnaissance drones.

While political considerations rendered their primary mission difficult in many cases, the *Talismans* served well throughout the early years of the war. Several of them eventually ended up in the service of ONI special operations teams and a study is underway to refit the others as advanced drone tenders. This would allow a division to hyper into a newly occupied system and set up an *ad hoc* perimeter security array on short notice. This capability is expected to be of most use in the new territories of the Star Empire of Manticore.

Illustrious-class light cruiser

Mass: 135,750 tons
Dimensions: 449 × 47 × 36 m
Acceleration: 517.3 G (5.073 kps^2)
80% Accel: 413.9 G (4.059 kps^2)
Broadside: 5M, 4L, 6CM, 6PD
Chase: 2M, 1L, 4CM, 4PD
Number Built: 26
Service Life: 1876–present

The *Illustrious* class was a product of the Enhanced Survivability Program undertaken by BuShips in the early 1860s. Unlike some of the other designs spawned by that program, the *Illustrious* class carried the concept far enough to compromise the offensive capabilities of the design, and most authorities consider the ship severely under-gunned. The Admiralty agreed with that assessment and shifted resources to the continued production of the older *Apollo* class rather than the newer *Illustrious*-class CLs.

The *Illustrious* design has been disparagingly referred to as the most expensive destroyer ever built. This is perhaps unfair, as the class has found several useful niches, but the RMN had hoped to use it as a more generalized light cruiser and hence overall it is regarded as a failure. Lacking the firepower to be a credible threat to any modern warship in its tonnage range, standard employment options for the class usually emphasize missions where its defensive armament is an advantage. Initially these deployments focused on situations where it was more likely to find a mismatch in its favor, either hunting pirates in Silesia or in an antiscouting role with the fleet. As the tempo of wartime operations increased, command groups with *Illustrious*-class cruisers attached have taken to detaching them to cover convoy elements while heavier elements have been tasked elsewhere. A related idea that saw *Illustrious*-class ships attached in division strength to deep raiding battlecruiser squadrons as supplementary defensive firepower met with some limited successes early in the war. Their conversion into light, fast-attack transports assigned to the RMMC is also under consideration.

Apollo-class light cruiser extension (Flight IV Apollo)

Mass: 128,750 tons
Dimensions: 441 × 46 × 35 m
Acceleration: 517.7 G (5.077 kps²)
80% Accel: 414.1 G (4.061 kps²)
Broadside: 5M, 4L, 6CM, 4PD
Chase: 2M, 1L, 3CM, 3PD
Number Built: 52
Service Life: 1886–present

After the *Illustrious* class failed to live up to its intended capabilities, another flight of *Apollos* was ordered. Over the course of several years, almost all of the original Flight I hulls were stricken and replacements were commissioned with the same names as the originals.

Recent experience with the *Talisman* class had emphasized the versatility of the basic *Apollo* hull form, and the decision was made to modify the class. Two beam mounts were removed from the broadside and replaced with a pair of counter-missile launchers and their magazines. This reduction in close combat ability was regrettable, but the new design was a welcome addition for task force commanders looking to thicken the defenses of their screen. Operational experience soon made it clear that the design was in many ways superior to the original *Apollo* class and a refit program was put into place to upgrade as many of the original hulls as possible.

At present, many surviving hulls of the original *Apollo* class have been upgraded to the Flight IV standard. At the beginning of its service life, this class was often referred to as the *Artemis* class, although officially they have always been carried on the Navy List simply as Flight IV *Apollos*. The distinction became irrelevant as the remainder of the older hulls were refitted to these standards.

Valiant-class light cruiser

Mass: 154,750 tons
Dimensions: 469 × 49 × 38 m
Acceleration: 516.4 G (5.065 kps²)
80% Accel: 413.2 G (4.052 kps²)
Broadside: 8M, 6L, 2G, 5CM, 4PD
Chase: 3M, 2G, 3CM, 3PD
Number Built: 83
Service Life: 1902–present

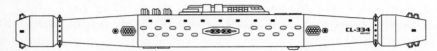

With half again the missile broadside of an *Apollo*, the *Valiant* class marks a departure in typical RMN light cruiser design. It is fourteen percent heavier than the *Illustrious* class and takes much of its design philosophy from the old *Courageous* class. The *Valiants* remain effective units even by today's radically changed standards, boasting a heavier missile broadside than any previous RMN light cruiser, energy weapons equal to those of an *Apollo*, and a respectable defensive suite. Another notable design feature is its heavy chase armament, although fitting in the three missile tubes and two grasers (plus the defensive mounts) required a substantial reworking of the internal hammerhead design.

Like the much smaller *Courageous* class, this capability comes at a price. Solid, reliable, and effective, the *Valiants* are shorter legged and more cramped than most of their contemporaries, despite their larger size. Enough *Valiants* have been built to completely replace the *Courageous*-class hulls as they are decommissioned, with many *Valiants* inheriting their names directly from the older ships.

Avalon-class light cruiser

Mass: 146,750 tons
Dimensions: 461 × 48 × 37 m
Acceleration: 749.9 G (7.354 kps²)
80% Accel: 599.9 G (5.883 kps²)
Broadside: 10M, 4G, 8CM, 8PD

Chase: 2G, 4PD
Number Built: 196+
Service Life: 1919–present

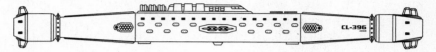

The *Avalon* class is the light cruiser variant based on the same design studies that created the *Saganami-B* heavy cruiser, and it shares many of the same advantages in terms of fire control, protection, off-bore launching and electronics. Although still categorized and deployed as a light cruiser, it is actually smaller than the *Roland*-class destroyer, a testament to the RMN's policy of classifying hulls based on role rather than tonnage.

Unlike its contemporaries the *Roland* and *Saganami-C*, the *Avalon* does not carry the Mk16 Dual Drive Missile (DDM). Instead it carries the same Mk36 Lightweight Extended Range Missile (LERM) as the *Wolfhound*. The Mk36 single-stage drive package is capable of significantly longer runtime and range than prewar missiles but remains considerably shorter ranged than the Mk16.

The *Avalon* admirably fills the role of a light cruiser as defined by the RMN. The class is being built in large numbers alongside the *Rolands* and *Saganami-Cs*, and many of them have been sent to Silesia, where their capabilities are badly needed at present.

Kamerling-class system control cruiser
Mass: 276,250 tons
Dimensions: 569 × 59 × 46 m
Acceleration: 741 G (7.266 kps²)
80% Accel: 592.8 G (5.813 kps²)
Broadside: 8M, 4G, 12CM, 12PD
Chase: 2G, 6PD
Number Built: 48
Service Life: 1921–present

While listed on the BuShips records as a light cruiser, the *Kamerling* class has the designation of "system control cruiser" and is in fact closer to a replacement for the *Broadsword*-class heavy cruiser.

One of the major disadvantages of the new RMN warship classes and their highly automated designs is that station commanders are finding more and more often that they lack the manpower and Marines to deal with boarding actions, prize crews, piracy suppression, and similar missions.

The *Kamerling* class was designed to address this problem. It takes advantage of the same level of automation and crew reduction as all modern classes, but in addition to the small Navy crew, it carries three companies of Marines, with support equipment and enough small craft lift capacity to move the entire contingent in a single flight.

While capable combatants against anything they are likely to encounter in distant stations such as the Silesian Confederacy, the *Kamerling*'s weapons fit is biased towards defense and, despite its tonnage advantage over both the *Avalon* and *Valiant* classes, its antiship capability is limited for its size due to the tonnage consumed by additional life-support. These ships were never intended to contest space control with another navy's units. Rather, they were conceived of as units intended to police commerce and restore the peacekeeping and humanitarian mission capabilities which had been lost in the low-manpower designs. However, the explosive increase in construction following the resumption of hostilities resulted in a shortage of building slips. Smaller slips were turning out *Rolands* and *Avalons* as quickly as possible already. Given the massive size of these ships, each one would displace the construction of a *Saganami-C*, so the original build numbers were cut twice.

Only forty-eight have been built and no more are planned until at least 1923. Nearly all of those have been assigned to Silesia.

HEAVY CRUISERS (CA)

For most of its history, the RMN relied on heavy cruisers—and later battlecruisers—as its primary offensive units. Commodore Edward Saganami refined this practice during the Ranier War, and his heroic actions at the Battle of Carson stamped it forever into the traditions of the Royal Navy.

The heavy cruiser is particularly well suited to commerce raiding. Operating in singletons or divisions, cruiser-class ships are easily able to overpower the traditional destroyer and light cruiser escorts and effectively force enemies to protect their supply lines with heavy units of their own, often at the cost of far more units pulled from the front lines than the expenditure of raiders.

While the nature of warfare has changed for many of the last generation of officers to serve King Roger III, moving from one of deep raids with nimble battlecruiser squadrons to the ponderous might of the wall of battle, the tradition has never been forgotten. Strategic planning even today still includes these pinpoint raids. Many in the Navy today believe no officer's capability has been truly tested until he or she has commanded a heavy cruiser.

Warrior-class heavy cruiser

Mass: 227,250 tons
Dimensions: 474 × 57 × 48 m
Acceleration: 513 G (5.031 kps²)
80% Accel: 410.4 G (4.025 kps²)
Broadside: 6M, 6G, 2CM, 6PD
Chase: 2M, 1G, 2CM, 2PD
Number Built: 46
Service Life: 1794–1906

While perfectly capable for the era in which it was built, the *Warrior*'s missile broadside is light by modern standards, a fact which was only partially offset by the quality of the RMN's missile penetration aids and seekers. On the other hand, it carried an all-graser broadside, which provided it with a powerful punch in close range combat. The defensive suite is typical of its time of construction, showing more point defense clusters than counter-missile tubes, a balance optimized against contemporary contact nuclear warhead missiles.

Despite these limitations, the *Warrior* proved to be an ideal frontier patrol ship for the Silesian sector. Its smaller size gave it a marginally better acceleration than newer, larger hulls, and, with the right initial geometry, it was capable of running down many light cruisers and even some destroyers. Its missiles gave it a reasonable attack against the lightly defended ships used by liberation front navies and pirates, and the generally low quality of Silesian equipment prevented its weaknesses in active defenses and armor from being a crippling disadvantage.

Although few remained in service by the start of the war, the *Warrior* class had always been a well-regarded platform, despite its age, and all ships in the class had received periodic electronic package upgrades throughout their operational lifetimes. Still, the era of battle for which these ships had been designed and in which they performed admirably was drawing to a close. Woefully insufficient in long-range defenses by current standards, the *Warriors* were low enough on the priority list that refitting them to a more balanced defensive suite was shelved in favor of designs that were more capable of fighting the People's Republic of Haven. While a few units saw combat at the opening of the war, the last of them were decommissioned less than a year later.

Truncheon-class heavy cruiser
Mass: 223,000 tons
Dimensions: 471 × 57 × 48 m
Acceleration: 513.2 G (5.033 kps^2)
80% Accel: 410.6 G (4.026 kps^2)
Broadside: 5M, 5L, 3G, 2CM, 6PD
Chase: 2M, 1L, 1G, 1CM, 2PD
Number Built: 77
Service Life: 1809–1905

The *Truncheon*-class heavy cruiser was designed in concert with the *Warrior* class as a less expensive option to make up total designated build numbers. Despite having been authorized and placed on the books a full year earlier than the *Warrior*, budget cuts delayed the first *Truncheon* for fifteen years after the *Warrior* class entered operational service. With several squadrons of the ancient *Acherner* class long overdue for retirement when the *Truncheon* finally did enter service, however, and in light of production problems with the *Warriors*, the original production run was lengthened in 1822 PD.

Two divisions of Flight I *Truncheons* were refitted in the early 1830s as marine operations support cruisers and redesignated with the prefix LCA. This refit reduced the broadside weaponry to make room for a full battalion of marines and support staff plus specialized command and control equipment. While sorely needed, the makeshift nature of the *Nightstick*-class conversion was never popular with the Corps. Plans were drawn up shortly thereafter for a purpose-built LCA, though several delays in that procurement kept the *Truncheons* in service decades longer than anticipated. When the long awaited *Broadsword* class was finally commissioned, two decades overdue, the converted *Truncheons* were finally decommissioned, much to the relief of the RMMC.

Prince Consort-class heavy cruiser
Mass: 246,500 tons
Dimensions: 487 × 59 × 49 m
Acceleration: 512.1 G (5.022 kps²)
80% Accel: 409.7 G (4.017 kps²)
Broadside: 8M, 3L, 2G, 5CM, 4PD
Chase: 2M, 1L, 3CM, 2PD
Number Built: 175
Service Life: 1851–1919

The *Prince Consort* class of heavy cruisers holds the record as the largest class of heavy cruisers in the Royal Manticoran Navy, though it is likely to be overtaken in the next flight of *Saganami-Cs* coming off the building slips in 1922 PD. The class was originally authorized as the *Crown Prince* class, but the name changed before the first was delivered.

Individually the *Prince Consorts* are powerful and effective units, but their design was a compromise in two ways. First, they were designed with just enough internal bridge volume to accommodate their original equipment, which caused a great deal of frustration as future refits and equipment upgrades had to be crammed wherever they fit, making for an even more cramped interior working space. Second, to get as much firepower into space as quickly and at as low a cost as possible, BuShips omitted a proper flag deck and its support systems in exchange for additional tonnage dedicated to broadside weaponry. Due to the shortage in flagships of any kind, this required *Prince Consorts* to be assigned to task force and fleet formations where other ships in the squadron could provide the space for a flag officer and staff.

Like most Manticoran designs, the *Prince Consort* enjoyed a healthy advantage in medium- to long-range missile duels against foreign opponents, where it could make the most of its superior seeker systems and electronic countermeasures. At closer ranges, where the disparity in missile qualities evened out, much of that advantage disappeared. While many of the class saw active service throughout the war, the growing numbers of more capable heavy cruisers being built gradually displaced the last of them.

Crusader-class heavy cruiser

Mass: 234,500 tons
Dimensions: 479 × 58 × 48 m
Acceleration: 512.6 G (5.027 kps^2)
80% Accel: 410.1 G (4.022 kps^2)
Broadside: 6M, 3L, 1G, 5CM, 4PD
Chase: 2M, 1L, 3CM, 2PD
Number Built: 25
Service Life: 1851–1919

The *Crusader*-class heavy cruiser was designed as a supplement to the *Prince Consort* building program. As the *Prince Consorts* did not have flag facilities, BuShips authorized a program which would have built the *Prince Consorts* in groups of seven and paired each group with a *Crusader* providing flag services to make a full eight-ship squadron. In addition to a flag bridge, the *Crusader* class mounts a full auxiliary command deck, in addition to a number of other system and habitability upgrades.

"Flag facilities" in modern naval parlance means the extra computational support, communications equipment, and watchstanders necessary to link a formation spread over tens of thousands of kilometers into a coherent tactical fighting force, as well as the long-range communications arrays necessary to coordinate the action of detached units across a star system. While any modern combat control system can perform this function at some level, dedicated personnel and facilities are required to optimize the use of a modern squadron's resources.

The original building program failed to allow for a realistic overhaul cycle, with the result being that at least twenty-five percent too few flagships had been projected from the beginning, and the Admiralty's decision to cut funding for them in the intervening years only made the problem worse. The shortage of *Crusaders* went largely unremarked at the time, but as the signs of war between Manticore and Haven grew, the forward redeployments of cruisers and battlecruisers as raiders highlighted the shortages of flag decks in heavy cruiser squadrons. The crucial importance of appropriate flagship facilities lay in the close coordination required of a modern squadron in combat.

As squadron flagships, the *Crusaders* performed admirably over their lifetimes. The weapons fit was weaker than that of the *Prince Consorts*, but even by modern standards this class had excellent command and control facilities, rivaling those of far larger ships. It was less capable in solo operations as it was not intended to operate outside a squadron. Aside from enhancements in targeting and penetration aids, the offensive power was comparable to that of the *Warrior*-class heavy cruiser, despite a more than ten percent increase in tonnage over the older class.

Additional advances in automation reduced the personnel and space required to build the same command and control capability into follow-on ships. With the *Star Knight* and *Saganami* classes and their variants being built in large numbers, the need for a class of lightly armed dedicated flagships was dwindling. Almost the entire class had been relegated to the Reserve by the time of Operation Buttercup, and it was finally scrapped during the Janacek build-down.

Broadsword-class Marine operations support cruiser

Mass: 268,500 tons
Dimensions: 531 x 59 x 49 m
Acceleration: 511 G (5.011 kps²)
80% Accel: 408.8 G (4.009 kps²)
Broadside: 8M, 3L, 2G, 5CM, 5PD
Chase: 2M, 1L, 4CM, 4PD
Number Built: 8
Service Life: 1873–present

The *Broadsword*-class marine operations support cruiser is built on an elongated *Prince Consort*-class hull, with a comparable weapon and defensive fit. The class fulfills two primary mission roles. The first is a rapid deployment ship for the RMMC in situations where a reinforced battalion will do the job but a full brigade or divisional Marine drop is too cumbersome. The second is as an orbital command ship for extended ground operations. In the first role, a *Broadsword* may be assigned individually or as part of a cruiser squadron, while in the second it will accompany a full Marine Transport Squadron. Given their specialized nature, *Broadswords* are rarely deployed as part of an offensive space control fleet element and usually do not arrive until the battle is over.

The *Broadsword*'s marine complement consists of a full battalion reinforced with a single assault company in addition to the heavy weapons company. With the newer Mk17 light assault shuttles, a *Broadsword* can drop its entire marine complement in a single wave. This class also carries a large number of containerized kinetic strike weapons, reconnaissance and communication satellites, planetary probes and other ground support equipment and has an extensive orbital command facility for coordination of Marine forces in the air, in orbital spaces, and on the ground. Additionally, the *Broadsword* is also equipped with hospital facilities comparable to those of a small station or forward base, making this class a welcome addition to any force.

Star Knight-class heavy cruiser
Mass: 305,250 tons
Dimensions: 523 × 63 × 53 m
Acceleration: 509.3 G (4.994 kps²)
80% Accel: 407.4 G (3.995 kps²)
Broadside: 12M, 6L, 3G, 8CM, 8PD
Chase: 3M, 1L, 5CM, 5PD
Number Built: 74
Service Life: 1893–present

The *Star Knight* is in all ways a revolutionary design, not simply for the Manticoran Navy but for the heavy cruiser type in general. This class was the first two-deck heavy cruiser in the service of any navy, though a careful disinformation campaign kept that fact from becoming obvious until well into its service life. The fourth and final design built on the *Prince Consort* hull, the *Star Knight* was designed to replace both the *Prince Consort* and *Crusader* classes. The design takes advantage of decades of research by the Weapons Development board in system miniaturization and it represents arguably the most notable achievement of BuShips in the nineteenth century. Its significantly increased armament, more powerful sidewall generators, heavier armor, better electronic warfare capabilities, and more numerous point defense systems make it at least thirty percent tougher than the *Prince Consorts*.

This improvement was due to the fact that the *Star Knight* was the first heavy cruiser designed from the keel out with the laser head threat in mind. The designers realized missile exchanges would begin to dominate, even among the lighter classes, and with half again as many missile tubes as a *Prince Consort*, the *Star Knight* could lay down an impressive volume of fire. While the number of beam mounts is equally impressive, the truth is that they are individually much lighter weapons than on some older classes, though the decisive edge in missile combat has blunted any criticism in that respect.

Despite this class' exemplary performance compared to its contemporaries, combat experience has shown that insufficient volume was allocated to offensive systems. This lack was largely due to one of the most controversial design choices: installation of a third fusion reactor as opposed to the normal two found on most ships of this size. Only a single reactor is required to carry the ship's combat load and the additional volume could have been used to mount a heavier broadside but, unable to find any way to mount ejectable GRAVMAK reactors and not entirely certain that their passive armor scheme could possibly protect the core hull from laser head strikes, the designers opted for increased power system redundancy.

Despite the exponential increase in lethality over the *Prince Consort* class, the RMN has come to consider the *Star Knight* a transitional design. Once wartime experience was factored in, the

RMN begun to develop an even more powerful and revolutionary heavy cruiser class as its replacement.

Edward Saganami-class heavy cruiser
Mass: 393,000 tons
Dimensions: 569 × 69 × 57 m
Acceleration: 592.2 G (5.808 kps^2)
80% Accel: 473.8 G (4.646 kps^2)
Broadside: 14M, 5G, 10CM, 10PD
Chase: 3M, 2G, 6CM, 6PD
Number Built: 46
Service Life: 1908–present

The *Edward Saganami*-class heavy cruiser was designed to improve upon the *Star Knight*. As the war progressed, the design underwent several major revisions, and construction was delayed by almost three years as the Manticoran designers studied innovations the Graysons developed for their *Alvarez* class and other small combatants. When the design was finally completed, the *Saganami* class became the RMN's first "all graser" ship since the *Warrior*. It mounted two additional missile launchers and fewer but more powerful grasers than originally planned, as well as major changes in crew structure using the new automation. Other improvements included significant electronics and systems upgrades, which greatly improved its passive defenses.

The lead ship, HMS *Edward Saganami*, bears little resemblance to the original design proposed in 1903 PD, and there are significant differences between all of the first flight ships. Indeed, in some ways, the Flight I ships may be considered a series of prototypes, as they were not all laid down simultaneously and the basic platform's design remained under development and refinement throughout their construction period. Later flights settled down into a more stable pattern. The Flight II *Saganamis* all carried first-generation bow walls, making them the first RMN warships larger than a LAC to use the new technology.

Saganami-B-class heavy cruiser

Mass: 422,750 tons
Dimensions: 583 × 71 × 59 m
Acceleration: 730.8 G (7.167 kps²)
80% Accel: 584.7 G (5.734 kps²)
Broadside: 19M, 10G, 16CM, 18PD
Chase: 2M, 3G, 6CM, 8PD
Number Built: 84
Service Life: 1917–present

Though it was billed as a block upgrade to the Flight II *Saganami*, the *Saganami-B* class is a radical departure from the original design, and the difference in armament led to its redesignation upon commissioning of the first unit.

Less than ten percent larger than a *Saganami*, the *Saganami-B* has a modified hullform to accommodate a broadside over fifty percent larger than that of the older ship. Its broadside of nineteen missile launchers and ten grasers more than doubles the armament of some older heavy cruisers still in service and, with active defenses equally upgraded, the *Saganami-B* is more than a match for most contemporary battlecruisers. On the passive side, electronics have been upgraded yet again, and the bow wall is joined by an equally powerful stern wall. The second-generation missile launchers are capable of limited off-bore fire into adjacent arcs, though the chase telemetry arrays limit them to realtime control of less than half the total salvo they could launch.

For all its improvements, the *Saganami-B* is another transitional design. It served as a testbed for new technologies and refinements of old technologies, all of which have led to the *Saganami-C* class.

Saganami-C-class heavy cruiser
Mass: 483,000 tons
Dimensions: 610 × 74 × 62 m
Acceleration: 726.2 G (7.121 kps^2)
80% Accel: 580.9 G (5.697 kps^2)
Broadside: 20M, 8G, 20CM, 24PD
Chase: 3L, 2G, 8PD
Number Built: 149
Service Life: 1920–present

The *Saganami-C* class is one of the few new classes BuShips managed to get approved under the Janacek Admiralty, which had focused all construction on LACs for system defense and lighter classes for strategic roles. Six of these were approved as an initial design study, although the first did not commission until after the war resumed.

The *Saganami-C* is uncompromisingly optimized for missile combat, with a total of forty missile launchers for the new Mk16 DDM. The third-generation launchers and missile allow them to fire off-bore up to 180 degrees, launching a forty-missile salvo into any firing arc, and telemetry arrays have also been upgraded, allowing full control of up to three "stacked broadsides" in any aspect not blocked by the wedge. Additional control channels in the broadsides allow the class to handle large missile pod loads in addition to the shipboard launchers. Its energy armament was reduced to only eight grasers, but each is significantly more powerful than those carried by the *Saganami-B*, with an output yield closer to the weapons some navies mount on smaller capital ships, and improved fire control modeling increases hit probability per mount significantly. Moreover, simulations indicate the larger beam diameters and larger plasma throughput of the new battery will actually increase the probability of kill against other heavy cruisers. It remains to be seen if combat experience will bear this out but early reports are promising.

Another advantage of the *Saganami-C* design are its two-phase bow and stern wall generators. A traditional endwall closes off the wedge at one end or another, reducing acceleration to zero for as long as it is active, but the two-phase generators carried by the *Saganami-C* allow the ship to produce what the RMN refers to as a "buckler." This is a smaller endwall projected across the throat or kilt but not directly connected to the wedge. Its arc of coverage is not as wide as a traditional endwall and leaves vulnerable gaps in some engagement geometries, but the ship retains the ability to accelerate and maneuver when it is active.

Combat experience has been limited to date but early reports have been extremely positive. These are the most modern, powerful heavy cruisers available to any navy, and, between the salvo size they can control and the range advantage granted by the Mk16 DDM, they could easily destroy at least twice their tonnage in older battlecruisers in a stand-up fight.

BATTLECRUISERS (BC)

For almost as long as there has been a Manticoran Navy, battlecruisers have been its primary tools for force projection. Even after the first battleship squadrons were built for system defense following the discovery of the Junction, battlecruisers were the main striking force of the Navy and remained so until the first superdreadnoughts began to be commissioned.

A battlecruiser is designed to outfight anything it can catch, and outrun anything that outguns it. Traditionally, BuShips' designers believed that any battlecruiser's life expectancy against ships of the wall would be brief and that battlecruiser-versus-battlecruiser actions would be short and sharp. As a result, BuShips believed it was better to throw more (and better) missiles faster and to incorporate an energy armament heavy enough to make the initial salvo of a beam action decisive. The traditional RMN battlecruiser therefore mounts cruiser-grade missile tubes in larger numbers (and with deeper magazines) than a typical heavy cruiser on a hull which masses two to four times as much as the cruiser's. In addition to a heavier weapons fit, that extra mass and volume also buy the BC a scaled-down version of a capital ship's protective scheme, with tougher sidewalls and heavier armor than a cruiser.

Battlecruisers have many roles in the Royal Manticoran Navy. The battlecruiser is envisioned as the minimum platform capable of performing long-range, extended patrol and interdiction, destroying commerce raiders (not necessarily the same thing as convoy protection), and projecting force against anything "below the wall." They are also useful for showing the flag, rear area security missions, and screening heavier ships and critical convoys. While the force balance and dynamics of warfare have caused certain roles to wax and wane over time, overall RMN battlecruiser doctrine has remained largely unchanged.

The Manticoran romance with the battlecruiser has taken on a different hue with the *Nike* and *Agamemnon* classes of recent years. As the balance of combat shifted, especially with the introduction of the missile pod for system defense and the reformed RHN wall of battle, these raids became more and more costly for the smaller ships. However, with the introduction of the *Nike* class in 1920 PD, the RMN apparently is moving back towards the traditional role for the type. It is a rather pointed commentary on the sheer destructiveness which missile combat has attained that the Navy feels that it requires a 2.5 million-ton platform to replace ships of less than one million tons put into service less than a decade ago.

Redoubtable-class battlecruiser

Mass: 784,750 tons
Dimensions: 686 × 87 × 78 m
Acceleration: 491.5 G (4.82 kps^2)
80% Accel: 393.2 G (3.856 kps^2)
Broadside: 18M, 8L, 6G, 9CM, 9PD
Chase: 6M, 1G, 6CM, 4PD
Number Built: 118
Service Life: 1786–1918

With over 125 years of service and four major deployed design revisions, the *Redoubtable* class is the longest serving battlecruiser class in the Royal Manticoran Navy. The *Redoubtable*'s birth dates back to the aftermath of the Ranier War and the Battle of Carson and the RMN's shift from a predominantly system-defense force to one that could perform power projection missions. A major new shipbuilding effort was required, and over the next century, the RMN's battlecruiser strength grew from a few dozen to over two hundred. The *Redoubtable* was the pinnacle of the Star Kingdom's battlecruisers during that early period.

Designed for closing engagements against lighter opponents and peers, the design had extremely heavy chase armament for its time, as well as heavy face-mirrored armor over the hammerheads. Even today the *Redoubtable*'s antiquated (by current Manticoran standards) fire control systems have proven to be more than adequate against most Havenite opponents.

Nonetheless, the *Redoubtables*, while a solid and frequently updated design, were clearly showing their age towards the end of the First Havenite War. Maintenance and reliability had become recurring issues as components last manufactured a century ago were replaced with modern substitutes, and ships of this class were retired from frontline duties as rapidly as *Reliants* could be commissioned to replace them. The last were decommissioned or sold to Alliance members shortly before the war resumed.

Homer-class battlecruiser

Mass: 834,000 tons
Dimensions: 700 × 89 × 79 m
Acceleration: 490 G (4.805 kps^2)
80% Accel: 392 G (3.844 kps^2)
Broadside: 20M, 8L, 8G, 1GL, 4ET, 9CM, 9PD
Chase: 4M, 2G, 4CM, 6PD
Number Built: 86
Service Life: 1863–present

Like the *Redoubtable*, the *Homer*-class battlecruiser was built as something of a brawler, mounting an extensive energy broadside, augmented (in later flights) with a grav lance and an array of energy torpedoes for extremely close engagements. Like many Manticoran designs, the *Homer*'s passive protection relied on sidewalls in preference to thicker skin armor, on the theory that sidewalls could be upgraded more readily than hull armor as technology advanced.

Because of experience with Service Life Extension Program refits for earlier classes, the *Homers* were built for ease of upgrade. Paradoxically, this was one of the principle justifications for the delay in their prewar refits, as the RMN knew it could be done comparatively quickly. Until the start of the First Havenite War, updates to the electronics and fire control systems were repeatedly deferred in favor of funneling more resources into the

Reliant-class building program. With the onset of hostilities, the *Homers* received defensive armament and compensator upgrades, to increase their ability to get in close, where their short-ranged armament could be used to greatest effect.

In operational service, the mixture of beams and missiles makes the *Homer* an unremarkable combatant outside of energy range, and only the pressing need for battlecruisers in the wake of the present resumption of hostilities has kept the class in service this long. All surviving units were pulled out of mothballs and quickly pressed into service in the wake of Operation Thunderbolt, even as building programs accelerated to build more modern units.

Reliant-class battlecruiser

Mass: 877,500 tons
Dimensions: 712 × 90 × 80 m
Acceleration: 488.7 G (4.792 kps^2)
80% Accel: 390.9 G (3.834 kps^2)
Broadside: 22M, 8L, 6G, 2ET, 10CM, 10PD
Chase: 4M, 1L, 2G, 6CM, 6PD
Number Built: 95
Service Life: 1896–present

The *Reliant* is only five percent larger than a *Homer* but is a far more capable platform. While perhaps not as revolutionary for battlecruisers as the *Star Knight* was for a heavy cruiser, they are still extremely capable warships and ideally suited to the fast, slashing tactics that the Royal Manticoran Navy has embraced for over four T-centuries. They are the first units below the wall fitted with fully integrated modern armor materials. While these materials offered improved laser/graser absorption and far better secondary mechanical and thermal properties, they are difficult to nanoform, requiring specialized coded chemical catalyst gear and careful environmental control to emplace or replace.

Designed from the keel out as a squadron flagship, the *Reliant* class has three boat bays with reserved visitor space for up to four additional pinnaces. Early in the First Havenite War, the few *Reliants* in service were most often found leading squadrons of older *Homers* and *Redoubtables*. As the wartime construction programs accelerated, they rapidly began to replace those earlier classes in frontline service.

Reliant-class battlecruiser (Flights III-IV)

Mass: 934,250 tons
Dimensions: 727 × 92 × 82 m
Acceleration: 616 G (6.041 kps²)
80% Accel: 492.8 G (4.833 kps²)
Broadside: 24M, 4L, 6G, 18CM, 18PD
Chase: 4M, 2G, 6CM, 6PD
Number Built: 73
Service Life: 1915–present

The *Reliant*'s combination of acceleration and firepower has made it a flexible, multi-role platform, but the original design did not age as well as others as the war progressed. Later flights became testbeds for a number of new technologies and doctrinal changes, and the Flight III *Reliants* show a significant evolution of the design, incorporating many lessons learned from observations of the GSN's *Courvosier* class.

While six percent more massive than the original *Reliants*, the incorporation of a third-generation inertial compensator has allowed them to make up any loss in acceleration, while their massively upgraded active defenses allow them to stand in the wall of battle far better than their predecessors. While they didn't move to the "all graser" armament preferred by the GSN, their beam weapons are fewer in number but much more powerful than the earlier flights, and the additional two missile tubes give them a slightly heavier broadside.

Any design has its critics and many have argued that the evolution of the battlecruiser as a type stalled with the *Reliant* class. This criticism is especially relevant when compared to the revolutionary designs BuShips has adopted for smaller warships. However, it has always been a solid performer and an additional three squadrons were ordered as part of the emergency wartime construction programs as a stopgap while the new *Agamemnon* and *Nike* classes were tooling up to go into series production.

Agamemnon-class pod battlecruiser

Mass: 1,750,750 tons
Dimensions: 815 × 118 × 110 m
Acceleration: 692.6 G (6.792 kps²)
80% Accel: 554.1 G (5.434 kps²)
Broadside: 10G, 30CM, 30PD
Fore: 4G, 12PD
Aft: 4MP, 4G, 12PD
Pods: 360
Number Built: 85+
Service Life: 1919–present

The *Agamemnon*-class BC(P) is one of the few new classes that Vice Admiral Toscarelli of BuShips managed to get approved under the Janacek Admiralty, though the design lagged behind the Grayson implementation of a similar concept. It was an effort to keep the battlecruiser a viable unit in the days of multi-drive missile (MDM) pod-based combat. The *Agamemnon* has a stern hammerhead designed around a pod core capable of deploying four-pod patterns. This design required significant alterations to the stern taper and aft impeller ring. As in the *Medusa* and *Invictus* classes, the pod core extends past the midline. Forward of the core the hull design is similar to a conventional battlecruiser, though to optimize pod storage the RMN has forgone any broadside missile launchers. In order to maximize salvo density rather than missile range, *Agamemnon* pods were usually loaded with the Mark 16 dual-drive missile. This design allowed BuShips to fit fourteen missiles into each pod and maintain actual missile densities per pattern close to that of a *Medusa* or *Invictus*.

Starting with the second unit of the class, HMS *Ajax*, BuShips began to send units already fitting out and in various stages of construction through a refit program to add the Mk20 Keyhole platform. Just over four squadrons were refitted, a process which eliminated half of the broadside graser mounts and resulted in significantly thinner armor over the primary fusion plant. It was originally planned to incorporate the design modification from the keel out in a Flight III build, but with evidence pointing to two of the three losses at Solon being due to reactor hits, that decision is being reevaluated and it is probable that any future Keyhole-capable BC(P)s will be more heavily redesigned to avoid the potential vulnerability of the Flight IIs.

This is a class whose time came too late in many ways. Against a Navy with no MDMs or pod-layers, it is a devastatingly effective platform, as even the Mk16s normally carried by the *Agamemnons* can be launched in quantities great enough to reduce any conventional superdreadnought to scrap well before it could get into its own missile range. Against a peer competitor, however, the limitations of the class quickly become apparent. Despite accepting a design with nearly twice the mass of a conventional battlecruiser, the designers were still forced to make fundamental sacrifices to fit in the pod core and other weaponry. The result is a design that can lay down an impressive weight of fire as long as its ammunition lasts, but which has limited magazine depth and is extremely fragile. In many ways the *Agamemnon* is even less suited to stand in the wall of battle than an older *Reliant*, despite its far greater firepower.

Nike-class battlecruiser

Mass: 2,519,750 tons
Dimensions: 1012 × 129 × 114 m
Acceleration: 674.3 G (6.613 kps²)
80% Accel: 539.4 G (5.29 kps²)
Broadside: 25M, 12G, 32CM, 30PD
Chase: 4G, 12PD
Number Built: 12+
Service Life: 1920–present

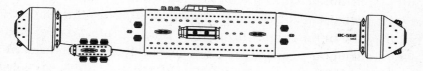

A single *Nike*-class battlecruiser was commissioned by the Janacek Admiralty as an operational prototype. For almost a year, HMS *Nike* (BC-562) was the only ship of her class in service, but the prototype's combat performance convinced the White Haven

Admiralty to proceed with mass production of the class. The first new-construction ships entered service in early 1921 PD.

Carrying fifty broadside launchers capable of off-bore firing the Mk16 DDM, the *Nike* can launch a salvo of fifty missiles into any aspect, and her magazines allow for over forty minutes of maximum rate fire. The class' improved compensators allow an acceleration rate thirty percent greater than that of the *Reliant* class, despite being over twice the mass of the older unit. While suffering from the greatest "tonnage creep" of any class in RMN history, the *Nike* well illustrates the RMN's policy of defining ships by their role and not by their tonnage. This has not prevented the size and classification from creating intense debate. In raw figures, these ships are five times the mass of a *Saganami-C*, with only a twenty-five percent increase in missile tubes. Accusations of poor design by BuShips and even outright incompetence are exacerbated by the fact that the *Nike* carries the same Mk16 DDM as the *Saganami-C*.

These critics overlook important difference in the capabilities of the two platforms and their designed missions. The *Nike* is designed to lead and survive independent long-duration deep-raiding missions in an era dominated by multi-drive missiles. The simple numbers of beam mounts, missile launchers and active defense systems belie qualitative per-mount differences. While a *Nike* and a *Saganami-C* may carry the same missile, each of a *Nike*'s launchers has four times the magazine capacity of her smaller heavy cruiser counterpart. A *Nike*'s grasers and point defense laser clusters are all superdreadnought grade. Their emitter diameter, plasma beam intensity, gravitic photon conditioning hardware, and on-mount energy storage capacity all rival the most modern capital ships. Finally, much of the *Nike*'s impressive mass is devoted to passive defense. Screening and sidewall generators have near-capital-ship levels of redundancy. The external armor system, internal mount compartmentalization, outer hull framing, and core hull construction are all designed to at least prewar superdreadnought standards. *Nikes*, finally, carry full flagship facilities and incorporate much greater Marine carrying and support capacity. The *Saganami-Cs*, while impressive space control platforms, have little or none of this capability.

The only reason, in fact, that a *Nike* might be less survivable than the prewar superdreadnought is the physical distance between the armor and the core hull. There simply is not enough depth to guarantee the same level of survivability to vital core systems as in a larger capital vessel. Early after-action reports indicate, however, that *Nike*'s survivability against her intended targets (heavy cruisers and other battlecruisers) has been extraordinary.

Above all other design elements, the addition of the Mark 20 Keyhole platform to the *Nike* class allows it a greater level of tactical flexibility than any other warship currently in service. This costs a tremendous amount of mass and creates interesting problems (which some commentators describe as weaknesses) in the armor system. But those costs buy the ability to tether the platforms outside the wedge, which, coupled with the off-bore missile launchers, makes *Nike* the one of the first warships that can fight an entire engagement with her wedge to the enemy. The telemetry repeaters allow full control of both missiles and counter-missiles, and the platforms' onboard point defenses thicken defensive fire. In addition, the Keyhole platform can act as a "handoff" relay, allowing a *Nike* to coordinate offensive and defensive missile control for another ship while both keep their wedges to the threat. This flexibility has resulted in vastly increased computational complexity in offensive and defensive engagement programming and helps to explain much of the class' survivability.

LAC CARRIERS (CLAC)

The first *Minotaur*-class LAC carriers were developed in secret along with the *Shrike*-class advanced LACs as part of Project Anzio. Experience with LACs as parasite craft in the *Trojan*-class Q-ships had shown they could be a powerful force multiplier when transported and serviced by a dedicated carrier, and the RMN set out to design a carrier that could keep up with the rest of the fleet and even survive in the wall of battle if necessary.

Original doctrine had the carriers launching their LACs and then staying far outside the range of the enemy wall of battle, screened by a cruiser squadron or other light units. This doctrine was intended above all to preserve the carrier, since it provided the only hyper-capable way to safely recover the LACs once committed to action.

On many raids and offensive actions this has proved to be a viable approach, but on major offensives or defensive actions the carriers are more likely to stay with the wall of battle, lending their active defenses to the other ships in formation and simul-taneously taking shelter under the wall's antimissile umbrella.

Minotaur-class LAC carrier

Mass: 6,178,500 tons
Dimensions: 1131 × 189 × 175 m
Acceleration: 428.2 G (4.199 kps^2)
80% Accel: 342.6 G (3.359 kps^2)
Broadside: 30CM, 28PD
Chase: 9M, 4G, 10CM, 10PD
LAC Bays: 100
Number Built: 18
Service Life: 1912–present

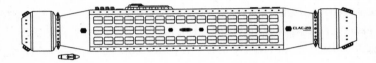

As the first operational unit of Project Anzio, The *Minotaur*-class LAC carrier can embark one hundred *Shrike-* or *Ferret*-class LACs in individual bays along the broadsides. Each bay is sealed by an armored hatch and can be completely pressurized if necessary to provide a "shirtsleeves" environment for hull maintenance, though that is rarely done for routine maintenance and operations. The LAC is held in place by a docking cradle, while an oversized boarding tube seals over the nose, allowing for easy access to the graser emitter and point defense for maintenance. Separate loading tubes run from the carrier's high-speed magazines to the LAC's missile and counter-missile launchers, allowing a LAC to be re-armed with a standard missile package in a matter of minutes.

Offensively, the *Minotaur*-class CLACs carry offensive weapons only in the hammerheads, with a heavy defensive weapons fit on the broadsides. The *Minotaurs* were the very first ships to be built from the keel out to fire the new (at the time) Mk41 capacitor-driven multi-drive missile, though they carry them in too few numbers to be more than a minor deterrent against anything larger than a heavy cruiser. The addition of the MDMs gave them the ability to harass any light raiding force dispatched to attack the carriers while the LACs were in-system, while the squadron would be forced to run from anything heavier.

The entire LAC complement of the carrier is organized into a single LAC wing, with a separate wing staff reporting to the wing CO, called the COLAC. The COLAC in turn reports to the carrier's commanding officer. Carrier-based support is provided by the LAC crews themselves, along with a core of specialists belonging to the wing. Much of the early doctrine was built by the crew and COLAC of HMS *Minotaur* during working up, with modifications for lessons learned at the Second Battle of Hancock.

Hydra-class LAC carrier (Flight II)

Mass: 6,145,750 tons
Dimensions: 1129 x 188 x 174 m
Acceleration: 428.5 G (4.203 kps²)
80% Accel: 342.8 G (3.362 kps²)
Broadside: 36CM, 36PD
Chase: 12M, 12CM, 12PD
LAC Bays: 112
Number Built: 94+
Service Life: 1914–present

While officially on the books as the *Minotaur-B* class, these ships are most often referred to as the *Hydra* class, after the lead unit of the new design. The *Hydra* class is slightly smaller than the *Minotaur* but carries twelve more LACs, extending the broadside length by sixty meters and cutting the chase magazine space in half.

While their active defenses are markedly lighter than those of the *Medusa* and *Invictus* classes, the *Hydras* have proved reasonably survivable in support of the wall of battle, especially when included in the defensive umbrella of the rest of the wallers.

Starting in 1920 PD, the Flight II *Hydras* have had their launch tubes and magazines configured to fire the Mk23 fusion-powered MDM rather than the much larger Mk41, and the elimination of all chase beam weaponry allowed them to increase the launch tubes to twelve, in addition to an increase in the defensive armament. This change reflects the operational realities of how little business carriers have in engaging in beam combat with ships of the wall, as well as providing them with a credible threat at extended range against anything below the wall.

DREADNOUGHTS (DN)

The RMN built two squadrons of battleships shortly after the first transit through the Manticore Wormhole Junction, and they served as the primary defensive component of Home Fleet, with regular overhauls, for nearly 250 years.

By the time the Navy began its expansion under King Roger III, the People's Republic of Haven had over two hundred battleships already in commission, and Roger flatly refused to build a warship that was qualitatively inferior to anything Haven had in service at the time. The last of the RMN's small battleship force was decommissioned in 1868 PD, when sufficient dreadnoughts had been built to replace them.

Unlike the People's Navy with their core of battleships for rear area support or the Imperial Andermani Navy with its "fast wing" of light superdreadnoughts, the RMN has historically kept all of its capital ships concentrated into heterogeneous squadrons and task forces filling the same doctrinal niche, the wall of battle. The natural consequence of this doctrine would have been for the RMN to begin building the more-powerful superdreadnoughts for the wall after inertial compensator improvements made the SD concept viable. Even with the strength of their economy, though, Manticore was unable to afford the number of hulls necessary, and hence continued to augment their superdreadnought force with new dreadnought construction.

The emergence of the modern missile pod, with its light-weight grav drivers, more numerous launch cells, and laser head-armed single-drive missiles, produced salvo densities which increased the relative vulerability of the already vulnerable dreadnought significantly. The type was increasingly relegated to rear area roles, and the introduction of the *Medusa*-class pod-layers of Operation Buttercup, armed with multi-drive laser head missiles, led to its outright demise. A dreadnought-sized ship of the wall simply could not support the mass and volume required to mount competitive offensive and defensive systems. Most of the remaining dreadnoughts were quietly retired by the Janacek Admiralty, and the last of them was decommissioned early in 1921 PD.

Ad Astra-class dreadnought (1878 refit)

Mass: 3,895,500 tons
Dimensions: 1064 × 154 × 144 m
Acceleration: 450.8 G (4.421 kps²)
80% Accel: 360.7 G (3.537 kps²)
Broadside: 18M, 14L, 12G, 6ET, 8CM, 18PD
Chase: 4M, 6L, 2G, 2CM, 8PD
Number Built: 11
Service Life: 1632–1913

The design of the *Ad Astra* class was refined over a few decades of operational experience with the *Manticore*-class battleship, a locally-built, Solarian licensed design. At almost twice the tonnage of the *Manticores*, they were the first Manticoran capital ships uncompromisingly designed for power projection as opposed to system defense. Reality fell somewhat short of expectations, however, as a succession of isolationist foreign policies resulted in a hyper-capable battle fleet that was firmly anchored to the Manticore system. Their first actual out-system deployment wasn't until 1674 PD, when they accompanied the First Battle Squadron to Silesia after the Battle of Carson to force the Confederacy to sign the Cherwell Convention.

Nearing three hundred years old when the first one was decommissioned in 1908 PD, the *Ad Astra*-class dreadnought was the longest serving single class in the history of the RMN. Subject to several major refits, and rebuilt virtually from the keel out in 1878, the ships decommissioned in the early days of the war bear little resemblance to the original ships laid down in the seventeenth century.

A full two squadrons (sixteen hulls) were originally planned, but only eleven ships were actually built. The first four ran afoul of cost overruns and multi-year delays in construction as the yards were expanded to handle hulls of their size, and a bitter budgetary debate in Parliament in 1651 PD suspended the entire program for almost half a century before the funding could be found to complete the class.

In the late 1880s, the entire class was modernized, despite the fact that the lead unit was over two centuries old. The original autocannon were replaced with modern point defense laser clusters, the armor was thickened in a few critical locations in response to the laser head threat, and electronics and missile launch systems were upgraded. Little could be done about the limited number of counter-missile launchers, a standard feature when these were built but a critical weakness in the era of the laser head.

Despite these shortcomings, the class continued well into the twentieth century, when the last units decommissioned midwar to provide crews for the final flight of *Bellerophons*.

Royal Winton-class dreadnought

Mass: 5,814,750 tons
Dimensions: 1216 × 176 × 164 m
Acceleration: 431.9 G (4.235 kps^2)
80% Accel: 345.5 G (3.388 kps^2)
Broadside: 20M, 18L, 16G, 6ET, 12CM, 28PD
Chase: 6M, 6L, 2G, 4CM, 10PD
Number Built: 21
Service Life: 1846–1916

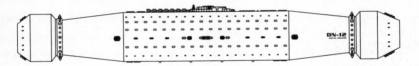

Over seventy years after the last RMN ship of the wall had been completed, the Admiralty realized at the turn of the nineteenth century that it needed to modernize Home Fleet. While the previous classes had all seen service life extension programs and heavy refits, two centuries of advances in naval warfare had rendered them obsolete, despite their modernized weapon systems.

The design study for the *Royal Winton* and *Samothrace* classes began in 1812 PD, building on the Navy's experiences with the existing wall of battle. The *Royal Winton*-class dreadnought was designed to completely replace the RMN's handful of battleships, joining the *Ad Astras* to provide a total of two active battle squadrons of dreadnoughts each led by a division of superdreadnoughts, with sufficient hulls to rotate through regular refits without any reduction in deployable forces.

Half again as massive as an *Ad Astra*, the *Royal Wintons* were nearly as large as the old *Manticore*-class superdreadnoughts and, by any objective standard, their combat ability was equal or better as well.

While nothing could compare to the glacial construction pace the *Ad Astras* had encountered, both the *Royal Winton*- and *Samothrace*-class superdreadnoughts suffered their share of "growing pains" as the Navy and civilian shipyards learned how to design a ship of the wall for series production. The class was broken into three distinct flights, each with a slightly different weapons fit, and even within a given flight no two hulls were exactly identical.

Gladiator-class dreadnought

Mass: 6,846,000 tons
Dimensions: 1284 × 186 × 173 m
Acceleration: 421.5 G (4.134 kps²)
80% Accel: 337.2 G (3.307 kps²)
Broadside: 22M, 18L, 24G, 1GL, 8ET, 18CM, 26PD
Chase: 6M, 4L, 6G, 6CM, 10PD
Number Built: 34
Service Life: 1868–1920

With King Roger's shipbuilding and infrastructure initiatives and the experience in building the *Royal Winton* and *Samothrace* classes, the shipyards had worked out most of the initial problems involved in building wallers by the time work began on the *Gladiators*, and both Navy and civilian yards were ready to embark on true series production.

The *Gladiator* class was built as a brawler, designed with an intentionally light missile broadside. Instead, it was equipped with the heaviest beam armament that could be fitted into a hull of this size, including an extensive suite of energy torpedo launchers and later refitted with the newly developed grav lance, a weapon capable of disabling a target's sidewall at extremely close range, in an early attempt to make a decisive wall engagement possible. The range limitation required a wall equipped with it to get close enough to actually use it, however, which (of course) meant that the primary effect of its introduction was simply to make fleet commanders across the galaxy even more cautious about close engagements.

The decision to greatly increase the *Gladiator*'s defenses, particularly the counter-missile launchers, proved prescient. The original rationale for the greatly increased area defense—even at the expense of the far more effective point defense clusters—was to allow the *Gladiator* to screen both itself and other units in the formation as they closed towards beam range. With the stand-off attack range of the laser head (first deployed by the IAN in 1872 PD), the utility of the short-ranged point defense clusters was critically reduced almost literally overnight, and the *Gladiator* was one of the few older classes to weather the transition.

Overall, despite the lost missile broadside, the *Gladiator* was a solid design, and remained in service a couple of years past the more modern *Majestic* class due to its better survivability and passive defenses. Plans were drawn up to substantially refit the surviving units with sufficient defenses to remain in the wall of battle even in the era of pod-based combat. The cease-fire and transition to the Janacek Admiralty scuttled those plans, however, and only a few *Gladiators* remained in service when the war resumed.

Majestic-class dreadnought

Mass: 6,750,500 tons
Dimensions: 1278 × 185 × 173 m
Acceleration: 422.5 G (4.143 kps^2)
80% Accel: 338 G (3.315 kps^2)
Broadside: 28M, 18L, 20G, 24CM, 24PD
Chase: 8M, 6L, 4G, 8CM, 8PD
Number Built: 40
Service Life: 1896–1918 PD

Following her father's death and the subsequent forcible annexation of the Trevor's Star System (and terminus) by the People's Republic of Haven, one of Queen Elizabeth's first actions was to reaffirm her commitment to her father's naval buildup, including a provision to more than double production of capital units within five years.

While the reasons behind the move to the *Majestic* class were many, the argument that the RMN could build a substantially less costly dreadnought class than the *Gladiators* was one of the primary drivers, and the class was sold to Parliament as having a per-platform cost seven percent less than a *Gladiator*.

There were other factors in play, however, including the fact that the Navy had to shift government contracts away from electronics providers that were under investigation for fraud and malfeasance.

Speeding up construction of a dreadnought (at least a dreadnought as capable as the *Gladiator*) proved to be a challenge, but the experience was to stand the RMN in very good stead in its ever-expanding wartime building programs. Ironically, though, while the *Majestic* had the virtue of being less expensive on a per-unit basis, the increased missile magazine size meant that the deployed cost of a fully equipped and armed *Majestic* dreadnought was nearly equal to the "more expensive" *Gladiator* it supplanted.

For all of that, the *Majestic* was never an entirely satisfactory design. Slightly smaller than a *Gladiator*, its heavy missile broadside was only possible at the cost of close combat capability, and despite the increase in active defenses, it had a far more fragile hull than the *Gladiator*. This relative frailty, despite far more numerous missile tubes during a time when beam combat was falling out of favor, was one of the reasons the entire class was decommissioned before the older *Gladiator*.

Bellerophon-class dreadnought
Mass: 6,985,250 tons
Dimensions: 1293 × 187 × 175 m
Acceleration: 420.1 G (4.12 kps²)
80% Accel: 336.1 G (3.296 kps²)
Broadside: 33M, 15L, 18G, 24CM, 24PD
Chase: 7M, 2L, 3G, 8CM, 8PD
Number Built: 38
Service Life: 1900–1921

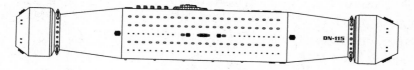

The *Bellerophon*-class dreadnought represents the pinnacle of Manticoran dreadnought design, incorporating lessons learned from all of the previous classes and the final prewar generation of RMN simulation data and doctrine. The *Bellerophons* were originally intended as inexpensive contemporaries of the *Gryphon*-class superdreadnoughts, to be built in larger numbers than the heavier ships and to support the SDs in battle. The originally projected building ratio for the two classes was reversed almost literally overnight once war began and the emergency construction programs reached their full potential, however. The class continued in construction at a slow rate for the first five years of the war, until the Navy's funding and infrastructure allowed it to begin building exclusively SDs for its line of battle, at which time the *Bellerophons* were honorably retired and phased out of service.

Massing just under seven million tons, the *Bellerophons* were in every way equal or superior to any of the early Manticoran superdreadnought classes and could give even the *Anduril* class a run for its money, especially given the predominance of missile-only combat in the later phases of the war.

However, no matter how advanced it was, there is no question that the *Bellerophon*, like every other conventional capital ship in the Manticoran Navy, was designed to fight the last war. When even the most advanced prewar superdreadnought was rendered hopelessly obsolete by modern standards, the cost and manpower were clearly better spent on building larger, more powerful, and more survivable ships to replace them. The majority of this class lies in mothballs and could potentially be reactivated, but the possibility that any of them will see service again is remote.

Nouveau Paris-class dreadnought

Mass: 6,331,500 tons
Dimensions: 1251 × 181 × 169 m
Acceleration: 426.7 G (4.184 kps^2)
80% Accel: 341.3 G (3.347 kps^2)
Broadside: 32M, 10L, 10G, 18CM, 20PD
Chase: 8M, 4L, 4G, 10CM, 10PD
Number in Service: 5
Service Life: 1905–1917

Several Havenite ships of the wall were taken into service during the early war, including five dreadnoughts during the First Battle of Hancock. None of these ships saw frontline service, but four of them spent some time as rear area security operating with captured Havenite superdreadnoughts. All of these units were scrapped by the Janacek Admiralty during the interwar period.

SUPERDREADNOUGHTS (SD)

Superdreadnoughts, along with their pod-carrying brethren, are the largest warships in any star nation's inventory. The classic prewar SD mounted a heavy missile broadside; had the sidewalls, antimissile defenses, and armor to shrug off most missile hits themselves; and served primarily as a platform for the massive beam weapons required for a decisive engagement at close range. For centuries, SDs have been the decisive units of the wall of battle, built to survive to reach beam range and then batter their opponent into wreckage at close range.

As the core units of the wall of battle, dreadnoughts and superdreadnoughts are rarely deployed in less than divisional strength, and far more frequently they are moved around at the squadron level, complete with screen and support ships. Their true strength is in the concentrated fire a battle squadron can create, and the existence of even a single battle squadron automatically propels a naval force into one of the top two dozen or so navies in the galaxy.

The RMN accumulated a great deal of operational experience with their early *Manticore*-class superdreadnoughts before they began to add any more to the order of battle. However, they had not developed much combat experience when King Roger began the naval phase of his buildup in 1860 PD, and BuShips was forced to develop, build, test and refine designs at an ever-increasing rate, all without the benefit of any battle experience. At the peak of production, the RMN saw a new superdreadnought commissioned every month and a new class every four years, with advances leapfrogging entire classes due to the frantic production schedule.

While the design of these massive ships was in a state of flux for years, their doctrine also had been refined over years of training and simulations. The RMN knew what to do with the type even as they were constantly refining how they were designed and constructed. Not even the RMN, however, truly appreciated in 1905 how close to the end of its long reign the classic SD had come.

Manticore-class superdreadnought
Mass: 6,515,500 tons
Dimensions: 1263 × 183 × 171 m
Acceleration: 424.8 G (4.166 kps^2)
80% Accel: 339.9 G (3.333 kps^2)
Broadside: 22M, 18L, 24G, 8ET, 12CM, 24PD
Chase: 4M, 2L, 6G, 6CM, 12PD
Number Built: 3
Service Life: 1742–1905

The original design requirements for the Star Kingdom's first superdreadnought called for a ship "fit to engage and defeat any ship of the wall now in commission or under construction," and for their time, their design proved more than sufficient in that regard. With greatly improved active defenses and twice the graser broadside of the *Ad Astra* class, the *Manticore* class was a powerful, modern unit that compared favorably to even the most advanced Solarian design of the day.

HMS *Manticore* and her sister ships *Sphinx* and *Gryphon* were commissioned over a period of fifteen years, while their old battleship namesakes were redesignated HMS *Thorson*, *Perseus* and *Bellerophon*, respectively.

The trio was originally intended to form the core of a modernized capable wall of battle along with the *Ad Astra*-class dreadnoughts. The initial units rode the tail end of the wave of construction that followed the Battle of Carson, and a total of nine ships was originally planned.

HMS *Manticore* was scarcely a decade old when she first saw combat, during the rather misnamed "San Martin War." Given that the war began and ended with a single battle, and an uneventful one at that, there was little to learn from the experience. Worse in some ways, the brief skirmish actually hampered additional efforts to secure funding, as victory had been achieved so easily and no navies in the region were viewed as a threat that warranted more than the three ships already in commission. Instead of the planned additional construction, the existing dreadnoughts and battleships underwent a modernization and service life extension program. The three ships of the *Manticore* class served as flagships for the two mixed battle squadrons of Home Fleet, with one in the yards for maintenance at any given time.

While an effective design for their time, the class was over 150 years old by the start of the First Havenite War. HMS *Sphinx* and *Gryphon* had already been decommissioned as their namesakes led new, modern classes, and while HMS *Manticore* had been refitted as a flagship and saw the opening salvos of the war, she was decommissioned in late 1905 and her name given to a brand new *Gryphon*-class hull.

Samothrace-class superdreadnought
Mass: 7,253,750 tons
Dimensions: 1309 × 190 × 177 m
Acceleration: 416.6 G (4.086 kps²)
80% Accel: 333.3 G (3.268 kps²)
Broadside: 28M, 22L, 18G, 6ET, 18CM, 26PD
Chase: 6M, 6L, 4G, 6CM, 8PD
Number Built: 7
Service Life: 1848–present

The *Samothrace* class was the second class of superdreadnoughts built by the Royal Manticoran Navy, and (not surprisingly, given that almost exactly a century separated the two classes) it was a marked improvement over the *Manticore* class. While the increased combat power was a decided advantage, the true reason for the construction of this class was, originally, to provide modern flagships for the two active battle squadrons of Home Fleet.

The plans called for a total of three hulls to be built to allow for regular maintenance cycles and still retain a division of superdreadnoughts in every squadron. However, the cost of these units, coupled with the actual and projected costs of the *Royal Wintons*, caused Parliament to cut funding, dropping the planned construction to a single hull.

However, the Navy had been steadily increasing the number of units below the wall for over a century since the discovery of the Matapan Terminus, with a major push by First Space Lord

Frederick Truman in the preceding few years. With both Parliament and the senior uniformed officers of the Navy focusing on the commerce protection mission, the so-called "Gun Club" advocates were outnumbered and outvoted.

When King Roger began his buildup shortly after his coronation, one of the first actions he took was to renew construction of the two cancelled hulls, plus allocate funding for four more while the builder's plans were finalized for the *King William* class. As one shellshocked member of the Opposition remarked following the King's remarkable success in this initial foray: "The Admiralty asked for three, we offered one, and His Majesty compromised on seven." It would not be the last armament battle that remarkable monarch would win.

In the late 1890s, the entire class was pulled from service and refitted extensively as command ships. Technological advances, even in the short time since their construction, allowed their defenses to be substantially upgraded while at the same time providing space for extensive command and control facilities. Many of these ships have seen wartime service as task force and fleet flagships, even after more modern classes had been placed in reserve, simply because of their command and control equipment.

King William-class superdreadnought
Mass: 7,170,750 tons
Dimensions: 1304 × 189 × 176 m
Acceleration: 417.7 G (4.096 kps²)
80% Accel: 334.2 G (3.277 kps²)
Broadside: 32M, 19L, 21G, 26CM, 28PD
Chase: 8M, 6L, 4G, 10CM, 10PD
Number Built: 25
Service Life: 1877–1919

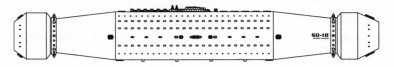

The *King William*-class superdreadnought was the first ship of its type to reach series production, after nearly a decade of design work and lessons learned from work on the *Royal Winton* and *Samothrace* classes. It was also the first ship built from the keel out to carry the new Mk19 Capital Ship Missile, then in development as the RMN's first laser head weapon, though not actually placed in service until several years after the first unit was commissioned.

Massing over seven million tons, the *King William* was designed to be a balanced combatant, giving equal weight to missile combat, beam combat, and defenses. The *King William*'s technological advances over the *Manticore* class resulted in a near fifty percent improvement in missile broadside strength, and the class established what was to become the standard Manticoran capital ship ammunition allocation of one round per minute per broadside launcher for a sustained period of two hours, known as the "1-for-2" rule.

While the *King Williams* proved a very successful design, they experienced their own share of growing pains during the course of construction. After the first eight of the class were completed BuShips realized counter-missile batteries were going to have an even greater prominence in missile engagements than originally realized, as laser heads increased the standoff distance of incoming missiles and reduced the effectiveness of point defense. A half-dozen point defense clusters were accordingly removed from the defensive weapon decks and replaced with counter-missile launchers.

Later refits brought the entire class up to a more consistent standard, leaving most of the remaining difference merely cosmetic. While the *King William* was eventually supplanted by the *Anduril* and *Victory* classes as the frontline Manticoran superdreadnought, a number of the *King Williams* distinguished themselves over the course of the war.

Most of the surviving *King Williams* were sold to Alliance navies during the Janacek build-down, including a full squadron transferred to the Erewhon Navy shortly before the resumption of hostilities and their subsequent exit from the Alliance.

Anduril-class superdreadnought

Mass: 7,506,000 tons
Dimensions: 1324 × 192 × 179 m
Acceleration: 413.3 G (4.053 kps^2)
80% Accel: 330.6 G (3.242 kps^2)
Broadside: 29M, 22L, 24G, 1GL, 8ET, 24CM, 32PD
Chase: 6M, 7L, 6G, 8CM, 12PD
Number Built: 14
Service Life: 1889–1918

The *Anduril* class was one of the shorter-lived designs of Roger's buildup, for two reasons. First, the older, cheaper *Gladiator*-class dreadnought had nearly the same capabilities for a considerably lower cost. Second, the Navy had come to the realization that missile combats were poised to become far more decisive than they had been at any time in the last two centuries, which moved the design trend towards more balanced combatants and away from brawlers like the *Anduril*.

While over four hundred thousand tons heavier than the *King William*, all of that extra tonnage was devoted to heavier armor and passive defenses. The *Anduril*'s distinction as the most heavily armored warship in the history of the RMN came at the cost of the offensive (missile) and defensive armament the Navy had come to value.

In addition, the heavy armor and internal compartmentalization had a hidden cost in terms of maintenance and downtime. Many systems, while well protected, were difficult to maintain, with too few accessways for movement of personnel and repair parts. Over the lifetime of the class, many pieces of equipment were simply abandoned in place rather than upgraded, due to the inability of the shipyard workers to install the new systems without cutting through a significant amount of hull armor.

The difficulty in upgrades, during a time when the Navy was undergoing generational changes in weapons systems literally every few years, was a death knell for the class. The *Andurils* were one of the first ships decommissioned during the Janacek build-down, and a number of them were sold to Erewhon with the *King Williams*.

Victory-class superdreadnought

Mass: 7,781,250 tons
Dimensions: 1340 × 194 × 181 m
Acceleration: 409.6 G (4.017 kps²)
80% Accel: 327.7 G (3.213 kps²)
Broadside: 35M, 20L, 19G, 6ET, 29CM, 27PD
Chase: 9M, 5L, 5G, 11CM, 9PD
Number Built: 36
Service Life: 1892–1918

With the *Victory* class, the RMN had finally hit its stride in superdreadnoughts. The construction woes plaguing the *King William* were a thing of the past, and the new design was a capable, missile-optimized platform that was a perfect match for the doctrine BuPlan had been perfecting since the advent of the laser head.

The class wasn't particularly large, as even at the time advances in capital ship design were progressing at breakneck speed. The entire series production run lasted no more than handful of years before it was superseded by the *Sphinx* class.

The disposal of the entire *Victory* class in early 1918 PD by the Janacek Admiralty was one of the most contentious decisions made by Second Lord Houseman. Every single remaining hull was sold to Grayson at scrap prices, despite the fact that the GSN couldn't possibly provide the manpower for all of those ships out of its own resources.

Benjamin Mayhew's decision proved to be fortuitous, however, as the RMN scrambled to reactivate every hull it had in mothballs after the resumption of the war with Haven. While the newer ships had been brought back into service first, BuShips has been negotiating with the GSN for the return of over half of the hulls over the next year. The remainder were crewed as GSN units with a higher than normal percentage of RMN "loaner" personnel.

Sphinx-class superdreadnought

Mass: 8,207,000 tons
Dimensions: 1364 × 198 × 184 m
Acceleration: 403.9 G (3.961 kps²)
80% Accel: 323.1 G (3.169 kps²)
Broadside: 36M, 21L, 19G, 6ET, 27CM, 31PD
Chase: 8M, 4L, 5G, 9CM, 12PD
Number Built: 67
Service Life: 1895–present

The *Sphinx* class was by far the largest SD class (in total hulls) when the war started. During the peak of the buildup these ships were entering service at an almost frantic pace of more than one every month.

In terms of weapons fit, the most visible feature of any warship, the *Sphinx* was merely an incremental update over the *Victory* class, with no truly revolutionary ideas. That was scarcely surprising given the pace of production and improvements in design and construction. The first *Sphinx* was laid down before the first *Victory* was even commissioned, so there was little time for lessons learned from one to propagate to another.

While the weapons fit was largely the same as the preceding class, the defenses were much different. In theory the RMN has always designed their capital ships to be able to survive their own fire; in practice, up until the war began, RMN simulation models were in an almost continual state of flux as the damage potential of the laser head warheads kept increasing, without actual real-world testing data to ground the sims.

The *Sphinx* class marks the turning point where enough real-world data had been accumulated for BuShips to fully understand the kind of armoring and compartmentalization a ship of the wall needed to survive the new environment. Weapon mounts were rearranged, internal bulkheads were strengthened, magazines were hardened, and compartments were arranged to protect critical systems with less critical equipment spaces, all leading to a ship that was far more survivable than any design yet in service.

Still, the speed of design and development had not slowed, and, in a short construction run of only six years the RMN built almost twice as many *Sphinxes* as the previous *Victory* class.

The *Sphinx* and follow-on *Gryphon* were the only classes spared in the Janacek build-down, though over half of both of these classes had been placed in reserve by the time the war resumed. They have been reactivated on a crash priority basis on the theory that any ship of the wall is preferable to none, especially with the loss of so many incomplete modern units at Grendelsbane.

Gryphon-class superdreadnought

Mass: 8,339,000 tons
Dimensions: 1371 × 199 × 185 m
Acceleration: 402.1 G (3.944 kps²)
80% Accel: 321.7 G (3.155 kps²)
Broadside: 37M, 19L, 22G, 8ET, 28CM, 30PD
Chase: 9M, 4L, 5G, 10CM, 10PD
Number Built: 163
Service Life: 1900–present

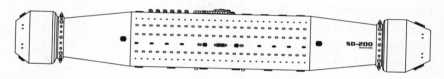

In many ways the *Gryphon* class was simply an evolution and continuation of the successful *Sphinx* class, as new construction began to incorporate lessons learned from the *Victory*-class testing and evaluation programs. The differences in weapons fit and evolutionary changes in design were great enough that BuShips redesignated them as an entirely new class, despite the fact that several of the later *Sphinxes* were all but indistinguishable from the earlier *Gryphon*-class ships.

Still under construction at the outbreak of the First Haven War, these represent the pinnacle of conventional superdreadnought design, and the demands of the war kept the class in series production with a minimum of changes for the next decade. They would have continued at that pace were it not for the fruits of Project Ghost Rider, and in fact, a number of the *Medusa*-class units were carried on the books as Flight III *Gryphons* to maintain secrecy on that project.

Most of the *Gryphon*-class ships were spared from the Janacek cutbacks, though many were placed in the reserve in line with the policy of leaving system defense to LAC wings and concentrating the Navy's striking power in the squadrons of pod superdreadnoughts already in commission.

During this period, a handful of *Gryphons* had been gutted and refitted with launchers capable of firing the new Mk23 Multi-Drive Missile from internal tubes. While plans had existed initially to refit all of the class with MDMs, the program proved prohibitively expensive and was bedeviled by technical and safety problems with the fusion-powered missiles, and only a small portion had actually been completed before the war resumed. Given the current strategic situation, the White Haven Admiralty has not been willing or able to pull the existing units off the front lines to continue the refits.

Duquesne-class superdreadnought

Mass: 7,187,250 tons
Dimensions: 1305 × 189 × 176 m
Acceleration: 417.5 G (4.094 kps^2)
80% Accel: 334 G (3.275 kps^2)
Broadside: 36M, 12L, 12G, 28CM, 24PD
Chase: 10M, 4L, 6G, 12CM, 12PD
Number Captured: 18
Service Life: 1906–1917

Exclusive of the original eleven donated to Grayson by Admiral White Haven, a number of Havenite superdreadnoughts were captured in the opening stages of the war, and the capture of several forward bases almost intact provided the RMN with enough ammunition and spares to bring them into service.

Along with the handful of captured dreadnoughts and smaller classes, these ships provided rear area security for a number of Alliance systems during the early stages of the war, but were relegated to mothballs as their crews were needed to man the new construction, while the ships in best condition were all sold at scrap value to Grayson in early 1917.

Haven-class superdreadnought
Mass: 7,816,250 tons
Dimensions: 1342 × 195 × 181 m
Acceleration: 409.1 G (4.012 kps²)
80% Accel: 327.3 G (3.21 kps²)
Broadside: 36M, 15L, 23G, 26CM, 32PD
Chase: 8M, 4L, 10G, 10CM, 12PD
Number Captured: 3
Service Life: 1907–1917

Similar to the *Duquesnes*, the few more modern *Haven*-class superdreadnoughts captured in the early days of the war served for several years as rear area security, freeing up hulls for the front. None of them saw battle against their sisters still in Havenite service, however, and the last were sold to Grayson along with the *Duquesnes*.

POD SUPERDREADNOUGHTS (SD(P))

The Royal Manticoran Navy began its operational experience with pod-laying designs with the *Trojan*-class armed merchant cruiser of Project Trojan Horse. While the initial designs were cumbersome, fragile, and inefficient, they still provided a huge force multiplier. They also proved the concept of the hollow-core pod-layer which certain officers in BuWeaps and BuShips had been proposing for some time. The *Trojans*' successful deployment finally routed most of the "traditionalist" opposition to the proposal, and BuShips was formally authorized to begin design studies on what became the SD(P).

Beginning with the *Medusa* class, the RMN took the concept of a pod-laying warship and began an entirely new era of warfare. For the first time since its inception centuries before, the ponderous formality of the wall of battle had been broken, as engagements were often decided in the opening salvos of missiles.

The simultaneous implementation of a practical multi-drive missile system gave the RMN a qualitative edge that was unparalleled, and drove the People's Navy to the brink of defeat in the few short months leading up to the ceasefire. Even though the

MDM was inherently inaccurate at extended ranges, the pod-laying designs could fire salvos of thousands, multiple times, so that even a low percentage rate of hits produced overwhelming numbers of them in absolute terms.

Almost unnoticed in the early stages of the developing doctrine was that the endurance of the missile pod allowed a single ship to stack multiple patterns of pods, allowing it to fire double or triple patterns (or more), up to the limits of its individual fire control. As a result, even an outnumbered force could put enough missiles into space to saturate a target's defenses in the opening salvo. The smaller force might still be wiped out in the end, but no longer would it go quietly.

With the introduction of the MDM and pod-layer on both sides of the conflict, the RMN has been forced to continually reevaluate its own doctrine for defending against the weight of fire a pod-layer can lay down. This reassessment is reflected in countless places, from new antimissile weapons, improved EW, and experimental defensive doctrine to the makeup of task forces and the formations adopted in combat, reflecting a time of rapid change in all areas of warfare.

Medusa-class pod superdreadnought

Mass: 8,554,750 tons
Dimensions: 1383 × 201 × 187 m
Acceleration: 502.8 G (4.931 kps²)
80% Accel: 402.3 G (3.945 kps²)
Broadside: 26M, 13L, 15G, 54CM, 52PD
Fore: 9M, 4L, 5G, 18CM, 22PD
Aft: 6MP, 4L, 5G, 14CM, 20PD
Missile Pods: 492
Number Built: 63
Service Life: 1914–present

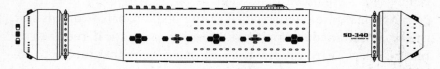

The *Medusa*-class pod superdreadnought was in secret conceptual development for over a decade prior to Operation Trojan Horse in

1909 while the Weapons Development Board and Project Ghost Rider worked to develop the weapon systems the class would eventually carry. The success of the prototype pod system in the *Trojans* threw the project into high gear, however, imposing a great deal of strain on BuShips' design staff.

Even before the first units were laid down, the RMN had begun a carefully crafted disinformation campaign, including a leaked "spring study" for the next generation (conventional) superdreadnought replacement for the *Gryphon* class. Thus the RMN diverted attention from the decrease in new *Gryphons* and gave the Havenite intelligence agencies a plausible explanation for the secret programs being conducted at HMSS *Weyland*.

Following the Graysons' lead, the class was renamed the *Honor Harrington* class to honor then-Commodore Harrington after her presumed execution. Following her dramatic return from Cerberus, the class name was changed back to the original *Medusa*. Deriving from the same joint design program, the *Medusa* is similar in design to the final *Harrington* class, the first units of which were commissioned over a year before the RMN managed to get the first *Medusa* into service.

As the first RMN warship designed from the keel out to deploy missile pods from an internal magazine, the *Medusa* faced some unique design challenges. The most obvious difference between it and any conventional ship of the wall is apparent from the broadside. All of the primary armament has been pushed into the forward half of the main hull to make room for the double rings of missile pod storage in the after section. The second most notable difference is the sheer number of surface arrays, which provide both fire control and telemetry uplinks for the hundreds of missiles these ships can launch in a single stacked salvo. Finally, the defensive armament, located at the upper and lower turn of the hull, extends along its entire length, and the number of point defense and counter-missile installations have been greatly increased over any previous design.

While massively enhancing the ships' first strike capabilities, the hollow-core filling the after third of the hull reduced its survivability in comparison to pre-pod superdreadnoughts. In addition, the need to mount armored hatches through which to deploy the pods forced the designers to sacrifice some of the after chase weaponry.

Despite the huge increase in offensive firepower, the *Medusas* contain a significant degree of automation in their design and require a crew less than half that of an older conventional design.

The pod rails on the *Medusa* class were designed originally for a modification of the old Mk10 missile pod, of which it could carry 564. Later pods were designed with the same rail attachment points and footprint, varying only in their depth. As deployed during operation Buttercup, the *Medusa* class carried just under 500 Mk11 missile pods, while currently deployed units can carry as many as 800 Mk17 series flat-pack pods.

Invictus-class pod superdreadnought

Mass: 8,768,500 tons
Dimensions: 1394 × 202 × 188 m
Acceleration: 562.6 G (5.518 kps²)
80% Accel: 450.1 G (4.414 kps²)
Broadside: 18G, 84CM, 62PD
Fore: 10G, 24CM, 22PD
Aft: 6MP, 10G, 14CM, 24PD
Missile Pods: 1074
Number Built: 53+
Service Life: 1919–present

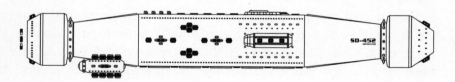

The *Invictus* class was on the drawing board at the end of the First Havenite War as the improved successor of the *Medusa* class, but construction of the first wave of ships had barely begun when the High Ridge Government agreed to a truce with the People's Republic. As per the drawdown of forces ordered by the new government, construction of the majority of units in the class was suspended and the unfinished ships were placed in storage in their building slips in the Manticore and Grendelsbane shipyards.

At the resumption of hostilities, only twelve *Invictus*-class ships were in commission, with a few more nearing completion in Manticore from previously suspended construction programs.

Dozens were lost in the Grendelsbane attack, and over a hundred were laid down as part of the emergency war construction program for completion over the next couple of years.

In many ways the *Invictus* is simply an evolution of the *Medusa* design, with a pod core extending half again as deep into the hull. In a departure from both traditional Manticoran and contemporary Grayson practice, all broadside missile tubes were eliminated to allow for the maximum extension of the missile core, which is capable of holding upwards of a thousand of the new flat-pack missile pods. Internally, the differences are even greater, however, as one of the major weaknesses of the pod-layer concept has been partially offset by armoring the interior of the pod core almost as heavily as the outer hull armor. Almost all of the tonnage advantage over the *Medusa* went into this new armoring scheme, which has greatly increased survivability.

Nevertheless, the greatest weakness of the design remains in the pod rails, and even with the new armoring scheme, a single lucky hit on the pod core can cause enough damage to jam up deployment of the pods "upstream" of the hit. Cross connecting rails, the ability to quickly jettison debris and destroyed pods, and a tractor system that can help the system "leapfrog" over broken rails all help mitigate the effects of this damage, but the incidence of mission kills in pod-layers with otherwise light damage remains potentially high.

By far the most significant improvement seen in the *Invictus* class, however, is the new Mk20 Keyhole platform. At least two versions of this versatile tethered platform exist, but both of them share a number of the same features. Although Keyhole was originally envisioned primarily as a means to improve active antimissile capability, conceptual evolution during development produced a very different end product. At their heart, Keyholes are telemetry relays, multiplying the number of telemetry links the ship can maintain, which in turn allows for even deeper stacked salvos, or a layered approach where conventional ships in the squadron can hand off their onboard and pod-launched missiles to an *Invictus* to centrally control.

In addition, the Keyhole platform extends the sensor reach of the host ship, both with dedicated offboard arrays as well as with the ability to deploy outside the wedge and relay information while the ship has rolled against the threat axis.

Finally, the platform not only replaces and enhances the traditional tethered decoy platform, mounting sophisticated jammers and ECM gear, but is very heavily equipped with point defense laser clusters of its own.

Although no more than two can be carried by even the largest of ships, they are still cheaper to replace than an entire warship, and their heavy onboard array of point defense laser clusters not only allows them a degree of self-defense far in advance of any previous tethered EW platform in Manticoran service, but also contributes significantly to the defense of the deploying ship.

While the *Invictus* is a new design, tested so far in only a few engagements, it is indisputably one of the most powerful and capable warships in existence.

ARMED MERCHANT CRUISERS (AMC)

While the Navy had long maintained the practice of installing defensive armament and sidewalls on its fast auxiliaries, the RMN had never operated Q-ships of any sort prior to Project Trojan Horse. Due to the mounting merchantship losses in Silesia resulting from the drawdown of forces in the Confederacy to replace losses on the Havenite front, BuShips and BuWeaps proposed to take a page out of the Havenite book and build auxiliary warships on essentially merchant hulls. The idea was to convert several of the RMN's standard *Caravan*-class support vessels from the Joint Navy Military Transport Command into armed merchant cruisers by incorporating some of the new concepts in development. The AMCs would both allow operational testing of some of the WDB's more radical new systems proposed and combat the growing piracy problem by deploying to the Confederacy as convoy escorts and independent patrol units.

While Trojan Horse as a whole succeeded in protecting commerce in Silesia, it was even more successful as a proof of concept for both LAC and carrier operations as well the internal pod rails and deployment that helped paved the way for the first *Medusa*-class SD(P) in 1914 PD.

Trojan-class armed merchant cruiser

Mass: 7,352,000 tons
Dimensions: 1199 × 200 × 185 m
Acceleration: 190 G (1.863 kps²)
80% Accel: 152 G (1.491 kps²)
Broadside: 10M, 8G, 10CM, 10PD
Fore: 6CM, 6PD
Aft: 6MP, 8PD
Missile Pods: 180
LAC Bays: 12
Number Built: 15
Service Life: 1909–1920 PD

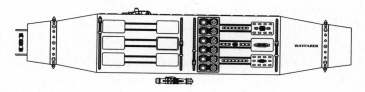

The *Trojan*-class armed merchant cruiser was a testbed platform in many ways, built on the hull of the *Caravan*-class freighter used by Logistics Command for rear area supply.

The armament of the *Trojan* class was unique at the time of construction. While the term "Armed Merchant Cruiser" belies the normal grade of weaponry found on a Q-ship, most of the examples seen in other navies are hybrid designs, able to carry limited cargo in addition to their disguised weaponry. BuShips decided to eliminate all cargo storage from the *Trojan* and use all of the volume freed up for a number of weapon systems, some more experimental than others.

Conventional broadside and chase armament consisted of the sort of missile broadside one might find on a heavy cruiser, except that the weapons in question, both missile tubes and energy mounts, were all superdreadnought-grade installations. Bottlenecks in capital ship construction, coupled with a surplus of weapon system components provided the systems in question, though the nature of the building queues resulted in different units of the class carrying a different balance of missiles and beams. The most common configuration was the ten missile launchers and eight grasers carried by the lead ship, but other ships in the class had mixed beam armaments, all lasers, and in some cases fewer missile tubes and more beams.

Unique to the *Trojans* at that time was an internal storage and deployment system for missile pods, making the *Trojan* the first ever pod-laying warship in service in any Navy. While outwardly similar to the more advanced system onboard the *Medusa* class, the prototype system had numerous inefficiencies and some out-right dangerous design faults that were fixed in later generations.

The second unique "weapon system" was the organic ability to launch a squadron of *Series 282* advanced light attack craft from internal bays. While its ability to service and rearm the LACs was somewhat limited, the *Trojan* was also the galaxy's first hyper-capable LAC-carrying warship.

After the early successes of the first four units, the class went on to serve well in the Silesian Confederacy for over a decade. The follow-on units became a common sight throughout Silesian space, and even though pirate groups learned to recognize them, they still provided a powerful deterrent effect, especially once the merchant cartels began to introduce more new-build unmodified *Caravan*-class freighters into the area.

While the Janacek Admiralty had written up plans to extend the class with an additional dozen units, those plans were scrapped with the onset of the Second Havenite War. With the need for manpower growing at an enormous pace, the *Trojans* were listed for disposal shortly thereafter, freeing up their overly large crews for the new construction starting to come off the building slips.

The Royal Manticoran Marine Corps

The Royal Manticoran Marine Corps was formally established in 1516 PD, but can trace its roots back to the Navy's Fleet Marine Forces, first created in 1438 PD shortly after the initial skirmish with the Free Brotherhood. Part of the process of transforming the Navy from a primarily civil defense organization into a true military organization, the Fleet Marine Forces grew from the core of cross-trained naval personnel who formed the original boarding teams and shipboard security.

Until the mid-seventeenth century, the Corps remained the only Kingdomwide armed service dedicated to ground or boarding combat. In 1665 PD, shortly after the Ranier War, a growing movement in Parliament called for a unified ground service encompassing both the newly created Army and Marines as a cost-efficiency measure. It made little sense, proponents argued, to maintain two separate forces, each with its own infrastructure needs and costs, when they performed so many overlapping roles and missions. While the new service was formally called the Royal Army due to the broad spectrum of official responsibilities the new service needed to meet, the majority of the senior officers came originally from the Corps. After a few generations, though, the drive to create "uniformity" in the name of efficiency became increasingly pronounced, eventually leading to much more emphasis being placed on planetary combat and less on the training in the shipboard duties like damage control and weapons crews which had always been part of the traditional Marine role. Increasingly, the Fleet found itself with soldiers assigned to its ships but not fully integrated into those ships' operations, which increased manpower costs—without Marines trained in shipboard duties more spacers were inevitably required—and decreased efficiency. Eventually, the nature of the problem was recognized and the Marines reemerged as a separate organization intensively trained to perform both shipboard and planetary missions.

Given the primacy of the RMN within the Star Empire, the RMMC has become the senior ground combat arm of the Star Empire. Originally tasked with providing boarding parties for naval units, the Corps' responsibilities are currently defined as follows:

1. Provide emergency landing parties, security parties, and boarding parties for the ship to which they are attached.
2. Provide shipboard police under the authority of a warship's master at arms.
3. Man shipboard duty stations at GQ or battle stations.
4. Provide garrisons, guards, and security detachments for Manticoran enclaves on other planets.

The Royal Marines are not responsible for sustained planetary combat, atmospheric support, or the garrisoning of entire planets. Those missions are the purview of the Royal Manticoran Army, which is specifically trained and equipped for these tasks.

Organization

A Marine rifle squad consists of thirteen members: a sergeant, two corporals, six riflemen, two grenadiers, and two plasma gunners. The basic tactical element, a section, consists of a plasma gunner covered by three pulser-armed riflemen and a grenadier, commanded by a corporal, while the sergeant exercises overall command. A Marine heavy weapons squad consists of a sergeant, two corporals, and six to ten riflemen, depending on the weapon the squad operates. Heavy weapons squads are "pure function" units equipped with either heavy tripod-mounted plasma guns, tri-barrel pulsers, man-portable SAMs, or mortars.

A Marine rifle platoon consists of a lieutenant, platoon sergeant, one clerk, and three rifle squads. In addition, each platoon has two assigned Navy Sick Berth Attendants (SBAs) to act as corpsmen. A heavy weapons platoon consists of a lieutenant, platoon sergeant, clerk, and four weapons squads (one of each type).

A Marine rifle company consists of a captain, four staff lieutenants, one first sergeant, three clerks, and three rifle platoons. Each company also has two additional permanently attached Navy SBAs and is normally paired with one of its parent battalion's heavy weapons platoons.

The primary maneuver unit of the RMMC is the battalion, which typically consists of a lieutenant colonel, one major (the exec), a ten-man staff, one sergeant-major, one color sergeant (a leftover from the Corps' earliest days now acting as the sergeant-major's noncommissioned exec), ten noncommissioned clerks, three rifle companies, and one heavy weapons company. In addition, each battalion should have an attached Navy doctor, assisted by five SBAs.

Approximately ten percent of the Corps' total battalions are "assault" battalions (indicated by adding [A] to their unit designations) in which all personnel are equipped with battle armor. An assault battalion has no "heavy weapons" company per se. Instead, an additional "rifle company" in battle armor takes its place. In addition, an assault company or battalion has a somewhat higher "teeth-to-tail" ratio than a rifle company or battalion because the Corps' attached Navy medical personnel are not trained in the use of battle armor and are not carried on the assault units' Table of Organization and Equipment (TO&E).

The largest permanent standing unit is the regiment, consisting of a command section leading three battalions. Regiments may be organized into brigades or even divisions, although this was seldom practiced before the Havenite Wars. Brigades are currently used as administrative organizations when a large Marine force needs to be deployed to a distant fleet station such as the Talbott Quadrant or Silesia. Deployment of units above regimental strength in a combat zone remains rare for two reasons: modern weapons and equipment mean that larger units are seldom required, and when larger units are required, the situation is almost always one which should have been handed over to the Army in the first place.

Equipment

The standard shoulder arm of the RMMC is the M32 series grav pulse rifle in 4×37 mm caliber. The M32A5, introduced in 1918 PD, is the latest variant of this versatile weapon system. The M32 has two magazine wells, each of which will accommodate a single hundred-round magazine. Pulser darts come in two basic varieties: a solid, non-explosive, antipersonnel round and a superdense, explosive round designed for antiarmor or general suppressive fire. A shorter carbine version, the M19, is designed for shipboard use. The standard sidearm carried by officers is the M7 pulser and its short-barreled variant the M9.

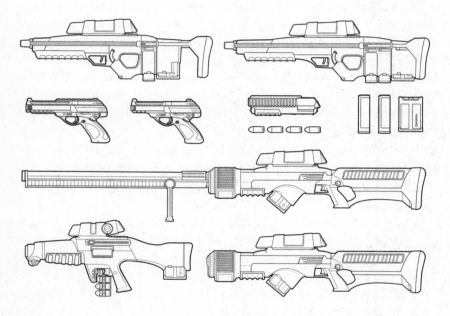

The M107 Plasma Rifle and M109 Plasma Carbine are the RMMC's standard antiarmor weapons. The M107 uses twin M13 power cells, while the M109 carries only one. Each cell is good for three to twelve shots, depending on power settings. Maximum effective range in atmosphere is about four thousand meters, but bloom and energy bleed begin reducing terminal effect very rapidly beyond twenty-two hundred meters. In vacuum, maximum range is usually line of sight, with minimal energy bleed.

Indirect supporting fire is provided by the M142 Grenade Launcher, a semi-automatic grav-launcher firing spin-stabilized

30mm grenades from forty-round belts or six-round box magazines. Maximum effective range is about eighteen hundred meters. The grenades can be fused for impact, delay, or air burst operation and the integrated targeting computer displays ranging data and kill zones on the scope or directly overlaid onto the Skinsuit HUD.

Heavy weapons squads are equipped with a variety of crew-served weapons, including the M247 Heavy Tribarrel, M271 Plasma Cannon, and M223 Mortar among others. These are tripod-mounted weapons carried disassembled by squad members and deployed in minutes to provide support fire to maneuver units. Variants of the M247 and M271 exist for battle armor, carried be a single assault marine and drawing from the suit's internal power cells.

Standard combat gear for the RMMC includes the Mk7 Armored Skinsuit. The underlying structure of the Mk7 is identical to the Navy's skinsuit, though the Marine variant trades comfort for protection and increased tactical features. For small arms protection, a series of armor plates covers the suit, providing adequate defense against light weaponry. The addition of weapon interlink ports allows the use of the helmet's heads-up display (HUD) in combat. The skinsuit is used in boarding actions, shipboard duty, hostile environment engagements and combat drops, while lightweight unpowered body armor is worn at other times.

Assault units are equipped with M21 Battle Armor, a combat suit with a powered exoskeleton and heavy armor plating, powered by internal power cells. The M21 Base Platform can be configured in a number of ways depending on mission requirements. In reconnaissance configuration, more power is stored at the expense of weapon loadouts, which increases endurance but leaves the trooper with nothing more than a standard pulse rifle, while in assault configuration, heavy weapons such as tribarrels and plasma cannon are carried.

The RMMC is a pure infantry force, with no organic vehicle components other than their (Navy-operated) small craft. The two most commonly seen subtypes are the Mk30 "*Condor II*" Pinnace and the Mk17 *Avenger* Assault Shuttle, though some units still carry the older Marine-optimized Mk26 *Skyhawk* Pinnace. All three are capable of company-level drops as well as fire support.

Aside from the dedicated *Broadsword*-class LCA and the new *Kamerling* class, interstellar transport was provided throughout the war by the aging *Rorke's Drift*-class Fast Attack Transports and the *Guadalcanal*-class Heavy Assault Transports. With the drawdown of onboard marine complements due to the increased automation onboard Manticoran Warships, a design study was put in place in 1920 PD for a new class of Marine transport. Designed to attach to a fleet to provide a centralized Marine support unit, the as-yet unnamed LPX (Attack Transport, Experimental) can carry three regiments plus support on a large battlecruiser-sized hull, with enough active and passive defenses to protect itself as part of the fleet train, and sufficient small craft capacity to deploy a full regiment in a single wave.

The Royal Manticoran Army

The Royal Manticoran Army was formally established by King Roger Winton II in 1648 PD and is the youngest of the Star Empire's three military services. Prior to that date, each planet in the Manticore system had its own Planetary Guard to provide for disaster relief, peacekeeping, and planetary security, but there was no perceived need for a Kingdomwide army.

With the growing merchant fleet and responsibilities of the Royal Manticoran Navy in the years following the first transit of the Junction, the Star Kingdom began to look toward gathering a military that was capable of force projection in addition to its historical role of providing system security and defense. The Royal Army was established as part of that initiative, merging the three Planetary Guard forces into a single service and starting a research and construction program to develop the equipment and doctrine to fight a major ground war if required.

The Army achieved two important "firsts" during the Ranier War: its first operational deployment and its first actual combat operations. The practical experience of several months of low-intensity combat in the Ranier System honed the skills the Army had developed through extensive training and wargaming. The Army's good performance was one of the factors cited to justify the century-long merger with the Royal Marines.

The Army's four primary mission roles are defined as follows:

1. Provide the mechanized "muscle" for sustained planetary combat.
2. Secure and maintain control of planetary surfaces and fixed ground defenses.
3. Maintain the peace against uprisings or unrest when called to do so by the Government.
4. Provide disaster relief and humanitarian assistance.

It should be noted that, despite the equipment and training, the Royal Army has never in its history been called upon to fulfill its primary mission. Any force that holds undisputed control of the high orbitals can force a surrender or can defeat even a superior enemy ground force without risking its own units with few exceptions. For those exceptions, the Star Kingdom has built an Army capable of sustained planetary combat, but the capability has not been needed to date. Instead, the Army has been tasked with peacekeeping and garrison duties on over a dozen captured Havenite worlds. Often the first Manticoran any of their population met in person was a member of the Army, and its training as peacekeeping and local police forces has served them well in that role.

Organization

The Royal Army is primarily a mechanized force, consisting of regular, armored, and assault infantry units; armored units; engineering units; heavy ground defense units; and aerial units, including both atmospheric and trans-atmospheric fighters (sting ships). The Army uses the term "armored unit" to indicate a unit equipped with armored fighting vehicles, which range from relatively lightly armored but highly mobile skimmers and infantry fighting vehicles to heavy tanks, capable of standing up to heavy plasma fire. In the unusual eventuality of really heavy ground combat, the Army usually provides heavy vehicles support for the Marines or completely takes over from them in the sustained combat role.

While the Army's "leg" infantry and few battle armored assault units operate with the same organization and doctrine as the

Marines, their armored infantry are organized a little differently at the squad level. An armored infantry squad fights dismounted, with two four-man fireteams (often called "quads") and a sergeant in overall command, supported by the two- to three-man team in their light skimmer or infantry fighting vehicle.

Armored infantry platoons consist of three squad vehicles plus a command vehicle. A tank platoon likewise consists of four tanks (three plus a command tank). Various support platoons exist at different levels of organization, but the core "three plus command" organization concept remains constant across this level of organization. A company, whether composed of infantry, armored infantry or tanks, consists of three platoons plus a command element. The command element will include a command vehicle for the staff, and often includes support vehicles (medical, engineering, air defense, etc.) depending on the mission.

A typical Army Battalion will consist of a command element, three standard companies, one support company (often a combination of heavy weapons and mission-specific support), and a fifth company that is normally detached for recruiting and depot duties, including vehicular maintenance and rear area security. Three battalions combine to form a regiment, which is the highest permanent organizational unit, similar to the Marines.

Pure function units above regimental size are not used, but when necessary, the Army will form mission-specific Regimental Combat Teams, typically consisting of one armored regiment, two armored infantry regiments, and one aerospace wing for transport and airspace control.

Atmospheric Command operates all of the Army's aerospace fighters and transports, and is organized into squadrons and wings. The unit organization changes to meet the needs of the mission, ranging anywhere from a cross-attached squadron for close-air support of an armored infantry battalion to a full transport wing to provide airlift for an entire regiment. Under the terms of the East Cay Agreement, Atmospheric Command is prohibited from operating extra-atmospheric vehicles at "interplanetary distances," which is interpreted to mean more than one light-minute from a planetary body. The East Cay Agreement was intended to prevent the design and procurement of competing assault shuttles, pinnaces, etc., by restricting the Army to stingships and similarly short-ranged extra-atmosphere combat vehicles. The East Cay

Agreement had been waived upon occasion, however, and Army stingships are designed to be capable of operating from Navy boat bays and Marine assault ships when necessary. Atmospheric Command personnel routinely train in joint operations with both the RMMC and the RMN.

Equipment

At the level of the individual soldier, the Army has a great deal of commonality of equipment with the Royal Marines, and its infantry regiments are equipped with identical gear across the board, with minor differences only based on mission focus. The Army has far fewer battle-armored assault units than the Marines, however, given the expense in both equipment and training to maintain them.

The primary combat unit of the armored regiment is the M11A2 grav tank. The M11 is a hybrid design, capable of short "sprints" on counter-grav, with conventional treads for stability and long distance travel. The primary weapon is a 120 mm plasma cannon, supported by a remote tribarrel pulser for anti-infantry defense as well as an automated point defense turret designed to rapidly engage and destroy incoming projectiles and missiles. Forward scouting is performed by onboard counter-grav reconnaissance drones, while an active and passive ECM suite works to defeat guided projectiles, as well as target locks from enemy tanks.

The M13 Infantry Fighting Vehicle is a lightweight variant of same hybrid pattern as the M11, but armed with a heavy tribarrel pulser in the turret and capable of carrying a total of twelve soldiers, including a commander, driver, gunner, and full rifle squad. Numerous specialty vehicles (command, engineering, air defense, artillery, etc.) are built on the M11 and M13 base platforms.

In comparison, the M27 Skimmer (often referred to as a "battle taxi") is a pure counter-grav vehicle that bears a closer resemblance to an armored aircar than a tank. Optimized as a fast reconnaissance vehicle, the M27 is capable of speeds up to nine hundred kilometers per hour at low altitude. Armament consists of a twin light tribarrel pulser turret to provide support fire to the embarked squad when necessary.

Atmospheric Command operates a number of aerospace craft, but the two most common are the M105 "Goliath" transport and the M116 "Viper" stingship. The Goliath is the primary heavy lift platform of the Atmospheric Command, and a Goliath Wing is capable of airlifting an entire regiment from one side of the planet to the other in less than twenty-four hours. The Viper is the standard single-seat stingship operated by the Army, a high-performance impeller-drive hypersonic attack fighter capable of operations from "treetops to low orbit," as well as limited space capability.

The Army has no interplanetary transport ability and must rely solely on Navy and Marine transport. The Star Empire is running chronically short of their fast attack and heavy assault transports, and the ones in service are worked hard. It is not unusual for Army regiments to find themselves loaded aboard civilian transport to reach their garrisons.

Queen's Own

The Queen's Own exists in order to provide physical security to the sovereign and to members of the royal family, and to provide area security for Mount Royal Palace and for other royal residences. More than mere bodyguards, the Queen's Own also has responsibility for certain support functions, such as intelligence, associated with protection of the Royal Family. While operationally part of the Army, the Queen's Own dates back to 1489 PD with the Coronation of King Roger I. Recognizing the need for a protective detail for the Monarch, given the influx of new colonists, the Manticore and Sphinx Planetary Guards each "donated" a company and a half of their troops to form the core of a battalion. Gryphon followed suit after its population reached a level to support its own Planetary Guard. The unit has grown in strength since then, and had already reached regimental size by the time it was merged with the Army in 1665 PD.

The Queen's Own (formally known as the Monarch's Own Regiment) is generally regarded as the elite of the Army, but its ranks are also open to Marines, and even the occasional naval officer. Before being accepted for service in the Queen's Own, an individual must first prove himself or herself thoroughly in one of the combat arms.

The Queen's Own consists of four "battalions," one for each of the three original planets of the Star Kingdom plus a "training battalion," which both trains new recruits and provides opposition forces for training at the Army's premier combat training facilities. The Queen's Own's battalions do not normally detach their "recruiting" or depot company. This means that, technically, the Queen's Own's official strength is 2,940 troops. In fact, it is usually somewhat understrength because of the high standards its personnel must meet. Like the Army itself, the Queen's Own contains its own atmospheric component of stingships and heavy transports. Most of its personnel, even on security detail for the Monarch herself, are normally configured as light infantry, but each battalion has its own integral heavy weapons company, and powered armor is available to it.

The Queen's Own is expected to contribute forces to frontline combat if the Star Kingdom is at war. This usually takes the form of deploying one of its three planet battalions to the active theater, leaving the other two planet battalions to hold down the Regiment's normal peacetime duties. Those duties include the personal security of the sovereign and members of the royal family, security at Mount Royal Palace and other royal residences, and intelligence functions related to the preceding two duties.

In addition to all of the above, the Queen's Own is the Army's premier ceremonial unit, as it has been a part of the Star Kingdom's military traditions dating back to the founding of the Star Kingdom itself.

The Protectorate of Grayson

My Lords, I do not intend to debate with you. It is the Sword's prerogative in time of war to instruct you, and such is my purpose today. I will entertain no discussion, and I will brook no defiance. Understand me well, and ignore my warning at your peril.

There has been much discussion in this Conclave over months past as to blame and responsibility. There have been countless whispers, and more than a few open arguments, that the time has come for the Protectorate of Grayson to walk away from the Star Kingdom of Manticore. It is not our job, I have heard too many of you say, to guard the back of a star nation which does not worry about guarding our own or consulting us on foreign policy as an ally should. It is not our responsibility to stand at the side of a star nation whose own policies, whose own internal political corruption and partisanship, have brought it to this deadly pass. It is wisdom to stand aside rather than fling ourselves between the Star Kingdom of Manticore and the Republic of Haven in this new and even deadlier war between them. We have paid enough standing there in days past; we will pay no more today.

Yes, My Lord Keys, I have heard you. The Sword has listened, as it is charged to listen. And now, having listened, the Sword will speak, and I will speak to tell you to be silent.

I know as well as any other man in this chamber—indeed, better than any other man in this chamber—how corrupt, how self-serving, how foolish and shortsighted and arrogant the High Ridge Government has been. I know how it has ignored consultation with its allies, how it has built down its own navy, paid no heed to the possibility that Haven might be acquiring equally advanced weapons. I know how it squandered the opportunity for outright victory which lay with in our grasp before the Duke of Cromarty and Lord Chancellor Prestwick were killed—murdered—right here at Yeltsin's Star by agents of the Committee of Public Safety. I know all of those things, yet they are not all I know, and unlike certain honored members of this conclave, I remember those other things.

I remember the Faithful on Masada. I remember their promises to destroy all we hold dear. I remember their plot, Haven's assistance to them, the way in which our Navy was destroyed by them. And, My Lords, I remember why they failed. I remember the men and women of a foreign, infidel star nation who never hesitated, never asked "Why?"—never even considered standing aside in a battle which was not theirs. I remember how many of those men and women died for us, when they did not even know us. When too many of our own people had systematically insulted them because of the difference of their beliefs. And I remember how much else we owe to those "strangers" who brought us modern medicine, interstellar trade, prosperity, safety. Who gave us the gift of the sons and daughters this hostile world of ours can now support. Who freed us from the curse which killed so many millions of our babies at birth. Who have fought and bled and died with our sons and our brothers because they are no longer "strangers," but have also become our brothers—and our sisters—by choice.

I will not hear a voice in this chamber which does not count them as much our own, as much the Tester's children, as any human being ever born of Grayson. Their government has made mistakes—grievous mistakes—but remember what the Intercessor said. Read our own history, see our mistakes, before you dare to cast that stone in your hand. The policy of the High Ridge Government was just that, my Lords—the policy of the High Ridge Government, not of the people or the Crown of Manticore. And I will assure you on my own honor as Protector of Grayson, that the Republic of Haven has lied about the contents of its diplomatic correspondence with Manticore. I do not pretend to know why, yet I have seen the Manticoran originals, and they do not support Haven's claims.

In the face of this fresh, undeclared, powerful attack upon the Star Kingdom of Manticore, one justified before the galaxy by lies and distortions, Grayson will stand by our brothers and sisters' side. We will remember our debt, our shared blood, all we have lost for one another's sake, and as the Tester is our witness, the sword we have drawn will not be sheathed once more until this time there is true peace and an end to the killing at last.

—Protector Benjamin IX of Grayson,
   addressing the Conclave of Steadholders,
   March 13, 1920 PD

Introduction

The Protectorate of Grayson is a feudal aristocracy consisting of a single system with one habitable planet and a significant space-based supporting ecosystem.

Grayson was founded in 988 PD by the Reverend Austin Grayson and his co-religionists of the Church of Humanity Unchained. The Reverend Grayson sought to take his followers away from Old Earth to the New Zion and its technology-free Garden of Eden. Upon arrival, however, the colonists found that their beautiful planet was so rich in heavy elements that survival without technology would be almost impossible.

Since the original intent of the colonization of Grayson was to build a New Zion without the evils of technologies used on Old Earth, the founders quite intentionally left behind a great deal of the knowledge and manufacturing capacity required for a technological base. The necessary reinvention and rebuilding of technologies on Grayson were very badly handicapped by that initial planned technology shortage and the need for much of the planet's labor resources to be dedicated to survival.

In support of that survival, Reverend Grayson made a radical change to the Church of Humanity Unchained's doctrine. He called for the rejection not of the machine but of the ungodly lifestyle which machine-age humanity had embraced. In time a religious schism between the technology-embracing Moderates and the technology-rejecting Faithful led to a bloody civil war

417

which ended only when the Faithful were exiled to a new colony on the neighboring Endicott System's planet of Masada. The rest of space-going humanity rediscovered the Yeltsin and Endicott systems in 1793 PD.

The Protectorate of Grayson fought the descendants of its exiles in the Masadan War of 1843 PD, the Long Crusade (a series of Masadan raids on Grayson) between 1848 and 1868, and the Second Masadan War of 1903. Following the Manticoran defense of Grayson from Masadan attack in the second war, RMN commander Honor Harrington was made the first non-Grayson and the first female steadholder. The war marked the Protectorate of Grayson's entry into the Manticoran Alliance and ended the Masadan threat but did not bring peace. Grayson fought as a member of the Manticoran Alliance in the next decade of wars with Haven, and the 1913 assassination attempt on the heads of state of both Manticore and Grayson was coordinated by agents with clear Havenite ties. The Protectorate of Grayson remains a strong ally of the Star Empire of Manticore.

Astrography

With a single habitable planet and a population of about three billion, the Protectorate of Grayson is one of many single-system nations in the Verge. Yeltsin's Star is a young F6 class main sequence star half again as massive as Sol. The system layout is remarkably similar to the Sol System, although the single habitable planet is much farther from the primary.

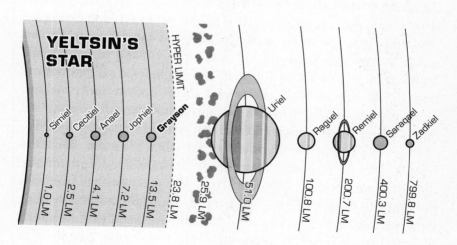

Grayson (Yeltsin V)

Radius: 6,242 km
Gravity: 1.17 G
Orbital Period: 681.61 T-days
Sidereal Day: 24.21 hours
Hydrosphere: 63%

The planet Grayson is significantly smaller than Old Earth, but is of approximately equal mass because it is a high-density world with unusual concentrations of heavy metals. None of its native plants or animals are safe for human consumption, due to the presence of those heavy metals. Population centers are primarily inland to avoid the toxicity of the planet's oceans. Early genetic engineering by the initial settlers resulted in a set of enzymes that allow native-born Graysons to sustain and survive degrees of heavy-metal contact that would kill unmodified humans. This genetic engineering has resulted in a live birth rate of females that is roughly triple that of males. Despite these modifications, heavy-metal toxicity remains an ever-present risk, and the population lives in air-filtered homes. Although able to sustain a "shirtsleeve" environment under many conditions, wind speeds which generate significant quantities of atmospheric dust require the use of protective masks, and gloves are frequently required when in contact with the natural environment.

The average temperature on Grayson is on the warm side by Manticoran standards, and limited hydrosphere and axial inclination do not help to moderate it very much. Unlike most planets, Grayson's orbital infrastructure contains a high percentage of orbital farms where the livestock and soil can remain uncontaminated.

Prior to joining the Manticoran Alliance, Grayson had very few exports or imports. Most products were produced for the domestic market only. While wartime construction has occupied most of the system's heavy industry, it has begun to export both light warships and merchant hulls to Alliance members. Although military needs have dominated and driven the development of Grayson's industry since 1905 PD, the infusion of modern technology and Manticoran investment funds have simultaneously provided for a huge leap in civilian manufacture, as well, at least in comparison to pre-Alliance levels. The planetary standard of living has risen quite remarkably over that timeframe as a result of the leaps and bounds by which productivity has increased.

The population as of 1921 PD was about three billion and expanding after a lengthy period of stagnant population curves, and the planet is experiencing a significant boom in space-based industry. Politically, the planet is divided into eighty-two steadings, each under the control of a steadholder. One consequence of the draconian population limitation Graysons were forced to accept due to their planetary environment is that no more than half of the entire planetary surface has actually been developed or organized into official steadings at this time. Harrington Steading, organized in 1906, is one of the youngest, but there remains much room for additional steadings as the Grayson population increases.

Asteroid Belt

The Asteroid Belt, which has never been given a name, provides the source of raw materials for the Grayson construction programs both orbiting Grayson and at Blackbird. Resource extraction ships move constantly between the processing nodes that are spaced equidistantly around the Belt. Refined materials are shipped from the nodes either in-system to Grayson or out to the Blackbird yards.

Blackbird Shipyards

The major Grayson Naval shipyard was built in orbit around the gas giant Uriel, and takes its name—"Blackbird"—from one of Uriel's moons. Blackbird was the site of a secretly constructed Masadan base during the last war with Masada and the shipyard's name was chosen as a deliberate memorial to the Graysons and Manticorans killed in the last Masadan attack on the home system. Heavy investment from the Hauptman Cartel of Manticore and Skydomes of Grayson was fundamental to the yard's initial construction. The Hauptman Cartel had been repaid in full by the time of the cease-fire of 1915 PD, but Skydomes remains a fully participating partner and major stockholder in Blackbird.

The shipyards consist of dispersed construction slips distributed around the Uriel subsystem, as well as an impressive dispersed defensive system consisting of both static and mobile assets.

History

The colonization of the planet Grayson represented an even greater leap of faith—in every sense—than the majority of pre-hyperdrive colony expeditions. Basic astronomic surveys had shown an apparently habitable world in the green zone for Yelstin's Star, with an atmosphere and surface temperatures permitting liquid water on most portions of the planet. Those bare facts were entirely correct, but for a planned self-supporting human colony the precolonization research was grossly and fatefully inadequate, for while the planet hosted no native sentient species prior to human colonization, it was an exceedingly hostile environment for humans.

The exclusive rights to the Yeltsin's Star System were acquired by the Church of Humanity Unchained, a religious group centered in an Old Earth polity known as the State of Idaho. While the Church's theology had Judeo-Christian roots, much of the Church's antitechnology doctrine was inspired by later Green and New Luddite teachings. Church leaders Reverend Austin Grayson and his deputy Oliver Mayhew hoped to build a new, more holy society far from the sinful technological temptations of Old Earth. Although Reverend Grayson's *Book of the New Way*, the core of the Church's new teachings, was actually less rabidly prejudiced against the evils of technology than many groups of the time, the combination of that prejudice with deep religious faith produced a zealotry which took them far beyond the range at which any truly detailed planetary survey could have been achieved in the belief that "God will provide."

Colonial Period, the Time of the Testing
988–1063 PD

On October 24, 988 PD (3090 CE), the starship *Gideon*, the Church's single cyroship, arrived in Yeltsin's Star System. The system's distant and isolated location, far beyond any other planned colonization efforts, had been a major factor in the colony planners' selection of their destination, and indeed it would be many centuries before any other ships would pass through that out-of-the-way corner of the universe.

Early records from just prior to landing name the colony planet as "Zion" and christen the other nine planets in the Yeltsin's Star System after Judeo-Christian archangels. A recording of the prayer made by Reverend Grayson prior to landing calls on God to ask the archangels to watch over their new colony just as the nine sister planets will patrol the heavens above Zion.

The name Zion was not to last. The planet's heavy-metal-rich surface proved sufficiently hostile to have tested human survival even in the most technologically advanced colony, far less one which had deliberately *discarded* technology. In the early days of the colony, heavy-metal poisoning caused horrific rates of miscarriage, with few pregnancies progressing to reach even a stillbirth. In the intense physical struggle for survival, a time when many of the colonists found themselves questioning what sin might have led God to test them so severely, the colonists balked at calling their home after the Holy City. During Reverend Grayson's lifetime, their planet became simply "the world"; after his death, it was formally renamed "Grayson's World" as a tribute to his leadership. Over the centuries, "Grayson's World" was shortened to the simple "Grayson" of today.

The hostile environment inspired a theological change as well. Reverend Grayson himself modified and extended the Church's doctrine to include the concept of the "Test" as God's way of refining and purifying His people. The doctrinal change faced minimal theological criticism during Grayson's lifetime and continued to evolve after his death, in accordance with Grayson's

teaching that God is never done teaching His people new ways
and new concepts. Born in this founding crucible, Graysons came
to speak of their God as the Tester and commonly held that the
human condition called for all good people to meet the Test set
before them.

Reverend Grayson had gathered the first-generation colonists
and served as the first planetary administrator, but he died only
ten years after landing, leaving no heir, and leadership devolved
on Oliver Mayhew, the Church's Second Elder, and Captain Hugh
Yanakov, *Gideon*'s commanding officer. Mayhew and Yanakov were
instrumental in creating the social and political structures the
colonists required to survive the Test presented by their planet.
It was clear they could *not* survive without technology, and
Mayhew completed a doctrinal evolution—begun by Grayson—
which held that the lesson of their Test was that it had been the
misuse of technology on Old Earth, not technology itself, which
had been evil. This cleared the way for the colonists to embrace
the necessary technologies, albeit in a cautious and circumspect
fashion. What the majority of the colonists were not told was that
Mayhew, with the blessing of the dying Reverend Grayson, had
also authorized a secret genetic modification project designed to
increase their heavy-metal poison tolerance.

The modification was initially (and covertly) tested on the
Mayhew and Yanakov families. Once it proved successful, it was
implemented across the entire population, but Mayhew recognized
that even if he were to posthumously reveal Grayson's blessing,
the modification would be highly controversial. A fervent, well
organized minority among the colonists, the progenitors of the
present day "Faithful" of Masada, continued to believe that faith
in God alone would heal the colonists. Though never more than
a quarter of the total population, that minority continued to
believe and to militantly insist that *any* reliance on technology,
even for medical purposes, was but the first step into the "Sin
of the Machine." Unwilling to risk a potentially deadly conflict
when the entire colony's survival hung in the balance, Mayhew,
Yanakov, and their inner circle decided to keep the genetic modification secret from the general public, propagating it throughout
the total population under the guise of a common cold.

Given the technology available to them, it was a remarkable achievement, but the modification was not perfect and an

unintended side effect caused a high miscarriage rate among male fetuses. The Church of Humanity Unchained had enshrined polygyny even before leaving Old Earth, and the sexual imbalance provided long-term social pressure to maintain that institution. In general, however, the modification proved very successful in mitigating the consequences of heavy-metal poisoning. While the miscarriage rate (especially among boys) remained tragically high, it nonetheless represented a vast improvement on the status quo. Knowledge of the genetic manipulation was so closely held, it was completely lost for a thousand T-years, until it was discovered by Dr. Allison Harrington in 1912 PD.

The Church's tendency towards patriarchy became increasingly pronounced after Reverend Grayson's death. This development was only exacerbated by the survival imperatives of the Grayson environment and the skewed birth rate, and despite efforts by Oliver Mayhew to prevent it, female social and legal rights began a steady erosion. In addition, the most ardent members of the Church, those who had most fervently opposed the easing of the Church's antitechnology tenets despite Reverend Grayson's approval, began to emerge as "the Faithful," an organized, minority sect which preached that the immediate struggle to survive had actually been a punishment, not simply a test. God had acted to chastise Man for failing to place his faith in Him rather than in technology, and if only the Church had remained faithful to God's *true* intent and rejected the Sin of the Machine, relying upon His power, He would have delivered them from their trials and transformed the Grayson environment into the technology-free Zion they had fled Old Earth to find. The Faithful's theologians grudgingly permitted the use of technology, regarding it as a necessary evil in a fallen world. Yet they argued that it was necessary *only* because of Man's "Second Fall" on Grayson, and the most ardent of them taught that if Man could be returned even now, fully and humbly, to God's original intent, God would relent and transform Grayson. In their theology the Test became a test of humanity's willingness to accept God's promise and return to His true will, despite the temptations of its fallen and corrupt existence, rather than a trial designed by God to refine those He loved and correct their original misunderstanding of His intent.

Consolidation, the Time of Learning
1063–1138 PD

After decades, the Grayson population finally achieved sufficient victories over its hostile environment that survival on the planet was no longer in doubt. Adequate locally produced technology became available to secure a minimum sustainable standard of living. The institution of the Steadholder had emerged as a hierarchical, authoritarian response to the demands of survival, expanding levels of population, and the technological cushion required for both. The doctrine of the Test was fully accepted by the mainstream Church, polarizing religious dissidents outside the mainstream into the still relatively small sect of the Faithful.

It should not be surprising that the original colonists, intent upon building a technology-free Eden, had brought very few tech manuals and textbooks with them. They were fortunate in that the technology they *had* intended to preserve had been heavily biased towards the life sciences and medicine, but they had under-estimated the extent to which those technologies depended upon a robust, diversified base of *other* technologies. While Grayson preserved pockets of advanced technology, especially in environ-mental capabilities, the planetary tech level as a whole regressed to one comparable to Old Earth's Victorian Era.

In one other area—spaceflight—a limited capability was pre-served largely as the work of one man: Hugh Yanakov. Yanakov succeeded in winning Grayson's approval for the preservation of *Gideon* rather than the complete cannibalization contemplated by the original colonization plan, which proved critical to the colony's early survival. *Gideon*'s sick bay was absolutely essential at more than one point in the struggle, and evidence suggests that the genetic modification was developed aboard ship. After Yanakov's death in 1018 PD, his eldest son took up the task of keeping a handful of the original shuttles operable and managed to do so for almost another fifty years, despite the powerful opposition of the Faithful and at least some of the mainstream Church.

Expansion, the Time of the Five Keys
1138–1261 PD

This period was generally one of optimism, of faith in both God and the future, and a broad sense of dynamism. The indigenous technology base improved in areas publicly acknowledged as direct and immediate needs, despite the Faithful's best efforts to prevent it. Even now, however, Grayson efforts focused on solving specific problems, rather than the pursuit of research for its own sake, and there were holes in Grayson's tech base which other planets would have found peculiar. The colonists had brought no lethal weapons with them, for example, and when personal weapons reemerged on Grayson, they took the form of swords and other muscle-powered weapons which were only slowly replaced by the reinvention of relatively crude firearms.

Following Oliver Mayhew's death, the steadholders (already coming to be known as the Keys) consolidated their political authority, creating the Conclave of Steadholders as a body of co-equal peers, presided over by the Protector, to consult with one another and support the formation of new steadings as population and wealth permitted. The formation of the Conclave was legitimized by the approval of the Church, yet the Church remained the true secular as well as temporal authority. Over time, power came to reside in the most powerful steadholders, known collectively as "the Five Keys." By the end of the era the five steadholders of the original Grayson steadings (Mayhew, Burdette, Mackenzie, Yanakov, and Bancroft) held effective control of the Conclave and through it, the planet. Anything like a true planetwide political state remained a purely nominal construct during this era, however.

Mayhew Steading, ruled by a direct patrilineal descendent of Oliver Mayhew, was Grayson's largest single Steading, and the Conclave's Articles of Establishment had provided that the Protector must be selected from all the adult males of the Mayhew line in perpetuity. This did not mean the planet had a single ruler, however. The Protector was *primus inter pares* ("first among equals"), responsible for presiding over the Conclave, administering its policies, and serving as the Conclave's formal interface with the Church, but forced to govern by forging consensuses or at least pluralities among the other Keys rather than through his own legal authority. The First Elder of the Church retained a mandatory seat among the Keys and was the ultimate arbiter of matters pertaining to the Church, which made him the true fountainhead of authority, but the Protector was envisioned as the executor and enforcer of that authority on Father Church's behalf.

By the end of the twelfth century, the life-or-death fight to survive on Grayson had stabilized in favor of survival, and by 1250 PD, sufficient resources had become available for the Five Keys to begin diverting a meaningful percentage of the planet's available capabilities to reestablishing the space presence which had lapsed in 1065 with the failure of the last of the original landing shuttles. The proposal to do so was carried (over the vehement opposition of the Faithful) on the argument that the exploitation of the star system's extra-planetary resources would repay the effort many times over. Ominously for the future, one of the Five Keys, Eustace Bancroft, Steadholder Bancroft, broke with his fellows to vote in opposition to the hotly contested decision.

Schism, the Time of Sundering
1261–1337 PD

The Faithful seized on this decision as "sin-filled and blasphemous," and their attitudes and doctrines began to harden, sowing the seeds for the eventual Civil War. Indeed, the official formation of the "Congregation of the Faithful" in 1261 PD as what amounted to an openly schismatic sect within the Church of Humanity Unchained was expressly justified by its founders' contention that in promoting a resumption of extra-atmospheric development, the Moderates had moved well beyond the technology absolutely essential to planetary survival and hence had returned to the "Sin of the Machine" against which Austin Grayson had preached.

Grayson society as a whole had by now acquired its highly consensual nature as a survival imperative, and Grayson remained a thoroughly theocratic state, but the Church enshrined a deep respect for individual belief, even when it conflicted with official doctrine, as a necessary and direct consequence of the Doctrine of the Test. Despite this, Grayson society had largely rejected the Faithful's beliefs, and social pressure had prevented their member- ship from spreading broadly. As their doctrine diverged further and further from the mainstream, the Faithful found themselves increasingly marginalized, regarded as shrill extremists when they were regarded at all.

This attitude began to change, though, as the degree of discipline necessary to ensure survival decreased. The extremists, no longer seen as a direct threat to necessary conformity, were less thoroughly ostracized, and a certain percentage of the Grayson population began to regard the Faithful and their leaders with at least grudging admiration. A mainstream Church clergyman of the period famously wrote, "I reject their beliefs, yet I have no choice but to respect someone who meets his Test by living his life one hundred percent in accordance with his beliefs, however unpopular they may be."

By the colony's three-hundredth birthday, this toleration had expanded to the point at which the Church of the Faithful first openly converted steadholders. Some personal journals of generally accepted provenance imply that, if not the steadholders themselves, members of the converting steadholders' families (and quite probably Eustace Bancroft at the time of the space program vote) had been secret members of the Faithful for at least a full generation prior to their open conversion.

Ironically, religious toleration was one of the areas where the Faithful diverged from mainstream norms, and as soon as those few steadholders publicly converted, they implemented a policy of enforcing their interpretation of doctrine in their steadings, with very little toleration for those adherents of the mainstream Church. Given the autocratic power and autonomy of the Keys, those steadholders were able to alter conditions in their own steadings very quickly, which attracted the immigration of more Faithful from other steadings (and prompted the emigration *from* their steadings of adherents of the mainstream Church). Many of the other steadholders were secretly relieved to see their own Faithful go, but although they were a clear minority planetwide, there were large absolute numbers of them, and the populations of the Faithful steadings grew rapidly. The Faithful steadholders became individually more powerful, as a consequence . . . and they also became increasingly insistent on exporting their own doctrine. The emergence of a distinct, aggressively proselytizing, increasingly powerful and militant "Faction of the Faithful" began to alienate the mainstream once again, and by the 1320s, the mainstream Church hierarchy was threatened with a steadily growing schism.

By the end of the thirteenth century PD, Grayson had rees-
tablished a substantial space presence, with private industry providing the lion's share of deep-space industry and the increasing
exploitation of the asteroid belt. The habitats orbiting Grayson
remained extremely primitive by present-day standards, heavily
dependent upon support from the planetary surface in many critical areas, particularly food and other life-support elements. Space
industry was providing benefits which clearly outweighed the support costs, however, and ambitious plans were afoot to construct
orbital farms to produce not simply sufficient food to support the
extra-atmospheric population, but also significant quantities of
foodstuffs free of the omnipresent heavy-metals contamination
which had such destructive effects for Grayson's *planetary* citizens.
The increase in private contractors and employees had inevitably
resulted in the need for both search-and-rescue capabilities and
law enforcement powers, and in 1286 PD, the Five Keys created
the Grayson Space Guard (GSG).

Civil War, the Time of Dying
1337–1351 PD

In 1337 PD, the Faithful launched a *coup d'état* against the Conclave of Steadholders, triggering the Grayson Civil War. Steadholder
Jeremiah Bancroft, an avowed member of the Faithful and one of
the Five Keys, had petitioned for a special meeting of the Conclave
of Steadholders, ostensibly to address some of the more contentious issues dividing the Faithful from the Moderates. Protector
John Mayhew II, with the support of Reverend Elkanah Timmons,
called the special Conclave and the steadholders attended with
their heirs. Steadholder Bancroft never arrived, but troops of the
Faithful massacred fifty-three of fifty-six steadholders and their
heirs. The other two survivors, Steadholder Oswald and Steadholder
Simonds, were also members of the Faithful. Reverend Timmons
was "accidentally killed" in the crossfire, the first patriarch of the
Church of Humanity Unchained to die by violence.

The Mayhew armsmen died to the man, fighting with Protector
John at their head, but by their sacrifice, they saved John's son
Benjamin, who escaped to claim the Protectorship as Benjamin
IV. The seventeen-year-old Protector, who was to become known

in the fullness of time as Benjamin the Great, fled to Mackenzie Steading and rallied the shattered remnants of the other Steadholders' Guards to him. Fighting was extraordinarily bitter and bloody, and the brutal measures the Faithful employed in an effort to suppress resistance in areas occupied by their troops was a key element in Benjamin's success in rallying and leading the military opposition. Damage to the planetary infrastructure, including its farmlands, was extreme, and almost forty percent of the total planetary population died.

One of the Faithful's first moves was to immediately terminate all support for the despised space industry and to demolish its ground-based component, throwing the fragile deep-space community back on its own limited resources. At the same time, the GSG promptly declared its support for Benjamin IV as the legitimate Protector and head of government, although there was little it could do at that time to assist him, given the need to divert every scrap of orbital and deep-space capability to simple survival, especially after the Faithful destroyed two of the three primary orbital habitats with surface-to-space missile strikes. The GSG was able to create an antimissile defense for the remaining habitat, but only at the expenditure of even more manpower and resources from a critically limited supply of each.

War is usually an impetus to research and development, and the bitterness of the fighting and the total incompatibility of the religious beliefs on either side led to the Faithful's creation and planned use of a doomsday weapon. Although the practicality of the threat, designed to crack the planet with a succession of powerful warheads, was questionable, there was no doubt that they would almost certainly wreak still more destruction on Grayson's remaining population centers. They might well also destroy sufficient of the farmland which had been slowly and painfully decontaminated over the past four centuries to threaten all remaining human life on Grayson through mass starvation. Faced with that threat, Steadholder Bancroft's senior wife, Barbara, defected. Warned by her of the Faithful's plans, Benjamin's forces found and defused the first of the doomsday weapons. The Faithful, however, continued building and secreted the weapons around the planet.

Some of Benjamin's advisers had seriously questioned his decision to "waste" desperately needed resources on off-world projects when they were fighting for their very lives on the planetary surface.

In their opinion, it would have been far wiser to withdraw the remaining human presence from space to the planetary surface rather than expend effort, money, and supplies on sustaining it. In the event, they discovered how wise Benjamin had been to reject their arguments when the GSG, given the vitally needed transfusion of resources and support he was able to provide, designed and built a kinetic bombardment capability. Available in 1349 PD, the ability to call in impossible-to-intercept, highly accurate, high-kiloton range kinetic strikes provided the critical edge Benjamin's still badly outnumbered but passionately loyal, skillfully led, and grimly determined army required to take the war to the Faithful. Another two years of bloody combat (and yet more damage to the farms and protected habitats necessary for survival) were required for the final defeat of the Faithful, but virtually every analysis of the Civil War has agreed that the GSG provided the margin which led to Benjamin the Great's ultimate victory.

Although the surface infrastructure on Grayson suffered terribly through the Civil War, the remaining spaceborne habitat was largely untouched after the initial missile strikes, as were the ships used to transport goods to and from this platform. The relatively minor nature of the damage to remainder of Grayson's distributed spaceborne infrastructure was to prove critical to ending the Civil War.

An impasse had been reached: the Faithful no longer had the ability to conquer the planet, but they could destroy its habitability once and for all. Benjamin, with the assistance of Reverend Baruch Gonzalez, Reverend Timmons' successor, ultimately brokered a deal with the Faithful under which Grayson's Moderates built short-range starships to transport the Faithful to an exile on Masada in the Endicott System in exchange for the locations of the hidden weapons.

Reconstruction, The Time of Healing and The Rise of the Sword
1351–1397 PD

The Grayson Civil War officially ended in 1351 PD, although the Faithful did not leave Grayson for the Endicott System until 1362, when the starships necessary for the trip had been constructed. Including the Faithful who departed for Masada, Grayson had lost almost fifty-three percent of its pre-Civil War population in just twenty-eight years and damage to the planetary infrastructure, while not total, had been catastrophic. Worse still, in some ways, the capacity diverted to building the starships required for the Faithful's exile had severely hampered early reconstruction efforts. Fortunately, the Graysons had lost none of the hardworking pragmatism that comes from living on a planet that is trying to kill you even in the good times. The same traditional goal-oriented R&D which had allowed Grayson to produce the capability to exile the Faithful to Masada was turned to the reclamation of the Moderates' home.

The political results of the Civil War proved far more lasting than the mere physical effects. The old order, defined by a relatively weak Protector serving as first among equals in a small group of leading steadholders, was completely turned on its head. One of the Five Keys and two other steadholders had turned traitor, the loyal Keys had been gunned down to a man, and Protector Benjamin (already beginning to be called "the Great") had rallied the leaderless steadings in defeating the enemy. Under Reverend Gonzalez, the Church had strongly supported Benjamin yet deliberately distanced itself from direct control of Grayson politics as a response to the religious fanaticism which had sparked the Civil War. Gonzalez continued to support Benjamin after the war, which, combined with his own achievements, gave him the opportunity to set up the new political system in whatever manner he chose, and that is exactly what he did.

The keys which steadholders wore around their necks were symbols of their power, and as "first among equals," the Protector had shared that symbol. Benjamin's new Constitution, however, promulgated in 1357 PD, formalized the political supremacy of the Protectorship, giving Benjamin and his heirs the *de jure* power that he had acquired *de facto* during the Civil War. Accordingly, the Protector's symbol became the Sword, rather than the Key, underscoring that supremacy and how it had been won. The steadings of the three treasonous steadholders were combined as the Sword Steading, the Protector's personal demesne, further cementing Mayhew dominance in the post-Civil War era. The original Mayhew Steading became the steading of the Protector's heir, thus effectively combining four of the larger steadings of Grayson in the direct Mayhew line.

Nor was that change the only dilution of steadholder power. The Constitution also created a second parliamentary house, the Conclave of Steaders. From the perspective of the exhausted steadholders, the common steaders had earned representation in a chamber of their own because of the way in which they had continued the fight even after their steadholders had been murdered or killed in battle. From the perspective of Benjamin IV (a shrewd politician, as well as a military leader of genius), the natural enemies and competitors for the Sword's authority were most likely to be found in the Keys, whereas a lower house would be inclined to ally itself with the Sword to protect its own prerogatives.

The cultural rebuilding of this era was made possible largely by the fact that the Faithful who wanted to leave the planet had done so. The lack of a defeated and disaffected former foe and the immediate needs of rebuilding, coupled with a general war-weariness, permitted a rapid and uncommon degree of religious reconciliation and healing. Madame Barbara Bancroft's remarriage to Protector Benjamin IV also helped Graysons of a more conservative religious perspective view themselves in full communion with the Church and sharing in the Protection of the Sword.

Even the setbacks were used to good effect. When an assassin murdered Madame Barbara Mayhew, members of the crowd tore the killer apart, and Protector Benjamin, with the full support of the Grayson steaders, used the opportunity to root out any remaining pockets of extremist groups unwilling to live at peace with their neighbors.

By the time of Benjamin the Great's death in 1397 PD, Grayson had largely completed the rebuilding process.

Maturation, The Time of the Protectors
1397–1703 PD

The nearly three centuries following the rule of Protector Benjamin the Great were a golden age for Grayson. The number of steadings continued to increase. The population continued to expand. The rate of growth was high for Grayson, considering the hostile environment. A sense of planetwide unity grew, particularly as the planetary data-net expanded and grew in complexity and capability.

In political terms, the authority of the Sword was wounded by the six-year dynastic war between 1418 and 1424 PD, which was sparked by Thomas II's assassination of his brother Caleb. Fortunately for the Sword's fortunes, Caleb's junior wife Patricia fled to her father, Steadholder Dietmar Yanakov. Unknown to Thomas (who became known to history as "Thomas the Usurper"), his sister-in-law was pregnant, and Yanakov and Steadholder Abner Mackenzie forged an alliance among a coalition of steadholders to depose Thomas and replace him with Caleb's posthumously born son, Bernard.

Barely twenty years had passed between Benjamin the Great's death and Thomas' coup attempt, and the Constitution (itself barely sixty years old) might well have foundered under such stress. Yanakov, Mackenzie, Reverend Ronald O'Day, and their allies among the Keys, however, recognized the potential for fresh civil war if that was allowed to happen. They stood unswervingly behind the infant Protector, and Yanakov and his daughter trained Bernard literally from the cradle up to rule and not simply reign. Under their rigorous, sometimes harsh tutelage, Bernard V emerged as a ruler almost as skilled as his great-grandfather, Benjamin IV, and strongly reasserted the Sword's authority after Yanakov's death in 1443 PD.

There were other setbacks as well. Perhaps the most egregious was the decision by three protectors in a row—Bernard VI, Peter, and Benjamin VII—between 1569 and 1655 PD to effectively turn their backs on further development of space. In fairness, all of them were focused on pressing planetary development issues, but many historians argue that their attitudes owed a great deal to how much of the existing space infrastructure had been created primarily to build the Faithful's exile fleet, which "tainted" it in the eyes of some of Benjamin IV's descendants. It was fortunate, however, that Protector Adrian (1655–1681 PD) reversed that trend when he did. Without his change in policy, Grayson would have found itself virtually defenseless in the face of the first Masadan attack on Yeltsin's Star.

While Grayson was focused on domestic affairs, however, the Faithful were rapidly expanding and consolidating on Masada. In one of history's greater ironies, Masada was a far more hospitable planet than Grayson, and without the checks of a hostile environment, the Masadan population grew rapidly. More ominously, had the Graysons known it, the Faithful's attitude towards technology had changed radically. While "the Sin of the Machine" remained anathema, the Masadan Church viewed the suppression of the "heretical" Church on Grayson as a holy mission laid upon it by God Himself. The Moderates had been the first to turn their backs on God; therefore, they and the entire planet which had been intended as His perfect world must be conquered and restored to God's will. All else must be subordinated to that end, and just as God had granted their ancestors the dispensation to use that technology absolutely essential to survival on Fallen Grayson, so He would grant them the dispensation to develop and use whatever of technology was required for the reconquest of Grayson.

However theologically inconsistent that doctrine might have been, it led to a fierce sense of Masadan identity and solidarity and an astounding reversal in the Faithful's attitude towards research and development. The first Grayson-Masadan War was one of the few interstellar wars fought without gravitic technology, but the fact that it could be fought at all within little more than three hundred years of the Masadans' exile speaks volumes of their determination and ability to transcend their antitechnology biases.

The initial series of raids were carried out entirely by sublight vessels, as neither combatant had the hyperdrive, the impeller, or the Warshawski sail. The GSG had expanded in step with the growth in industrial capacity and population, and electronic listening posts and remote observatories were established outside the system's Kuiper belt to monitor (as well as possible) events in Endicott, since no one on Grayson was foolish enough to believe the Faithful did not cherish a burning hatred and desire for vengeance following their defeat. Those monitoring posts had been neglected under Adrian's predecessors, though, which, coupled with well thought out Masadan measures to conceal the nature of their preparations, might well have proved fatal. Fortunately, however, the signatures of the attack force's fusion drives and the electromagnetic noise of their passage through the interstellar medium gave sufficient warning—barely—for defensive measures to be taken prior to the first Masadan strike on Grayson in 1672 PD. The GSG's existing cutters would have been thoroughly inadequate to defeat that attack, but Protector Adrian had been given sufficient warning to commission a force of hastily converted ore-carriers and personnel transports to meet it.

The fighting was furious, bloody, and costly. To quote from Andrew Preston's *God's Warriors: Masada and the Endless Crusade*:

"Modern analysts are uniformly shocked by the suicidal obsessiveness of the Masadan raiding parties. The huge ramscoop fusion carriers that made the multi-year journey to 'cleanse' their ancestors' homeworld were fueled by hydrogen isotopes. Their crews, though, were fueled by religious fervor and a searing hatred, worked to a razor's edge over three centuries of careful preparation by the Elders of the Faithful. By the time the first Masadans returned to Yeltsin's Star they saw themselves as chosen instruments of God, guaranteed salvation, on a one-way mission to fight the forces of Satan at the gates of Hell itself. They did not even bother to establish a refueling complex for a chance at returning home. They just fought and died, willing to do anything to purge a planet none of them had ever seen, let alone set foot on, of a people with whom none of them had any personal experience."

The Faithful were defeated, but the cost was heavy and it was evident to all Graysons that Masada would not accept that defeat as final. As a recognition of that fact—and also as a well-earned tribute to its services—the GSG became the Grayson Space Navy on November 1, 1675 PD, becoming an independent, coequal of the Grayson Army, a status it has maintained ever since.

The follow-up attack in 1696 PD assumed the same flavor, with the Graysons enjoying the advantages of years of warning and a defensive position. The Masadans had realized that, since surprise was impossible, a base of operations in the outer Yeltsin System was necessary, but the increasingly capable Grayson Space Navy prevented the establishment of such a base.

Rediscovery and Modern Warfare
1703–1750 PD

In 1793 PD, the Havenite merchant ship *Goliath* contacted both Yeltsin's Star and the Endicott System, reestablishing contact between the descendants of Austin Grayson's colonists and the rest of humanity. Although additional contacts with the galactic mainstream were sporadic and infrequent, to say the least, the effects of rediscovery were profound. New technologies, whose possibility had never occurred to any Grayson or Masadan, were revealed, and a period of frenetic R&D ensued, driven by the longstanding hostility between the two star systems. Although neither Grayson nor Masada could obtain more than bits and pieces from their occasional visitors, both were aware of the dire consequences of falling behind their enemies, and both introduced domestically engineered versions of the hyperdrive, impeller drive, and Warshawski sail in remarkably short order. The locally produced iterations of those systems were both crude and outmoded compared to more modern systems, yet in the process of essentially reinventing technologies the rest of the galaxy had enjoyed for centuries, Grayson researchers opened several promising lines of development which had not occurred to anyone else.

More important in the short term, the Rediscovery advanced Masadan and Grayson interstellar warfighting technology drastically in a short period of time. Within less than forty years, the Masadans had developed the ability to attack with no warning and with the massive payloads that Warshawski hyperships made possible. The first attack of what came to be known as the Third Masadan War was launched in 1736 PD, thirty-three years after the Rediscovery. The GSN—by this time, a highly professional military force that had been effectively continuously at war for the better part of a T-century—had developed its first hyper-capable warships primarily for rapid response in system defense rather than to project power beyond its home system and decisively defeated the fresh Masadan attacks. Masada's much larger system population allowed it to allocate roughly two to three times more resources to its military than the Graysons could afford to allocate to the pre-Alliance Grayson military, however, creating a losing proposition for Grayson. With interstellar distance no longer equalizing the equation, the situation was grim, and the Navy's strategists soon realized that they would need to destroy Masada's interstellar capability if Grayson was going to survive

The first true interstellar warships of the GSN were laid down in 1742 PD, and The Fourth Masadan War began seven years later with a GSN strike on the starship construction infrastructure in the Endicott System. The Grayson captains were scrupulously careful to avoid any possibility of an Eridani Edict violation, but their attack completely surprised the Masadans (who had neglected system defense in favor of offensive forces) and wreaked havoc on Endicott's deep-space infrastructure.

Triumph and the Decline of the Sword
1750–1848 PD

Protector Michael II had made the construction of the GSN's starships and the destruction of Masada's war-making capacity his life's work, and he succeeded. Although the planet itself was too heavily defended to be attacked without committing an Eridani violation, centuries of orbital infrastructure were wiped out during the attack. Unfortunately, Michael died in 1753, before he could drive the war through to a conclusion, and his heir, Robert I, was a very different Protector. Without his father's aggressive energy, lacking in political insight, and more interested in the fine arts than in matters military, Robert declared victory, recalled the Navy from Endicott, reduced its strength, and turned his attention to domestic concerns.

The respite won by Michael's strike on Endicott permitted Grayson to survive Robert's policies, but many of the Keys recognized that would not be true forever. In the power vacuum created by Robert's vacillation and disinterest in governing, the Conclave of Steadholders began to chip away at the Sword's authority and prerogatives. Robert I's protectorship was short, but when his son, Robert II, replaced him in 1766, he proved no stronger or more politically adroit than his father had been.

The erosion of the Sword's power continued as a political structure reminiscent of the Time of the Five Keys reemerged. A power bloc of steadholders who eventually came to be called the Great Keys gradually assumed primacy. By the end of the era, the Great Keys controlled the government of Grayson, and over the next century, the *de facto* power of the Protector was reduced to little more than figurehead status.

The Long Crusade and Cold War
1848–1903 PD

The bill for the succession of weak protectors came due in 1848 PD when Masada, having rebuilt its infrastructure—and its navy—launched the Fifth Masadan War, which came to be known as the Long Crusade. The initial attacks took the GSN by surprise and almost succeeded in reaching Grayson's planetary surface. Defeated at heavy cost, the Masadans withdrew, but only to reorganize and launch a fresh assault four years later. The GSN launched a counterattack, only to encounter powerful Masadan system fortifications and take heavy losses of its own. The fighting continued, see-sawing back and forth, until Masada ultimately *did* get through to Grayson with a series of planetary nuclear strikes in 1868. Casualties were severe, although Grayson's heavily protected environmental domes held them to a much lower level than Masada apparently expected, and under the Great Keys, a heavily reinforced GSN took the war back to Masada in a series of bitter battles. The Long Crusade guttered down to a state of cold war in 1875, but neither side was so foolish as to believe the longstanding war was at an end, and the interval was marked by occasional skirmishes, Masadan commerce raids, and Grayson reprisal strikes when the raiders became overly blatant. By 1892, however, the rising tensions between the People's Republic of Haven and the Star Kingdom of Manticore, coupled with Yeltsin's Star's and Endicott's strategic position between the PRH and the Manticoran Alliance, had drawn the two warring star systems into the toils of great power politics.

The Mayhew Restoration
1903 PD–PRESENT

Both Endicott and Yeltsin's Star are located along a direct hyperspace route between Haven and Manticore, and, as the likelihood of a conflict between the Star Kingdom and the People's Republic increased, so did the strategic value of the two bitterly hostile star systems. The growing alliance between Grayson and Manticore may prove to be the most important outcome of the last twenty years, given its major contribution to the survival of both star nations at least to date. Many Grayson political analysts, however, would argue that the political implications of the rise of Protector Benjamin IX, the so-called "Mayhew Restoration," and his domestic policies have even greater significance for the people of Grayson.

Of course, these events are not independent, as the restoration of Benjamin the Great's Constitution has been closely linked with the alliance with Manticore. The Courvosier Mission, Manticore's initial attempt to bring Yeltsin's Star into the Manticoran Alliance, would have ended in unmitigated disaster if not for a Royal Manticoran Navy squadron commanded by then-Captain (subsequently Steadholder) Honor Harrington. Harrington's desperate and costly defense of Grayson against the so-called "Maccabeus Campaign" launched by Masada with Havenite support, created the political climate in which Protector Benjamin Mayhew IX could reassert the Sword's ascendancy and restore the Constitution. In public statements, Protector Benjamin has acknowledged that the absolute power of the Protectorship may need to be reduced in the fullness of time. His actions, however, imply no intention of giving up any of his authority in the near future. Opinion polls of steaders in the last several years show powerful majority support for his continued power and policies, despite periodic complaints from individual steadholders in the Conclave. While it seems likely his heirs may face a gradual transition to a genuine limited monarchy, most Manticoran constitutional scholars and Grayson historians agree that too precipitous a transition could prove disastrous because of the nature of the Protectorship itself. Every steadholder is recognized as a sovereign head of state and absolute ruler, limited only by the citizens' rights clauses of the Constitution and the fealty he owes to the Protector. Until and unless the power of the individual steadholders can be reduced, any attempt to limit the *Sword's* powers is all too likely to result in a return to something very like the Time of the Great Keys.

Government

The Grayson's form of government evolved as the result of the challenges that faced its colonists. Although the Civil War and the Constitution that followed provide a convenient dividing point in its development, the Protectorship and Steadholderships both predate them. The Protector was originally called "Protector of the Faith," but that was changed to the present title in 1822 PD after decades of debate. The Time of the Five Keys is the term used to describe the period when the Protectorship was legally no more than the first among equals, elected from the Mayhew dynasty by the majority vote of all steadholders and subject in almost all ways in secular matters to the paramount authority of the Conclave of Steadholders. This all changed, beginning in 1337, with the start of the Civil War. At its conclusion, as the triumphant leader of the Moderates following the Civil War, Benjamin Mayhew IV instituted the Constitution of 1357 (deliberately promulgated on the twentieth anniversary of the Faithful's initial coup) which established the primacy of the Protector and the general form of government that remains in effect.

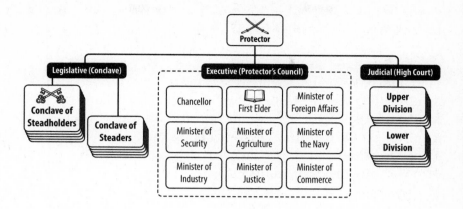

The Protectorship

The Protectorship, also known as "the Sword," is passed through the male Mayhew line, and can be traced directly back to the original Oliver Mayhew. Prior to the Civil War, the Protector was elected from all adult male Mayhews; since the Civil War, the Protectorship has passed in unbroken patrilinear succession from Benjamin the Great to the current holder of that office. The Protector serves as both the head of state and head of government for Grayson, and the Constitution grants him far more executive power than is typically seen in constitutional monarchies. All military oaths are sworn directly to the Protector and he has the power to issue direct orders to any military personnel. With the exception of a steadholder's personal armsmen, no other Grayson armed forces are allowed to recognize a different commander in chief. He is also the only person on Grayson who has the right to organize full-scale military units out of his personal vassals.

Because religion and public life are inseparable on Grayson, the Sword is also responsible for upholding the authority of the Church of Humanity Unchained. It is the Sword's responsibility to enforce the decisions of the Church if necessary. By extension, the Sword is also responsible for enforcing judicial decisions of the High Court.

The reigning Protector of Grayson is Benjamin Mayhew IX, a direct descendant of Oliver Mayhew, the First Deacon of the Church of Humanity Unchained. His son, Bernard Raoul Mayhew, is his heir.

The Sword is assisted in his duties by the Protector's Council. Its membership is composed of:

Chancellor: Lord Floyd Kellerman
First Elder: Reverend Jeremiah Sullivan
Minister of Foreign Affairs: Brother Uriah Madison
Minister of Security: Hiram Bledsoe, Steadholder Seneca
Minister of Agriculture: Gregory Mandalow
Minister of the Navy: Truman Womack
Minister of Industry: Brother Jacob Inman
Minister of Justice: Aaron Sidemore
Minister of Commerce: Francis Maxwell, Steadholder Redmon

The Council supports the Protector by serving as his advisory panel, and assists in the high level organization and operation of the government and its bodies.

With the exception of the First Elder, who is automatically on the Council, all Ministers are chosen by the Protector and serve at his pleasure. Although the Constitution does not require him to abide by the advice and consent of the Great Conclave, the Keys and Steaders hold the power of the purse and may refuse to fund a particular ministry if they disapprove of the individual chosen to head it. Prior to the Mayhew Restoration, the Conclave of Steadholders, having taken advantage of a succession of weak Protectors, was able to use this power of the purse to effectively control both the Council's membership and its policies. That situation ended with Benjamin IX's reassertion of the Sword's prerogatives.

The Great Conclave

The Great Conclave, or planetary legislature, is composed of two houses. The senior house is the Conclave of Steadholders, also known colloquially as "the Keys." The lower house is known as the Conclave of Steaders, collectively referred to as "the Steaders." As a legislative body, the conclaves are rather more circumscribed than those of other star nations. Because of the Constitution and the almost feudal supremacy of the Sword, the conclaves may not propose or introduce financial bills. National budgets and taxation policy are formulated by the Protector, and the Great

Conclave is restricted to an up-down vote to approve or disapprove. Although there is no formal amendment procedure for money bills, the practice of "remonstrance" allows either chamber—or both jointly—to set forth what portions of a proposed money bill they find objectionable, inviting the Sword to craft a compromise acceptable to them. Aside from money bills, the Great Conclave does have the power to create national law and legislation, and the Constitution specifically grants the Great Conclave the power, by majority vote of both chambers, to defund any ministry as a means of avoiding tyrannical rule by the Sword.

The Conclave of Steadholders is composed of the heads of every steading on Grayson and dates from before the Constitution. Members are immune from prosecution in most instances unless the Protector can provide proof of treason, or the Conclave sustains a two-thirds vote of impeachment. The Sword, however, holds the right to remove any Steadholder from office upon his sole discretion for acts of treason. His decision takes immediate effect and may not be contested or resisted, though it may be subsequently appealed to a joint session of the Great Conclave, where a two-thirds majority vote, after presentation of evidence, may reverse the Sword's decision. A steadholder condemned by the Sword also holds the ancient right of an immediate challenge to trial by personal combat and, if he is victorious, is permanently exempt from any punishment on the charge for which he was condemned. The Keys share the right of legislative veto with the Protector, where a two-thirds majority can override the Protector's decision. The Conclave of Steadholders also has the right to approve the heir to a steading whose succession is in doubt as well as to approve a regent for any minor heir.

The lower house is the Conclave of Steaders. Unlike the Conclave of Steadholders, it was created by the Constitution, ostensibly as a check on the Conclave of Steadholders. It is an elected body with proportional representation based on population. Realistically, for many years it had been reduced to irrelevance by the power of the steadholders. Since the Mayhew Restoration, it has become a source of strength for the Sword, as a solid core of its members, even those uncomfortable with some of Protector Benjamin's social reforms, are Mayhew loyalists. Like the Conclave of Steadholders, they can introduce legislation but approval must be by both Conclaves.

Following the establishment of the Constitution, the Sword was clearly ascendant. After several centuries, however, a series of weak Protectors allowed the steadholders to reverse that ascendancy by the end of the eighteenth century PD. Prior to the Mayhew Restoration, the Keys acted with *de facto* powers through its ability to dominate the important ministries and, thereby, the government, yet the *de jure* powers were reserved to the Protector. Benjamin IX succeeded in reasserting the primacy of the Sword over the Conclave, due in no small part to the fact that the High Court held that the Constitution had never been changed, that it did not provide for ministerial rule, and that the powers enumerated in it—and thus real power—were therefore still vested in the Sword.

Although the Great Conclave can directly exert only a limited effect on the behavior of the Sword, it does have its own weapons and represents a source of opinion the Protector must take into account. Moreover, because the steadholders are ruling lords within their own steadings, a concentrated opposition among the Keys must always be a source of concern. Opposition by the Conclave of Steaders serves as an index of general public opinion.

Local Government

The Protector maintains authority over all of Grayson's surface which has not been bestowed to a steading. Only the Sword may initiate the process to create a new steading from unallocated land, although the Conclave has the right of approval. The process is known as a Grant in Organization. Once a steading has been created, it may not have its status revoked except under the most extraordinary of circumstances, such as general insurrection or treason. Because all steadings are autonomous on creation, they are considered national units under the overall umbrella of the Protectorate of Grayson. This makes a steadholder an actual head of state, unlike other aristocratic systems like the Star Empire of Manticore or the Andermani Empire where territories are administered in the name of a higher authority.

Steadholders, as absolute monarchs within their own steadings, have virtually unlimited powers. Even the Sword may not interfere with the purely internal functioning of the steading. The only limitation on legislation within the steading is that it may not conflict with either the Constitution or national legislation. The Constitution guarantees Grayson steaders' civil rights, including freedom of speech and freedom, protection from unreasonable search or seizure, protection from arbitary arrest, and protection from self-incrimination, but that constitutes only the planetary baseline and a steadholder may extend greater rights to his subjects than are provided by the Constitution. Because personal armsmen are sworn to the steadholder, they are required to follow any order given by the steadholder, even if the action ordered is illegal under the Constitution. The steadholder who gave the order may be held liable, impeached, tried, and convicted of a crime committed by one of his personal armsmen at his command, but the fact that it was the order of his steadholder is a complete defense to any charges against the *armsman*, civil or criminal, resulting from his actions.

Judicial System

Due to its origins in Idaho in what had been the United States of America on Old Earth, the Grayson judiciary and legal systems are based on the American system as it existed at the time. As such, it is a common law system with legal precedent being the most important consideration.

The judiciary system is at once very simple and very complex. It is simple in that there is a single planetary level court known as the High Court. It is complex in that each Steadholder holds not just executive but also judicial power within his steading.

The High Court can be thought of as the secular extension of the Church of Humanity Unchained. While the Church, in the aftermath of the Grayson Civil War, renounced secular executive authority, it retained sole responsibility for training the planet's jurists. Thus, while sitting judges are barred from holding a position in the Church, the opinions of the Church still influence judges. In addition, the Reverend has a veto over nominees to the court.

The process of filling a vacancy on the Court involves all three of the major centers of power on Grayson. The Protector compiles a list of at least six nominees. The Reverend, with the assistance of his legal staff, reviews these nominees and is allowed to reject anyone on the basis of their qualifications. This decision is final but he does have to justify it. Once the vetted list has been approved by the Reverend, it is passed to the Conclave of Steadholders, which may also strike names from it upon a two-thirds majority vote. The Protector then chooses one nominee from the vetted list. Under the Constitution, if the Conclave rejects *all* of the Protector's nominees then the Protector may make his choice from any name on the original list, as approved by the Reverend.

The High Court is divided into an Upper and Lower Division. Each steadholder holds the power of high, middle and low justice within his own steading, and with virtually feudal powers, each can create laws applicable to his own steading. Because there is no uniformity of law among the steadings, disputes that cross steading lines, or that implicate choice of law questions, are heard by the Lower Division of the High Court. In that sense, the High Court's Lower Division courts are the trial courts and courts of original jurisdiction for these cases. The Lower Division of the High Court also hears criminal cases where planetary law has been violated. Cases that do not meet these criteria are tried in a steading's own courts, which are the courts of local jurisdiction.

The Upper Division of the High Court is the court of final appeal for cases that originate in the Lower Division. There is no appeal to the High Court from the courts of individual steadings. The High Court also hears cases regarding the Grayson constitution. The number of judges on the Upper Division of the High Court is fixed by the Constitution at nine members.

The steadholders hold the power of judicial appointments to the courts of their own steadings. Although all the steading-level court systems are based on common law, the variations in law and procedure that have grown over the years would require an individual examination of each steading. What the systems have in common is that they are structured as three level systems: trial courts, appellate division courts, and steading supreme courts. Steadholders have the right to institute any laws within their own steadings (indeed, their decrees have the force of law) as long as these laws do not conflict with planetary law or impinge on any of the Sword's prerogatives, as well as the power of commutation and pardon.

It is not legally possible for a steadholder's decrees to be "unconstitutional" within his own steading unless they conflict with planetary law or impinge upon the Sword's prerogatives. The constitutionality of steadholder decrees of law may be challenged only if the Lower Division of the High Court agrees to hear the challenge. Once accepted by the Lower Division, either party to the appeal challenge may appeal to the Upper Division, but the choice to *hear* the appeal is solely within the High Court's discretion. Lawyers admitted to practice in one steading are generally accorded the privilege of appearing in courts of any other steading, although there are some exceptions.

Church of Humanity Unchained

The people of Grayson are not required to be members of the Church of Humanity Unchained, but nearly all of them are. Well over eighty percent of all Graysons are active members of a local church or cathedral. Aspects of religious observance and customs in living out the faith vary between steadings, but the core doctrine and the primacy of the First Elder as chief interpreter of the holy text remain the same.

The church is unified on a planetary level by the Office of the Sacristy which is headed by the First Elder. Sub-denominations within the Church of Humanity Unchained may hold entirely opposing views, yet the Church is clearly hierarchical.

The Church is a creedal religion which is clearly part of the Christian tradition, as is obvious from the Austinian Creed which contains the key points of its doctrine. These are essentially those of mainstream Christianity, but the Sacristy further requires universal acceptance of the two primal doctrines unique to the Church of Humanity Unchained: The Doctrine of the Test, and The Doctrine of Toleration. Serving members of the clergy are further required to abide by the instructions of the First Elder and their ecclesiastic superiors in matters of observance, scriptural interpretation, and instruction.

The Doctrine of the Test teaches that God, the Tester, places certain challenges before all human beings, as a means of instructing and strengthening them, but has also granted them the strength and ability through grace to meet those challenges. The Doctrine of Toleration teaches that it is for the Tester alone to judge how any human has risen to his or her individual Test. Any child of God has not simply the right but the absolute obligation to meet

his or her Test in accordance with his or her individual interpretation of God's will, yet the Church, as the corporate body
of all believers, is responsible for teaching right doctrine and
providing coherent instruction in the understood will of God.
Any serving priest of the Church is therefore required to live
and teach in accordance with the Sacristy's rulings and scriptural
interpretations on major points of doctrine and Church discipline.
If he cannot in good conscience do so, he cannot be condemned
for his refusal, which is enshrined in the Doctrine of the Test,
but neither may he retain an active office of the Church until
the conflict between its teachings and his own beliefs has been
resolved. Note that on several occasions in Grayson history, the
conflict has been resolved when the Church accepted that the
dissident's beliefs had been correct, rather than the reverse.

The Reverend Austin Grayson founded the Church, led the
colonization of the planet, reformed the faith around the Doctrine of the Test, and was canonized as the Church's first saint.
Believers do not worship Grayson himself, but he is honored as
an exemplar who met the Test placed before him. The Church
of Humanity Unchained draws divine inspiration from not only
the Old and New Testaments of the Judaeo-Christian tradition
but also from *The Book of the New Way*, a collection of writings
by Reverend Grayson. The writings include texts written on Old
Earth, in orbit, and after landing. All are considered sacred as
they show how even a man as obedient to God as First Elder of
the Church wrestled with the challenges of planetary survival,
feared failure and abandonment, and yet rose to meet the Test by
recognizing his own failures and seeking redemption for himself
and all of Father Church's children through grace and good works.

People

The people of Grayson are the product of their environment and have developed distinctive religious and cultural imperatives in response to their hostile homeworld's survival requirements. Theologically, this shows most clearly in the Church of Humanity Unchained's doctrine of the Test which undergirds a religion which is simultaneously intensely conservative and yet highly adaptive. Culturally, the colonists' need to live together in close holdings, shielded from the environment, led to the institution of the steadholders as the autocratic leaders who, in times of crisis, were obligated to select who among a holding's citizens would be euthanized to ensure that it had sufficient purified air, food, and water to survive. In addition, the high mortality rate and skewed gender distribution reinforced and preserved the practice of polygynous marriage.

While the desperate days of the founding are long past, these traditions remain in modern forms. Steadholders continue to rule their steadings as autonomous states, and while they no longer have the need to decide who lives and who dies on a daily basis, they retain much of their original power.

Grayson's views of women and their roles in society are in the process of changing, as well. Polygyny remains the standard form of marriage, but the societal view of gender roles has changed with increasing dominance over the Grayson environment and interaction with outside cultures. Over the last two decades, women have been permitted to own property, enter the workforce, and exercise the franchise, and inheritance laws have been modified to permit female succession to steadholderships. Despite this, traditionalists still maintain that women suffer most from the harsh nature of Grayson's environment, and that men therefore should serve as their protectors from all other stresses of life outside the creation and nurturing of families.

Bagwell, Frederick
Rear Admiral, Grayson Space Navy

Frederick Bagwell served as Admiral Harrington's staff operations officer as a commander in the First Battle Squadron. As a captain, he commanded GNS *Honor Harrington* as Vice Admiral Brentworth's flag captain. Promoted to rear admiral in 1919 PD, Bagwell is currently CO, Battle Division 4.1, GSN.

Benson-Dessouix, Harriet
Rear Admiral, Protector's Own

Harriet Benson, a captain in the Pegasus System Navy, became a Havenite POW when her system was conquered and she spent sixty-five T-years imprisoned on the planet Hades. Transferred to Camp Inferno after leading a passive resistance movement against StateSec atrocities, she was a key participant in Honor Harrington's escape from Hades and commanded the captured battlecruiser *Kutuzov* in the Battle of Cerberus. Married to Henri Benson-Dessouix, who was imprisoned with her on Hades, she is now a Grayson citizen and commands the Protector's Own's Carrier Squadron 1.

Benson-Dessouix, Henri
Colonel, Harrington Steadholder's Guard

Henri Dessouix, imprisoned on Hades with Captain Harriet Benson, played a major role in Honor Harrington's escape from Hades. Now a Grayson citizen married to Harriet Benson-Dessouix, he resides in Harrington Steading and serves in the Harrington Steadholder's Guard.

Brentworth, Mark
Vice Admiral, Grayson Space Navy

Commander Mark Brentworth served as Honor Harrington's liaison officer during the battles of Blackbird and Second Yeltsin. His subsequent commands included GNS *Jason Alvarez*, GNS *Raul Courvoisier*, Battlecruiser Squadron 1, and Battle Squadron 2. He is currently CO, Blackbird Yard.

Brentworth, Walter
Vice Admiral, Grayson Space Navy (retired)

Walter Brentworth was a commodore during the final war with Masada. Promoted to rear admiral, he served as CO, BatDiv 1.1 under Admiral Harrington in the Third Battle of Yeltsin. Promoted to vice admiral in 1911 PD, he served as CO, Office of Shipbuilding, retiring from that post in 1915.

Candless, James *(deceased)*
Corporal, Harrington Steadholder's Guard

James "Jamie" Candless, the second ranking of Honor Harrington's three original personal armsmen, died during Harrington's extraction from solitary confinement onboard PNS *Tepes*.

Caslet, Warner
Rear Admiral, Protector's Own

Warner Caslet served as an officer in the People's Navy. Defeated by Honor Harrington in the Battle of Schiller, he was reassigned as Admiral Thomas Theisman's staff operations officer and personally assigned by Cordelia Ransom to escort Harrington to Cerberus for execution. Captured by Alistair McKeon during the escape from PNS *Tepes*, Caslet accompanied Harrington to the surface of Hades and, eventually, served as Harrington's XO aboard the battlecruiser *Farnese* during the Battle of Cerberus. He accompanied her to Grayson, where he became a Grayson citizen and currently commands Battle Division 2.1, Protector's Own.

Clinkscales, Carson
Commander, Grayson Space Navy

Carson Clinkscales, nephew of Howard Clinkscales, became Honor Harrington's flag lieutenant and was captured by the People's Navy with her while he was an ensign. He was instrumental in Harrington's escape from PNS *Tepes* and in the later escape from Hades. He is currently CO, GNS *Erastus*.

Clinkscales, Howard Samson Jonathan *(deceased)*
Regent, Harrington Steading

Howard Clinkscales began his career as a Sword Armsman, attaining the rank of brigadier in Palace Security by age thirty-six. As a general, he commanded Planetary Security at the time of the Courvoisier Mission to Grayson. He later served as Steadholder Harrington's regent and as CEO of Grayson Skydomes, Ltd., until his death in 1920 PD at the age of ninety-two. He is survived by his wives, Bethany, Rebecca, and Constance, and by his children, Howard, Jessica, Marjorie, John, Angela, Barbara, and Marian.

Fitzclarence, William *(deceased)*
Steadholder Burdette

William Fitzclarence used his steadholdership to plot against Protector Benjamin Mayhew's reforms and against Steadholder Harrington in association with Steadholder Mueller and Brother Edmond Marchant. Fitzclarence ordered Harrington's assassination in 1907 PD. Accused of treason, he demanded trial by combat and was killed by Steadholder Harrington in her role as Protector's Champion.

Gerrick, Adam *(deceased)*
Chief Engineer, Grayson Skydomes, Ltd.

Adam Gerrick, a Grayson engineer, proposed the construction of crystoplast, hermetically sealed domes to protect cities and farmland from the toxic planetary environment. That key technology was funded by Steadholder Harrington through the creation of Grayson Skydomes, Ltd., with Gerrick serving as chief engineer. He analyzed the catastrophic collapse of the Winston

Mueller Middle School Dome, successfully demonstrating that it was due to sabotage, then was killed when Steadholder Harrington's pinnace was shot down on the orders of William Fitzclarence, Steadholder Burdette.

Gutierrez, Mateo
Lieutenant, Owens Steadholder's Guard

Mateo Gutierrez immigrated to Manticore as a child following the PRH's conquest of San Martin. He enlisted in the Royal Manticoran Marine Corps and rose to the rank of platoon sergeant aboard HMS *Gauntlet* during the Tiberian Incident in 1918 PD, where he served as Midshipwoman Abigail Hearns' senior Marine. In 1919, he transferred from the RMMC to Owens Steadholder's Guard with the rank of lieutenant, and serves as Abigail Hearns' personal armsman.

Hanks, Reverend Julius (deceased)
First Elder of the Church of Humanity Unchained

Reverend Hanks, as the spiritual head of the Church of Humanity Unchained, was a firm supporter of the "Mayhew Restoration's" reforms and of Steadholder Harrington. In 1907 PD, he was aboard Harrington's pinnace when it was shot down on William Fitzclarence's orders. Although Hanks survived the subsequent crash landing, he gave his own life to save Steadholder Harrington when he threw himself between her and an armed assassin.

Hearns, Abigail
Lieutenant, Grayson Space Navy

Abigail Hearns is the third daughter of Steadholder Owens and is the first Grayson woman to graduate from the Royal Manticoran Naval Academy on Saganami Island. She has since served exclusively in the RMN, beginning with her midshipwoman's cruise aboard HMS *Gauntlet*, where she demonstrated both leadership and courage in the Tiberian Incident. As assistant tactical officer, HMS *Hexapuma*, she was the acting squadron tactical officer at the Battle of Monica in 1921 PD.

LaFollet, Andrew
Colonel, Harrington Steadholder's Guard

Andrew LaFollet, after completing training and service in Palace Security, served as Steadholder Harrington's senior personal armsman from 1906 until 1921 PD, when Harrington made him her son and heir's personal armsman.

LaFollet, Miranda Gloria
Chief of Staff, Harrington household staff

Miranda LaFollet first entered Steadholder Harrington's service as her personal maid on the recommendation of her brother, Andrew LaFollet. She currently manages the Harrington House staff and, with her treecat companion Farragut, works with Dr. Adelina Arif in the development of treecat sign language and the integration of treecats into human society.

Matthews, Wesley
High Admiral, Grayson Space Navy

Wesley Matthews was, as Commodore, the senior surviving Grayson officer in space at the First and Second Battle of Yeltsin's Star. His open-mindedness and ability to coordinate with the Star Kingdom of Manticore served him well when he was subsequently promoted to High Admiral, the uniformed Commander-in-Chief of the GSN, in 1903 PD following the death of High Admiral Bernard Yanakov. He has held that post continuously since that time.

Marchant, Solomon
Commodore, Grayson Space Navy

Solomon Marchant served as XO, GNS *Jason Alvarez*, in 1911 PD. He accompanied Steadholder Harrington aboard HMS *Prince Adrian* and was captured with her by the People's Navy. After playing an important role in the escape from Hades and commanding the battlecruiser *MacArthur* in the Battle of Cerberus, he returned with Harrington to Grayson. Promoted to captain in 1912 and to commodore in 1915, Marchant currently commands Cruiser Squadron 6, GSN.

Mayhew, Benjamin Bernard Jason
Protector of Grayson

Benjamin Mayhew IX graduated from Harvard University's Bogotá Campus on Old Earth before becoming Protector of Grayson in 1898 PD. In 1903, Captain Honor Harrington and her treecat Nimitz saved Benjamin's family from assassination and he, in turn, saved Harrington's life in the same fight. He is a political moderate, a close friend and advocate of Honor Harrington, a proponent of Grayson's societal modernization, and a firm ally of Queen Elizabeth III of Manticore. He is married to Katherine Elizabeth Mayhew and Elaine Margaret Mayhew, with whom he has seven living children: Rachel, Theresa, Jeanette, Alexandra, Honor, Arabella, and Bernard.

Mayhew, Bernard Raoul
Steadholder Mayhew

Bernard Raoul Mayhew, Steadholder Mayhew, and heir apparent to the Sword, was born in 1913 PD of Benjamin Mayhew's senior wife, Katherine.

Mayhew, Michael

Although Michael Mayhew, younger brother to Benjamin IX, no longer holds the title of Steadholder Mayhew, he remains second in the line of succession to the Sword. Educated at Anderman University, New Berlin, and King's College, Manticore, he is a senior technical consultant to the Grayson Space Navy and frequently serves his older brother as a personal representative and special ambassador.

Mayhew, Rachel
Midshipwoman, Grayson Space Navy

Midshipwoman Mayhew is the eldest child of Protector Benjamin and Katherine Mayhew and the second Grayson to be adopted by a treecat. She is bonded to Hipper, one of the Harrington treecat colonists, and is currently entering her second year at the Saganami Island Naval Academy.

Mueller, Samuel *(deceased)*
Steadholder Mueller

Samuel Mueller, Steadholder Mueller, was an ally of William Fitzclarence, Steadholder Burdette, and a member of Fitzclarence's conspiracy against Benjamin IX and Steadholder Harrington. Despite his association with the plot, including his direct involvement in the sabotage of the Winston Mueller Middle School Dome, he escaped detection at that time and was not legally implicated. In 1915 PD, however, he was blackmailed by Masadan agents into participating in their attempt to assassinate Elizabeth III and Benjamin, although he was unaware of their full intentions. In 1916, after being successfully impeached in the Conclave of Steadholders and convicted of treason, he was executed.

Paxton, Gregory
Director of Sword Intelligence (retired)

Gregory Paxton, with doctorates in history, economics, and religion, served as Steadholder Harrington's intelligence officer when she commanded the First Battle Squadron in 1907 PD. In 1911, Dr. Paxton resigned from naval service to accept the post of Director of Sword Intelligence for Protector Benjamin and held that post until his retirement in 1920.

Prestwick, Lord Henry *(deceased)*
Chancellor of Grayson

Henry Prestwick became Chancellor of Grayson in 1897 PD and remained in that office following the Mayhew Restoration of 1903, serving Benjamin IX loyally and well. In 1915, Lord Prestwick, along with many other Manticoran and Grayson government officials, died in the destruction of HMS *Queen Adrienne*.

Sullivan, Reverend Jeremiah Winslow
First Elder, Church of Humanity Unchained

Jeremiah Sullivan succeeded Reverend Julius Hanks as First Elder of the Church of Humanity Unchained following Hanks' assassination in 1907 PD. Although by nature more conservative than Hanks, Reverend Sullivan has continued and reinforced his

THE PROTECTORATE OF GRAYSON

459

predecessor's policies in support of the Mayhew Restoration and its social, religious, and medical reforms. He is a close personal friend of Steadholder Harrington and her parents.

Yanakov, Bernard (deceased)
High Admiral, Grayson Space Navy

Bernard Yanakov was the uniformed Commander-in-Chief of the GSN at the time of the Courvoisier Mission in 1902 PD. He forged a personal friendship with Admiral Raoul Courvoisier, took a leading role in the diplomatic negotiations with the Star Kingdom, and died commanding the Grayson-Manticoran combined fleet in the First Battle of Yeltsin.

Yanakov, Judah
Admiral, Grayson Space Navy

Judah Yanakov, the nephew of High Admiral Bernard Yanakov, continues his family tradition of service. As a rear admiral, he served as a divisional commander in the First Battle Squadron under Steadholder Harrington in 1907 PD. In 1913, promoted to admiral, he commanded the Grayson contingent of Eighth Fleet at the Second Battle of Basilisk. Since the resumption of hostilities, he has commanded Task Force 82, Eighth Fleet, under Admiral Harrington.

Yu, Alfredo
Admiral, Protector's Own

Alfredo Yu was part of a covert "exchange program" between the PN and the planet of Masada, as a captain in the People's Navy. As the commander of MNS *Thunder of God*, he attempted to prevent Masadan atrocities and resisted Masadan plans to use his ship to bombard the planet of Grayson. The Masadans, however, seized his ship and attempted to attack the planet. Yu managed to escape with a significant portion of his Havenite crew. Following the destruction of *Thunder of God* by HMS *Fearless* (CA-286), Yu requested and was granted political asylum by the Star Kingdom of Manticore. After intensive debriefing and service in support of the Royal Manticoran Navy's Office of Naval

Intelligence and the Grayson Office of Shipbuilding, he requested Grayson citizenship and was subsequently granted a GSN commission and served as Steadholder Harrington's flag captain aboard GNS *Terrible* in the First Battle Squadron at the Fourth Battle of Yeltsin. Upon Steadholder Harrington's return from Cerberus and Protector Benjamin's creation of the Protector's Own in 1914 PD, Yu formally transferred from the GSN to the Protector's Own as Steadholder Harrington's second-in-command and *de facto* CO.

Treecats

A total of forty-two treecats now live full-time on Grayson. Those not bonded reside permanently in Harrington Steading, while those who have bonded accompany their adopted humans. Nimitz (Laughs Brightly of Bright Water Clan) is bonded with Steadholder Harrington and mated with Samantha (Golden Voice of the Sun Leaf Clan; bonded to Hamish Alexander-Harrington), with whom he has four treekittens: Jason, Cassandra, Achilles, and Andromeda. Eight other adult treecats from the Bright Water Clan originally immigrated to Grayson. Of the original immigrants, Farragut is bonded with Miranda LaFollet of Harrington Steading, and Hipper is bonded with Rachel Mayhew, daughter of Protector Mayhew.

Xenologists were originally divided on whether this move should be considered the first colonization of another world by the treecat species. Nimitz and others did participate in space travel and visit other worlds prior to the birth of Samantha's litter and the immigration of the eight members of Bright Water Clan. However, the archives of the Xenology Institute of Sphinx, which makes a special study of treecats, had no prior instance of so many females leaving Sphinx together or of treekittens being raised outside of a Sphinxian treecat range.

After the communication breakthrough by Dr. Arif, the treecats themselves were able to answer the question definitively, and two follow-on groups have immigrated from Sphinx in the intervening years.

The Grayson Space Navy

While the GSN was officially founded in 1675 PD (3777 CE), it traces its origin to the founding of the Grayson Space Guard in 1386, making the GSN one of the galaxy's older navies.

The GSG was envisioned more as a civilian law enforcement and SAR organization than as a military force, equipped with a modest force of small, lightly armed patrol craft and a handful of longer-ranged "cutters" (essentially, reaction-powered equivalents of what the rest of the galaxy now calls light attack craft). The GSG was never really big enough or sufficiently well-funded to perform its various missions over so vast a volume, yet it succeeded in doing so anyway, establishing a tradition of adaptive innovation and resourcefulness which was to serve it and the Grayson Space Navy extraordinarily well over the ensuing centuries.

After thirty-five years of police and SAR duties, the GSG's first combat action occurred in 1422 PD, when it supported Benjamin the Great's forces by launching kinetic strikes against the Army of the Faithful during the final years of the Civil War, but it came truly into its own in 1672, when it defeated the first Masadan attack on Yeltsin's Star. Shortly thereafter, in recognition of its service to the Protectorate and as an acknowledgement of its future role, the GSG formally became the Grayson Space Navy.

For most of its history, the GSN has been at war or preparing for war with Masada, and during that time the Navy of the

461

Faithful has cycled several times in capability, from barely space-worthy to a near-peer competitor with the GSN.

From the early days of converted ore haulers and GSG cutters, the GSN had grown into a small, but respectable force of cruisers, destroyers, and light attack craft by the time Grayson joined the Alliance. Since the Protectorate of Grayson's admission to the Manticoran Alliance, it has become one of the largest, most modern, and most powerful navies in existence.

Organization

The GSN has historically been organized into a three-tier system. In the first tier are the Offices, roughly equivalent to the Bureaus of the RMN. Each office is run by an Admiral and is broken into divisions that focus on different aspects of its area of responsibility. The second tier consists of independent Commands, unique in that they report directly to the High Admiral, though they may work closely with one or more Office. Finally, in the third tier are the administrative units, smaller staffs that provide support in specialized areas.

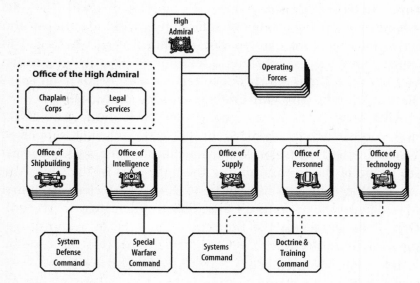

This organizational scheme worked quite well when the GSN was a small system defense force with no more than a half-dozen hyper-capable ships in its order of battle. Scaling this organization to run one of the five most powerful navies in the galaxy has been difficult, though the Graysons, with their combination of stubborn adherence to tradition and flexible attitude towards change, appear to have made it work.

Office of the High Admiral
High Admiral Wesley Matthews

Every layer of the Navy has historically reported directly to the High Admiral, and the formal tables of organization still reflect this polite fiction. However, over almost two decades of explosive growth, the office of the High Admiral has grown to encompass a number of smaller administrative units as well as a staff to manage the day-to-day inputs from the Offices and Commands. Encompassed in the Office of the High Admiral are both the Chaplain Corps and Legal Services, tasked with caring for the Navy's spiritual and secular well-being. These offices have traditionally dealt with sensitive issues requiring direct access to the High Admiral.

Office of Shipbuilding
Admiral Cornelius Browning

The Office of Shipbuilding is responsible for all aspects of starship construction, from stations and small craft to superdreadnoughts. While every part of the Navy has expanded since Grayson joined the Alliance, the Office of Shipbuilding has probably had the most growth, responsible for the design and construction of no fewer than twenty-two warship classes (both Grayson-designed and locally constructed RMN designs) in the twenty years since joining the Alliance.

Office of Intelligence
Admiral Austin Roberts

The Office of Intelligence coordinates all of the Naval/Military Intelligence-gathering activities into one cohesive whole. It works closely with Sword Intelligence and Manticore's Bureau of Planning. This office has the distinction of being the oldest organizational unit of the GSN. It is descended from the group that controlled the original "Watcher" platforms built to monitor the status of the Masadan colony expeditions during the Exile. While the platforms themselves have been transferred to System Defense Command (SDC), the Office of Intelligence retains its original function and works closely with SDC to identify threats to the Yeltsin's Star System in enough time to counter them.

Office of Supply
Rear Admiral Carlyle Jones

The Office of Supply encompasses the logistical side of the Navy as well as the Ordnance Command and is responsible for all munitions, drones and other expendables carried aboard warships. It works in tandem with the RMN Logistics Command to form the Joint Navy Military Transport Command, the fleet of fast commercial freighters that has been the core of rear-area logistics throughout the war. Armed fleet auxiliaries operating in conjunction with Grayon's forward deployed wall of battle also report to the Office of Supply.

Office of Personnel
Vice Admiral Justin Ackroyd

The Office of Personnel is responsible for manning requirements as well as all administrative issues surrounding personnel management (payroll, benefits, promotions board, leave, etc.). It has worked heavily with Alliance partners to find homes for allied personnel in GSN service.

The Office of Personnel has also had the unenviable task of navigating the minefield of forming a gender-integrated Navy, with the introduction of female Grayson personnel into what has always been a male Navy. The GSN's experience with female personnel "on loan" from the Royal Manticoran Navy has been a godsend in this respect, but the process of integrating even those experienced, trained women into their all-male service was not without problems. Integrating Grayson-born women has been even more challenging, given the Grayson tradition that women are to be protected rather than exposed to danger, and there has been considerable friction, especially in the early years of the process, but the GSN appears to be coping.

Office of Technology
Admiral William Gaffney

The Office of Technology grew out of the alliance with the Star Kingdom of Manticore and the need for the GSN to quickly incorporate the wealth of new technology and data coming into the system. Taking a page from the RMN, the Office of Technology works closely with corporate and shipping concerns both in Grayson and Manticoran space to gather technological news from across explored space.

By 1921 PD, the Office has moved into more of a pure R&D role, working closely with the R&D programs in Systems Command. Pressure to merge the two groups into a single office started when the Janacek Admiralty shut down all coordination between the navies in the interregnum between operational phases of the war, but bureaucratic inertia, present even in the GSN, has so far resisted the merge. During the locust years of the Janacek Admiralty, the Office of Technology began to form its own relationships with Alliance navies and had established robust channels of communication independent of the RMN by the time the war resumed.

System Defense Command
Admiral Leon Garret

System Defense Command (SDC) maintains the long-range detection arrays, border sensors, and several squadrons of quick reaction forces to identify and respond to possible threats. It is the oldest formally integrated organization in the GSN and is also in charge of the "fixed" defenses of the system, including orbital fortresses, missile pods and planetary defenses. In the event of an attack on the home system, the mobile force commander works closely with SDC.

Admiral Garret is one of the last of the original GSN admirals to survive the War, and he has been instrumental in organizing and coordinating the home system defenses for longer than much of the current crop of Grayson officers has been alive. He continues to work tirelessly despite his advanced age and calls from some quarters for his retirement. He runs his Command as a personal fiefdom but, despite any personnel management peculiarities, his results have kept him in charge. His style is seen by many as abrasive but this defect has been matched by the near total success of his defensive measures. Admiral Garret has publicly acknowledged the successful defense of the Yeltsin's Star System as his personal Test and has been quoted in the 'faxes as saying, "God will let me know when it's time for me to go. Probably when my heart stops beating."

Doctrine and Training Command
Rear Admiral Michael Reston

Doctrine and Training Command (DTC) works closely with the Office of Personnel and has been instrumental in keeping pace with the rapidly evolving theory of warfare in the Alliance as a whole and GSN in particular.

For the first decade after Grayson joined the Manticoran Alliance, all GSN officers attended the RMN Academy on Saganami Island, and the majority of them continue to do so. In 1920, however, the revamped Isaiah Mackenzie Naval Academy, the traditional source of the GSN's officer corps, reopened with a thoroughly modernized curriculum and up-to-date training facilities. DTC has been deeply involved with coursework design for Saganami Island from the very first, and was instrumental in designing the new Mackenzie curriculum and in recruiting visiting Manticoran professors. In addition, DTC bears primary responsibility for local enlisted personnel training, and it has also been instrumental in some of the changes in command and control structure on Grayson warships, rippling down from flag staff to individual bridge crews.

Systems Command
Vice Admiral Thomas Albert

Systems Command has been the Navy's research and development shop since long before the Alliance. All of the home-grown technology updates the Navy had put into place before the first Masadan attack after the Exile were developed here. Systems Command provided the original work on the improved compensators and fission reactors and has worked very closely with the RMN's Weapons Development Board on many aspects of Alliance technology.

The original intention was to replace Systems Command with the Office of Technology once the influx of new tech from Manticore grew from a trickle into a flood, but High Admiral Matthews, with the firm support of the Protector, overruled the decision. He argued that Grayson must not rely on foreign efforts to develop new technology and should continue its own development, incorporating but not slavishly following Manticoran tech and practice. Thus, Systems Command retains its research and development role while coordinating closely with the Office of Technology to screen for useful ideas from across the human galaxy.

Special Warfare Command
Lieutenant General Gerald White

Special Warfare Command (SpecWar) is the smallest Command in the GSN and also one of the older ones. The hyperdrive, and exposure to the rest of humanity, brought both the GSN and their Masadan opponents a limited ability to conduct covert operations in each other's star systems. SpecWar was the organization that grew out of the Office of Intelligence unit tasked with covert operations in either star system. As such, it gathered a substantial amount of information for the Alliance forces that occupied Masada.

Protector's Own Squadron

Protector Benjamin Mayhew IX established the Protector's Own in 1914 PD, using as its core the warships and volunteers of the Elysian Space Navy. The crews of the Elysian Space Navy were former State Security prisoners of war who escaped the Cerberus System under the command of Admiral Harrington. Every member was offered a position in the Protector's Own, and nearly one hundred sixty thousand accepted. Like service members in the Grayson Space Navy, members of the Protector's Own are entitled to Grayson citizenship following six years of honorable service. While the initial service members of the Protector's Own were foreign, and in some cases decades out of practice in the art and science of space combat, that core group and the Grayson-born members who have joined it have become the most skilled force in the already elite Grayson service.

The Protector's Own is personally financed by the Protector of Grayson. The squadron's new ships are built in Grayson Space Navy yards. The Protector's Own Squadron, currently nearer to a fleet in size, generally shares doctrine, training, maintenance, and upkeep facilities with the GSN. Service members of the Protector's Own are uniformed in the Mayhew gold and maroon. They are paid on a scale set by the Protector. As of 1921 PD, that rate is 115 percent of GSN pay for the same grade.

In recognition of Fleet Admiral Harrington, its commanding officer, the emblem of the Protector's Own is a flame-enshrouded salamander. Because of her other duties, Admiral Harrington relies on her second-in-command, Admiral Alfredo Yu, to serve as the acting commanding officer in her absence. Though many of the members of the Protector's Own are foreign born, service is open to all spacers (foreign or steaders) who meet the qualifications standards and choose to compete for a position. Most of these service members become Grayson citizens. Additional members of the Protector's Own, as needed to maintain force strength, have been enlisted and commissioned from Grayson. Most maintain residences in Harrington Steading. All Protector's Own officers and general spacers make their oath to the Protector, as do all members of the GSN, but the Protector's Own has been established as a separate service branch, legally coequal to the Grayson Space Navy, the Grayson Army, and Grayson Planetary Security. A recruitment office run at the direction of the Protector on Mayhew Steading reviews applications and administers qualification testing quarterly.

Uniforms and Equipment

OFFICER'S SERVICE DRESS

The Grayson Space Navy's officer's uniform consists of a medium blue hip-length tunic with lapels blending into a collar that opens towards the neck. The tunic is sealed with three buttons and has pocket flaps bilaterally on the breast and hips with silver buttons. Service badges, ribbons and awards are worn above the left pocket flap, and a nametag and unit awards are worn over the right. Officers assigned to a particular ship wear the ship's patch on the shoulder of the right sleeve, while the GSN crest is worn on the right shoulder. Rank insignia pins are worn on both sides of the shirt collar and duplicated on the shoulderboards. Traditional cuff rings are worn as well, with the exception of lieutenant senior grade which also has a Grayson sword above the single gold ring.

The shirt worn under the jacket is, for some reason, referred to as an Oxford shirt. It is white with buttons up the front and buttons holding the points of the collar, which is folded down over an old-fashioned navy blue necktie.

The trousers are dark blue and come down to the tops of the black boots. As an option, and thanks to the efforts of the Bancroft Society, the GSN Uniform Board has made skirts an option for the dress uniform and split skirts for working uniforms for female GSN personnel. The skirts are the same color as the trousers.

The officer's cap is generically referred to as a "wheel cap." The cloth portion of the cap is the same dark blue as the trousers. The band around the head is black, with a black strap secured by silver buttons at the sides and a black peak, carrying gold braid "scrambled eggs" for senior officers and flag officers. A silver badge with the GSN crest adorns the front of the cap. In a tradition borrowed from the Manticoran Navy, starship commanders wear a white band on their cap.

ENLISTED SERVICE DRESS

GSN enlisted personnel wear a short jacket that seals up the front in the same medium blue as the officer's tunic. It opens toward the top to lapels that blend into a collar. The sleeves terminate at the cuffs in a wide knit band for comfort. There are pleated pockets on both sides of the chest with silver buttons on the pocket flaps. Similar to officers, awards and decorations are worn over the left pocket and an identification tag is worn over the right. The Oxford shirt and necktie are the same as worn by officers. Shoulder decoration is the same as the officer's uniform. Rating insignia is worn on the left sleeve while service hash marks adorn the right, one for every four years of service.

The trousers are similar to the officers', but in the same medium blue as the tunic, terminating at the black boot tops. Like officers, female enlisted personnel also have the option of wearing a skirt.

The hat is a fore and aft cloth cap in azure blue with a narrow black band around the base.

SKINSUITS

Graysons use state-of-the-art skinsuits imported from the Star Kingdom of Manticore. Markings on these Grayson-issue skinsuits are similar to their Manticoran counterparts, but there are noticeable differences.

Like the RMN, skinsuits used by the GSN mark an enlisted spacer's department in a large color-coded area along the arms and legs. Unlike the RMN markings, the Graysons prefer to leave most of the chest area white, coloring only the shoulders and the front helmet attachment piece in a fashion that slyly resembles their duty uniform's ancient necktie.

Markings on the left arm of the enlisted suit include the Grayson roundel (a six-pointed star over crossed swords) reversed from the department color in white. Below that is the wearer's rank, also in white. The spacer's name is worn in his department color on the right breast. Like the RMN, Graysons also color the enlisted helmet's visor with the wearer's department color, reversing out their name in white. Rank is displayed above the name for enlisted spacers.

The Grayson officer's skinsuit utilizes department-neutral coloration, favoring a navy blue accent around the shoulders instead of the black of RMN officer skinsuits. Rank is displayed on the helmet, on the collar, reversed on the shoulders, and on the sleeve of an officer's skinsuit. The name is displayed on the visor of the helmet and on the right breast.

Both officers' and enlisted spacers' skinsuits display the hull number and unit name on the right shoulder. The officer's skinsuit also displays the Grayson roundel on the left shoulder.

Order of Battle

The Grayson Space Navy was defined by its wars with the Faithful. The GSN's sudden and rapid adaptation of modern interstellar warfighting technology, successful conclusion of its conflict with Masada, and ascension to its role as a senior Navy in the Manticoran Alliance is a testament to the flexibility of the force and a telling reminder for those who would see Graysons as backwards. In Grayson parlance, the modern GSN met and surpassed the Test for which it was created.

At the time that they were recontacted by the rest of humanity, the Graysons had the capability to build fission- and fusion-powered reaction drives, create large spaceborne structures, and conduct a great deal of their society's industrial business off-world. They accomplished this with no gravitic technology, completely ignorant of nanofacturing techniques that had been industrial standards in the rest of the explored galaxy for centuries. Their accomplishments were aided, somewhat ironically, by the natural abundance of heavy elements through which their world daily tried to kill them. For example, their development of nuclear fission reactor technologies to previously undreamed of levels was largely due to the abundance of the needed fuels in their rocks, soil, and groundwater. The radioisotopes required less infrastructure to extract and a lower level of capability to burn than safer and cleaner fusion fuels.

This particular issue famously led to revolutionary developments in light attack craft (LAC) powerplants when the Grayson industrial base familiarized itself with modern fabrication techniques. However, it also created a host of problems as the Graysons tried to build their first modern fusion-powered hyper-capable warships. Simply put, pre-Alliance Grayson fusion plants were not gravitically/electromagnetically compressed (as are GRAVMAKs). They operated purely on electromagnetic principles and were enormous when compared to a modern GRAVMAK of similar output. Pairing their plasma output with hyperdrives, impeller nodes, sidewalls, and other gravitic devices strained Grayson ingenuity to its limits before it joined the Alliance.

Given a technically literate populace, a robust space infrastructure, and the motivation of the coming Manticore-Havenite War, the nascent Grayson space industry rapidly learned how to overcome many of these technical issues as they license-built their first Manticoran designs during the prewar naval buildup. The large number of space workers in Grayson service, coupled with new manufacturing techniques and processes brought in from Manticore, combined to create explosive growth in Yeltsin's Star's space population and manufacturing capability. This infrastructure and the generation who built it have become some of the most accomplished shipwrights in the known galaxy by any standard. Thoughtful understanding of technical principles and a continuous search for better ways of accomplishing their tasks are hallmarks. The GSN's methodical approach to modern starship design has surprised the known galaxy, enemies and allies alike, with innovations from the first years of the Alliance up to the present day.

LIGHT ATTACK CRAFT (LAC)

Before the Protectorate of Grayson entered the Manticoran Alliance, the GSN boasted twenty-one locally built light attack craft in its order of battle. The influx of military and spacecraft technology that followed Alliance admission rendered these early Grayson LACs obsolete even for their original sublight system defense mission. The GSN summarily halted all construction and decommissioned the units in service.

When Project Anzio kicked off production in 1912 PD, the GSN rapidly constructed a number of the new advanced LAC classes as part of the military building push in advance of Operation Buttercup. These more capable and reliable units performed the system defense mission and remained close to home during the initial attacks. Later GSN fleet exercises evolved to more closely integrate LAC operations within GSN doctrine.

Grayson architects improved on Manticoran designs in their production of LACs for the space superiority role. They used the cancelled RMN Space Superiority LAC Program for initial designs, but followed through with superior designs of their own. Grayson's latest LAC class, the *Katana*, is in service in both the RMN and GSN as a dedicated "LAC killer."

Faith-class system defense unit
Mass: 11,250 tons
Dimensions: 138 × 23 × 21 m
Acceleration: 409.3 G (4.014 kps²)
80% Accel: 327.5 G (3.211 kps²)
Broadside: 12M, 1L, 1AC
Chase: 1L, 1AC
Service Life: 1891–1907

The *Faith*-class unit's formal designation in Grayson service was "system defense unit" rather than "light attack craft" because it was actually the primary sublight system defense platform for the primitive, pre-Alliance GSN and massed barely twelve percent as much as a contemporary Grayson cruiser. However, those units were widely regarded as LAC analogs by other navies, given their mission requirements.

The *Faith* class was divided into at least three distinct subtypes, but the weapons fit between them is nearly identical. The major changes between subtypes are in the sensors, electronic warfare packages, and fire control systems. Like many pre-Alliance GSN units, the *Faith* class were protected by point defense autocannon, as the smallest pre-Alliance Grayson beam installation was far too large and slow firing to be an effective missile defense system. The designs are crude compared to modern units, but the *Faith* class performed well in the final Masadan attack.

Fission power plants driving plasma accelerators for gravitic conversion were standard in these units, and the inability to refit more modern Manticoran gravitic radscreens into their power-plants was a major factor in their retirement. The GSN initially considered upgrading them to modern GRAVMAK fusion plants similar to those used in RMN LACs, but decided against it. The tradeoffs revealed in that study convinced the GSN to propose the combination of Grayson fission reactors with Manticoran shielding materials and screen generators that ultimately resulted in the *Shrike*'s powerplant, however.

Another significant presage of the *Shrike* design were the *Faith*'s spinal laser weapons. While most impeller drive warships mount their largest weapons in their chase batteries, the *Faith*-class mounts were unusually large compared to their broadside mounts, requiring a dedicated plasma accelerator to feed them from the fission pile. The *Faith*-class' designers realized that the platform needed improved turn rates if its crews were going to survive to use these weapons and gave it larger maneuvering gyros and more wedge torque than previous designs. All of these features provided valuable experience for designing the *Shrike* around a single spinal beam.

Shrike-B-class light attack craft
(for specification, see RMN Shrike-B-class LAC)
Service Life: 1915–present

While involved heavily in the initial *Shrike* research and development, Grayson lagged behind Manticore by several years in operational LAC and carrier deployment. A number of early *Shrikes* were in service with Systems Command as research and development testbeds, but the first advanced LAC class in GSN service was its own *Shrike-B* variant. The differences between the models are minor and each can operate from the other's carriers as necessary.

Katana-class light attack craft
Mass: 19,500 tons
Dimensions: 71 × 20 × 20 m
Acceleration: 640.4 G (6.28 kps²)
80% Accel: 512.3 G (5.024 kps²)
Forward: 5M/CM, 3PD
Aft: 6PD
Service Life: 1917–present

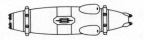

Originally designed as Grayson's answer to the *Ferret* class, the *Katana* does everything Grayson wanted a *Ferret* to do without trying to fill the antiship role. The Graysons realized early on that the primacy of the LAC in the antiship role was time-limited and began looking for ways to create a space-superiority fighter with enhanced dogfighting capabilities. The cancellation of the RMN's own Space Superiority LAC Program under the Janacek

Administration made the *Katana* class the only functional space-superiority LAC in the Manticoran Alliance.

The *Katana* carries five high-speed launchers capable of launching either standard Mk31 counter-missiles or the Mk9 Viper anti-LAC missile. These off-bore launchers are capable of launching into virtually any open aspect, including directly aft.

With no provision to carry the larger shipkillers, magazine levels have been increased over even that of a *Ferret*. The *Katana* also carries a trio of heavy superdreadnought-grade point defense clusters forward, optimized for antimissile defense but powerful enough to be used against other LACs in close combat. Aft, they carry a standard ring of light point defense clusters like the *Shrikes* and *Ferrets*.

The *Katanas* are slightly smaller and substantially more maneuverable than any of the other *Shrike* variants, with improved electronic warfare capabilities as well as the new two-phase "buckler" bow wall. Their multipurpose launchers fire the Viper missile, which can be used in either counter-LAC or counter-missile mode. Used in the second mode, the Viper remains an extremely capable counter-missile, matching the antimissile performance of the cheaper dedicated Mark 31 counter-missile from which it was derived.

In addition to its dogfighting role, the GSN and RMN have recently begun to use the *Katana* to supplement fleet missile defense, especially in the kind of MDM environment Alliance ships have faced against Haven's new wall of battle post-Operation Thunderbolt.

DESTROYERS (DD)

With the explosive growth of the Grayson economy and the matching growth of naval responsibilities following Grayson's membership in the Manticoran Alliance, the Grayson Space Navy found itself in desperate need of light units. The fact that none of its officers had ever commanded a warship heavier than a light cruiser and that they had no experience with extended deep-space hyper operations also gave Grayson good reason to begin by increasing the number of smaller ships in its Navy.

Like the rest of Grayson naval doctrine, Grayson destroyer design evolved nearly independently from the rest of the explored galaxy's conceptions of naval power. Already at war continuously for several hundred years prior to their rediscovery, the first GSN "destroyers" were really just the lower level of two tiers of hyper-capable Grayson warships, used defensively to intercept Masadan raiders in the Yeltsin's Star system and offensively as support units on Grayson raids into the Endicott System. Unlike most other navies, limited interstellar trade meant that GSN destroyers were not needed in the traditional commerce protection role common across the rest of human explored space.

Grayson's Alliance membership changed the roles of its destroyers as it changed many other things. For the first time in living memory, the GSN no longer had to worry about an existential threat a handful of light-years away. Instead, it faced the potentially much larger threat of Haven and began concentrating on the development of interstellar combat power. Not content to accept "received wisdom" from their Manticoran partner, the Graysons responded with their hallmark inventiveness and reexamined their naval doctrine across the board. The end result was a concept of operations for their destroyer forces that essentially ignored traditional commerce protection missions. Instead, the forces are designed for three fleet missions: scouting, antiscouting, and screening.

First and foremost, GSN destroyers scout for a deployed battle fleet both while in hyper transit and in normal space. The new doctrine calls for a substantially larger scouting force, spread across multiple hyper sub-bands to maximize sensor performance. This increase in demand, combined with the relative ease in incorporating Manticoran technology in the smaller shipyards and a need for small-ship command billets to train the first generation of capital ship commanding officers (COs), explains the rapid initial buildup in destroyer numbers in the early days of the Alliance.

Second, and closely associated with the scouting mission, is the antiscouting mission. GSN destroyers engage light enemy scouting units as they are found, both to support their own scouting mission and to prevent enemy scouting.

Finally, once the main enemy formation is located and its composition determined, GSN doctrine calls for the destroyer force to fall back to the main body of the fleet and integrate itself into the wall of battle, augmenting the battle fleet with its sensor and antimissile capabilities.

Ararat-class destroyer (pre-Alliance)
Mass: 62,500 tons
Dimensions: 341 × 40 × 23 m
Acceleration: 526.6 G (5.164 kps^2)
80% Accel: 421.2 G (4.131 kps^2)
Broadside: 3M, 2L, 2CM, 2AC
Chase: 1L, 1PD
Number Built: 1
Service Life: 1874–1903

GNS *Ararat* was the oldest ship in Grayson service at the time of the battles of the final Grayson-Masadan War. As the first vessel built from the keel up to take advantage of the locally developed inertial compensator, *Ararat* could in many ways be considered the first modern GSN warship.

Like all of the pre-Alliance warships, *Ararat* mounted few broadside missile launchers, with even fewer chemical-burning counter-missiles for area defense. On the broadsides she still mounted autocannon for the point defense role but had recently been refitted with crude, but longer-ranged laser clusters to cover her vulnerable hammerheads. *Ararat* was destroyed with all hands during the Masadan War.

Zion-class destroyer (pre-Alliance)
Mass: 65,250 tons
Dimensions: 346 × 41 × 24 m
Acceleration: 525.5 G (5.154 kps^2)
80% Accel: 420.4 G (4.123 kps^2)
Broadside: 4M, 2L, 2CM, 3AC
Chase: 1L, 2AC
Number Built: 3
Service Life: 1879–1905

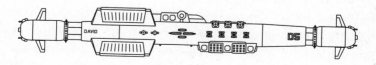

The *Zion* class was designed as a follow-on class to GNS *Ararat*. The most significant change was to add a fourth broadside missile

launcher. Unfortunately, the lack of room for additional missile storage reduced the number of salvoes per launcher from eight to six.
Defenses include dual gravitically driven point defense autocannon
as chasers and an additional autocannon on the broadsides. These
autocannon were imported ex-Solarian weapons. Grayson industry
was as yet unable to construct such weapons, but the GSN was able
to acquire them from Solarian reclamation yards as the SLN converted to laser clusters in more recent construction. Although the
autocannon were more volume intensive than the cruder, electromag-
netically driven Grayson weapons, they required much less volume
and a lower energy budget than laser clusters would have, while
their higher rate of fire and muzzle velocity remained more than
adequate for dealing with then state-of-the-art Masadan shipkillers.

The class was scheduled to receive the same defensive upgrades
as *Ararat*, but the onset of the final Masadan War disrupted those
plans. GNS *Saul*, the only member of the class to survive the War,
was decommissioned in 1905 PD after the first wave of the Alliance Technological Exchange Program ships arrived. Her survival
in combat was directly attributed in official reports to an increased
volume of defensive antimissile firepower and the dramatic improvement that her autocannon represented over the older electromagnetic
guns on *Ararat*.

Jacob-class destroyer
(for specification, see RMN Noblesse-class DD)
Number Purchased: 7
Service Life: 1903–1921

These are former RMN *Noblesse*-class destroyers that were shipped
to the GSN instead of being scrapped. Initially outdated by RMN
standards, their electronics were upgraded before delivery. Complete fits of modern point defense weapons alone made them far
superior to any pre-Alliance Grayson-built destroyer.

By the middle of the first war with Haven, they were mostly
relegated to training duty or System Defense Command. Few of
them saw action, though some were assigned as convoy escorts.
They were modernized again in late 1911 with upgraded sensors
and electronic warfare (EW) systems. However, given that the
youngest was over seventy T-years old when they entered Grayson

service, their impellers and compensators in particular were difficult to maintain. Preferring to spend scarce maintenance resources on more modern units, the GSN retired the *Jacob* class with a sense of relief as the first of the *Paul* class were commissioned.

Joseph-class destroyer
(for specification, see RMN Chanson-class DD)
Number Purchased: 3
Service Life: 1903–present

As part of the Technological Exchange Program offered by the Star Kingdom of Manticore that gave them the retired *Nobelesse*-class destroyers, three brand new Flight IV *Chanson*-class destroyers were sold to Grayson between 1903 and 1904 PD. Renamed the *Joseph* class when they entered Grayson service, these destroyers joined with the seven older *Jacob*-class destroyers as the early modern units of the GSN before the first locally built destroyer was commissioned in late 1905.

While GNS *Joseph* was lost in one of the early battles of the war, her sisters, *Manasseh* and *Ephraim*, have served the Navy well in the intervening years. Though not as capable as the newer construction, they are well suited to the picket duties and other tasks to which they are assigned. Many serving GSN flag officers had their first taste of extended deep-space hyper operations onboard one of these ships.

Joshua-class destroyer
Mass: 79,250 tons
Dimensions: 369 x 44 x 25 m
Acceleration: 548.9 G (5.383 kps²)
80% Accel: 439.1 G (4.306 kps²)
Broadside: 3M, 3L, 5CM, 4PD
Chase: 2M, 1G, 2CM, 2PD
Number Built: 44
Service Life: 1905–present

The *Joshua*-class destroyer is the first ship of its type designed specifically with GSN doctrine as its guide. While the original inspiration was the Flight IV *Chanson*-class DD, the Office of Shipbuilding had its own ideas about warship design from the review of operational data received from the RMN. Somewhat to the consternation of their new allies, the Graysons made several significant changes to the *Chanson* design before putting it into production and still managed to complete the first unit over a year before their Manticoran advisers would have believed possible.

The GSN had already begun planning for its transition from a strictly system defense force to a force able to project power outside the Yeltsin's Star system, and the *Joshua*-class plans reflected the first steps of the evolution of current Grayson doctrine for well-protected light units to provide layered defensive support as part of a screen for the wall of battle. Indeed, the GSN committed to the *Joshua*-class designs almost immediately after joining the Alliance, well before the completion of their first locally produced capital ship in 1908.

The *Joshua*-class destroyers were constructed at a time when Grayson designers and shipbuilders were still getting themselves up to speed with the technological changes the alliance brought to Grayson shipbuilding. Notionally they were built in two flights, with Flight II units carrying an additional point defense cluster in each broadside, more repair remotes, larger hydroponics bays, improved maintenance capability, and the myriad other upgrades experience had proved necessary to operate on remote stations with a wall of battle. In practice, the design was in a constant state of evolution as the Grayson engineers rapidly gained confidence. These constant changes made for some interesting times for *Joshua*-class crews. New hardware was frequently the only example of its type in GSN service and the only training to be had was in the simulations and technical manuals installed with the hardware. RMN and builder technical support staff did their best to be everywhere at once but these personnel have always been in short supply in Manticoran service. Any *Joshua* crew member has at least one story about how he caught himself up by "a few hundred years" with only the installed simulations and his own wits to help him.

The GSN never had enough of these hulls to go around, and even while almost every single one of them was assigned to a screening squadron, they were constantly stripped off for independent scouting duties. With the outbreak of the war and the emergency construction programs, the GSN laid down another two squadrons. As screening units, they were quite capable, though most of their additional defenses came at the cost of cruise endurance, offensive capability, and other factors valued in independent command. As good a "first effort" as seen in any navy, construction tapered off as the *Paul* class began coming out of the distributed yards.

Paul-class destroyer
(*for specification, see RMN Roland-class DD*)
Number Built: 17+
Service Life: 1921–present

The *Paul of Tarsis*-class destroyer (known in service as the *Paul* class) is similar in design and identical in mission to the Manticoran *Roland*-class DD. Built from the same base plans, the unique preferences of the GSN produced several subtle differences between the two classes. The most notable internal difference is the split berthing that the GSN has built into all of their new construction to accommodate mixed-gender crews. Most other changes are minor, reflecting differences in sensor and electronics between the two navies.

Operationally, the GSN expects to use these ships in much the same way the RMN uses the *Rolands*. They have the stowage for extended operations for deep-raid or commerce protection missions. This represents a change for Grayson destroyer doctrine, one made possible only by the tremendous increase in mass and volume of these units.

LIGHT CRUISERS (CL)

Modern GSN light cruisers are the direct descendants of the "cruiser" type of hyper-capable warship used by Grayson in its wars with Masada after the rediscovery of Yeltsin's Star but before the Alliance with Manticore. The larger of the two GSN hyper-capable designs, these ships were the largest locally produced units before the Alliance and served as the centerpieces of GSN combat formations during the last Masadan War.

Post-Alliance Grayson light cruisers serve as strategic scouts, commerce raiders/protectors, and screening elements for the wall of battle. These roles are often filled by destroyers in other modern navies, but the Graysons, as is typical for them, elected to go their own way. In this case, their decision was that the light cruiser was the smallest vessel they would build for extended-duration, independent operations. For that reason, Grayson CLs typically have proportionally larger hydrogen bunkers, more onboard repair facilities, and greater supply storage than their smaller DD consorts, because DDs are designed to travel with, and gain support from, the wall of battle's support train.

GSN light cruiser commands thus serve much the same role as battlecruiser commands in other services. As such, assignment to command a light cruiser is an indication to a GSN officer that he is being considered for higher positions.

Glory-class cruiser
Mass: 83,000 tons
Dimensions: 381 × 40 × 30 m
Acceleration: 519.9 G (5.098 kps²)
80% Accel: 415.9 G (4.078 kps²)
Broadside: 4M, 3L, 2CM, 3AC
Chase: 1M, 1L, 1AC
Number Built: 1
Service Life: 1869–1903

Referred to simply as a "cruiser" when commissioned, GNS *Glory* was the first power projection unit of what most consider the modern GSN. Boasting an inertial compensator of home-built design and a true broadside missile battery of first-generation impeller-drive shipkillers, she was the largest and most powerful ship in the Navy for over a decade.

By the standards of the rest of the galaxy, she was hopelessly antiquated even before she was launched, with short-ranged ship-killing contact nuclear missiles, rocket-propelled counter-missiles, autocannon point defense, and a myopic beam armament. However, by the standards of the war with Masada, she was a powerful ship, well suited for duty as the system defense flagship for Yeltsin's Star and finally capable of true power projection into Endicott.

Damaged during the First Battle of Yeltsin's Star, *Glory* was decommissioned shortly after the first of the Alliance Technological Exchange program ships began to arrive.

Austin Grayson-class cruiser
Mass: 91,750 tons
Dimensions: 394 × 41 × 32 m
Acceleration: 519.4 G (5.094 kps²)
80% Accel: 415.6 G (4.075 kps²)
Broadside: 5M, 3L, 3CM, 3AC
Chase: 1M, 1L, 1CM, 1AC
Number Built: 2
Service Life: 1880–1904

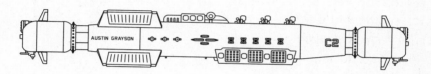

GNS *Austin Grayson* and GNS *Covington* comprised the remaining two indigenously built cruisers in service at the start of the Alliance. While both are listed as the same class, several minor differences appeared in layout and weapons fit between the two vessels, as each of the three light cruisers in GSN service was rotated through refits at least once during its operational lifetime. Weapons fit was similar to GNS *Glory*, and equally obsolete by the standards of the rest of the galaxy at the time.

Austin Grayson was the flagship of the GSN and was lost in the initial Masadan ambush at the First Battle of Yeltsin's Star, while GNS *Covington* survived the battle only to be decommissioned by necessity along with *Glory* when the first modern units began to arrive from Manticore. *Covington* remains a museum ship in close orbit over Grayson at the time of this writing.

Matthias-class light cruiser
(for specification, see RMN Courageous-class CL)
Number Purchased: 9
Service Life: 1902–1921 PD

RMN *Courageous*-class light cruisers were presented to the GSN as part of the Technological Exchange Program on a similar basis to the *Noblesse*-class destroyers. Given the number of interoperable parts and the remaining stock of Mk50 shipkillers carried by both classes, there were plenty of spares to maintain them.

The *Matthias* class served the GSN well early in the war, when they were desperate for light units; but, like the *Jacob*-class destroyers, these were reassigned to the Polar Reaction Squadrons for System Defense Command by the time of Operation Buttercup. Three of the class were converted to interim early-warning system ships pending the completion of the GSN's first large space surveillance platforms. All remaining units were placed in reserve by 1917 before complete decommissioning and materials reclamation in 1921.

David-class light cruiser
Mass: 130,500 tons
Dimensions: 443 x 46 x 35 m
Acceleration: 517.6 G (5.076 kps²)
80% Accel: 414.1 G (4.061 kps²)
Broadside: 6M, 5L, 6CM, 4PD
Chase: 2M, 1G, 3CM, 3PD
Number Built: 18
Service Life: 1904–present

The *David* class was the locally built variant of the Manticoran *Apollo* class, though benefiting from two decades of miniaturization advances and influenced by the Grayson's stubborn refusal to uncritically accept any shipbuilding concepts even from its closest ally. Externally, the two classes are similar, though the

Graysons replaced one broadside laser mount with a sixth missile tube and upgraded the chase energy mounts to grasers. Hull space constraints would not allow the total missile loadout to be increased, so each launcher dropped from twenty to sixteen missiles. The *David*-class light cruisers were much better armed than the *Joshua* class, but the defenses were not much better than those of the smaller ship. This fact was not lost on the critics of the platform, especially those who thought all small classes should be effective screening units first, with less emphasis given to other duties.

The *David* class, however, really shone operationally in the other independent duties to which the GSN would not assign destroyers. Its defenses were more than adequate for its primary roles of commerce protection, commerce raiding, anti-piracy, and picket work; and its operational endurance was superior, even for a light cruiser. The GSN has worked the few units of the *David* class hard over their lifetimes. By 1921, almost every senior commander had spent a few years of his early career in command of one of these ships on one of Grayson's few detached duty stations.

Glory-class light cruiser
(for specification, see RMN Valiant-class CL)
Number Purchased: 7
Service Life: 1906–present

The growth of the GSN's wall of battle consumed more local shipyard production capacity than was predicted. This led to particular difficulties in procuring lighter units, as the new battle fleet would create a desperate need for strategic scouting. Over the course of two years, seven new *Valiant*-class light cruisers were purchased from Manticore. The *Valiant* was a powerful unit for its time, well suited for deep raids and strikes, part and parcel of the prewar doctrine of the RMN. Its heavy broadside and average defenses are not quite as well suited to the missions the GSN prefers for light units, but the ships have still been well received. All of the *Glory*-class ships still in service are currently serving in the Protector's Own.

Neophyte-class light cruiser
Mass: 145,000 tons
Dimensions: 459 x 48 x 37 m
Acceleration: 516.9 G (5.069 kps^2)
80% Accel: 413.5 G (4.055 kps^2)
Broadside: 8M, 5L, 6CM, 4PD
Chase: 2M, 1L, 3CM, 2PD
Number Captured: 2
Service Life: 1913–1916

Two of the Havenite *Frigate*-class light cruisers were bought into GSN service after Admiral Harrington returned from Cerberus with her fleet of captures, and both were assigned to the newly created Protector's Own squadron shortly after arrival. While cutting-edge technology for Havenite warships at the time, Grayson found little to learn from the designs, and unlike the *Warlord* and *Mars* classes brought with them, these light cruisers had limited ammunition stowage and no interoperability of weapons between them and their larger brethren.

Both ships were relegated to training service shortly after being replaced with new-build *David*-class units and were decommissioned soon thereafter. Their hulks were towed out to the asteroid belt and used as target vessels during workups of the *Paul*-class destroyers.

Disciple-class light cruiser
(for specification, see RMN Avalon-class CL)
Number Built: 52+
Service Life: 1919–present

The *Disciple*-class light cruiser is almost a clone of the RMN *Avalon* class, locally built by the GSN. With numerous small differences in internal space allocation and electronics, the basic weapons fit between the two classes is identical. This faithful GSN reproduction of a Manticoran design is not so much a case of the GSN changing its design philosophy as of the RMN changing its own, as the RMN has begun to follow the GSN lead in terms of the "all graser broadside." Production of the new class was just beginning when the war resumed in 1919, and the planned first flight was doubled in size as part of the emergency measures.

While the *Disciple* class as a whole has seen limited combat, individual units have more than proved their worth, both as independent operators and as members of the screen. Their off-bore capability in particular has been well received, given that it has multiplied their effective broadside.

The *Disciple* class also has the distinction of being the first of the smaller GSN warships to be built from the keel out to handle mixed crews, with space set aside for gender-segregated berthing facilities in keeping with Grayson social practices.

HEAVY CRUISERS (CA)

The GSN built its first heavy cruisers in the light of the realization that their new Havenite opponents had something the Masadans lacked: a dependence on an extended, potentially vulnerable trading network. The GSN recognized that their light cruisers were capable of conducting commerce attacks but wanted a platform capable of operating for long periods of time hundreds of light-years away from support. The same endurance characteristics that enabled heavy cruisers to hunt down merchantmen on distant stations naturally helped them convoy merchantmen to and from those same stations.

Battlecruisers could have been used, as in the RMN, but the desired characteristics of a deep raiding battlecruiser differed substantially from the fleet support battlecruisers the GSN already had in mind and would have necessitated the construction of two different classes. At this point, the necessary number of yards big enough to produce the desired number of battlecruisers of two types simply were not available when the need arose. Making a virtue of necessity, the Grayson heavy cruiser has thus come to fulfill much the same role as the battlecruiser in Manticoran service and has acquired the same romantic aura: long-range independent deep-space commands both beyond help and absolute master of their own destiny.

Berilynko-class heavy cruiser
(for specification, see RMN Warrior-class CA)
Number Donated: 3
Service Life: 1904–present

These three old Manticoran *Warrior*-class heavy cruisers marked for disposal were diverted to Grayson in 1904 as part of the Technological Exchange Program. While these ships appear to be named after a Grayson steading, they are actually named after a famous army general who made notable contributions during the Civil War.

Analysis of both Manticoran and Grayson experience with laser heads clearly demonstrated that the primary shipkiller had become the missile, but the traditional energy-range combat scenario clearly could not be ruled out, as Captain Honor Harrington's engagement at Blackbird Base and against the Masadan battlecruiser *Thunder of God* indicated. Both the GSN Office of Shipbuilding and Doctrine and the Office of Training Command concluded that the high volume of fire which had been a major requirement in pre-laser head capital ship design had become far less relevant than sheer hitting power, however. Missiles had become even more effective at knocking down sidewalls before the energy engagement, improving targeting resolution and capability during the energy engagement, which reduced the need to saturate the potential target zone in order to secure hits. This led to the conclusion that the graser was a superior choice for shipboard energy mounts, despite the weapon's mass and volume penalties in comparison to the laser, given its greater destructiveness and range, and the Grayson Space Navy conducted extensive simulations to test that conclusion. The simulation analysis was validated in operational practice and played a major role in the GSN's preference for an all-graser broadside armament in everything from cruisers to superdreadnoughts.

Alvarez-class heavy cruiser

Mass: 319,500 tons
Dimensions: 531 × 64 × 54 m
Acceleration: 508.6 G (4.988 kps²)
80% Accel: 406.9 G (3.99 kps²)
Broadside: 14M, 5G, 8CM, 8PD
Chase: 3M, 1G, 5CM, 5PD
Number Built: 12
Service Life: 1904–present

The *Alvarez*-class CA is similar to a *Star Knight*-class CA, with specific GSN changes, most notably the all-graser broadside offensive beam armament. An even larger missile broadside and armor features better designed to counter laser heads also figure in the class' larger mass. The emphasis on the missile as opposed to beam combat is taken by some as an indication that the GSN was quicker than the RMN to recognize the family of technologies which, combined, ultimately revolutionized space warfare during the Manticore-Havenite Wars. This view gives the GSN too much credit. The *Star Knight*, of course, is widely recognized now to be a revolutionary but transitional design, and the Grayson designers had the advantage of the better part of a full decade in deployable technology, plus the benefit of the hard-won combat experience both they and the Royal Manticoran Navy had amassed since the Manticoran class was first designed. The *Alvarez* design merely advances down the path *Star Knight* began, incorporating far heavier grasers in her reduced energy armament and using individually more capable point defense laser clusters.

The *Alvarez*-class CAs were the first locally built Grayson heavy cruisers and the largest mobile space structures the Graysons had built at the time of their completion. The importance of the heavy cruiser in Grayson service, similar to the RMN's battlecruisers, makes the choice to name this class after a foreign officer a poignant reminder of the respect with which Commander Alvarez's sacrifice is viewed.

Alliance-class heavy cruiser
(for specification, see RMN Star Knight-class CA)
Number Purchased: 5
Service Life: 1904–present

These were *Star Knight*-class ships directly purchased from Manticoran builders. They were largely unmodified in Grayson service and often served in mixed squadrons with the *Alvarez* class.

Protector Adrian-class heavy cruiser
(for specification, see RMN Edward Saganami-class CA)
Number Built: 36
Service Life: 1908–present

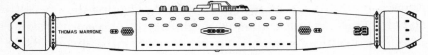

Originally on the books as simply the *Alvarez II*, this class was formally named the *Protector Adrian* class once the lead unit was commissioned. The RMN learned a lot from Grayson's experiences with the *Alvarez* class, and the design for the *Saganami/Adrian* classes was a joint RMN/GSN project. These units represent in many ways the peak of cooperation between the RMN and GSN shipbuilders and were identical to the RMN *Edward Saganami* class in most respects. They are the largest production run of heavy cruisers in Grayson history at the time of this writing.

As built, these vessels corrected the biggest problem that the GSN had with the *Alvarez/Star Knight* line in operational service: their acceleration. Improved compensators, and the more powerful nodes required by a larger hull improved acceleration by nearly ninety gravities. This change shifted the balance of GSN heavy cruiser deployments, with the older *Alvarez* CAs moving into convoy escort roles and the Flight II's forming the bulk of independent deep-raiding squadrons toward the end of the war. Remarkably, the number of GSN cruiser losses decreased during this period, due almost entirely to the nimbleness of the *Adrians*.

Proselyte-class heavy cruiser

Mass: 477,250 tons
Dimensions: 607 x 73 x 61 m
Acceleration: 501.1 G (4.914 kps²)
80% Accel: 400.9 G (3.931 kps²)
Broadside: 11M, 12L, 12CM, 10PD
Chase: 3M, 3G, 4CM, 6PD
Number Captured: 4
Service Life: 1913–present

These four *Mars*-class heavy cruisers were part of the StateSec forces that Admiral Harrington captured during her escape from the Cerberus system. While too antiquated to serve in a frontline role in an age of multi-drive missiles and too heavily built to be economical to refit, the four together were renamed the *Proselyte* class and have served for several years in the Protector's Own.

Larger and more modern than any of the early captured specimens of Havenite hardware, they have reportedly received special Grayson-designed inertial compensator upgrades. This, ironically, makes them the only units of the *Mars* class to receive the necessary compensation hardware to make use of the full power capability of their impeller drives. Substantial performance gains have been made, though Grayson technicians report that the ships remain difficult to maintain. Unfortunately, most of the captured hardware consists of early production run units and extensive computer modeling and new plant operating software were required to bring the ships' notorious Goshawk-Three fusion reactors up to GSN acceptance specifications. Nothing short of complete replacement could render the reliability of the plants completely satisfactory, however, and the expense has been too great up to this point. In the meantime, the fusion plants are reportedly known as "the Bombs" by their crews.

Burleson-class heavy cruiser
(for specification, see RMN Saganami-C-class CA)
Number Built: 17+
Service Life: 1921–present

Named for one of the first GSN captains to conduct an attack on the Endicott System, this class is an indigenously produced version of the RMN's *Saganami-C*-class CA. While there have been some positive reports from the Manticorans on this design, none of the *Burlesons* have yet seen combat.

BATTLECRUISERS (BC)

GSN doctrine uses battlecruisers very differently from the RMN. This is one area where the two nations' disparate strategic and operational needs clearly show in their tactical decisions. Independent of the need to protect a far-flung trading network and desperate to add mass to their wall of battle, the GSN initially saw battlecruisers as the centerpieces of heavy strategic and tactical scouting/antiscouting formations. As envisioned, battlecruiser missions included coordinating subordinate formations of cruisers and destroyers, concealing the exact makeup of the wall of battle using their powerful electronic warfare suites, hunting down and destroying enemy scouting forces attempting to determine that formation, and finally thickening the wall's offensive or defensive firepower after battle had been joined. Twenty years of warfare have not fundamentally altered this doctrine, though the introduction of the pod battlecruiser has been seen by some as a move in a new direction, towards short, intense combat and limited individual survivability.

Tomkin-class battlecruiser
(for specification, see RMN Redoubtable-class BC)
Number Purchased: 16
Service Life: 1903–present

The RMN donated two full squadrons of old *Redoubtables* between 1903 and 1906 PD to bolster Grayson's local defense forces. Like the smaller ships provided at the same time, these were refitted with modern electronics before delivery. Experience with the mixed laser/graser offensive energy battery in simulation and GSN fleet exercises helped form the Grayson opinion that mixed energy armaments were not optimal for their uses, in light of their requirement for battlecruisers to augment the wall and conduct heavy screening duties. In the Grayson view, quickly overwhelming a smaller target's sidewalls with massed graser fire was more valuable than the theoretical antimissile capabilities of a dual-purpose laser weapon unable to fire fast enough to repel the salvo densities common in wall-of-battle engagements in even the early 1900s.

Like all imported ships, these were renamed upon delivery. GSN battlecruisers are named for deceased admirals and war heroes: Admiral Isaiah Tomkin died repelling the first Masadan hypership invasion in the last century.

Courvosier-class battlecruiser

Mass: 903,750 tons
Dimensions: 719 × 91 × 81 m
Acceleration: 514.7 G (5.048 kps²)
80% Accel: 411.8 G (4.038 kps²)
Broadside: 26M, 8G, 16CM, 16PD
Chase: 4M, 2G, 6CM, 6PD
Number Built: 47
Service Life: 1904–present

The *Courvosier* class is in many ways a clone of the RMN's *Reliant* class. It is somewhat larger, mounts a somewhat heavier broadside, and has greater defensive capabilities. Like other GSN designs, it cut the beam broadside almost in half in terms of mounts, but those that remained were grasers with larger plasma beam emitter diameters and more powerful grav-lenses than previously installed on a battlecruiser in any navy.

The *Courvosier* class was in many ways as revolutionary for a battlecruiser as the Manticoran *Star Knight* was for a heavy cruiser.

Uncompromisingly optimized for what was then regarded as high-volume missile combat, these ships have proven themselves to be powerful units, and they have clearly set the pattern for the GSN and the Alliance as a whole when it comes to smaller combatants. Although they have become much more vulnerable in an era of pod-based missile salvoes, they have served well throughout the war. With the resumption of hostilities, an emergency construction program ordered another four squadrons of this well-tried, reliable class, the last of which was delivered in late 1920.

The lead ship of this class, GNS *Raoul Courvosier*, was built with a slightly reduced broadside to free up mass for a flag staff and full-scale fleet CIC and communications network. She served for several years as the flagship of the Grayson Space Navy until eventually supplanted by GNS *Vengeance*, the first of the refitted *Duquesne*-class superdreadnoughts.

Hill-class battlecruiser
(for specification, see RMN Reliant-class BC)
Number Built: 3
Service Life: 1905–present

Like the *Star Knight* and *Redoubtable* classes, a few *Reliants* were purchased from the Star Kingdom outright while the Grayson shipyards retooled to produce large modern warships. The trio has been seen as the "odd men out" in Grayson service. They tend to operate alongside the *Courvosiers* most of the time, given their similar performance characteristics in missile combat, yet their mixed laser/graser beam fit is ill-suited to GSN doctrine. All three of these ships are attached to the Protector's Own Squadron where their unique characteristics are closer to the nature of their operational deployments. These ships are typically and (for Grayson) uniquely often employed as flagships for small independent detachments.

Convert-class battlecruiser

Mass: 918,750 tons
Dimensions: 723 x 92 x 82 m
Acceleration: 487.4 G (4.78 kps²)
80% Accel: 389.9 G (3.824 kps²)
Broadside: 26M, 6L, 6G, 16CM, 12PD
Chase: 6M, 2G, 6CM, 6PD
Number Captured: 5
Service Life: 1913–present

Five of these units, all older first-generation *Warlords*, came back from Cerberus and were taken into service with the Protector's Own Squadron. Along with the ex-*Mars*-class units and the material they brought along with them, the GSN had enough spares to keep these ships operational, though they are decidedly second-class units today and are earmarked for early retirement.

Courvosier II-class pod battlecruiser

Mass: 1,763,500 tons
Dimensions: 817 × 118 × 110 m
Acceleration: 678.4 G (6.653 kps²)
80% Accel: 542.8 G (5.323 kps²)
Broadside: 6M, 6G, 26CM, 24PD
Fore: 4M, 3G, 8CM, 12PD
Aft: 4MP, 4CM, 12PD
Pods: 360
Number Built: 40+
Service Life: 1919–present

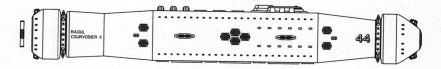

The *Courvosier II* class is a Grayson pod battlecruiser, the first unit of its type developed by any Navy. Its conventional missile broadside is reduced by eighty percent to allow it to mount superdreadnought-sized energy weapons. Under GSN doctrine, the massive salvo size of the pod battlecruiser serves to augment the all-important first salvo in an engagement, after which the BC(P)s retreat to less exposed positions in the formation. The ships then support the wall's missile defense and continue to augment its offensive salvoes while coordinating the hunt for opposing scout platforms throughout the engagement. In more recent fleet problems, the GSN has reportedly experimented with tying CLACs and BCs together to provide improved protection for both.

Almost double the mass of previous battlecruiser classes, they are also among the first Grayson units to benefit from the wholesale use of automation to reduce crew size and can operate with as few as three hundred spacers. In addition to their central missile cores, these ships also mount broadside missile tubes.

The GSN has been criticized for the decision to retain broadside mounts as an unusual act of conservatism on its part which compromises the pod-laying function, and this criticism would appear to be justified. It does, however, provide at least some limited self-defense missile capacity following exhaustion of the type's limited pod capacity as well as a backup in the event of a mission kill of the pod core. Development of the ability to fire off-bore missile from broadside tubes has also allowed broadside fire to be integrated with pod salvoes, and Grayson practice has been to use the broadside weapons to augment and replenish EW platforms used to aid in penetrating enemy antimissile defenses.

LAC CARRIERS (CLAC)

While there is no doubt that early experience with the prototype HMS *Minotaur* drove some of its design decisions, the GSN began to reevaluate LAC carrier (CLAC) design with its customary independence by looking at commercial impeller drive asteroid mining operation ships. These ships hosted numerous subordinate mining craft and were a natural place to look for inspiration when designing a LAC-carrying ship. The GSN designers quickly realized, however, that a large mobile hangar could not reasonably be made survivable and decided early on that the LAC carrier had no place in the wall of battle. Thus, Grayson doctrine declares that a GSN CLAC's primary offensive weaponry is carried by its LACs, and the offensive armament on planned Manticoran designs is wasted space. They designed their first and only CLAC to date with this doctrine in mind.

Minotaur-class LAC carrier
(for specification, see RMN Minotaur CLAC)
Number Purchased: 6
Serice Life: 1914–present

While the GSN was heavily involved in the original design of the *Shrike*-class LACs, they let the RMN take the lead on initial carrier design. Six *Minotaur*-class carriers were ordered from 1914–1915 PD while the *Covington* class was still working up.

Covington-class LAC carrier
Mass: 6,244,250 tons
Dimensions: 1135 × 189 × 175 m
Acceleration: 476.7 G (4.675 kps²)
80% Accel: 381.4 G (3.74 kps²)
Broadside: 30CM, 28PD
Chase: 12CM, 10PD
LAC Bays: 124
Number Built: 30+
Service Life: 1915–present

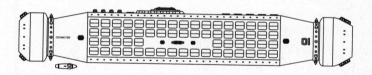

While only slightly more massive than a *Minotaur*, foregoing all offensive missile and energy armament allows the *Covington* class to carry almost twenty-five percent more LACs. The Office of Shipbuilding decided that the increased operational flexibility was desirable, even if doctrine required two squadrons of LACs to be held back to protect the carrier. The professional disagreement between GSN and Manticoran designers applies only to offensive armament, as the *Covingtons* retain defensive capabilities fully comparable to the Manticoran counterparts and, if necessary, can protect themselves quite well.

In 1917 PD, several of the Flight I *Covingtons* underwent minor refits to their ammunition handling machinery to rearm and service the new *Katana*-class LACs with the Mk9 viper anti-LAC missile. The Flight II units are being constructed from the keel out with new ammunition handling machinery to more efficiently store both the shipkillers and counter-missiles for the *Shrikes* as well as the Vipers carried by the *Katanas*.

SUPERDREADNOUGHTS (SD)

The GSN is not unique in using its superdreadnoughts for one thing and one thing only: controlling the space around its stars and the stars of those who would oppose it. As with their battlecruiser force, the differences between Manticoran and Grayson strategic problems can be seen in several areas. Lacking numerous wormhole termini and distant stations to protect, the GSN opted for concentrated combat power in its purest form. The GSN is alone amongst Alliance space forces in never having built battleships or dreadnoughts. Their first true power-projection force consisted entirely of captured, donated, and newly built superdreadnoughts.

Manticore's Gift-class superdreadnought
(Note: Specification reflects base class only)
Mass: 7,187,250 tons
Dimensions: 1305 x 189 x 176 m
Acceleration: 417.5 G (4.094 kps^2)
80% Accel: 334 G (3.275 kps^2)
Broadside: 36M, 12L, 12G, 28CM, 24PD
Chase: 10M, 4L, 6G, 12CM, 12PD
Number Captured: 28
Service Life: 1906–present

The original eleven units of this class were *DuQuesne*-class super-dreadnoughts captured at the Third Battle of Yeltsin, turned over to the GSN by Admiral White Haven and heavily refitted on a crash basis, using a mixture of cannibalized parts from wrecked

Havenite ships and Alliance equipment. As a result, their specifications differ from the original People's Navy configurations, and the haphazard nature of their refits resulted in eleven unique units, each with a slightly different weapons fit.

The units that survived the Fourth Battle of Yeltsin were refitted to a more consistent standard between 1910 and 1911 as the early *Steadholder Denevski*-class SDs were being commissioned.

Seventeen more ex-Havenite superdreadnoughts were added in 1917 PD when the remainder in RMN service were decommissioned by the Janacek Admiralty. Despite tensions between the two navies, Second Lord of the Admiralty Houseman was more than willing to defray expenses in that year's budget by selling them to Grayson for scrap value.

These ships are remarkable in that their spacious designs made them relatively easy for the Graysons to repair, maintain, and modify, especially after they had been refitted with compact Alliance equipment. As a result, they frequently act as testbeds for new GSN equipment. The hulls still in service have been split equally between Systems Command for use as testing platforms and System Defense Command as part of the ready reserve squadrons.

Steadholder Denevski-class superdreadnought

Mass: 8,352,250 tons
Dimensions: 1372 × 199 × 185 m
Acceleration: 402 G (3.942 kps²)
80% Accel: 321.6 G (3.154 kps²)
Broadside: 37M, 34G, 28CM, 30PD
Chase: 9M, 8G, 10CM, 10PD
Number Built: 22
Service Life: 1908–present

The *Steadholder Denevski*-class superdreadnought represents a uniquely Grayson take on capital ship design, much like their versions of smaller ships. The original pattern was the Manticoran *Gryphon* class which, at the time, was the most advanced superdreadnought in service anywhere in space. The most notable Grayson change included the complete elimination of all lasers on the broadside, in favor of additional grasers.

Built with the advantage of several years of battle experience, these ships were designed with a full understanding of the combat environment they were likely to face. They are some of the best-protected ships in space, with area and point missile defenses fully adequate to the pre-pod laser head threat. Intense study of Havenite weapon characteristics allowed the armor designers to take full advantage of face mirroring techniques designed to better protect against the known X-ray wavelengths.

Incorporation of new technology as a result of all this recent combat experience had at least one unintended consequence. The construction of two of the *Denevskis* was delayed by eight months when critical parts were diverted to meet construction deadlines for the first unit of the *Honor Harrington*-class pod superdreadnought. Along with the RMN *Gryphon* class, they are considered the best pre-pod SD design in existence, although they have been relegated increasingly to secondary duties, particularly since the Havenite acquisition of multidrive missile capability.

Benjamin the Great-class command superdreadnought

Mass: 8,517,750 tons
Dimensions: 1381 × 200 × 186 m
Acceleration: 468.3 G (4.592 kps²)
80% Accel: 374.6 G (3.674 kps²)
Broadside: 38M, 32G, 30CM, 34PD
Chase: 9M, 8G, 10CM, 10PD
Number Built: 3
Service Life: 1911–present

This class was originally designed as an advanced variant of the *Denevski* class, but with the secret SD(P) program already starting up, the ships were modified after laydown into dedicated command ships. The hull was extended an additional nine meters, and two grasers were removed from the broadsides to accommodate an advanced command deck, room for flag staff, larger and more sensitive sensor arrays, more extensive communication equipment, and a significant increase in active defense.

While they have, arguably, the finest flag deck of any ship in commission anywhere and are still highly sought after in the GSN, they are beginning to show their age, and dedicated command variants of *Harrington*-class pod superdreadnoughts have begun to supplant them.

Protector-class superdreadnought
(for specification, see RMN Victory-class SD)
Total Purchased: 34
Service Life: 1917–present

This class consists of all of the remaining RMN *Victory*-class ships scheduled for disposal after the First Manticore-Havenite War. Protector Benjamin took a personal interest in the acquisition of these units because he was convinced that the RMN under the Janacek administration would find itself critically short of capital ships if hostilities resumed. As with the Havenite superdreadnoughts in Manticoran service, Janacek was convinced that maintaining these ships was a waste and was more than happy to sell them to Grayson for their material reclamation value.

The original intention was to place the ships immediately in mothballs as a ready reserve for both Navies, since the GSN lacked sufficient crews to man them at the time. However, when the war resumed and the Janacek Admiralty collapsed, instead of transferring any back to the RMN, the Office of Personnel and BuPers arranged to loan Manticoran crews as they came back from civilian life to supplement the GSN crews who were themselves returning to active duty. While all of these ships officially fall under the GSN, operationally they are part of the Alliance fleet and serve under RMN and GSN command as necessary.

POD SUPERDREADNOUGHTS (SD(P))

While the Grayson Space Navy was the first fleet to place pod-laying superdreadnoughts in commission, the SD(P) actually originated as a top-secret project of the Royal Manticoran Navy.

The GSN, lacking a huge long-term investment in a traditional wall of battle and already engaged in a revolutionary rethinking of established tactical doctrine, were more able and more willing than even the RMN to quickly adopt a technology that would radically challenge current practices. In short, the GSN had nothing to lose and everything to gain. Moreover, their procedures for authorizing new construction were more flexible and adaptive than Manticore's because they had so recently created a modern fleet effectively out of nothing. The combination of those factors allowed the GSN to lay down the very first "podnoughts" and to complete its first units a full year ahead of Manticore. This speed in turn pushed the pace of Manticoran construction of its own *Medusa* class.

The essential technological elements enabling viable podnoughts are the laser head, the multi-drive missile, and the missile pod itself. Operationally, the pod superdreadnought fulfills much the same role as the superdreadnought. It simply relies on a different main battery weapon to control the space around it.

Some theorists regard the retention of energy weapon batteries as wasteful, given the primacy of missile warfare. In the Alliance's eyes, however, it provides a degree of security in the admittedly unlikely event of an enemy attaining energy-range in an "ambush" scenario, as well as providing at least limited ship-to-ship combat capability once the SD(P)'s ammunition has been exhausted. In addition, it is seen as providing a highly useful anti-infrastructure and space-to-ground capability. Expenditures of missiles against infrastructure targets are wasteful, less precise, and carry more risk of collateral damage than energy weapon fire. Additionally, the frequency and power of a graser beam give it substantial through-atmosphere capability against ground targets once a ship controls the high orbitals. Kinetic strike weapons are, of course, preferred because high-power space-to-ground beams require direct line of sight to the target. The ability to select the yield of a graser strike, however, has proven useful.

Harrington-class pod superdreadnought

Mass: 8,629,250 tons
Dimensions: 1387 × 201 × 187 m
Acceleration: 498.5 G (4.889 kps²)
80% Accel: 398.8 G (3.911 kps²)
Broadside: 32M, 22G, 54CM, 52PD
Fore: 10M, 8G, 18CM, 22PD
Aft: 6MP, 6G, 18CM, 22PD
Pods: 492 Mk11/798 Mk17
Number Built: 104
Service Life: 1913–present

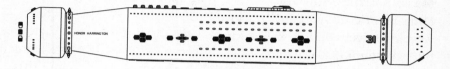

The *Harrington* class is the Grayson counterpart of the RMN's *Medusa* class. In addition to a huge increase in offensive firepower, it is far more automated than pre-pod superdreadnoughts, requiring smaller crews. The chassis and pod rails are identical to those of the *Medusa* class, but the broadside and chase armament reflect the GSN preference. While the RMN still includes a mix of lasers and grasers, the GSN accepts fewer, but more powerful, grasers and more missile launchers. This power actually improves the utility of the broadside batteries in their secondary space-to-ground role, in addition to the anti-shipping role. The benefits of this arrangement were not lost on the RMN, which subsequently adopted it for its follow-on *Invictus*-class pod-layers.

As with LAC carriers, the professional difference of opinion between Manticoran and Grayson designers is largely limited to offensive armament, with the defensive armament of the *Harrington* class being identical to the *Medusa*'s.

GNS *Honor Harrington*, the lead ship in this class, had the distinction of being the galaxy's first warship designed from the keel out as a pod-layer, commissioned one year to the day after the reported death of Admiral Harrington. The GSN's Office of Shipbuilding actually has a policy forbidding the naming of ships after living persons, which produced some consternation after Harrington's return from Cerberus. An official exception was adopted and the class retained the name, much to the her reported embarrassment.

During the interwar years, while the Janacek Admiralty was rapidly cutting back on the RMN's own SD(P) construction, the GSN was accelerating its program, a fact that proved prescient after the Haven sneak attack when the Alliance's "junior" member had more of these ships in service than Manticore.

Harrington II-class pod superdreadnought
Mass: 8,779,250 tons
Dimensions: 1395 × 202 × 188 m
Acceleration: 561.9 G (5.511 kps^2)
80% Accel: 449.5 G (4.408 kps^2)
Broadside: 24M, 24G, 64CM, 62PD
Fore: 12M, 6G, 16CM, 24PD Aft: 6MP, 6G, 16CM, 24PD
Pods: 984 Mk17
Number Built: 61+
Service Life: 1919–present

This design is similar to the *Invictus* class and, like the *Invictus*, it carries a Keyhole II platform and can launch Apollo missiles. Unlike the *Invictus* class, however, this design sacrifices some pod-core volume in order to retain internal missile tubes on the broadside. The RMN built the *Invictus* with only beam mounts and no integral missile launchers at all, but the GSN was concerned by the potential for catastrophic loss of combat capability if a single attacking missile successfully completed a stern-aspect attack that breached and crippled the pod core. Internal armored doors in the pod core were considered but were found to slow down pod deployment, consume mass, and complicate the arrangement of engineering systems in the after taper to an unacceptable degree. Hence, the GSN gave the second flight *Harringtons* internal tubes and modest ammunition storage for them.

The Grayson Army

The Grayson Army can trace its roots back to 1337 PD, the date young Benjamin Mayhew rallied the shattered remnants of the other Steadholders' Guards in Mackenzie Steading and forged them into the army that defeated the Faithful. When the Constitution was ratified after the war was over, those units formed the core of the Grayson Army, operating under the direct command of the Protector.

Prior to the fourteenth century, each Steadholder's Guard had owed personal and direct allegiance to its own Steadholder, answering to no higher authority and hence representing a perpetual and serious check to any Protector's power. Benjamin's creation of a unified Grayson Army was thus also intended as part of a comprehensive package of reductions in the Steadholders' collective power vis-à-vis the Sword. The next reduction in their power was to limit a Steadholder to a maximum of fifty personal armsmen, referred to as the Steadholder's Own. The older Steadholders' Guards continued to exist, at least in theory, but now consisted of those fifty armsmen plus all members of the Steading's police and emergency services and included no regular military units at all. The Steadholder's Own, despite its small size, remains extraordinarily powerful, as its members are exempt from the legal consequences of any act performed at their Steadholder's order; the other members of the Steadholder's Guard, however, are not. In addition, all member of the Steadholder's

505

Guard other than the Steadholder's Own hold regular commissions or enlisted ranks in the Grayson Army as well, allowing the Protector to summon all of them to active Army service in the event of a conflict.

In addition, while a Steadholder remains in direct command of any other Army units based in his Steading, by longstanding policy the Army has made an effort to rotate units, and avoid situations where the majority of personnel in a given Army unit come from the Steading in which the unit is based. This assures that, even with the possible defection of the Steadholder's Guard, the Protector will still be able to take control of the garrisoned troops. In addition, the oaths of all members of the Grayson Army and Navy are directly to the Protector, whose military authority is supreme and overrides that of any Steadholder. Thus Steadholders act as the Protector's deputies and their orders may be countermanded by him at any time.

The primary mission of the Grayson Army has always been planetary defense, with secondary focus on the traditional roles of emergency services, disaster relief and occasional police duties. Prior to the Manticoran Alliance, few Army units served aboard regular Navy ships, though some specialized units were trained for boarding actions and were carried on specialized transports.

When Manticore began providing the GSN with warships, the Navy realized that it was unable to provide the troops necessary to fill the traditional role of the RMMC onboard a Manticoran warship. Instead, they revised the berthing arrangements and duty stations to split apart the traditional roles. On-mount crew, corpsmen and damage control teams traditionally filled by Manticoran Marines were assigned to naval crew, while a much smaller core of Army troops were embarked purely as shipboard security and boarding parties. The Grayson Navy has always taken an active role in boarding parties, and the expectation was that naval troops would fill any gaps where necessary. This transition has not been without its rough spots, but overall the process has been a success.

The Army has never been tasked with force projection, heavy planetary combat or occupation duties, as until recently Grayson's only foreign policy related to Masada, and no military planner had ever seriously suggested occupation of Masada as a viable post-war policy.

Organization

The Army is primarily a light infantry force, with a large Corps of Engineers and a much smaller mechanized force. Its heavy armored cavalry units have been drawn down in the centuries since the civil war, though they have been slowly building up that capability in the last few years. In the Grayson Army, the term "mechanized" is used for any vehicle-embarked infantry, while the archaic term "cavalry" is still used for tanks. "Armored" infantry now refers to battle-armored infantry units. These differences in terminology and usage have caused some confusion with other Alliance ground forces, who typically adopt Manticoran customs, but the Grayson Army still has refused to change in this respect.

A standard Army rifle squad consists of thirteen men: sergeant, three corporals, six riflemen, one grenadier, one plasma gunner, and one tribarrel gunner. The squad is divided into three fireteams, which serve as independent maneuver units. Each fireteam is led by a corporal and carries one of the three heavy weapons. The sergeant is in overall command. A heavy weapons section consists of nine to twelve men armed with heavy crew-served tribarrels, plasma cannon, mortars or man-portable SAMs.

Three rifle squads and a command section combine to form a rifle platoon. A rifle company consists of a command element, three rifle platoons, a heavy tribarrel section and a number of additional mission-specific heavy weapons sections. The most common configuration adds a mortar section attached to the command element but antiair or antiarmor sections are added when required, all cross-attached from the battalion's heavy weapons company.

An armored infantry company is equipped with battle armor and is organized like a standard rifle company. A mechanized infantry company retains the same basic organization, but each squad is carried in two lightweight counter-grav-equipped infantry fighting vehicles.

From the battalion level on up, the organization follows Alliance standards. A command element, three rifle companies, and a heavy weapons company make up a battalion; three battalions plus a headquarters unit form a regiment. Most of the cavalry units are organized into companies of thirteen tanks and cross-assigned much like their heavy weapons companies on the battalion level where needed. Air units are likewise considered to be cavalry units and are organized accordingly.

Equipment

The Grayson Army, like the Grayson Navy, uses Manticoran equipment almost exclusively, a state of affairs that lasted up until the High Ridge cease-fire. During the interwar years, development was started on a new pulse rifle, compatible with Alliance magazines and power cells but of Grayson design. The PR-18 is a conventional design similar to the Army's pre-Alliance rifle and has seen limited service in some ground units since 1918 PD, but widespread rollout was delayed indefinitely with the resumption of hostilities. The majority of the Army's weaponry, battle dress, skinsuits and battle armor are all current Manticoran issue, with the exception of the M136 light tribarrel (no longer in service with the Royal Manticoran Army) and the Grayon Army's standard sidearm, a locally produced variant of a Manticoran civilian-designed pulser.

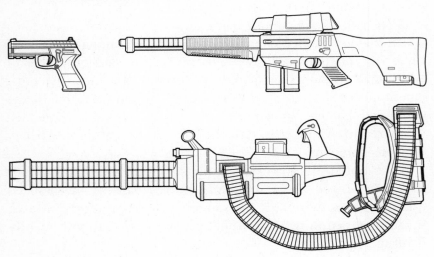

The M136 is a man-portable light tribarrel firing the standard 4 x 37 mm darts used by the PR-18 and M32 pulse rifles. Capable of a sustained rate of fire of up to two thousand rounds per minute while the ammunition in the backpack-worn ammo tank holds out, it is a devastating light support weapon. Given the weight of the weapon, it is designed to be fired from the hip with a stabilized harness, the weapon's range-finding and sighting system feeding directly into the operator's helmet display. While used in some Manticoran units, the Royal Manticoran Army has been phasing out the M136, and most of the inventory was sitting in a warehouse when the Grayson Army made their request for the weapon.

The Manticoran M11 grav tank and related variants are in service in a limited capacity, but the Army has designed its hybrid infantry fighting vehicle to meet their needs, with a design that is faster than the M13 but carries fewer troops. Stingships and trans-atmospheric transport are all Alliance issue, however, as are the pinnaces and assault shuttles operated by the Navy. The Army lacks any kind of interstellar transport, and the few times units have been deployed in support of Alliance occupations they have traveled on Manticoran hulls.

Afterword

✦ ✦ ✦ ✦ ✦

Building a Navy in the Honorverse

DAVID WEBER AND CHRISTOPHER WEUVE

Introduction

Building a navy is a complicated endeavor, whether one is bending steel or turning phrases. Doing it right depends on understanding a set of key parameters that will define the structure of the navy. These parameters can be broken into six major areas:

1. Strategic Assumptions
2. Strategic Goals
3. Fleet Missions
4. Fleet Design
5. Force Size
6. Force Management

Each of these major categories builds on the one preceding it; conversely, a failure at a later step may require rethinking earlier steps, because sometimes "you can't get there from here." Each of these areas can be broken down into sub-topics.

By answering the questions implicit in all of these topics, you can define a navy. In this essay, David Weber teams up with a naval analyst formerly on the faculty of the US Naval War College to do just that.

Strategic Assumptions

The Strategic Assumptions are the essential starting place, the place where you define the context in which a navy operates. There are two essential parts—the Security Environment (the general threats to be countered) and the Fiscal Environment (the resources available to pay for it).

The nature and laws of interstellar warfare had evolved over several centuries, following the invention of the Warshawski sail, which made interstellar commerce—and warfare—practical. The weapons available were easily capable of sterilizing any inhabited planet and, with some disturbing episodes from the early days of interstellar warfare as examples, the "rules of war" reverted to an earlier model which attempted to limit the incredible destruction "total war" could wreak upon inhabited worlds. Planetary combat power per se was effectively insignificant in the conflicts that emerged; all hinged upon the space-going naval power available to the combatants, since any fleet that controlled a planet's orbital space was, in fact, in a position to destroy any target upon that planet. The rules of war therefore required a planet to surrender when a hostile fleet had established control of the volume of space around it. If it failed to surrender, the enemy fleet was entitled to use kinetic or other bombardment against military targets on the surface of the planet until the planetary government yielded. Genocidal attack, attacks on nonmilitary targets, and "demonstration" attacks or terror attacks on population centers were forbidden, although it was accepted that in attacking military targets, collateral damage might well result to nonmilitary targets, as well. These rules were designed to protect planetary populations from indiscriminate attack, but the attacker was allowed a substantial degree of flexibility in the event that surrender was not forthcoming, on the theory that he was not obligated to suffer avoidable casualties among his own personnel if the defenders defied the accepted customs of war. The use of biological, lethal chemical, and weaponized nanotech attacks against inhabited planets were also precluded, however, and "legitimate military targets" did not create any exemptions for those weapons classes under any circumstances.

To at least a limited extent, the Solarian League (see below) also exercised a general interstellar peacekeeping function, in the form of the "Eridani Edict," to see to it that the rules of war were observed. Incorporated into an amendment to the Solarian League Constitution, the Edict obligated the Solarian League Navy to punish—effectively, to destroy—the government of any star nation guilty of genocidal attack (including any use of proscribed biological, chemical, or nanotech weapons) or planetary bombardment of nonmilitary targets. In the case of pirates or brigands guilty of the same offense, the Eridani Edict classified them as "general enemies of all mankind" and authorized SLN warships and officers to summarily execute the offenders. In the case of "rogue states," the government responsible for authorizing the Eridani violation was to be dissolved and replaced with one overseen and administered by the Office of Frontier Security until such time as the League could be confident the offense would not be repeated. Individual members of the government that authorized the violation were subject to arrest and prosecution in Solarian courts, and faced imprisonment and even execution. By 1800 PD, many non-Solarian star systems had come to the view that the Solarian League was utilizing its role as guardian and enforcer of the Eridani Edict as a tool to empower its own imperial expansion. The League, needless to say, rejected that view.

The tools of naval warfare had likewise evolved over that same period, but along a remarkably stable, incremental track. Navies were built around ships of the wall, the heaviest combatants in space, considered capable of "lying in the wall" of battle against their foreign counterparts and armed primarily with heavy, relatively short-ranged energy batteries, backed up by much lighter missile armaments. The wall was seen as the queen of battle, and it was commonly accepted that the only thing that could stop a solid, energy-armed core of dreadnoughts or superdreadnoughts was an equivalent force of the same classes of ships. Missiles were relatively ineffective against ships of the wall with properly designed and coordinated antimissile defenses, and the nature of the ships' propulsion had a marked effect on combat in general. Since the ships impeller drive created an "impeller wedge" whose stress bands were impenetrable to any known weapon, it had become traditional by the early eighteenth century PD for a wall of battle which realized it was outclassed to break off the action, roll to present the impenetrable aspect of its impeller wedges, and retreat behind that shield before taking crippling damage. As a consequence, tactics had become increasingly sterile and the art of naval warfare focused on strategies by which an opponent could be compelled to retreat rather than on tactics that might permit an opponent's destruction.

Lighter warships—battlecruisers and below—possessed lighter armor and weaker antimissile defenses and, due to their smaller size, were far less capable of absorbing damage. Those lighter classes made much greater use of missile armaments, particularly with the emergence of the laser head in approximately 1872 PD. The laser head significantly increased the damage missiles could inflict and simultaneously increased the standoff range at which they could attack their targets, making them much more difficult to intercept before they inflicted damage and thus far more dangerous. Even so, it was generally accepted in 1900 that ships of the wall remained effectively invulnerable to missile attack due to their massive defensive capabilities.

Warships smaller than destroyers (that is, generally massing less than approximately eighty thousand tons) were no longer regarded as effective combatants and were in the process of being rapidly phased out of all first-line navies. Systems and particularly valuable point targets, such as wormhole junctions or termini, might be further protected by permanently deployed fortresses (in effect, massive, slow-moving, sublight vessels with defenses and armament heavier even than ships of the wall could mount) and/or minefields (permanently deployed short-range missiles equipped with heavy contact nuclear warheads—or the more recently developed laser heads—which could be programmed to automatically attack any vessel not positively identified as friendly). Planets were seldom if ever armed, given the constraints of the accepted laws of warfare, but might be protected by orbital weapons platforms and/or minefields.

From the perspective of the Royal Manticoran Navy, the security environment (pre-1850 PD, approximately) was characterized by a large, central sphere in which the Solarian League (as the paramount economic, industrial, and military power of the explored galaxy) reigned supreme and security threats consisted primarily of pirates and the occasional "rogue state." Pirates were regarded as a police function, rather than a truly naval function, and "rogue states" (normally consisting of independent star nations within the Solarian League's sphere) were dealt with by Frontier Fleet and the Office of Frontier Security. The Solarian League was distant, overwhelming, and largely stabilizing, and as a result the Solarian League and its navy did not really factor into the SKM's security calculations.

Outside the Solarian League, the security environment was divided between a relatively small number of multi-star system polities and a very large number of single-system star nations, the result of various colonization expeditions. The Star Kingdom of Manticore lay in the area that the Solarian League had labeled "the Haven Sector," because the Republic of Haven (consisting of the Haven System itself and a handful of Haven's daughter colonies) had by the seventeenth century PD become the center of a wealthy, dynamically expanding cluster of inhabited star systems anchored and supported by access from the Solarian League via the Manticoran Wormhole Junction. Unfortunately, by the middle of the nineteenth century PD, the situation in the Haven Sector had changed considerably.

From the Star Kingdom's perspective, the significant political entities in a position to affect its security and strategic interests were, in order of size and/or military/industrial power (and exclusive of the Solarian League):

1. The People's Republic of Haven
2. The Andermani Empire
3. The Republic of Erewhon
4. The Silesian Confederacy

Taking these in reverse order, the Confederacy was, in fact, larger in both spatial volume and population than the People's Republic of 1850, but its central governing authority was essentially defunct, turning it into a "failed state" on an interstellar scale. Incapable of policing its own internal volume, it represented no direct threat to its neighbors except in so far as its weakness invited exploitation that might bring competing neighboring star nations into collision.

The Republic of Erewhon was a Solarian ally, although beginning to move away from that alliance in the face of the People's Republic's expansion and an Erewhonese perception that the Solarian League was unlikely to protect it against Havenite aggression, given the current relationship between the Solarian League and the People's Republic. Erewhon's uneasiness with the Office of Frontier Security's increasingly open encroachment on independent star nations within the League's self-defined sphere of interest also played a part in the progressive chill in Erewhon's relations with the Solarians. The Republic's military capability was restricted primarily to that of a system defense force, with a significant amount of firepower and access to current-generation, export-grade Solarian military technology, but without a significant power projection capability of its own.

The Andermani Empire, relatively removed from immediate proximity to the Star Kingdom of Manticore, was nonetheless a competitor with Manticore for influence, trade, and potential territorial expansion into the Silesian Confederacy as it crumbled. Its naval power was smaller than either the People's Republic's or the Star Kingdom's, but still significant; it had a potent military tradition; and its location on the opposite side of the SKM from the People's Republic lent its military capabilities a disproportionate strategic weight as a dangerous distraction from the primary threat.

The People's Republic, after more than two T-centuries of disastrous economic policies and political corruption, had embarked upon an ambitious policy of interstellar expansion (under the so-called "Duquesne Plan") in an effort to acquire the resources and economic muscle required to support its tottering, statist economy. Although the Haven System lay over 250 light-years from the Manticore Binary System, the Star Kingdom's wealth and the strategic prize of its wormhole junction (see below) meant that Manticoran strategists must consider the threat which the expanding borders of the People's Republic posed to their own security. The People's Navy, despite several significant internal weaknesses (see below), was by far the largest and most experienced navy in the Haven Sector. Moreover, by 1900, it possessed a "tradition of victory" and confidence in its own capabilities bolstered by almost sixty T-years of steady, uniformly successful expansion through conquest.

The Star Kingdom itself was unique in the explored galaxy: a single-system political unit with no less than three inhabited planets and the location of the largest and wealthiest wormhole junction known to exist. Although its population density remained low, the Manticore Wormhole Junction conferred upon it a wealth and a political and economic "reach" which were quite astonishing. The Manticoran merchant marine was the largest single-system merchant marine in the galaxy, and in the mid-nineteenth century PD, it was expanding at a rapid rate. The Junction also turned the Manticore Binary System into a primary financial hub, supporting a very robust banking industry and stock market, backed by an extensive and sophisticated manufacturing sector. The Star Kingdom's *per capita* income and standard of living were actually higher than those of the Solarian League's core worlds, which explains what might make it a tempting target for Havenite expansion.

In terms of relative industrial and economic power, the People's Republic of Haven and the Star Kingdom of Manticore were clearly the two preeminent star nations of the Haven Sector. On a *per capita* basis, there was no comparison between the output and economic strength of the two star nations, yet the sheer size of the People's Republic meant that despite its relative economic inefficiency, its total industrial capability—and, particularly, the percentage of its industrial capability devoted to military purposes—was significantly greater than that of the Star Kingdom. Nonetheless, Manticore was in a far better position than any other non-Havenite star nation to match the power and strength of the PRH's military establishment. Manticore also possessed a significantly more developed and capable domestic technology base than Haven, which, combined with the leadership of the House of Winton, made the Star Kingdom the logical focus for any interstellar alliance and/or collective security agreement aimed at restricting or limiting future Havenite expansion.

Strategic Goals

The Strategic Assumptions phase defines both the need and the resources available; in the Strategic Goals phase, those two ideas are brought together to define the strategic outcome the navy is attempting to achieve, and the role the fleet has in the larger strategic picture.

The Royal Manticoran Navy's strategic goals and responsibilities, as of 1900 PD, in order of priority, were defined as:

1. The defense and security of the Manticore Binary System, its planets, its population, and its industrial base.
2. The defense and security of the central terminus of the Manticoran Wormhole Junction and the industrial and economic base associated with it.

3. The protection and security of the secondary termini of the Manticoran Wormhole Junction.
4. The protection and security of Manticoran commerce and the Manticoran merchant marine.
5. In conjunction with 4, the enforcement of the Cherwell Convention for the suppression of the interstellar genetic slave trade.

Although the Navy's strategic requirements had been defined as above for more than three centuries, actual emphasis for many years had been much more focused on the fourth goal than any of the three responsibilities that preceded it. In large part that was because, during that period, no realistic threat to the Manticore Binary System itself, to the Junction, or to the Junction's secondary termini seemed to exist. This had freed the Navy to concentrate on the commerce protection/anti-piracy portion of its mission, and it was uncompromisingly oriented in that direction at least until the middle of the reign of Queen Samantha II (1802–1857 PD). By the end of King Roger III's reign (1857–1883), a fundamental realignment of naval policy and emphasis had occurred in response to the threat of the steadily expanding PRH and Roger's personal leadership in face of that threat. The RMN's wall of battle had been significantly augmented, commerce protection had been downgraded in importance to match the Royal Navy's longstanding official strategic hierarchy, and operational doctrine and training had been uncompromisingly reoriented to emphasize realistic (and rigorous) training for fleet actions and combat tactics. During that same period, a major R&D effort was put in place as part of a consciously designed RMN policy of offsetting its numerical weakness vis-à-vis the People's Navy with a qualitative superiority in weapons technology and training.

Fleet Missions

The first step, Strategic Goals, defined the navy's role writ large; this second step defines the navy's role *vis-à-vis* other services, and in general terms what the fleet does in support of its missions. In this step, there are three sub-steps.

SERVICE ROLES AND MISSIONS

The first is Service Roles and Missions. What services exist, and which parts of the larger strategic puzzle are allocated to each service? What type of mission does each service consider a core capability? Note that these roles do not have to be rigid. The US Marine Corps entered World War II, for instance, with a heavy service emphasis on conducting amphibious landings, but the US Army conducted plenty of amphibious landings, too, even in the Pacific where the Marines were concentrated.

In the case of the Star Kingdom of Manticore, the Navy is unquestionably the senior military service. Both the Royal Manticoran Marine Corps and the Royal Manticoran Army come under Navy jurisdiction and control in war time, and the RMMC is placed directly under the operational control of the First Space Lord in peacetime, as well.

The Navy is tasked to provide combat, support, and logistic functions for its own operations and for those of the Marines and/or Army when operating outside the Manticore Binary System. For this purpose, the Navy has established a small number of official "fleet stations" outside the Star Kingdom itself (usually in areas where it is conducting sustained commerce protection operations or there is a perceived need to support an allied star nation's security and a permanent, forward deployed presence seems necessary).

Prior to the year 1890 PD, the RMN's entire wall of battle was organized into "Home Fleet," which remained in the Manticore Binary System, positioned to defend the system and its planets or the Junction against any aggressor. Lighter units were more often assigned to fleet stations to project power and presence into areas of particular importance to the Star Kingdom's commercial posture. In addition, a very significant portion of the RMN's cruisers and destroyers were routinely assigned to convoy protection and piracy suppression missions, especially within the Silesian Confederacy. By 1900–1905, as the situation *vis-à-vis* the People's Republic of Haven worsened and as the collective security system known as the "Manticoran Alliance" grew, individual squadrons or even small task forces of capital ships came to be assigned to the more significant fleet stations, many of which were by then being organized as strategic nodes within the Manticoran Alliance rather than primarily as trade protection nodes.

The Royal Manticoran Marine Corps is a flexible organization whose members are crosstrained to perform integral functions aboard the warships to which their detachments are assigned. Marines man weapons systems, perform damage control functions, provide the ship's security and boarding detachments, constitute an organic landing force capability, and are often deployed on humanitarian missions in the face of natural or man-made disaster. In addition, the Royal Marines are the primary offensive planetary combat arm of the Star Kingdom, operating in up to brigade strength from specially designed transports and assault ships at need. Such expeditionary forces (prior to 1905, at least) were seldom required, and the SKM maintained sufficient assault vessels to mount no more than three brigade-level expeditions simultaneously. With the outbreak of open hostilities against the People's Republic, the RMMC underwent significant expansion, but generally continued to operate only in brigade-level strength or below. The Royal Navy is responsible for the Marines' transport, logistics, landing craft, and fire support.

The Royal Manticoran Army as of 1900 PD was primarily a domestic security force. The term "Army" represented something of a misnomer, in that the Army was a unified service responsible for all planetary combat—that is, for atmospheric and maritime combat, as well as land combat. The Navy was tasked to provide space-to-surface fire support and landing capability as and when the Army required it, but there was no great expectation that naval support would be required, and joint operational doctrine remained woefully underdeveloped in that regard. With the outbreak of hostilities between the Manticoran Alliance and the People's Republic of Haven, the RMA began a steady, relatively rapid expansion, as it was tasked to provide planetary garrisons for Havenite systems as they were occupied and to provide security forces for Allied planets whose own infrastructure limitations prevented them from raising and equipping modern planetary combat forces of their own.

FLEET CONOPS

The second sub-step is Fleet Concept of Operations, or CONOPS. In general, what do you envision the fleet doing? When and where will the fleet execute the missions defined in the last step? Will the fleet fight near home, or will it fight in enemy territory? Is it offensive in orientation, or defensive?

Prior to the Havenite Wars, as the conflict between the Star Kingdom of Manticore and the People's Republic came to be known, no one had fought a major interstellar war in over three hundred years, and war-fighting doctrine was sadly underdeveloped. The People's Navy, the senior armed force of the People's Republic of Haven, had more combat experience in 1900 PD than any other navy, including the Solarian League Navy, in the explored galaxy. Virtually all of that experience, however, had been gained against relatively small, single-system star nations, none of whom had been able to build a navy capable of mounting a sustained or serious resistance to the People's Navy.

In general terms, the Solarian League Navy, because of its preeminent status, was taken (remarkably uncritically) as the doctrinal and operational model for the rest of the galaxy. The fact that no one else in the galaxy had the sheer size, industrial capacity, and manpower of the SLN was, apparently, lost on most independent navies of the time. SLN doctrine called for a remorseless, unstoppable, system-by-system advance towards the home star system of any opponent. It was an attritional strategy, designed to compel the enemy to confront the Solarian wall of battle by threatening objectives which had to be defended, creating a series of engagements in which superior Solarian numbers and (in theory, at least) war-fighting technology would grind the opposing fleet into dust. This was a doctrine that emphasized steady, incremental advances, destroying and/or occupying enemy fleet bases and star systems, rather than any sort of misdirection or deep-strike missions.

The possibility of such deep strikes always existed, however, particularly in the case of star nations that had only a single system to lose. That described the Star Kingdom of Manticore quite well, and that threat had to be defended against. As a consequence, Manticoran strategic doctrine emphasized the absolute necessity of maintaining sufficient strength in Home Fleet to protect the

Manticore Binary System and Wormhole Junction against attack. Offensive operations could be carried out only with that portion of the Navy available after the home star system's security and essential infrastructure had been provided for. Within that limitation, the RMN's strategists sought persistently to take the offensive against the People's Republic, although always with an eye towards their own forces' lines of supply and rear area security.

The People's Republic of Haven's strategic doctrine mirrored that of the Solarian League Navy, and it had worked well for the People's Navy prior to its collision with the Star Kingdom of Manticore. The technological capabilities of the Royal Manticoran Navy came as a very unpleasant surprise to the People's Navy, but even more significant in the early stages of the Havenite Wars was the revolution organized against the Legislaturalist regime by Robert Stanton Pierre and his followers. Dismayed by its losses in the opening engagements against Manticore, the People's Navy's officer corps found itself under attack domestically, as well, and the Pierre Purges, ruthlessly carried out by Pierre's Committee of Public safety, cost the PN an enormous percentage of its senior officers. That loss of operational experience, coupled with rigid political oversight by "People's Commissioners" with little or no naval experience of their own, greatly inhibited Havenite operational flexibility. Unconstrained by such rigid political control and without such grievous, self-inflicted losses among its officer corps, the RMN enjoyed a much steeper learning curve during the first several years of the Havenite Wars. Coupled with a steadily increasing technological edge, the Manticoran concept of operations became far more sophisticated than that of the People's Navy, with significant consequences for the People's Republic.

In particular, Manticoran strategic thinking evolved steadily away from the incremental, predictable, step-by-step advance prescribed by Havenite (and Solarian) doctrine in favor of deep strikes, well behind the enemy's front lines, to destroy his war-making infrastructure and to engage his system defense forces in isolation from his main battle fleet, defeating them in detail and inflicting a steady stream of attritional losses. It was, in fact, in many ways an elaboration and further development of the original concept that both Manticore and Haven had borrowed from the Solarian League.

FLEET POSTURE

The final sub-step under Fleet Missions is the Fleet Posture. Is the fleet forward deployed or based outside of the home system(s)? Is it garrison-based, i.e., homeported in the home system(s)? Does it conduct frequent deployments or patrols, or does it largely stay near home space and only go out for training? Pre-World War II, for instance, the US Navy was garrison based; until right before the start of the war, the battlefleet was homeported in the continental US. It spent a lot of time training at sea (garrison-based does not imply inactive), but generally the fleet stayed close to US territory, and the trips were generally short. Post-World War II, in contrast, the US adopted a policy of forward deploying some forces in overseas ports, and extended deployments in areas the US considered critical. Fleet Posture is not where the fleet units are based—that step is yet to come—but how it is based and how forward-leaning it is.

Manticoran strategic doctrine was considerably more sophisticated than its Solarian and Havenite antecedents, and in many ways it turned the Star Kingdom's single-system vulnerability into a relative advantage. Prior to the First Haven War, the Star Kingdom had only two absolutely critical targets to protect: the Manticore Wormhole Junction and the Manticore Binary System itself. Even after active conflict began, Manticore had far *fewer* such vital defensive requirements, with the exception of two or three critical systems which were to be taken along the way, such as Trevor's Star. That meant it could deploy a larger percentage of its smaller fleet to adequately meet its rear area defensive needs.

Because of the nature of hyper travel, "rear areas" in the classic sense of a zone protected from attack by a "front line" did not truly exist, of course, since attacking forces could readily evade detection or interception on their way to their targets. Instead, "rear-area" targets were defined as those objectives far enough behind the volume of active operations as to take some time for strike forces to reach and sufficiently important for industrial, logistic, or economic reasons to be worth reaching and attacking in the first place. The far larger People's Republic had many more such vulnerable points, and providing adequate security for its vital areas drew off a far greater proportion of its fleet strength. Not only that, but it was literally impossible for the People's Navy to provide strong enough system defense forces everywhere to prevent the RMN from amassing crushing numerical superiority at points of its choice, resulting in a steady, grinding flow of Havenite losses.

Fleet Design

In the preceding steps, the environment has been described and the fleet's general role in that environment has been defined. We've also fleshed out the missions of the fleet, including where it is based and where it expects to fight. To this point, though, we have only talked about fleets. Now we start to discuss the ships that make up the fleet.

FLEET CAPABILITIES, SIZE, AND MIX

The military (both uniformed and civilian analysts) often talk about both capability (what you can do) and capacity (how much you can do). So, Fleet Capabilities are the tasks that the fleet can do, as embodied in its platforms. Modern US Aegis ships, for instance, can provide area-wide air defense against air and missile threats. Most can embark helicopters and conduct operations against enemy submarines and other surface vessels as well. Fleet Size is the total number of ships in the fleet. Fleet Mix describes how many of each different type of ship. Between Fleet Capabilities, Fleet Size, and Fleet Mix, the capabilities and capacity of the overall fleet have been explained.

Prior to the end of the nineteenth century PD, the evolution of warship types and functions had been remarkably stable (see above), and had generally sorted itself into the following ship types, from largest to smallest.

The ship of the wall, usually a superdreadnought massing between seven and eight million tons, was essentially an energy weapons platform. It was designed and armored to bring its energy batteries into range of an opponent and stay there until that opponent was destroyed, and it had no other function. Maneuverability and acceleration capability were totally secondary; protection and brute firepower were the primary considerations.

The superdreadnought had supplanted the dreadnought for the same reasons the dreadnought had supplanted the battleship. As gradual improvements in inertial compensators allowed steadily larger hulls to be accelerated at acceleration rates in the "capital ship" zone (roughly 350 to 450 gravities), those larger hulls gained a decisive qualitative advantage. A designer could simply put more weapons—and more active and passive defenses—into the larger unit, which exerted a gradual, slow, but inexorable upward pressure on the mass of ships considered fit to "lie in the wall of battle."

Dreadnoughts were simply superdreadnoughts writ small—lower displacement units, massing between four and seven million tons, with the same design function and philosophy as the superdreadnought. They continued to be built after the emergence of the superdreadnought by cost-conscious navies (like the RMN) that wished to expand the number of units in their wall but could not afford to standardize on the larger vessel. Individually, they remained superior to any lesser opponent than an SD and technological advantages could go far towards equalizing the playing field even against the larger ship, yet by the mid-nineteenth century, they had become a clear second-choice decision for major navies.

Battleships, massing between one and a half and four million tons, had once been the galactic standard for ships of the wall. By the end of the nineteenth century, however, they were thoroughly obsolete, simply because they were far too fragile to survive a "proper waller's" fire long enough to make their own lighter, less numerous weapons effective. They were, however, used, especially by the People's Republic for rear area security. The SKM itself built two squadrons of battleships as part of the initial force buildup to protect the home system after the discovery of and first transit through the Junction. By the time the RMN needed a proper wall of battle, however, dreadnoughts had already entered the picture, and all Manticoran battleships had been decommissioned by the time of the First Havenite War.

Battlecruisers, massing between five hundred thousand and a million tons, were the fast, powerful screening and raiding units of choice. Designed to destroy anything they couldn't outrun, they were envisioned as commerce-raiders *par excellence* and (especially by the People's Navy) as antimissile screening units for the wall of battle. Unlike ships of the wall, their offensive weapon suites tended to allocate far more tonnage (proportionately) to missile tubes and magazines, in keeping with their role as "space-control" units.

At the outbreak of the Havenite Wars, cruisers and destroyers were also considered suitable for use as screening and light antimissile escorts for the wall of battle. Experience, and the increasing lethality of missiles (especially Manticoran missiles), demonstrated that this was no longer in fact true—that such light units were simply not survivable in fleet combat scenarios. They were, therefore, increasingly designated for convoy work, commerce raiding, patrol duties, sensor pickets, etc., and released from fleet combat duties.

In 1900 PD, the People's Navy's cumulative tonnage was approximately twice that of the Royal Manticoran Navy, but the RMN, which found it necessary to provide security for a far smaller total number of star systems, could concentrate a higher percentage of its total available tonnage in ships of the wall. At the start of the war, the RMN had 188 superdreadnoughts and 121 dreadnoughts in commission, while the PN had 412 superdreadnoughts and 48 dreadnoughts, backed up by 374 battleships for rear area security. As the Havenite Wars continued, the percentage of tonnage devoted to ships "below the wall" in both navies plummeted as the unsuitability of those lighter units for fleet combat became increasingly evident.

The introduction of missile pods near the beginning of the war fundamentally altered naval tactics. No longer would ships of the wall slug it out in protracted duels that might begin at long range but must culminate in the inevitable short-range pounding match. Instead, with the massive opening salvos made possible by the pods (themselves largely unarmored and hence vulnerable to destruction), the opening salvo of an engagement was often the only salvo. Initially, pods were towed on tractors behind existing ships, but beginning in about 1910 PD, the Manticoran introduction of the multidrive missile, married to the use of pods, completely transformed the nature of combat and hence of the platforms best optimized for it. With the arrival of the MDM, the energy-armed superdreadnought became hopelessly obsolete, and the resulting total redesign produced the "podnought," or SD(P): a hollow-cored design intended to deploy pods of very large, very capable, very long ranged, and very lethal missiles in the largest possible numbers. The possession of that weapon and those ships gave the RMN an overwhelming advantage, which brought the first phase of the Havenite Wars to a disastrous conclusion for the People's Republic in 1914–1915 PD.

FLEET LAYDOWN

The final element of Fleet Design is the Fleet Laydown. Where are the parts of the fleet located? How many bases exist, and how many/what type of ships per base are located at each base? Before World War I, for instance, the Royal Navy concentrated its battlefleet in bases in the northern United Kingdom, to better position itself to engage the German High Sea Fleet. This meant that the most powerful navy in the world was often underrepresented on some of its far-flung naval outposts.

As Manticore repositioned itself to confront the Havenite threat, its deployment patterns changed. Historically, the Manticoran wall of battle had always been kept concentrated in the home system in order to protect the Star Kingdom's inhabited planets, its infrastructure, and the Manticoran Wormhole Junction. On the occasions—such as the dispatch of capital ships to Silesia after the Battle of Carson or the short "war" with San Martin—when capital ships had been employed outside the Manticore Binary System, they were dispatched directly from First Fleet for the specific operation but remained administratively attached to First Fleet and returned to it as promptly as possible.

A redistribution of forces was a fundamental part of Roger III's planning, although that was not perhaps immediately apparent. First Fleet was officially redesignated Home Fleet as a clear indication of its function and also additional numbered fleets were soon to be organized. As the size of the Manticoran wall of battle increased and as the Manticoran Alliance acquired additional members, detachments of ships of the wall were permanently deployed to critical naval stations like Grendelsbane and Hancock or to the support of Allied star systems such as Alizon and the Caliphate of Zanzibar. Such detachments were normally accompanied by appropriate scouting and screening units, although in the case of the system like Alizon light local naval units might be assigned for that purpose.

Home Fleet's responsibilities were somewhat simplified by increasing the number of fortresses deployed to protect the Junction.

Although the total manpower cost of the Junction forts was high in absolute terms, it was substantially lower in terms of manpower per unit of fire, given the forts' powerful armaments and defenses. The forts served two functions: first, to protect against a conventional attack through hyper-space; second, to prevent a surprise attack through the Junction itself. In many ways, the latter threat was a graver concern for Manticoran analysts than the threat of a conventional attack, particularly before the introduction of the laser head. Wartime experience and steady improvement in both missile and mine laser head technology were to demonstrate that the fear of an attack through the Junction had been grossly overinflated, but no one in the Admiralty was aware of that in the last quarter of the nineteenth century. Once Manticore had captured Trevor's Star, the vast majority of the Junction forts were speedily decommissioned, leaving only a sufficient number to serve as command platforms for the heavy numbers of system defense missile pods deployed to protect it against conventional attack. This liberated large quantities of trained personnel for duty aboard the ships of the steadily expanding Manticoran wall of battle.

Additional fleet stations—such Hancock Station—were established to provide fleet concentration points and advanced repair and maintenance nodes in accordance with the traditional strategic doctrine which required defensive depth against the steady, incremental advance contemplated by most fleet planners. Several years of active wartime operations and the gradual evolution on Manticore's part of the doctrine of the deep strike would eventually suggest that Manticore had actually established too many of those advanced bases. While the provision of logistics nodes closer to the scene of active operations was convenient, the same support was available from the Fleet Train of fast freighters and repair ships which could operate with fleet units far from home. Moreover, each of those isolated fleet stations became a defensive liability in its own right, tying down and dispersing combat power which might otherwise have been concentrated into offensive striking forces. By the end of the First Havenite War, Admiralty thinking had hardened toward the abandonment of all but the largest and most important of the fleet stations. In theory, the disestablishment of the more peripheral fleet stations would permit the forces normally tied to them to be redistributed to better protect the truly critical ones. The redeployment had only begun at the time of the ceasefire, however, and the Janacek Admiralty predictably failed to complete its implementation before Operation Thunderbolt.

One consequence of the Navy's redeployment, coupled with procurement plans which of necessity concentrated on the construction of capital ships, was a steady drawdown in the numbers of lighter units previously available for commerce protection in the Silesian Confederacy. Destroyers and cruisers were required to scout for and screen the battle squadrons, and they were being built in smaller numbers. Accordingly, the policy of maintaining light units semi-permanently on station "visiting" Silesian star systems had to be discontinued in favor of rotating patrols and convoy escort. The new policy allowed the Navy to economize on platforms but provided a lower level of security and protection for merchant traffic in Silesia.

The long, arduous, and eventually successful campaign to capture Trevor's Star had major strategic consequences. The Royal Manticoran Navy's prewar operational planning had emphasized the need to secure Trevor's Star in order to neutralize the threat of any attack through the Junction. By the time Admiral White Haven's Sixth Fleet actually captured Trevor's Star, the realistic threat of an attack through its terminus of the Junction had been effectively nullified (if it had ever actually existed at all), but the Navy's strategists had not yet realized that was the case. In the event, Trevor's Star's greatest value to the Star Kingdom lay in the advanced, secure base it provided. Two hundred and ten light-years from Manticore, deep into what had been the Havenite sphere, Trevor's Star was only a single transit from the Manticore Binary System itself, and transit through the Junction provided not only a huge savings in time but also complete security against Havenite commerce-raiders. It shortened the operational loop for offensive Manticoran operations and freed up large numbers of light units which would otherwise have been required to escort the shipping supporting it. The formation of Third Fleet to protect it did not dilute the Navy's striking power as one might have anticipated. Indeed, in many ways, Third Fleet became a ready reserve for Home Fleet (and vice versa), freeing the newly formed Eighth Fleet for what ultimately proved decisive offensive operations against the core star systems of the People's Republic of Haven.

Force Size

The fleet is more than just ships—it also consists of people and infrastructure. On the people side, what is the fleet's Manning Strategy: How many guys do you need to man the fleet, and how do you get them? Are they conscripts or volunteers, and how qualified is the base of people you draw upon? Do you fully man the ships in peacetime, or do you maintain just a cadre to be augmented with new recruits if there is a war? What sort of reserve forces are there, and how and when do you "call up the reserves"? What's the ratio of officers to enlisted (do you even break it down that way?), and does that ratio change depending on whether you are at peace or at war? Do you automate to decrease the number of people you need, or have large crews to improve flexibility?

Traditionally, the Royal Manticoran Navy is manned by volunteers: professional, long-service officers and senior noncoms who choose to make the Navy a lifetime career form the backbone of the service. Prior to the Havenite Wars, the standard enlistment term was for six Manticoran years (approximately seven T-years); following the outbreak of the Havenite Wars, enlistment became "for the duration of hostilities."

Throughout the period of hostilities, the RMN made strenuous and largely successful efforts to meet its manning requirements through voluntary enlistments. It succeeded in large part because of the high premium the Star Kingdom's citizens placed upon military service and the preservation of their independence after the long, agonizing buildup of the sixty-year-long "Cold War" between the People's Republic and the Star Kingdom and its allies. Good pay, good benefits, significant technical training opportunities, and the opportunity for promotion and advancement inherent in the steadily expanding Navy also helped attract quality personnel. By 1914, the Navy was seriously considering conscription, but the adoption of increased shipboard automation drastically curtailed manning requirements, which eased much of the pressure. There were countervailing pressures, of course, including the adoption of large numbers of new, highly capable light attack craft, but the enormous ships' companies required by prewar ships of the wall had become a thing of the past, and the Navy's ability to stand down the forts covering the Manticoran

Wormhole Junction following the liberation of Trevor's Star freed up a very substantial manpower pool.

It should be borne in mind that the enormous size of the Manticoran merchant marine provided both major advantages and disadvantages when it came to manning the fleet. On the one hand, the merchant marine provided an enormous pool of experienced spacers, and somewhere between a third and a half of all merchant officers held in reserve Navy commissions, as well. That equated to a reserve of trained, capable manpower no other navy in the galaxy probably could have matched. The existence of that merchant marine, however, was also a major factor in the economic and industrial power of the Star Kingdom. Manticore literally could not afford to draw down its merchant marine—indeed, it needed its merchant marine to continue to expand—if it was to meet the economic and industrial demands of war against an opponent the size of the People's Republic of Haven. So even though the merchant marine represented an enormous theoretical manpower reserve, the Admiralty was in fact constantly aware that it could not draw too heavily upon that reserve except in the most dire of emergencies lest it destroy the Star Kingdom's long-term ability to sustain the war.

It would be difficult to overstate the Star Kingdom's qualitative advantage when comparing RMN personnel to those of the People's Navy, particularly after the Pierre purge of the Havenite officer corps. Unlike the RMN, the PN had depended upon conscription from the very beginning. Although there was a solid core of professional officers and NCOs prior to the Havenite Wars, that experienced cadre suffered brutal losses as the combined result of combat against an equally professional navy with superior weapons and doctrine, on the one hand, and of political purges, on the other. This was particularly unfortunate in the People's Navy's case because the educational level of the People's Republic was far lower than that of the Star Kingdom of Manticore. In essence, the People's Navy's recruits required much more training and, even after that training, tended to be less individually capable than their Manticoran counterparts. Duties which in the RMN would have been routinely carried out by junior enlisted personnel were the province of senior NCOs in the People's Navy, which meant the loss of those senior NCOs had a serious impact on the PN's combat capability. On the other hand, because of its reliance on conscription, the People's Navy could always meet its manpower numbers, even if it could not match its opponent's manpower quality.

ORGANIC SUPPORT FUNCTIONS

The fleet is more than just ships—it also includes shore facilities and perhaps capabilities and capacity "borrowed" from other providers. Organic Support Functions are those functions the fleet does for itself, such as providing tankers that are assigned to the fleet. Shore Infrastructure are those services that are not located with the fleet, such as shipyards and fleet depots.

The RMN's "shore establishment" in 1920 PD is concentrated, as it has been for the past sixty to seventy T-years, in the Star Kingdom's major space stations: HMSS *Vulcan* (Sphinx orbit), HMSS *Hephaestus* (Manticore orbit), and HMSS *Weyland* (Gryphon orbit). These are enormous aggregates of fabrication, building, and maintenance capability, with a level of sophistication and capability unmatched anywhere else in the explored galaxy. *Weyland*, orbiting the secondary component of the Manticore Binary System, is the site of most of the RMN's critical research and development activity.

The Navy maintains an extensive Fleet Train, consisting of supply ships, fuel tankers, maintenance and repair vessels, mobile shipyard modules, personnel transports, etc. The majority of the Navy-crewed vessels belong to Fifth Fleet and the Joint Navy Military Transport Command, and are equipped with military-grade impellers, inertial compensators, hyper generators, and particle screens in order to permit them to maneuver freely with the fleet units they are tasked to support. In addition to the JNMTC, however, the RMN routinely charters civilian vessels for transport and service duties in rear areas and where the ability to "keep up" with fleet units is not a critical factor.

In Manticoran practice, fleet stations are permanent duty assignments outside the Manticoran home system. Fleet stations may range from as little as a handful of destroyers to as much as an entire task force or even fleet of ships of the wall, and organic fleet support is assigned to each station as appropriate. Generally, any fleet station will be provided with at least one major repair ship and at least a pair of missile colliers, since by their very nature such stations do not normally possess local capability to meet the Navy's needs in those respects.

This basing doctrine contrasted sharply with Havenite doctrine. The People's Navy's practice was to establish numerous major nodal bases distributed throughout the large volume of the PRH. Fleets units were relatively "short legged," tied to the nodal bases to which they were assigned, and with limited organic support capability. Havenite strategic doctrine envisioned the dispatch of powerful task forces and/or fleets in short, sharp, heavily weighted and rapidly decisive campaigns, after which the fleet units would be withdrawn to the nearest forward base for repairs, servicing, and training while occupation and pacification forces secured the newly occupied territory. (The basic conceptual model for this doctrine was the Solarian division of the SLN into designated Battle Fleet and Frontier Fleet units, although the demarcation between the units assigned to each task was not so sharply and formally drawn in the PN as in the SLN.) This was a major factor in both its fleet structure and logistic planning. (See below.)

Force Management

Force Size decisions determine how you get your navy manned and supported; Force Management describes how you keep the force in fighting trim.

PERSONNEL POLICIES

First, there's the issue of Personnel Policies. How much personnel turnover do you plan for? The US Army, for instance, assumes that a substantial number of enlisted soldiers will make the Army their career. The US Marine Corps, on the other hand, is designed on the assumption that very few Marines will go career. (Take a look at their respective commercials sometime, and notice the difference in emphasis regarding the long term.) What's the "personnel tempo" for the force, i.e., how often are the people deployed, away from their families. PERSTEMPO issues have a high impact of personnel retention.

The modern RMN is a well-paying, professional force built around well-educated, well-trained, and long-serving personnel. Four factors define the pool of available people from which the RMN draws. First, Manticore has always had a first-rate educational system. Coupled with the educational and training opportunities presented by the RMN itself (gravitics techs, for example, receive training equivalent to several years of undergraduate education), the end result is that, rate for rate, RMN personnel as a group are probably the best trained and most competent in the galaxy. Second, the RMN has been expanding for the last sixty T-years. This means that not only is the Bureau of Personnel constantly hungry for new recruits, but that the RMN is seen as a place where advancement is not only possible, but required. Third, Manticore's large merchant marine functions not only as a limited manpower reserve, but also as a place for follow-on employment—in other words, it makes the RMN more attractive because a recruit knows that, worst case, they have a fallback where RMN-taught skills will be highly valued. Moreover, since the RMN is in effect "always hiring," merchant spacers often maintain reserve status, knowing that they can always return to active service if need be. And, finally, the RMN has established a reputation for producing victory after victory against numerically superior forces which endows it with a "mystique" few military forces in history have matched and none have exceeded.

The cumulative effect of these factors is a system where the RMN is viewed both as an excellent career and as a good place to start, and RMN personnel policy is based on the assumption that the average new recruit is probably going to stay in the navy for decades, even if not in a single unbroken stretch. Of course, in this way like many others the RMN is unique—few other star nations are experiencing such booming growth, and few other navies have expanded at such a precipitous rate.

Personnel Tempo (PERSTEMPO) is a strong determinant of retention rates. Higher PERSTEMPO means more time away from family, and hence a high peacetime PERSTEMPO negatively affects retention. Currently, RMN PERSTEMPO is running high, as it always does in wartime. Given that enlistments these days are "for the duration," it has had no negative impact on retention rates.

LOGISTICS CONCEPT

A second Force Management issue is the Logistics Concept. How do you provide for the fleet? Do you maintain large depots forward deployed, or large depots well to the rear? Do you have small depots and depend on just-in-time logistics?

In the case of the Royal Manticoran Navy, logistic concepts are quite flexible. The degree to which resources—supplies and maintenance/support resources—are forward deployed depends on the nature of the fleet station or base. Given the fact that the prewar RMN had only a single home star system to worry about, the vast majority of its important depots and supply ships were (and are) maintained in the Manticore Binary System. Many of those depots are located aboard or in close proximity to the major space stations, but critical components—like ammunition depots, in particular—are also stockpiled at discrete, widely separated points within the star system in order to protect them in the unlikely event of an enemy attack on the system itself.

RMN warships are normally provisioned and supplied for minimum six-month deployments, and are supported by fleet or chartered freighters. Given the lift capacity of a four-million-ton freighter, the quantities of supplies which can be forward deployed on shipboard are very, very high, and the Fleet Train is usually capable of sustaining necessary levels of provisions, spare parts, ammunition, etc., without undue strain. Obviously this is not always the case under wartime conditions, but it is the ideal.

The RMN is built around the concept of "underway replenishment." That is, its Fleet Train and logistics tail is designed to take supplies to forward deployed ships as necessary, rather than returning those ships to base to resupply. This is in distinct contrast to prewar Havenite practice (see above) and the flexibility it provided contributed significantly to the Manticoran evolution of deep-strike doctrine. With a far greater number of star systems, the People's Navy was able to establish a widespread system of depots, centered around Duquesne Base in the Barnett System for operations against the Manticoran Alliance. The operational concept called for Havenite ships to return on a rotating basis to those depots to resupply as needed, and facilities to provide the maintenance the undertrained, conscript crews weren't truly capable of providing out of their own resources, were also located in the depot systems. What was intended to provide a dispersed, flexible, widespread support net, however, turned out to be a limiting factor on wartime operations. The People's Navy had been oriented around short, intense campaigns against relatively small opponents without the military strength or strategic depth to long resist the sort of overwhelming power the People's Republic could deploy against them. Against an opponent which failed to oblige by collapsing quickly, the Havenite prewar logistics and depot concept proved woefully inadequate, and throughout the period from 1905 to 1915 PD, the People's Navy was never able to match the Royal Manticoran Navy's strategic and operational mobility because of its lack of an equivalent Fleet Train to keep its units supplied and maintained "on the move."

LEVEL OF READINESS

The third issue in managing the force is the Level of Readiness, both Afloat and Ashore. Are the forces ready to fight immediately, or do they need to ramp up? Are their stockpiles of materiel in place, or do they need time to build up? Between the World Wars, for instance, Great Britain explicitly adopted a "Ten Year Rule," a codified assumption that the next war would not occur for at least ten years. Such assumptions can be dangerous—it requires an awful lot of prediction to notice changes that far in advance, and domestic considerations can lead to the assumption taking on a political life of its own.

By the time the Star Kingdom of Manticore and the People's Republic of Haven actually met in combat, both sides had been actively preparing for over half a T-century. In theory, the level of readiness—both for the fleet and for its "shore establishment"— was very high on both sides. Indeed, the peacetime ammunition loadout for the Royal Manticoran Navy was identical to its wartime loadout, and from 1880 PD on, personnel strengths aboard Manticoran warships were maintained at one hundred percent of wartime manning requirements. The People's Navy was at a lower level of manning, and although it was theoretically at the same level in terms of matériel, it was, in fact, probably at no more than eighty-five percent of Manticoran levels of readiness prior to about 1904 PD. At that point, in the Legislaturalists' deliberate buildup to hostilities against Manticore, readiness was increased to very nearly the same level as in the RMN. One effect of the increase in personnel, however, was to dilute the experience levels of its units on the very verge of war by the introduction of so many newly trained personnel. This was exacerbated by the PRH's educational deficiencies, since it took a proportionately longer time for Havenite personnel to acquire the necessary expertise.

The Star Kingdom of Manticore, however, had a significant advantage in terms of its fixed-support infrastructure. It had fewer fully developed bases and depots, but those it possessed were much more capable and tended to be considerably larger. They were maintained at that level by a rigorous system of training exercises, drills, and inspections intended to ensure (largely successfully) that when the inevitable hostilities against the People's Republic of Haven began, the fleet's support structure would be as close to one hundred percent readiness as was humanly possible. In terms of mobile logistical support, there was no real comparison between the two navies. The RMN's organic logistical command was far more highly developed and capable, and the sheer size of the Manticoran merchant marine gave the Admiralty a far deeper pool of "ships taken up from trade" which could be used to augment the Navy's own personnel and supply lift at need.

ACQUISITION STRATEGY

Finally, there's the question of how you go about buying the stuff you need for your navy, especially given that a warship is a significant capital investment with a long design cycle and construction cycle.

The Royal Manticoran Navy's acquisition strategy and requirements were greatly eased by the size and capability of the Star Kingdom of Manticore's industrial base. The fact that the Star Kingdom's home industries built and maintained one of—if not the—largest merchant fleets in the entire galaxy gave it a basic "heavy industry" capability no other single star system could have matched. The possession of the Manticoran Wormhole Junction, coupled with the size of the Manticoran merchant marine, provided a cash flow for the Manticoran government of prodigious size. Even a minor increase in Junction transit fees generated a major increase in revenues, and Manticore was in a position to leverage its status as a major financial and investment center into the sale of war bonds and other investment instruments to support its war effort. Despite that, and even with unprecedented levels of taxation, the Star Kingdom was forced into a pattern of deficit spending that was distinctly alien to its traditional fiscal policies. This resulted in a significant level of inflation for the first time in modern Manticoran experience, although by the standards of most wartime economies, Manticore's managed to avoid "overheating" through a combination of wise fiscal management, the continuing expansion of its merchant fleet and carrying trade, aggressive pursuit of still more foreign markets for civilian goods as a means of maintaining and expanding its general industrial base and economy, and the enormous "natural resource" provided by the Junction.

As the war continued and emphasis shifted more and more drastically toward missile combat with the introduction of the multidrive missile, platform costs came to be dominated by ammunition costs, and enormous missile production lines were set up. Strenuous efforts were made at every stage in the process to rationalize weapons design in a way that would permit the most economical possible volume production. Given the sheer scale of that production, the per-unit cost of not simply expendable munitions but of warship hulls and components fell drastically as the war continued. Despite the much greater size and lethality of the MDM, the cost of a late-generation multidrive missile was actually lower for the Star Kingdom than the cost of a late prewar single-drive missile had been, largely because of the relatively small numbers in which those prewar weapons had been purchased and manufactured and because the "bells and whistles" of their design had not been nearly so ruthlessly rationalized. One of the outstanding achievements of the Star Kingdom's military industrial base throughout the Havenite Wars was the ability to introduce new and even radically upgraded weapons without major disruptions of output, largely as a legacy of Roger III's insistence on prewar planning towards exactly that end.

In contrast, the People's Republic was never able to match the efficiency of Manticoran industry and ship building, nor did it have a resource remotely like the Manticoran Wormhole Junction as a revenue generator. It did, however, have a command economy that was over a century old when the war began. In many ways, the PRH was less constrained by fiscal policy than Manticore because its domestic economy was a largely closed system which the government could manipulate in whatever fashion it chose. Ultimately, the strain was ruinous and unsustainable, but in the short- and midterm, the government was in a position to direct and control resources and trained manpower in a way Manticore simply couldn't have matched. The coercive power of State Security and the other revolutionary police and spy organizations set up under Oscar Saint-Just at Robert Pierre's direction also helped enormously in providing "direction" to the Havenite war effort. And, last but not least, the sheer numbers of political prisoners held by the PRH provided Haven with a massive supply of slave labor which required no wages whatsoever.

Under the circumstances, Pierre's ability to actually reform the PRH's currency, rationalize taxation, reduce the Basic Living Stipend, and reintroduce the notion of wage-based labor was little less than miraculous. It would never have been possible without the iron support of StateSec and of the People's Commissioners assigned to the PRH's military forces and it was accompanied by a degree of disruption and civilian hardship which required often brutal measures (see the Leveller Revolt in 1911 PD), but that should not be allowed to take away from the sheer magnitude of the accomplishment.

Despite that, it is questionable how much longer Pierre or Saint-Just could have sustained the PRH's war effort if the introduction of the MDM in 1914 PD had not brought the first phase of the Havenite wars to a crashing halt. It is indisputably true that the Star Kingdom proved far more capable than Haven of transitioning back to a peacetime economy in the wake of Thomas Theisman's overthrow of the Committee of Public Safety, and the ongoing economic strain of the Havenite civil war between Theisman's supporters and those still loyal to the Committee of Public Safety or seeking to carve out their own empires came very near to undoing Pierre's accomplishments. The sheer size of the PRH came to the restored Republic's rescue, however, proving once again that with a sufficiently large population and resource base, even a relatively inefficient economy can generate large absolute revenue streams.

Putting It All Together

The model we have described is shown in the figure below.

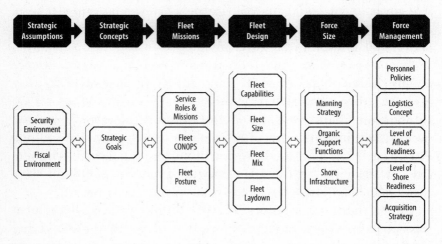

These, then, are the sorts of things one needs to think about when designing a navy. The answers to each of these questions do not exist in a vacuum—not only do earlier decisions set the stage for later decisions, but there is a lot of interrelatedness between the issues under discussion. Those feedback loops have been omitted from the illustration for sake of clarity, but they are there.

Sometimes it might become apparent later in the process that an earlier decision has created an untenable situation downstream. In the real world, this mismatch is an indication that the process needs to be rethought, usually because the original plan was too ambitious. An author has a bit more leeway, and can change "ground truth" to provide the answers he needs for narrative purposes.

This model comes from the "Naval Metaphors in Science Fiction" talk that Chris often does at science fiction conventions. He observes that most science fiction does not cover the whole model; at best it might cover Fleet Missions and Fleet Design in detail, with most other areas only vaguely defined. It would be disingenuous to say that David went through each and every one of these steps as presented when he defined the navies of the Honorverse. But, one thing Chris noted when he showed David the illustration above was that David had a ready answer for each and every one of these sections, answers that were obviously the result of long and careful analysis of both real-world history and the setting he had created. In the real world, these are questions that must be answered. In a fictional universe, an author at least needs to know these questions exist, and to have thought about them, even if only in general terms.

The view presented here is obviously not the final word on the topic, as each and every one of these subheadings could be an essay in and of itself, for each navy in the Honorverse. In addition, there are a lot of elements that we've only glossed over. First, there are a lot of important issues below that are not discussed, such as the political will to build a navy. Second, a navy is a dynamic thing—it changes with time. Sometimes this is because technology changes, but oftentimes it is because other factors change: The strategic situation gets better or worse; new missions get added, old missions get subtracted; the education level of the population changes, affecting the navy's personnel requirements, etc. Science fiction authors have the luxury of a clean sheet of paper, but real policymakers do not, and sometimes tomorrow's navy is defined not by the navy they want but by the navy they have today. Third, this model does not discuss the importance of doctrine and tactics, techniques, and procedures (TT&P). Doctrine describes what you want to do, and TT&P describes how you use your stuff to do it, so generally doctrine is an important input into the design process, and TT&P is an important output. (For our purposes, you can think of doctrine and tactics as being part of the fleet you are buying.) Finally, the entire process is permeated by a discussion of the potential threat. Threat is part of the strategic environment, it determines the usefulness of individual ship design, it affects basing and force sizing decisions, etc.

In other words, there's plenty more ideas to explore!

Frequently Asked Questions

DAVID WEBER

What are the other sentient species and how do they interact with humanity?

I regret to say that we aren't going to answer this question in any detail at this time. I will say that there are additional sentient species in the Honorverse, at least one of whom has been "uplifted" to current human levels of technology and trades with humans. I have taken the position in the Honorverse, however, that it is unlikely for there to be numerous species at comparable or near comparable levels of technological development at any given moment. And, since I chose to write about a human-versus-human conflict, humanity had to be the primary star-traveling species. By default, that moved most of the nonhuman species to pre-space and/or primitive technologies. The reason I'm not going to answer this question in detail is that while I have several species roughed out, I don't intend to introduce them into the books anytime soon, and as a storyteller, I need to keep my options open on reworking or modifying my rough notes in order to best suit my needs at the time I do introduce them. Assuming, of course, that I do!

Where is Amos Parnell as of 1921 PD? What is he doing and, most important, what does he think of the resurrected Republic of Haven?

Amos Parnell is still living in exile in the Solarian League. He is in something of an ambiguous position, given his prewar rank in the People's Navy and his status as one of the few surviving members of a truly prominent Legislaturalist family. He is on very friendly terms with the new, restored Republic's government, but Eloise Pritchart is just as happy to have him safely out of the domestic political mix, for several reasons. The biggest one is that despite the restoration of the Republic, people hankering for the "glory days" of the conquering People's Republic of Haven still exist, although they are an enormously marginalized fringe at the present time. She has no desire to bring home Legislaturalist émigrés who might, willingly or otherwise, serve as a rallying point for the lunatic fringe. On the flip side, Parnell is the most visible, most senior surviving member of the Old Regime of the Legislaturalists. If he were to return home, his life would be in permanent danger at the hands of people who still have grudges, very well deserved grudges, in many instances, against the Legislaturalists. He sees the resurrected Republic as his birth star nation's last and best chance at redeeming its soul, and having seen the corruption of the Legislaturalists from inside the belly of the beast and having experienced the brutality of the Committee of Public Safety firsthand, he is a strong and powerful supporter of the effort to restore the pre-PRH Republic. At the moment, however, his best opportunity for doing that (and surviving in the process) is to speak for it from abroad.

What are the larger political entities outside the Solarian League and how large are they?

There aren't very many "larger political entities" outside the Solarian League, the Andermani Empire, and the Republic of Haven. Remember that even though the People's Republic of Haven had only a teeny tiny number of member star systems compared to the League, it was the largest extra-Solarian political unit. After the League, the Silesian Confederacy was closest to the PRH in terms of inhabited star systems, but calling the Confederacy a star nation would have been too generous by the seventeenth century post diaspora. It had already become a failed state at that point. The truth is that the Manticoran Wormhole Junction had an enormous amount to do with the emergence of the Republic of Haven, its transformation into the People's Republic of Haven, and its eventual restoration. Although it was called the "Haven Sector," that was more an example of Solarian arrogance hanging a label that suited its perceptions on the region. The true focal point of the quadrant's interaction with humanity in general was the Junction, which gave access to the region directly from Beowulf at the very heart of the Solarian League. However, the Star Kingdom of Manticore was a kingdom, a monarchy, and it was an article of faith in the League that monarchies (which were not members of the enlightened Solarian League, at any rate) were automatically primitive neo-barbarians, which is one reason they have appended that label to Manticore so persistently. The fact that Manticore is fabulously wealthy and refuses to kowtow to the League only strengthens that Solarian attitude towards the Star Empire... especially now that it has become, in very truth, an empire. Haven, on the other hand, had a robust, capitalist economy, was busily expanding and exporting its citizenry and its institutions to other star systems in the vicinity, and was a republic. As such, it was far more acceptable to the League and *ipso facto* became the "dominant power" of the quadrant even before the PRH turned conquistador.

It was, however, actually the access available through the Junction which drew outside wealth, migrating populations, and ever-increasing and ever-denser trade to the "Haven Sector," with the result that outside the heart of the Solarian League itself, that region became the wealthiest and most densely settled one. And out of that density of population, that concentration of wealth, and that attractive effect on additional wealth and people, emerged the multi-system star nations in the vicinity. It may be best to think of the Haven Sector as an outlying lobe of human expansion that leapfrogged over the intervening space courtesy of the Junction. The Verge, the sort of surrounding crater ringwall of independent star systems between the League's member systems and the Haven Sector, consists almost exclusively of single-system star nations, with here or there two or three star systems which may have leagued together into a minor local power. It is the absence of local power blocs which could be considered true star nations which makes the Verge so vulnerable to the Office of Frontier Security's steady encroachment. The fact that the Star Empire of Manticore is creating such a local power bloc in the Talbott Quadrant, thereby preventing an option to ingestion by OFS or its minions, explains another layer of the Solarian League's hostility towards Manticore.

There were several modest-sized star nations within two or three light-centuries of Sol in the first couple of centuries after the creation of the Solarian League prior to about 1400 PD. In the roughly 125 to 150 T-years following the development of the impeller drive and the Warshawski sail, however, the League expanded to incorporate those star nations into its membership. Aside from a handful of mini-Leagues (in the sense of economic unions) like the Rembrandt Association, however, there are very few true multi-system star nations outside the League. That is not to say that there aren't other relatively wealthy single-system star nations (like Erewhon) or entities which would like to be star nations but which haven't been allowed to coalesce because of OFS' policies (like Smoking Frog), simply that there aren't any larger political entities, which was what the question asked about.

Before the Republic of Haven became the PRH and embarked upon the Duquesne Plan of conquest, what was the tone of relationships between the RoH and the SKM?

Prior to the emergence of the People's Republic of Haven, the Star Kingdom's relations with Haven were actually very good. While it was the Junction which accommodated so much of the population movement into the Haven Sector, Haven was actually settled around a century before the Star Kingdom, thanks to the emergence of the impeller drive and Warshawski sail, which allowed the initial Haven colony expedition to overtake and pass the sublight Manticore colony ship *Jason*. It was a well-financed expedition, the quadrant contained a higher than average concentration of desirable star types, it established a vigorous economy and an attractive political system, and it aggressively and actively sought to bolster and support follow-on waves of settlers. As a consequence, it was seen as the "Athens of the Verge" by many, including the Star Kingdom of Manticore. Manticore had never had the population Haven did and, prior to the discovery of the Junction, was essentially an out-of-the-way star system which didn't go out of its way to draw attention to itself or (after the Plague

Years, at least) actively seek to promote immigration. By the time the Junction was discovered, Manticore had become accustomed to thinking of Haven as the "way of the future," and it took some centuries for the Star Kingdom to begin to recognize the true nature of the commanding economic and strategic advantage the Junction conferred upon it. There was no Manticoran merchant marine, really, before the Junction was surveyed in the 1580s, and by 1650, the Republic had begun its slide into the People's Republic, although that didn't become readily apparent to the outside galaxy for quite some time and immigration into the Republic actually increased rather dramatically once the Junction gave access to Beowulf. During that seventy-year window, the Star Kingdom became an ever more potent economic force, building its merchant marine and coming to decisively dominate the carrying trade of the Haven Sector (including the transport of quite a few of those Haven-bound immigrants). What was not immediately apparent to either Manticore or Haven was that in the process, the Star Kingdom was replacing the Republic as the region's dominating economic power.

Throughout the period prior to 1750 (that is, for a period of very nearly two hundred T-years following the discovery of the Junction) Manticore and Haven traded with one another, joined with Beowulf in endorsing the Cherwell Convention, cooperated in piracy suppression and the suppression of the slave trade, and were, in fact, the two poles of the economic engine of the Haven Sector. However, the truth was that the Star Kingdom could be, and would have been, a major economic power even if the Republic of Haven had never existed, given the existence of the Junction. Following the Havenite Economic Bill of Rights in 1680, a gradual cooling of the relationship set in. By the time Haven promulgated the Technical Conservation Act in 1778, the once close relations between Haven and Manticore had largely disappeared. The growing resentment of Manticoran prosperity among Havenites, and especially among the growing Dolist class, as the Republic's economy stalled and then began to contract, only made that situation worse. The new Constitution of 1790 was the frosting on the cake as far as Manticoran admiration of Haven was concerned, and by the time the Duquesne Plan was formulated, the People's Republic already recognized that its greatest potential stumbling block would be the Star Kingdom.

If the revolution hadn't happened, is it fair to say that the Peeps would have had a very good chance of beating the Manticore Alliance?

I don't think I'd go so far as to say that the Peeps would have had a "very good" chance of beating the Manticoran Alliance. I will say that they probably would have had at least an even chance of victory if the Revolution, the Committee of Public Safety, and the Pierre purge of the Legislaturalists (and, of necessity, the officer corps) hadn't intervened. Their fleet was bigger, they actually had more experience in combat operations than the RMN, and their economy, although much less efficient, was much larger than Manticore's. In order to win, however, they really would have had to overpower the Star Kingdom in the first rush, the way they had all of their earlier victims. With time for Manticore to absorb the shock of the initial attack and fully mobilize its economic and industrial power, the numerical odds were bound to begin to equalize, because unlike Manticore, the PRH had very little "slack" in its economy and industrial sector. In effect, Haven was already running at wartime production levels, whereas Manticore was still running essentially at peacetime production levels, with significant capacity for increasing its output. Moreover, the R&D programs which had been put in place by Roger III in the forty years or so leading up to his assassination had unbalanced the playing field more than anyone (including Manticore) realized at the time. It would have come down to a question of whether or not the PRH would have been able/willing to pay the cost in very high casualties to overwhelm the SKM's already developed and deployed qualitative superiority before the even greater qualitative superiority inherent in Manticore's R&D came into play. By the standards of the later period of the Havenite Wars, the casualties involved probably would have been no more than moderate, but no one knew that in 1905, and I would say that it's probably unlikely the Legislaturalists would have risked the scale of losses involved, once they realized what that scale was, because of the implications it would have had for the internal stability and security of the PRH. In many ways, Pierre's successful coup, which owed a great deal to the PN's initial losses, was simply a demonstration of what probably would have happened at some point fairly early in a protracted war between the Legislaturalist regime and the Star Kingdom if the PRH had decided to wage a war of attrition against the SKM's superior weapons systems, 1905-style.

To what extent are planets in the Honorverse dependent upon food import from other planets?

That depends entirely on the planets in question. Grayson was something of an extreme case of a planet finding it difficult to feed its own population because of environmental circumstances, but for all intents and purposes, the orbital farms could be said to be a sort of surrogate for food imported from other planets. There are other worlds which for various combinations of reasons have found it more economically advantageous to import food in substantial quantities rather than producing it locally. The relative cheapness of interstellar transportation in the Honorverse is such that it is viable to rely on out-system sources of food, but most planets get nervous if their total food supply depends on imports. It is much more common for imported food to consist of luxury items or staples which happen not to do very well in their local ecosystem. Beef from Montana, for example, commands a very good price on the import market. There are also planets whose populations have simply grown to a level at which supplementary food sources from out-system are necessary to sustain a comfortable nutrition level. Old Earth falls into that category, at least at the present time, because the inhabitants of Old Earth have chosen not to produce food in the quantities needed to sustain their diet from internal sources. Partly that's because the planetary population is so large, partly it's because land values are so high that people can always find a "better use" for it than as cropland, and partly it's because imported food supplies are simply cheap enough that it would be extraordinarily difficult to compete with them pricewise given land costs, material costs, and wage costs on Old Earth. That doesn't mean the planet couldn't produce enough food on its own surface to feed its population; it simply means it hasn't chosen to produce food in those quantities. As a very rough analogy, it costs less to truck commercial quantities of lettuce in from Florida than it does to grow it in roof gardens in Manhattan.

Are there any sublight colony ships still in transit to very distant destinations at the time of the Honorverse novels? Likewise, have there been exploratory or colonization missions far beyond what is considered human settled space?

I don't know (he said innocently). Are there?

What is the most popular sport in the Star Kingdom?

That depends. On Manticore itself, it's soccer, closely followed by grav skiing. On Sphinx, it's hang-gliding, closely followed by hockey. On Gryphon, it's skiing, closely followed by skiing, with skiing in third place. The Star Kingdom doesn't really have a single "trademark" sport the way Grayson does with baseball or Haven does with lacrosse. Rather it has what you might think of as a broadly diversified sports landscape.

What kind of beer is Old Tilman's?

Old Tilman doesn't actually have a precise terrestrial analog. The best way to think of it would be as a hoppy oatmeal stout with a touch of honey added for sweetness. What gives it its distinctive flavor, and the reason there isn't a precise terrestrial analog, is that it is brewed exclusively on Sphinx using both oats and hops which have mutated/been genetically altered to suit their new environment. As a consequence, the oat-based malt has a fuller, sweeter flavor with a hint of almond and the hops are milder, not quite so bitter flavored. It's really quite good, but I'm afraid I'm not prepared to share my personal stock of it with anyone else at this time. Sorry.

I don't get the feeling from the books that there was a real sense of "being at war" in Manticore. The feeling I get is best portrayed by the famous whiteboard picture saying: "America is not at war, the Marine Corps is at war, America is at the mall." Is that an accurate assessment?

No, that isn't an accurate assessment. The problem is that one cannot draw too tight a parallel between the economy and society of the Star Kingdom of Manticore and historical experience. There are parallels, of course; don't get me wrong. But there are also ways in which I have deliberately "broken" the historical model by altering bits and pieces of it.

Warfare in the Honorverse, at least prior to the end phase of the Havenite Wars, is generally very "civilized," at least where "first world star nations" are concerned. What happens to the locals when the Gendarmerie battalions arrive to do Frontier Security's bidding, or what happens when the local President for Life decides the opposition element needs to be wiped out, is quite another thing, of course. However, for "civilized parts," where the threat is from another star nation, standing fleets are the key to survival in the Honorverse and the accepted rules of war (reflected, in part, in the Eridani Edict) mean that if your fleet is defeated, you are defeated. The People's Navy crewed its ships using conscription, which was a comfortable fit with its statist economy and command society. The Royal Manticoran Navy crewed its ships using voluntary recruitment and drawing upon its merchant marine as a seed bed for experienced spacers.

Perhaps a workable (although flawed) analogy would be Great Britain during the Napoleonic Wars. The analogy is flawed because the UK confronted an adversary whose military power was land-based while its military power was sea-based, but the sense that Manticore itself was safe from Peep depredations as long as the Navy was able to guarantee the security of the Manticore Binary System and the Manticoran Wormhole Junction was very much a part of Manticoran thinking and attitudes. At the same time, Manticore's carrying trade was virtually completely secure from Havenite raiding because it passed through the Junction and went to places far beyond the People's Navy's reach. (Recall the nature of Javier Giscard's mission to Silesia, and the reasons for it, in *Honor Among Enemies*.) So the economic stability of Manticore, aside from the fiscal demands of building and maintaining the Navy, was also secure as long as the RMN protected the home star system. That doesn't mean Manticorans didn't follow the war closely, that people who have families and friends in the Navy weren't agonizingly aware of their losses, or that the Star Kingdom took the war lightly. It simply means that the strains were distributed differently from, say, our own experience in World War II. And, of course, much of the Manticoran attitude during the first fifteen years or so of the Havenite Wars has been changed forever following Operation Beatrice and Oyster Bay.

Given the population density possible with residential towers in the setting, how is the land on a planet like Manticore used?

There are several factors to consider when looking at residential patterns and land-use on a high-tech planet in the Honorverse. First, these are incredibly productive economies, by any standard with which we are familiar. Consider how someone living in first-century Rome might regard a twenty-first-century shopping mall, for example. They are also, with the exception of planets like Old Earth herself, worlds with relatively (note that I said relatively) low population densities compared to the present day. If you can imagine an entire planetary population with a twenty-first-century American standard of living, you'll begin getting close to visualizing Manticore. One of the consequences of this is that what is considered an acceptable amount of living space has actually increased significantly between now and then. Residential towers, with their huge height and amenities, make it possible for an "average family" to enjoy very expansive and comfortable space in an urban environment. At the same time, routine supersonic transport by air car, electronic networking, virtual workplaces, etc., mean that many of the factors driving urbanization in our own experience no longer apply. This can be seen in Stephanie Harrington's story or the Harrington freehold in Honor's time.

What this means is that planets can be far more flexible about where people live, how they live, and what use is made of the land. By and large, population per square mile is very, very low compared to our standards, and even in an urban environment, population per cubic mile (bearing in mind the sheer size of the towers involved) is low compared to someplace like New York City or (far more so) someplace like Shanghai or New Delhi. Vast amounts of the planetary surface of a world like Manticore or Sphinx is left fallow, undeveloped, available for recreational use, perhaps, but not built over or farmed. Nor, given access to asteroid belts, gas giants, moons, etc., is it generally necessary to mine planetary surfaces or exploit fossil fuels, while Honorverse civilizations' energy budgets are stupendous . . . and cheap . . . and have very little environmental impact.

This may not have answered your question entirely, but I hope it moves in the direction of an answer. Of course, given the diversity of planets and (especially in the Verge) of the technology actually available to a given star system or world, conditions can vary greatly from star system to star system, and the lower the tech level available, the more negative impacts are likely to be felt by the local planet and its ecosystem.

About BuNine

BuNine is short for "Bureau Nine," and is both a play on the Royal Manticoran Navy's bureau structure as well as an indication of the number of founding members.

BuNine got started in a group of science fiction fans that coalesced around Ad Astra's *Saganami Island Tactical Simulator* and its designers, Tom Pope and Ken Burnside. David Weber is himself a former game designer, and was quick to recognize both the necessity for game designers to pick his brain to get the game right, and the advantage to him in having a group of people double-checking and extending his work. The so-called "Great Resizing," for instance, came directly out of the game designers realizing that they couldn't make the math work under the assumptions they were given.

BuNine is not just a group of Honor Harrington fans. About half of us have some sort of connection to the US military, mostly the Navy, in either a civilian capacity or in uniform. Those who don't are artists, lawyers, computer specialists, and the like, all accomplished experts in their fields. What sets us apart is that not only are we fans, we are fans with day jobs that directly or indirectly relate to our hobbies. If you read a BuNine article about the evolution of Manticoran law concerning treecats, for instance, you'll discover the author is a practicing attorney. As one of our members says, "In my day job, I'm a naval analyst. My hobby is that I analyze navies that don't actually exist."

Over time, BuNine went from a loose collection of people to a more formal organization, usually because of events involving other people working with the Honorverse. When a would-be motion picture developer needed help thinking about how the bridge of a starship would be organized, we adopted our current name and started having annual meetings. When Toni Weiskopf at Baen suggested to David that the twentieth anniversary of On Basilisk Station warranted a companion volume, David said "I know just the people to write it"—thereby forcing us to actually create a legal entity to go with our group identity. Along the way, we've designed ships, drawn blueprints, invented doctrine, asked probing questions, and done the math to fill in the elements around which David has built stories. BuNine is not a club; if anything, it's closer to an invitation-only professional society or a technical consulting organization.

This book is the result of many, many people, both inside BuNine and out, working long hours. None of us could have done it alone; all of us enjoyed doing it together. We hope you enjoy reading it as much as we did writing it.

About the Authors

Most of the authors are members of BuNine, and many of us have day jobs involving employers who are sensitive to people conflating our day jobs and our BuNine work. An incomplete set of biographies is below.

Scott Akers
Treasurer—Treecat name is "Keeper of the Nerds"
Scott is the Director of Financial Operations for a bulk fluids trucking firm in Seattle, Washington. Scott has an eclectic background. He served in the Navy as an enlisted navigator, worked as a ranch foreman, sold printing supplies and products, was a Series 7 stockbroker, spent five years as an executive for the Boy Scouts of America, and worked as an instructor on Middle Eastern Culture for a defense contractor at the Army's National Training Center on Ft. Irwin. He has spent the last seven years as a financial professional. His background provides BuNine with skillsets ranging from history to finance to naval analysis to comparative political thought.

Scott Bell
History Student
Scott is a medieval historian, with a focus on warfare, who reads both fantasy and military science fiction. Scott was recruited

to work on the Star Kingdom of Manticore awards, decorations and all things peerage and royal. This has expanded to include the SKM government and all awards and decorations of all the star nations.

Ken Burnside
Exobiologist in Residence

Ken is a freelance writer and award-winning game designer. He co-authored, with Tom Pope, *Saganami Island Tactical Simulator* and both of the *Jayne's Intelligence Review* volumes, which indirectly inspired this project when David said "I like these, and I think Baen Books might like something like this as well." On this volume, he did climatology, geology, speculative biology, some factoring of orbital mechanics, stellar brightness, and energy output from stars. When not purveying recreational mathematics, he does graphic design and editing and teaches Western Sword.

Derick Chan
Jack-of-All-Trades

Derick is a computer programmer working in the state of Ohio. A relative newcomer to the BuNine, he has helped with behind-the-scenes research, and contributed to a number of articles in the *Honorverse Companion*. Derick also is responsible for moderating David Weber's forums on his website, www.davidweber.net. During what little free time he has left, Derick is an avid video and board gamer, particularly in the strategy and RPG genres.

Pat Doyle
Chief Pilot, BuNine Flight Operations

Pat has spent the previous fifteen years as a commercial pilot, from flight instructor to airline captain. He will head up BuNine's Flight Ops Department . . . just as soon as we can afford an Mk28 Condor. Pat has published a wargame and has a strong interest in military history, tactics and strategy. Pat's geek superpower is starship combat. He is a four-time national champion for a popular starship combat game and is writing the Tactics Manual for that game. His contributions to the Honorverse are in helping to define the operational level of war and he is working to design a fleet starship combat game within the Honorverse.

Bill Edwards
Systems Analyst, Design, and Engineering

Bill is a systems engineer working for the US Department of Defense (DOD). He began this effort as an Electronic Warfare specialist, integrating that with various weapon, communications, and sensor systems, and serving as a naval warfare instructor, program manager, and senior systems engineer for multiple DOD programs. Bill describes his fandom superpower as being able to correlate real-world physics and technology with science fiction's questions on "how might such a device actually work?" which he does in collaboration with his BuNine peers in support of the underlying foundations of the Honorverse.

Rob Graham
Concept Artist, Designer and Jack-of-All-Trades

Rob is a trained digital artist, leaning toward 3D modelling and teaching with a lot of mostly useless knowledge picked up from reading way to many university papers and other sources. He originally joined BuNine to work on moving the Honorverse map into the 3D realm, but since has shifted gears to become a jack of all trades, tackling just about any job that's been thrown at him, including developing new uniform concepts, the Grayson sword, and even ship designs. He hopes to one day to make the trip across the Pacific from the land of Oz to meet many of the people he's worked with, including David.

Mark Gutis
Attorney (his wife makes him own up to being one)

A praticing attorney, Mark was recruited by BuNine because, while he knows nothing about space hardware and can't understand math, he *can* index and write about stuff like legal systems and governments.

Richard Hanck
Systems Integration and Sounding Board

Richard is an ex-Navy Electronics Tech with experience in communications and nuclear hardware operation, troubleshooting, and repair. Currently working in physical security while attending college, he was recruited to BuNine from the wild, with a general specialization in "rough out" 3D work and 2D rough concepts. Richard mostly plays backup for the more skilled artists and techs, providing ideas and commentary on new production, research and math backup, and helping to flesh out the structure under the skin of the ships and other tech. He hopes to one day completely and accurately model an entire SD(P).

Bryan Haven
BuNine Chief Information Officer (Ok . . . Secretary)

Bryan is BuNine's Secretary. He is a retired Navy Submariner who went on to work for NASA and then Apple, Inc., before taking over as general manager for Atlantis Games & Comics in Norfolk, Virginia. His contributions include general organizational support and the pointed question now and again.

Robb Jackson
Retired Police Officer

An amateur historian and historical reenactor covering three hundred years of American military history (as well as a few out-rider eras), Robb was recruited as a freelancer to BuNine to work on making the Royal Manticoran Army more than a few vague references. He also helps run The Royal Manticoran Navy: The Official Honor Harrington Fan Association, Inc., with—you guessed it—the Royal Manticoran Army.

Arius Kaufmann
Human Terrain Analyst

Arius recently graduated from the University of Virginia with a degree focusing on East Asian history. A jack of all trades, he has been a defense analyst, a software engineer, a political campaign staffer, and a wargame developer for the US Navy When he's not trying to bring about The Singularity, he's reading Supreme Court decisions or conserving angular momentum. In the Honorverse, he's interested in government structure and bio-sentient continua. In real life, he likes using fancy words—sometimes appropriately.

Martin A. Lessem, J.D.
Regulatory Attorney

Martin is a regulatory affairs professional who has worked for a variety of pharmaceutical companies doing everything from regulatory CMC to labeling to advertising and promotions review. He is an occasional contributor to medical blogs with information on how medical regulatory agencies work. In his spare time, he runs The Royal Manticoran Navy: The Official Honor Harrington Fan Association, Inc., and tries to assist BuNine in liaising with fandom in general. His pet cat, Nimitz, is a constant source of inspiration.

Thomas Marrone
Illustrator

Forged in the fires of graphic and web design, Thomas recently made the transition to user interface and concept designs for video games. He is currently working as a UI Artist for Cryptic Studios on the MMORPG Star Trek Online. Within BuNine, Thomas works with other BuNine artists and authors to create and develop concept illustrations from initial sketches all the way through print-ready art.

Barry Messina
Naval Analyst

Barry is a military analyst working for a federally funded R&D center. He has recently completed twenty years of service as a civilian, following twenty years of Navy active duty as a nuclear machinist's mate, an ELT, and a SWO (TAO-qualified on three different classes of ships no longer in service), with degrees in nuclear engineering and operations research. He is a generalist specializing in tactical development, concepts of operations, the interface between submarines and special forces, and command and control. He has an unshakable conviction that nearly everything the US Air Force believes is wrong, and a fervent unwillingness to believe that members of the Senior Executive Service and Flag and General officers are always correct by divine right. He has been reading science fiction since discovering Andre Norton and Robert Heinlein in fourth grade. He is making very slow progress in his self-imposed Honorverse tasks of translating the International Regulations for Preventing Collisions at Sea into Interplanetary Regulations for the Prevention of Collisions in Space and then rewriting Multinational Maritime Tactical Instructions and Procedures Volumes I and II into tactical doctrine for the RMN and allied forces. He is incapable of remaining within imposed limits on the number of words that may be used in any publication, including this one.

John O'Donnell
Virtual Builder

A former US Air Force bomb loader now working for an entertainment provider that delivers red envelopes to their customers' mailboxes, John does 3D modeling for BuNine. He works strictly on hardware; humans are not a factor. He has been interested in science fiction for thirty-nine of his forty-seven years, having first read Jules Verne's *A Journey to the Centre of the Earth* at the ripe age of eight. John also enjoys classic progressive rock, especially with an SF angle, such as Rush and Yes.

Tom Pope
Ninth Space Lord

Tom is an IT support staffer at the Institute for Software Research at Carnegie Mellon University. He has an eclectic mix of programming, graphic design, and print production skills mostly learned on-the-job either at CMU or freelance or both. Tom is the official head of BuNine, which makes him both the head cat herder and the guy who did the most work to keep the project organized and on track. His knowledge of the Honorverse is encyclopedic, and his research into areas with which he has no formal experience (e.g., naval display systems) means he can usually hang with the professional naval types as well. His one glaring weakness is an inability to write about himself, which is why he outsourced his own bio. Tom is married to Diane, the most patient woman in the world.

Gena Robinson
"Designated Adult"

As David Weber's personal assistant, schedule keeper, first reader, web master, on-line store clerk, promoter and travel planner, fixer of broken computers, and sometimes wrangler of three kids, Gena Robinson is assured that no day at work is ever boring or monotonous. As a long-time reader of the Honorverse who has worked for David for ten years, she offers a unique view on the series, focusing on characters and the histories of the nations. Away from work, Gena enjoys writing for her active blog, contributing articles to jewelry trade journals, making said jewelry, and cavorting at Cons.

Kay Shelton
Copy Editor

Kay has a bachelor's and a master's degree in English Literature, supplemented by additional experience and professional workshop training. With a particular affinity for science fiction and fantasy, she describes her work for BuNine as "the comma wrangler."

Joelle Presby
Geek at Large

An accidental world traveller, Joelle has lived in France, Cameroon, California, Cameroon (again), Ohio, Maryland, California (again, but not the same part), Japan, South Carolina, New York (for a week but all her stuff came with her and got completely unpacked and repacked so it counts), South Carolina (again and the same part), and Virginia. She has been in Virginia for nearly five years and refuses to leave the state in spite of repeated hurricanes attempting to force her to decamp. Joelle also knows that France, Cameroon, and Japan are countries while the others are not, but she already used too many parentheses as is. (Besides, it is funnier to tell it this way. Just call her an American. Everyone else does.)

David Weber

David Mark Weber is an American science fiction and fantasy author. He was born in Cleveland, Ohio, in 1952. He started writing poetry and short fiction in the fifth grade, and a lifetime of reading, writing, and studying has given him a love of storytelling that shows in his work. In his stories, he creates a consistent and rationally explained technology and society. Even when dealing with fantasy themes, the magical powers are treated like another technology with supporting rational laws and principles. Many of his stories have military, particularly naval, themes, and fit into the military science fiction genre. He challenges current gender roles in the military by assuming that a gender-neutral military service will exist in his futures, and by frequently placing female leading characters in what have previously been seen as traditionally male roles, he has explored the challenges faced by women in the military and politics.

Christopher Weuve
Naval Analyst

Chris is a naval analyst working for the Department of Defense. He spent six years at the Center for Naval Analyses as a naval exercise analyst and wargame designer, and five years on the faculty of the Naval War College as a wargame designer and analyst. In addition to wargaming, his specialties include command and control and antisubmarine warfare. He describes his fandom super-power as being able to talk about real-world navies and science fiction navies at the same time. In the Honorverse, he's interested in command and control, and naval tactical and operational doctrine.

Greg Whitaker
Game Designer, IT Manager, Wargamer

A six-year US Navy veteran and CG plankowner, Greg is currently an in-house service delivery manager supporting enterprise data storage and protection systems to a Fortune 500 bank. He has over twenty years in the wargames industry including but not limited to being a playtester for Wizkids and a contributor to Ad Astra Games' SITS game supplements. In his off-time, Greg reads science fiction and plays just about any wargame that has dice.

Marcus Wilmes
Tax Adviser

Marcus was recruited by Tom Pope at the German Honor Harrington Forum as the in-house Andermani expert. Before his career as Andermani expert, Marcus received training to be a Steuerfachangestellter (tax consultant) and worked for several Steuerberater (tax advisors) in Germany. To satisfy his curiosity regarding business and economics, he enrolled at a university and received the grad of Diplom Kaufmann in Betriebswirtschaftslehre (business administration) with the main focus on business informatics from a university of applied science. At the moment, he is employed at a German ambulance service.